SHADE

SHADE

JAMIE BEGLEY

Shade

Young Ink Press Publication
YoungInkPress.com

Copyright © 2015 by Jamie Begley
Edited by C&D Editing, and Hot Tree Editing
Cover Art by Young Ink Press

All rights reserved.

ISBN-13: 978-0692414651
ISBN-10: 0692414657

Life is eternal; and love is immortal; and death is only a horizon; and a horizon is nothing save the limit of our sight."

— Rossiter Worthington Raymond

PROLOGUE

Shade watched from a seat in the darkened corner of Evie's living room, as she came through the front door, her startled eyes meeting his as she stepped into the room.

"Shade?"

Shade stared back at the woman who had been his friend since high school. Evie, her boyfriend at the time, Levi, and he had been an unbreakable trio that had gone on to join the military together. He and Evie had remained close friends throughout the years, even after Levi's death. When she had made it known that she intended to join The Last Riders, he had tried to dissuade her, knowing it was a emotional reaction to losing Levi. Meeting her now husband King, Lily's father, had been good for her. Every day, he saw a little more of the woman she used to be, before she had been raped and lost Levi.

"We need to talk." Shade kept his face impassive. It was because of their friendship that he was there in her home.

Shade watched as Evie carefully placed her purse down on the coffee table. "I guess I don't need to ask what about. How's Mag?"

Shade's expression didn't alter at her question. Mag was Cash's grandmother, who was recovering in the hospital after unknowingly eating poisoned beans intended for Lily, at the yearly town festival.

"Better. She'll be at the hospital for a couple more days," he said grimly.

"I'm surprised Cash didn't come with you."

"I told him it was my problem to deal with. He doesn't agree. He wants to take Brooke out himself, but I told him no." Shade got up from the chair and walked to the window, staring out at the small town. "He doesn't need the death of a woman with a small child on his conscience."

"You're not worried about your own?" Evie asked.

"I don't have one." Shade shrugged.

"Shade, you have feelings. I don't know why you think you don't. Lily shows you're capable of loving someone."

"She's the exception."

"I don't believe so, or you wouldn't be here," Evie said softly.

Shade turned to face her. "I'm here because you're a Last Rider, and we've always been honest with each other, Evie. Brooke's not going to stop until she hurts Lily, or I stop her." He stared into her eyes, seeing the flash of pain she couldn't hide.

"She's my fraternal twin; I grew up with her and know her better than anyone else…" As Evie paused, taking a deep breath, Shade braced himself for her to ask for mercy on her sister's behalf. "There is nothing redeemable inside of her. You think you have no con-science and can't feel for anyone?" Her lips gave a mocking twist. "I begged my father for a cat when I was younger, and he finally allowed me to pick one out from the shelter. I was surprised when Brooke actually seemed to like it. She played with it all the time and even let it sleep curled up against her. We had that cat for six years, and it ended up being more hers than mine.

"One night, a boy she had been dating for a couple of weeks came over and had an al-lergic reaction to the cat. He wouldn't come inside after that. A month later, the cat disap-peared. I searched all over the neighborhood for it, kept going into the backyard thinking it would come back. I finally noticed a mound of dirt had been dug next to our garage. I dug it up and found my cat. Its throat had been slit, and it was wrapped in the blanket it always slept on. When I told Brooke, she never shed a tear and never admitted she had done it, but I knew she was the one who had killed it.

"Believe me, she's the true psychopath. Do what you have to do."

Shade gave a brief nod before asking, "What about your nephew?"

"He'll still have a father, who'll be better off without Brooke. Besides, it's only a matter of time before she hurts one of them if they get in her way."

"I can't wait long. It's not going to be easy to hold Cash back."

Once Evie nodded, showing she understood her sister's death was imminent, Shade went to the door.

"Shade…?"

He turned back to face her.

"Let Cash handle Brooke. You don't need her death on your conscience."

Shade gazed back impassively at Evie. "Cash is the one with a conscience. Me? I won't feel a thing when I pull the trigger. I never do."

Shade saw the doubt in Evie's eyes.

"Your love for Lily shows you're not as emotionless as you say."

"Brooke claims she loves me. That's why she tried to destroy you and kill Lily," Shade mocked.

"You're nothing like Brooke."

"Aren't I?"

ဆ ∞

The cold had been getting to him lately. I must be getting soft, Shade thought wryly to himself. He would have to remedy that soon; he couldn't afford to be soft.

Protecting Lily kept him on his toes. He had never known a woman who managed to always be in the wrong place at the wrong time as often as her. She needed his skills and strength to keep her safe, and keeping Lily safe was his number one priority. Without her, he didn't want to think what life would be like for him or others who would be unlucky enough to be near.

He stomped the snow off his boots before going inside the small office building. It was late enough that there wouldn't be anyone to see him enter.

Making his way to the office of Knox's wife, he bent over the lock, taking a few minutes to open the door. Then, sliding inside, he made his way into her private office and went to the window which gave him the view he had come to observe.

As he watched Brooke lay her son down in his crib to sleep, in hindsight, Shade thought he should have known Lily would change his life. It had taken two women to satis-fy him the night after seeing her for the first time and then hours before he could purge her from his mind enough to sleep. And that had only been the beginning.

Standing in the darkness, staring at the church across the street, his mind played back over the series of events that had led him to that place in time…

Chapter One

"What are you staring at?" Razer asked, turning away from the sheriff who was pretending he didn't know them while inspecting their motorcycles.

Shade nodded toward the two women standing on the sidewalk across the street. His dick grew hard while staring at the young woman delicately eating an ice cream cone, imagining her tongue flicking against his cock as she sucked on him.

A low whistle had Shade glancing at Razer, who was staring as avidly as he was.

A reaction he had never had before flooded through his bloodstream. At first, he didn't recognize it, but the longer Razer stared, the feeling became stronger.

Possession.

Shade managed to gather control long enough to notice the details of the woman who had stopped his breath. Her long, black hair fell in waves down her back, almost touching the curve of her ass. She was tall and slim, which was different from the women he usually fucked. He liked curvier women. They didn't break as easily from his demands. He also preferred large breasts, which the woman seemed to have from what he could tell under her loose dress. What held his attention, though, were the violet eyes which seemed to hold a wealth of pain he wanted to soothe away.

"Damn, I need to take that ice cream away and give her something better to lick," Razer hissed in a lust-thickened voice.

Shade stared at him sharply, about to slam his fist into his face.

"Wonder if that blond hair is real or if she dyes it?"

Shade's fury evaporated at his question. He had barely noticed the blond. The women were complete opposites—one as fair as the other was dark.

"Those two are hands-off." The sheriff's quiet remark drew his attention. "That's Beth and Lily Cornett."

Shade's stomach sank. They were the women responsible for them being in Treepoint, Kentucky. When Cash, a brother from The Last Riders, had asked Shade's father to check on the women, it had led to the club taking an interest in the town. Then he had learned the innocuous town was a vital part of a highly sophisticated system of drug trafficking, and Viper, their club president, had sent his brother Gavin in to set up a factory, which they would use as a front to establish

1

themselves in community. At the same time that was going down, Lucky had been instructed to go undercover with the ATF, further increasing their odds of stopping the drugs flowing through the town. The result had been something none of them had anticipated.

Gavin had been murdered.

The Last Riders moved into the large home, and Viper was determined to find his brother's killer. Each of the brothers had his role to play in the small community until Viper had the information he wanted, one being the secrecy of Shade's relationship with his father, who happened to be the sheriff.

Shade saw the blond glancing furtively at Razer, but the dark-haired one never looked in his direction.

"Which is the one with dark hair?" Shade didn't take his eyes off her.

"Lily, and she's too young for you. She's only seventeen."

Shade didn't do kids. He forced his gaze away, not looking back at the young woman again despite the constant pull he felt.

They followed the sheriff into his office for their new motorcycle licenses while Shade reminded himself she was too fucking young to deal with a man of his experience and desires. By the time he came back outside, the two women were gone.

Razer climbed onto his bike, not looking any happier than him.

"Which one did you have your eye on?" Razer asked casually.

"Does it matter? You heard what the sheriff said."

"Not going to make a move on her, just curious." A casual shrug couldn't hide the fact Razer was just as interested in the blond as he was in the dark-haired one.

"Lily." Shade felt a chill slide down his back as her name left his mouth.

"Cool." Razer started his bike.

He gave a short laugh. "You don't stand a chance with her."

Razer gave a grin. "It's a small town. Sooner or later, I'll see her again."

"And when you do?"

"She's not underage, so there's no reason I can't talk to her."

"You mean fuck her."

"You think I stand a chance?"

Shade remembered the furtive look the blond had shot at Razer. "Yeah, but a woman like that doesn't play like we do," he warned. "Bitches like that get serious after they get your dick in them."

"I'll cross that bridge when I come to it." Razer ignored his warning as he pulled out of the parking lot.

Shade started his own bike, thinking he wouldn't interfere with Razer going after Beth Cornett. Because, despite his best intentions, he *did* want to see Lily again, and letting Razer pursue her sister just might give Shade the opportunity.

He rode his bike back to the clubhouse, parking next to Razer. Both men were quiet as they entered the front door. The other members were sitting around, talking and drinking.

Shade watched Sam get up from Memphis's lap when she saw Razer, sidling up next to him. The blond slut had found her way into the club by getting friendly with one of the women members then started fucking her way through both the males and females.

Razer's hand went to her ass, pushing her toward the steps as Sam stupidly giggled.

"You miss me while you were in town?"

Razer didn't reply, following her up the steps.

"Coming, Shade?" Razer paused on the steps as Sam turned around to twine her arms around his neck, trying to kiss him. Razer didn't let the woman have his mouth; instead, he picked her up and tossed her over his shoulder.

Shade chose to follow them and as he entered the doorway, Razer already had Sam's shorts off and was bending her over the side of the bed. Shade watched as Razer put on a rubber then pounded his hard dick into the moaning bitch. Then he walked farther into the room, taking off his clothes before climbing onto the bed where he knelt in front of Sam as Razer pounded into her from behind.

Sam licked her bottom lip as she watched him take his cock in his hand, sliding it up and down his shaft.

"Want it?" he taunted her as his thumb slid over the crest, smearing a drop of his semen.

"Yes," she moaned, lowering her head.

She licked at the top of his dick, causing Shade to groan as he pictured a darkhaired woman over him instead of the one using her experienced mouth to make him harden further. He thrust in and out of her mouth as she sucked, using the skills she had perfected on the other brothers in the club to have him coming in her mouth.

"You never come that fast," Sam moaned as his cock slipped from her lips.

He didn't reply as he sprawled back on the bed to watch Razer come in her greedy pussy. Her screams filled the bedroom as she orgasmed, making him wince, and Shade almost climbed out of the bed to leave, but he was already getting hard again.

3

When Razer pulled out and went to the bathroom, Sam lay down next to him, her hand going teasingly to his cock.

Shade jerked her hand away. "You know the rules. You don't touch without my permission."

"I'm sorry." Sam pouted.

"You don't look sorry." Shade narrowed his eyes on her unrepentant face. "But you will be. Go downstairs to my room and get my flogger."

She jumped off the bed without bothering to put on any clothes and was out the bedroom door in a flash.

Razer came out of the bathroom. "She doesn't seem too worried," he laughed.

"She likes to be flogged as much as she likes to fuck. You up for another go-around?"

"Might take me a couple of minutes, but I'm game."

Sam came bounding into the room minutes later with the flogger, handing it to him. He watched as she climbed on the bed, getting on her knees and thrusting her ass up to him.

He used the flogger on her sparingly because she simply got too much enjoyment from it, and he enjoyed not giving her what she wanted. He waited to fuck her until she was begging for his dick, and then he fucked her until she begged him to stop.

He didn't let himself come inside her, though. Even with a condom on, he never let himself come inside any of the women.

When he was finished, he turned to Bliss who had entered the room to wait her turn.

"Want to take a shower?"

"What do you think?" She grinned, pulling off her clothes then following him into the bathroom.

Shade showered, letting Bliss run her soap-covered hands over his body, washing the scent of sex off. Then she kneeled at his feet and sucked him off; she had managed to get him hard again. The brothers called her Bliss because that was what it felt like when you fucked her. Shade personally thought she was just as good giving a blowjob.

Shade wrapped a towel around his hips, leaving both women in bed with Razer as he went to his own room. Lying in the bed, he stared up at the dark ceiling for hours before he finally managed to find sleep.

CHAPTER TWO

Razer had been right; it was a small town, and he saw her again much sooner than he had expected. The weather was warm, and several of the brothers wanted to go for a swim at the nearby lake. The women packed a couple coolers with beer before they headed out.

Shade was starting his bike when Sam climbed on behind him. He almost told her to get off then noticed the other brothers already had bitches on the back of their bikes. He would have preferred Evie or Jewell; at least they wouldn't cling to him like a fucking leech. Regardless, the ride to the lake relaxed him despite Sam's presence.

As Razer slowed down, making the turn onto the isolated spot where they could party in private, Shade was surprised to see Beth Cornett kneeling on a blanket while her sister swam.

He climbed off his bike without taking his eyes off Lily, who had frozen when she saw the motorcycles pull into the small lot. Shade swallowed hard as his eyes slid down the curves of her body while she merely stood in the water, her hands going to her breasts to cover the flesh left exposed by the pink bikini she was wearing. He was grateful the sunglasses he was wearing were dark enough to hide the lust he was sure would be visible, until he saw the terror in her beautiful face.

With so many eyes on her, she was petrified.

"Mind if we join you?" Razer asked as he walked up to Beth.

"Not at all, but as you can see, we're about to leave." Beth looked worriedly at Lily.

"We can't tempt you to stay?" Shade heard Razer ask.

"No. We've been here awhile, and the sun is getting to us."

"I bet that isn't all that's getting to you," Sam said snidely, brushing up next to Razer. Her sharp gaze was pointed at Beth's swimsuit top.

Everyone noticed how Beth blushed.

"Ignore her. She's a bitch, but I'm sure you know that since you've lived around her longer than I have. Hi, I'm Evie."

Shade was thankful for Evie and her kindness. They needed to know the people who lived in the town. It was the only way to gain trust and, therefore, answers.

"Hi," Beth acknowledged while continuing not to take her eyes off Lily.

Standing, Beth pulled on her shorts self-consciously and was about to reach for her T-shirt when Razer made his move, already bending down to get it then holding it in his hand, playfully not letting go at her sharp tug.

"Everything all right?" Razer was staring at the still-frozen Lily.

"Yes, everything is fine." Beth got a hold of her shirt then put it on.

"She okay?" At Evie's question, Shade looked around at The Last Riders and saw the looks of concern they had for Lily, who was beginning to tremble.

"Hey, we can leave," Razer offered, which Shade was part glad about, not wanting to scare the poor girl any further, and part sad because he wanted to watch her, talk to her, hold her, chase her fears away.

"No...No, it's fine." With the blanket in her hands, Beth walked slowly toward her sister. "Lily, I finished packing everything. Are you ready to leave?"

Shade watched as Beth tried to coax her out of the water.

Lily shied away from her, back into the water, and Beth stopped.

"Lily, please. They won't hurt you. They haven't even started drinking yet. You have nothing to be afraid of. Have I ever let any harm come to you?"

A small moan passed Lily's trembling lips as she took a hesitant step toward Beth, and Shade felt a primal urge to protect her at the sound.

"That's it, sweetheart," Beth praised.

"For Heaven's sake, leave, bitches. No one wants you here anyway." Sam's loud mouth had Shade clenching his hands into fists. He wanted to shut the stupid bitch up, but he didn't want to make a sudden move that would frighten Lily further.

"Shut up," Evie hissed quietly.

"Why do I have to shut the fuck up? That skinny slut thinks she's better than us—"

Fortunately, Evie smacked Sam on the mouth, silencing her. "I told you to shut up."

The other women surrounded her, moving Sam away from the water so Beth would have a clear path to get Lily to their car.

"Beth..." Hearing Lily's broken voice for the first time, Shade knew he would never forget it.

"Come on, sweetheart; a few more steps."

Lily walked within reach of Beth as Shade motioned the brothers back, giving the women even more room. He gritted his teeth as Beth wrapped Lily protectively into her arms and pulled her from the water. She was almost paralyzed with fear, her eyes blank and focused on the terror in her mind.

Shade easily recognized the signs of someone who had been traumatized. Having fought overseas, it wasn't the first time he had seen an incapacitating panic attack. He wanted to snatch the woman from her sister's arms and be the one to protect her. However, he forced himself to stand still as Razer said something to Beth before she drove away.

"Let me go." Sam tore her arm away from Evie's tight grip. "I don't know why you're all acting like pussies around those stuck-up bitches." She kicked off her tennis shoes before removing her shorts. "I'm going swimming. Any of you going to join me?" She ran into the water, her white ass jiggling until the water covered her.

Train and Rider both jumped into the water as the other women took off their own clothes.

Shade made no move to join them; instead, going to the cooler to pull out a beer. Taking a long swallow, he sat down on his bike and watched the others skinny-dip and get drunk.

No one tried to coax him into participating. When he wanted to join in, he would. If he didn't, he would remain alone, watching over them to make sure they were all safe and no one was hurt from partying too hard. Right then, he wasn't interested in getting shit-faced; he was too busy analyzing his reaction to a girl who was too young for him.

No one had ever made him feel the least amount of emotion, and he had been that way for as far back as he could remember. His first memory was of when his mother had reached out to stroke his hair. He had seen the hurt in her eyes when he had pulled away.

She had blamed his father for his being detached because he was constantly gone on deployment and moving them whenever the military gave him a new assignment. His father had tried to bond with him yet couldn't reach past his emotionless barrier. Eventually, the fights between his parents had escalated until it had resulted in divorce. They had given him a choice of who to live with, and he had chosen his father for the sole reason that he didn't try to hug or get into Shade's physical space.

When his father had remarried, Shade was older and had learned to plaster a fake smile on his face and have other kids over to play, pretending to be normal. When Penni had been born, he had said "ooh" and "ahh" like everyone else, having learned what reactions to portray. He had watched and observed others, perfecting the mask he showed the world while inside, he had remained cold and unattached to everyone.

As he had grown older and matured, he had realized there was something seriously fucked-up with him. He felt no attachment to anyone. The deaths of relatives meant nothing to him. Watching others cry and grieve was as foreign to him as those who fell in love. If he had been raised by someone less caring or in an abusive home, he would have probably turned out to be a monster who went off the deep end and eventually took innocent lives.

Thankfully, his stepmother had been kind and treated him as her own, pushing him toward sports and finding true friends. Evie and Levi had been as close as he could let anyone in, though. Ultimately, between his family, Evie, and Levi, he had felt the only emotion he was capable of—loyalty.

It was why he had joined the military, which ultimately had saved him. He had been trained to do what he was born to do—kill. The military had taught him how to fine-tune his "talent" until there were very few who had his expertise. He could take out a target and not feel one fucking thing. He could kill someone and eat dinner an hour later without feeling the slightest bit of remorse.

He had *never* felt any spark of emotion until he had seen Lily. He could control his own heartbeat, yet it had sped out of control when she had glanced in his direction while she was in the water. She had stared through him as if he didn't exist, and he hadn't, until then. She had made him real. She had made him human without saying a damn thing.

Shade ran a hand over his hair, trying to make sense of what was happening.

"What's up? Why are you glaring at Sam like you want to strangle her?" Razer asked, opening a beer.

"I'm getting sick of the bitch."

Sam cast him a wary glance. She was too far away to hear his words, but she was smart enough to interpret the cold face staring at her.

"Didn't seem that way the other night when she was sucking your dick."

"She's not the only woman who sucks dick."

"That's true, but none of them have her father. You know Viper wants us to find out what we can about Vincent Bedford. Neither the president of the local bank nor the good citizens of the town are going to give us the information we need, but Sam might. Come on, relax. What's got you so uptight anyway?"

"Nothing."

"You sure?"

"I'm sure. Now quit busting my balls and leave me alone," Shade snarled, throwing his empty bottle in the trashcan then grabbing another one.

"Okay." Razer laughed, taking a drink of his own beer.

"You going to make a move on that blond bitch?"

"Beth?"

"Yeah."

"Probably. I haven't made my mind up yet."

"When you do, make sure you keep me out of any conversations with her."

"Brother, your business has always been your own."

"Good. Let's keep it that way."

Chapter Three

"Want another refill?" Shade turned his attention from Train at the question, his eyes sliding down the waitress's body in the tight uniform. She had conveniently left several of the buttons undone, giving a generous view of her tits.

"No, thanks. I've had enough." His cold voice left no doubt of his double meaning. He had fucked her a few times, enough to know her pussy wasn't all that remarkable.

Her mouth dropped in disappointment as she refilled Razer and Train's cups, leaving when neither man responded to her smile.

"Going to have to find a new place to eat breakfast."

"Why? The food's good," Shade asked, drinking the last of his coffee.

"Don't want a horny waitress spitting in my food because she's pissed at you," Razer commented as the door to the restaurant opened and people flooded inside.

"Church's out," Train said, still eating the large breakfast he had ordered.

Shade sensed when *she* came in the door.

As Lily walked across the restaurant, snagging one of the last tables, he didn't have to remind himself she was too young for him. The other kids with their fresh faces and immature bodies confirmed that he was too fucking old for her.

One pimply-faced punk plopped down next to her, handing her a menu. Her sister sat at the end, watching them in amusement. Shade didn't know what she found so fucking funny.

He wanted to break the punk's hand every time he tried to take Lily's in his. She unconsciously would move it away, but it didn't lessen the anger he felt.

"Lucky's coming in the door."

While the Pastor stopped to talk to his faithful parishioners, Shade could tell Lucky only wanted to sit and eat.

Shade's own amusement died at Lucky's frustration when he heard Lily call him to their table. There was an easy familiarity between the two as he talked to Lily and her friends before giving his attention to Beth. Then the bastard managed to snag an invitation to sit and eat breakfast with them.

"I'm done. You ready?" Train asked, reaching for the check.

"No," Shade answered at the same as Razer. "I want another cup of coffee." He motioned to the waitress.

After she refilled his coffee, he and Razer unashamedly eavesdropped on Lily's table, learning she was going away for the weekend on a youth trip.

Shade frowned. Why the fuck was Beth allowing her sister to go away for the weekend with a bunch of randy kids?

Shade could only hear bits and pieces of the conversation going on at the table. Regardless, he did catch the end when Lily stood up, preparing to leave.

"We better be going," Lily told her sister. "I'll be home by ten."

"Finish your project. Don't worry about the time, but remember you have school in the morning."

Shade gritted his teeth at Beth's mischievous look. What the hell? What kind of guardian was she to let Lily stay out late? She was practically giving them permission to fuck.

Shade saw the boyfriend put his arm around Lily as they left, the tension easing in his stomach when he saw her pull away from the touch.

Razer stood, watching Lucky flirt with Beth and then leave her to go pay the check.

"Let's go," Razer snapped as Beth left the diner.

Shade rose, already knowing what Razer had planned. He grinned when Razer picked up the tab for all three of them.

"What's the hurry?" Train asked as they followed a rushing Razer outside.

"Shut up and get in," Shade told him, getting in the truck.

Razer caught his eyes as he drove the truck out of the diner's parking lot. Instead of speeding up on the small, two-lane road, Razer drove slowly.

"She's not going to give your ass the time of day," Train spoke up from the backseat, showing he wasn't as clueless as Shade thought.

"Yes, she will." Razer threw them a confident grin.

Shade didn't smile back. He didn't want Razer to become friendly with the pretty blond. He had a bad feeling in his gut. They should avoid any contact with either of the sisters, who lived the complete antithesis of the life The Last Riders led.

Instead of arguing against the upcoming interaction, however, he found himself speaking up. "There she is."

Razer pulled up alongside where Beth was walking. "Want a ride home?"

"Yes." The look on her face was composed, but Shade didn't miss the hesitation in her eyes.

Shade didn't give her time to change her mind, jumping out of the truck to let her climb in before getting back in himself.

"I live down Pine. It's just—"

"I know where it is," Razer cut her off before introducing them to her.

Shade saw her looking over his tattoos before lingering on his sunglasses.

"What's so funny?" Razer asked, probably noticing her smile instead of focusing on driving.

"I was just wondering how you decided what your name was; if you chose it or someone else."

"Depends," Razer answered.

"On what?"

Razer shrugged. "A lot of things. It's usually because we're good at something."

"So because Shade wears sunglasses, he was given that name." She smiled at him.

"You think I'm called Shade because I wear sunglasses?" He couldn't hold back his laughter. Her naiveté was unbelievable.

He had been given the name while in the military, and it sure as shit wasn't because he wore sunglasses.

"Then why do you think they call me Razer?"

"Because you like to shave?" A tinge of red covered her cheeks when Train laughed at her that time. Even Razer had a hard time holding back from laughing in her face.

If the woman knew how Razer had earned his nickname, she would jump out of the moving truck. The brother had become an expert at shaving the women's pussies. The man had a fetish about having the women cleanly shaven, and if they shared his bed and hadn't taken care of it, Razer would pull out his long-handled razor and shave them himself. Shade had witnessed it for himself many times over the years. Razer shaving the women was erotic as fuck and made the women hornier than hell.

Razer pulled into Beth's driveway, where she further showed her innocence when she didn't ask how they had known where she lived. Honestly, he and Razer had often found themselves driving by the house after the day they saw the sisters eating ice cream.

Shade didn't get out of the truck, giving Razer his opportunity to be alone with Beth after he had let her out his door. Shade observed her uncertainty as she talked to Razer in front of her door.

"Think she'll go out with him?" Train's voice was skeptical.

"Yeah." She might have been uncertain, but Shade also saw curiosity.

When Razer was back in the truck, Train asked, "Well?"

"We're going for a ride on my bike." Razer put the truck in reverse, pulling out of the driveway.

The speed he drove them back to the clubhouse showed how anxious he was. Shade had never seen Razer so eager to hook up with a woman. Usually, he was laid back, and all a woman had to do to get Razer's attention was spread her legs. For once, Razer was having to chase tail. Although, Shade didn't know how long that would last, since Razer had a short attention span whenever pussy was involved.

Shade climbed out of the truck when Razer brought Rider's truck to a stop by his bike.

Razer tossed him the keys. "Give these to Rider for me."

"Sure thing. Have fun."

"I will." Razer gave him a casual wave as he started his bike.

Shade went up the long flight of steps to the clubhouse sitting on the hill. Finding Rider inside at the bar with his arm around Jewell, Shade slid his keys across to him.

"I thought you weren't going to be gone long?" Rider questioned.

"Something came up." *Razer's dick*, Shade thought wryly, deliberately trying not to remember his own desire to sit and watch Lily.

Shade went behind the bar he and Knox had built the first week they had moved into the large clubhouse. It had been meant to be a bed and breakfast for buyers coming to see the factory which was being built, but that had all gone to Hell when Gavin had disappeared when it had come time to buy the equipment. Everyone in the town believed Gavin had taken the investment money and disappeared. Everyone except The Last Riders. They all knew in their heart he was dead, but they were determined to give him the proper burial he deserved.

Shade poured himself a whiskey, thinking he would return to Ohio and never look back after they had found out what had happened to Gavin and Lucky finished his investigation.

"I have to go run an errand for Viper. Later." Rider left Jewell and him alone with Knox and Train, who were playing pool.

Shade studied Jewell's black hair as he drank his whiskey. "Take off your top."

Shade kept his eyes on hers as she pulled off her grey T-shirt, exposing her breasts since she wasn't wearing a bra. Her breasts weren't large, but they were firm with brown nipples.

Shade wondered what color Lily's nipples were then immediately felt guilty for having dirty thoughts about an underage girl. He poured himself another drink.

"Lose the jeans."

Jewell slid the jeans down her hips and thighs before stepping out of them.

"Sit on the stool." Shade kept his instructions short, watching as her stomach quivered at the tone of command in his voice.

She lifted herself to sit on the stool as Shade walked over to her, spread her thighs until he had a clear view of her pussy, and then sat down in a chair facing the stool.

Knox and Train quit playing their pool game to watch.

"Play with yourself."

While Jewell's fingers started to eagerly rub her already wet pussy, he sipped on his whiskey, stretching out his legs to give his dick some room in his jeans.

"Don't come," Shade warned as her breasts shook from her escalated breathing.

Jewell nodded, keeping her finger on her clit while Shade unbuttoned his jeans, releasing his engorged cock.

"Come here."

Jewell hastily slid off the stool, coming to stand in front of him.

"You want my dick?"

"God, yes," she moaned.

Shade reached into his back pocket for a condom, ripping it open and sliding it on. Then he reached forward, taking a nipple between his two fingers to tug her closer to him.

As Jewell placed her knees on each side of his hips, her pussy hovering over his dick, Shade smiled at her approvingly.

"May I please fuck you?" she begged seductively.

"Yes."

Her hot pussy slid down easily over him while Shade leaned forward and took the brown nipple into his mouth.

"Fuck me," he ordered.

Jewell began sliding up and down his dick, whimpering as he leaned back against the chair, making her do all the work.

"What's wrong? Not enough for you?" Shade questioned.

"I need more." Shade knew she meant she wanted him to pound into her, but he wasn't ready to give her what she needed.

"She needs more, brother." Knox dropped the pool cue onto the pool table, coming to stand behind Jewell who was fucking Shade's cock like a piston.

When Shade took her ass cheeks in his hands, spreading the globes wide, Knox unzipped his jeans, pulling out his cock then hurriedly putting on a condom.

"I need to get some lube." He hesitated with his cock pointed at her ass.

"No!" Jewell shouted.

"She likes the pain. Don't you?" he asked, seeing the lust blazing out of her eyes.

"Yes!"

"Put it in, Knox," Shade told him.

Knox leaned forward, rubbing his cock through the juices seeping from her cunt, and then Shade felt her cunt become even tighter as Knox worked his cock into her tight asshole.

"Damn. Fuck," Knox groaned, his hands clasping her tits from behind. Shade's fingers went to her clit to give her the added stimulation as Knox fucked her from behind.

Shade rubbed a tendril of her black hair between his fingers, letting his mind pretend his dick was in another woman, another pussy.

"Train."

"I'm here." Shade heard his voice from behind his chair.

Train moved to the side of the chair as Shade removed his fingers from her clit. Going to her mouth, he placed a wet finger against her lips, using it to open her mouth.

"You going to leave Train hanging?"

"No." Jewell sucked Shade's finger as she unzipped Train's jeans and took out his cock.

Train stepped closer to make it easier for the woman who had no room to maneuver between the three men.

Shade removed his finger, letting Train replace it with his dick, and slid his hand to the back of her head, holding her steady. He then began to move, shoving his dick forward as Knox moved backward.

Shade's head fell back as he felt his climax building. Closing his eyes, he let his imagination go until he was unable to hold back his climax. Then he lifted Jewell enough to slide out of her before thrusting a finger inside of her as his climax played out.

"You done?" Train grunted.

"For now," Shade said.

Train took his seat, sliding Jewell toward him.

Shade drank his whiskey, watching the two men fuck the woman between them as he threw the condom away and shoved his dick back into his jeans.

When the men finished coming, they gently placed a wrung-out Jewell back on the floor. It took a few minutes before she moved to pick up her clothes.

15

"Don't bother." Shade took the clothes away from her. "Go take a shower, grab Bliss, and then meet me downstairs in my room."

"Okay." Her face lit up again as she moved toward the stairs.

Shade picked up the whiskey bottle and a couple of glasses while Knox and Train went back to playing pool. He made his way next door where his room was. Then he showered before sitting down on his bed naked, running his hand over his still-wet hair. He turned when he heard the women entering the room.

"I thought I would use your shower." Her disappointed pout showed she wasn't happy he had already taken one.

"Help yourself," he said, making himself comfortable on the bed. "Bliss can keep me occupied until you get back."

Bliss grinned as she jumped onto the bed.

While Jewell went into the shower, Shade let Bliss suck his semi-hard cock into her mouth, feeling himself already lengthening. This was what he needed to keep his mind off Lily. He would also avoid her and quit driving past her house. She was too young and innocent for him to focus on. He would drive her from his mind, using every bitch in the club. They didn't need to know he played out his fantasies for another woman by using their bodies.

"You got room for me?" Jewell asked jokingly, coming to stand by the bed.

"What do you think?" Shade growled, rolling to his side, careful not to let his cock slip out of Bliss's mouth. "I can do two things at once."

Chapter Four

Shade picked his glass up, taking a long drink. He had just finished a long shift at the factory. He hated working there; the close confines wore on his nerves. He could sit out in the freezing cold for days and be content, yet a nine-hour shift behind a desk had him pouring a drink as soon as he walked in the door.

He leaned a hip against the kitchen counter as Evie came in through the kitchen door carrying several empty beer bottles.

"Aren't you coming out?" she asked with a raised brow, throwing the empties away in the trash can.

"In a minute. I'm going to grab a sandwich first."

"Need your energy for the night ahead?" Her teasing had his lips curling into a smile. "The club's packed tonight, even for a Friday. Razer's new piece is about to faint from shock."

"Who?" Shade asked.

"The preacher's daughter."

Shade straightened away from the counter, going to the door and slightly opening it until he could see into the clubroom. Evie was right; the room was packed, and the party was already going strong.

Beth was sitting on Razer's lap on the chair Shade had fucked Jewell on the previous week. Train was sitting next to them on the couch, getting a blowjob from Stacy while her sister was sucking on Train's neck. Beth looked like her eyes were going to pop out of her head.

"Go talk to her."

"Why?" Her question had him closing the door and turning back to her.

"Because I want you to show her we're not all sex-crazed bikers."

"Why should I give a shit what she thinks about us?"

"Because I asked you to." His expression went hard, letting her know he wasn't really asking.

"Okay, okay. I'm going." As Evie put out her hand, opening the door and going into the other room, Shade backed away so Beth couldn't get a glimpse of him.

He decided to forego food, taking his drink downstairs to the bedroom he'd recently claimed, instead. He stayed alone in his room, not participating for the first time during a Friday party. He had no desire to fuck in front of Lily's sister.

He had done what he could for Razer. Unless Beth calmed down, she would run from the club and Razer by the time Train finished with Stacy's mouth.

He dozed off, waking in the morning to a growling stomach. Taking a quick shower, he then went upstairs to the kitchen. On Saturday mornings, everyone fended for themselves for breakfast, the members usually too hungover to eat. As a result, Shade fried himself a couple of eggs and made some toast.

He was sitting at the table eating when Razer and Evie came in looking like death warmed over. Razer looked like he hadn't slept, and Evie's face was pale. She kept shooting looks at Razer as she poured them coffee.

"How did the night go with Beth?" Shade asked, curious despite himself.

He didn't miss the glance Razer and Evie shared before Razer answered.

"It was fucked up. I should never have tried to hook up with her. I took her up to my room last night, and she looked at me like I was about to attack her. The woman gave me a blowjob last week, but she acted like she didn't know what a dick was last night," Razer grumbled. "So I took her ass home and came back to the club."

"Then what's wrong? I'm sure you managed to find someone to keep you occupied last night," Shade said sardonically.

"I did. Evie and Bliss more than made up for what Beth wasn't putting out. Train, Sam, and Knox decided to join in, too."

"So what's eating your ass, then?" Shade stood up from the table, carrying his dirty dishes to the sink.

"She came back. Sam went to get some lube and saw Beth. The fucking bitch opened my door, and Beth saw me and Train fucking Evie. She took off running before I could get my dick out of Evie."

Shade sat back down at the table. "Did you go after her?"

"No, but I used the number she gave Evie to try to talk with her. She refused to see me, though. Fuck it. I had already made up my mind that I wasn't going to see her again, anyway. Too much of a hassle for some pussy." While Razer shrugged, Shade could tell from his expression he was more upset than he was pretending.

"She offered me a job, and I was supposed to go see her Monday. I won't be getting it now," Evie said.

"Why not?" Shade questioned.

Evie rolled her eyes. "Because she saw me fucking a man she wanted. Just because we share doesn't mean it doesn't freak other people out. She probably hates my guts right now."

"Maybe, but she hates Razer more. Go see her Monday."

"Nope, I'll find a job somewhere else."

"Go see her. She was raised in the church, and they love to have an excuse to forgive. They eat that shit up."

Evie's eyes stared directly into his. "What's going on, Shade? First you want me to be friendly with her, and now you want me to take a job with her. What's up?"

Razer looked up from his coffee cup. "It's the sister, isn't it?"

"Who?" Evie asked, staring back and forth between Razer and him.

"Beth's sister, Lily. I think Shade's got a boner for her."

"Shut up, Razer." Shade cast Razer a warning look.

"Lily's a looker, but she's too young," Razer told Evie, ignoring Shade's glare.

Evie turned to him. "I see, you want me to get closer to Beth so I can find out more about Lily."

"Yes." Shade saw no reason not to tell the truth.

"But, if she's too young...you know the club rules," Evie needlessly reminded him.

Club rules or not, he wouldn't touch an underage girl.

"She won't be underage forever."

Evie grinned at him. "No, she won't," she agreed. "What's it worth to you for me to go suck up to Beth to get the job?"

"What do you want?" Shade's jaw clenched.

"You have to pull my shift at the factory twice a week. It will be hard to hold down two jobs. If I tell Viper you'll work two of my shifts, it will make him happy, and I won't have to listen to the others who will have to pick up the slack."

"Okay."

"But you hate working in the factory," Razer reminded him. "Shade...?"

"Stay out of it, Razer. I don't need your advice."

"Wasn't going to give you any. I was just going to tell you I'm going to Ohio for a few days. Wanted to see if you cared to ride along."

"What do you think?" Shade said, standing up.

"There's a few bitches who've been waiting on our votes," Razer laughed.

"Let's not keep them waiting then. I'll be ready to ride in an hour."

CHAPTER FIVE

Nine months later…

Shade drank his beer while listening to Knox and Rider argue back and forth about who had made Natasha come the most the previous night. Razer was standing at the bar, talking to Mick, while the other brothers took up two tables. The bar had been almost empty when they had walked in the door.

Bored out of his mind, he decided to go back to the clubhouse to find Natasha and prove to both men *he* held the record for making a woman come. Then the door opened, and Viper came in looking furious.

Only one person could bring out that level of frustration in the president of The Last Riders, and that was his father, Ton.

"Mick, have you seen Ton? I just got back in town this morning, and when I went home, both he and the truck were gone." Viper's angry comment had Shade sighing.

There went his fuck session with Natasha. Viper would probably make them search for his father.

"I haven't seen him today." Mick's answer escalated Viper's anger.

"Mother fucker! I'm going to strangle him with my bare hands when I find him!"

Viper's cell phone rang just as Shade was about to offer to go look for Ton. From his expression, he had found his father. As he ended the phone call, all the fury on his face was replaced with concern.

"I found Ton."

Shade stood up, moving closer to the bar so he could hear.

"He was in an accident. He broadsided Beth Cornett's car on Ivy Hill. They've both been taken to the E.R."

"How bad is she hurt?" Viper and Mick both looked at Razer, surprised by his reaction.

Shade wasn't the only brother who knew Razer hadn't forgotten the blond. He quizzed Evie as often as Shade did about what was happening in the women's lives.

"Don't know. That was the only information dispatch would tell me. The sheriff told them to contact me and to have me meet him at the hospital."

His father would have told dispatch to call rather than himself handling it, as if he didn't know Viper personally. Even when they were alone in public, they were to keep up the pretense of not knowing each other; his father would be able to give them information. That was the only way they had to find Gavin's murderer and to help Lucky bring an end to the traffickers.

Once Viper ran out of the bar with Razer hot on his heels, Shade went outside to see Razer jump in Viper's car as he was peeling out. Shade climbed on his bike, determined to follow. Unaware the other brothers were doing the same, Shade wondered if Lily had been contacted about her sister's accident.

He hadn't seen her for months. Even though she'd already turned eighteen, she was still too young and innocent for him. Therefore, he had made sure to stay away from places he would see her when she was home from college.

Evie had informed him of the day she was leaving. He had parked his bike on her street in the shadows that morning, watching as the sisters had gotten into the already packed car.

Lily had looked beautiful as hell, but her expression had been unhappy. Her violet eyes had held even more pronounced shadows than usual. Shade had wanted to ask her why she was leaving if she really didn't want to go. However, he had moved farther back into the shadows when he had seen her glance in his direction.

He was sure she couldn't see him, since he was too good at hiding in plain sight, but she had somehow sensed she and Beth weren't alone. If she had sensed a predator was near, she'd been right.

He had remained long after they had left before he had returned to his bike, heading back to the clubhouse where he could douse his desire to chase after her with whiskey and Bliss.

Snapping out of the memory, Shade parked his bike next to Viper's car then followed the men inside, standing back in case Lily was there. He didn't want anyone observing him when he saw her; he wanted privacy while he gauged his own reaction to seeing her for the first time since she had left.

Maybe he was no longer attracted to her. Honestly, he hoped his interest in her was gone.

He didn't have to worry about attention, though; everyone was watching Ton fight the nurse to see Beth.

"Let me go, woman. I have to check on that little girl."

The nurse argued back, trying to keep Ton in his wheelchair. Then Viper tried to calm his father, too, but the man was too upset, trying to convince his son he had not been drunk when he had hit Beth's car.

Shade felt the air hit his back as the electric door slid open. As Ton demanded Viper shoot him for hurting Beth, Shade was shocked to see Beth come to a stop nearby before moving forward. Shade didn't understand. Beth was right there, trying to calm Ton down. Then her words hit Shade like a bullet.

"You have to calm down. Remember your blood pressure. You don't want me to be worried about you, too, do you?"

Shade didn't hear anything else as he realized only one other person would have been driving Beth's car—Lily.

Shade forced himself to stand still as Beth convinced Ton to go with the nurse. Then the sheriff walked out of a room down the hall, drawing everyone's attention.

"How is she?" Beth asked.

"Lucky. She has a concussion, a sprained ankle, and she is going to be sore as hell for a couple of days, but all that research you put into purchasing a safe car paid off."

Shade went outside, sucking in a deep breath. He didn't have to question if his attraction to Lily had lessened or not. He had his answer.

Shade paced back and forth outside the E.R. door, trying to keep from going in and demanding to see with his own eyes that Lily was all right. The brothers and his president would look at him like he was crazy, and he was at the moment. Although he had never even spoken to the young woman, she had his insides twisted into a knot.

Since when did he care for anyone? It wasn't in his emotionless soul to give a fuck, yet something inside her spoke to him. She made him feel human, as if he was real and not a man who lived constantly in the shadows.

Razer strode outside, pausing when he saw Shade. "You know about Lily?"

"I heard. How is she?" Shade asked despite himself.

"Beth is with her. She told the sheriff her brakes didn't work. It could have been much worse; Beth drives all over the county in that car. She could have driven off a mountain." His hoarse voice showed Shade wasn't the only one who was coming to the realization that he cared about someone.

"Let's get out of here."

"You want to go back to the clubhouse?" Razer asked, getting on his bike.

"Fuck no. I'm going to have a look at Beth's car."

వ ౪

Shade sat next to Razer near the entrance to the hospital.

"There they are," Razer said unnecessarily, since Shade had seen them the instant they came outside.

After Razer pulled forward, bringing the dark blue car to a stop in front of the hospital, Shade opened the door and got out to see both sisters staring at them in surprise.

"Your chariot awaits, ladies." Shade grimaced at Razer's lame comment. He was trying to ease the women's tension, but it sure as shit hadn't worked.

"But Evie is picking us up," Beth protested, standing still.

Lily's eyes darkened in fear as her gaze went to Razer coming to a stop next to him. He felt a jolt of electricity as she looked at him, taking in the tattoos that covered his body. He had never pretended to be the boy next door.

"Evie was, but Loker called. He rented this car until yours is repaired. He asked us to drop it off to you."

"He shouldn't have done that. Ton wasn't responsible for the accident."

"You can take that up with him. Loker didn't want to leave Ton alone, so he asked me. I wasn't busy, so here I am. Now, are you ladies ready to roll?"

Shade held back as Razer took the wheelchair away from the orderly. He wanted to be the one to help Lily into the car yet could see from her terrified gaze that Razer came across as less threatening to her.

Shade watched as Razer and Beth helped Lily into the car. When she was in and Razer had moved away, Shade knelt down beside her, removing his sunglasses so he could see her clearly.

"You good?" he asked.

"Yes." At the tremble to her voice, something twisted inside of him, relishing the fear he felt emanating from her in waves.

She wasn't like other women who would stare at him. He was well aware of his attraction to them, knew they fantasized about having sex with a bad boy, and he did his best to make their dreams come true. When Lily stared at him, though, he was her worst nightmare.

She smoothed down the dress which had ridden up her silky thighs when Razer and Beth had helped her into the vehicle. Shade's eyes followed her movement, a sexual aura hanging around him despite his attempt to tone it down. He tried to soften his facial features, to lower his voice to place them on a more intimate level.

However, the woman wasn't reassured. She saw right through him, her discerning gaze shifting slightly away along with her body so he wasn't as close to her.

Shade lithely stood, closing the car door then getting in the front seat. Razer talked to the women during the drive, but Shade wasn't paying attention. He was studying Lily in the rearview mirror as she talked about college.

Razer pulled up in front of their house much too soon for Shade, and they got out of the car. While Razer grabbed Lily's bag out of the trunk, Shade opened Lily's door, stepping away as Beth handed Lily her crutches.

Her sister helped her get out of the car, and Shade didn't miss Lily's wince as she placed the crutches under her arms.

"I guess I'm still a little stiff." Lily tried to laugh it off.

When she took a step forward slowly, a whimper escaping from her pursed lips, Shade expected her to stop and ask for help; instead, she attempted another step. Her face was filled with pain, which was unacceptable to him.

"For Christ's sake," he finally exploded.

Unable to watch any longer, he swept her off her feet and into his arms. The crutches fell to the ground as she arched her back, trying to throw herself out of his arms as if his touch were burning her flesh.

He knew Beth didn't like him touching her pretty little sister. He saw her take a step forward, but Razer held her back as Lily continued to struggle.

"Wait, I can walk on the crutches." Lily tried to reason with him.

He gave her a small toss into the air, as if he was going to drop her, causing her to circle her arms around his neck, holding on to him.

"Be careful, you don't want me to drop you." He laughed, trying to ease the tension. However, the feel of her breasts against his chest had him clenching his teeth until she leaned away from him as he packed her into the house.

"Where do you want her?"

Beth motioned to the couch, where he gently laid her down on it, making sure her back was propped up with a pillow and another under her sprained ankle. He then went outside to get her crutches without explanation, afraid his hoarse voice would give away how her nearness had affected him. He went back inside without knocking, taking the crutches to lay them within her reach. When he saw her face turn up to him, her lips parted as she tried to catch her breath, Shade turned on his feet immediately and got the hell out of there.

Closing the door behind him, he worked to slow down his breathing.

"Fuck." He was in trouble.

Chapter Six

The car door opened, and the sheriff slid into the front seat of his cruiser. He was about to start the car when he glanced into the rearview mirror.

"Shit, Shade, you trying to give me a heart attack?"

"No, I just wanted to give you a heads-up. Checked out Beth's car, only thing wrong was cut brake lines. Looks like someone was trying to hurt, if not kill her."

"You could have told me this in a phone call without scaring me to death," his father snapped.

"I could have, but that wouldn't have been as much fun." Shade gave his father a wry smile before becoming serious. "Call Beth in for a talk. Try to find out who would want to hurt her, and tell her to be careful. Make sure she understands that someone wants her dead."

"I don't want to scare her," his father argued back.

"If she doesn't take you seriously, Lily will be put in danger again. If you tell her the truth, she'll watch Lily closer or keep her away entirely."

"Lily's the one you're concerned about? What's going on with you two?" Concerned eyes met his in the mirror.

"Nothing." Shade looked out the squad car's windows before opening the door to slide out. "Have your deputies do patrols around her house, too."

"Anything else?"

"Tell Rachel I said hi." Shade hadn't been able to visit his stepmother lately, and he was getting tired of her text messages asking him to come by.

Shade quickly disappeared into the trees bordering the sheriff's office. He had one more stop to make before he could return to the clubhouse.

He watched the church until he was sure no one was inside except Lucky. The dumb fuck left the doors open until he went to bed at night, in case a parishioner wanted to stop by for a chat. Shade had warned him that, if his cover was blown, anyone out for revenge could walk right in to take him out, but he wouldn't listen.

Shade didn't knock on Lucky's office door; he simply went in and closed the door behind him.

Lucky wasn't surprised to see him, either.

"Is that all you do, play Peeping Lucky when you're bored?" Shade took a seat in the chair in front of Lucky's desk.

"I don't have a lot to keep me occupied," Lucky replied, turning away from the window. "How's your dad?" The comment let Shade know he had seen him get out of his father's car.

The windows behind his desk faced the sheriff's office, the ones on the left faced office buildings behind the church, and the windows to the right faced the diner. He had the whole town under his surveillance without leaving his fucking office.

"He's fine. I was just telling him someone cut Beth's brake line." That time, it was Shade watching for Lucky's reaction.

"Do you know who did it?"

"No, they didn't leave a calling card behind," Shade answered sharply.

"I gave Razer his chance. Has he used it?" Lucky decided to change topics and acknowledge the elephant in the room. "I've avoided her and her calls, but I'm not waiting forever for Razer to make up his mind."

"He waited for you. When the other men in the unit left your ass in that village, Razer waited. You kept him waiting for three days while you helped that sick family. Razer got you back to the unit safely when no one else gave a fuck. He put his life on the line for you."

"I don't need you to remind me; I remember. What am I supposed to do, just pretend I don't care about her?"

"Let's be real, Lucky; you don't. She's a beautiful woman, and you haven't had any pussy for a couple of years. I told you to pretend to go on a sabbatical for a couple of days and visit the Ohio clubhouse."

"I won't do that."

Shade shook his head. "Then, brother, I suggest you pull out the soap and grab a shower, because Beth isn't going to be the one to help you with your blue balls. Razer will make his move."

Lucky took a seat behind his desk, picking up a pencil to hold in a tight grip. "What did you come here for, Shade?"

"Don't be mad at me, brother. You want a pretty woman to keep your bed warm while you find your pipeline? Find someone else."

"She's perfect," Lucky said unhappily.

"What were you planning on doing with her after the investigation is over?"

"It might have worked out, and we would have had a long and happy marriage."

"Yeah, and pigs might fucking fly. You and Razer are just alike. You both like variety in your beer and pussy."

"I would have stayed faithful," Lucky snapped.

"If you had married her, of that I have no doubt. Once you make a vow, you always keep it. That's why you want to get married, so you don't break your holy vow before you get done with your case. But what about afterward? You keep saying you're leaving the church when it's over. Beth would be left behind along with the church."

"Churches allow divorces now."

"Leaving you a clear conscience to divorce her. Jesus, save me from hypocrites."

"I'm not a hypocrite. Our marriage could have worked out." The pencil broke in his hand.

"I guess we'll never know, will we? She's Razer's." Shade made sure Lucky heard the finality in his voice.

"Why did you come here?" Lucky repeated.

"I need a favor."

Lucky burst out laughing. "You want a favor from me after pissing me off? What do you want?"

"I want you to keep an ear out for anything you hear about Charles."

"Lily's boyfriend?"

"He's not her boyfriend," Shade snapped.

"*Now* who's pissed?"

"Just do it." Shade stood up from the chair.

"Why should I help you out? I don't owe you any favors," Lucky mocked.

"Not yet, but you will. Sooner or later, everyone eventually needs my help. Think of it as insurance for the future."

Lucky studied him steadily. "All right. I'll let you know if I hear anything."

"You do that." Shade walked to the door, opening it.

"When I need a favor."

Shade slammed the door behind him. The pious bastard would make him pay a high price for any information he found out, but Shade believed in preparing for the future. He wanted information to use against Charles if he ever needed it.

Shade had learned to be a good judge of character, and he had a feeling church boy wasn't as squeaky clean as he pretended.

80 03

Shade sat at the bar drinking his whiskey. He moved slightly to his left, trying to discern through the dim lighting exactly how close Lily's sister was letting the brothers get. When she scanned the crowded room to see if anyone was watching, he made sure to drop his gaze to his drink. The last thing he wanted to do was frighten her off. He wanted to draw her closer.

One thing he had learned since becoming interested in Lily was that the sisters were close. Where one went, the other did, too. It was what he was counting on.

His lips quirked when Razer and Beth stood up to leave together, but then Shade's smile disappeared seconds later when he heard shots from outside.

"Outside, now! I heard gunfire!" Shade yelled, running out the back door of the bar, where he had heard the shot coming from the surrounding mountain. When he didn't see or hear anything he ran to the front of the parking lot where he saw Razer standing by Beth's car.

Razer motioned for him to stay with Beth, as he disconnected from a call and took off into the woods with Rider and Knox.

"Stay down!" Shade snapped when he saw Beth's head begin to rise.

His experienced gaze studied the wooded hillside. He wished he had been standing outside when the shot had been fired; the flash would have shown him where the shooter had hidden. From the direction Razer, Rider, and Knox had taken off, the shooter had chosen the best view of Beth's car. She had been the target.

Razer came out of the wooded hillside, looking aggravated, followed by Knox.

"Did you find anything?" Shade asked, knowing the shooter was already gone.

"No. Rider is still looking."

"Who the fuck would be brave enough to piss Viper off by taking a hit out on you?" Knox questioned grimly.

"Don't know." Shade remained silent at Razer's words, not enlightening them that Razer hadn't been the target.

"Cops here." Knox's warning didn't come as a surprise with the blue lights flashing.

Shade stood silently as his father approached while Razer opened the car door for a shaky Beth.

"Who called the police?" Beth asked.

"I did," Razer answered. "Didn't want them thinking we were the ones out here with a gun."

"Beth, Razer." The sheriff nodded toward him and Knox. "What happened?"

"Beth and I were by her car when someone fired a shot at me," Razer began explaining.

"Don't expect it was you they were shooting at," the sheriff corrected with a look toward Beth.

"What do you mean?" Razer looked at the sheriff in confusion.

"I thought I told you to be careful?" The sheriff leveled a look at Beth.

"I was, but how was I supposed to know someone would be crazy enough to shoot at me in front of witnesses?"

"Someone is trying to kill Beth? Why?" Razer asked, clearly confused, before his eyes met Shade's accusingly.

Shade had wanted to see if Beth would tell Razer that Lily's car accident was really an attempt on her life, and his question had just been answered. He had thought she would behave like most women would—freaking out with the news someone was trying to kill her. But she had proven she would keep things hidden from Razer, which meant he couldn't only use him as a source of information on the sisters.

"I'm still investigating," the sheriff responded.

"You're investigating? Since when?"

"Since I discovered her car's brakes had been tampered with. I haven't been able to find any prints or witnesses to the tampering. I have the deputies keeping an eye on her. She was supposed to be home like she usually is when she's not working. Someone either had to follow her here or knew she was going to be here. Did you notice anyone following?"

"No, but I wasn't paying attention," Beth admitted.

"Show me where the shot came from, Razer. Beth, get back in the car."

Beth did as she was told.

Shade leaned against the car door while the other men talked. When they finished, Knox went back inside the bar and Razer came back toward him.

His angry gaze warned he wasn't happy Shade hadn't told him about Beth's brakes being tampered with, since they had been together when Shade had examined the car. Shade met his gaze directly, stepping away from the car as Razer got in beside Beth.

Shade waited until the car had left the parking lot before he headed for the hillside. Only two men in the club were good at tracking. He was one, and Cash was the other. He was hoping he would find something the others had missed.

He really didn't give a shit what Beth had become involved in to make herself an enemy, but it placed Lily in danger, and *that* he wouldn't tolerate.

CHAPTER SEVEN

Shade drove his bike into the club parking lot. Pulling to a stop when he saw the door open at the house, he looked up and saw Beth. Even from where he was sitting, he could see the pain on her face.

Quickly, he took out his cell, punching in Razer's number.

"Beth is leaving the house. From her face, I would say she knows what went down this morning."

"Keep her there. I'll be there in five." The line disconnected.

Shade positioned himself in front of Beth's car door.

"Hi, Beth."

"Shade." Beth paused, probably because Shade wasn't budging from her car door. "Excuse me, Shade. I would like to get in my car."

Shade remained where he was.

"Oh, going somewhere?" Shade knew it was a dumbass question, but he was trying to buy Razer time to get there.

"Yes. Do you mind?" She tried to maneuver around him, but he remained still.

"Actually, I do. Razer will be here in a minute. He wants you to wait for him."

"But I don't want to wait for Razer," Beth argued.

"Take that up with him." He shrugged.

"To do that, I would have to be here, which I don't want to be. Now, would you please move out of my way?"

"Too late." Shade gave a nod toward Razer as he blocked Beth's car with his bike. He then backed off, going up the steps to the clubhouse, letting the two fight it out.

When he went inside the door, the women were standing at the window, watching the show.

Natasha turned her head when he entered. "She's pissed off at me, isn't she?"

Shade didn't know how to answer; it was something Razer and Beth would have had to deal with sooner or later.

Seeing the hurt in her eyes, Shade told the woman, "I'd say she's more pissed at Razer right now. Does it really matter, though? I thought I told you to keep becoming a member on the down-low after Viper left this morning?"

"You did," Natasha said miserably. "But she saw the bandage covering my tattoo."

Shade's face hardened. "Go downstairs to my room. I'll be down in a minute," he ordered the shivering woman, seeing more desire than fear in her face.

Natasha took off running toward the kitchen.

"You really going to punish her for an accident?" Evie asked.

"No, but I plan on taking her mind off whether or not Beth is mad at her."

The door opened, and the amused group watched as Razer packed Beth upstairs. A minute later, his bedroom door slammed shut.

"I accidently bumped Natasha. That's how Beth saw the tattoo," Ember confessed with a grin.

Shade's cold blue gaze went to Ember. "Then I guess you get to share her punishment."

80 C3

Shade felt like shit warmed over when he walked through the back door into the kitchen after cleaning the remains of the party from the backyard. He had been up all night fucking. He'd pulled clean up duty as punishment for not telling Razer about Beth's brakes.

Determined nothing was going to stop him from going to sleep, he paused when he found Beth and Razer in the kitchen. Deciding to let his rolling stomach settle down before going to bed, he sat down next to Razer and swiped the coffee he had been about to drink.

"Hey, Shade, where were you last night?" Beth asked.

Shade paused, wincing when Beth laughed at his reaction.

"Yeah, Shade, where were you last night?" Razer joked as Beth set down a new cup of coffee in front of him.

Shade wanted to punch Razer in the face for aggravating him. "I was visiting a sick friend," he said with a straight face.

"That was kind of you. Do they need any help? I could go down before we go for a ride," Beth offered.

"No, thanks," Shade managed to get out.

The innocent woman would run screaming from the house if she saw the sick friend of his still tied to his bed downstairs. He planned to untie her and send her away before going to sleep.

"Are you all right? You sound as if you're coming down with something. Is your friend contagious?"

"No. If I need any help, I'll ask Evie. They know each other very well."

"You do that. Evie will stay on top of the situation."

"Yes, she will," Razer heartily agreed.

Shade's shoulders slumped. He wanted to pound Razer into the ground because he liked to brag that Evie's favorite position when she fucked him was being on top.

"Why are you both up so early?" Shade questioned while wanting his sunglasses to dim Beth's blinding smile.

"Razer is taking me for a ride this morning."

Shade stared down at the plate of food Beth set in front of him.

"I thought you might be hungry."

Shade almost lost the contents of his stomach at the sight. He started to slide the food away yet stopped when he saw her disappointed expression. Instead, he picked up the fork, gingerly taking a bite.

Seeing Razer in his riding clothes, he had been curious as to where they were going, but by that point he was wishing his boots had kept on walking.

"Where to?"

"If it's okay with Razer, I thought we could ride to see my sister."

"Cool with me," Razer said as Shade almost vomited up the bite he had taken. Razer saved him the humiliation when he slid the plate toward him and began eating Shade's food.

"Mind if I ride along?" Shade asked, trying to keep the small bite of egg he had forced down to stay in his heaving stomach.

"I don't mind, but..." Beth frowned, trailing off.

"What?" Shade asked.

"Don't be surprised if my sister is a little nervous around you."

Shade's lips tightened. Had Lily told Beth she didn't like him after he had carried her into the house?

"Any reason why?" Shade probed, his stomach twisting tight.

Beth's face went blank. "Probably the whole biker aura."

He relaxed. His appearance intimidated a lot of people; as a result, it wouldn't surprise him if a girl as young and innocent as Lily was frightened of him merely from seeing his tattoos.

"Finish eating, Beth, so we can get on the road. Lily will be fine. She needs to get used to the biker aura. The sooner, the better."

Amen to that, Shade thought to himself.

Shade finished his coffee then got up. "I'll meet you at the bikes. I need to get my sunglasses from my room."

Razer gave him a mocking look as he went downstairs to get his sunglasses and untie Bliss who pouted at him when he did and tried to tug him down to her.

Shade pried her hands loose. "Let go. I'm going for a ride with Razer."

"Can I go?"

Shade picked up his sunglasses and wallet from his nightstand. "No."

He left without giving her any further explanation. All the women knew their place with him—it was in his bed, not out of it.

Once outside, Shade climbed on his bike and started the motor. He was bat-shit crazy to be going out as tired as he was, but the opportunity to see Lily up close was too good to pass up.

Within a few miles, the sleep fog disappeared with the wind hitting him in his face.

As soon as they rode past the city limits, Shade heard Razer's yell. "Wide fucking open, brother."

Shade increased his speed, riding beside Razer's bike on the narrow, two-lane road. A little ways later, Razer motioned down at his tank as they neared a gas station.

Shade got off his bike to pump the gas.

"I need to go to the restroom," he heard Beth say; however, Shade wasn't taking his eyes off the bikers pulling into the station as they parked to the side of the building, wearing their colors.

"Fuck," Razer grunted when the women got off the bikes and followed Beth into the store.

"Be prepared," Shade warned as the over-bloated bikers managed to get off their bikes and then came toward them.

"This is the Destructors' territory. Why are you wearing your colors through our town?" one dumbass said who Shade thought actually believed he was Dwayne 'The Rock' Johnson.

"We're just passing through. We're not looking for a challenge." Razer tried to prevent the fight he could see brewing. Shade could have told him it was a wasted effort, though.

"Then take off your colors until you're out of our territory."

"That's not going to happen," Shade said, taking the nozzle out of his gas tank.

"It is, mother fucker, or we'll take them. It's your choice."

"The choice is yours. Go back to your bikes and wait for your bitches, or I'll shove my boot up your ass," Shade warned.

"Fuck you."

Three of the five men took him on while two went for Razer. Shade wondered why the larger numbers always went for him when Razer was the bigger of the two of them.

Cars in the lot started peeling out when they saw the fight break out. Shade felt his lip sting as one of the bikers managed to slam a fist into his face while he was taking down the fat-ass Dwayne.

Pinning the dumbass down with his boot on his throat, Shade swung his fist at another one, knocking him back long enough to grab the third one by his neck, twisting him until his back was to Shade's front. He wrapped his arm around the biker's throat then twisted his neck until he cried out in fear.

"Tell them to back off, or I'll break his fucking neck."

"Ace?" the one he was holding whined down at the one he had pinned to the dirty concrete.

Shade lifted his foot just enough to let him gasp out the order. "Back off!"

The bikers all pulled back except the two Shade had in control.

"Razer?" Shade didn't take his eyes away from them as Razer moved to where he could see them.

Pulling his gun out of his saddlebag, Razer motioned for the men to leave. Then Shade threw the one he was holding away while lifting his boot. The fake Dwayne shakily gained his feet, holding his throat.

"You going to leave us alone, or do I need to finish things?" Shade moved his hand to his side, slightly lifting the side of his vest enough to show the butt of his pistol.

"Like you said, we don't want any trouble." Ace backed away, leading his men back to their bikes.

After Shade climbed back on his bike as Razer put his weapon inside his saddle bag, the bikers avoided glancing in their direction when the women came out together.

Razer and Shade started their bikes as soon as Beth planted her ass on Razer's. Thankfully, the rest of the trip was uneventful.

Shade memorized the small campus as they rode through it to Lily's dorm, stopping his bike next to Razer's as Beth went inside to get her sister.

When the women walked outside hand in hand, Shade could only stare. He was just as awestruck by Lily's beauty as he had been the first time he had seen her. The difference between the two was stark. One sister was so light and golden, her smile as bright as the sun, her loving nature obvious as she held her sister's nervous hand. The other, a dark enigma who only let her guard down when she looked at her sister.

The male students walking by stopped, appreciating the beauty walking among them. The female students, on the other hand, were not as appreciative.

"Bet you a six pack those bitches hate her guts," Shade muttered.

Shade let his gaze catch several of the men and women and they all soon hurried on their way, smart enough to know they were out of their league.

Beth smiled at Razer and Shade.

"Lily, you remember Razer and Shade."

"Hello."

"I told Lily we could go eat lunch. Maybe a little shopping if it won't put you guys out."

"Not at all. You girls climb on the bikes," Razer answered.

Beth immediately went to Razer's bike and climbed on, but Lily stayed frozen. Shade wasn't going to put up with it. He kept his focus on Lily, ignoring Beth trying to get off the bike to help her and Razer telling her to stay put.

"Come here, Lily," Shade ordered, easily recognizing the wounded look in her eyes as Lily's body went taut and she threw a wild look at her sister. His stomach clenched in fury. He had seen the same look before after Evie had first been attacked.

Before Beth could do anything, Shade threw his extra helmet into Lily's grasp. The only way to get her on his bike was to distract her from her fear.

"Get on the bike. I'm hungry. Move that sweet ass, or I'll put you on the bike myself."

Lily hesitantly followed his order, getting on the bike, putting on the helmet as Shade started it up, and then they pulled out with a roar of motors.

The restaurant they chose was small with a family atmosphere. They sat talking after they had eaten until the waitress started throwing them dirty looks. Afterwards, they drove to the small strip mall where the sisters wandered around arm in arm, window-shopping and occasionally going inside one of the small stores. Razer and Shade sat on their bikes, keeping a close eye on the women.

They came out of one shop with several bags. Shade noticed Lily's laughter die when she saw him, not paying attention to Beth's frown.

"What wrong?" Razer asked.

"How are we going to get the bags to campus?" Beth asked.

As Razer and Shade split the load between them, stashing the bags of clothes into their saddlebags, one bag dropped and a waterfall of colorful underwear fell to the pavement.

"Oh." Lily immediately bent, hastily putting the clothes back inside the bag.

One bright red pair fell by Shade's boot, and before Lily could pick it up he had the silky material in his hands, his dick hardening behind his zipper when he felt the soft material, imagining the panties covering her pussy.

With a face as red as the underwear she had just purchased, Lily could only mutter her response. "Thanks."

"No problem." Shade's response was just as strangled as he regained control over his body. As a Dom, he always had control of his dick. He couldn't remember the last time he'd had an erection, which was beyond his ability to control.

Shade had to grit his teeth all the way back to the campus. Her arms circling his waist and her breasts pressed against his back made him want to keep riding when Razer pulled up in front of Lily's dorm room. Shade wanted to grab her hands as they fell away from his waist, feeling as if the sun had moved behind a cloud.

Shade pulled out Lily's bags as the sisters said their goodbyes.

He kept his face impassive when he heard her soft voice addressing him.

"Thank you for bringing Beth. Goodbye."

Shade's heart sank further with every step she took away from him.

"Brother, she's too young."

Shade turned his mirrored gaze to Razer. "You think I don't know that? It's the only reason I'm letting her go back inside," Shade admitted. Loyalty ran deep with Shade; he wasn't going to lie to another brother. "I can wait."

"You sure?" Razer's doubt-filled voice questioned.

"I'm sure. I won't touch her until she's twenty-one," Shade promised, seeing the dubious look didn't disappear from Razer's face. "Have I ever gone back on my word?"

"No, but I've never seen you look at a woman the way you do Lily."

"I can wait," Shade repeated his words. "But when she turns twenty-one, despite whatever is going on with you and Beth in the future, I expect you to keep out of my business with Lily."

Razer's hands went up in surrender. "I wouldn't think of interfering. Besides, I won't even be seeing Beth then. That's years away."

Shade didn't reply. His intuition told him the blond had Razer by the balls, but if Razer didn't realize he was in ass-deep with Beth, Shade wasn't going to be the one to tell him. He didn't stick his nose in other brothers' business, and he didn't want them in his.

Shade was going to miss sharing a woman with Razer, but he saw the advantage of Razer forming a deeper relationship with Beth.

Shade wouldn't have to lure Lily into the club. Beth would.

CHAPTER EIGHT

Shade was woken up by a rough hand shaking his shoulder.

"Beth's disappeared." Shade was instantly awake at Knox's words.

He slid from his bed, taking his jeans off the chair and pulling them on before tugging on his boots. His hand reached for his shirt as Knox strode from the room, and then Shade pulled it on over sore muscles as he followed him up the steps. It had been a while since he had fucked so many women in one night, and his body was feeling the after-effects.

"Who saw her last?" Shade questioned, coming to a stop in the kitchen where all the members were gathered.

"I did," a pale-faced Razer told him, running a hand through his long hair. "I packed a couple of boxes to my room for her. She said she was going to organize them for Mrs. Langley. I went for a run and when I came back, I went out back to get the work schedule before going to my room to take a shower. She was gone."

Shade studied the occupants of the room. "Anyone else missing?"

The members stared at each other, trying to figure out who wasn't there.

"Where's Sam?" Shade asked sharply, knowing Knox had been with her until late in the night.

"I don't know." Knox frowned. "I haven't seen her since breakfast."

"Find her," Shade ordered. "Evie, call the sheriff."

They were about to search through the house when Razer's cell phone rang. Shade froze at Razer's response to whatever was said to him.

"We'll be there as fast as we can. Wait for us." He disconnected the call.

"Viper saw Sam force Beth inside a house he was watching with Bedford in it. Sam had a gun on her," Razer warned as they ran from the house to their bikes.

Razer took the lead with a trail of bikers following.

As they passed the sheriff's office, he saw his father running to his patrol car. They rode by in a burst of speed Shade knew it would take him valuable time to catch up.

He nearly lost control of his bike when he turned down an unpaved driveway. The brothers parked their bikes at the end of it, taking off at a dead run. Then they saw Viper and Cash giving the signal to be silent and the brothers lined up beside the house, waiting for Viper's orders.

Once Viper pointed at him, Razer, and Cash, they moved stealthily to the back of the house, going up a short flight of steps. Viper reached for the doorknob yet paused when the loud voices could be heard clearly from the outside.

"I didn't have time. The box was closed when I went in the room. How was I supposed to know she was smart enough to take the papers out?"

Shade twisted his body so he could look through the dirty window. It looked like the box in question was sitting on a table.

"You check!" Vincent Bedford screamed at his daughter.

"I can go back and get the papers." Sam turned to Beth and smacked her across the face. "What did you do with them?"

Shade watched as Beth touched her stinging cheek, refusing to answer. He was surprised she was strong enough not to give in to their demands.

"I will shoot your kneecap. I can look if I have to, but it will be quicker and less painful for you if you tell me where they are," Bedford threatened.

"I put them in the closet." Shade could tell Beth was lying, and they knew it, too.

"She's lying."

"No shit," Sam snapped back at her father.

Furiously, she hit Beth again with the gun in her hand and Beth fell, barely managing to catch herself by grasping the end of the table. When her hand cupped her cheek, Shade saw blood on it, and so did Razer. Cash and Shade had to hold him back from storming inside the house. They needed to know what Bedford wanted from Beth. If they stopped it too soon and he was arrested, he would lawyer up. Then they might never have the answers they needed.

"Now, where are the fucking papers? This is the last time I am going to ask before I leave. If I search your room and someone comes in, I will shoot. Do you want to be responsible for someone being hurt?" Sam screamed at a dazed Beth.

A rough hand in Beth's hair jerked her toward Vincent Bedford. "Tell me where you put the papers. I will put a bullet through your brain if you don't." Bedford placed the barrel of the gun he was holding against her temple.

"I put them in a brown shoe box in the closet." Shade had to admire her bravery when she lied again.

Bedford slammed the gun into her head, and that was when Viper used his booted foot to kick in the door as Bedford threw Beth to the kitchen floor.

Shade saw his father coming around the corner of the house as Viper, Razer, and Cash went inside.

"Back off; let them handle it." Shade placed a hand on his father, preventing him from interfering with what was happening.

His father nodded, and then both of them turned to watch the fight taking place.

While Cash restrained Samantha, who fought like a wildcat trying to get away from him, Viper pulled two knives, one in each hand, and started cutting Bedford to shreds. The older man was covered in blood and trying to defend himself against a man whose skill with those knives was unmatched.

When he turned to flee, Viper kicked him in the back, forcing him to fall forward onto the floor. The man attempted to crawl away from the revenge-driven biker, but Viper stepped on his hand, stopping his forward momentum.

Razer was bent over Beth as she attempted to stop Viper.

"Loker, stop."

Viper ignored her, bringing his boot back, about to plant it in the screaming Bedford's face.

"Please, Loker, stop. I have all the proof you need to convict him back at the clubhouse."

That time, Viper stopped and looked at her.

"Cover him," Razer said to Shade.

Shade lifted his gun, pointing it at Bedford's face, wanting to pull the trigger as Razer tried to comfort Beth.

"How did you find me?"

"Loker was watching Bedford, and when he saw Sam come in with you, he called us."

It was up to Viper when he would drop his alternate identity. Until then, they would keep his secret.

"I had to. He threatened to kill my baby. He gave me no choice." Sam hung pitifully in Cash's arms, all the fight drained out of her. "He paid someone to take my baby. I don't even know if it was a boy or girl. He took the baby while I was unconscious after the delivery. He won't tell me where my child is or even with whom." The whole room went quiet, listening to Sam's heart-rending cries. "It was Gavin's child."

"You lying bitch!" Viper yelled. He went to Sam, his hands circling her throat. "Lie again, and I'll kill you."

"I'm not lying. I swear."

The sound of the sirens came from outside.

"Loker, let me deal with her. The deputies are here, and I'll find out the truth."

Viper thrust Sam away from him and into the sheriff's custody.

"You better, or I swear I will tear this mother-fucking town apart until I find the answers I want."

CHAPTER NINE

Shade listened to Razer tell Beth it was over in less than gentle terms while he strummed his fingers on the bank statements Razer had found in his nightstand.

When Sam had told them what Bedford was searching for, she had cut herself a sweet deal for the information, leaving her father to fend for himself.

Razer walked into the room with Bliss in his arms, dropping her onto the bed.

"That seemed unnecessarily harsh. Did you really have to humiliate Beth in front of the whole club?" Shade set aside the documents.

Razer shut the bedroom door. "I had to make it seem like I was finished with her until we find out who Bedford's accomplice is. Your dad get any more information out of Sam?"

Shade shook his head. "He said he would call."

He swiveled his chair and saw Bliss strumming her fingers over her clit to ease the fire Razer had started.

"You going to take care of that?" Shade nodded toward Bliss.

"No," Razer said sharply before opening the bedroom door and leaving.

"You like having Razer's fingers on your pussy?"

Bliss moaned, "Yes."

"Spread your thighs wider. If you're going to play with yourself, do it right."

Bliss followed his commands, showing Shade a view of her glistening pussy.

Standing up, he unzipped his jeans before taking a condom out of his back pocket.

"Why should I put out a fire another man started?" Shade questioned. This was what he loved about sex the most—tormenting the women with desire until he decided to give them the relief they needed.

"Please, Shade. I'll do anything you want."

"You're a naughty bitch, aren't you?"

Bliss frantically nodded against the bed.

"Suck on your fingers," Shade ordered, shifting her body until her thighs hung over the side of the bed. Taking her hips in his hands, he lifted her until his cock was nestled against her opening. He watched as she sucked her wet fingers into her mouth, her tiny tongue laving her juices off her fingers. "What do you want?"

"Your cock," Bliss begged.

Shade nudged his cock slowly into her greedy cunt, feeling her silky flesh glide over his hard dick. He loved the feeling of first entering a tight pussy, gradually loosening it un-til they could take the force of his thrusts.

Bliss tried to arch her hips to make him go faster and Shade pulled his cock away, stepping back from the bed.

"Shade," Bliss whimpered in frustration.

"Did I tell you to move?"

"No."

"You know that's against the rules?"

"Yes," Bliss admitted.

"Then I guess you don't want my dick, do you?"

"I want it so…bad."

"Do bad girls get my cock in their pussies?"

"No," Bliss's tear-filled voice answered as she sat up on the side of the bed.

"No, they don't, do they? Not until they're punished for being bad. Go down-stairs and get my paddle."

"Okay." Bliss stood up, going to the doorway.

Shade turned the clock on the desk to face her then used his finger to tap it. "Every minute it takes you will be one stroke."

Shade easily read the heightened desire in Bliss's expression when she slowed her pace as she walked toward the door. Bliss enjoyed their games as much as he did.

Turning back to the paperwork Bedford had tried to murder Beth over, his eyes nar-rowed over a certain account number. Shade had almost perfect retention—that was how he had proved so successful as a sniper—and he was familiar with the account number.

Picking up his cell phone, he called his father.

"Hello."

Shade didn't take the time to repeat the greeting. "Ask Sam about Memphis. Call me back when she admits he's the accomplice. I'm going to be busy, though, so you may have to let it ring a while."

"You sure it's Memphis?"

The bank account number of the brother who had betrayed them was staring back at him.

"Yeah, I'm sure." He disconnected.

"Did I take a long time?" Bliss came back into the room, setting the paddle down on the desk in front of him.

"You took just long enough," Shade said, picking it up.

CHAPTER TEN

Shade stood hidden in the shadows, waiting as a lone figure came down the staircase. The previous night's party had been a large one with the brothers from Ohio in town, which Viper had sent for. With all The Last Riders in one place, it would provide the perfect opportunity for their betrayer to make a move. The trap had been set, and like the rat he was, he had fallen for it and was scurrying for the bait.

The brothers had bedded down for the night on any available furniture sturdy enough to hold their weight. Several had even thought ahead, bringing a sleeping bag and finding an open piece of floor to crash on.

The figure methodically came down the steps, careful not to make a sound to alert anyone they were all about to be killed in their sleep. Shade, who had a keen sense of sight in the darkness, saw he held something in his hand as he headed for the door.

Shade flipped the switch, the sudden burst of light blinding the brother he was staring at coldly.

Memphis paused for a second, their gazes meeting. Shade let him see the death in his lethal eyes. Startled, Memphis spun around to see Viper, Razer, and Cash standing by the door.

"Hey, man, you're going to wake everyone. Douse the lights." Shade's lips twitched at Memphis's attempt to squash any suspicions.

"Everyone is already awake. What are you doing awake? Last I saw, you were upstairs with Evie." Viper's harsh voice belied his casual stance.

Memphis shrugged. "She's asleep. I thought I'd go for a ride."

"Sounds good; care if we join you?" Viper asked.

"I was wanting some alone time, if you don't mind?" Memphis started to move forward, but the three men blocked his path.

"We do mind."

Memphis turned to leave through the backdoor yet found his way blocked by the members he had thought were sleeping. Outnumbered, he tried to brazen his way out.

"What's up, Viper? Since when does me going for a ride become club business?"

"It becomes our business when you're planning on blowing us to smithereens on your lone ride."

"I don't know what the fuck you're talking about." Memphis's eyes darted back and forth between the brothers, making sure he didn't meet Shade's again. The fucker knew he wouldn't find any sympathy from him.

"Search him, Razer," Viper ordered.

When Razer stepped forward, Memphis bolted, attempting to force his way through the men blocking the door. However, his face was quickly shoved into the wall and his arms held high behind his back. When he tried to fight free, Viper smashed his face into the wall using his hair.

"Stay the fuck still."

Cash searched Memphis clothes. "Well, look what I found." He pulled the detonator out of Memphis's pocket, lifting it where all the members could see.

Razer flung Memphis across the room, and Knox grabbed him then threw him down on the couch.

"It took three fucking years of my life to figure out who betrayed my brother. You sorry piece of shit, you killed him for fifty grand. I would have given you the fucking money if you had asked, you motherfucker."

"I would have done it for free." Memphis shrugged, showing his obvious death wish.

Viper lunged at him, but Razer and Cash held him back while Shade merely shook his head at the prick's stupidity.

"He's just trying to piss you off so you'll kill him quick. Find out your answers first," Razer reasoned.

"First, answer my question then I'll answer yours. How did you finally figure it out?" Memphis questioned, now trying to delay the inevitable.

"Sam. We promised protection and no jail time if she told us who her father paid to kill my brother," Viper answered.

"She didn't know. Bedford swore he wouldn't tell. He was scared enough of me to keep his mouth shut."

"Sam followed her father to one of your meetings. She recognized you when she started hanging around the house."

"Damn slut," Memphis muttered.

"I answered your question, now answer ours," Viper demanded.

"I killed Gavin because he was a pain in my ass. I was dealing drugs on the side, and he was going to tell you at the next meeting. I would have been out. I couldn't have that going down. I had a plan and was going to stick to it no matter what happened. Him being dead distracted everyone enough that I was able to move a lot of the patents to my name, and with the money I made off them, as well as the insurance policy on everyone, I would have been a rich man."

The insurance policy had been taken out between the eight friends when they had started their survival business. That way, if anyone was killed, the business would not be affected because the insurance was made out to the surviving group members. The bomb he had planted and planned to detonate would have killed a large number of them, including those carrying the larger chunks of stock.

"What did you do with my brother's body?" Viper braced himself for Memphis's answer.

"I buried him behind the Road Demon's clubhouse."

Viper struck out at Memphis, no one trying to stop him that time. He pulled back and landed a final jab to his jaw which sent Memphis down to the floor, groaning and curling into a ball.

"Tomorrow, I'll ask for a meet with the Road Demons to try and get Gavin's body. If it's not there—"

"I'm telling the truth. What are you going to do with me?"

"Keep you alive long enough to bring Gavin home. After that, the club will deal with you one by one."

All the brothers knew what that meant. Each of the original members would stand in a circle with Memphis positioned in the middle. The members would then each have the opportunity to give him a killing blow. It wouldn't matter if he were dead after the one chosen to go first. In that case, because it was Viper's brother, he would be allowed the first strike. After each had their turn, he would be disposed of just as he had with Gavin. The only difference was Gavin would finally be coming home to a proper burial.

"We're going to show you the same mercy that you showed my brother." Viper's promise was deadly accurate.

Shade and Cash took Memphis to the basement and chained him against the wall in Shade's bedroom where they would guard him until they found Gavin.

ᔬ ᔪ

Shade stood in the junk-heaped backyard with its broken-down motorcycles, glad they had waited to kill Memphis. Shade hoped there was a piece of him still alive when it was his turn.

A large black Suburban rolled to a stop and a tall, muscular man climbed out, going to the back and raising the hatch to let a massive German Shepherd jump out.

Shade saw the looks the Road Demon brothers gave each other.

"The dog's being given Gavin's scent. We're not here to get in your business," Shade assured the brothers who were worried about their own dark secrets being exposed.

Their postures relaxed as Cash greeted his friend. The two men shook hands before Colt pointed to the backyard.

As the nose of the dog was rubbed with Gavin's colors, Shade recalled the day all the original Last Riders had gone to the leather shop to pick up their individual vests.

"Seek!" The dog took off, going to several parts of the backyard.

Shade had worked with cadaver dogs before and recognized the signal each time the dog smelled a body, but it didn't bark to show this was the one they wanted. It took twenty minutes for the dog to find Gavin and sit down on top of an old couch cushion.

Viper nodded toward Train and Rider, who moved forward to dig. Even Shade, despite the numerous lives he had taken, felt a momentary twinge when they pulled Gavin from the hole that had been dug.

As Viper walked over to his brother's body, more than one brother had to blink back tears when they heard his words before the medical examiner team came in to transfer the body to the morgue.

"It's time to come home, brother."

CHAPTER ELEVEN

"She still there?" Shade questioned Razer as they sat on their bikes at a red light in town.

The club had already buried Gavin, but The Last Riders had gone to Ohio to declare Gavin dead and take care of the legal bullshit needed with his part in their survival business.

Finally, they were back, and Razer had called Lucky to ask him to get Beth to the diner, figuring it would be easier to talk to her without her being able to slam a door in his face.

It was just getting dark when they rode their bikes into the diner's lot. They watched as Beth didn't hesitate in her footsteps as she crossed the parking lot, walking with her head down until she almost ran into Razer's bike.

Shade blocked her retreat, pulling in behind her and pinning her between the two bikes. Shade and Evie each gave her a nod as he and Razer cut their motors. The sudden silence was a relief.

"Beth."

"Razer."

"How have you been?"

"Good."

"You don't look so good."

Beth shrugged. "Appearances can be deceiving."

Razer nodded while Beth stared at her car parked behind him. When he cleared his throat, Beth's head snapped back to him.

"Yes, they can. That's why I want to talk to you. Can we go somewhere to talk? I would like to explain some things to you."

"No explanations are necessary. You got your message across clearly the last time I saw you." Beth took a step to the right, trying to get to her car.

"Beth, let him explain. I want to tell you how sorry I am for the way things went down. If you would listen..." Evie trailed off as Beth stopped and turned, meeting her eyes. Shade felt Evie flinch at his back.

"I don't need explanations, Evie. I provided employment for you until the factory opened. It's not your fault that I misinterpreted it and thought we had become friends."

"We were friends…No, we *are* friends. Beth, listen to me—"

With a sad smile, Beth shook her head as she spoke over Evie once again. "No, Evie, you are no friend of mine. You left me in that hospital to wake up alone, scared and not knowing what had happened. I kept thinking you would come by and bring me a few magazines or a couple of things I could have used. You never did, though. Then, when I came to the club and was humiliated in front of everyone by a man I cared about, did my friend stand by me? No. She ignored me and cut me deep by quitting when I needed her the most. Did my friend come by and see me to let me cry on her shoulder? No, you didn't. A friend would have been there for me. I would have been there for you." When Beth finished in a soft voice, Shade squeezed Evie's hand, knowing she would be hurt by Beth's justified outburst.

Again, Beth took a step forward to leave.

"Beth, wait…I can explain." Razer's hand snapped out and caught her arm, keeping her from leaving.

"Razer, explanations are not necessary for the simple reason that they won't make a difference to how I feel about you. You were wrong that night at your house. I wasn't beginning to care for you; I had fallen in love with you. I knew you didn't return my feelings, and I let it happen anyway. I've had a few bad weeks since then, but I am getting over you. If the explanations you want to give me end with you wanting to be friends, that won't work for me. It would be too painful for me to see you with other women and not touch you myself." Razer went to speak, but Beth raised a hand to stop him. "Let me finish. On the other hand, if you are hoping these explanations lead to us being back together again, that no longer is an option. You are incapable of giving me the relationship I need to be happy, which involves trust, fidelity, and love. Even if you swore to do all three, I would never, ever believe in you again."

That time, when Beth took a step forward, Razer's hand dropped to his side. Both Shade and Razer's bikes sat immobile as Beth carefully maneuvered her SUV around them, pulling out onto the road without a look back.

෫ ෬

"We fucked up bad." Evie's head fell forward onto Shade's back.

"More like crashed and burned," Lucky said, stepping out from behind a parked van.

"Back off, Dean. You had no business eavesdropping."

"I had every right. I handed you that girl on a silver platter, and what did you do? You screwed her over so badly that now, not only don't *I* have her, but *you* don't have her, and it's not looking like you ever will," Lucky ruthlessly threw Beth's words back in Razer's face.

"She'll come around; she'll forgive me. The girl is incapable of holding a grudge."

"Did you even make an attempt to get to know her?" Lucky asked in disbelief.

"What does that mean?"

"It means, she is not going to forgive you. You hurt her too badly. She won't put herself back in that vulnerable position again, with either of you."

"Come with me." Lucky left the parking lot without another word, walking toward the church across the street.

"You two go on back to the club."

Shade nodded as Razer rode across the street to the church.

Shade dropped Evie off at the clubhouse before going inside the factory to take care of the orders which had come in since they had been gone, finding Crash had done a good job keeping everything up to date.

Shade finished those which hadn't been processed then went to the clubhouse. He grabbed himself a beer before going quietly into the kitchen, coming to an abrupt stop when he saw Razer already back and sitting on the couch watching the TV screen. He had hooked a VCR to it and had a box of tapes sitting on the coffee table in front of him.

Shade's hand froze as he was about to lift the beer to his mouth, recognizing a much younger Beth on the screen. A tall, thin man with wire-framed glasses stood behind the pulpit.

The preacher gave a blistering sermon that would have put the fear of God into any grown man, much less the tiny girl sitting on the front pew. It was a thing to shrink a grown man's balls with Hell and damnation used as threats. Beth was sitting quietly and still by a rigidly stern woman who amened constantly in agreement as the long-winded sermon droned on.

Razer fast-forwarded through much of the tape, stopping it when a movement from Beth's father motioned Beth to stand up in front of the large congregation.

"Now, we come to the part of service where I give everyone a chance to repent their sins and take their punishment to be forgiven of them. My daughter will begin. Beth?"

Beth stared straight ahead as she stood before the congregation.

"I am pleading for forgiveness from my Lord to forgive my tardiness to dinner twice this week. My mother works hard to make the meal, and my father works hard to provide it. I should be more appreciative and show my respect by being on time."

"Beth, do you repent your sins?"

"Yes, Pastor Saul."

"Then kneel before your peers and take your punishment."

Beth got to her knees as her father stood behind her, carrying a leather strap.

"REPENT!" he screamed and the strap struck out, hitting the girl on her back.

The church members yelled back, "Repent!"

Three more times, the leather struck her on her back before her father allowed her to resume her seat.

Horrified, Shade set his beer down on the counter, moving closer to the couch Razer was sitting on. When Evie entered the room, Shade motioned for her to be quiet as she came to stand next to him.

Clumsily, Razer removed the tape and put in another one. He fast-forwarded through six more tapes, each with Beth getting strapped for little or no reason. Not a single member among the so-called Christians spoke against his treatment of a young child, nor did they volunteer to repent their own sins. Each merely sat like fucking sheep as Beth took beating after beating. The room began getting crowded as the brothers came to get dinner and ended up becoming engrossed in the tapes being played.

Cash was one of the last ones to come in, standing shakily beside him as one particular tape began. It was different from the rest; instead, it seemed as if they were in a smaller church, and the parishioners were standing around chanting.

Shade's brows rose as the church members danced in place and chanted in an unrecognizable language.

As a large, bearded man went behind the podium and pulled out a snake, Beth, who had been stepping slowly back and forth between her parents, was pushed forward as the snake was held out. She didn't speak; she simply continued moving, holding out her frail, little arms. The snake slid up her forearm as a no more than nine-year-old Beth whimpered, a look of pain across her face as the snake reared back and struck her in the upper arm.

"Praise God." The man pried the snake's teeth from her arm and then she fell to the floor, crying as the parishioners circled around the whimpering child. Suddenly, the tape ended, as if the machine taping it had fallen to the floor.

"I remember that day. I tried to get to her and knocked the camera over," Cash explained.

Shade and Cash had shared several horrific missions together in the service, but Shade had not once seen the tortured expression in Cash's eyes that he saw at that point.

"What the hell was that?" Jewell said in shock.

"Snake handling. Her bastard of a father would take us into the mountains once a year to a sister church. Every year, I watched the same scene. Didn't Beth tell you when you saw the scars on her arms?" Cash asked Razer.

"No."

"Did they take her to the hospital? Why didn't someone call social services?" Bliss questioned.

"No, they never took her to the hospital. The proof of faith is when she doesn't die. So no medical treatment, no one reported it to social services, and the sheriff back then was a member of the congregation who couldn't have given a shit. The congregation prayed over her all night while her little body was wracked with pain till morning. It was the last time I ever prayed." Cash's hands clenched the back of the couch.

"The next year they went, they didn't make her do it again, did they?" Viper asked.

"As far as I know, from what my grandmother told me, yes. A couple of times, it was a close call, but she survived. The members took it as a sign of their faith, but I would say it was more likely that she built up an immunity to the venom. I wouldn't know; I left town the next day and enlisted in the Navy. I never went back to that church."

Razer went to the next box and picked a tape from a couple years later. Beth was older in that tape, looking age eleven or so. It was more of the same, except the beatings became worse. She continuously begged for God's forgiveness, never her crazy-assed father, no matter how many times the leather struck her back.

The next tape had Lily in it. Shade sucked in a deep breath at the first appearance of the small, underweight girl with those haunted shadows already in her eyes. Shade wanted to kill someone for whatever had made Lily the way she was before she had been adopted.

In the video, she was brought forward as they explained the charity they'd had to give to a child in desperate need of a home. No mention was made of where she had come from, though.

Several tapes were gone through before the minister ordered Lily forward for a punishment. When she would have stepped forward, Beth pulled her back, explaining it was her fault Lily had committed what had been deemed as a sin. The pastor, thwarted in his desire for new prey, took it out on a blank-faced Beth. This continued on until a tape where the pastor once again ordered Lily forward and Beth was denied when she would have stepped forward.

"You will sit, Beth. Lily will take the punishment for letting you influence her, and then I will punish you for your part in it. It is time that Lily learned not to let you force her from the path of righteousness."

Shade easily recognized the signs that Lily had been beaten on a regular basis. She didn't look frightened. Instead, a look of peace came over her as she clasped her hands in front of her. Her silky, black hair fell forward as she repented in a strong voice. When the leather struck her, she didn't flinch or move and her voice remained the same monotone as before.

"I am going to throw up," Natasha warned.

Fury exploded inside of Shade. He walked forward and jerked the tape out of the VCR, throwing it at the television, which burst with sparks flying. However, not one member chastised him for doing so.

Shade had seen a lot of sick shit in his life, but seeing Lily in a submissive pose she had obviously done many times in her young life was possibly the sickest. It churned his gut that such a beautiful young girl hadn't been protected by those who were supposed to keep her safe.

"Did that shit continue until the bastard got killed?" Razer asked Cash.

"No, by then the new sheriff was in town, and from what my grandmother wrote me, he had heard of what was going on, but no one would talk. Beth and Lily were home-schooled, so he couldn't get the girls alone to talk to them, either. It wasn't long after he was appointed that Beth disappeared for an afternoon. When her parents searched for her, they found her at the restaurant across from the sheriff's office where she was sitting, eating a sundae. Granny wrote she was frightened for Beth that following Sunday until the new sheriff showed up before church and had a talk with Pastor Saul. After that, the sheriff was there every church meeting, rain or shine. The girls both entered school the next school year, too."

"The sheriff probably threatened them with social services," Bliss guessed.

Cash gave an evil grin. "Bet he threatened to kill him if he touched them again."

"She won't forgive me, not after what I did. I humiliated her in front of everyone, just like he did. She was hurt, and I ignored her just as those people stood around and didn't do a damn thing." His hands clenched into fists. "She begged me to talk to her in private..." Razer didn't continue.

The women's smothered sobs could be heard in the silence of the room while the men moved to stand by their brother who sat staring sightlessly at a broken television.

Shade witnessed Razer's laid-back attitude disappear and a new man appear, one who realized he might have lost the woman he loved for good. The Last Riders gathered closer to Razer's side, doing what they always did when one of their own needed support—come up with a plan of action to save his ass.

The young Beth they had seen treated cruelly on the television screen had needed a hero to protect her when she was younger, and no one had stepped forward. The woman she had become was one who would have your back for the rest of her life.

CHAPTER TWELVE

"Going somewhere?" Shade asked Razer when he saw him grab his leather jacket.

"Going to The Pink Slipper."

"What the fuck for?"

"To get something that belongs to me," he answered grimly, putting on his leather gloves.

The other members stood and started getting ready, as well. They weren't sure exactly what was going on, but they never let a brother go alone into what obviously was going to be some kind of battle. Razer only wore his gloves when he was going to whip some serious ass.

Razer took the lead with thirty club members at his back. When they turned into the Pink Slipper's lot, Shade saw just as many bikes already parked.

Beth was sitting at a large table with four biker chicks sitting close to her while the rest of the table and chairs were filled with angry bikers and others stood blocking the table. Beth couldn't hide her frightened expression as the other women started arguing with the men.

Razer came to a stop at the table as Shade and the rest of the Last Riders followed behind. Shade noticed half of the patrons at the bar started motioning the waitress for their bills; the other half were raking cash out of purses and wallets, throwing it down on the table without waiting for their tickets. Shade couldn't blame them for not wanting to get caught between the two clubs.

Shade gave a mocking smile to the bikers he recognized from the gas station.

"Beth."

Beth's eyes widened. "Razer?"

"Let's go."

"Bitch isn't going nowhere with you or your men. Y'all need to get back on your machines and leave us to our fun," a bitch with her hair teased and crazy eyes answered for Beth.

Shade had always told The Last Riders they were lucky they didn't have any female members who liked to bust their balls. He had a feeling those bitches were about to prove his point.

"Beth, let's go. I'm not telling you again."

Beth's eyes narrowed in anger. "You don't have the right to tell me shit. Crazy Bitch is right; you guys need to leave us alone. We were minding our own business until everyone interfered."

"Minding what was in the pants of those pussies you bitches were dancing with when we showed up is more like it," Ace from the gas station spoke up.

"Yeah, I don't care what you think, Ace. We came to celebrate my shop opening Monday. The same one you, or any of you assholes, didn't want to help paint or do shit to help with. I don't want you guys here tonight; you don't deserve to be part of our party."

"I didn't see that douche bag whose throat you had your tongue down doing any hammering there, either."

"Yeah, well, he was going to do plenty later tonight."

Shade didn't pay any attention to the woman talking, looking for an opportunity to grab Beth and get her out of there before the verbal fight escalated into a physical one. However, the other bikers were standing too close.

"Was he or were they?" He jerked his head toward The Last Riders. "Did you plan on hitting their clubhouse next?" Ace asked in a menacing voice.

Shade could have answered that question for him. Fuck no.

"You kidding me? We were going to fuck around, not betray the club. If we were going to do that, we would have picked one worth the punishment of breaking a rule."

"Did she just put us down?" Knox asked.

Shade wanted to punch the brother for being so slow on the uptake.

"Yes, she did, dumbass," Sex Piston mocked.

Evie, Dawn, Jewell, and Natasha pushed to the front of them, standing by their club members.

"What the fuck are you doing here?" Viper questioned.

"Loker James?" Beth questioned.

Shade thought wryly that the secret was out when he heard a gasp from a nearby table. Everyone turned to see Winter Simmons, who Viper had been pretending to date since he had come to town, staring at Viper in recognition.

"He's Viper," Evie explained.

"Well, that's none of my business, is it?" Beth said, picking up her drink with a trembling hand.

"To answer your question, if Beth was in trouble, we were going to be here to help," Evie answered Viper's question and ignored Beth's.

"Who the fuck are you?" a snide voice asked.

"Evie," she answered in her toughest voice.

"You're the bitch who left Beth high and dry! Damn, girl, you got balls to stand there after you fucked her man then watched her man fuck these other bitches."

The other club was beginning to look at The Last Riders' members with dawning respect.

"How'd you manage that, man? My bitch would cut my balls off in my sleep if I touched another bitch."

Shade didn't doubt the biker's words.

"We did it to protect her. We had a brother who was a crazy fuck, and the only way we could protect her was to put space between us," Razer answered.

"Yeah, was the hand that was playing with that girl's titty imaginary? Any one of these fucks do that to one of my bitches, I'm gonna cut his hand off." The bitch looked mean enough to do it, too.

Evie tried to make up some lost ground. She was losing to the biker bitches, and she was getting more and more pissed off.

"No, it wasn't imaginary. Razer had to prove she meant nothing to him. Memphis had already tried to kill her twice. We had to make him believe he was in the clear after Bedford was arrested, or he would never have made a clear move against us. We had to have proof he betrayed the club. We couldn't take someone outside the club's word as proof without evidence," Evie explained in front of everyone. Talking club business in front of others was breaking a rule, but they owed Beth an explanation, and she hadn't given them the opportunity. Truthfully, no one really blamed her, though.

"So, instead, you betrayed Beth. She's not club, so she didn't matter," the bitch threw the explanation back in Evie's face.

"She matters." That time, it was Razer who spoke.

"Not enough," another bitch gave her unwanted opinion. "But I have a question I need answered." Turning to Beth, she asked, "The one with all the tats, he do anything to hurt you? Because my fingers are dying to see how far down those tats go."

Shade just stood there, ignoring the woman while keeping his expression bland. He didn't want that crazy-looking bitch anywhere near his dick.

He was startled at Beth's defense of him.

"No, he is the best of the bunch. Never saw him laying a hand on the women. Never drunk, didn't see him at the parties. I have no problem with Shade."

Shade's eyes narrowed on Beth when she gave him a saccharine smile. She had told him she would pay him back for stopping her from leaving the house that day. It had taken a while, but she had gotten her revenge.

The Last Riders' mouths dropped open. Even though they knew she was throwing Shade under the bus, they could tell she believed what she had said.

Natasha couldn't prevent the laughter bubbling from her throat, and the other women from the club started laughing, too. "Are you serious? He's the wor—"

"Shut up," Shade said, his tone promising retribution if one woman spoke another word.

"Damn, you had to go and blow it, telling her to shut up. Don't let him talk to you that way, bitch. Still, if you fuck as good as you look, I could always tape your mouth shut." If anyone was going to be taped, it would be her.

Shade was about to break his silence and tell her she couldn't handle the way he liked to fuck. Her ass would be bright red when he finished with her.

"You aren't going to be touching nothing of his, bitch. Get on the back of my bike; we are leaving!" a biker behind Ace yelled.

"I'm not going anywhere with you, Joker. We're going to Beth's house after we get done here. Sex Piston is going to cut her hair."

Shade studied the bitches at the table, easily guessing which one was named Sex Piston.

"No, she's not," Razer and Beth spoke at the same time.

Throwing a dirty look at Razer, she told her friends, "I was going to make an appointment next week, remember?"

"I'm going to save you the trip," Sex Piston said, slamming her drink down on the table, which caused what little was left to slosh over the side of the glass.

"She's going home with me. You're not touching her hair," Razer warned.

"I'm not going home with you," Beth argued.

"Yes, you are," Razer said between gritted teeth.

"No, I am not."

"Beth is not going anywhere with you." The crazy-looking one put her arm across the back of Beth's chair while the rest of the biker bitches also scooted their chairs closer to Beth.

"Back off," Evie cautioned.

"Listen to the bitch," the crazy bitch taunted the men.

"I was talking to you," Evie said, stepping closer to the woman who was practically sitting on Beth's lap.

"Evie." Natasha tried to pull Evie back.

"Who are you?" Sex Piston asked.

"Natasha."

"What kind of name is that?"

"I haven't really been given a nickname yet."

"You the new member Viper fucked a couple of weeks ago, and you let Beth think it was Razer?"

Natasha flushed, letting Evie's arm go. "Viper didn't want anyone to know he was in town."

"Instead, it was easier to stick a knife in Beth's back. I can think of several names for you, but first there is something I wanna know, been wondering ever since they walked in the door. He fuck as good as he looks?" She pointed to Viper.

Natasha laughed. "Better."

"Damn."

"It don't matter how he fucks; none of you bitches are going to find out. Hell, he's keeping his own clubhouse of pussy warm; he's not getting mine. Now get on the fucking bikes!" Ace's face turned a mottled red.

It was The Last Riders looking at the other club in sympathy as the women just sat at the table, ignoring the men, which finally pushed Ace over the edge.

"That's it." Ace moved forward to grab Sex Piston, who threw her glass at him. When he dodged it, he accidently shoved Knox, who shoved back. Taking it as an aggressive move, one of Ace's men punched Knox. From there, the shit hit the fan.

The two clubs began fighting, taking their frustration with the women out on each other. Beth was almost thrown out of her chair when Evie ripped Crazy Bitch's arm off her, and the two women began fighting.

Shade knocked one biker back as he swung at him, seeing Beth jump up when Sex Piston grabbed Natasha by the hair and slammed her face on the table.

"Which of these bitches is Bliss? I'm going to take care of her tonight, too," Shade heard Sex Piston ask.

Shade wondered why they were interested in Bliss.

"Lucky bitch. I'll have to deal with her later, then."

He would have to warn Bliss to stay close to the clubhouse. She would be no match against those thugs disguised as women.

When Ace came at him with a vengeful look, Shade snapped out his boot, kicking him in the balls and bringing the asshole to his knees. Cash was fighting off a couple of bikers, so Shade headed toward him when he saw Viper trying to get Winter and her friends out the door. Shade moved forward to help, leaving Cash to deal on his own. One of the women was almost pushed down by a Destructor, but Shade managed to catch her in time, guiding them to the door.

"Get the fuck out of here," Viper ordered Winter.

"We're trying to."

Viper was on one side of the women while he was on the other. His attention on pushing the other women out the door, Shade didn't have time to react when two of the other bikers he had fought at the gas station came at him. Joker slammed a drink tray into his face.

Shade didn't know which was more aggravating: the Destructors' bitches or the brothers who were trying to beat him to a pulp. As he blocked the doorway, preventing the fight from spilling into the parking lot to give Razer time to leave with Beth, who was thrown over his shoulder, the sound of sirens started coming from the other side of the door.

Shade ducked when a bottle of whiskey came flying toward him, crashing against the door. That pissed him off. Barreling forward, he took down three Destructors, pummeling them and not giving them time to regain their senses with him on top of their prone bodies.

"Ace, get him off me!"

The one who yelled got his fist, and Shade felt the skin on his knuckles split.

"Stop, Shade."

He ignored the hands trying to tear him away. It took two sets for him to realize one was his father.

"Arrest them all." The sheriff glared at Shade as he yelled his command to his deputies.

"You've got to be fucking kidding me!" Shade yelled. "They fucking started it!"

"I Do. Not. Care!" The sheriff turned to grab Ace by the collar who was trying to resist arrest by his deputy.

"Every last one of you are spending the night in jail!" While he handcuffed Ace then threw him through the doorway to his deputies, Shade saw Viper being handcuffed by another officer.

"You're not putting cuffs on me," Shade said between gritted teeth.

The sheriff wasn't in the least fazed by Shade's anger. "Then you better get your ass in the backseat of my squad car."

Shade knew when he was beaten. He couldn't argue with his father in front of the others.

"I'm going."

Razer is going to owe me big-time for this, Shade thought as he strode angrily out of the bar, going to the sheriff's car.

"Slide the fuck over," Shade told Viper who scooted over to let him in. "This was a fucking mistake," he told his president. "We should have waited until they came out and took care of them in the parking lot."

Viper looked as bad as he did. His lip was split, and blood was oozing out of his nose.

"Your nose is broken," Shade said, leaning back carefully against the seat.

"No shit, Sherlock."

⁖ ₳

Shade limped through the club room, following the rest of The Last Riders to the kitchen where the women were already pulling out the contents of the freezer and handing them out for everyone to use.

"Give me the ice," Evie snarled at Natasha, who hastily handed it to her. "Were those bitches even fucking women?" she asked Shade.

"Don't know. Don't want to know."

Evie dumped the ice tray into a bowl, wincing as she climbed onto a stool. Gingerly, she lowered her swollen hands into the ice. Jewell took the remaining ice, Shade didn't object. The women had faced the deadlier adversaries.

Dawn and Ember began trying to clean everyone up, and Viper's harsh obscenities had Shade's brow going up.

"It hurts like a mother fucker. If the sheriff had let me go to the hospital, it would have already been set," Viper excused himself.

"He might have let you go if you hadn't thrown his deputy on the floor when he took off the handcuffs," Shade reminded him, handing him one of the raw steaks he found in the freezer, keeping the other for himself and leaving the frozen vegetables for the rest of the brothers to use as ice packs.

Bliss came into the room with ibuprofen, passing the useless painkillers around. The beer she was handing out with it would do more good.

Beth and Razer opened the kitchen door, coming inside to survey the damage that had been left in their wake. Shade saw the content look on the brother's face and knew they had made up. He grunted at that. *At least one of the brothers will be getting some; the rest of us will be too sore to fuck for a month...make that a week,* Shade thought resentfully.

"I think we better order some pizza," Beth told Razer.

"Did the Destructors look as bad?" Razer asked.

"The men did," Viper said, taking a beer from Bliss.

"The women?" Beth asked hesitantly, twisting her hands together.

"We don't know. They were sitting at the bar drinking when the sheriff and his men arrested us," Shade said, glaring at Beth.

"You were taken to jail?" Razer asked in surprise, staring at Viper.

"We all were. Held us until bond was posted an hour ago. Tried to call you, but you weren't answering," Shade stated through gritted teeth.

"Figured you were kind of busy," Evie said with a hesitant smile.

"Where was Bliss?"

"We didn't call her. Beth's new BFFs were waiting outside the sheriff's office to jump her," Shade said in a voice promising retribution.

"Sheriff thought it would be better for everyone's safety if she stayed here," Viper cut in.

"She could have relayed the message to me."

"They wanted you, too. Those bitches weren't very happy with the way you packed Beth out of The Pink Slipper."

"Why didn't the sheriff just arrest them?"

"He did. He put us in one and the Destructors in the other."

"So who posted bail?"

"An impartial party."

"An impartial party? Who?"

"Pastor Dean. The sheriff figured they wouldn't attack a man of the cloth." Shade took another beer from Bliss with a shaking hand. "The crazy one asked for his number."

"Crazy Bitch?" Beth asked, pleased.

The bottle Shade was lifting to his busted mouth froze. "That her name?"

"Yes." Beth nodded.

"And you made frien—"

Razer cut him off. "Don't go there; you won't like the answer."

Shade took a long drink of his beer before putting the bottle down carefully on the counter with a still shaking hand. All eyes were on him, tensely waiting, except Beth who was handing Train a paper towel to wipe the blood away from his dripping nose.

"I am going to bed."

Beth nodded. "I'm sure you'll feel much better after getting some sleep."

Shade's lips tightened into a thin line. Limping slowly to the doorway, he stopped by Beth, who looked up from holding pressure to Train's nose. Razer, Cash, and Knox shifted unobtrusively closer to Beth.

"Is your sister like you?" Shade asked.

"No, we're the complete opposite of each other."

Thank God! Beth had managed to ignite a free-for-all between biker clubs, and those bitches weren't done with them yet. They had threatened them all the way to their motorcycles.

"Good." He continued to the doorway. He needed a shower.

"Everyone always assumed I was the troublemaker, but I was the one always having to get Lily out of some trouble she managed to get herself involved in before she went to college. Actually, her being away is giving me a break. Of course, I would never admit that to her."

Shade's shoulders slumped. Stopping by the counter full of liquor bottles that were used to restock the bar, he grabbed a bottle of whiskey before leaving, his mind on car accidents, red panties, and long, black hair.

CHAPTER THIRTEEN

Four Months Later...

Shade held his phone to his ear, listening to the ringing on the other end.

"Hey, bro, what's up?"

"Why does anything have to be up for me to call? Can't I call and check on my little sister?" Shade tried to insert warmth into his voice. His relationship with his younger half-sister was as close to normal as he was going to get.

A snort sounded through the line. Clearly, he hadn't fooled her.

"How is school?"

"Good. Would have been better if Mom and Dad would actually let me go without having to live at home." Penni hadn't been able to come up with a valid argument for leaving home when they lived within a few miles of the University of Ohio.

"I could help convince them to let you go to an out of state college."

"What's the catch?" Suspicion laced her voice.

"It has to be the college of my choice."

"What's the name?" Penni asked excitedly.

"Breckinridge College."

"Don't recognize the name. Let me check it out on the web. Hang on."

Before he could protest, the phone was set down. It didn't take long before she came back on the line.

"No, thanks." All excitement was gone from her voice.

"Come on, give it a chance."

"No."

His snort could be heard over the line this time. "What will it take?"

"A car, a generous allowance, and a vacation of my choice every summer." Damn, the little vixen knew he could afford it, too.

"Okay. Do the paperwork. I'll talk to the parents."

"That's not all."

"Penni..." he warned.

"A reason?"

64

He stared across the church yard at Lily as she filled her plate with food. She was the only reason he had come to the lame Fourth of July picnic.

"Someone needs a friend."

"Deal."

Shade hung up the phone as Beth and Lily approached the picnic table he was sitting at, waiting for everyone to return from the buffet.

"Where's Razer?" Beth asked.

"Getting the drinks."

As the two women sat down on one side of the table with filled plates, Lily didn't look any happier than before she had left the picnic table. She had spent the last hour trying unsuccessfully to convince Beth to let her switch colleges.

Razer set drinks in front of everyone before sitting down next to Beth, who promptly gave him her shoulder. Shade wondered why the blond was giving Razer a hard time now.

"How long you going to stay mad?" he asked, picking up his hamburger.

"At least past that date you had tatted on your razor knife."

"Still can't understand why you're so mad. I thought it would make you happy," Razer said in his own defense.

"Most women get engaged with a romantic dinner and a ring, not the guy pointing to a tattoo then saying 'let's do it'."

"No sense in putting it off with a bun in the oven." Razer shrugged.

Shade almost burst out laughing when she nearly choked on her hamburger.

"I am not pregnant," she told Lily, who was unable to hold back her own amusement.

"You will be if we miss that date," Razer threatened. "Take a drink before you choke to death."

Beth reached inside her paper cup, pulling out a diamond ring.

Razer took it from her, sliding it on her finger, then kissed her until Lily turned red watching the couple.

"Is this romantic enough?" Razer asked, brushing the tears off Beth's cheek.

"It's perfect."

"I'm so happy for you both!" Lily jumped up from the picnic table, giving them both hugs from behind as the brothers behind them began cheering. Shade nearly crushed his own cup in his hand as he watched Lily's breasts press against Razer's back when she hugged him. Lily was so happy she didn't notice Shade giving Razer a warning look.

Razer hastily stood up, moving to shake the brothers' hands while Shade couldn't prevent the jealousy storming through him. His hand trembled with fury at the sight of Lily gradually opening up with Razer, spending time with him when she visited from college on the weekends. He wanted her to grow closer to *him*, not Razer. On the other hand, he had no desire to develop the brotherly bond Razer was forming.

Shade tried to look interested when Beth flashed her ring to the others standing around, using the opportunity to stand closer to Lily and smell the soft fragrance she used.

Lily glanced up at him warily before gripping her sister's arm. "I'm going to go help Winter with the kids."

"Okay," Beth told her happily.

Shade watched her skitter away like a doe sensing danger. He stood with the brothers, keeping her within eyesight as she began playing freeze tag with the children. She stopped suddenly when she saw a young couple arrive with twin boys.

"I'm going to go fix some more punch. It's beginning to get low," Beth commented.

"Don't take long," Razer told her before she left, going inside the church.

As Winter talked to the couple, Lily took one of the twins and placed it on her hip.

Shade felt a lump in his throat at seeing true joy on her face for the first time. Lily being carefree and happy was a sight he didn't want to end, but then her attitude changed when the man who considered her his approached, handing her a cup. Charles took the cup back when she finished, putting his arm around Lily possessively and giving the impression of a future Shade was determined wasn't going to happen. It was going to be his and Lily's.

Blind fury overtook Shade. Dropping his own cup to the ground, he moved to rip the fucker's arm out of its socket.

Razer, who was standing next to him, saw his reaction. "Don't do it, brother," Razer warned.

Shade didn't answer him, too fueled with possessive rage.

Razer placed a hand on his chest, trying to hold him back, but Shade raised his fist, smashing it into Razer's face. Train and Rider butted in next, at first simply trying to break up the fight.

"Stop him," Razer told them, putting a hand to his bloody lip.

Shade didn't feel any remorse, wanting the others to feel the pain he was feeling at watching Lily and Charles together. He managed to break away from the brothers. Then Viper tried to stop him. Getting madder every second that Charles touched Lily, he swung his foot out and nailed Viper in the balls. As Viper hit the ground, Shade stepped around his prone body, and Rider and Train tried to interfere again. He just smashed them together.

Unfortunately, Razer had recovered and, with Knox's help, managed to slow him down long enough for Rider and Train to get a good grip on him.

"Shade, calm down. He's moved away from her," Razer hissed close to his ear.

"Fucker touches her again, I'll kill him," Shade snarled, seeing Razer was telling the truth and Charles was going to a car in the parking lot.

"Let him go," Razer said.

Shade felt the hands holding him back drop away.

"What in the fuck was that all about?" Viper asked, his face pale and his own anger evident.

Shade nodded toward Lily. "See her?"

The brothers all turned to look at Lily who was once again playing with the children, the twin child still on her hip.

"Beth's sister?" Viper asked.

"She's mine. I'll kill anyone who touches her."

"You have to be fucking kidding me, Shade. She can't be yours. She's messed-up, brother." Razer took a hasty step backward, his hands raised in surrender at the look of murder in Shade's eyes. "I didn't mean it to be cruel, just stating a fact. You haven't said more than three words to her, so how can you claim her before you've even had her?"

"I'm telling every brother here, she's fucking mine, and I'll kill anyone who tries to take what's mine, brother or not."

"He's bat-shit crazy," Knox stated.

"Shade…" Razer began.

"I told you I'd wait until she's older before I make a move on her, and I will," Shade grimly broke him off. "But I won't stand around like a pussy while someone else does," he warned.

Razer nodded, his eyes going toward Lily.

"Son of a bitch."

Lily had been playing horseshoes with the children. However, instead of throwing the metal horseshoe toward the sandpit, she hurled it at a young man arguing with his girlfriend, striking him in the back before running toward the couple despite the anger she had incited in the man who had spun around when he was hit.

Shade took off running, Razer and the others following behind. He heard Lily's words as he silently approached, coming to a stop behind her.

"Don't touch her," Lily hissed.

Shade hadn't been aware Lily had a temper, much less the spunk to stand up to a man. She stood with the baby on her hip, her black hair disarrayed from playing and running around with the kids, and her breasts were heaving as she tried to catch her breath. Shade wanted to reach out and smooth her tangled hair, to find out if it was as soft as it appeared.

"What business is it of yours?" The punk was about to get his ass whipped if he kept trying to intimidate Lily.

"I am making it my business. You were hurting her," Lily replied.

"Perhaps, Jake, you could take a breather until you calm down," Viper's supposed girlfriend, Winter, tried to divert the punk.

"You two cunts need to back off."

Shade was going to kill him with his bare hands. He just didn't want Lily to see how he was going to do it.

Viper, who was standing next to him, didn't seem any happier.

"We can do that. Lily and I were just going to get the kids a drink, and we could use some help. Carmen, would you mind?"

"She isn't going anywhere. We're leaving." The punkass pulled the young girl to his side, shoving Winter out of his way.

Viper almost knocked Shade over to catch Winter, his arm going around her waist, holding her steady until she was able to regain her balance.

Shade motioned The Last Riders into position to protect the women.

"That was a mistake," Viper said as Winter quickly moved away from him, disappearing in the gathering crowd.

"You need to let the girl go and take a walk with me." Shade gave the one and only warning he was going to give as he stepped in front of Lily.

"What's going on?" Lucky hurried toward the group with Beth at his side.

Shade didn't break eye contact with the punk, letting him see his imminent death. He heard Beth whispering to her sister as the parents came to claim the child Lily was holding.

Winter reappeared, taking the hand of the punk's girlfriend in hers before tugging her away. Shade read the boy's intention to stop her so he moved forward an inch, holding his gaze steady, and the little shit stood still, letting his girlfriend be led away.

"Razer, perhaps you should take Beth and Lily home," Lucky suggested.

Razer led the girls away while Lucky dispersed the crowd, assuring them he had the situation under control.

The little shit tried to hide his fear, yet his eyes darted back and forth between the brothers.

"How old are you?" Shade asked him.

"Why, you want to fuck me?"

Shade gave him a sinister smile. "No, because I don't kill kids."

The next thing the punk knew, he was falling to his knees, holding his stomach. Shade reached down, taking a handful of hair in his hand and jerking his head back until he could stare into his face.

"Your dick isn't old enough to be treating a woman the way you were. Does it get you hard when you mistreat that little girl? She's too young to know how to deal with you and put up with your disrespect. And you don't call my girl a cunt. Ever. I'm going to beat the shit out of you, but you'll be able to crawl away when I'm done. If you go near her again or even look in her direction, you'll be carried away in a body bag. You got me?"

"Yes..." Shade's fist didn't let another word pass his busted lips.

Lucky finally pulled him away when he was barely conscious. "He's had enough unless you've changed your mind about the body bag."

When Shade backed away, Lucky knelt down to help the kid to his feet until he stood, swaying, Viper knocked him back down on the ground.

"You don't help that fucker," Viper ordered when Lucky would have tried to help him again.

"Viper, he's had enough! Someone is going to call the police," Lucky warned.

Viper glared at Lucky before walking away. Shade followed, now that Lily was gone there was nothing left for him there.

CHAPTER FOURTEEN

Shade carried his coffee to the front door of the clubhouse. He hated supervising the factory yet had drawn the punishment from the bag for beating the brothers at the picnic. He had another month to endure before Viper took it back over. Viper disliked the job as much as him, but Shade was a night owl and the job required early mornings, so it was his idea of Hell.

Opening the door, he stepped onto the front porch then closed the door behind him. He was about to go down the steps when his gaze skimmed across the parking lot. Shade's foot hovered over the step before backing up onto the porch.

He held his coffee, drinking it as he rested his hip on the banister. Viper had a tire jack in his hand and was smashing his bike to pieces then throwing the separate parts across the parking lot. Shade knew from experience that whatever had caused that rage was bad, and Viper needed to release it.

He saw no need to interrupt Viper until the man went to his knees next to what was left of his bike. Leaving his coffee cup sitting on the banister, he went down the steps, coming to a stop next to his president.

"If you're done, I'll clean up the mess," Shade offered, not asking him why he had trashed his bike.

Viper lifted his head, staring back at him with vacant tear filled eyes until Shade finally saw reason return. Then his president rose to his feet, looking around the parking lot.

"No, I'll get Rider to do it. I want you to call Cash and meet up with him. He's searching for whoever nearly beat Winter to death last night at her school. The bastard left her to fucking die."

"How bad is she?"

"The sheriff doesn't think she's going to make it. I'm going to the hospital." Viper turned toward his bike then stopped, realizing he had destroyed his means of transportation.

Shade pulled his bike keys out of his pocket, handing them to Viper. "Take mine. I'll take one of Rider's, and we can switch later. I'll call Cash and find out where he is, but I want to stop at the high school first and see if I can find anything."

"Okay." Viper went to Shade's bike, taking a seat before starting it up. Gunning the engine, he took off at a speed which made Shade think he would be lucky to get his bike back in one piece.

He went inside the factory's office, taking a set of keys on a peg nailed to the wall, then headed back outside. Shade found the bike he was looking for at the end of the row. The club always kept several extras for the brothers to use—someone's bike would break down or one would crash, but the extras kept everyone mobile.

Once Shade reached the high school, it was easy to see where Winter had been attacked since it was still taped off. The amount of blood on the pavement didn't faze him, but it did give him an indication as to how severe her injuries were. Winter was lucky to still be alive.

Shade went over the school grounds thoroughly, finding an oil spot that was still fresh. It was away from the student and faculty parking and gave the best spot for watching Winter's car unobtrusively. He also found several ashes on the ground before his keen gaze noticed something in the grass a few feet away near a large tree.

He walked closer, using the toe of his boot to move the grass. A cigar butt lay on the ground. Shade used a stick to pierce it, picking it up from the ground then packing it back to his bike where he took a napkin from the saddlebag. He wrapped the cigar butt and placed it in the saddlebag before taking out his cell phone to call Cash.

"Where are you? Viper thought you might need some help."

"Nah, this fucker was easy to find. He left a trail my grandmother could have tracked."

"Who was it?" Shade asked curiously.

"Jake. Remember the kid Lily hit with the horseshoe?"

"It was him?" He was surprised the kid had possessed the balls to touch another woman after the beating Shade had given him. He had thought the punk came off as a poser, pretending to be worse than he actually was.

"Yeah, he stopped at his girlfriend's house first and set it on fire. Luckily, no one was home. The girl's parents had taken her to stay with a relative. It's what set him off and made him crazy enough to set the fire and attack Winter. Seems Winter was the one who gave the parents a heads-up to the kid mistreating their girl."

"They sure it was him?" Shade asked sharply. Lily had also been involved in getting the girl away from the kid, and he didn't want the punk getting out of jail and going to look for her.

"The sheriff has witnesses seeing him running from the house."

Something didn't feel right to Shade. He would drop the cigar butt off at the sheriff's office then head back to the clubhouse. He didn't see a kid Jake's age smoking a cigar, so whoever had been smoking it might not have been the one who had beaten Winter, but he had been watching her.

CHAPTER FIFTEEN

Two Months Later...

Shade stared out the factory window, watching Viper, Knox, and Razer as the car they had been waiting for pulled up and came to a stop. He went outside to see if they needed more help than they had anticipated.

Razer opened the car door, pulling Beth out of the driver's seat. It had taken Razer and Viper weeks to convince her to what essentially was kidnapping. Although she had lived, Winter had been left with injuries severe enough to be unable to care for herself for some time. While still in the rehabilitation center, she had asked Beth to help once she got home. Viper had other plans, though.

He had finally invested in the gym the brothers had been asking for, building it in the basement. However, he hadn't done it for them; it was to aide in Winter's recovery. Viper was a tightwad when it came to hanging on to the profits of their company in order to reinvest and expand, but he had purchased the best equipment for her, even putting in a whirlpool when he had heard it would ease some of her pain.

Needless to say, Winter had no idea Beth would be bringing her to the clubhouse, expecting to return to her own home instead. Beth had called thirty minutes before to give them a heads-up they were near, which was why they had been waiting in the parking lot. Shade knew Winter's reaction wasn't going to go down well for the soft-hearted Beth.

Shade was proved right when Beth burst into tears. Razer put his arms around her before leading her away while Viper opened the back door.

"Hello, Winter," Viper said.

"Take me home. This isn't going to happen, Viper. I am not going to stay here."

"I'm sorry, Winter, but I am not giving you a choice." He carefully lifted her into his arms. When she would have struggled, he held her in a firm hold and talked to her in a voice which had her going still. "I know right now you're mad as hell and I understand, but I am not going to let you hurt yourself. Stay still or else I will make you sorry."

"You're going to hurt me to keep me from hurting myself?"

Her attention turned to Knox who was opening the trunk, taking out her suitcases while Razer walked away from Beth to lift out the wheelchair.

When Beth would have gone to Winter, Shade stopped her with a hand on her arm.

"I wouldn't lay a hand on you, but you would get my message." Viper carried her up the long flight of steps without stopping, and the brothers packed Winter's belongings while Shade followed along with Beth.

Evie opened the door as they approached. "Hi, do you remember me from church? Believe it or not, I'm a nurse. I also worked with Beth for a while, so you'll be in good hands while you're here."

When Winter didn't return her greeting, Viper continued through the entry, going to the stairs not far from the door and then carrying her up another flight of steps. Shade watched as Winter stared toward the club room until Viper turned down the long hallway.

Shade tried to keep Beth from following, but she gave him a look which dared him to stop her. Shade gave her a mocking smile in return, pulling back enough to let her go upstairs. He would keep an eye on her, though. If she tried to interfere between Viper and Winter, he would remove her. Shade let her get as far as the doorway before motioning for her to stop.

They watched as Viper gently lay Winter down on his king-sized bed. The room of the president of the Last Riders was the largest in the house, with a couch and two chairs in a small sitting area. A desk and chair took up space along one wall with a dresser and chest on another.

"I am not staying here, Viper…"

Viper ignored her, walking out of the room and leaving her alone with Evie, who began opening Winter's suitcases which Razer and Knox had set on the floor.

"Thanks, guys," Evie thanked the men before both left without a word, closing the door behind them.

The group stood in the hallway, easily listening to what was going on behind the thin door, until the room went silent. Then Beth stared at the men surrounding her with anger.

"I'm not going to just leave her in your care. I'm going to check on her every day, and if I feel she really needs to leave, I'll carry her out of here myself."

"Beth, I only want to help her. She has to have constant care, and there's no way you can provide it unless you let your other patients suffer," Viper tried to sooth Beth's fears.

Shade had seen a change in his president since Winter had been attacked. He had stayed at the hospital, sitting in the waiting room until she had awakened, and only leaving then because the sheriff had forced him to see reason. He had gone back, though, every day until she had been discharged to the rehabilitation center. He had gone missing several times after that, asking Shade to keep supervising the factory during his absences. The business credit card statement had showed he was buying gas on the road to and from where she was recovering.

Shade went downstairs with Knox and Rider, leaving Viper talking with Beth and Razer. One thing was for sure—with Winter in the house, things were going to change even more. The brothers were just getting used to having Beth around during the time Lily was in school, and from that point on Winter would be there, as well. It was going to be interesting to see how Winter adjusted. He was just happy he could hand the reins of the factory back over to Viper.

The next morning, Shade was enjoying his first breakfast in a long time, hanging out in the kitchen with the members, when Viper came in carrying Winter. She was tiny against Viper's muscular body, her frailness evident in the fine lines of her face.

He sat her down at the round table.

"I'll fix you a plate," Viper offered.

Shade ignored her stare while Knox and Razer returned it with one of their own.

"Hello," Winter muttered.

They merely gave nods. None of the brothers talked much before noon.

Viper set a plate down in front of Winter before sitting next to her as Evie sat next to him with her own plate.

"I need a plate like hers. I can't eat all this," Winter protested.

"Eat," Viper told her before addressing Razer. "Razer, you get Becker's order finished?"

"Yeah, I checked the area it's from and pulled a couple of things. The humidity would have affected them, so I replaced them with similar items that would hold up better. I also included a couple of freebies for his organization to try out. Figured, if they liked them, they would order more."

"Good idea."

Shade went on to give him a rundown on an order which was only half completed. Their survival business was booming, and it was becoming harder to keep up with the demands.

75

"They are talking about a big order going out tomorrow. That's why everyone is up today, working an extra shift at the factory next door," Evie explained to a listening Winter.

When Winter pushed her barely touched plate away, Viper pulled the plate to him, finishing what remained.

"You need to use the restroom?" Shade felt a tinge of compassion when Evie asked Winter the personal question, and Winter blushed bright red and shook her head.

The doorbell rang, producing a huge smile from Evie. "That must be your therapist."

Shade didn't like the look on Evie's face and found out why when she returned.

"Winter, this is Conner Stevens, your physical therapist," Evie introduced.

The women in the room could only stare in awe at the man who had entered, while the brothers weren't happy with a new male breaching their territory. Shade, on the other hand, didn't give a shit. Let the pretty boy make them wet; he and the brothers would be putting out the fire. Viper was the most displeased, not trying to hide his jealousy, but Winter didn't notice, her eyes pinned on her new physical therapist.

"Tell Beth she kept her promise. I forgive her," Shade heard her whisper to Evie.

What the fuck did she mean by that? Shade thought.

"Are you ready to get started?"

"Yes," Winter answered, lifting her arms.

Conner laughed, coming to her side and lifting her easily.

"I'll show you the way." Evie guided them through the doorway which led to the basement.

"Wow," Dawn breathed.

"Holy moly." Jewell moved behind his back, rubbing his shoulders.

Shade took a drink of his coffee, already enjoying the benefits of the women wanting what they couldn't have.

"Beth was alone with him for two hours when she interviewed him. I thought it was taking too long when she kept me waiting at the diner for her," Razer complained. "I see why now."

Viper was still staring at the closed door until his chair suddenly scraped back and he stood. Shade could read his intention.

"Evie will stay with them. She's not going to let anything happen," Shade consoled, leaning back as Jewell's hands slid down his chest.

"He's gotta go," Viper stated.

"Yes, he does," Razer agreed.

"Damn, you two quit being pussies. Evie will give a heads-up if she feels Winter wants more than his skills as a therapist. Jesus, never thought I'd see the day my brothers would be jealous of another man." Shade shook his head at his brothers' downfall.

"This comes from the man it took practically the whole club to hold back when a man put an arm around Lily," Viper barked back snidely.

Shade grinned. "I haven't fucked her yet. When I do, she won't be looking elsewhere when I can give her what she needs," Shade bragged.

"Think so? Brother, you're headed for a fall," Razer warned.

Shade ignored him, standing up. "You all need to get to work if we're going to get that order out."

The members then all filed out, but when Jewell started to go through, Shade placed an arm around her shoulder.

"You can be late. Viper owes me." Viper's lips tightened at Shade's words.

"You have an hour," he reluctantly told Jewell.

Shade's hand went to Jewell's ass. "Make it two. You know I like to take my time."

He felt Jewell tremble under his arm.

After Viper paused before giving his permission, Shade gave him a grin as he guided Jewell out the door, not able to resist his parting shot. "Razer, Beth give you any after she interviewed her new employee?"

He left before Razer could reply, but he could still hear him from behind the door.

"I want to kick his ass."

"I'm in," Viper agreed.

Chapter Sixteen

Shade sat at the kitchen table with Winter sitting across from him. He and the brothers were watching the television in the back room, which could be seen easily from the table. Winter was watching Rider and Evie argue over the best way to make sweet potatoes. When Evie made gagging noises after Rider mentioned marshmallows, Winter's responding laughter brought a smile to Viper's lips.

The brother has it bad, Shade thought.

Winter had gradually accepted staying at the clubhouse. Rider had told him of her escape attempt after Viper had yelled at her, but she had settled down and was growing stronger every day from the physical therapy with Conner. She was actually progressing much faster than anyone had expected.

On the downside, the news of her progression put Viper in a bad mood.

"They are like this every holiday," Bliss explained the argument.

Razer and Beth came in as they were about to eat.

"I thought you would have dinner with Lily?" Winter asked.

Beth smiled. "This is the first Thanksgiving we have spent apart, but a friend from college invited her to spend the holiday with them, and she accepted."

Shade already knew that, which was why his ass was sitting there instead of at his family's table.

Winter raised a brow. "As overprotective as you are, I am surprised you let her go."

Beth laughed, turning red. "Lily is old enough to make her own decisions now—that was the whole point of her going away to college—but I did ask Razer to check them out for me. He assured me it was safe," Beth confessed.

Winter caught the unguarded look on Razer's face as he stared at Shade across the table. Shade kept his face expressionless, aware Winter was watching. That woman could see through anything.

"How long has she known this girl?" Winter questioned Beth.

"They met at the first of the school year. Next year, they are thinking about being roommates. It's great for Lily. I was about to break and let her come home, but I didn't want her driving back and forth to the nearest college. This girl has made college life bearable for her. We'll have to invite her one weekend."

As expected, Lily had become good friends with Penni. Hell, a rabid dog wouldn't be able to resist Penni. He had been relieved when Penni and Lily had become friends, because there was no way he could have stayed away if she had returned to Treepoint.

Razer's face twitched at Beth's words. The brother didn't like misleading his woman. However, Shade remained expressionless, continuing to eat his meal under Winter's scrutiny.

"I would wait a while. Finals will be coming up then Christmas. Besides, you have a wedding to plan after Christmas. I'm sure Lily can explain that it will be several months before you can return the favor." Her response drew his eyes, having no doubt Winter knew something wasn't as it seemed with Lily's new friendship. She somehow knew Razer and Shade were involved, proving the woman saw entirely too much.

"Perhaps you're right. I'm going dress shopping in Lexington after Christmas. We could make a weekend of it, just us girls."

"That sounds like a good plan."

Neither Razer nor Shade hid their relief.

The food was gone in a fourth of the time it had taken the members to cook it. Afterward, Shade helped clean the table, handing Bliss the dirty dishes to load in the dishwasher, brushing her body with his when he was sure Beth and Winter weren't watching.

Shade grabbed himself a beer when he saw her nipples peak before going to find himself a seat on the crowded couch. While the men easily eavesdropped as they watched the game, the women sat at the kitchen table, planning Beth's bachelorette party.

It wasn't long before Razer and Train began yelling at the game, and Shade relaxed back with his team winning.

"That's settled then," Shade overheard next. "Winter, I bought an outfit for you to wear to tomorrow's party. I hung it in your closet before coming downstairs."

Shade decided it would be one Friday night he would miss. He was smart enough not to let Beth and Winter see anything that could come back to bite him in the ass.

"That was sweet of you, but I'm sure I had something that would have been fine," Winter voiced her thanks.

"I seriously doubt that," Beth deadpanned. "I want to explain about the parties, Winter. The first one was a shock for me."

"I have been to several parties, Beth. I am not a social butterfly, but I don't think I'll embarrass myself."

Shade was willing to bet Winter had never been to anything like the one she would be attending the following night.

"That's not what I mean, Winter. What I meant is that the parties can get a little carried away; you may see some things that will shock you."

The brothers began to lower their voices, amused at Beth's attempt to warn Winter about their parties. They were hiding their laughter as nothing was going to prepare Winter. It was like being a virgin; until you fucked, there was no way to describe how good it was.

"For Heaven's sake, Beth, I think she's seen a naked man before. Hell, she dated Viper for two years," Jewell interrupted, exasperated.

"I never saw Viper naked when we dated. We never had sex," Winter confessed to the women.

Shade lifted a brow at his president, who actually turned red at Winter's admission.

Rider yelled out at a touchdown, and Knox elbowed him in the ribs so they could hear.

"You dated Viper for two years and never fucked him?" Evie asked, just as surprised as the rest of them.

Rider and Train were giving Viper pitying looks.

"No. At first, my mom was sick, so I thought he was being understanding. Then Mom died, and I still thought the same thing. That excuse lasted about a year," she said, opening another beer. All the women at the table watched the movement.

"What about the other year?" Bliss asked.

"We went to church together," Winter said.

"Yeah, so?" Jewell asked what everyone was thinking.

"Oh, I understand," Beth stated.

Shade was glad someone did because he sure as fuck didn't.

"Well, fucking explain it to us," Jewell demanded.

"It's our Christian belief not to share sex before marriage. Many couples in our church don't even kiss before their wedding day." By that point, Beth was as red as Winter.

"So you thought," Jewell started in a strangled voice, "that Viper shared your Christian values?"

Shade nearly dropped his beer at that answer. Lily belonged to the same church her sister and Winter did. Who in the hell waited for marriage to fuck? Nobody waited. They might *pretend* to wait, but they fucked. *Everyone fucks*, Shade tried to convince himself.

As the women burst out laughing, only Viper's glare at the brothers prevented them from joining in.

"What about the last months you were together?" Stori asked.

"I thought he was gay."

Viper choked on his beer and started to jump off the couch, but Knox and Shade held him down. The women turned at the sounds of the scuffle.

"What happened?" Winter asked.

"I think the other team got the ball," Evie said, laughing.

"Oh, then I was at a football game and saw you guys walk by, and I realized he wasn't gay," Winter went on explaining.

"How did that make you realize he wasn't gay?" Bliss asked.

"I saw him look at you. No man who is gay looks at a woman's ass like that."

The whole table got quiet, and Shade watched Viper's face pale at Winter's words.

"That's when I realized he just saw me as a friend."

"Ouch," Shade muttered. Viper didn't appreciate his snide remark and elbowed him in the ribs.

"Damn." Jewell's voice let the brothers know the women didn't appreciate the way Winter had been used to gather information on her relative.

"Back to tomorrow's party. I am sure I am a big girl, and if I see anything I can't handle, I can get Viper to take me to my room."

"I am sure that won't be a problem. Uh, maybe you should stay away from Rider and Knox tomorrow night, to be on the safe side."

Knox and Rider both looked disappointed at Beth's advice.

"Why? Do they drink too much?" Winter's innocent question had Viper smiling.

The woman was good for Viper. Shade hadn't seen him smile so much since before Gavin had disappeared.

Shade saw Viper looking over his shoulder to where Winter sat rubbing her back. He rose from the couch. "Time for bed." He said taking Winter into his arms, carrying her out of the room.

Silence filled the room as the swinging door closed behind them.

"I can't believe she thought Viper wasn't fucking her because she's a Christian," Jewell muttered.

"I can't believe she thought he was gay," Evie said.

"There are still women out there who are innocent," Beth said, taking up for her friend. "Winter is one, and my sister is another."

Shade disagreed. Those shadows in Lily's eyes didn't come from being innocent; they came from seeing too much.

Shaking off his thoughts of Lily, he thought Winter had to have known Viper wasn't interested in her sexually. That was why she had made up so many excuses. Women saw only what they wanted to see. Shade was counting on it.

CHAPTER SEVENTEEN

Shade lifted the whip, letting the tip touch the tip of the pink nipple with a slight sting as his cell phone started to ring on his nightstand. Ignoring the woman chained to his bedroom wall, whimpering in frustration, he answered the call.

"Yes?"

"I need a favor." Shade could barely hear Viper's low voice.

"Already giving you two." Shade's eyes went back to Natasha, who was wiggling her ass against the mat hung on the wall, then switched to where Ember was tied to his bed.

"I told you I would pay you back. Conner leave?"

"About an hour ago. He thinks he's going to be a Last Rider."

"He wouldn't live through the initiation."

"I don't know; kind of liking the benefits of having him around."

As Natasha's hand on her thigh started to inch toward her pussy, Shade pulled the whip back then snapped it forward so it almost moved in slow motion, striking the back of her hand. She slid it back down to rest on her thigh.

"Shade? You there?"

"Yeah, I'm here. What's wrong with your voice?"

"Winter's sleeping, and I don't want to wake her."

"So, what's the favor?"

"I need you to guard the stairs and make sure Winter doesn't try to escape."

"I take it Winter didn't enjoy her first party."

"Oh, she enjoyed it, too much. She's going to try to bolt, but I want her to stay right where she is. That's where you come in."

"I'll do it, but it's going to cost you."

"What do you want?"

"For two favors, I was willing to settle for a week off. For three, I want your marker."

"I don't give out markers," Viper refused. "Pick something else."

"You gave Beth your marker," Shade reminded him.

"That was different. I thought Dad was responsible for Lily's accident."

"So, Winter's staying here isn't as important?" Silence from the other end of the call had Shade pushing the boundaries of what his president would allow. "Get Rider to do it."

"He's drunk off his ass."

"Get one of the prospects to do it."

"They're young enough that Winter will intimidate them into helping her."

"Where's the rest of the brothers?"

"They all decided to take a midnight run."

"Sounds like you're shit out of luck. Why don't you do it? Watch some TV?"

"I'm tired, and I'll be putting in a lot of overtime since I promised you those days off for being the women's reward if they kept Conner away from Winter. I'm worried she'll sneak out of bed without me knowing," Viper snapped.

"Sounds like you have only one option left."

"I could order you to do it."

"You could," Shade agreed.

"Fuck you, Shade. What do you need my marker for?"

"I like to be prepared," was Shade's only response.

"All right, then, but she better be here when I wake up," Viper warned.

"She will be," Shade promised, his eyes returning to the two women in his bedroom. "Give me twenty minutes before you go to sleep. I have to finish with these favors first."

Viper hung up on him.

ॐ ⊛

Shade heard the bedroom door open and the sound of metal scraping. Viper must've been getting old not to have woken up with the racket Winter was making. He waited for the little runaway to make her way down the hallway to where he was hidden at the top of the steps.

Winter gave a startled scream when she finally saw him.

"Going someplace?" he asked casually.

"Breakfast?"

Shade lifted a brow at her show of fake innocence. "No one is up yet."

"I can make my own."

"How were you going to get down the steps?" he asked coldly.

"What are you doing here?" Winter asked impatiently, ignoring his question.

"Viper had a feeling you would try to make a run for it after last night." Shade shrugged. "Seems he was right."

"He asked you to stand here all night?" she asked in disbelief.

"Yes. Need a lift downstairs, or do you want to go back to bed?"

"Downstairs, please."

The doorbell rang just as he was about to lift her.

"Your accomplice?" Shade asked as he saw Viper striding down the hallway.

"Who is it?" Viper asked.

"Pastor Dean."

Shade's and Viper's eyes met over Winter's head, and Viper grinned. "Could be worse. Shade, answer the door while I get Houdini."

Shade went down the steps to open the door.

"Hey, Dean."

"Shade, you look like you enjoyed your Friday night."

He glared back at the fresh-faced Lucky who wasn't trying to hide his amusement. "Fuck off."

Lucky brushed by him. "I don't know why you're so cranky; I'm the one who missed the party," he mocked.

Viper reached the bottom of the steps carrying Winter.

"Viper, Shade, Winter, it's good to see you all again."

Lucky's pastor persona made Shade want to vomit up the whiskey he had drunk last night.

"Want some coffee?" Viper asked, carrying Winter to the kitchen and sitting her down on a chair at the table.

"Sounds good to me." Lucky sat down at the table next to Winter, giving her a reassuring smile.

It never failed to amaze Shade the way Lucky could turn the two sides of his identity on and off. *And everyone thinks* I'm *the psychopath*, Shade thought wryly.

"Going to bed, Viper."

"Thanks, Shade."

He left without a word to Winter or Lucky, feeling her glare on his back. He almost hung around to watch the show Viper and Lucky would put on in front of Winter yet then decided he really didn't give a fuck.

He went into his empty bedroom where he meticulously cleaned the equipment he had used on the twins, even washing down the mat before sliding it under his bed. He then went into his bathroom to turn the shower on.

When steam began filling the room, he went under the hot spray. Picking up the shower gel, he began to clean himself as thoroughly as the equipment, wiping away the memories of the women he had fucked the night before.

His body should have been satiated; instead, it was as if he hadn't had a woman in months. None of the women were Lily.

He felt his cock hardening, surging upwards along his lean belly. He could have called any of the women and they would have run downstairs to relieve the hard-on, yet Shade didn't want them—he would only have to take another shower to wash their touch from him.

Shade lathered his hand with the gel then slid it down to his cock, his thumb gliding over the tip. He braced his other hand on the tiled shower wall as he began to slip his hand up and down, imagining Lily spread before him with desire in her eyes, the shadows of fear gone. He imagined her playing with herself as he stroked, his balls tightening as he imagined her arching, lifting her hips toward him. His cum burst out, giving him a brief moment of relief from the desire, which constantly rode him for Lily.

Shade laid his head on the shower wall. It would be three more years before he could make his move on her. He was never going to last that long.

CHAPTER EIGHTEEN

It was nearly noon when Shade woke up, stretching his naked body on the sheets. He had always been lucky that a few hours of sleep refreshed him, waking up without feeling groggy.

He dressed then went upstairs, deciding to get something to eat, to find the kitchen empty except for Rider, who was sitting at the table with his head in his hand and a cup of coffee in front of him. Shade didn't say anything to the brother, seeing he felt like shit.

Everyone was used to fending for themselves on Saturday, since the parties on Friday made them too hung-over or tired to cook. However, he could tell a meal must have been made earlier, even if it was gone by that point. Probably Viper cooked some shit for Winter since she had decided to sneak out at the ass crack of dawn.

The kitchen door opened, and Razer came in.

"Want a sandwich?" Shade offered, about to pull the lunch meat out of the refrigerator.

"Fuck no. We all ate a big breakfast this morning. Plus, I'm going into town to eat lunch with Beth. She took Winter Christmas shopping. Want to go?"

"No."

"Lily will be there," Razer said.

Shade shut the refrigerator door. "I'll ride along."

Rider's chair scooted back. "I'll go, too. Maybe the fresh air will make me feel better."

"Figured you would," Razer taunted.

"Couldn't hurt," Shade said, slapping the hung over brother on the back.

Both Shade and Rider punched Razer for being in such a good mood. Laughing, he held his hands up in surrender as they left the kitchen.

The brothers had just sat down on their bikes when Razer's cell phone rang. Shade started his bike, waiting for him to finish his call. He spoke briefly before disconnecting.

"What's up?"

"Lucky called, said he's at the church and looked out the window toward the diner. Ton's trying to take on some bikers and the women are with him."

"Dammit." Shade gripped his handlebars, taking off in a rush and nearly losing control as he pulled onto the road.

Razer and Rider sped along behind, trying to catch up.

The sound of motors racing down the street didn't stop the fighting or the men who held Beth and Lily. Shade, Rider, and Razer pulled into the diner's parking lot and surrounded the fighters. Lucky had failed to mention Viper was there, already taking on a couple of the men. He had also failed to mention the fact that Sam seemed to have made new friends, from the looks of it.

Razer gunned his bike toward Beth and Lily, startling the men into letting Beth go. However, the one who had Lily tightened his grip around her waist, turning her to face the group of angry bikers.

Beth ran straight to Razer as he climbed off his bike. Shade kept his attention on Lily, who was frozen in terror, her dress torn off one shoulder. He wasn't worried in the slightest over whether Viper could handle the bikers he was fighting.

Once Shade and Rider climbed off their bikes, Rider began to move forward, but Shade gave a hand signal for him to back off. The one who dared to touch Lily was all his.

Shade didn't rush the biker; instead, he took off his sunglasses and jacket, leaving him in his long-sleeved, black T-shirt. When he took Lily from the asshole, he didn't want anything encumbering him.

The biker holding Lily tightened his grip on her, smart enough to know she was the only thing keeping him alive.

Shade maneuvered himself closer to his target, each incremental inch forward putting him within striking distance.

"Let her go." Shade's voice came out deadly.

One of the men Viper was holding yelled out, "Slot, let her go."

"Let me get on my bike and get out of here. Then I will let her go. She your bitch?" The man ignored his biker buddy, smart enough, at least, not to take his eyes off Shade.

"She is no man's bitch." Shade kept himself still.

"She's yours. Just let me go. No trouble."

"You had trouble the second you looked at her." Shade motioned for Rider to move back when he caught him sneaking forward. He wasn't about to give the brother a piece of the guy who had touched Lily.

Slot looked at Rider, but Shade didn't take advantage of the man's lack of attention; instead, drawing it back toward him, which wasn't easy. His eyes were darting back and forth between The Last Riders, trying to figure out who posed the biggest threat. When his eyes returned to stare into his, Shade knew he had figured it out.

"Have you heard of The Last Riders?" Shade tried to provoke the biker into lowering his guard.

"Yeah, but I ain't afraid of you. You guys fuck more than you fight."

"That's because the other motorcycle clubs have learned not to mess with us, which gives us more time to fuck. Did they tell you how we got our name?" Shade replied in a manner that said the biker's opinion didn't matter, and it didn't. It was easy to see from their dirty clothes and cheap bikes they spent more time sitting around doing drugs than riding.

"No." The biker was becoming more agitated. Shade could practically see the scared shit shaking.

"See that wheelchair over there with the woman sitting in it?" Shade nodded his head toward Winter.

"Yeah."

"I'm going to give you one just like it. They call us The Last Riders because, if you fuck with us, we fuck you up so bad you will never be able to ride again. Slot, you have taken your last ride."

Shade released his control, unleashing the blinding fury only Lily could rise in him. Only she could take him from the cold, emotionless pool he lived in to the fiery height of emotions which allowed him to feel the rage storming through his body.

He moved left, smashing his fist against Slot's face while using his other hand to push Lily toward Razer. None of the brothers made a move to stop him, not wanting to take him on.

Shade was unaware of the sheriff and his deputies swarming the parking lot at that point. It took two deputies and the sheriff to pull him off the whimpering biker, and if the sheriff wouldn't have been there, Shade would have ignored the deputies.

He managed to kick the biker one more time in the face before letting himself be pulled away.

"Let him go," his dad ordered as soon as they had managed to put enough space between Shade and Slot. "You cool enough for me to arrest them?"

"Yes," he snapped back, turning to see Beth holding Lily, the look of terror still frozen on her face. Whatever Beth was whispering to her had no effect; she was lost in her own world of nightmares.

"Does she need to go to the hospital?" Winter asked in concern.

"No, I need to get her out of here and go home," Beth answered. Shade wanted to rip Lily from her sister's arms, yet he had to stay back and let Razer handle the women.

"The sheriff will give us a ride home, and we can come back tomorrow for your car," Razer said, moving close to Beth and Lily protectively. The whole time, Lily didn't seem aware of what was going on around her.

The sheriff's car stopped next to them, and his dad got out to open the door for the three of them.

Shade hurried to his bike, ignoring the sheriff when he said he needed to give his statement to one of the deputies. He was behind the sheriff's car the whole way to Beth's house and was already by the back door before Razer or Beth could get out.

The sheriff got out of the front seat, observing Shade's reaction as he opened the door for Beth. Razer slid out the other side, coming around the back of the car for Beth.

Shade crouched down next to the car with Lily still inside.

"You going to sit in here all day?" he asked softly.

"Shade," Beth tried to interrupt. "Let me. She's used to turning to me when she's scared."

"She doesn't need to be scared. That shit's over."

Lily didn't even seem to hear him.

"Shade"—Beth placed her hand on his shoulder—"she needs me."

He stood, stepping aside as Beth took Lily's hand and sat with her in the car for almost an hour before she was able to coax her out and lead her inside the house.

"I need to get back to the station," the sheriff stated, getting inside his car.

"I better not see them on the street anytime soon," Shade warned.

After his dad nodded, closing his door, Razer and Shade went inside the house, finding the downstairs empty.

"I'll fix us some lunch. We never did get to eat. Beth usually keeps some frozen meals." Razer went to the small kitchen, opening the freezer.

"I'm going to kill them."

Razer didn't pause at taking out a pizza. "Let me know when you decide to do it, and I'll help."

CHAPTER NINETEEN

Shade handed Viper a beer as he put steaks and burgers on the grill. He enjoyed being out of the house, in the backyard again. It was still the beginning of spring, the warm day drawing everyone outside.

Shade had spent the previous few weeks doing recon on The Blue Horsemen Club, forgoing Christmas with his family. He had made an excuse during that time to stop by Beth's house to see Razer while checking out how Lily was doing.

The woman acted as if being almost raped hadn't happened. Razer had told him Beth had convinced Lily to see a psychologist. Shade didn't have much faith in it working yet was glad they were recognizing something needed to be done about Lily's panic attacks.

Shade set down his beer, helping Viper flip the steaks before they all became burned when Evie approached with a natural seductiveness the other brothers all appreciated. Both men turned, already well aware of her motive thanks to the mischievous gleam in her eyes.

The woman loved steak. She would eat it every night if she could. She was too late this time, though. He had already laid claim to the largest one sizzling on the grill.

Evie leaned into Viper, who put a casual arm around her waist.

"Don't forget, I like my steak rare, and I want the biggest one on the grill."

Viper laughed. "You'll have to fight Shade for it. That's the only reason he's helping out."

Evie reached out, running her finger teasingly down his arm. "Come on, Shade. I was the one who went to the store to buy the steaks in the first place."

"I was the one who lugged the bags up those fucking stairs. You can have the one Viper picked out," he offered without remorse, feeling as if someone was watching them.

His years as a sniper had kept him in the shadows to the extent that he had grown sensitive to being the center of someone's attention. When he searched the backyard and saw no one paying them attention, he lifted his gaze to the house, finding who was observing them.

"Like he'll give it up to me. Winter's the only one who stands a chance of stealing that bad boy away from him. Next time, I'm going to make Knox do the grill. At least then I could stand a chance of getting a decent-sized steak."

Shade moved back from Evie's friendly, teasing touch. He had never touched Evie sexually. Not only had he known her before they had become Last Riders, but she was anything other than a submissive, like the woman staring at them from the house.

"Everything cool between you and Winter?" Shade asked Viper, turning back to the grill.

"Yeah, why?"

"No reason. It's just that she's been watching us for the last five minutes."

"She's probably just hungry," Viper joked.

Viper and Evie looked toward the house.

"I talked to her before coming downstairs. She said she would be eating with us tonight." Evie shrugged. "She seemed fine then."

"She seems pissed off to me," Shade contradicted. He had been at the other end of similar glares from women too many times to misinterpret its cause. "Brother, watch your ass," he warned.

Viper nodded. "I'll go check on her. Maybe she needs some help getting down the steps."

"Possibly," Shade agreed, but he didn't think so. Winter was finally walking without having to be packed up and down the steps.

Shade took the steaks and burgers off the grill, placing them on two large platters. Then he set one on each of the two large picnic tables before sitting down at the one where Evie, Bliss, Dawn, Rider, and Viper, who had already returned from checking to see if Winter was ready to eat.

"I've died and gone to Heaven," Bliss said, her fork stabbing a hamburger.

"That's what I say every time I come in your pussy," Rider grinned, taking his own hamburger as everyone at the table laughed.

As Shade saw the back door opening, his instincts shifted to alertness, aware that Viper had also realized something wasn't right.

Winter walked out, using her cane to stab the ground as if she was on a mission.

She had gone through several changes since she had begun living with them. Her hair had grown out, brushing the top of her shoulders and gleaming with health. The green sweater she was wearing matched her emerald-colored eyes, which were sparking with a mixture of anger and hurt. She had lost weight after the attack yet had regained most of it, looking fit and healthy instead of sick and frail.

She took a seat at the opposite end of the picnic table he and Viper were sitting at, next to Dawn with Bliss seated across from her.

Stiffening, Shade didn't like the insincere smile she gave the women.

"Let me get you a plate," Viper offered as he started to get up.

"No, thanks, but I will take one of those beers." She pointed to the cooler at the end of the table.

Shade reached in and pulled one out, passing it down the table until it reached her. Opening it, she took a long drink as the members began eating and talking again while they finished their food.

After dinner, Knox and Stori stood up from their table, beginning to dance to the music Train had set up to play in the backyard.

"Bliss, I like your top. The color suits you," Winter complemented as everyone sat relaxing around the table with full stomachs.

"Thank you. I got it with the gift certificate you gave me for Christmas."

"I'm glad you were able to find something you liked," Winter said then casually asked, "I was wondering something. I noticed all the women members have tattoos with different numbers on them."

Evie's and Dawn's tops were barely there, so anyone could easily see their tats on the curve of their breasts.

"Yes, we can pick which tattoo we want and put the date on it," Evie explained. "Some, like me, just have the date tatted."

"I see."

Shade noticed Beth shoot Razer a concerned look from the other table as she took another sip of her beer. Even she was beginning to realize her friend was up to something.

"Does everyone have the same date?"

There it is, Shade thought, figuring out exactly what had the high school principal so upset.

"No," Evie spoke cautiously, beginning to suspect the trap.

Viper stiffened in surprise at the turn of the conversation, turning toward Winter. He was no fool; he knew where the question was leading.

"What determines the date that goes on the tattoo?" Winter asked, her breathing unconsciously deepening.

"It's the date we became a member of The Last Riders," Evie explained slowly.

"I see. How do the women become members?" Winter asked.

Evie looked around the table, willing someone to jump in and take over the discussion, which Shade wouldn't touch with a ten-foot pole.

Being president of the club and Winter's old man, Viper managed to step in with a grim look.

"Ask what you want to know, Winter."

"I just did. What's the big secret?"

"No secret, it's just club business. Only the members or potential members need to know, but I will tell you. The women become members by fucking or causing six of the eight members to have an orgasm."

As her hands tightened on the beer bottle, Shade expected her to throw it at Viper. She let him have her sharp tongue, instead.

"Well, doesn't that make it nice for the male members? How do *they* become members? By fucking a certain number of women? What is it, a hundred?" she said snidely.

"No, the recruit who wants to become a member and join us must pick four of the original members."

"Male members to fuck?"

Shade almost laughed out loud at the angry glares Winter was receiving from the brothers.

"No, they pick four of the eight members to beat the hell out of them. Then, if they fight well and aren't hurt too bad, they become members."

It was a harsh initiation none of the brothers would apologize for. When they were fighting, they needed to know each of the brothers could carry their own weight. A weak link during a life and death battle could get several men killed. If anyone who wanted to join The Last Riders wanted to be babied, they needed to stay home with Mama.

"You guys have a thing for numbers, don't you?" Winter asked.

"We have to know that a man we are making our brother can handle himself and have our back. Going on beer runs and dumb shit like that won't be of any help to us when another club wants our cut."

"Well, your club has worked out all the details. So, the women get the tattoo after they fuck their sixth original member?"

"Basically, yes." Viper's firm voice held no apology.

"I can see by the women's tattoos that they are very proud of their accomplishment."

The women at the table stiffened, as did Shade and the other brothers.

Evie was the first to break the stunned silence. "We don't deserve that attitude. You might think that is a large number of men to sleep with, but *we* happen to think we are very selective. I have girlfriends who aren't in The Last Riders who go out to party every weekend and fuck a couple of different guys a month, knowing shit about them. I know everything about these men, who, I might add, have lugged your ass around for the last few months and been nothing except polite to you."

"I agree. I apologize for any affront I may have caused. All of you have been more than kind to me, and I shouldn't repay your kindness by being a bitch."

After a few moments of silence everyone started to relax, but Winter ruined it by asking, "I don't see your tattoo, Bliss? May I see it?"

Bliss stiffened in her seat, looking toward Viper and silently asking what she should do.

"Show her," Viper ordered.

Bliss reached out and pulled her top back, leaving the curve of her breast bare and giving a clear view of the tattoo. The date she had earned her vote was tatted, which also happened to be the day Winter had been attacked.

"Who gave you the last vote you needed?" Winter asked, not moving her eyes away from the glaring proof of what Viper had been doing while she was being attacked.

"I did," Viper admitted.

"Now I understand why you said what you did to Bliss today, Rider."

Everyone looked at the two members who sat in confusion, not understanding what she was referring to, but Winter was about to remind them.

"I heard you tell Bliss that you guys could get back to normal after I leave, like Viper told you. If *that* is any example"—she pointed to Bliss's tattoo—"I bet you can hardly wait until I am gone. Viper told you two weeks; I am not going to cramp your style. I am leaving tonight. My bags are packed, and my ride should be here any minute. I would like to thank each of you for your help this last month."

She turned to Viper, who stared back at her impassively except for the burning fury in his eyes. "You put yourself out for nothing. They said you were still playing me, hoping Vincent would tell me something about the baby. You were way off-base. Sorry I couldn't have been more help, but at least this time you didn't have to waste two years of your life."

"I see that Rider and Bliss were a fountain of information for you."

Both of them sat as still as statues, while Bliss had fear on her face.

"They didn't know I was even there. I was in the hallway, and they were in the hot tub."

"But they were discussing my business?"

Winter wisely didn't answer his question. "Bliss and Rider didn't do anything wrong; I was the one eavesdropping."

Viper ignored her defense of the members. "So, who did you call to come get you this time?"

"The sheriff."

Viper motioned to Shade, who immediately stood, pulling his phone out of his pocket before going inside the kitchen to call his dad.

He answered on the second ring. "What do you want?"

Shade gritted his teeth, knowing his father was still angry he hadn't showed for Christmas. "Where are you?"

"Headed toward the clubhouse. Isn't that why you called?" he mocked.

Shade knew his dad was getting tired of only getting called when it involved The Last Rider's business. "As a matter of fact, yes. Don't bother. Winter was angry at Viper. She's over it now."

"You think I'll take your word for it without checking for myself? I'll be there in five."

Shade had ten minutes. It would take his dad another five to make it up the long flight of steps at the front of the clubhouse.

He put his cell phone back in his pocket as he went outside again, easily finding Viper stalking Winter toward the gazebo.

He stealthily moved to the other side of it so Viper could see him, motioning for Viper to take her upstairs. Viper shook his head, though.

Shade leaned against the tree as the yard darkened, letting the shadows hide him as he listened to Viper and Winter's argument.

"I could have fucked you silly as Loker James, but I wanted you to know who I really was before I put my dick in you. I won't always be so nice. I am not a nice person. Never was, don't want to be. Nice people get fucked over. My brother was an example of that."

Winter started to interrupt, but Viper talked over her. "You're a nice person. I fucked you over, but deal with it because I am *done* trying to make amends. I never led you to believe there was more to us than there actually was, and until you come to grips with that, you are going to stay pissed at me. But I can deal with pissed; actually, it makes me want to fuck."

His hand went to her chest, pulling down her sweater and bra, leaving her breasts bare. When Winter looked around to see if anyone was watching and ended up dropping her cane as she tugged her shirt back up, Shade backed farther into the shadows. Viper's back blocked her from everyone's view except his.

Viper brought her hands upward, knotting soft cords around her wrists that Shade had nailed there himself. He used the gazebo often when Beth was around. Razer would keep her in the club room while he partied outside or in his bedroom.

"You guys are prepared for everything." Winter struggled against the restraints.

Viper laughed. "We try." Viper lowered his head, capturing her mouth in a kiss that made her quit struggling briefly before tearing her mouth away from him. Ignoring her obvious protests, he tugged her top back down and took her nipple in his mouth,

Shade saw the flash of Viper's teeth as he teased her flesh while Viper's other hand once again uncovered her breasts completely, squeezing one from bottom to top. Winter's head fell back against the gazebo.

"Do you know how many times I imagined you like this? With your breasts just waiting for my mouth, your nipples for me to suck them until you scream for mercy? I fucked every woman here the last two years pretending it was your pussy I was inside."

"You fucking liar. I bet you didn't think of me that night with Bliss once. There were four daisies. Does that mean she fucked four members that night?"

"Yes; Cash, Evie, and me. We fucked all night long." Viper unbuckled her jeans, spreading them open before sliding his hand inside. Winter kicked out at him but he stepped between her legs, making her attempt useless.

"Careful, I don't want you to hurt your back. More importantly, I don't want you hurting something of mine I plan to be using in a few minutes."

"You go to Hell. If you think tying me up—"

"You don't like it? That's all you had to say." With a twist of his hand, the cord around her wrist was loosened before giving away. "We don't need safe words—a simple no will do—but your wet pussy is telling me no isn't on your mind."

When Shade saw his father come outside with Evie, he moved sideways noiselessly until he could leave the trees without the couple seeing him.

"I want to see Winter," the sheriff demanded.

Beth stood up from the picnic table, throwing Razer an angry glare.

"I don't think they want to be interrupted," Shade told him as he approached.

"Now, Shade."

Shade shrugged, leading the sheriff to within a few feet of the gazebo.

Beth, who was following along despite Razer trying to stop her, came to an abrupt stop herself, giving a low gasp.

Viper's head was lowered over Winter's breasts, and his hand was moving underneath her jeans as she arched against him.

"Still want to talk to her?" Shade asked in a low voice.

His father turned bright red and started backing away at the low whimper of desire coming from the gazebo. "That's okay. Tell Winter I don't have time to be running back and forth from town when she and Viper get in a fight," he snapped.

"I'll make her aware you weren't pleased with having your time wasted," Shade smoothly lied.

"You do that." Giving a sharp nod, he turned on his polished heels and left.

Beth gave Razer an embarrassed smile before tugging him away from his interest in the couple being intimate only a few feet away.

Shade snagged a beer from Evie's hand as they both unashamedly listened.

"There was someone else, but he doesn't like his business talked about any more than I do."

No, he didn't. Shade was glad Viper knew when to keep silent.

"I never told Rider fuck about when you were leaving because you are staying right where you are, in my fucking bed." With that, Viper lifted her into his arms, packing her into the house, and she didn't even notice Shade had to move before he was knocked over.

"Want to dance?" Shade stiffened as Bliss's arms slid around his waist, sliding her hands to sit intimately against the zipper of his jeans.

Shade tipped the beer to his mouth, finishing it and then tossing the bottle into a trashcan. He took one of Bliss's hands, pulling her around until she was pressed against his chest.

"When was the last time we played in the gazebo?"

"Last summer," she breathlessly reminded him. "I don't exactly remember which night it was."

"Let me refresh your memory."

CHAPTER TWENTY

Viper and Winter were in the kitchen eating as the rest of The Last Riders came in to fix breakfast. Shade microwaved the already-cooked bacon, heating it up as Beth scrambled some eggs and Razer made himself useful making toast. Jewell nudged everyone out of the way as she made coffee and poured glasses of orange juice. The members quickly made breakfast as a synchronized unit, having become used to the routine.

"Couldn't manage to fix yourselves something decent?" Jewell asked, sitting down with a glass of juice.

Winter looked embarrassed, but Viper just casually slung his arm around her shoulders.

Razer and Shade sat down at the table as Beth served Razer his breakfast.

When Winter eyed his plate of food in longing, smiling, Beth slid one just like it in front of her.

"I love you," Winter said fervently.

Beth smiled before taking a seat with her own plate. Viper eyed hers before getting up to fix his own plate.

"How is Lily doing?" Winter asked.

Shade sat chewing a piece of bacon, waiting for Beth's answer.

"Good. She goes back to school in two weeks. She and her friend are planning on going on spring break together."

"Where are they going?" Winter asked.

"They're having trouble making their minds up. Penni wants to go on a mini cruise, says it's the perfect place to meet guys without the party atmosphere of the beaches on spring break."

Shade frowned. Razer had neglected to give him that piece of information.

"Does Lily want to go?" Winter asked the question that was on his own mind.

"Actually, she wants to go to Arizona."

Shade's frown changed to a smile, much happier with that answer. The Grand Canyon was in Arizona. He could see Lily enjoying the rugged canyon.

"To see the Grand Canyon?" Winter asked.

"I asked the same thing." Beth laughed.

"What did she say?"

"She said Arizona has cowboys. Seems she has this thing for them; has the impression they are all macho, protective, and are gentlemen. She thinks they are sexy."

Shade's smile disappeared once more. What the fuck did Lily know about men? Hell, if a man came within ten inches of her, she panicked.

The women laughed good-naturedly at the young girl's fantasy. Shade didn't think it was funny, though. His fork viciously stabbed his eggs.

"Doesn't Arizona have tornados?" Winter asked casually.

Shade actually thought of high-fiving Winter.

Beth's laughter stopped. "Really?"

Shade and all his brothers nodded.

"Spring break is right in the middle of tornado season," Winter confirmed.

Hell fucking yeah. He was unaware he was still nodding his agreement.

"I'll have to tell them. Maybe a cruise would be better."

Shade wasn't any happier. He was going to have to bribe Penni, and it was going to cost him a fortune.

He was trying to think of the states which had the lowest male population when Winter came up with an idea.

"Perhaps you might convince them to stay a few days in Lexington—spring meet will be on at Keeneland. Then you could bring Lily back with you, and we could have your bachelorette party on that Friday."

Beth seemed to consider it for several minutes. "I think that's a great idea. Thanks, Winter."

Winter smiled at Beth, ignoring the narrowed stare of Shade.

It was better than a fucking cruise with the girls running around in bikinis, but Lily would still be around men and horses. Shade wondered if Lily found short men attractive.

"I'm looking forward to the bachelorette party. Evie talked to Mick; he said to let him know the date, and we could have the bar for the night. It's going to be nice with just us, no men," Jewell said, lying through her teeth.

"Well, us and a few of my other friends," Beth clarified, hesitantly.

"Like who?" Evie asked suspiciously, sitting down at the table with her food.

"Crazy Bitch, Sex Piston, Killyama..."

Shade was instantly glad he wouldn't be there. He might ride his bike to Lexington and keep an eye on Lily and Penni then stay on a few days until it was safe to return to Treepoint.

Evie raised her hand. "You have got to be shitting me. Tell me you're not seriously considering inviting them to your party."

"I have to invite them. It will hurt their feelings if I don't."

"Those bitches don't have any feelings. Not normal ones, anyway," Shade butted into the conversation.

Beth sent Shade a reproachful look, which he ignored. The woman was blind where her friends were concerned.

"There is a problem with them coming," Evie reminded Beth. All eyes turned to Bliss who was unashamedly listening from the kitchen counter.

Beth shook her head. "No, that is all forgotten. They'll be cool, they promised."

Shade wasn't the only one in the room looking at her doubtfully.

"May I make a suggestion?" Winter put in. "Suppose we have the party at eight until two. Tell your biker friends it starts at eleven. If Bliss wouldn't mind, she could leave a few minutes earlier than when they would arrive."

Bliss smiled in relief. "That works for me."

Beth didn't seem as happy as Bliss, and if Beth wasn't happy, Razer wasn't.

"Okay, if that makes everyone more comfortable," Beth conceded.

Winter and Viper left the room before the rest were finished.

Jewell smirked in Shade's direction before leaning forward in her chair.

"Lily found any young college boys to date?"

Shade had been about to get up from the table but he sat back down, deciding to finish his coffee.

"Actually, no. Lily doesn't seem interested in any of the boys she's met at college, and with Charles running his father's restaurant, they practically never see each other anymore. She says they're just friends, anyway."

"I think she's attracted to older men. When I interviewed Conner, I almost couldn't get her out of the room."

Shade choked on his coffee.

"He's from Texas, and he promised to teach her to ride a horse. Now that the weather is getting warmer, I'm sure he'll keep his promise. I'll be happy for her to spend some time with the opposite sex, and I like Conner. He's a nice guy. I checked all his references myself. Lily will be thrilled when Conner takes her riding."

"I bet she will be. I know I would." Jewell snickered.

Shade's chair scraped back from the table. He walked away, taking his dirty dishes to the sink, not caring that his coffee cup broke from the force. He then strode toward the kitchen door.

"Where you going, Shade?" Razer taunted with an evil smile.

"I need to buy a plane ticket. Someone I know needs to go home as soon as possible."

"Oh, I hope it isn't serious?" Beth's voice was filled with concern.

"It's a medical emergency," Shade replied, going out the door.

⮵ ⮴

Shade leaned nonchalantly against the kitchen counter, waiting for the club meeting to begin. He wished Viper would give them their punishments instead of making them draw them weekly.

"Where's Viper?" Shade had been late for the meeting because he had been held up finishing an order at the factory, making up time for being late that morning.

He was fucking tired. His nights were getting longer, and nothing seemed to be working to keep Lily off his mind. And he had tried it all.

"He's in the backyard, fighting with Winter," Bliss explained. She was standing on the opposite side of the counter.

"What over?" Shade asked without turning around.

She lowered her voice so only he could hear her in the crowded room. "She seems to think either Razer or Viper are the reason I've been late to work at the factory lately."

Shade's face darkened. He liked to keep his business private, especially from Winter and Beth, but he didn't expect his brothers to take the blame for something he had done. He was about to go outside when they returned.

Winter sat down at the table, and Bliss took an empty seat as Viper went into the large room connected off the kitchen where Cash handed him the red punishment bag.

"Bliss," Viper called.

Bliss got up from the table, going to Viper. He held the bag out to her, and Bliss put her hand out and dug inside the bag. When her hand came out, she was holding a folded piece of paper.

"Rider." Rider, who was leaning on the kitchen counter next to him, walked to Viper. He also pulled a piece of paper from the bag.

Viper repeated the procedure seven more times. "That's everyone." Viper handed the bag back to Cash before going to the counter to grab himself a beer while everyone read their punishments.

Shade unfolded the slip of paper he had drawn.

"I got the worst one," Bliss complained.

102

"What did you get?" Natasha asked.

"Laundry for two weeks." She pouted.

"That's not bad. I got dishes for three weeks. Want to switch? I don't mind the laundry if it's for two weeks," Natasha bargained.

"I don't want to pack everyone's laundry up and down the stairs for two weeks. I may be willing to switch."

"Seed inventory," came from Winter, and Natasha and Bliss switched papers.

Nobody wanted seed inventory.

"Mine seems the easiest."

Shade almost felt sorry for Winter. If he wasn't such a bastard, he would offer to switch with her. However, he was, so he held onto his own punishment.

"Dinner's ready," Evie called.

Shade got in line behind Evie and Stori.

"I'm surprised Viper made her pull a punishment after she found out from her aunt that Sam's baby isn't Gavin's," Stori remarked.

"Viper plays fair." Evie shrugged.

"Have they been able to find any trace of the baby yet?" she asked.

"No. Viper said the sheriff is working to find out, and he ordered the brothers to help run down the clues," Evie answered.

The line moved fairly quickly with Shade and Rider last in line.

"You want to go over today's orders?" Shade asked Rider.

"Yeah, give me a minute," he said, going to the table Winter was sitting at.

"What punishment did you get?" Rider asked Winter.

"What did you get?" she asked first. Winter was a fast learner.

"Cooking, two weeks," Rider answered. Winter looked at Shade.

"Cleaning the stove, fridge, and pantry," Shade answered, despite having already made up his mind. He wasn't switching punishments with her.

"I got seed inventory."

Shade turned away when Rider did.

CHAPTER TWENTY-ONE

Shade and the original members stood outside, waiting for the brothers to eat their dinners. Many had started riding from Ohio right after work on Viper's orders.

"You better be right about this, Shade, or we'll be walking into a trap in the morning," Viper warned.

"I've checked out The Blue Horsemen's president. Stud keeps the club clean of drugs, but he does run a chop shop which is lucrative. His brother Calder is the wild card; he has a bad habit which Stud is trying to help him break. I don't think he's going to succeed, but it's his brother, and he's not the type of man to turn him out in the cold.

"Like he told you this morning, those assholes belonged to The Blue Horsemen until they robbed a grocery store in West Virginia. Then they were cut loose, but they didn't return their colors and kept bragging about belonging to the club. That club may be a lot of things, but they don't condone their men attacking women."

"We'll stick with the plan, then." Viper paused before he continued. "There's another piece of business we need to discuss before we go inside."

"What?" Cash asked.

"Joy." Shade waited impatiently for Viper to get to the point, and then understanding came when he and Razer exchanged looks.

"The votes?" Shade asked intuitively.

Viper nodded his head. "She has Rider's, Knox's, and Cash's. She needs three more to become a member."

Shade leaned his hip against the picnic table. Joy required six votes from the original eight members to become a full fledged member of The Last Riders. She needed three more from either Shade, Train, Lucky, Razer, or Viper.

"Razer told me he wants to relinquish his voting rights."

"That's not a problem. That still leaves enough men for the women to get six votes," Train reminded Viper. Train didn't get what Viper was beating around the bush about instead of coming out and saying it.

"I want to relinquish mine also, and since Lucky won't vote while he's committed to his job, right now that leaves us one short of voting in new members."

"Fuck," Knox growled.

Rider didn't look any happier. The men both enjoyed breaking in the new members.

"You could always give them your markers," Shade suggested.

"I don't like giving out my markers for new recruits. We came up with this idea so we would know the women were loyal to the club, not just a few brothers they fucked. It's about building trust and loyalty."

"Then give them your votes." Shade shrugged. "I don't see the problem."

"I won't betray Beth," Razer snarled, taking a step toward Shade.

"I won't betray Winter," Viper said grimly.

"Settle down. There are two ways to give them your vote; do I need to remind you? You could both fix it that you're near with your women when another member is giving their vote. From what I hear, both Beth and Winter like to watch." Shade could tell Rider, Knox, and Train liked that suggestion. Those three were the biggest show-offs in the club. Cash didn't look like he gave a shit.

Razer and Viper relaxed.

"That might work," Razer agreed reluctantly. "But what if it doesn't? I'm not going to jeopardize my relationship with Beth to watch Joy get fucked."

"Then one of you needs to give their marker or pass your voting rights to another member. Crash would be a good choice. He's been in the club since the beginning. The only reason he wasn't an original member is because he was the last to get out of the service." Shade's booted foot swung back and forth as he talked.

"I'll give him my voting rights until Lucky is willing to resume his," Viper agreed. "With Crash being able to vote, Knox, Rider, Cash, Shade, and Train make six."

"Thank fuck that's settled. I'm hungry." Cash left with the others following behind.

Viper and Razer were also about to leave as Shade straightened.

"Remember, a marker can count as a vote. That's how Beth was made a member," Shade reminded them.

Viper and Razer both turned back to face him.

"Why's it so important to you?" Viper snapped.

"When I own something, I like to know what it's worth," Shade stated. He had worked hard to earn Viper's marker, and if it couldn't be used the way he planned, it was useless to him.

"You want it for Lily, don't you?" Razer asked, stepping closer to him.

"I don't see her fucking six members to get their votes, do you?" Shade asked, not backing down.

"I don't see her in the club at all." Razer's hands clenched by his sides.

"I do." As soon as the words were out of his mouth, Razer swung at him.

Shade caught his fist mid-swing, and then Viper pushed them apart, placing his body between them.

"It's okay for Beth to become a member, but not Lily?" Shade snarled.

"There's a fucking difference!" Razer yelled back.

"You think I'm stupid? I know there is. You wanna tell me why? What happened to Lily to screw her up so badly?"

Razer's shoulders slumped in defeat as he began shaking his head. "I honestly don't know, brother."

"Then shut the fuck up."

"She doesn't even know you exist."

As Shade closed down, turning his back to the two men, Razer's harsh breathing gradually slowed down.

"I'm sorry, brother, but it's the truth."

"Don't call me brother." Shade walked to the door.

"Shade…My marker will count as a vote."

He didn't stop at Viper's words, going through the door with the two men behind him.

After Viper gave Evie the signal to take the women in the other room, leaving the kitchen and TV room filled with the brothers, he came to a stop in the middle of the room. The room went quiet as he began to speak.

"I want to thank everyone for being here. I know you put in a hard week at work and spent the night riding up here. First off, I would like to tell everyone that, with Winter's help, we were able to prove Gavin didn't disrespect the club rules by fucking Sam. The bitch lied, just as we all knew she had. We still haven't been able to locate the baby, but the sheriff is continuing to investigate. We offered our assistance if he needs it. Evie and the women have been given permission to do what is necessary if Sam makes any further attacks on the club, but as of now, we are done with the bitch."

Murmurs of approval filled the air before they quieted down with Viper's next words.

"I wanted to handle this a few weeks ago, but Shade cautioned me to hold my hand. The group Sam has attached herself to are one-percenters, and he didn't want us to strike out before we were ready. We are now prepared, and that's why I sent for you. We planned on hitting their club tonight, but they called for a meet this morning. My guess is they have someone watching the house and are aware we are about to strike.

"I was not happy they wanted a meet, but did so because Shade urged me to at least talk to them. I'm glad I listened. The president of The Blue Horsemen informed me that the four men who attacked Beth and Lily are outlaws, no longer associated with their club. They have been trying to get their colors back, but they have been outrunning their enforcers. We offered our help, and they accepted.

"Shade has put in motion a set-up for tomorrow that they won't be able to resist. We won't need a show of force, but I am not an idiot. I won't send you back to Ohio until our business with them is complete.

"Enjoy yourselves tonight, and we'll take care of business tomorrow morning. If everything goes as planned, you can be back home tomorrow night."

After the meeting broke up, the brothers spread out, making themselves comfortable. Viper and Razer went in search for their women in the other room.

Shade went to the kitchen cabinet, taking a bottle of the good whiskey and a glass, carrying it downstairs to his room. He wasn't in the mood to hang out with the brothers.

He stared down into the glass of whiskey he poured, seeing Lily's image. She had dragged him from his emotionless shell, and it was affecting his relationship with the brothers. Hell, he was probably planning for something which was never going to happen.

A knock drew his attention.

"Come in," Shade said, not bothering to straighten from his sprawled position on the bed.

"You in the mood for some company?" Joy came strutting in the room.

Shade swallowed the remainder of his whiskey. "I'm in the mood to have my dick sucked." Shade reached out and set his glass on the nightstand.

"I can do that." She licked her bottom lip.

Shade stretched as the woman climbed on his bed between his sprawled legs. Her head bent toward his mouth, but Shade moved his hand to the back of her head, taking a handful of her hair.

"Did I say I wanted your mouth on mine?"

"No." A look of fear flashed in her eyes.

"The only place I want that mouth is on my dick."

A smile widened her lips. "Okay." Her hands went to his jeans, unbuttoning them and sliding down his zipper. Then her mouth slid down the expanse of skin she had exposed as she pulled his cock out.

"Raise your skirt so I can see your ass," Shade ordered.

She wiggled her hips as she raised her skirt, not lifting her mouth from him as she exposed her ass with the tiny red thong.

Shade heard her gasp as his cock hardened even further. The hand still in her hair pressed her farther down on his surging cock as he lifted his hips.

"Bitch, this is going to be one vote you'll never forget."

Chapter Twenty-Two

"What makes you think Slot and the rest will show up?" Stud, the president of The Blue Horsemen, asked.

"They'll show." Shade didn't shift in his seat as the others did, waiting impatiently for the five bikers to arrive at the wrecker yard just outside of town.

They watched the painfully thin tow truck driver drop a car he had towed in next to the dilapidated garage. For the last ten years, Lyle, the tow truck driver, had hated spending more than ten dollars on anything other than liquor.

An old pick-up drove onto the lot, coming to a stop. Greer climbed out of the truck and was slamming the door when five motorcycles turned into the parking lot.

"Damn." Stud whistled low. "How the fuck did you figure this out? We've been trying to find them for the last three months." Stud threw two men sitting on their bikes nearby a disgusted look.

Shade merely shook his head, unwilling to give his source away.

The Greer brothers were assholes and wouldn't give information out on their clients. However, being the one to buy the weed for the club had provided him with an invaluable source: Rachel. Their younger sister who had gone to school with Lily had offered to help when Shade had asked for information on the men who had attacked the women.

"Wait for Greer to leave," Cash cautioned. "He keeps a rifle in his truck, and if he sees us coming, he'll pick us off like sitting ducks."

The men watched as Greer returned to his truck and drove away. Then the bikers remained talking to Lyle until one shoved him hard against the side of the garage.

The clubs started their bikes, riding down the old, paved road on the hillside no one used anymore. The renegade bikers tried to scatter when they saw them coming yet were surrounded, finding their exits blocked.

Viper and Stud rode their bikes to the front of the line.

"Slot, Timber, Marsh," Stud mockingly greeted his former brothers, not bothering to address the two who had taken off running on foot.

Rider and Train brought one back while Knox dragged another by his leg, after he'd run him down on his bike.

"Hey, Stud, we haven't seen you in a while. How you been doing?" Slot spoke as the others remained silent.

"I've been doing well," Stud began conversationally, leaning forward on his bike. "You were supposed to give your colors to Pike. Any reason you didn't?"

"We never saw him, and—"

"You forget where the clubhouse is?"

"No, but figured we wouldn't be welcome."

"You're right about that," Stud spoke through gritted teeth. "Since we're all here, being friendly and shit, I'll be taking them." The renegade bikers took off their vests, handing them to a large Blue Horseman.

"You robbed Deaton's grocery, and he's a friend of mine." Fear clouded Slot's and the other's faces at Stud's words. "The Last Riders said you also tried to kidnap and rape two of their women."

"We didn't know they were with The Last Riders. Who knew they could have such pretty women?" Slot's lame joke fell on a humorless crowd of bikers out for revenge.

"You always did think you were funnier than you actually are. Look around; nobody's laughing, you dumb fuck."

Slot tried to run when Stud got off his bike yet was held immobile by Crash and Razer.

"I made a deal with The Last Riders that, if they helped us find you, they could keep two, and I could take two. That way, everybody's happy," Stud explained.

"But there's five of us," Slot whined.

"We decided to share one."

Once Stud's fist slammed into Slot's belly, knocking him to his knees, he pulled his pistol out from behind his back, bringing it down on the side of Slot's head.

"Stud, remember my half," Shade reminded him as he got off his bike.

"Which half do you want?"

"The part I bury."

෨ ෬

Shade forced himself out of bed the next morning, going up the steps to the kitchen. The punishment of cleaning the kitchen was a pain in the ass, but it was better than doing seed inventory. He snickered to himself, thinking of the tedious job Winter had drawn.

He opened the door to see the object of his sarcastic humor sitting at the kitchen table with a cup of coffee in front of her.

He poured himself a cup, taking a sip of the coffee to bolster his flagging energy before he moved toward the stove. Opening the oven door, he stared at it for several minutes before closing it.

Shade then went to the kitchen closet, gathering cleaning supplies and filling a bucket with soapy water. He went to the refrigerator, opened the door, and within seconds, he was slamming it shut. Turning green, he hastily moved away to lean on the counter.

With the amount of whiskey he had consumed the previous night about to make an appearance, he decided he was going to call the local appliance store and have them bring a new stove then take the one in the kitchen. There was no way in Hell he was going to clean that mess.

"The punishments are a bitch, aren't they? I thought mine was bad, but at least I don't have to clean that oven or the fridge," Winter remarked conversationally.

Shade looked back and forth between the offending appliances. There was no way you would think the refrigerator could be worse than the oven, but it was. Shade internally debated the price of a new fridge. He could buy one that had a water and ice cube dispenser on the door, and the brothers would thank him.

"I would start with the oven. Give your stomach time to settle. It's a little early to clean something that smells so bad." Winter stood up, freshening her coffee as she stared at him.

By that point, he was seriously debating the cost of the appliances against his pride at Winter seeing him act like a pussy. Shade had one weakness other than Lily, and that was vomiting. He hated to vomit. When you vomited, you had no control over your body, and control was everything to Shade.

"Of course, I could help you with your problem."

He turned to face her, his eyes narrowing in on her innocent expression. The witch had somehow guessed he had a stomach which was a wimp when he had been drinking.

"I could clean the oven, fridge, and pantry for you."

His eyes went to the pantry door, but he made no move to see what condition it was in. Everyone knew it was a close second to the seeds in punishments. He could buy a new oven and fridge, but he couldn't buy a new pantry, and the women hated to clean worse than he did. They wouldn't be bribed into doing it for him. Besides, they would tell Viper on him.

"What do you want?" he asked grimly.

"It's going to take me at least a couple of hours to scrub that oven down. In case you didn't know, that's cheese on the bottom. The fridge is even worse—it smells like Armageddon—and the pantry has an ant infestation," she told him before taking another sip of coffee.

"What's your price?" he demanded through clenched teeth.

"I want your vote. Look at it this way; it's going to take several hours of work to clean this mess up. If we had sex, it would take ten minutes. You're getting a better deal. Besides, we both know you're not going to vote me in with sex, anyway."

Shade stared at her before shrugging. It was a no-brainer for him. "It's all yours." He poured himself another cup of coffee, giving her a smug grin. "I'll have to tell Viper he must be getting old if you think sex lasts ten minutes."

He went to sit at the table as she opened the refrigerator door. Shade almost dropped the coffee cup as he practically ran without stopping until he was back in his room, dragging in deep breaths of clear air.

Viper's woman was proving to be as resourceful as he was. Shade didn't like being the blackmailed; he much preferred being the blackmailer. She was cleaning up a mess he didn't have the stomach for, for no reason. He had already planned on giving Viper his marker for Winter's vote, even though she certainly didn't need it. She had secured five votes on her own, and Razer would have been cajoled by Beth—he was sure—for the sixth she would need.

Shade whistled as he took off his clothes and went to the shower. He was the master of maneuvering people to do what he wanted. Winter needed to be taught by someone who really knew how to play the game.

As soon as he had showered and his stomach had settled down, he would find Viper. They needed to have a talk.

Shade grinned evilly to himself. Winter was going to become a student once again. He was going to teach her not to fuck with him.

CHAPTER TWENTY-THREE

Dressed in workout shorts, Shade found Viper already in the gym finishing up a set. Picking up a couple of hand weights, he started up the treadmill to a steady run.

"Where's Winter?"

"Upstairs talking to the lawyer from the Teacher's Union."

"She still trying to get her job back as principal of the high school?"

Evie had told him the school board had given Winter's job away while she was recovering from her injuries, citing moral turpitude as the reason. Shade personally thought it was small-town bullshit, she'd have a battle on her hands, trying to fight the hypocrisy of the residents of Treepoint.

He pressed a few buttons so that he ran on an incline.

"Do you have to do that while I'm working out?" Viper grunted, dropping the weights onto the mat.

"Do what?"

"Show off."

Shade grinned. "I have to stay in shape."

"Fucker."

"Who's her lawyer?"

"Ms. Richards," Viper mimicked the snooty woman's tone.

"She's new in town," Shade commented.

"You know her?"

"No, just make it my business to know all the lawyers in town. I wouldn't be much of an enforcer if I didn't know the best way to protect the brothers if any of them get in trouble."

Viper nodded in acknowledgement. "I talked to Cash. Winter spoke with Carmen, Jake's girlfriend, and she's convinced Jake is innocent."

Shade had felt something wasn't right himself.

"The sheriff ran the DNA on the cigar butt I found; it wasn't a match."

"Get the sheriff to let you talk to Jake. Take Cash and Razer with you. The three of you together might be enough to get him to confess. If he doesn't, we'll look into it further."

"Cash will be enough to scare that kid."

Viper frowned. "Shade, Razer didn't mean anything by what he said. He's trying to protect Lily."

"He doesn't have to protect her from me. I'm not going to make a move until I know she's old enough to handle it."

"Brother, that woman has problems age isn't going to fix."

"Not with everyone wrapping her in cotton. Overprotecting her can get her hurt."

"It isn't up to you to make that decision," Viper cautioned.

"Not yet."

"You always were a patient bastard."

⁎ ⁎

Shade passed out beers to the brothers as they watched the women get ready to leave for Beth's bachelorette party at Rosie's. The brothers were complaining that the women looked to hot to leave the house without them.

Shade eyed Bliss who had been one of the first downstairs. She would be coming home early with the Biker Bitches coming after she left. *I'll have to make sure she doesn't feel left out when she returns,* he thought in anticipation.

"Let's go!" Natasha's yell had doors from the upstairs banging open as the women rushed to answer her summons.

It wasn't long before the women were all waiting at the bottom of the stairs for the happy couple to come down the steps. As they did, Razer kept his arm around Beth's shoulders, who was wearing a pink 'Bride to be' T-shirt and a modest blue jean skirt. The couple didn't try to hide their happiness from the large group watching them.

A couple of months had passed since his and Razer's argument and since then, Razer had tried to make friendly overtures, which Shade had rejected. He wasn't nursing hurt feelings like a pussy, but he resented the lack of faith Razer had him, thinking he would make a move on Lily while she was still so young.

"They are perfect together," Shade overheard Winter's comment to Viper.

"Let's go, or Bliss is going to miss the party." Evie nudged everyone out the door.

Viper swept Winter into his arms, following the women who were excitedly rushing outside.

"He's fucking whipped," Knox groaned.

Rider laughed. "Better not let Viper hear you say that, or you'll be the one getting your ass whipped."

Knox shrugged, the huge biker clearly not worried about anyone giving him an ass-whipping. "What are we going to do with all the women gone?" he whined for the fourth time.

Shade took a seat at the card table, shuffling the cards. "Let's play poker until Bliss gets back."

Knox took a seat in front of him. "What good is one woman going to be with so many brothers waiting?"

"We're talking about Bliss," Shade reminded him, dealing the cards as Razer sat down. The other brothers fought for the remaining chairs. Then the ones who hadn't claimed a seat found solace at the pool table, getting drunk off their ass.

Viper came back into the room, going to the pool table. He was a lousy poker player.

Shade hadn't even noticed how much time had passed until Bliss came through the front door, and was immediately attacked by both Rider and Train. She giggled as they hauled her ass up the stairs. Shade sighed, thinking it would be at least two hours before he got his turn, for which he would ask Knox to follow them down to his room to join.

Shade had a pile of cash in front of him and was looking forward to winning another hand while Razer dealt the cards. He was dealing the last one when Viper's cell phone rang.

Shade caught Viper's frown as he stared at the caller ID before answering.

"Hello?" The expression that came to his face had Shade's blood running cold.

"We're on our way." Viper snapped his pool stick in two by slamming it on the corner of the pool table. "That was one of the Bitches. They were on their way to the party when they saw Winter on the side of the road about a mile from Rosie's being attacked. She said Lily took off into the woods."

Viper, Shade, Cash, and Knox were running out the door while Razer ran upstairs, calling for Rider and Train to get their asses moving. Shade was the first on his bike with Cash and Viper right behind him.

The bikers sped down the mountain road, unconcerned for their own safety. They came around a curve and to a scene which brought them to a stop a few inches away from Beth's SUV.

As he climbed off his bike, Shade took in what was going down. Winter was surrounded by the biker bitches, one with a gun in her waistband and holding a baseball bat. One of the sheriff's deputies Shade instantly recognized was lying on the road, unconscious.

Viper got off his bike, running directly to Winter. "What happened?"

Shade studied the nearby hillside while impatiently waiting for Winter to explain.

"The deputy pulled us over. He's crazy, Viper. He's the one who attacked me at the school, to pay me back for almost getting him fired. When he knew I recognized him, he hit me. He was going to kill me, but I fought him off. Lily managed to get away." Winter broke down in tears. "He shot at her twice before she ran into the woods."

Viper took command. "Sex Piston, take Winter in Beth's vehicle back to Rosie's. Don't open your mouths about what happened. You never stopped. You came directly to Rosie's after you left your home. Understand me?"

"You going to finish this motherfucker, or do you need me to stay and help?" the scary one named Killyama asked.

"I think we can handle this piece of shit from here. Go on to the bar, get drunk, and have some fun. Forget this happened." Viper's eyes bore into the biker bitches' faces.

Getting the message, all the women except Sex Piston and Winter climbed back in their vehicle, the tires screeching as Crazy Bitch's car peeled out.

"Razer, call Beth, tell her what happened and not to tell anyone. You tell her we'll find Lily. Winter, get in the SUV and go with Sex Piston. You need to keep Beth calm."

Sex Piston was behind the wheel before Viper finished talking. Winter shakily walked to the passenger door, getting inside with Viper's help. Then Winter and Viper exchanged a few words, and Sex Piston did a U-turn before driving off in the direction of the bar.

"Cash, Shade, Rider, find Lily."

The men moved, each going to their bikes where they pulled out what they needed before running into the dark woods.

"Slow down, Shade; give me a second to find her tracks," Cash ordered.

Shade forced himself to move slowly. Cash was an excellent tracker, probably the best there was, but Shade was good, too. Both men separated themselves by a short distance, trying to find a clue as to the direction Lily had run, while Rider stood still, not wanting to damage any of the tracks.

Expertly, Cash shone his flashlight back and forth across the ground. They were lucky because it took them less than fifteen minutes to find her first track.

"There it is." Shade flashed the beam of his own flashlight on the overturned rock.

Moving apart a few feet, they began a search grid, steadily working their way closer to Lily. Cash was familiar with the mountain and instantly began searching for areas it would be easier for her to run.

Shade soon found a ripped portion of her dress with blood on it. He gripped the torn cloth tightly in his hand as they moved forward, changing direction slightly.

"We're fucked," Cash said, obviously recognizing a nearby marker.

"What?" Shade snarled.

"We're on Porter land."

"So?"

Cash shook his head, squatting down by a tree. "She rested here, someone found her, and then she left with them in that direction." He pointed at an area to their left.

"How the hell do you know all that?" Shade asked, staring at the ground.

"Because whoever found her was riding a mud puppy. The good news is it left us a trail a blind man could follow."

Since they had easier signs to follow, it didn't take them long to come to the large house built into a clearing.

"Son of a bitch." They hunkered down as close to the house as they could get without being seen from the occupants within.

"Let's go," Rider said when they saw the four-wheeler they had been tracking parked in front of the house.

"Get down," Cash hissed.

"Why? Let's just knock on the fucking door," Rider tried to reason.

"If you knock on their door, the coroner will be scraping what brains you have left off the front porch. Listen to me; the Porters are the biggest weed growers in the county," Cash said, trying to explain the danger they were in.

Shade didn't need to be told—he knew what kind of arsenal was behind that house's door. You didn't just walk onto a weed dealer's property in that area of the county, and it wasn't his first visit to the Porter's.

Shade stealthily crossed the yard, blending into the dark night. This was what he was used to—becoming invisible until he made his presence known. He was at the side of the house when Cash came striding toward the front door.

He didn't make it far before the door opened. One of the Greer brothers came out of the front door holding a shotgun pointed at Cash. Shade was constantly telling the brother he needed to learn how to be more covert, but Cash was the type of fighter to barrel into a fight.

"Get off my land."

"Greer, it's Cash Adams."

"I can see who you are, fuckwad. Get your ass off my property." Greer didn't raise his voice; the shotgun got his message across.

"My friend's fiancée's sister found herself in trouble tonight and took off into the woods. We're trying to find her."

"Haven't seen anyone tonight other than you and that chicken shit you have hiding over by that tree," Greer said, cocking his shotgun.

"Rider, come out." When he didn't, Cash knew where Dustin was.

"Dustin, you better not hurt him, or you're going to have deal with The Last Riders. You won't have anything except scorched earth left to grow that weed you're so proud of."

"Shut the fuck up, Cash," another voice spoke as a third man pressed a gun muzzle against the back of Cash's head.

"I was wondering where you were, Tate. Will you tell your crazy-assed brothers to back off? We just want Lily and we'll go," Cash tried to reason with the oldest brother.

Shade used the opportunity to move around the house, looking through the windows to find Lily.

"There isn't any woman here!" yelled Greer.

The fucker was lying; Shade spotted her in the back bedroom.

Taking the knife from his boot, he used it to pry the locked window open. He was halfway in when the window was lifted the rest of the way up, making it easier from him to climb inside.

Rachel Porter's critical gaze studied him.

"You better make them see reason, Tate. You don't want trouble with The Last Riders." Both of them heard Cash's yell from outside.

"I better get out there." She turned toward the doorway.

"You're just going to leave me with her?" he asked, somehow disappointed.

Rachel cocked her head at him. "Yes. You won't hurt her."

She left him alone with Lily, who was sitting on the floor in the corner of the bedroom with her forehead on her knees, her arms wrapped around herself, rocking back and forth.

Shade leaned against the wall, evaluating the situation before making a move toward Lily. The red rubber band the counselor had given her was on her delicate wrist. Penni had told him the counselor had instructed Lily to snap it against herself when she became too frightened to deal with a situation. Penni had also told him that, at first, she would see Lily snapping it constantly, but it had begun tapering off to only a few times a day. He only wished Penni could get Lily to open up about what was causing the attacks, which she hadn't been able to do so far.

"Lily?" Shade tried to soften his harsh voice. He had seen her that way a couple of times. Beth had told Razer that only time itself would draw her out of the self-induced trance Lily used as a defense mechanism. However, Beth either didn't know or wouldn't tell Razer the reason for the attacks in the first place.

Shade slowly walked toward Lily, hunching down in front of her rocking form. "Lily." That time, his voice was more forceful, commanding her attention, and the rocking stopped.

Coming to a decision, Shade reached out, lifting her into his arms. It wasn't the smartest choice, however, as he found himself with a wildcat in his arms. The unexpected fury of the woman had him forcing her against the wall to gain control of the nails going for his eyes. Pinning her there with his body, he didn't try to grab her hands, merely blocking her moves.

"Lily, stop it now!" he said in a firm voice. "Aren't you worried about Winter? She's worried about you. She was crying she was so worried, Lily. Beth is probably scared out of her fucking mind." Shade kept her pinned against the wall as he kept repeating Beth's and Winter's names.

Finally, he saw a light of reality break through her blank expression.

"Shade?" her voice whimpered.

"Yes, baby."

As Lily sucked in deep breaths as if her chest was going to explode, her hand wiped at the tears on her face. "Is Winter safe?"

"Yes. Beth's friends stopped and helped. Winter is waiting with Beth. They are both waiting to hear from us. You okay?" Shade asked, worried about the blood he had found on her clothes. His eyes searched her body, finding a scratch with drying blood on the underside of her forearm.

Lily nodded, still trying to catch her breath.

"Lily, breathe slowly," Shade ordered in a hard voice.

Lily jumped, but her breaths gradually slowed and he took a step back, giving her some room.

"Can we go now?" Lily asked, her soft voice gaining strength.

"Yes." Shade backed away more, allowing her to slide by him. Then he opened the bedroom door, letting Lily go ahead of him before following her outside.

Lily walked out the door and came to a sudden stop when she found the yard filled with The Last Riders.

When Beth jumped off Razer's bike, running to her sister and nearly knocking her down, Shade placed his hand on Lily's back, holding her steady.

"Are you all right?" Beth asked.

"I'm fine. I'm sorry I couldn't help Winter. I shouldn't have pan—"

"Don't you dare apologize. You were smart enough to run. Winter said he shot at you twice. I would have run, too. Anyone would."

Lily shook her head. "Even when Rachel found me, I couldn't tell her what happened. Her brothers could have helped."

Beth smiled softly at her sister. "Winter had plenty of help. Sex Piston and her crew showed up. They took a baseball bat to the bastard."

"Really?" Lily asked as they walked toward Razer's motorcycle.

"Yes."

"Winter's okay?"

"She's on the back of Viper's bike."

Shade saw her finally relax, knowing Winter was safe.

Shade got on his own bike, starting it as he saw Knox sitting uncomfortably behind Rider. He owed the brother a favor for bringing his bike.

Once Viper also fired his engine, The Last Riders waited as one for their brother to leave. Razer's new family was now their own.

Shade rode his bike up next to Lily.

"Lily." He used the same tone of voice he had used with her inside.

Lily didn't appear to want to be parted from Beth. He didn't think she truly would feel safe until she was home.

"Razer, could you call and ask Mick if he would drive my SUV here?" Beth asked.

"Get on, Lily. I'm taking you home." Shade's firm voice had Lily moving reluctantly toward him.

Beth paused.

"Get on, Beth. She's safe with Shade." Razer and Shade's eyes met as Lily climbed on behind Shade, holding his sides with her legs, her trembling hands taking his helmet.

As soon as it was on, Shade throttled his engine, and Viper pulled out in the lead with the others following down the winding road. Shade saw Beth turn around, checking to make sure Lily was okay. Beth had a long way to go with learning to trust him with Lily, but Shade had seen that night what Razer had been trying to tell him. It wasn't about what anyone wanted to do for Lily; it would always be about what was best for her, and Shade could live with that.

CHAPTER TWENTY-FOUR

Shade was sprawled in one of the chairs at Rosie's, enjoying a lap dance from the stripper Knox had hired for Razer's bachelor party. He was wearing blue jeans and had pulled off his T-shirt in the hot bar.

She seductively ran her hands down his naked chest, grinding her pussy down onto his cock which was about to burst his zipper. "God, please. Shade, please." Chastity's face was a tortured mask of desire.

"What you want, bitch?"

"Your cock. Please, Shade," she whimpered.

"Where you want it?"

"My pussy."

"Can't give it to you now." Shade wasn't about to fuck the woman with Winter at the front of the bar. "If you come back to the clubhouse, I'll give it to you all night." Shade bragged, half-drunk and horny.

The woman nodded frantically.

"Go give my brothers their dances. If you want to give them anything else, you can give them your mouth. Save your pussy for me." If the dances hadn't already been paid for, Shade would have dragged her to his bike already.

The woman shakily moved off Shade, heading toward Knox who was eagerly waiting his turn. She tugged off the flimsy, pink robe she was wearing, pressing her bare breasts against Knox's chest as she went to work, grinding on him.

Shade half-stumbled toward the bar to get another bottle of whiskey. The counter was a large circle so Shade stood at the back part, hidden from view by the massive wooden shelves that held the liquor bottles.

Bliss was standing next to Train, who had become tired of waiting for the stripper and had removed Bliss's top. "I heard you promise Chastity your cock."

"You think I don't have enough for the both of you?" As his fingers cupped her tit, tugging roughly at her nipple, Bliss moaned, pushing her hips toward his.

"I know you do. It just depends on whether you want to give it to me. Train has me too horny already, and I don't want to beg for what you might not give me." Bliss pouted.

"When have I ever not satisfied your greedy pussy?" Shade tilted his head until he could see around the wooden shelf and saw Winter arguing with Viper at a table where they sat with Razer.

Shade took a seat as Chastity came over to them, like she had somehow heard her name mentioned.

With his lap dance abruptly over, Knox shot him a middle finger, and Shade grinned back.

Bliss hadn't bothered with panties, and her shaved pussy beckoned his drunken mind as she sat down in his lap, straddling him. "Please, you always wait until we beg."

Chastity came up behind him, groping his throbbing cock. "I'm already begging."

Cash, who was standing at the bar, slammed his beer down onto the counter, drawing his attention before walking hurriedly toward him.

"Lily's here."

It onl took that one word to have Shade out the chair, practically knocking Bliss into Train, who managed to catch her as she gave a small scream.

"Damn, Shade, be careful."

He tried to shake off the fog surrounding his mind, when he noticed the wall of brothers between him and Lily, giving him precious seconds to get out of the precarious position.

"Sorry," Shade apologized to the two. "What in the fuck is Lily doing here?"

"I don't know," Train said, giving him a hard shove. Usually, Shade would have returned it, but he let Train get away with it that time, figuring he deserved it.

Shade moved closer to the brothers who hid him from view as he tried to listen in on the conversation at Razer's table. He was barely able to catch a glimpse of her between Knox's back and Cash's shoulder.

She was sitting at Razer's table, flicking that fucking red rubber band.

Shade motioned for Mick to turn the music down.

"Razer, you know I love my sister."

"I know that you two are very close." Razer's eyes were watching Lily's hands.

"We are. Our parents adopted me, but Beth and I are as close as if we shared the same parents. We tell each other everything," Lily confessed, not noticing that Razer was becoming tenser. "When you and Beth broke up, she came to my dorm and shared with me how badly she was hurt."

Shade tried to edge closer, but the wall of bikers wouldn't move.

"Move, Knox. I'm going to ask her to dance."

Knox just rolled his eyes, which pissed Shade off. Why shouldn't he ask Lily to dance? It sure as fuck would take her mind off the red rubber band he was going to rip off her fucking wrist.

"You're fucking drunk off your ass, Shade. Back off."

While Train snorted at Knox's words, Shade saw Lily's eyes had gone to Bliss, who was dancing with Rider. They weren't dancing as erotically as they usually would be, but Bliss couldn't hide the sexy outfit she was wearing, her shirt back on at that point.

"I don't want to see her hurt that way again," Lily said miserably.

Razer suddenly leaned across the table, his hand covering her wrist. Everyone could see the bright red flesh of her skin from torturing it with that rubber band.

"Lil' sis, you're breaking my heart. Please stop."

Lily's hand became still under his.

He nodded toward Winter. "You trust her?"

Lily turned her head to observe Winter before turning back to Razer. "Yes."

"Do you trust her enough that she would tell Beth if I'm stepping out on her?"

"Yes."

"She's attached to my hip the rest of the night. When she leaves, I leave."

"Okay." Lily smiled at Razer in relief.

Damn it to Hell, she is fucking beautiful, Shade thought.

"I am marrying Beth because I love her, which means I'm not going to do stupid shit to hurt her again. Beth has learned to trust me, and I want you to, also." He moved his hand, touching the rubber band. "You don't need this anymore to keep from being afraid, lil' sis." Razer leaned farther across the table. "I swear on my life, I'll never let anyone hurt you again."

Lily gave him a heartwarming smile before getting up from the table and hugging him. Razer hugged her back, and that was when Shade tried to lunge between the brothers, but they knocked him back. Razer quickly set her away from him by several inches.

"Now, let's get you out of here. You have another year before you can legally be in a bar," Razer joked. "Mick made an exception for Beth's bridal shower, but he might get pissed off if we start making a habit of it."

Lily laughed. "He can't get in trouble. I turned twenty-one on my last birthday. I thought Beth told you. Everyone just thinks I'm a year younger because Mom and Dad were so concerned I was behind in school when they adopted me."

Hearing that sobered him right up and immediately he was filled with a murderous rage. Beth had lied about Lily's age, and he knew instinctively that Razer had known, despite pretending he hadn't.

He was done fucking around. He used his boot to kick the back of Cash's knee, forcing him to drop out of his way. Then he started toward Lily, only to find Train blocking him.

"Shade..." Train warned.

Shade saw Razer hustling Lily toward the door, realizing she was getting away from him.

She was twenty-one; he didn't have to wait for her any longer. He didn't have to go home and fuck two faceless women when the one he really wanted was finally within his reach.

He went berserk when he saw Lily about to go through the doorway.

Evie and Dawn screamed when he picked up a chair and threw it at the bikers standing in front of him.

"Move!"

The brothers stayed where they were, so Shade quit being nice. He grabbed Crash by the T-shirt, using him as a battering ram as he took out four of the brothers.

"Shade, she's gone. Stop!" Viper's order fell on deaf ears as Shade reached for the beer bottles sitting at the counter, using them as missiles to clear a path.

"Fuck!" Rider ducked, the beer dousing him as the bottle nearly hit him, breaking the glass mirror at the bar.

"Shade, I'm going to kick your ass!" Mick came toward him, but Viper pushed him out of the way as a beer bottle struck him in the chest.

Angrily, Viper charged toward Shade, punching him on the jaw.

Shade used the side of his hand to strike Viper's shoulder, grinning in satisfaction at his groan of pain. Leaning over, he used his shoulders in a maneuver he had learned when he was in high school, flipping Viper over his back. He was finally managing to get closer to the door.

"Hold him back!" Viper yelled furiously from the floor. "I'll kick anyone's ass who lets him through."

"Mother fucker, move out of my way." Shade shoved Knox and Train into a table, their combined weight causing it to give out and break into pieces.

"Shade!" The door opened, and Razer came back inside.

Lily was gone.

Before anyone could stop him, he had Razer by the throat. "You fucking liar! You kept throwing her age up to me, and the whole time, you knew she was twenty-one instead of twenty!" Shade snarled.

"I didn't, Shade. I swear." Razer slammed his arms down, breaking the hold on him. "Brother, I'm telling the truth—"

"I told you not to call me brother!" Shade pummeled Razer in the stomach.

Knox came up behind him, pinning his arms to the side, and he slammed his head back. Knox quickly released him.

Before Shade could attack Razer again, Viper, Train, and Razer came at him, pinning him up against the wall.

"Listen to me!" Razer yelled. "I'm telling you Beth didn't tell me, but it doesn't make a difference, Shade. Did you not see her snapping that fucking rubber band? How's she going to deal with a crazy mother fucker like you? Let him go," Razer ordered.

Shade shrugged their hands away, storming toward the door.

"What are you going to do, Shade? Fuck her up even more?" Razer yelled at his back. "You don't give a shit about Lily."

Shade turned around, rushing at Razer until he was the one pinned against the wall, his arm across Razer's throat.

"Don't *ever* say that again. I'll make you disappear before Beth can marry you."

"It's the truth, Shade. If you cared about Lily, you would see she's incapable of a relationship right now. You can deny it all you want, but in that cold heart of yours, you have to know it's the truth."

Shade wanted to strangle Razer to shut him up; instead, he released him, stepping back using deep breaths to regain his control.

"You don't know what it's like," Shade confessed. "Can you imagine if Beth didn't ever give you the time of day, if she jumped every time you came near her, if you could see she was screaming for help in her eyes and no one was listening to her? I see that in Lily. She's not getting better; she's getting worse. And I'm standing back, watching her fade away more inside herself every time I get to see her."

"I don't know what to say, Shade. I really don't."

"There's nothing *to* say." Shade ran his hand wearily over his closely cropped hair.

"The most important thing to Lily and Beth is that she finishes college. She dreams about becoming a social worker. Let her finish school, and I won't stand in your way. I'll make sure you can be around her, slowly get her used to you being a part of her life. You don't want to become another nightmare she has to live with, do you?"

"No."

"I'll help, but we have to do it my way. Can you do that?" Razer asked.

"I have no choice, do I?"

"No, brother, you don't."

Shade wanted to yell at Razer not to call him brother, but stopped when he saw the torn expression on Razer's face.

He was trying to protect Lily for Beth. Shade couldn't fault the brother for his loyalty. It was the one feeling he understood.

Shade left the bar, ignoring Winter who hastily stepped back from the door, went to his bike and took off toward town. He passed the street Lily lived on, keeping to the speed limit until he reached the county line. There, he opened his bike up, full throttle. He needed to put some distance between him and Lily until he could think again, until he could breathe again.

CHAPTER TWENTY-FIVE

Shade stood at Razer's side as he spoke his vows to Beth. The wedding was in the backyard of the church. Tables had been set up on the other side of the yard, away from where the ceremony was being performed.

While everyone's eyes were on the happy couple, his were on Lily. Her gaze briefly met his before dropping to the bouquet she was holding, the faint trembling of her hands betraying her calm facade. Shade turned his head, pretending to watch Lucky perform the wedding. He bet Beth's father was rolling over in his grave at the man who had taken his position over in the church.

The ceremony didn't last long, but afterward, the pictures of the wedding party took forever. There were several photos taken in various positions. First, the whole bridal party, then the bridesmaids, then groomsmen, and then the groomsmen and bridesmaids.

The brothers began getting antsy when they saw the guests going for the buffet tables.

"They're going to eat all the food," Knox muttered.

"Let's finish this up," Razer warned Beth, seeing the men's threatening glares.

"All right, all right. Just a few more," Beth soothed.

Shade was in no hurry, managing to put himself in several pictures with Lily. The photographer decided to take pictures of them together, exactly like the others had during their pictures.

"Last one," the photographer said, moving to a different position.

Hearing the photographer, Charles moved closer, waiting for Lily, who gave him a sweet smile. Shade's eyes narrowed as he slid his arm around Lily's waist, bringing her flush against his side. Lily stiffened within Shade's grasp, her hand going to his chest. Though she didn't pull away, her body went taut against his.

While her smile became more nervous, Shade's became a different matter, giving a clear warning to the young man standing beside Winter.

"Let's get something to eat." Charles led her away to the buffet tables, giving Shade a gloating smile over his shoulder.

Did that little pissant think he was going to get away with that smug smile? Shade was going to rip him a new asshole.

Winter moved to block his path. "Hey, Shade. It was a nice ceremony, wasn't it?" Winter used a saccharine sweet voice which scraped at his nerves.

He took a deep breath, reminding himself she was Viper's woman.

"Beth and Lily looked beautiful, didn't they?"

Shade's eyes went to Razer and Beth standing together as their friends congratulated them.

"Yes," he growled out.

"They all are so happy; Beth with Razer and Lily finally settling into college. Their lives are merging, yet still fragile. It could be hurt irreparably if Beth feels Razer's putting a friend's wants over her sister's needs."

Shade's body stiffened.

"It's not like you're deprived of female companionship. Lily will be out of school in two years with a degree she's wanted since I've known her. By then, you might not even want her anymore."

Shade gave her a look that had her taking a step back. Then he stood back and watched Charles with Lily. The man considered her his even though they hadn't dated in months. Charles had every intention of marrying Lily someday. It wasn't going to happen, though. Shade would see to that. If he had to wait five years for Lily, he would. He turned back to Winter, letting her see the conviction in his eyes.

However, she was right, no matter how much he hated to admit it. If he tried to initiate a relationship with Lily at that point, it would create a rift between Razer and Beth. Razer needed time to cement his marriage to Beth, and he needed to place Razer over his need for Lily. *For now.*

Seeing Winter had received his silent message, he went to fix himself a plate. After the food was eaten, he sat at his table, watching the dancing. He was about to get up and leave when Beth, Razer, and Lily walked up to him.

"You leaving?" Razer asked.

"Yes," Shade answered. He couldn't take another minute of watching Lily with Charles.

"Dance with me before you leave." Beth grabbed his hand, dragging him to the dance floor, laughing as she turned to face him before stepping into his arms.

Razer followed with Lily, dancing with her as soft music began to play.

"This is my favorite song. Do you mind if I dance with Razer, Lily?" Beth asked as Lily and Razer danced next to them.

"N-no." Lily stood stiffly as Shade moved sideways, taking her into his arms.

Casting a quick glance toward Razer, he seemed as surprised as Shade was by Beth's maneuvering.

As Shade moved slowly, bringing her closer to him, Lily didn't try to move away, but she didn't look up at him, either.

"How's school going?" Shade asked.

"Good," she answered softly then cleared her voice. "Do you remember the first time we met?"

Shade almost stumbled at her question.

"Yeah, I remember," he answered hoarsely.

"They were just beginning to know each other, and now they're married." Her face lifted to his. "I want to thank you for helping me into the house that day and for that night at the Porter's."

"You're welcome."

Lily slid her hand to his shoulder as she relaxed, enjoying the dance. As the song ended, she gave him a sweet smile before going back to Razer and Beth's side.

She had remembered him. He might make her uncomfortable, but she had noticed he was slowly becoming a part of her life. He was gradually coming out of the shadows, becoming visible to her. He might not be who she wanted to see, but she knew he existed in her world. Shade could settle for that until she was ready to handle more.

CHAPTER TWENTY-SIX

Shade drove through town, heading back to the clubhouse. He had gone to the auto store to pick up a part for Rider's truck.

He was passing the local motel when he saw the sheriff and the coroner's cars out front. Slowing, he drove his bike nearer, parking along the street.

A body bag was wheeled outside on a stretcher with the sheriff and coroner both talking as they exited the same room. Shade waited until the coroner had driven off with the body before approaching his dad.

"What's up?" Shade asked as a couple of the deputies went inside the room.

"A motel worker found a body in the room when they went in to clean."

"Anyone I know?" he asked curiously, doubting anyone he knew would stay at the motel.

"Sam Langley." The sheriff's grim response shocked Shade.

The young girl was a bitch who had hung out at the club when they had first come to town, sharing several of the brothers' beds during the weekends as they had tried to find clues to Gavin's death. When she had tried to kill Beth, she had dodged going to prison by claiming to have had Gavin's baby. Winter's Aunt Shay had told the truth, and the whole club had been relieved to find out that baby wasn't Gavin's.

Since then, no one had seen Sam other than the day she had been with the bikers who had attacked Beth, Winter, and Lily at the diner.

"She was hanging around with some renegade bikers the last time I saw her."

"I'll have to find out if she was still with them. They never showed for their court appearance. Their bail bondsman and I have both been trying to find them."

"I heard they left town." Shade shrugged.

"They're not the only ones. Deputy Moore is missing, and his father is raising hell."

"Don't know him." Shade stared back impassively at his father.

The sheriff nodded grimly. "I have a few witnesses to talk to. I'll talk to you later."

Shade watched his father walk toward an older woman who stood in front of the hotel, upset.

He walked back to his bike and started the motor. Pulling out, he rode back to the clubhouse. He would find Viper and tell him Sam was dead. Shade, despite the fact he had fucked the woman several times, felt no sorrow for her death. Her

130

actions outside the diner that day had made her his enemy, and he had planned to pay her back for her part in the attack. Looked like someone had saved him the trouble, though.

›› ❦❧

"You're going to be late," Viper warned as Shade came down the steps.

Shade paused, going out the front door of the clubhouse. "I have five minutes. Besides, the boss isn't there yet," Shade stated, reminding Viper he wasn't the only one not at the factory.

"I'm on my way. I need to grab a cup of coffee first." Viper's eyes narrowed over Shade's shoulder.

He turned to see who he was staring at and saw the sheriff standing grimly in the doorway.

"Viper, Shade, can I come in?"

The formal tone the sheriff was using raised Shade's instincts. Something was wrong. Shade opened the door wider, letting him come inside.

"I'm here on official business to question Knox."

"What for?" Viper asked. "He get drunk and bust up another bar? I'll write a check—"

"Money isn't going to solve this problem, Viper. I'm here to question him about Sam's murder."

"Sam's?"

"Yes, unless there's another murder that's happened in town that I don't know about," the sheriff barked back.

Shade's mouth snapped shut as Viper took out his cell phone to call Knox.

The sheriff glared at Shade as Viper disconnected the call. "You need to get him a lawyer, and fast."

"What evidence do you have?" Shade asked warily.

"He was seen leaving the hotel room Sam was found inside. There's evidence that they'd been intimate."

Both Shade and Viper became angry at hearing Knox had been with Sam.

"This is bullshit. Knox didn't touch that bitch!" Viper's voice rose. The club had banned any members from seeing Sam.

"Calm down, Viper. Let's hear him out," Shade reasoned.

Knox came down the steps as they watched his approach.

"What's up?" Knox asked the Sheriff.

"Samantha Bedford's body was found this afternoon at the motel," the sheriff replied while watching his reaction to the news.

Knox stiffened, as if sensing where this was going.

"Knox has had nothing to do with that bitch since she attacked Beth; none of us have. She wasn't allowed back here at the clubhouse, and after the stunt she pulled with Winter, Beth, and Lily at the diner, we haven't seen her."

The sheriff didn't say anything, just merely continued staring at Knox.

"I saw her yesterday. She stopped her car after I crashed my bike."

The silence in the room became tangible.

"What happened then?" the sheriff probed.

"We went back to her hotel room and fucked. When Viper called, I left. She was breathing just fine when I walked out that door." Knox stared back at the sheriff.

"Damn it, Knox," Viper said angrily.

"You're not going to say anything I didn't say to myself."

Shade wanted to punch the brother for letting his dick get him in this mess.

"There are enough women here that you didn't need that bitch. What were you thinking?" Viper asked the question on Shade's mind.

"I wasn't. She pulled out my dick and went down on me," Knox said wryly.

"I have to take you in for questioning, Knox. There's no way around it; the newspaper is involved. A witness saw you leaving her room and told the reporter."

Knox nodded, stepping forward. "Let's go."

Viper took his arm. "Don't answer any more questions. I'll get you a lawyer."

As Knox nodded again and went out the door with the sheriff following him closely, Viper and Shade stared after him grimly.

"Find the best lawyer in Kentucky and hire him."

"I'll take care of it." Shade took out his cell phone.

It took fifteen minutes before he could report back to Viper.

"Marc Harris is on his way to see Knox now. He's good, the best in Kentucky, and he happens to live in Treepoint."

"At least that's some good news. Maybe he can use his connections to get bond for Knox."

"Possibly," Shade said doubtfully.

"You don't seem so sure. I thought you said he was the best?"

"He is," Shade assured him. "The problem is, he's an asshole, and Knox is an asshole. The two might not get along."

"Go to town and warn Knox to play nice," Viper ordered.

"Will do, but it isn't going to work. Knox doesn't know how to play nice."

CHAPTER TWENTY-SEVEN

"I won't be talked to that way by anyone! Did you hear what he told me to do?" Marc was practically screaming at Viper and Winter.

"Mr. Harris, Knox didn't mean for you to take it so literally. He's just—" Winter tried to placate the older man.

Shade wanted to tell Winter she was wasting her time. The courthouse was busy that day, and the lawyer had lost his cool enough to not care who could be watching. One person who had stopped to listen had caught his eye. Tilting his head to Viper, he nodded toward Diamond Richards, the lawyer who had managed to get Winter's teaching license restored, enabling her to become the principal at the alternative school.

"I don't care. You can find another lawyer, one who can deal with that asshole."

"But—"

Harris stormed across the lot to his car. All of them except Shade were still staring when he pulled out with a screech of tires. Shade's eyes were on the lawyer who had been observing them since she had come out of the courthouse.

"Ms. Richards could handle the case until we find the evidence to clear Knox," Shade stated.

"Ask her to talk to us."

Viper had spoken to Winter, but Shade could tell from Ms. Richard's horrified expression that she had already figured out their next move.

Swiveling on her high heels, Diamond took off down the street at a brisk walk, and Shade didn't waste time going after her. Winter called out to her, which resulted in the woman speeding up, practically running down the sidewalk as she tried to avoid them.

Shade cut across the courthouse parking lot, managing to reach her before she turned the corner. He stepped out in front of her, bringing her to a sudden stop.

"Ms. Richards, we need your help," Winter began when she had managed to catch up with Viper, Rider, and Train trailing behind.

They hadn't seen the need to rush; Shade wouldn't let her leave until they had their say.

"I'm not taking on any new cases." The lawyer refused before Winter could even ask if she would represent Knox.

"That isn't what your sister said. She said you're having a hard time finding clients, and that was why you moved to Treepoint from Jamestown. Please, can we just go somewhere to talk for a few minutes?" Winter pleaded.

The stuck-up lawyer didn't like being reminded of her relationship with Sex Piston. Shade wouldn't claim her, either, if she was his sister.

Diamond grudgingly gave in, though. "My office is just around the corner.

The Last Riders entered her office behind her. A young woman was filing papers in the cabinet when she turned to see who had come in. Her mouth fell open when she saw the bikers.

"Holly, I'll be in my office if you need me."

Her secretary nodded while clearly begging silently not to be left alone.

Rider and Train took seats in the lobby as Shade, Viper, and Winter went inside her private office, leaving the door open. It made Shade wonder if she was afraid to be left alone with them or if she wanted to keep an eye on her secretary.

Ms. Richards went behind her desk, placing her briefcase on the neat surface before taking a seat.

"What's going on, Winter?"

"One of our members has been arrested in the murder of Samantha Bedford," Viper answered her question.

"I am going to save us both some time. I don't have the experience to defend a murder case." She started to rise to her feet.

"The best criminal defense lawyer in the state of Kentucky just walked out on us. That asshole will defend anyone for the right amount of money. Knox pisses everyone off. There's not a lawyer who won't become angry and quit with his attitude. I don't want to be looking for a new lawyer every day. We need someone who isn't going to run away the first time Knox gets angry and scares the shit out of them."

"I'm sorry."

The stuck-up bitch doesn't look sorry, Shade thought.

"I'll pay whatever fee you want," Viper stated, looking around her inexpensive office.

"If money is no object, then you can afford any lawyer you want," Diamond protested.

"Money didn't prevent Harris from walking out on us," Viper said in disgust.

"How much money are we talking about?" Diamond asked, a gleam she couldn't hide appearing in her eyes.

They had her. Money always made The Last Riders more palatable.

"Let's cut to the chase. You prove Knox is innocent, I'll give you five hundred thousand dollars."

Shade cocked a brow at Viper offering such an exorbitant price yet then reminded himself it was Knox she would be defending. The woman would be demanding more before it was over.

"I take it you believe Knox is innocent?" Diamond queried.

"I know he is," Viper stated without pausing.

"You can't be so sure. Everyone has a breaking point, and from what you're telling me, Knox isn't the sweetest man in the county. Perhaps they got in an argument—"

"If he had killed her, Ms. Richards, no one would have found the body."

Diamond's eyes widened at Viper's calm reply while Winter winced.

Shade saw Diamond studying them, watching for their reactions. All the brothers believed in Knox's innocence, not because he wasn't capable of killing her, but because he would have told them and the mess would never have happened.

Viper stated, "Of course, if you quit on us, I won't pay you one fucking dime."

Her mouth turned down in disappointment.

"All right, you have a deal." Her eyes went to the front lobby.

Shade watched Rider get up from his chair and go to the secretary's desk, leaning against it as he tried to sweet-talk the curvy woman. The whole club knew Rider was a man who could appreciate good tits, and the secretary had a set which would make any man's dick stand up.

The sound of a chair hitting the wall sounded from the outside room right before the flustered woman came rushing into Ms. Richards's office to stand behind her boss's chair with her face flaming red.

Rider came to stand in the doorway, watching with a predatory gleam in his eyes.

"Ms. Richards, your next appointment is due in ten minutes."

"Stop it, Rider. Go on outside," Winter snapped at the man who then turned and walked away with a final wink at Holly.

The rest of the brothers laughed at Rider's failed attempt. Not many women turned Rider down.

"Thanks, Holly." Ms. Richards stared hard at Viper. "After I'm finished with my next client, I'll go down to the sheriff's office and see what they have on him. I'll keep in touch. Get a bail bondsman ready for a call. I'll see what I can do about getting him out. Is he going to be a flight risk?"

"Knox wouldn't run if you pointed a gun at him. It's not in him; he's a soldier. He stands and fights."

"Good to know because, if he takes off, I'll still expect my money, and you can find yourself another lawyer."

"Deal," Viper said, leaving the office with Winter, Shade, Rider, and Train trailing behind.

"That was a fail," Rider complained, giving the secretary a wink, which she ignored as they closed the door.

"You came on too strong," Shade enlightened.

"It's the only way I know," Rider bragged. "It always worked before."

Shade agreed; not many women refused to at least flirt with Rider. He was easily the best-looking in the group, the easiest going, and the most liked. The only thing that grated on the brothers' nerves was his arrogant attitude toward women. He believed no woman could resist him, and up until then, he had been right.

Holly was young and obviously shy. She should've been ripe for Rider's plucking; instead, she had rushed from him as if he was about to have her for lunch. Something about the woman didn't add up, but as long as it didn't affect The Last Riders, Shade didn't give a shit.

৪০ ৫৪

The Last Riders were waiting for Knox's release when he came out of the courthouse with his lawyer. Bliss was the first one to greet him, throwing herself into his arms.

"Keep him out of sight and whatever you do, don't let him get into any trouble. The Commonwealth's Attorney won't hesitate to throw him back in jail," she told Viper and Winter.

Her caustic comment grated on Shade.

"I'll make him stay at the clubhouse," Viper promised.

"What's next?" Winter asked Ms. Richards.

"A trial date will be set. I'm going to look into the case and hopefully find something to prove his innocence before then. It's our best hope."

"Is that safe?" Winter asked.

"Yes. If Knox didn't kill her, then we have to cast some doubt. The best way to do that is to prove someone else had a motive. I'm mainly going to be talking to Sam's friends."

"Good luck with that; she didn't have any," Evie spoke out. She and Sam had hated each other on sight.

"There has to be someone in town who knew Sam well. I'll find them. I need to get back to my office. Like I said, keep him out of sight." She cast a last look at Knox, who had Jewell locked to his side.

"No problem."

Diamond threw Viper a doubtful glance, and then turned on her heel, leaving.

"She didn't seem too happy, did she?" Winter commented in a speculative voice.

"She's a stuck-up bitch," Shade said as the lawyer walked huffily down the sidewalk.

Winter laughed. "I won't disagree with the bitch assessment, but how can someone with the name Diamond be stuck-up?"

"That her first name?" Knox asked in surprise.

"Yes."

Shade agreed her name didn't seem to fit. It sounded like a stripper name.

He slapped Knox on his back as they got on their bikes. "So am I right or wrong; is she a stuck-up bitch?"

Evie climbed on behind Knox.

"Brother, she is so stuck-up you can see the stick hanging out her ass."

As the brothers all laughed, riding out onto the road and forcing cars to wait their turn, Train flipped off one driver who dared to blow their horn.

As they passed Diamond, Knox turned his head in her direction. Shade caught a flash of interest and was surprised. The lawyer was the opposite of the women Knox liked to fuck. Maybe Winter was right, though; a stuck-up bitch wouldn't care that Knox had a woman on his bike. Diamond cared.

CHAPTER TWENTY-EIGHT

When Knox came down the steps the next day, dressed to ride, Shade was playing pool with Rider yet laid down the pool stick.

"Going somewhere?"

"Been cooped up long enough. I want to go for a ride."

Shade could understand. Even though it had only been a day since he had been released, Knox hadn't been on a ride since he had been arrested.

"We'll keep you company."

"Suit yourselves. Let's get something to eat at the diner first."

"Sounds good to me. I'm hungry," Rider said, laying down his pool stick.

The others all stood, going outside to get on their bikes. It was a pretty day. The sun was hot, but it wasn't humid.

The diner's parking lot was almost filled with several motorcycles lined up in front when they got there.

"The Blue Horsemen are here," Viper said to Shade as they entered the door.

Shade stayed in the rear of the group to watch everyone's back, making sure no one snuck up on them and caught them unaware.

They came to stand behind Diamond.

"You having problems?" Viper asked Diamond.

Before she could answer, the leader of the other club spoke. "She doesn't have a problem; we do. We've asked her twice to leave, and she's ignored us both times."

"That true?" Viper turned to Diamond.

She stared back at Viper. "I need to find the men who were with Sam that day outside in the parking lot. They belong to The Blue Horsemen. You want me to clear Knox?" Diamond stared pointedly at Knox.

Stud leaned toward Diamond, losing his casual appearance. "I don't know where the fuck they are, and I don't know a damn thing about their families. They aren't Horsemen anymore, and they weren't when they pulled that stunt with Sam."

"Stud, I think she got your message," Knox said, taking a step forward.

"Good. Then maybe she'll get her ass away from our table," Stud snapped.

"Ms. Richards. Let's go," Viper ordered.

"Ms. Richards? When the hell did you become so polite?"

The Blue Horsemen around the table laughed.

"You laughing at Viper being polite, Bear?" Knox came back with his own smart-ass remark. Tension filled the restaurant that time as the tempers of the men from the rival bike clubs began to escalate.

Diamond rose to her feet.

Ash looked at Knox. "No."

Bear's lips tightened at his brother, most likely because he had backed down for Bear. "I'm finished. Sorry for the interruption." Diamond broke the heightening tension, leaving the diner without looking back. However, she was brought to a stop outside when Knox grabbed her by the arm.

"What in the hell were you thinking?" Knox angrily asked her while Shade and Viper chased after him, not wanting him to get arrested again before he could go to trial.

"I thought I might try to find out who killed Samantha. It's what Viper hired me to do," Diamond answered, jerking her arm out of his grasp.

"I didn't tell you to take on a motorcycle club. You should have called me or the sheriff who could have found out the information you needed," Viper said.

"I didn't need your help. I was safe. What were they going to do in a restaurant across from the sheriff's office?"

"Were you planning on staying in there? They would have followed you home." Knox stared at her like she was stupid.

"It doesn't matter; it's over." Turning on her heels, she strode to her car.

"It isn't fucking over. You're on their radar now. They're going to watch and make sure you don't drag their club into being investigated," Knox said, striding after her with the rest of them following.

"How do you know that?" Diamond snapped.

"Because it's what we would do," Knox answered, slamming his hand on her car door when she tried to jerk it open.

"Back off, Knox," Viper stated calmly.

Knox stepped away, removing his hand from her car door.

Diamond swung around to face the brothers. "If you want me to find out who killed Samantha, I'm going to have to step on some toes. Are you going to give me shit every time?"

"We're not giving you shit. The men Samantha associated with were dangerous, and those are the ones we know about. Obviously someone killed her, so eventually, you're going to come into contact with the person who did. The best way to handle this situation is to keep someone with you who can keep an eye on the situation so you won't get hurt," Viper cautioned her.

"I don't need someone to watch my back. I can take care of myself."

"I'm sure you can. We'll merely provide you with back-up if you need our help," Viper reasoned.

"I can't find out what I need to know with you guys following me around," Diamond argued back.

"You won't need all of us; one will do. Knox and Rider can take turns keeping an eye on you." Viper crossed his arms over his chest, his mind made up.

Shade was simply glad he wasn't the one who had to watch over her.

"Hell no." Diamond refused to have either of the men following her.

"Why not?" Knox asked. "I should be helping. It's my ass that will be back in jail if we don't find out who killed her."

"Fine. The next time I want to talk to someone who is in a motorcycle club, I'll give you a call." Diamond opened her car door, slid in, and slammed the door closed.

The men moved out of the way as she reversed and pulled out of the parking lot.

"Knox," Viper ordered.

Knox nodded and headed to his bike to follow the stubborn attorney. Whether she liked it or not, he had just become her shadow.

"I give it a day," Shade commented.

"On what?" Viper asked.

"Before she quits."

❧ ❦

Shade was sitting on the chair in the club room, talking to Viper with Winter cuddled next to his president's side when Knox came in.

"What are you doing back so early?" Viper questioned.

"She's in for the day," Knox answered. "I'm going to grab a shower. Then I'm going to Rosie's."

"I'm in for that," Rider said, coming into the room.

By the time Knox was ready, several others had decided to tag along. Shade decided to go, as well; he was bored with sitting on his ass.

"Stay out of trouble," Viper warned.

When Knox gave him the finger as he walked out the door, Shade nodded toward his president, acknowledging he would keep Knox close.

Knox, Rider, Train, Cash, and Shade all headed to the bar with several of the women riding at their backs. As they pulled into the lot, Shade recognized Diamond's car.

"Isn't that Diamond's car?" Rider asked Knox as they parked their bikes.

"Yes, it is," he answered grimly.

Knox didn't look too happy that his lawyer was there. Shade could tell the brother wasn't going to listen to Viper about staying out of trouble. The way he strode in that bar said he was going searching for it.

Knox slammed open the door to the bar, and then The Last Riders filed in. He strode across the floor toward Diamond who looked like she was about to leave. If they had been five minutes later, they would have missed her.

Shade would ask Mick later what questions the woman had wanted answered.

"What the fuck are you doing here?" Knox asked angrily.

Diamond's back stiffened. "Drinking a beer. What business is it of yours?"

"Since when do you hang out in biker bars?" Knox inquired.

"Is this a biker bar? I wasn't aware of that. There weren't any motorcycles out front, nor were there any signs saying 'Assholes only,' " Diamond mocked.

"She was asking about Sam," Mick interrupted.

"What did Viper tell you about letting us know when you were going to be snooping around?"

"*You* might have to bow down and kiss Viper's ass, but I'm not one of your members, so I don't actually give a damn what he wants."

Shade leaned against the bar, picking up the drink Mick had automatically set down in front of him.

"He the one who pays you?" Knox asked the question everyone in the room already knew the answer to.

"Yes." Diamond was trapped by her own answer.

"Then you better be worried about what he wants."

"It doesn't matter; I'm done here."

"Since you're here, you might as well stay and have another beer." He turned to the bartender. "Mick, get her another beer on me."

Mick turned around, reaching for the beer.

"I don't want one." Diamond started to slide off the seat, but Knox placed an arm around her waist, planting her back on the barstool.

"But I want you to stay. At least then I'll know where you are." His body blocked hers from getting off the stool.

Giving in, the stuffy lawyer took a drink of her beer. Shade was about to tell Knox to back off, that Viper would kick his ass if she quit, but then she relaxed, turning her face toward Knox and giving him a venomous smile.

Shade leaned against the bar, enjoying the show. This was worth an ass-whipping.

"You think your macho attitude is going to send me running? You're just pissing me off, Knox. I'm trying to find out who killed the woman you're going to go to jail for murdering, unless I catch a break and find out who did."

"What did you think you would find out here?" He reached for his own beer, his chest brushing against her shoulder.

"I thought I would find out if there was someone else in town she was sleeping with who might have a motive. Until I can find the men who were with her that day at the diner and find out if they could be responsible, then your ass is still the best suspect the jury will have."

"They weren't responsible for Sam's death, so if that's your only lead, you need to start searching somewhere else."

"How can you know that for sure?" Diamond questioned.

"Because they're not in town. If they were, the sheriff would have them locked up. Find someone else."

"It's not that easy," Diamond snapped.

"If it was going to be easy, Viper wouldn't have hired you."

Shade almost smiled at the look Knox was giving Diamond. The lawyer was turning bright red in embarrassment.

"Let's dance." Knox didn't give her a chance to refuse, taking her hand and leading her to the dance floor where he turned Diamond into his body, pulling her hips close.

Diamond instantly struggled to put some space between them.

"That's like oil and water, isn't it?" Mick asked as they both watched.

"More like dynamite and nitro. Put them together, and you have Armageddon."

"Fuck, Shade, I didn't know you could crack a joke," Mick laughed.

"I wasn't joking." Shade watched Diamond and Knox dancing together. The same look Shade had seen on his face the day before was there again.

Knox had intended to pay Diamond back for not following Viper's orders, but the brother was on a slippery slope, not realizing his own danger.

Bliss was grinding against Rider while Evie danced with Cash. Stori and Raci were dancing together, giving Knox fuck-me looks over Diamond's shoulder. When the music ended, Knox let her leave the dance floor, placing her back on the stool.

"I need to be going." Diamond placed her empty beer bottle on the bar top.

Knox moved closer to her side. "Want another beer? I can give you a ride home."

Shade rolled his eyes at Mick as they made fun of his attempted seduction. That woman needed more than a fuck-me stare.

"No, thanks. I've had enough."

When she would have jumped down from the stool, Knox leaned forward, placing his hand between her thighs. The lawyer froze in place.

Shade subtly moved closer to Knox's back, unable to see what the brother was doing. Knox gave him a warning glare over his shoulder, and Shade placed his hands in the air. Backing away an inch, he moved so he could watch them in the mirror behind the bar.

"I think you should stay and party with us. We can show you a good time."

Shade thought she seemed to already be having a good time by the way her body was trembling.

Knox flashed the metal ball on his tongue, and the sight must have scared the shit out of her because she jerked his hands away from her thighs

"If you don't move your hand, I'm going to drop your case and keep the half million Viper owes me without giving a damn that your ass will be sitting in jail for a crime you didn't commit."

Knox was smart enough to remove his hand, standing back up straight to lean against the bar. He picked up his beer and took another drink.

"How do you know I didn't kill Sam?"

Rider came to stand by Diamond's side, motioning to Mick for a drink. When Mick gave him his beer, Rider remained, obviously listening to their conversation. The brother needed to learn to be more subtle.

Shade shook his head. Diamond thought Rider was just eavesdropping, but Rider was really feeling out the situation with Diamond. The two brothers loved breaking new women in together. Shade could have told Rider he was shit out of luck, though.

"I drove through the neighborhood you crashed your bike in before I came here today. It's a shortcut to the road that leads out here then to the clubhouse, so I know why you were on the road."

"So I was taking a shortcut? What the fuck does that have to do with me killing Sam?"

"I couldn't understand how you wrecked your bike on such a little road with barely any traffic. I saw by the skid marks you obviously crashed to avoid hitting something."

Knox shrugged. "So, a car pulled out in front of me."

"Nope. There was no parking where you wrecked, and it's a one-lane road. As I sat, trying to think how such an experienced rider had wrecked, I saw several interesting things."

Knox stiffened, throwing Rider a dirty look. "Don't you have something better to do?"

"Not right now. This sounds too good to miss. You never did tell me how you busted up your bike."

"Fuck off," Knox said, taking a drink of his beer while glaring at Diamond.

Rider's grin widened as he took a seat on the stool next to her. Shade was suppressing his own grin, interested to know what had gotten Knox so uncomfortable.

"I saw a beautiful neighborhood filled with older homes that had an abundance of trees. The yards also had several squirrels. I think you swerved to miss a squirrel. You couldn't kill Sam if you wrecked your bike to prevent killing a squirrel."

"I didn't wreck my bike to keep from hitting a fucking squirrel."

Shade choked on his drink because Knox's red face showed he was lying.

Diamond burst out laughing. "You're a marshmallow."

"You actually wrecked your bike to keep from killing a squirrel?" Rider said in disbelief.

"No, I didn't," Knox barked back sharply.

"You fucking did." Rider burst into laughter.

"Marshmallow." Diamond nodded at Rider.

"I am not a fucking marshmallow!" Knox yelled as he slammed his beer down on the bar.

"You better go; the marshmallow is about to explode," Rider joked.

Shade set his drink down on the bar, prepared to hold Knox back.

Diamond grinned back at Knox. "I'm going." Sliding off the stool, she left as Rider continued antagonizing Knox.

"You're a fucking marshmallow, na, naa, na," Rider crowed in a brutal attempt at a sing-song voice.

"Shut up, Rider. I'm warning you!" Knox threatened.

"So, Knox, did you miss the squirrel?" Rider slapped his hand down on the bar, bursting into laughter.

Shade's drink was knocked out of his hand when Knox reared his arm back to punch Rider, knocking him to the floor. Knox reached down, pulling Rider to his feet, ready to pummel him when Shade grabbed his arm, pulling him away. Cash and Train then wisely helped Rider get away.

"Mick, get Knox another beer." Shade slapped Knox on the back. "Don't worry, brother; no one's going to mistake you for a marshmallow."

Knox picked up his beer, taking a long drink.

"By the way, brother, did the squirrel live?"

CHAPTER TWENTY-NINE

Shade rolled over in his empty bed to pick up his ringing cell phone.

"Get upstairs now!" Viper ordered.

Instantly alert, Shade didn't ask questions. He hurriedly dressed before running upstairs.

The living room was filled with The Last Riders. Winter and Viper were the only ones dressed, standing next to Knox who only had on a pair of jeans he hadn't bothered to button all the way up. Rider was wearing only jeans, too, as were most of the other brothers. Evie was wrapped in a blanket, and Bliss was in a sheet.

Shade heard a racket coming from upstairs. It sounded like the house was being torn apart.

"What's going on?" Shade asked.

"The sheriff and the state police are searching Knox's room. They have a search warrant."

The sheriff came down the steps. "Knox, you're under arrest. They found what they were searching for."

He placed the handcuffs around Knox's wrists while Shade stood there silently. It was Viper who argued they were unnecessary. With the state police watching, Shade knew the sheriff had no choice other than to put the cuffs on him and lead him out the door.

Diamond came downstairs, packing Knox's clothes and boots.

"Diamond? Why are they arresting Knox again?" Viper yelled angrily.

"Someone called in a tip last night. They found what they were looking for. That's why they're taking him back in. Don't worry; the court is just going to raise his bail. The quicker you let me get out of here, the sooner I can get him out."

"Go," Viper answered begrudgingly. "When you're done, I expect to see you."

Shade and all The Last Riders went out on the porch to watch Knox be taken away.

Bliss wrapped her arm around Shade's waist, sniffling. "Is he going to be okay?"

"Yes," Shade replied between gritted teeth. He would make sure of it.

Jerking away from Bliss's arm, he went to his bike, not waiting for Viper's order. He rode to town, waiting outside the sheriff's office in a spot he knew he wouldn't be seen.

It was almost two hours before he saw all the troopers leave, and then the sheriff headed to his car. His father spotted him, coming to stand next to him under a tree. No one looking outside would see them.

"What the fuck?" Shade asked as soon as he drew close.

"I didn't have time to warn you. David Thurman, the Commonwealth's Attorney, showed up with the state police, and they stayed by my side the whole time. Your fucking lucky they let me call Diamond. The only reason they did was so she wouldn't be able to get any of the evidence obtained thrown out of court."

"What were they searching for?"

"Jewelry. Mrs. Langley had given Sam a necklace and two rings, and they were missing from her room when her body was found."

"They found it in Knox's room?"

"All three pieces," the sheriff confirmed.

"Fuck." It was beginning to look bad for Knox.

"Any idea why they were in his room?"

"No, but I know he didn't take them."

Knox didn't need the money from the jewelry; he was rich enough to buy a jewelry store if he wanted. Someone in the house had hidden them in his room, but none of The Last Riders would have done it. Shade had no doubts about any of their loyalty. That meant whoever had done it had managed to breach the clubhouse.

Shade rode back to the clubhouse and told Viper and Cash what he had found out from the sheriff.

"One of the hangers-on could have hidden them," Cash suggested.

"Possibly," Shade agreed yet didn't think so.

Even though the hangers-on weren't checked out until they decided to become a member, they weren't supposed to be left upstairs alone.

"The sheriff said someone called the tip in to the state police. Whoever did it must have known the layout of the house and where the jewelry was hidden. They also didn't call it into the sheriff's office so he could warn us."

"Fuck." Viper ran his hand through his hair. He looked exhausted.

"What's our next move?" Cash asked.

"Diamond will get Knox out of jail. Shade, have the women straighten up Knox's room. I don't want him coming home to that mess."

Shade nodded, turning to get the women started.

"Shade, should we get a better lawyer? Is she capable of saving him?"

Shade remembered the look on Diamond's face at the bar as well as her packing his boots and socks down the stairs.

"She may be his only hope," he said cryptically.

Chapter Thirty

Shade followed Razer into the diner with the rest of the brothers behind him.

Beth smiled as soon as she saw Razer. "Diamond, this is my husband, Razer. Razer, this is Diamond. She's representing Knox."

Razer gave her a smile before taking a seat next to Beth, placing an arm over her shoulder while the empty seats on her side of the table were taken by Rider and Knox. Viper took a seat on Winter's side of the table.

"Diamond, I think you know everyone here except Shade and Train."

Shade and Train both gave her a nod before sitting down. As Shade sat next to Lily, he interpreted Winter's leery look as the same one she gave every time she caught sight of him.

"What have you women been doing?" Viper asked Winter.

"Nothing. I finished what I needed for tomorrow. Sure you're not going to change your mind and leave me at the altar?" Winter teased.

"I'm sure," he replied, putting his arm around Winter's shoulders.

The men ordered their lunches, and Diamond's lips twisted in amusement at Knox and Rider's big orders.

"What's so funny?" Knox asked.

"I think you guys are as hungry as I was. I bet you could have eaten two more pizzas last night."

"Make it three, and you'll be more on target," Knox said, sliding her a sideways grin.

"I need to get back to my office." Diamond stood abruptly before leaving the diner.

"She find a roach in her food?" Viper asked as the women smiled to themselves at her quick exit.

"I think she found something scarier than a bug." Beth and Winter laughed as they stared at Knox.

Shade turned his attention to Lily. The blue dress she was wearing made her look too young for his taste.

He slid her half-eaten plate closer to her. "You need to eat all your vegetables if you're going to grow up strong and tall." He used the voice he had heard adults use when they talked to children, and Lily's eyes flashed purple fire at him.

Shade ignored it, though. If she wanted to dress younger than she was to protect herself, she didn't know men, and he wasn't going to let her hide from the fact that she was a desirable woman.

"I'm finished," she told him.

"You sure?"

"I'm sure."

Shade slid the plate in front of him, eating the rest. It was an intimate gesture, which Lily turned away from, concentrating on Winter discussing her wedding at the clubhouse the following day.

It wasn't much longer before he saw the sheriff come into the diner and head toward their table.

"Viper," he greeted, nodding his head at the rest of the table.

"Want to join us for lunch?" Beth offered.

"I wish I could, Beth, but I'm busy. I called my order in."

"What has you so busy?" Shade asked, sensing his dad hadn't stopped by for a friendly visit.

"I was at Diamond Richards's office just now. Someone broke in and trashed the place. From the looks of it, I'd say more than one person is responsible."

The women and the other Last Riders were up and heading out the door while Shade threw down some cash on the table.

"Call me later," Shade told the sheriff as he quickly caught up with the others.

It was a short walk to Diamond's office.

"Do you think it has something to do with a client?" Shade heard Diamond's secretary ask as they walked down the hallway. Diamond had left her office door open.

"I don't know, although whoever wanted me distracted succeeded."

Diamond's voice sounded upset, and Shade couldn't blame her. The office was a mess.

"No, they didn't," Knox said, entering her office.

Diamond and Holly both turned as the office filled with The Last Riders, followed by Winter, Lily, and Beth, who were staring in shock at the vandalized surroundings.

"I'll help," Lily offered as she went down on her hands and knees to pick up the papers.

"We all will," Winter said, taking out her cell phone. "Evie, could you and a couple of the women come down to Diamond Richards's office? Someone broke into it, and she needs help cleaning up. Thanks."

"That's unnecessary; both Holly and I can handle this," Diamond protested.

"Really? I think I'd be interested to see you try to lift those filing cabinets and desk," Knox said, moving forward with Rider to lift the heavy cabinets back into place while Shade, Train, and Viper went into her office to lift the heavy desk.

"It took a couple of people to create this damage. The sheriff came into the diner after you left. He told us your office had been vandalized. He thinks more than one person was responsible for the damage, also," Knox said, righting the end tables while the others restored order to the rest of the furniture.

Winter, Beth, and Holly joined Lily on the floor.

"When the others get here, we can get them back in order," Beth said.

"Please stop, Winter. You're getting married tomorrow; I'm sure you have things you need to take care of. I can handle—"

A sharp gasp from Lily had everyone's attention going to her. She raised her hand with blood dripping from a wound.

"Beth…" Lily whispered, turning toward her sister and giving another gasp of pain, reaching for her knees. Blood seeped onto the papers she was kneeling on.

Winter and Beth immediately moved toward the young woman, but before either could reach her, Shade was lifting Lily from the floor into his arms. Lily tried to struggle free with her eyes on her bloody hand.

"Where's the bathroom?" Shade snapped at Diamond.

When she pointed to the door outside her office, Shade strode from the room with a still-struggling Lily.

"Beth…"

Shade didn't slow down at Lily's whimper.

"Stop it, Lily," Shade said, sitting her down on the closed toilet seat.

Her eyes remained on her bloody hand as her eyes started to roll back into her head. A sudden shake had her eyes traveling back to Shade.

"Eyes to me, Lily," he snapped. "Don't look at your hand again."

"It hurts."

Shade's lips tightened. He had almost protested when Lily had gone to her knees to pick up the messed-up office, yet he hadn't wanted to interfere. He was angry at himself for not following his instincts. He was getting fucking tired of the fine line he was walking to keep everybody happy, especially since Lily was invariably the one getting hurt because he was unable to protect the accident prone woman.

"I'll get the glass out and get it cleaned up, and then the sting will stop."

"Beth is a nurse; she can do it, Shade. I want Beth," Lily replied stubbornly, refusing his help. Shade knew she was reacting to being in the close confinement of the room with him.

"I'm sure you do. Do you think Beth can pull out that glass with you crying and acting like a baby?" he said, hoping her anger would arouse her fighting instincts.

While Lily stiffened, Shade could see her trying to gather her composure as her eyes tried to sneak a peek at her still-oozing injury.

"Eyes on me," Shade snapped again, wetting paper towels and gently picking out the fine shards of glass.

He could instantly feel her gaze on his face. She hadn't argued against his commands, even though he had been a bit harsh. The same nearness of the restroom, which was unnerving her, was straining his control.

As he finished her hand, he heard a knock on the door and Razer telling him he had a first-aid kit. When he opened the door, a silent message passed between the two men before the door closed once more.

Shade opened the box, finding sterile gauze for cleaning her knees. One particular shard had become imbedded there, so he took great care in removing it; however, Lily's dress had ridden up her silky thighs, rattling his concentration. Shade's hands shook as he finished cleaning her knees, wiping them with an antiseptic and starting to wrap them with bandages. He felt her tremble as his hands touched the soft skin behind her knees, trying to clench her thighs together.

"Open your legs. I need to wrap your other knee."

He felt her legs open a scant amount so he wrapped it softly, stroking the sensitive flesh behind her knee. When she would have pulled away, Shade rose to his feet, letting his hand slide across the top of her thighs with a delicate touch the innocent girl would think was accidental.

Taking her hand, he applied the antiseptic to it then wrapped it, taking his time once more, enjoying her eyes watching his every move. Unable to prolong the inevitable any longer, he took a step away.

"You're done."

Her eyes immediately broke from him, and she practically ran from the restroom.

Shade picked up the first-aid kit, meticulously replacing the items he had taken out. Going to the sink basin, he washed his hands and sprayed cold water on his face, wondering how much longer he could resist reaching out and taking what he was determined would be his.

The glass had been swept up by the time Lily reentered the room with wild eyes. Shade watched from the bathroom as she immediately went to Beth. Her sister rubbed her back, easing her tension until Lily calmed and sat on a chair to begin organizing the papers The Last Riders were picking up.

Shade's eyes remained on Lily when he came back into the room. He started gathering the papers while taking in Lily ignoring him. He didn't like being ignored by her. She hadn't even bothered to thank him before running out of the room, either. He could still feel her soft skin under his fingertips.

Shade was unaware the brothers had formed a circle around him until he looked up and saw himself surrounded.

Evie, Dawn, Jewell, and Raci arrived then, lessening the tension in the room. All of them brushed aside Diamond's protests and began organizing her paperwork. Holly put them back in the cabinets when each folder was completed.

What would have taken a week to reorganize took just one afternoon with everyone's help.

"Damn, any idea who did this?" Evie asked, handing Diamond the last sheath of papers.

"No, but I think it involved Knox's case. It's too much of a coincidence with the search warrant for the jewelry and now this. Someone wants me to stop."

"I agree; they're escalating. This is becoming more dangerous than I anticipated. I don't want you going anywhere without back-up, Diamond," Viper ordered.

"I'll be careful, Viper," Diamond said.

"You better be," Knox stated sternly.

Evie and the other women paused at Knox's words, looking stunned while Diamond turned away and busied herself by putting the rest of the folders back in the cabinet.

"We're done here. Holly can replace the sofa for me Monday. Thanks, everyone. It would have taken several days for us straighten this mess out," Diamond said gratefully.

"No problem. We're glad we could help," Winter said with a smile.

She, Lily, and Beth stood.

"I'm sorry about the cuts, Lily," Diamond apologized.

"I shouldn't have overreacted; it was just a few scratches. We'll see you tomorrow." Lily shook off her apology with a smile.

Beth took her hand, leading her out of the office while Razer and Shade followed.

"I left my SUV at the diner," Beth said as they stepped outside.

"You two stay here with Razer. Give me your keys, and I'll go get it." Shade held his hand out for the keys.

"I can walk," Lily protested but snapped her mouth closed at his cold glance, taking a step closer to Beth.

Beth handed the keys to Shade.

"You can walk with Shade and get your bike, Razer. I'll stay here with Lily until Shade brings my car."

Razer and Shade both shook their heads.

"An office in this building was just broken into a few hours ago, and they haven't been caught; it's not safe to leave you alone. I'll be right back." Shade strode away, taking deep breaths, easily identifying Lily's perfume in the air.

Being confined in the small space for hours had gotten to him. He had seen her darting, fearful glances whenever any of the brothers had come too close, especially him. He had hoped, with the few times she had been around him, she would begin to feel safe. Instead, he was seeing the same fear in her eyes as when she had first seen him at the lake. She just managed to hide it better.

He opened the door to Beth's vehicle and climbed in. Then he put it in reverse to pull out, and as he did, he saw a blue ribbon which must have fallen out of Lily's hair. He straightened the wheels and put the car in drive before his hand went to the seat, picking up the silky ribbon and touching it to the side of his face. He wished it was her fingers on him, instead. He slid the ribbon into his jean's pocket before pulling out onto the road, driving to Diamond's office where he stopped the SUV in front of them, getting out to hold the passenger door open for Lily as she said her goodbyes to Razer.

Beth kissed her husband before getting behind the steering wheel.

Lily hesitated before climbing in, giving him a shy smile. "Thanks, Shade. I'm sorry I was such a baby."

Shade had to swallow the lump in his throat, glad his sunglasses hid his eyes. He managed a brief nod before closing the door. As he stepped back, Razer came to stand next to him.

"Do you ever wish you hadn't seen her that day?" Razer asked softly.

The first day he had seen Lily was the first day he had actually felt alive. Before then, he had merely existed; there were no highs or lows, no thinking about her constantly—if she was all right or if she was ever going to care about him. All the emotional bullshit he had suffered through would never have happened. Her purple eyes, smile, and gentle beauty filled his mind.

"Not once."

Chapter Thirty-One

Shade watched Viper and Winter's ceremony as far away from Lily as he could sit. There was only so much he could stand before he reached his breaking point.

He had called in all the IOU's he had earned playing poker and from the betting pool he had started on whether Knox's squirrel had lived or died. They had used Evie to get Knox drunk off his ass then questioned him. The squirrel had survived, and Shade had made a bundle of cash, giving the money to Viper to give to Winter with the idea of redecorating the club room so Lily wouldn't be smacked in the face with their lifestyle when she entered the first time.

He made sure he was one of the last in line after the wedding. He even sat at another table and was carrying his dirty plate to the sink with every intention of passing the table where Lily sat, without even looking her way.

Evie and Bliss were getting up from the table, excusing themselves to wash dishes as Diamond and Lily started to rise to go help.

"Let them take care of it; it's their punishment." Knox stopped Diamond with a hand on her arm.

"Punishment?" Diamond questioned.

Lily's eyes widened at Knox's words.

"They screwed up an order that went out last week. The kitchen is the punishment they drew."

"You punish them when they make a simple mistake?" Lily questioned.

"It wasn't a simple mistake; a customer was kept waiting for the supplies they needed. They gave us a bad review and took their order somewhere else," Shade said, pausing by their table.

"Then write them up," Lily snapped back. "But punishing them like children is ridiculous."

"Is it?" Shade said. "Do you think a written paper telling them they made a mistake is as effective as making them wash all the dishes and clean the kitchen for a week?"

"For a week?" Lily asked. "They should report you to OSHA."

Shade's lips twisted into a smile. "It was handled as a club punishment, which is different than what we would have done if they had been one of the hired employees."

"What would you have done to a hired employee? Make them mop the floors for a month?" Lily asked with fight in her eyes.

"No, we would have fired their asses," Shade answered.

Shade could see the wheels turning behind her eyes.

"Do you have to take punishments like that?" she asked her sister.

When Beth didn't answer immediately, Lily drew taut beside her sister.

"Then you don't need to belong to the club anymore," Lily declared.

"She's Razer's; she belongs to him and the club," Shade said bluntly.

Lily stared at her sister, wanting her to deny their ownership.

"We'll talk about this later, Lily," Beth said, taking Lily's hand. "But I love Razer and you do, too, and you know it. The Last Riders are a big part of his life; he considers them family. I did know he was in a motorcycle club when I fell in love with him, and it's not like it's an overly harsh punishment. The worst thing that could happen is dish-pan hands."

Lily gave her sister a rueful smile. "I'm sorry I overreacted. I just couldn't stand the thought of you taking any punishment for any reason." The women shared a private moment. "Besides, it's your life, and I know for a fact you're very happy."

"Yes, I am." Beth smiled.

Shade once again started to walk on until Lily's next words stopped him dead in his tracks.

"We need to go to Arizona. They have cowboys, Diamond," Lily said to her mischievously.

He almost tripped spinning back around so quickly.

"Cowboys?" Diamond asked, not understanding the abrupt subject change.

"I'm going to marry a cowboy. They're gentlemen, kind, and protect their women," Lily said with authority.

"They do?"

Lily nodded.

Shade gritted his teeth. The only man who was going to be in her life was him. Cowboy? Fuck, he could outshoot any of those mother fuckers.

Beth laughed at her sister's idea of a perfect husband. "Our father wouldn't let us watch television. The only shows he would take us to every now and then were cowboy movies. Lily has been infatuated with them ever since," Beth explained.

Shade's hands itched to show her exactly what a real man could give her instead of those dreams she had built around cowboys. He was about to ask her how far she had gone with the imaginary cowboy of her dreams when Winter came up behind him.

"Shade, Razer is waiting on you."

Shade leaned over Lily, reaching for Diamond's empty plate. "You think cowboys don't know how to punish their women, Lily? They have whips and spurs they use on their horses."

A terrified look came over Lily's face, and her hand went to the wrist with the red rubber band. Shade's hand covered the wrist before Lily could touch it, his chest brushing her shoulder. He had bent low enough that his breath whispered over her neck.

"I'll take that to the kitchen for you, Diamond. At least when *I* punish someone, I don't leave a mark," he said suggestively, rising with Diamond's plate in his hand before leaving the quiet group behind.

"That wasn't nice." Evie smiled as she came up behind him, setting the dishes in the sink.

"I'm not a nice guy."

"Yes, Shade, you are." Evie shook her head when he would have spoken. "No one else was there when I needed them. I don't know what kind of shape I would be in today without your help. You helped me keep my sanity in a time I didn't want to hold on to it. It meant more to you than it did me. So, yeah, you're a nice guy. You're much better than a cowboy; you're a knight in shining armor."

"I wouldn't take it that far." Shade snorted. "This knight's armor was tarnished long ago."

Evie looked toward Lily. "Sometimes, all it takes is someone to care enough to polish it and make it shine."

Shade shook his head at her romanticism. He was no knight; he was what nightmares were made of, with a fascination for a woman who didn't need another monster in her life.

He went outside to the backyard where the brothers and women were dancing. Shade walked to a tree, leaning against it as he watched Lily come outside and take a seat. Razer and Beth went to the dance floor while Lily watched them with a wistful look.

Shade left his spot to move to the dance floor where Jewell and Bliss were dancing together. He began dancing with them until Jewell eventually began dancing with Train. Shade didn't trust himself to dance with her; however, he wanted Lily's eyes on him as she looked at the dance floor.

A few of the brothers began to feel uncomfortable that Lily was the only one not dancing; even Razer was glancing her way frequently. Shade gave him a warning look. Brother-in-law or not, Shade didn't want to see her dance with anyone except him. He knew he was being a selfish bastard, but he had agreed to give Lily time to graduate college. Of course, that didn't mean he had to stand back and watch her have fun with another man.

When Knox and Diamond stood up to dance, Knox walked to the dance floor while Diamond snatched Lily's hand with hers, saying something to her.

Lily's expression took Shade's breath away. He missed a step before righting himself, apologizing to Bliss for smashing her foot under his.

Knox gave him a wary glance as Diamond pulled Lily onto the dance floor. Diamond's stubborn expression showed she wasn't giving the brother a choice other than to dance with them both.

The only thing that saved him from Shade decking him was he danced close to Diamond's side, staying as far away from Lily as the crowded floor would allow.

Lily stayed on Diamond's other side, dancing with youthful enthusiasm. She was good, her lithe body moving to the music as a rosy glow crept onto her cheeks, her purple eyes sparkling with joy. She twirled when the music ended, laughing at Diamond's astonishment at her skill, missing Shade's own awe.

"You're very good," Diamond complimented her.

"Beth and I used to dance in our bedrooms when we were little. We were terrible, but it was just us, so we didn't care," Lily confessed.

"You're not terrible now; you're really good."

"My roommate has been teaching me. She likes to go to some of the college parties, and she makes me go with her." Her voice was a little loud, so he could easily hear over the music.

Shade decided he was going to deduct from Penni's allowance for taking Lily to parties.

She twirled again, and that time, Shade was waiting. Lily immediately tried to shy away from him, but Shade held her close with his arm around her waist.

"You dance with guys at these parties?" Shade asked.

"No," Lily said, trying to break away.

Shade loosened his grip, letting Lily put some space between them.

"Dance with me," he said persuasively, loosening his hold.

As Razer and Beth came to dance next to them, Beth sent Lily an encouraging smile. Shade had expected Beth to make an excuse for her sister and provide an escape from him, not encourage her.

Lily slowly began to dance to the music, yet she didn't regain the fluidity of before. Her hand went to her wrist, but Shade sent her a warning glance and she removed it. As soon as the music was over, she fled from him, leaving him standing alone on the dance floor. He followed slowly.

"It's time I leave. I'm going back to school tonight. My roommate is picking me up at my house. She's visiting a family friend. Beth didn't want me to drive back in the dark." Lily accepted her sister's over-protectiveness without complaint herself before they could reach their chairs. She hugged Beth and Razer goodbye. "See you in a couple of weeks."

"Bye, little sis," Razer said with his arm around Beth's shoulder.

Lily turned to Diamond, giving her a quick hug. "It was nice seeing you again, Diamond."

"You, too, Lily. Drive careful."

"I will," Lily murmured, stepping toward the door, avoiding Shade's sharp gaze. Each time she left, it was torture for him.

Arms circled his waist as Bliss pressed her breasts to his back. "Can we finish dancing now?"

"I don't feel like dancing." He removed her hands from his waist and went inside.

ಬಿ ಲ

The motorcycle drove steadily up the mountain road, taking the curves at maximum speed. He passed Rosie's bar on his way back to the clubhouse, and there was a patrol car beginning to pull out of the parking lot. Seconds later, he saw the flashing blue lights in his rearview mirror. Slowing down, he pulled carefully off the road.

Shade turned off his motor as he watched the sheriff get out of his car. The thought struck him that he was walking slower and his face had become more lined since the last time Shade had seen him, which had been only the week before.

"What are you doing out so late?" The sheriff greeted him with the gruff question.

"Couldn't sleep."

"Knox just passed ahead of you. Something going on I need to know about?" The sheriff always tried to stay alert to possible trouble involving The Last Riders.

"No."

The sheriff stared at him silently, patiently waiting for more information.

"Nothing's going on. Knox took his woman home and was going back to the clubhouse," he explained, knowing he would worry.

"Anyone I know?" he asked curiously.

"Diamond Richards."

The sheriff whistled. "Never would have guessed that one."

"You're looking tired."

"I am. I'm a deputy short." The sheriff sighed, raising his hand to rub his eyes. "When Cash asked me to come up here and check on Beth and Lily, I never expected to stay this long."

"I know."

"Rach wants to travel. Lost one wife not listening to what she wanted, don't plan on getting another divorce in this stage of my life."

"She won't divorce you. Maybe stop cooking for you, but she wouldn't leave you."

"I asked Lucky, if I retired, if he would take over," his dad said, looking up the dark road ahead.

"What was his answer?"

"He told me to shove it." The sheriff didn't try to hide his disappointment at wanting to turn the reins of the sheriff's office over to someone he could trust.

His dad turned the conversation back to the reason he had made the stop. "Penni stopped by to see us. She was pretty upset about you calling her to jump on her ass."

"She doesn't need to be going to parties, and she damn sure doesn't need to take Lily with her."

"Go home and go to bed, Shade. You're looking tired yourself. You're not going to find what you're looking for on this mountain road." The Sheriff turned to walk away, but then turned back. "And slow your ass down."

"I will. Night, Dad." Shade started his motor, pulling out onto the road.

"Night, son."

No, he was not going to find what he wanted in the mountains; she was sleeping in her room at college. Shade had begun driving down a couple times a week to check on her. Every time he got on his bike for a ride, he swore he wouldn't go there, yet he would inevitably find himself sitting outside her dorm. It had even gotten to the point he had hoped she saw him.

Penni had come out tonight while he had sat there on his motorcycle.

"Shade, if you don't leave, someone will call campus security."

He shrugged. "I'll tell them I'm here visiting you."

"Is this how you want her to find out you're my brother?"

"No," he admitted.

"Then go home, Shade. Lily's sleeping, so go home and get some yourself. You look like you haven't had a good night's sleep in weeks."

Penni hugged him as Shade sat stiffly, keeping his hands by his side until she slowly released him then turned to go back inside.

"Penni?" She turned back to face him. "Don't take her to any more parties."

CHAPTER THIRTY-TWO

"Where you two going?" Shade asked Knox and Razer, who were leaving the diner as he was entering.

"Diamond called, said she had some news about my case. I'm going to her office. Viper wanted Razer to tag along." He nodded to where Viper sat, eating in the back.

"You finish lunch?" Shade asked Razer.

"No, the waitress just brought my food," Razer answered grumpily.

"Go eat. I'll eat later."

"You sure?"

Shade nodded, going with Knox.

"Diamond say what it was about?"

"No, only that it was good news."

Shade hoped so. He let Knox enter the office first while he picked up a UPS box sitting outside her door. He was placing it on the desk of Diamond's secretary when he saw Diamond run across her private office, throwing herself into Knox's arms. Shade backed away toward the door, not wanting to interrupt them.

"The Commonwealth's Attorney's office dropped the charges against you. Samantha had a genetic kidney disease; that was the cause of death."

"What?"

"It's true. Even if they find evidence of an argument between you, which they won't," Diamond added hastily, "they would have to do involuntary manslaughter, and that would be hard to prove unless someone actually saw you inflict the injury on Samantha."

"It's over?" Knox asked, relief filling his voice.

"Yes. I'm still going to try to find who attacked her because I don't want that hanging over your head, but you're free now."

Shade heard the shuffling of feet.

"Want to go back to my apartment and celebrate? I don't have any cases this afternoon."

Shade was about to leave when Sex Piston barged by him before he could stop her. On her way by, she tossed him a look, daring him to interfere. Shade stiffened,

162

tempted to meet the bitch's challenge, but he didn't want Diamond to be able to testify against him after he strangled her sister.

"Have you lost your fucking mind, Diamond?" Sex Piston snarled.

"What are you doing here?" Diamond's confusion was apparent at her sister's sudden appearance.

"I came to see why in the hell you haven't returned any of Ma's and Pop's calls. Now I see why. You're giving them shit while you're screwing that fuckwad."

"Don't talk about him like that, Sex Piston," Diamond snapped angrily at her sister.

"You're taking up for him? You've been fucking him after throwing up your high and mighty morals to me for years. I don't think so, bitch. You're letting someone fuck you who *I* wouldn't let touch me."

"Shut up."

"Why? You don't want to hear what I got to say? Too fucking bad. I've put up with your shit for years." She nodded in Knox's direction. "If you've been fucking him, then you've done Rider, too."

"What are you talking about?"

"They're the welcoming committee to The Last Riders. They double-team the women who are joining the club. He tell you how the women become members?"

"Like Pop's club; you become a member's old lady or fuck buddy."

"Don't tell me you're that fucking stupid? None of those women belong to any of the members. They *are* members."

"How do they become members?"

Knox remained silent at Diamond's question.

"There are eight original members. The women who want to join fuck six out of the eight. When they've accomplished that milestone, they go get themselves tatted with the date they got their final vote. Now, isn't that too sweet?" Sex Piston said harshly.

The bitch could have broken the news to her sister gently; instead, she had smacked her in the face with her knowledge of The Last Riders. Shade didn't have to figure out it was Beth who had spilled the information, and Beth was going to earn a punishment for the mess before him.

"You been to one of their Friday night parties?" Sex Piston asked.

"What?"

"It's their weekly fuck-fest where they swap sex partners and decide if any new women are going to become members." She nodded toward Knox. "I heard he has a regular smorgasbord every week.

"If you didn't make it to one of their Fridays, then he has no interest in you joining. You're less than those women; you're just a temporary fuck."

"Get out," Diamond demanded.

Sex Piston's mouth closed with a snap. Throwing both of them dirty looks, she stormed from the office, slamming Diamond's office door as she left.

Shade backed away from the closed door and a furious Sex Piston.

"You get your rocks off watching others, don't you?"

Shade narrowed his eyes on the woman. "Be careful, Sex Piston. I'm not Knox or Razer. I don't give a fuck if you're a woman."

For a brief second, fear flashed in her eyes before she lowered her lashes, giving a sharp nod then turning on her high heels and leaving.

Shade also left, returning to the diner to give Viper and Razer the news about the charges being dropped.

"I hope Knox took the news better than you," Razer said, noticing his angry expression.

Shade told Razer what he had overheard.

Razer's face went taut. "Beth and I both will both draw a punishment this week. Obviously, I didn't make it clear enough not to talk about club business. I'll apologize to Knox, too. He should have been the one to tell her when he was ready." Razer began to get up.

"Sit down," Shade told him. "Wait until you get back to the clubhouse. Give him some time to think."

"About what?"

"If he gives a fuck," Shade answered.

CHAPTER THIRTY-THREE

Shade straddled the chair at the kitchen table next to Knox. The brother had never been a big talker, but since his fight with Diamond two months ago, he didn't talk much at all. The conversation went quiet around the table when Beth's cell phone rang. Her monosyllabic replies were short, and the call didn't last a full minute. Then Beth sat, staring at her phone with a hurt expression on her face.

"Who was that?" Razer asked.

"Diamond Richards," she said, glancing at Knox.

"What did she want with Lily's number?"

Shade and Knox both stopped eating at Razer's question.

"I don't know. She hung up before I could ask."

Razer and Beth kept eating until Razer couldn't ignore the looks both Shade and Knox were throwing.

"Maybe you should call and find out," Razer suggested.

Beth picked up her phone and called her sister while the men waited impatiently for several minutes until Beth hung up.

"What did she want?" Knox asked before he could.

"She wanted to know if there was a boy in her and Sam's class who would freak a parent out if their daughter became involved with them."

"Was there?" Knox asked while all Shade could feel was relief that nothing was going on with Lily.

"Yes."

"Who was it?"

"Dustin Porter."

&⁢ ᘐ

Shade used hand movements to show the brothers which positions by the house he wanted them to take. They had left their bikes at the bottom of the hill and ran to the house, missing Tate, Greer, and Rachel entering by moments. Diamond was already inside with Dustin.

He, Viper, and Knox, edged silently closer to the door. Once there, Shade put his finger to his lips then raised it to show he wanted the brothers to wait. Voices could be heard on the other side.

Shade stared into a small window covered by a curtain, finding a small part which wasn't covered and gave him a small glimpse of what was happening inside. He then raised a finger, showing someone inside had a weapon.

"I'm not going to press charges," Diamond was saying.

Rachel was standing next to her while Tate and Greer stood by a table with Dustin.

"I'll pay for the damages," Rachel burst out.

"That's not necessary," Diamond said. "The couch was the only thing I had to throw out, and I like my new one."

As the other brothers stared at each other, Shade realized the Porters had been the ones responsible for Diamond's office being trashed.

"What are we going to do? She's going to go to the sheriff," Greer asked his brothers.

"No, I'm not. We're going to the sheriff together." Diamond kept her voice firm. "Dustin will always be looking over his shoulder for the rest of his life if he doesn't. He's going to face it and get it over with then start over."

"My brother isn't going to jail," Greer said angrily.

"No, he's not. Samantha died because of her kidneys, not the blow to her head. I can get the charge dropped to involuntary manslaughter. I'll talk to Caleb to see if we can work out a deal."

"Listen to her, Greer," Rachel said, going to her brother and trying to take the gun from him.

"They're not going to offer him a deal! They've been trying to lock one of us away for years, and all because of that slut, they're going to get one of us!"

"I told you not to call her that!" Dustin said.

"You were always blind where that bitch was concerned! I told you to stay away from that stuck-up pussy, and did you listen to me? Hell no! Now look at the mess we're in all because you had to have that slut!"

Rachel attempted to take the shotgun away from Greer again before her brothers came to blows, and Diamond went forward to get Rachel back when the gun went off.

Everyone froze in shock. Diamond took a breath of relief when she realized the shot went through the back of the sofa.

"Thank God," Rachel said.

With that, Shade gave the signal, letting Knox crash open the door. As The Last Riders came into the room, Knox went straight to Diamond.

"Are you okay?" Knox asked Diamond.

She batted his hands away. "I'm fine. Why are you here?"

"Beth called Lily to see what you wanted. Knowing your track record about going at things alone, I had a feeling you would come here," Knox explained angrily.

"I didn't need anyone's help. The gun went off accidently," Diamond snapped back.

"Guns don't fucking go off by accident if you're not holding one," Knox said, looking at Greer who was staring guiltily at his sister.

"I'm sorry, Rachel," Greer apologized to his sister.

"I've told you that temper of yours is going to get someone killed," Rachel told her brother.

Shade wanted to beat the shit out of the three brothers for being stupid enough to fight over a weapon with women nearby. One of them could have been killed. However, from their pale faces, they already realized their mistake.

"Diamond, take Rachel outside and wait for me," Knox ordered, staring at Greer with deadly intent.

"We're not going anywhere." Diamond refused to leave as The Last Riders spread throughout the room.

Rider and Razer were by Dustin, Cash and Viper were next to Tate, and Greer had Train and Crash standing by him. Rachel was shaking, still standing next to Greer, while Shade stood by the door, making sure the Porter brothers didn't make a run for it. He was always the last means of defense because *no one* got past him.

"I didn't ask." Knox lifted her off her feet, turning toward the door.

"Stop it, Knox. You don't even know what's going on. I'm Dustin's lawyer, and I came out here to discuss his court case with him."

"Which one? The one where he sold pot to an undercover cop or for Sam's death?" Knox mocked her.

"Put me down!"

Cash took Rachel's arm, moving her away from Greer.

"Don't fucking touch her!" Greer yelled, moving forward, but Viper had him in a second, held immobile as Rachel struggled against Cash.

"Stop it, and listen to me. He didn't mean for the gun to go off. Rachel tried to take the gun from him. You know he wouldn't hurt his sister. Knox, calm down and listen to me." Diamond quit trying to struggle against him, letting her body go pliant. Turning against him until she was plastered against his front, she took his face in her hands, drawing his furious gaze back to hers. "They had no intention of hurting me."

Knox released her.

"Let her go, Cash," Viper ordered.

Cash freed a still struggling Rachel who turned, planting her foot in his balls. Cash went immediately to his knees.

"Don't ever fucking touch me again." She started for the downed man again.

Shade laughed, moving forward to save the brother by blocking Cash.

"I think he got the message, Rachel," Shade told her.

Rachel pulled her shirt down, which had ridden up her flat stomach, before planting her hands on her hips.

"You're going to buy me a new door, Knox." She turned around and pointed her finger at Greer. "You're going to get your ass out of bed in the morning and buy me a new couch." Turning to Viper, she let him have it, too. "Next time you come to my house, fucking knock first." She looked around at a smirking Shade to see Cash trying to get to his feet.

Shade offered him a hand, but was met with an angry scowl.

"You have a whole club of women to haul around, so don't touch me again or the only thing you're going to be able to touch them with are your damn fingers."

Taking a deep breath, she turned to Diamond. "Now, can you help Dustin or not?"

"Yes," Diamond said softly. "I'll go with him to the sheriff's office to make a statement. I'll talk to the Commonwealth's Attorney to try to work out a deal, but he knows he doesn't have much of a case. I sent for the coroner's report from Frankfort; Samantha Bedford was in bad shape. She needed a kidney transplant and wasn't even aware she had a problem. I talked to her grandmother; it could have possibly been what killed her mother. It was a genetic condition the family was unaware of."

"Could my kid have it?" Dustin asked.

Shade whistled silently to himself, realizing the kid they had been searching for was Dustin's. Vincent Bedford wouldn't have been happy when he found out Sam was pregnant by one of the Porters. They supplied practically the whole state with weed.

"Possibly. Dustin, right now we have to deal with Samantha's death. I'll do what I can to see how I can get more help for you to find your child, okay?"

"All right. I don't have a choice, do I?" Dustin said unhappily.

"No. I'm sorry, you don't. Samantha made several bad decisions, but I do think she cared about you, Dustin, and if she did, she would have seen your child was taken care of. You have to hold on to that hope."

Dustin nodded. "Let's get this over with."

"Wait a minute, who planted the jewelry in my bedroom?" Knox asked.

The Porters stopped, looking at each other.

Greer faced Knox. "I paid Tara and Stacy to plant it for me. I gave them a month's supply of pot for doing it and then to tell me which room was yours. Then I called the state police."

Shade nodded evilly. He had the perfect punishment in mind for the twins.

"Who are Tara and Stacy?" Diamond asked, confused.

"They're twins who are hangers-on. They come to the clubhouse every Friday," Viper explained, not able to look her in the eyes.

Diamond walked toward the door, keeping her face averted from Knox and The Last Riders.

The Porters started to follow her until Knox took a step forward and punched Greer in the face. Tate managed to catch his brother before he fell to the floor, and then Tate started to move toward Knox, but Viper's words stopped him.

"If it wasn't for Diamond and Rachel, we would have had a different outcome tonight. Don't press your luck. Get your asses to the car before I change my mind and don't care if they see us get even."

The Porters didn't hesitate, going out to the front yard which was also full of The Last Riders.

Diamond went to her car, ignoring Knox, while Shade and Viper went to stand next to him.

"I'll meet you at the sheriff's office," she told the Porters.

She looked toward Viper, who silently acknowledged her thanks with a nod of his head. With that, Diamond got in her car and drove down the mountain road.

"Looks like Dustin's in a shit-load of trouble," Shade commented.

"Diamond will get him out of it. She's good at her job," Knox said, still staring at where Diamond's car had disappeared.

"She took it pretty good with the Porters shooting at her. She didn't get hysterical. Seems to me she would be easy to talk to, being a lawyer." Shade looked down at his boots.

Knox's mouth twitched. "You trying to give me advice?"

Shade started walking. "I don't offer advice—that's for pussies. I give suggestions."

CHAPTER THIRTY-FOUR

Shade closed his bedroom door following Raci and Jewell down the hallway and up the steps to the kitchen. He had only bothered to pull on his jeans, and his hair was still wet from the shower he had taken with the women. He didn't have to worry about appearances since Winter and Beth were both in bed with their husbands at this time of night. Jewell and Raci were only wearing T-shirts with nothing on underneath, both flushed with red faces. He had worked up an appetite.

Jewell opened the door, and they went into the kitchen to see Diamond and Knox sitting at the table with Cash and Evie. Diamond had paused with the sandwich in her hand, her eyes following them. His eyes met her open-mouthed stare as he closed the door behind him.

The silence in the room was tangible as the two women went toward the refrigerator to make their own snacks while Shade walked to the liquor sitting on the counter. He grabbed one of the bottles then went to the cabinet to get a glass, coming to take a seat across from Diamond who had managed to take a bite of her sandwich.

His gaze went to Diamond and Knox.

He should have known she was still there at the club, although anyone not a member was supposed to be out by two. He had called Viper the night before on his cell phone when he had heard the commotion upstairs, but he had been busy with another job Viper had given him. His president had told him Diamond had showed up with Sex Piston and her bitches to make up with Knox. Then he had told him Stud had showed up for Sex Piston and her crew which hadn't wanted to leave. It had sounded like a clusterfuck to Shade. He didn't know why Diamond hadn't just given Knox a blowjob. That was all she had needed to do to achieve the reconciliation she had wanted, and been less aggravating to the whole club.

Shade liked his business kept private. He didn't want loose lips damaging a relationship with Lily before he could begin one.

"You going to need my vote?" Shade asked, his gaze on Knox.

Knox stared back. "Yes."

"Then handle it," he said, getting up from the table and taking the whiskey and glass with him.

Looking back at Evie, he asked, "Coming?"

Evie grinned, standing up to take her dishes to the sink before going to Shade who was waiting. She went down the stairs, giving Knox a final stare.

"I'll take care of it," Knox said, showing he had received the unspoken message that Diamond wasn't allowed to talk club business.

Closing the door behind him, Shade walked down the steps and towards his bedroom door where Evie was waiting impatiently, practically bouncing on her heels.

Shade opened the door for her to enter, and she went inside bursting into laughter.

"You made them watch you fucking Jewell and Raci all night?"

"Yep," Shade said, climbing onto the bed. Stacy was chained to his wall naked, and Tara was chained to the bottom of his bed. Both women's hands were bound so they couldn't get off, as they watched him pleasure Raci and Jewell.

"I played with them first while Raci and Jewell partied upstairs, and then I let them come downstairs. I think they enjoyed themselves. What do you think? Tara? Stacy?"

"You fucking bastard. Shade, please, I can't take it anymore. We didn't think they would actually arrest Knox," Tara whined, still attempting to reach her pussy.

Her groan of frustration irritated him.

"Get them down and out of here," Shade told Evie. "Either of you touch your cunts before you get home, I'll chain you back up."

Evie released the women then handed them their clothes, and as soon as they were dressed, Evie held the bedroom door open for the twins who were anxious to leave.

They were halfway out the door when Shade's voice stopped them. "Don't come back to the clubhouse again. You're no longer welcome."

Both women burst into tears.

"Knox know to get Diamond back upstairs?"

Evie smiled. "I warned him when she was watching you get your whiskey. I'll be right back."

Shade was on his second glass of whiskey when Evie returned. She wrinkled her nose at the smell in the room.

"Need me to clean up?"

Shade nodded, rolling off the bed.

Evie changed his sheets while he cleaned his equipment, tossing most of it into the trashcan beside his bed. Evie watched him yet didn't say anything. She walked out to place his dirty sheets and the dirty wash clothes he used to wipe down the mat and equipment in the washing machine in the other room.

He was sliding the mat under his bed when she came back in. He didn't try to hide his weary expression as he climbed back onto the bed, picking up the whiskey bottle to pour Evie a large amount into the glass. He took a long drink from the bottle as he used the remote control to turn on the television.

Evie sat down on the bed next to him, placing a couple of pillows at the top for her to lean back on before picking up her glass.

"So, Knox and Diamond are a couple. Never figured he'd find someone after Sunshine."

Shade shot her a look. "You know none of that was your fault…it was out of our control. You can sit there and wish you hadn't been attacked, and I can sit here and wish I had been there when Levi got in that fight, but it wouldn't matter. It's not going to come true."

"I know, but sometimes I just wish it could have been me. You think that Knox…"

"No, I don't fucking think Knox ever wished it had been you." Shade said harshly.

"Okay…okay. I'll stop. Guess now he's with Diamond I won't be getting a taste of him anymore," Evie said, lightening the grim mood. Shade lifted the whiskey bottle, taking another long drink.

"How much longer you going to be able to go on this way, Shade?"

"Another year," he sighed. "Probably more."

"Talk to Razer. Maybe he can work it out so you can begin seeing more of her. Maybe he can invite you over to dinner one night when she's in from college."

"It wouldn't work. If I started seeing her, I wouldn't be able to stop."

"Yes, you would. I know you—"

"Not where Lily's concerned you don't. Leave it alone. Let's just watch television."

They watched a comedy on a group of teenagers running from the police.

"Remember when Levi and I stole Dad's Jeep? We were already drunk off our asses by the time we picked you up."

"I remember," Evie said softly, scooting lower in the bed to lay her head on his shoulder. "Levi was laughing his head off, and you were driving around base, trying to pick up girls."

"I never did get one that night."

"They were too scared of you. You scare everyone."

"Lily most of all." Shade's arm covered his eyes as he lay back on the bed.

Evie caught the whiskey bottle before it could spill.

"Go to sleep, Shade. You haven't slept in two days."

"Evie, you think it's possible Lily will ever like me?" Shade's voice slurred between the whiskey and lack of sleep.

His breath deepened as he dozed off before he could hear her soft answer.

"I think she's going to love you."

Chapter Thirty-Five

Shade, Knox, and Viper were on their way to the diner when they saw Diamond enter the police station carrying a kid. The sheriff was holding the door open for her while the deputies followed with her secretary and a man Shade had never seen before.

"What the fuck?" Knox said, swinging his bike toward the police station, and a car horn blared.

Shade and Viper turned in when the pissed-off motorist had passed. Knox was already inside as Shade and Viper entered the station.

"I'm all right, Knox!" Diamond was yelling, trying to get Knox's attention while he attempted to strangle the man in handcuffs.

Shade and Viper pulled him off, backing him away, as the deputies rushed the man out back.

"Knox, if you don't stop, I'm going to arrest you," the sheriff threatened.

Knox took a deep breath, going toward Diamond.

The little boy burst into tears.

"Holly!" he cried out with big tears sliding down his cheeks.

Shade was no expert on kids, but the one Diamond was holding didn't look well.

"Sheriff, please let me hold him," Holly cried, trying to take a step forward, but the deputy held her back.

"Sheriff, I already told you I'm not going to press charges. You have no reason to arrest her. She had his legal mother's permission to care for him," Diamond added her own plea.

The sheriff gave a sigh, going to Holly to release her handcuffs. "You should have brought the child forward. I wasted a lot of man hours searching."

"I know. I regret that I didn't. I should have contacted you when I found out Sam was dead, but with Vincent Bedford in prison, I was afraid he would be put in foster care. I've taken care of him since he was born."

Diamond handed the little boy to Holly.

"I didn't know Mitch had a gun. I just wanted Sam's autopsy report so I could find out why Logan is sick all the time," the frightened woman explained. "I'm so sorry, Diamond. I should have asked for your help instead of listening to Mitch's idea of breaking into your office."

Shade caught the warning look Diamond shot Holly.

"I told you it wasn't a break-in if you had a key."

"Well, we need to get this little guy to a doctor, and then I'll take him to Mrs. Langley. She's his only relative left," the sheriff said, taking out his cell phone.

Diamond stopped him.

"No, she isn't."

⁝ ⁞

Diamond and Knox came downstairs. Shade watched her eyes widen when she saw Jewell between Rider's legs, sucking on his cock.

He was standing at the bar, talking to Bliss and Evie, when they stopped next to them.

Evie handed Diamond a beer.

"Thanks, Evie."

"Did you eat dinner?" Knox asked, taking a drink of his own beer.

"Yes, I picked something up at the diner."

Shade tilted his head to the side when Diamond met everyone else's eyes except his.

"Let's dance." Knox broke into the strained silence, leading Diamond to the dance floor.

"You scare the crap out of her." Bliss laughed.

Shade silently agreed. In the month Diamond and Knox had been together again, she still appeared nervous around Shade. She was friendly with Beth and Winter, but she didn't gossip. Shade liked that about her. He liked it a lot.

Diamond had a good head on her shoulders, and she was concerned about other's feelings. She had seen to it that Dustin was given custody of his son while ensuring Mrs. Langley was able to see her grandson. Her secretary was still employed with her, and Diamond had talked Dustin into letting Holly stay near his son, despite his older brothers' anger from Holly having kept the child from them. Everything had been smoothed out by Diamond.

He and Evie were still standing at the bar later when Knox carried Diamond up the steps.

"When do you think it's going to dawn on her that she's the new member being voted in tonight?" Evie laughed as they both watched Train go upstairs.

"In about two minutes," Shade replied as Cash left the dance floor with Bliss in tow.

"You change your mind about joining in?" Shade asked her.

"No. I said I would help you. Are you almost ready?"

Shade set his unfinished beer down on the bar counter.

Rider, seeing them heading to the door, left the dance floor. "Let me grab my keys, and I'll meet you at my truck."

Shade nodded, going out the door.

Crash turned off the music as the rest of The Last Riders followed them out the door and down to the parking lot. The women climbed in the front of Rider's truck, which was filled to the brim with everything from Diamond's bedroom that Knox and the other's had taken from her apartment while she had been at work, while those who didn't fit jumped on whichever brother's bike was near.

Shade rode down the road alone, letting the fresh air hit him in the face, waving to his dad in his brand new truck as they passed on the winding road.

As the bikes pulled into the driveway of the house Knox had bought, Rider and Shade went to the tailgate of his truck where everyone grabbed something to pack in. Shade and Rider carried in the heavy mattress, setting it down inside the front door, since everyone else seemed to be waiting at the bottom of the steps for Shade's orders.

"Everyone, let's try not to make a mess of the new carpet. Women, we'll pack everything up the steps, and you tell us where you want it. Knox wants the bedroom perfect when he brings Diamond over in the morning.

"What do you want me to do with this, Shade?" Evie walked in the doorway carrying Knox's new sheriff uniform.

"Hang it on the bottom of the stairs so he'll see it in the morning when he gets here. He wants to surprise Diamond."

She nodded, hanging it over the banister.

Shade and Rider picked up the mattress again.

"Get busy, brothers. Knox is depending on us."

CHAPTER THIRTY-SIX

Shade, Razer, and Rider were walking by the front window of the diner. Anxious to see Lily for the first time in several weeks, he looked inside and then came to a dead stop, causing Razer and Rider to nearly collide into him.

"Watch where you're going, Shade," Rider snapped.

Shade ignored him, narrowing his eyes on Razer who was trying to keep a straight face. "Mother fucker, why didn't you tell me who Beth and Lily are having lunch with?"

Shade didn't give him time to answer. Turning on his boot, he began walking back to his bike.

Rider peeked in the window and took off after him.

"Shade, wait." Razer caught his arm then Rider's. "You guys are supposed to be my brothers. You can't desert me in my time of need," Razer begged.

"Pussy," Shade snapped, getting back on his bike.

"Come on, it wouldn't be so bad if it was just one or two of the bitches, but four of them are in there." Seeing he was making no headway with Shade, Razer turned to Rider who had always been the sucker of the group. "Rider, you're bragging all the time that you're the toughest brother. You can brag you took on Sex Piston and her crew while Shade ran."

Shade could tell that appealed to him. The big chump's ego had fallen for Razer's load of crap, hook, line, and sinker. Shade started his motor.

"Lily's going back to college tonight. You really want to miss being able to see her until the end of the term? She has finals…"

Razer gave an unholy grin when Shade turned his motor off and stood back up.

"Let's go," Shade growled at his former brother.

When they returned to the clubhouse, Shade was going to make Beth a widow. He would be able to hold Lily at Razer's funeral while she cried on his shoulder. Shade's imaginings ended when Razer held the door of the diner open for them.

Rider started to enter then stopped. "Since Shade's going in, I won't be able to brag about—"

Shade pushed him inside the diner, ignoring his frightened expression.

Razer bent and kissed his wife on the cheek.

"Got anything left?" he teased, looking down at her empty plate.

"No, you'll have to order your own."

Shade and Rider each grabbed chairs and pulled them up to the table. Once Shade had maneuvered his chair between Beth and Lily's, Rider sat down on the other side of Lily, giving Crazy Bitch and Killyama's side of the table a wide berth. Razer sat down next to his wife, placing his arm over the back of her chair.

Killyama looked unhappy with the seating arrangement. She took turns alternating between pursuing Shade and Rider. Thank fuck she was usually on Rider's case more than his, but that was only because he was better at dodging her.

"What you been up to, Shade?" He winced when Killyama's usually abrasive tone turned seductive.

He didn't take off his sunglasses, but his head turned in her direction. Shade kept the sunglasses on so he could stare at Lily without making her uncomfortable; he didn't care what everyone else thought.

"Nothing much," he responded before ordering himself a coffee from the hovering waitress.

Razer and Rider both ordered burgers and fries.

"Not hungry, Shade?" Sex Piston asked.

"No. I already ate," he said with an expression that dared her to question him further.

As they waited for Razer and Rider's food, Beth and Crazy Bitch talked about Crazy Bitch getting her GED and starting beauty school during the summer.

"You going to let me do Beth's hair?" Crazy Bitch asked Razer.

"No." Razer didn't try to soften his answer. He was wearing a bandana on his own head of long, dark hair.

"I'll let you do mine," Lily offered, finishing her lunch.

"No." Shade's dark sunglasses landed on Lily.

Lily turned to Shade with a stubborn look on her face. "If I want her to do my hair, then she can do my hair. You don't tell me what to do."

"You still wanting that summer job?" he asked in a soft voice.

Shade saw a glimmer of stubbornness as she refused to back down.

"Yes." She stiffened in her chair, staring defiantly back at Shade.

"Then she doesn't touch your hair," Shade said. "It's fine the way it is," he supplied as an afterthought.

He had plans for that hair. He had fantasized too many times of fucking her while he held it gripped in his hand.

"She's going to need someone to practice on, and I was thinking of getting it cut anyway."

Shade stiffened, not in anger as everyone thought because of her arguing with him, but that she was learning not to be afraid of him.

He decided to push a small amount, just to see just how much better she was becoming in dealing with her panic attacks.

"Then think again." Shade's hand went to hers on the table.

Her delicate wrist wore no jewelry, but the damn red rubber band was still there. Placing his hand over her wrist, he turned more fully toward Lily, leaning into her space. He lifted his other hand to her black hair, twining a curl around his finger and pulling it taut.

"You want your hair cut? Don't you know men like long hair, especially cowboys? I, on the other hand, think short hair is sexy."

Lily's body leaned as far away from Shade's as she could without falling out of her chair. His heart sped up when she didn't stand up and run from the table.

"I kind of agree with Shade," Sex Piston butted in. "Your hair is beautiful; leave it alone. It just needs a little trim. Stop by my shop during spring break, and I'll trim it for you."

"Okay."

Shade stared at Sex Piston, perfectly aware she had known he didn't want Lily's hair cut and had sought to change Lily's mind.

He released Lily's hair, letting it slide from between his fingertips. He had wanted to know how her hair felt since he had first seen her. At that point he had to concentrate on lifting his coffee cup and not reaching out to touch it again.

"I can give you a new look, but not have to cut much off the length."

"Do you think you could introduce me to Pike while I'm in Jamestown?"

Shade's satisfied look disappeared at Lily's request, and he stiffened in his seat. "Who's Pike?"

"Someone Sex Piston and Fat Louise know. They said he's from Arizona," Lily said, waiting for Sex Piston's answer.

Fat Louise started to answer, but Sex Piston cut her off. "I'm afraid you're going to have to wait until you move to Arizona to meet a cowboy, Lily. Pike has a girlfriend, and I don't think she would appreciate me introducing him to you."

Shade's hands clenched on his coffee cup. He had been walking on eggshells around her for three fucking years to make sure she could deal with a relationship, and she was actually asking Sex Piston to set her up?

He opened his mouth, about to tell her the only way she was going to see Pike was at his funeral.

"When you going to give me a ride on that bike of yours, Shade?" Killyama asked.

Shade's chair screeched as he slid it back from the table. "I'll wait for you outside, Razer."

He threw some cash down on the table then strode outside, wanting to hit something or someone.

A minute later, Rider joined him. "I don't know which of those bitches is the worst."

When Shade didn't answer, taking a seat on his bike, Rider threw him a wary look, getting on his own bike as Razer came out next, his face pale.

Shade didn't wait for him to start his bike before he was peeling out of the parking lot toward the clubhouse. As he parked, Razer pulled in next to him.

Shade got off his bike, but Razer caught his arm. "Shade, you can't be angry. She doesn't know you're interested in her. If she did, she wouldn't have said anything. Lily didn't mean to hurt you."

"She's a woman, and she has wants and needs. Lily is trying to tell you both she wants someone in her life. Whether you and Beth realize it or not, she's ready to face her fears so she won't be alone. I'm not jealous; I'm about five fucking seconds from getting back on my bike and showing her she doesn't have to be alone."

Razer shook his head. "She wants a figment of her imagination that she wanted when she was a little girl—a cowboy."

"She wants someone to protect her, to hold her, someone she can be safe with. *That's* Lily's cowboy."

"She's not ready," Razer denied. "She'll be finished with school next year then—"

"She only has half a semester left. I want her to start getting to know me now, before she gets herself hurt trying to find what isn't out there anymore."

"Beth and I both think it's best if you wait until she graduates," Razer replied stubbornly.

Shade was done talking, leaving as Rider drove in, passing him without a word to climb the steps to the clubhouse. He wasn't going to change Razer's mind, and Beth would help Lily stay away if he tried to move in too soon.

He opened the door to the clubhouse and went inside. The brothers and women were sitting around, enjoying their afternoon off. The orders from the factory had been filled that morning, leaving them with free time.

Shade went behind the bar, taking down a bottle of whiskey while ignoring the curious looks from the others.

Bliss came to sit on a stool in front of him. "Can I have one?"

While Shade reached for a glass, filling it half full, Razer came to the bar and leaned against it. "Since you're playing bartender, can I have a beer?"

Shade wanted to tell him to fuck off; instead, he set a beer down in front of him. "What has you two looking so pissed off?"

Shade remained quiet, drinking his whiskey.

Bliss sidled closer to Razer. "Come on, Razer, you can tell me." She ran her hand up and down Razer's arm, and he jerked it away.

"Back up."

Bliss made a pout with her lips, taking a step back. "I was just trying to make you feel better."

"You were trying to get laid," Shade corrected her, "which I can take care of."

"I'll go to your room." Happiness shone out of her eyes.

Shade shook his head. "I haven't finished my drink, so sit on the chair."

Bliss walked toward the chair and took a seat.

"Spread your legs."

"I'm out of here. I have some work that needs to be done on our house. When you get done, you could come and help." Razer said, setting the beer down on the counter.

"When I'm done, I don't plan on being in any shape to do anything."

Razer gave a sharp nod before leaving through the kitchen door. Shade then directed his attention back to Bliss who was sitting with her legs sprawled out.

"You know what I like?"

Bliss nodded. She began touching herself, parting the lips of her pussy to slide her finger against her clit.

Shade carried his whiskey to the card table. "Anyone up for a game of cards?"

Once Rider, Cash, and Train took chairs at the table, Shade began dealing the cards, talking to the brothers and ignoring Bliss as they played.

They had finished playing the first game, which he won, and Rider began shuffling the cards as Bliss's moans gradually escalated.

"If you come, you won't get my dick," Shade warned her.

She bit her bottom lip.

"Raci, turn some music on."

The woman turned the music on then came toward Shade.

"Can I play?"

Shade picked up his cards, scooting the chair back slightly from the table, and she sat down on his lap. Shade's free hand slid down to her belly before he unzipped the pair of shorts she was wearing, sliding his hand inside and finding her already wet. Raci trembled as his fingers slid through her slick warmth.

"Pull your top off."

After she did, showing her bare breasts, Shade leaned down to take a red nipple between his lips as his finger plunged inside of her cunt.

"Your turn, Shade." Rider's hoarse voice reminded him.

Using his thumb, he discarded the card he didn't want before bringing his mouth to Raci's other nipple. She squirmed on his lap as he finger-fucked her, her hands going to his shoulders to hold on to him. His cock hardened under her ass, making her squirm more in need.

"Raise."

Shade laid his cards down then threw some cash into the pot as Raci moved her hips so she could fuck back against his hand.

"Call," Shade said, turning the cards over as Raci moaned, dropping her head against his chest, shuddering.

"You win, Shade."

He lifted his head as he removed his hands from her pussy then wiped his wet fingers on her shorts before buttoning and zipping them back up. Then she shakily rose off his lap while Shade reached forward, raking his winnings toward him.

Shade looked toward Bliss as Cash began shuffling the cards, seeing her withering on the chair, her hands going slowly over her swollen clit. Cash dealt the cards as Shade took a long drink of the whiskey, feeling the burn at the back of his throat.

"Come here, Bliss." Shade picked up his cards as Bliss approached, her tiny black skirt around her waist. Glancing at them briefly, he laid the cards back on the table. "Fold."

He reached into his back pocket and took out a condom then unzipped his jeans. He ripped open the condom before sliding it on his hard length. When he was finished, his arm went around Bliss, bringing her closer. Lifting her leg, he helped her to straddle his lap, but when she would have sunk down on his cock, his hands went to her hips.

"Make a play for Razer, Knox, or Viper again, and you'll never have my dick again, understand me?"

Bliss nodded, fear in her eyes.

"If they want to break their marriage vows, that's on them, but you don't need to be throwing it in their faces. There's more than enough brothers here to keep your cunt satisfied. Right, brothers?"

"Yeah." "Yes." "Hell, yes," the men around the room chorused as Shade jerked her down onto his cock.

Bliss's head fell back as he filled her greedy pussy. She was so wet he slid easily inside of her.

Shade leaned to the side, using his legs to scoot the chair farther away from the table before arching his hips, giving her every inch of him. His hands went to her ass, lifting her until she was sliding up and down his cock. Shade then stood up, holding her as he turned and laid her down on the wooden card table, fucking her harder.

"Anyone want to place a bet on who can last the longest? I bet I can last through Bliss giving all three of you a blowjob."

"Fuck, I'll take that bet." Cash threw a twenty down on Bliss's stomach.

"No, only markers." Shade flipped the twenty back toward Cash.

He stood silently, watching Shade's cock slide in and out of Bliss. "Why do you want our markers?"

"Because I do. You just going to stand around and watch, or are you going to place your bet," Shade jeered.

"Son of a bitch." Cash went into the kitchen. Coming back with a pad of paper and pencil, he scrawled his name then tore the paper off before laying it on the table.

"I bet he only makes it through two of us." Rider picked up the pad of paper, scrawling his name then ripping it off and placing it on her stomach.

He was always a sucker, Shade thought as Bliss's thighs circled his hips.

When Cash pulled out his cock, going to Bliss's head, she opened her mouth then sucked his cock deep into her throat as the brothers gathered around to watch, placing their own bets.

Cash played with her nipples as he gave her his cock. "It's a good thing I didn't bet on how long I'd last. I never could hold out very long with her sucking me off," he groaned as she managed to twist her upper body so her hands could reach his balls, squeezing them as she sucked him off.

Cash stepped back when he finished, letting Rider take his place.

From his expression, Rider was going to attempt to outlast him. Rider pumped his cock into Bliss's mouth, placing a hand on each side of her shoulders.

Shade slowed his speed as his hand went to Bliss's clit. It only took a few strokes before she came, sucking furiously on Rider's cock as her hips fucked Shade back, trying to draw out her orgasm.

"Damn it!" Rider groaned, coming in her mouth.

"My turn." Train took Rider's place at the head of the table when Rider shakily moved away, sliding his cock into Bliss's waiting mouth.

"God, I'm going to come again," Bliss moaned around Train's cock.

Shade fucked her faster, helping her over the edge she was fighting for as she swallowed Train's cock, making him hiss.

"She wants him to win," Train accused, taking a nipple between his fingers and pinching it as the woman's head rose and lowered.

"The fucker isn't even breaking a sweat," Crash said, moving closer to watch.

Train moaned, placing a hand on the card table to brace himself. Sweat broke out on his face, and his T-shirt began to get damp. His teeth showed as he gritted them, trying to hold off.

"Fuck!" Train shuddered, losing the bet.

Shade grinned as Train removed his limp dick from Bliss's mouth. He finally let his control go, sliding Bliss closer so her clit would feel it every time his cock slid into her. He let her enjoy the ride a little longer before pulling out and letting himself come.

He straightened from her then removed the condom and tossed it in the trash can. Taking the slips of paper off Bliss's stomach, he placed them on top of his already-large winnings and then Shade helped a thoroughly satisfied Bliss off the table, smoothing down her skirt.

"I need a drink."

Shade handed her the almost-empty whiskey bottle he had been drinking out of, sitting back down in his chair and sliding it back to the table.

"Whose turn is it to deal?"

CHAPTER THIRTY-SEVEN

Friday

"Fuck! " Shade braked hard, barely managing to hold the bike upright.

The car in front of him had stopped suddenly while coming out of a curve. Neither of them had seen the long line of traffic going in the direction of Jamestown five miles away. There must be some serious shit going on ahead for the traffic to be so long. No cars were coming from the direction of Jamestown, showing traffic wasn't getting in or out. The tension Shade had felt all day increased; that was why he was on the damn road in the first place.

Penni wasn't at college anymore; she was on a job out of town, leaving Lily alone at a nearly deserted campus during spring break. He had been planning on keeping an eye on her until she left to go on her internship in the morning. He had spent the previous night watching her then left after she walked to her car to head to her job. He was on his way back to make sure she was okay after working and to watch her through another night. He would have to get a new bike soon if he kept putting so many miles on that one.

He was beginning to get aggravated with the dead-stop traffic when his cell phone rang. Reaching into his leather jacket, he took it out.

"What do you want?" he snapped, still angry at Razer for refusing to acknowledge that Lily was ready at least to talk to him.

Razer laughed. "I thought I would do you a favor, but never mind." He hung up on him.

"Fuckwad," Shade snorted, pressing a button.

Razer answered on the first ring.

"Why did you call other than to bother me?"

"I thought I would give you a heads-up. Lily called Beth and told her, since she was so close to Treepoint, she would drive in and spend the night. If you are where I think you are, it's a waste of time."

Shade started cussing, beginning to turn the wheel of his bike to head back to Treepoint. At least he would be out of the traffic.

"Hang on a minute, Shade. Lily's calling."

Shade stopped turning his bike, worried Lily might have been hurt. Could the traffic have been caused by an accident she had been involved in? Had she had a flat tire? Different scenarios ran through his mind as he waited impatiently for Razer to return to the call.

"Shade." He could tell from Razer's voice that what he was about to tell him wasn't good. "Lily's...in trouble. Her phone is on, and from what I can figure out, she's at Sex Piston's shop. She and the bitches have been taken hostage. From the voices, I think there are two men. I'm going to get the brothers and leave immediately. How far away are you?"

Shade had to clear the wrenching agony from his throat before he could answer, staring at the massive traffic at a standstill. "Five minutes."

"I'll call Stud and have him meet you there then call the police. Brother"— Shade heard something in Razer's voice he had never heard before—"please save her."

"I plan to." Shade put his phone back in his pocket.

Giving his bike gas, he used the oncoming lane, going seventy miles an hour. If a car came, he would have been a dead man, but he didn't care. He went faster until he came to where he had to take a left to Jamestown, where fire trucks and police cars blocked the road.

Shade decreased his speed, finding a space to ride his bike through. The smoke-filled sky was coming from a house near the railway tracks. He could barely see as a cop tried to stop him by waving a sign.

Ignoring him, Shade leaned to the side, forcing his bike through two fire trucks. Firemen leapt out of the way as he passed without slowing down. When he finally managed to get through the smoke and saw the road ahead, he gunned his motor to pick up speed again. He was almost there.

It wasn't long until he slowed and flicked off his headlight when he turned into the small strip mall where Sex Piston's shop was. Parking his bike at the end where it couldn't be seen from inside the store, he was getting off when Stud and the Destructors came running from behind the building.

"Who's inside?" Shade asked.

"All the women, Lily, and Dale and Joker," Stud informed him grimly.

"Weapons?"

"Dale and Joker each have one. Razer had Crash transfer the call to Bear's cell phone. We can hear what's going on inside; we just can't get inside without making noise—both front and back are locked."

Shade was unable to see into the beauty shop from where he was standing. "They in the front?"

"They took them in the back."

Shade had been hoping they would be in the front of the shop. He would have been able to take them out with a bullet.

"They're coming out. He's making Sex Piston take him to the bank to get money," Bear whispered, covering the cell phone.

"Spread out," Shade ordered. "No one moves until I signal."

Sex Piston could be seen unlocking the front door. The woman paused before stepping out, surveying the parking lot.

"Lock the door back up," Dale ordered loudly.

The dumb-fuck was confident no one was around. *The same confidence is going to get him killed*, Shade promised himself.

"Move," Sex Piston demanded, telling Dale to get out of her way before turning back toward the door.

After she locked it, he jerked her away and pushed her toward the car everyone knew was hers at the side of the building. The pitch-black parking lot allowed them to stay out of sight as they walked past, and then Shade and Stud moved in from behind.

When Sex Piston opened her car door, forcing Dale to take a step back, Stud reached out, jerking Dale back by placing an arm around his neck. The slow bastard didn't have time to react as Shade closed his hand over the gun, wrenching it from his hand expertly. Then Shade pointed it at Dale while Stud squeezed Dale's throat until he passed out.

As soon as Stud let him fall to the ground, Bear moved out of the shadows, picking up Dale as the other brothers from the club followed him out of the darkness.

"Put him somewhere and leave two men watching over him," Stud told Bear.

Shade was happy that, for once, Sex Piston's mouth remained closed as she watched the men drag Dale away.

"You okay?" Stud asked.

As she nodded, Shade could see she was shaken up and worried about her friends, but the tough woman remained calm.

"Joker has the others in the back of the shop, Stud. He has a gun pointed on them," Sex Piston told them.

"We know." Stud grimly moved toward her to take her in his arms, holding her close. "How?"

"Lily. We've been listening in on her cell phone," Shade answered.

"Thank God."

"Stay here." Stud released her after giving her a tight squeeze.

"I'm going with you. I can go in the door first and distract him," Sex Piston argued.

"You're staying here," Stud demanded, turning away, but Sex Piston reached out and grabbed his arm.

"You've never been inside my shop. He has a gun on my friends. You go through that door first then Joker might shoot. Please, Stud."

Shade was becoming impatient listening to the two argue, but he knew Sex Piston was right. He could also understand Stud wanting to keep his woman out of trouble.

"Let her go. If he starts shooting in a small room, any of those women could be hit by a bullet. If she could get his back to the door, then we can take him," Shade said grimly.

Stud hesitated before agreeing.

Sex Piston went to the door alone and unlocked it. Then, holding it open, the men moved silently into the shop, hiding behind the counter, trying to keep their reflections from the mirrors.

At Shade's nod, Sex Piston walked toward the back of the shop while Shade and Stud maneuvered themselves closer to her, trying to stay out of Joker's line of vision.

Stud had a gun in his hand while Shade's remained empty, but he wasn't worried about it. He wanted his bare hands on the mother fucker, and with the deadly look in his eyes, he was every bit as frightening.

Joker jerked the pistol toward Sex Piston when he saw her in the doorway. Shade managed to see past her to where Crazy Bitch was kneeling on the floor, her lip bloodied and a bruise forming on her cheek. Killyama was holding Lily protectively, Lily's hand a mangled mess. Joker must have found the cell phone lying on the floor. T.A. and Fat Louise were standing on opposite sides of the room.

The amazing thing to Shade was that none of Sex Piston's crew were showing fear. Shade, during the time he had been in the military, had seen men break down under pressure, whereas those women were holding it together.

"Looks like you've been busy, Joker," Sex Piston smarted off.

"Where's Dale?" he asked, his eyes going to the doorway behind her.

"He said to tell you to go fuck yourself and took off," she taunted the man.

"You're lying!"

"No, I'm not. When we got outside, he took off." Sex Piston shrugged, looking at one of the women in the room. "I always told you he was a pussy."

Joker moved toward her, and Sex Piston tried to shift to the side so she could get his back to the door, but Joker was too lost in his anger. Reacting violently, he grabbed Sex Piston.

However, before he could do anything, Killyama was on him. She picked up one of the break chairs and crashed it down on the back of his head.

Stud and Shade were already running in, but they couldn't get past Sex Piston fast enough and into the small room before Joker fired his gun.

As the women screamed, Shade had to force himself to go for Joker, despite his first instinct to rush to Lily.

He managed to grab the gun away from Joker. Turning it to point directly at him, Shade fired a bullet into the side of Joker's abdomen. When he killed the fucker, it wasn't going to be painless—Joker was going to suffer the terror Shade had felt trying to reach Lily.

"That will keep you busy," Shade's voice was cold.

Shade ran past Crazy Bitch who was getting to her feet while Lily shakily scooted closer to Fat Louise as T.A. rushed over to them. Fat Louise was lying on the floor with blood pouring from her leg. T.A. grabbed some towels from the shelf to try to stop the bleeding as Lily sank down next to her, taking Fat Louise's hand with her good one. Her other hand fell uselessly to her lap as Bear and Pike came in the door.

"The state police are outside, and an ambulance is on the way," Bear informed them.

Shade stood, letting Lily comfort the woman while fighting off the need to reach down and take her into his arms.

"You're going to be okay," Sex Piston told her friend.

Fat Louise nodded, trusting her friend's judgment without question. Shade had never witnessed the depth of friendship the women shared. The Last Rider's women were friends with each other and got along well, but those five women would die for each other.

The women finally moved away as the ambulance technicians came through the door. It was too cramped in the small room, so everyone was forced to move outside to the front of the shop as they worked on Fat Louise and checked on Lily, who was turning pale. The red rubber band on her broken wrist was a reminder that she might not be handling the situation as well as she seemed, and Shade wanted nothing more than to be with Lily.

He was about to go back to the room where she was being treated when two state troopers came into the shop. They had waited until the technicians had cleared out. If he made a fuss, he knew they would arrest him, and Shade didn't want to be locked up behind bars when Lily needed him.

One approached Sex Piston, asking questions, while the other came to him. He told them the story from being on the call with Razer when Lily called to disarming Joker.

Part of the way through being questioned, Shade noticed Killyama was moving toward Sex Piston, but Shade stopped her with a hand on her shoulder, ignoring the officer.

"I saw you putting yourself in front of Lily." His hard face stared at the obnoxious woman. "Then you tried to take that bastard out before we could touch him. If you still want that ride with Rider, it's yours."

Killyama's face broke into a vindictive smile. "I'll take you up on that, Shade."

Shaking his head, he turned back to the man questioning him.

The trooper had just finished questioning Shade when a stretcher with Lily on it was rolled out. He quickly followed them out the door, daring anyone to try to stop him. His hands clenched at his sides as he saw her face had become even paler.

There were two ambulances outside. The EMTs lifted Lily's gurney into the back of the one not holding Joker, and Shade followed in.

"You can't ride in here." The EMT gave him a stern look, which he returned with one of his own.

"I'm family." Shade took a seat on the bench next to Lily who was staring at him with wide eyes at his answer. After they put an emergency splint on Lily's wrist, Shade reached out, gently touching it.

"You doing okay?"

"Yes." Her lips trembled, and she began shaking. Her violet eyes darkened as they stared up at him. "I'm not acting like a baby this time; did you notice?"

"I noticed." His voice was hoarse. He knew the signs of shock, and Lily was beginning to exhibit them.

"Get an IV in now!" Shade snapped at the EMT who was making notes on his pad.

The man jumped, laying the pad down then looking at her blood pressure.

Shade scooted off the bench to lean over her gurney. "Lily, did you get hurt anywhere else?"

"I bumped my head when I fell."

Shade looked at her blood pressure. "Get the fucking IV in now, or I will."

As the EMT reached into the cabinet, taking out the IV bag, his eyes met Shade's, both of them aware of what was happening. A few seconds later, she slipped into unconsciousness.

Shade yelled out to the driver, who turned on the siren and picked up speed. The EMT worked on her while Shade backed out of the way.

The ambulance came to a stop at the emergency room entrance and Shade jumped out of the back, already getting Lily's stretcher before the driver could get out to help.

"Go wait in the lobby. Someone will be out to talk to you soon."

Shade tried to follow them inside the entrance, but two security guards blocked his path. Shade wanted them concentrating on Lily, not him, so he backed off until he heard Lily's scream of pain outside the door. Shade lost it at the realization that she had come to, was in pain, and he wasn't with her.

Shade tried to get inside where the patients were being treated, but the two guards held him back, threatening to place him under arrest. He just slammed the men together, knocking them on their asses.

"Shade." Sex Piston tried to intervene, but when he turned angrily toward her, she hastily backed away.

She didn't have to worry. Shade wasn't going to touch her; he only wanted her to back off so he could bust down the door separating him from Lily.

The sliding doors opened behind them and Stud, Viper, and Razer entered, seeing him banging on the door with his booted heel.

Razer and Viper tore Shade away from the door while Stud helped the security guards to their feet. He wanted to knock them back down again, but Stud moved them farther away.

Shade shook off Viper then rounded on Razer, throwing him up against the wall, his forearm pressed against Razer's throat. "I'm fucking done. You hear me, Razer?"

Razer managed to nod against the pressure Shade was exerting against his throat.

"That woman in there could die, and I haven't even been able to touch her yet, feel her against me, or even fucking kiss her, because I've let what little conscience I have left and my friendship with you stop me. No more. You deal with Beth however you want, but I'm done with everyone telling me to stay away from her. Do you fucking understand me?"

Again, Razer nodded.

Shade stepped back, moving away from both Viper and Razer, who stood watching while he fought for control. Running a shaking hand over his short-cropped hair, he finally managed to gather himself before turning back and catching sight of Sex Piston.

The sudden blaring over the intercom calling a code had his eyes going wild again. Shade took a step toward the closed door when Sex Piston blocked his path, grabbing his shirt in a tight grip.

"You need to get your shit under control," she said between gritted teeth. "Beth will come in that door any minute. Lily will not be happy to have her sister upset any more than she already is. So calm your ass down."

Shade found himself listening to her. She was right; Lily would want him to protect Beth the way Razer protected Lily. The brother's face was filled with anguish, yet Razer was keeping his shit together.

Shade took a steadying breath, focusing on Sex Piston and not the code blaring through the hospital and the running of feet.

"I see what you see in her. She comes across as this frail-as-shit wimp until you look in her eyes. She's strong, Shade. Strong enough to survive whatever Hell that's been given to her. She *will* pull out of this. She will never forgive you if you hurt anyone she cares about."

"You can't be sure she'll be all right!" he said harshly as he watched through the windows of the ER's doors as several hospital staff ran into the room Lily was in.

"Yes, I can." She lifted her shirt at the hem, baring her tattoos to his gaze. Her finger touched the two butterfly tats, drawing his gaze to her side. "I was stabbed twice when I was in the seventh grade, Shade. I coded twice. I'm standing before you now, telling you that beautiful girl is not going to die." No doubt was in her gaze.

When Shade calmed as he leaned back against the wall for support, Sex Piston gave him a sharp nod. "You cool now?"

"Yeah, I'm cool," Shade said with his eyes on the doorway, but he made no more attempts to go inside.

The sliding doors opened again and Killyama, Crazy Bitch, and T.A. came in. Shade had forgotten that Fat Louise had also been hurt until he saw the women.

"We don't know anything yet. Did you call her mother?"

"Yes, she said to call her when we know something."

Shade was disgusted that the woman's mother wouldn't be coming to the hospital.

The sliding glass doors opened again as Beth along with The Last Riders' women and brothers came into the waiting room. Diamond and Knox entered last. He must have been on duty because he was wearing his uniform.

Beth went directly to Razer. "How is she?"

"She coded a few minutes ago. We don't know what's happening inside."

Beth crumbled, almost falling to the floor before she was caught against Razer and held tightly against his body. She sobbed as she pressed her face against his chest.

They eventually took the chairs in the lobby, filling the room with The Last Riders and The Blue Horsemen.

For two hours, Shade sat in a chair with his eyes on the door, willing Lily to live, until a tired doctor came out to talk to them. Shade rose to his feet, unsure whether he wouldn't crumble like Beth had if it was bad news.

"Lily is going to be okay, but it was close. She had an epidural hematoma. We relieved the pressure, and she's stable for now. If she had been a minute farther away from the hospital, she wouldn't have made it." The doctor ran a hand over his face, exhaustion apparent. "Her hand is broken in two places. We've stabilized it for now, and we'll put a cast on it in the morning." His words let everyone know she was still in critical condition.

"How about Fa—" Crazy Bitch cleared her throat. "What about Louise?"

"She's in surgery to remove the bullet, but it did little damage." The doctor turned to go back into the room. "Only two family members can go in to see Miss Cornett before she's moved to the ICU. Make it quick. She isn't conscious, but I'm sure you're anxious to see her." With that, the doctor went back into the emergency room.

Beth went to the door the doctor had already gone through, opening it before turning back. With tears rolling down her cheeks, she held out her hand toward Shade. Disbelieving, he took a step forward, grasping her hand. They went into the E.R. together, the door closing and leaving a stunned silence behind them.

The emergency room was busy as a nurse led them down a long hallway. Shade let Beth go first as he followed her into the room. His first sight of Lily had him leaning on the wall for strength as Beth burst into tears, going to her sister's side.

Shade's eyes watered at seeing her still form lying on the bed. He took a faltering step forward, reaching down to graze her pale cheek with his knuckles.

"Lily," he whispered, "I love you." That was why he had fought so hard to see her. He hadn't wanted that beautiful woman to leave the world without knowing she was taking a piece of him with her.

Shade didn't know how Knox had borne it when his first wife had died. In that moment, he felt Knox was a stronger man than him.

When Beth moved away from the bed, leaving them alone, Shade memorized Lily's face with her dark lashes lying against the paleness of her cheeks. She had a bandage on the side of her head near her temple. Her new haircut had hidden it from view when the EMT had checked her out, and she hadn't wanted to come across as a baby, so she hadn't complained. His words had almost gotten her killed.

"Don't, Shade. None of this was your fault."

Shade looked at Beth, startled that she seemed to have read his mind.

"I've known you for some time, Shade, and you take responsibility for every-thing—the club, the men, the women."

"I called her a baby when she cut herself at Diamond's office. She didn't tell us she had hit her head because of that."

Beth gave a wry smile. "Lily's matured a lot these last few weeks. She's stronger. She's learning to stand on her own. It's why I sent her off to college. It's likely she was more worried for Fat Louise than herself."

"Beth, I'm in love with her."

"I heard."

Shade stared at her in confusion. "You're not worried?"

"About you?"

As he nodded, Beth came to stand by his side, touching his arm. "Razer told me you helped save her."

"Stud was also there."

"You were there when it was over, too. You rode in the ambulance, and you didn't want to leave her side even when security tried to stop you."

"Razer told you everything, didn't he?" He wasn't only referring to the events of tonight.

"Yes. He told me months ago, Shade."

"You going to ask me to wait some more?"

Beth shook her head. "Why would I do that? I've been praying for you since she was a little girl. What's taken you so long?"

CHAPTER THIRTY-EIGHT

Saturday

"Shh…baby, you're going to be fine."

Shade stood in the corner with Razer standing tensely by his side. He knew Razer had come to care a great deal for his sister-in-law.

Both of them were watching with grim expressions as Lily tried again to get out of the hospital bed. Beth prevented her with a soothing voice, murmuring words over and over again that neither men could hear over Lily's cries. The trauma combined with the pain and medication had left her disoriented.

Every cry and whimper, which passed her lips, increased his resolve to take his vengeance out on the two men who were responsible for her injuries. Shade had every faith the judicial system would release them on parole, and he would be waiting for them, just like the biker who had dared to touch her and the deputy from Treepoint. Both had disappeared just as Joker and Dale would.

Lily finally slipped into a fitful sleep, tossing and turning on the hospital bed while Beth continued sitting by her side, holding her hand.

Shade stepped forward. "You should both go and get some sleep. I'll stay until you get back."

"I'm not leaving her," Beth protested.

"Go and get a couple hours' rest at Sex Piston's parents' house; it's just a few blocks away. I'll call as soon as she wakes."

It was another hour before exhaustion had Beth leaving reluctantly with Razer.

After they left, Shade sat down in the chair by Lily's bed.

After the night before, when Lily had coded, there wasn't anyone who didn't know he had reached his limit. He was done waiting. He had sworn that, if Lily survived, she would be his. No more waiting, no more fucking around. He planned to get Lily the way he would have taken on one of his missions in the SEALS. It was why, behind closed doors, he was known as the deadliest sniper in the US armed forces with over two-hundred twenty-six confirmed kills. Those were only the ones they knew about, not the privately contracted ones by the government he still carried out when the price or the reason was motivating enough. He had been given the nickname Shade because of his ability to blend into the shadows, hitting his targets with cold-blooded precision others considered impossible.

Part of what made him so successful in taking out his target was learning everything about them, knowing their strengths and weaknesses. Especially their weaknesses.

To gain Lily's trust, he had to find out her weakness. He had always known she and her sister had secrets they hid from everyone, refusing to talk about Lily's past. No woman had as many anxieties and fears as Lily without a reason. To reach her, he would have to overcome those fears.

Each time he had tried to find out about the cause of her panic attacks, he had been thwarted. Neither had she confided in Razer, Penni, or her therapist, who was shitty for a therapist, something else Shade intended to change. The only thing the woman had done was put that fucking rubber band on Lily's wrist, teaching her to give herself pain as a way to relieve her anxieties. Shade had every intention of teaching Lily the same thing, except in a more enjoyable way.

He sat by the bed, watching Lily sleep as the day slipped into night. When the nurses checked on Lily and tried to get him to leave the room, his cold gaze intimidated them into silence, sending them scurrying.

When the outside had been completely swallowed by night, Shade got up from the chair, going to the door and closing it after the nurse. Determined to find out Lily's secrets, he only had one option left.

Lily was beginning to wake; he had noticed she had begun to move about beneath the covers. He prayed the drugs would keep her disoriented enough that, when he was finished, she wouldn't remember what he was about to do.

Shade's fingers flipped the light switch, plunging the room into darkness. He knew from Razer that Lily always slept with a nightlight. Otherwise, her terrified screams could be heard throughout the house. Maybe those screams would give him the answers he was looking for.

At first, all he heard was her breathing.

"Beth!" Lily began shaking the rail of her hospital bed.

Shade immediately went to her, pressing her down onto the bed. He wasn't about to let her damage herself. She began crying and whimpering. Then she began screaming.

"Sh..." He had meant to be reassuring; instead, her screams stopped immediately.

"Please don't hurt me. Please...Please. I'll do what you want, just don't hurt me anymore."

She was disoriented, not understanding why she was in so much pain; therefore, she had connected it to a time in her past when she had experienced the same helplessness.

Shade remained silent as Lily began talking between whimpers.

"Please don't hurt me anymore, Mama. I'll do what you want. Please, don't make me drink it. It makes me sick, and I won't be able to play with Sawyer and Vida. They promised to let me take a turn playing with Vida's new doll."

As Lily began making gagging noises, Shade hastily raised her up, wanting to give her a drink of water, but he was afraid it would become too much for her if she felt something pressed against her lips.

Shade listened as she went back and forth between adult and child. The child described the atrocities she had lived with while the adult was ashamed she was still frightened of her past. She was literally being torn apart by the two.

Her mother had given Lily alcohol to make her more complacent to do what she wanted until Lily must have quit fighting her to keep herself from being drugged. Lily, for all her appearance of virtue, had never known innocence.

"Don't want to remember. Don't want to remember…Now I lay me down to sleep, I pray the Lord my soul to keep…"

Shade couldn't bear any more. He gently lifted her, carrying her to sit on the chair where he gently rocked her until she quit crying, the drugs in her system making her drowsy again.

"Are you my daddy?"

Shade stiffened.

"No, I'm not your daddy," he answered gruffly.

"I've always wanted one. Do you have a daddy?"

"Yes."

"Is he nice?"

"Yeah, he's nice."

"I'm glad." Lily laid her head on his shoulder. "Are you a cowboy?"

"No, I'm not a cowboy."

"Then who are you?" she asked in a whisper, as if she was afraid to hear the answer.

"I'm nobody; you're dreaming."

"You feel real. Besides, this can't be a dream." She yawned.

"Why not?"

"Because I don't have good dreams."

Shade rose with her carefully in his arms, carrying her back to her bed where he laid her down, covering her up. She had already slipped back to sleep.

"You will, Lily. I promise, I'm going to make all your dreams come true, even if you don't want me to be a part of them."

Shade waited until her breathing deepened before turning the light on by the doorway. It would reassure her if she woke up again, yet it was not bright enough to wake her.

He sat back down in the chair to wait for her to be more alert. That time, he didn't mind waiting; he needed the time to think and plan how he was going to insert himself in her life.

It was time to begin his pursuit of Lily.

Chapter Thirty-Nine

"Lily." Shade stood in the doorway of the factory office, watching Lily stiffen as soon as she saw him. He almost smiled as he watched Lily's reaction to having to share lunch with him every day.

As she drew closer, Evie came out, giving her a friendly smile. She had brought their lunch.

"How's it going today?" Evie asked.

"Fine," Lily replied, smiling back.

"Cool. You two enjoy your lunch."

"Why don't you stay and have lunch with Shade today? I'm not very hungry."

Shade didn't say anything as he stared down Evie. She knew the answer: no one was to interfere. If they did, he would take it as a direct challenge, and he would respond in kind.

"I've already eaten. I'd better get back; I left Rider doing lunch by himself," Evie said, leaving before Lily could make up another reason for her to stay, not that it would work.

It never did, although she had been very inventive at trying to keep out of his way.

Lily slipped by Shade, who made no effort to move away from the door, forcing her to brush her body against his. She then took a seat on the chair, sitting next to his desk. He had moved the chair there purposely so she could become used to him being in her space, and he could smell the delicate hint of her perfume.

Shade closed the door then took a seat at his desk. Handing her one of the plates with baked chicken and vegetables, he began eating his own food.

As long as he didn't try to stray from the boss/employee relationship, Lily felt overwhelmed by him but not afraid. When she was forced to eat lunch with him, she didn't like being near him. For that brief period of each day, she wasn't able to hide from the fact that he was an attractive male, and that was enough in itself to terrify her.

Seeing the thoughts swirling behind her eyes as she tried to devise yet another way out of their lunches, Shade tried to distract her to calm her nerves.

"How's your arm doing since the cast came off?"

"Fine. The doctor said it was healed."

"When does school start back?"

"In a month."

"How many classes are you taking?"

"Four. They're pretty simple ones. I already completed the coursework in my major area. The only courses I have left are just to give me enough credits to graduate."

Shade continued eating his food silently. He almost grinned, relieved her college days were almost over.

Clearing her throat, she played with the food on her plate. "I know you and Razer are friends, and I appreciate the club giving me a job for the summer, but I— you don't have to eat lunch with me every day, Shade. I can eat outside with the rest of the workers." She released a deep breath, as if she was proud of herself for getting through the obviously rehearsed speech.

"Don't you want to eat lunch with me?" Shade questioned, his gaze steady on her. He wanted her to learn to be honest with him about her emotions.

"No. Yes. I don't want you to feel like you have to keep me company because of Razer and Beth being your friends."

"Do I seem to be the type to do anything I don't want to?"

"No."

"Good, then that's settled." *Let's see her get out of this one.*

Unless she came out and said she didn't want to eat lunch with him, she was stuck, and Lily hated hurting anyone's feelings. The beautiful woman didn't understand he didn't have any feelings to hurt.

After asking about job applications, Shade took a step further and insulted Lily's lack of taking care of herself and getting into situations that could have gotten her seriously hurt, or even killed. He was setting her up and she was falling right into his trap.

"I can take care of myself just fine," Lily snapped.

"You could if I taught you how," Shade said, leaning back in his chair.

"What? How?"

"I could teach you self-defense. That is, unless you change your mind about being a social worker."

"I'll make a good social worker. I—"

"Good, that's settled. Monday, when you come to work, bring some workout clothes. I'll work with you an hour every day at the end of your shift."

"But—"

"If you're finished, could you ask Train to come here?" He wasn't going to give her an attempt to get out of his trap.

Lily stood up, going out the door and closing it behind her. Train came in his office minutes later.

"What's up?"

"I want to know why the orders to Darrel Finley were late." Shade hated managing the factory, but Viper had asked repeatedly for him to take on the position full-time, and if he took the job on, he was going to do it right.

Train pointed to the spreadsheet, explaining the difficulty in getting some of the products on time for the shipment due to the high volume of orders. For the next hour, they talked over which items to increase production of.

When they finished, Rider came in, leaving his door open as Train left. Rider gave him the spreadsheet of the orders which had been filled for the day, then talked about the new bike he was thinking of buying as they waited for Lily to finish her last order.

As they saw Lily struggling to place the large order in the mail cart, Rider stood and said, "I'll go help her."

"Let her do it. She needs to regain her strength in that arm."

Rider nodded before going outside to wait while Lily cleaned down her workstation.

Meticulously cleaning his desk, he saw the time. Closing the desk drawer, he stood and stretched, loosening his taut muscles.

Going to the door, he saw Lily reaching down to pick up a pair of scissors. Her perfect bottom pointing in his direction had him wanting to stride across the room to bend her over the table and fuck her from behind.

When she turned at feeling his gaze on her, her fingertips grazed over the red rubber band on her wrist; however, she was smart enough not to snap it with him watching. Anytime she felt sexual interest, she would go for the fucking rubber band. In a sense, it was a tell, showing when she was feeling desire she didn't want to feel, because it frightened her.

Her trembling hands smoothed down her knee-length dress instead, and Shade almost praised her, though he didn't think she would appreciate it. Yet.

"I'm done for the day, Shade." Her eyes avoided his, going to Rider who was sitting on one of the tables nearby.

The other factory workers had left over a half hour before, yet her speed hadn't increased by much since her cast had been removed earlier in the week. Beth had told him it would take time for her to regain the dexterity and strength she'd had before.

As she quietly stood there, Shade wondered what had caused the brief flash of pain he saw cross her face.

Rider was looking pointedly at the clock, anxious for their Friday party to start. He wanted Lily gone so they wouldn't have to monitor their raucous behavior. With the factory empty, if Lily wasn't here, Rider would already have a beer in his hand while he waited for him, but because alcohol terrified Lily, Shade had made it a rule that they weren't allowed to have it out until she was gone.

"Hot damn. Let the good times roll," Rider said, jumping off the table.

Shade threw Rider a warning look for wanting to get rid of her.

Lily picked up the scraps of paper lying on her table, throwing them in the trashcan before going back to the table and picking up her purse.

"See you guys Monday." Lily headed out the door.

Shade frowned as Bliss passed her in the doorway.

"Finished for the day?" Bliss smiled warmly.

"Yes. Have a good weekend, Bliss."

Bliss's smile disappeared when she saw Shade wasn't happy. The woman knew she and the other women weren't allowed to flaunt their bodies when Lily was there. Not only was Shade not ready for her to discover the sexual relationship the men shared with the women, but Beth and Razer wanted her kept in the dark for the time being.

He smoothed out his expression when Lily turned her head.

Lily waved goodbye, closing the door behind her.

"I'm sorry. I thought she was gone," Bliss apologized as she moved toward them.

"No, you didn't. Her car is still outside."

Shade didn't care about her hurt expression. He hadn't touched Bliss for the last three months since Lily had been hurt and nearly died. He wouldn't have touched her the last time if he hadn't wanted the brother's markers to use to make Lily a member. He was a manipulative bastard, but Bliss had known the rules when she became a Last Rider. The sex they enjoyed didn't equal a relationship, and the sexual relationship they had shared was over. The only thing she aroused in him anymore was anger when she pushed at his limits. Bliss was not going to be allowed to hurt Lily the way Winter had been hurt when she had seen Viper's unguarded reaction to her overt sexuality.

"I think you're missing being punished." Shade ran his fingertips across the tattoo she was so proud of. It had the day she had become a member of The Last Riders with a daisy chain circling it. His finger tapped one of the daisies. "Don't make me regret giving you my vote."

"I'm sor—"

"I told you I don't want to fuck you anymore, and do you really think, after all the time you've known me, I'll change my mind?"

"No, but—"

Again, Shade ruthlessly cut her off. "You thought you would tempt me?" Shade shook his head at her. "I have no desire to punish you, but I think Rider does." He lifted a brow at Rider as he took a step behind Bliss, his hand going to her belly.

Rider lowered his head, teasing the side of her neck. "Shade may not want to paddle that ass of yours anymore, but I have one which will make you just as wet," Rider promised.

Shade enjoyed watching Rider when he let his dominant side out. The brother didn't show it often, and when he did, he wouldn't usually allow observers. Bliss, on the other hand, enjoyed being the focus of the men. The more she had, the more excited she became.

He was enjoying the show when the light from the doorway caught his attention. Lily had come in the door, abruptly halting as she watched them.

Shade froze at her expression, having no doubt she had seen the sexual excitement on their faces. He wanted to throw something. He hadn't been going to participate; he had been about to leave and go to his room to take a shower.

"Uh...um." It took her a second to speak again. "Rider, Beth's car is broken down at Mrs. Langley's house. She needs you to bring the trailer. Excuse me." With that, she turned and ran, her hand hitting the metal door rail on her way out. The door flew open, and Lily ran to her car.

"Mother fucker!" Shade strode to the door with Bliss and Rider following.

Lily was already reversing out of the parking lot by the time he was outside. She waved at them, trying to appear normal, but there was nothing normal about Lily's expression when she had seen them.

"Shade..." Both Rider and Bliss spoke at the same time.

"Stay away from me, Bliss."

Shade went to his room, ignoring the members as he passed through the clubhouse. Once in his room, he took out his cell phone to call Razer.

"We're on our way to the clubhouse, can it wait? Beth's car isn't—"

"I fucking know her car isn't working," Shade snapped. "Lily went back in the factory after I thought she had left. Rider and Bliss were there."

"What did she see?" Razer asked furiously.

"Rider was holding Bliss, and I was watching," Shade answered truthfully.

"If you can't keep your dick in your pants, then stay the fuck away from Lily," Razer told him.

Shade spoke between clenched teeth. "Don't talk to me that way! You know damn well I haven't touched anyone since she was hurt."

"Where is she now?"

"I assume, from the way she took off, she was heading home."

"As soon as Rider picks the car up, we'll go check on her."

"Call me and let me know how she is."

Razer sighed. "I will, but Shade, you have to be more careful. I won't let her be hurt."

"Rider was going to punish Bliss." Shade lowered his guard enough to explain.

"Fuck." Razer paused. "He was going to let you watch?"

"Yeah."

"Damn! You think he'll do it tonight since he was interrupted?" Shade heard the humor return to Razer's voice.

"I don't know. Why don't you ask him when he gets there?"

"I will. Beth hasn't seen him in action yet."

"Later." He really didn't want to hear about how much Beth would enjoy the performance. She and Razer would fuck all night if they were allowed to watch. Shade had plans of his own, though.

CHAPTER FORTY

Shade stood in the doorway of the factory as Lily walked across the parking lot. He heard her greet Train and Kaley, who had become a regular hanger-on. From Lily's concentration on the two, she knew her.

He held the door open for her as she approached.

"Good morning, Shade." Lily smiled.

"Lily." His eyes went to Lily before moving over her shoulder to Kaley and Train.

Lily brushed by him without stopping while Shade motioned for Train to get Kaley out of sight before closing the door. He didn't want a repeat of Friday; therefore, he was going to have a talk with the brothers. The bitches needed to stay in the clubhouse unless they were working or going into town while Lily was at work.

Shade walked toward his office, seeing Lily studying the board where orders were posted.

He had spent Friday night with her instead of partying at the club, under the ruse of returning Beth's fixed car and ordering food that couldn't be delivered to the clubhouse. It had been the first step toward coming out from behind Razer's shadow. Up until then, she had seen him as Razer's best friend, whereas at the factory, she saw him as a boss. Friday night, however, he had wanted her to see him as a man.

He wanted her to learn to talk to him without being afraid. He had used the lunches so she could get used to them being alone. Now, he wanted her to get used to him in her home. He had every intention of being there frequently.

"I've been to Alaska," Shade had commented.

"You have?" Lily asked, staring at him in surprise. "Is it as beautiful as the pictures?"

"Yes, but I was too busy freezing my ass off to appreciate it at the time."

Lily had laughed as he had wanted her to.

He had flipped the pages of the book, describing the places he had been to in Alaska. They talked about his family, growing up with a dad in the military. Overall, the night had been comfortable, and after a while, Lily had seemed to relax and enjoy being around him, until she blacked out.

It had scared Shade half to death, but then she recovered quickly, explaining it was just a headache and she had had one earlier that day, after catching him, Rider, and Bliss in the factory, though she hadn't needed to say that. Shade ended up sleeping on her couch, leaving early the next morning before she woke and before Razer and Beth came home.

Shade snapped out of the memory of Friday night when he saw Hardin come up behind Lily.

"Going to save one for me?"

She laughed, stepping to the side.

"I might if you weren't so slow," she joked back. She never fucking joked around with him so naturally.

Hardin took one of the orders off the board. "Why don't you take one of the work stations next to mine, and I'll show you how it's done."

Shade didn't give her time to reply. "Lily's work station is the one I put her at; yours is going to be at the unemployment office if you don't get busy."

Hardin hurried to his workstation at the sharp comment, while Lily gave him a reproachful look from her violet eyes.

"Don't look at me like that, Lily. He deserved it. Get to work," Shade snapped before going to his office. He barely restrained himself from slamming the door, leaving it open to keep Lily in his sight. That was why he had assigned her that particular workstation; he had a clear view of it from his desk.

Shade kept busy answering emails until Bliss came in carrying his and Lily's lunch. She closed the door with her foot then set the tray down on his desk.

"Can I get you anything else, Shade?" Bliss stared down at him with her fuck-me smile.

He leaned back in his chair. Bliss was like a rapacious puppy which couldn't understand why her master didn't want to play.

"Yes. When you get back to the clubhouse, tell Train he better play it cool when he's in public with Kaley."

Bliss nodded. "Okay."

Shade stood up and Bliss went taut, her nipples showing under her thin shirt. He opened the door for her to leave while she hid her disappointment, giving him a smile as she left, waving at Lily.

"Lily."

Lily set down the box she was working on, going to Shade's office. Shade sighed to himself at seeing her determined stride and clenched hands. *Here we go again.* Shade was curious what her new excuse would be to get out of sharing lunch with him.

She took the seat next to his desk as he closed the door and resumed his, handing her one of the trays with a grilled chicken salad. Lily ate her lunch quickly while he ate his more slowly to annoy her.

"What's the rush?" Shade asked.

Lily finished chewing the bite in her mouth. "I think it's better if I eat lunch with everyone else," Lily delicately began.

"No." Shade took a bite of his own food while Lily sat stunned. It took her a second to recover from his denial.

"But—"

"Did you bring a change of clothes?" he asked, looking at her pink dress.

Lily flushed as his eyes lingered on the tiny buttons at the front of her dress. "Yes."

Shade kept eating while Lily ate more slowly now, chewing her food thoughtfully.

"Why didn't you eat lunch at the diner yesterday?" Shade asked the question which had been bothering him since Beth had shown up after church at the diner without her.

"I wasn't hungry," Lily snapped.

Shade's stern mouth twitched in amusement. "If you didn't eat lunch in here, what would you do for lunch, Lily?"

"I would eat lunch outside with the other workers."

"You don't need to eat lunch with them. You would become too friendly with them, and they would start to take advantage." Shade gave her the partial truth.

"That's ridiculous."

"Is it? They all are aware that your sister is married to one of the owners of the factory."

As Lily finished eating her salad in silence, Shade placed his plate back on the tray.

"I would never use my connection to Razer."

"I think it's better to not put you in that position. Is it so hard to keep me company for lunch?"

"I don't think you lack for company, Shade," Lily teased him wryly as she got to her feet.

"Really, what makes you say that?" His eyes bore into hers.

She speculated, "I'm pretty sure that any of The Last Riders would join you for lunch, not to mention the other women who work here. Several of the women are interested in you. They ask me constantly if you're seeing someone."

"Tell them to mind their own business," Shade snapped, seeing no jealousy in her eyes.

Lily laughed at his disgruntled expression.

Opening the door, she glanced back. "I can't do that, Shade. I wouldn't presume on my relationship with you to speak for you." She closed the door before he could say anything else. The seductive witch had actually managed to one-up him.

Shade leaned back in his chair, smiling.

୫୬ ୦୪

Shade stood when he saw Hardin go out the metal door. Lily had left for break a few minutes before, and it didn't take any of the skills he had acquired in the military to figure out what the man was after.

He went outside, seeing Hardin had made his move and was talking to Lily as Shade strolled to where Rider was working on his bike.

"What's up?" Rider asked, picking up a wrench.

"Nothing," he said, watching the expressions cross Lily's face. *She has no problem talking to Hardin*, Shade thought sarcastically.

Rider laughed, shaking his head. "I'll never understand you, Shade. You have every woman in town wanting to fuck you, and most of the women in the clubhouse would rather be in your bed than anyone else's. But you're working a job you fucking hate just to even be near her. I wouldn't put that much effort into buying a bike, much less a woman," Rider bragged.

"That's why your bike is broken down all the time," Shade told him as Georgia walked up to Hardin and Lily.

The floor supervisor was a bitch. Rider had promoted the single mother when he had been managing the factory, and Shade had to put up with the evil bitch because of Rider's bad decision.

He waited until break was over before going into his office. It wasn't long before Georgia came in after briefly knocking, placing her clipboard on his desk.

"We're going to need an extra truck today. We have too many orders."

"I'll take care of it," Shade replied, not looking up from his computer.

"I overheard Hardin asking Lily out."

Shade took his eyes off the computer. The bitch seemed absolutely giddy about spreading gossip.

"Why would I care who my employees see in their free time?"

"I just thought…It seemed like you were interested in Lily." She became wary when Shade's expression darkened.

"It's been a long time since I've had to deal with tattletales, Georgia. I don't feel the need to encourage gossip, either. Mind your own business, or I'll transfer you back to the production line to keep you busy."

"Yes, sir." The woman hastened out of his office.

He picked up his cell phone as soon as her ass was out.

"What do you need?" Viper hissed.

Shade smiled. He had seen Winter's car pull in the parking lot. It was Viper's birthday, and his doting wife was probably at that moment giving Viper his present. From the moans he heard in the background, he had interrupted one or both of them coming.

"I need to hire a new driver."

"We hired one a week ago. We don't need to hire a new driver; just have them make another trip."

"That doesn't work for me. I like to stay on schedule. Besides, we don't have to hire a new employee; I have the perfect person in mind, and he already works for us. We'll just increase how much he gets paid."

"No, I want to stay on budget."

Shade grinned evilly. "I have Winter's IOU from last night. I'm thinking of cashing it in because Bliss likes that new purse Winter's been packing."

"Son of a bitch!" Shade didn't know if Viper had just come or if he was insulting him. "Go ahead. Do what you want, but I want that IOU at dinner tonight."

"Will do. Oh, and Viper, I have a brand new paddle that hasn't been broken in yet if you want to borrow it."

"Fuck off."

Shade waited until the end of the day before calling Hardin into his office.

"In your employment application, you stated you have your CDL license. That true?"

"Yes, but I also said I was tired of driving. I drove a coal truck and—"

"Is the license still current?"

"Yes, bu—"

"Good. We need another driver, and Viper doesn't want to hire a new one. You can start tomorrow."

Hardin placed a hand on his desk, leaning toward him. "I don't want to drive a truck," he said angrily.

"Then I'll have to fire you so I can hire someone who does. It's your decision." Shade shrugged.

"It's not my decision, or I wouldn't have to drive a fucking truck."

Shade remained silent.

"Fine, I'll drive the truck. I have child support payments to make, and I'm two months behind. I can't afford to be late on another payment, or my ex will take me to court."

"I'm glad that's settled." Shade went back to work on his computer. "Make sure you stay away from Lily while you're loading the trucks, or I'll call your ex and tell her about the extra cash you're making helping Razer build his house."

As Hardin's face turned a ruddy red and his hands clenched by his side, Shade stood up, coming around his desk. "Are we going to have a problem?"

Shade pinned him with a deadly look. The slimy fucker wasn't going to slide into home plate with Lily after he had waited years for her. Shade didn't believe Lily would be attracted to Hardin, but he wasn't going to take a chance. Shade had seen too many killed in the service by not being careful.

"No, I don't have a problem. I'm sure I'll enjoy my new job," Hardin said, jerking the door open.

"Is everything all right?" Shade heard Lily ask Hardin.

He didn't speak to her, merely walked past her to leave the building at the same time Shade came out of his office.

"Is everything all right?" she asked Shade instead.

"Everything is fine," Shade said, losing interest with the man when he walked out the door.

"Why was Hardin upset?"

"That's none of your business." When Lily would have said something else, Shade forestalled her. "But I'll tell you, anyway. I gave him a promotion. We need another driver, so he's going to be working on the trucks from now on."

Lily looked out the window as Hardin sped out of the parking lot. "He doesn't seem to be very happy about his promotion."

"I'm sure he's not," he said grimly. "Are you ready?"

Lily nodded, following him outside.

"I need to get my clothes."

Shade waited by the steps as she grabbed her small travel bag out of the back-seat of her car.

"Where are we going to work out?" Lily asked as she came to stand by him.

"In the gym in the basement." Shade walked up the path. The concrete path had taken them a couple of months to lay and led around the house to the backdoor, making it easier for Winter to walk up instead of using all the steps.

Instead of going in through the kitchen door, Shade opened another door at the side of the house which had been added when the path had been made. He wanted Lily to be able to come and go from the basement without going upstairs. That way, Lily couldn't see anything he didn't want her to, and The Last Riders could still have their freedom while Lily was downstairs. Shade and Razer had both told Beth when they had agreed for her to work in the factory that the upstairs was off-limits.

She looked around curiously, and Shade saw what she was seeing: a large room with exercise equipment, the pole Rider and Train had installed for the women to give shows to the brothers, a large couch placed against one wall, and a flat-screen television.

"You can get changed back here." Shade walked across the room, opening the door which led to a hallway. "That room has the hot tub." Shade pointed to the door on the left. "That's the restroom where you can get changed. The door at the end is my room. I'll wait for you in the gym."

Shade left her standing in the hallway, going to his room to change into a pair of shorts and a T-shirt. Then he stood outside the bathroom door to wait for Lily.

When she opened the door, his mouth almost dropped open at what she was wearing. She had changed into sweat pants and an oversized sweatshirt he thought was big enough to fit Knox. Lily had gathered her dark hair into a tight ponytail, which highlighted her high cheekbones and violet eyes, making her beauty stand out among other women. Her outfit, though, was horrible. Shade wanted to rip it into shreds.

"What kind of workout clothes are those?" he asked without waiting for an answer, striding to the mats he had laid down before going to work that day.

"It's what I always wear," she said.

"Then you need to get some different ones. Those won't do." Shade motioned for her to stand on the mat.

As Lily came to stand in front of him, her eyes flitted nervously over his body, lingering on his tattoos.

His cock stirred under his shorts as he distracted her, having her warm up by stretching, which he also did. Then Shade showed her how to kick out at him, which he blocked over and over again.

"Come on, Lily; you can do better than this."

Lily repeated the move, striking out with her foot several times.

"That's enough," he said when she stopped to catch her breath. "At least you're in good shape physically, but you need to do some weight training."

"I agree. Thanks, Shade."

"When we're in here, you call me Sir." He stared deep into her eyes, determined to lay the ground rules from the beginning.

"Okay."

She picked up her bag to leave, and then Shade held the door open for her before walking with her to her car.

"Bye, Shade."

"Later." Shade closed the car door and watched as she pulled out of the parking lot.

He was always watching her leave, but he was beginning to see a light at the end of the tunnel. One day in the future, he would give her a reason to stay.

CHAPTER FORTY-ONE

"Anything wrong?" Shade asked.

She had been picking at her lunch for ten minutes.

Lily shook her head, picking at her hamburger and fries. "No."

"Are you sure?"

"Yes," Lily said glumly.

Shade's lips twisted. "You're very emotional, aren't you?"

Lily stiffened in her seat. "I'm sorry if I can't be emotionless like you. I get a little upset when people run like the plague when I approach them."

"Who's running?" he questioned, barely able to hide his amusement.

"The other workers. If I try to talk to them, they ignore me and move away."

"I'm sure you're exaggerating," Shade said, eating his own food with a hearty appetite. He was glad the men who worked in the factory had understood his silent message of getting rid of Hardin for getting too friendly with his woman.

"I'm not exaggerating. I asked Gaige if he knew where the pocket flares were, and you would have thought I had asked for condoms. I asked Trent to help me find a packet of seeds, and he walked off while I was still talking to him. And, in case you didn't know, Georgia is a reincarnated Attila the Hun."

Shade burst out laughing and saw Lily's hurt feelings disappear a little. His breath caught when he saw a hint of attraction for him on her face. Then, curiously, her eyes went blank and her hand went to her wrist, snapping the red rubber band.

"Why did you do that?" He knew why yet wanted to see if she did or if she would tell him.

Lily handed him her partially untouched plate, preparing to get to her feet.

"Sit down."

His hard voice had her bottom immediately returning to her seat, her eyes going to her hands on her lap.

"Eyes to me, Lily," Shade ordered firmly.

Lily's eyes reluctantly returned to his.

"Answer my question. Why did you snap the rubber band?" he gently probed.

"I don't know. It's just a habit. Sometimes I do it without knowing why," Lily said softly.

"I see. I only give instructions once, Lily. The next time you snap that rubber band around me, you better be able to explain why. Do you understand me?" Shade stared directly into her eyes.

Her hands clenched as if she wanted to defy him, yet she managed to keep still.

"I need to get back to work," Lily said, standing up and leaving his office.

Shade stared after her contemplatively. If she had felt a spark of attraction for him, it was time to start building on that foundation.

At quitting time, Shade was about to leave the factory, anxious to spend the next hour alone with Lily, when Georgia asked him about her brother getting a job at the factory.

"He really needs the job. He has good work references." She smiled at him flirtatiously, as if that would help make up his mind. It didn't.

"I've already told you no, Georgia. Rider and Train have, too. We don't want two family members working in the factory, especially when one is already in a supervisor position. If you want to step down, then maybe…"

"No! No. I love my job."

Shade knew the woman used her forceful personality to intimidate the other employees. He had already decided to talk to Viper about moving her back to the production line.

He was leaning against the doorway to his office while Georgia talked to him about how much the raise had helped with providing for her children when the door to the factory opened, and Lily came back in with her workout bag. She didn't interrupt, waiting patiently for their conversation to end.

"Georgia, I'll see you tomorrow." He broke into her description of her daughter, leaving her standing to walk toward Lily.

"What has you looking so guilty?" Shade questioned the look he had caught on her face.

"I was thinking that you and Georgia would make a nice couple."

"Really?" If she had felt a spark of attraction for him earlier, would she be talking up another woman to him?

"That's when I felt guilty. In case you didn't know, she's really not a nice person."

"I think I can handle Georgia," he said, walking to the door of the factory and holding it open for her. He could handle three Georgias. Of course, they would all be tied up with their mouths gagged.

"That's good to know. Then I think you should go for it. She obviously has a thing for you," Lily said helpfully.

Shade stopped in his tracks. "Lily, have I given you the impression that I want to be your BFF?"

"Noo…"

"Good."

Lily followed behind Shade's quick strides.

He was angry with her for throwing another woman at him while he would kill another man over her. When he opened the door to the basement, waiting for her to enter, Lily avoided his eyes as she went inside.

"I'll go get changed," Lily said, heading straight to the restroom.

Shade changed into his workout gear and began on the weights while he waited for Lily.

He paused when she entered the room, his eyes going to her new workout outfit. Shade didn't say anything, but he wanted to ask why she was determined to wear clothes three sizes too large. The black leggings were hanging off her, and the spandex top was also too large with long sleeves.

Shade placed his weights down.

"Come here," he said, coming to a decision. He was going to find out once and for all if she was ever going to feel attracted to him. If she didn't, he would be wasting his time.

Lily moved toward him, and he showed her the weights to use then returned to his own workout. He had to stay in shape since he was still called for specialized jobs from the government when targets needed to be eliminated. He had to be ready to leave at a moment's notice, so his body had to be at its peak performance level to go into the dangerous situations he had been placed within.

Shade spent the next hour with her weight training, making sure the hand which had been broken started with minimal weight.

"Two more, Lily." She was lying on the bench, lifting weights, when Shade's hand went to the inside of her thigh. "Keep your legs straight."

As Shade's hand guided her leg to where he wanted it, Lily stiffened. Touching her lightly—not enough to frighten her, but to make her aware she was a woman and he was a man—her arms trembled under the weights she was holding.

"Keep your arms steady." His hand glided up the length of her arm, steadying it. He wanted to surround her with his presence to heighten her femininity.

His hand lay flat on her stomach, well aware of how sensitive she would be there and that the thin material of her shirt wouldn't provide a barrier against the warmth of his hand.

"Breathe, Lily."

While Lily took a deep breath then released it, her chest shuddered and her little nipples poked through the material of her bra and workout shirt.

He had his answer.

"That's enough for today." Shade straightened, standing above her. He took the weights from her as she hastily got to her feet, her face flushed, eyes wild.

"Two days a week, we'll work on weight training. The other three, we'll work on your defense moves." He brought her back down gently, taking the focus away from a body she didn't recognize as being aroused.

"That sounds good," Lily said, not looking at him as she picked up her workout bag. "I appreciate your help, Sir."

Shade watched her run out the door, letting her leave. He was concerned her reactions might have been more than she could handle.

Shade sighed. There was no going back to the clubhouse, just as there was no going back with Lily.

CHAPTER FORTY-TWO

"I'm making a liquor run into town. Need me to pick anything up?"

"No, I'm good." Shade was talking to Train when Lily came out of the backroom where the seeds were kept refrigerated. Gaige had followed her in a few moments before, and Lily's reaction was one Shade recognized. The bastard had done something to upset her.

She was trying to blank out, like she had the day at the lake and the day the bikers had attacked her and Beth. She had her cell phone to her ear, since whenever she was frightened, she always wanted one person: Beth. Her sister was her security, and she clung to that tightly when she was afraid. Shade wished just once she would turn to him. He was more than capable of protecting her.

Lily went to her workstation.

Even from inside his office, he heard her whimpers. Either Beth was unable to calm her, or she wasn't answering.

As the front door of the factory opened and Razer walked through, Lily took a step toward him, still whimpering.

"Lily!" Shade moved around Train, coming to the doorway of his office.

Lily had stopped when he said her name, her hands going to her hair.

He was afraid she would tear it out if he didn't calm her down. "Lily, come here. Now!"

Lily's feet changed direction, and she moved toward him.

"Go take your chair." She needed a safe zone; her submissive side was begging for direction.

"I need Beth," she said between chattering teeth.

"Go take your chair," Shade repeated, his expression hard. He took her jaw in his hand. "What did I tell you about me repeating instructions?"

"Shade?" Razer wanted to help Lily, but the way he and Beth were handling Lily's problems wasn't working.

She had to learn to build herself up to where she was strong enough to calm herself. Razer had to learn Shade wasn't going to put up with any interference with what he thought was best for Lily, and it was just as good a time as any.

"I will handle this, Razer." He maintained eye contact with Lily, giving her the strength she didn't have for herself.

Seeing Lily's whimpers had stopped, Razer backed off.

Shade's hand dropped from her face before giving Train a quick look. Train had also seen Gaige go into the back room.

"I'll take care of it," Train acknowledged his silent order.

Shade came inside the office and shut the door.

"Go stand in the corner, Lily." When she didn't move right away, he snapped, "Now." The more authority he used, the more she responded.

Lily was a natural submissive. Her abuse as a child by a figure of authority had fucked her up, though. He had to teach her that, if she followed his instructions, he would give her the care and affection she craved without harming her.

Lily immediately went to the corner where she stood, facing the office while Shade took his seat back at the desk and resumed doing his paperwork as if she wasn't there, giving her traumatized mind time to recover.

He heard her take a deep, shuddering breath then saw her lean her head on the wall. Shade wanted to hold her close and soothe her, but he made himself wait; she needed him to have the control she didn't.

"Stand up straight." Shade didn't take his eyes off his paperwork, pushing a few buttons on his computer before making more notes.

Lily straightened, her hand going to her wrist.

"No." That time, he looked up, daring her to snap the rubber band.

Her hand reluctantly fell to her side. Then her breathing gradually slowed, and her pale face returned to a rosy glow.

"Come here, Lily." She came to his side as he pushed his chair back from his desk. Reaching out, he grasped her hand, jerking her down to sit on his thigh.

Lily started to go wild.

"Sit still," Shade ordered, and she instantly followed his directions. He wanted her to see she would be rewarded.

Shade didn't attempt to touch her further, his hand going back to the computer screen, moving the cursor to begin going through the emails.

"The Farthings ordered three more cases of MREs. I think they're planning for World War III." He went down the emails, checking them off one by one. Sometimes he would make a remark, and sometimes he wouldn't.

"So, what happened to get you upset?" Shade finally asked as he scrolled down the list for the next email.

"When I was in the back room, Gaige came in. I was bent over the refrigerator, and he slid his hand underneath my dress."

"I would be upset if he tried to touch my ass, too," Shade remarked, still working and not looking at her.

Lily laughed.

"Did he try to stop you from leaving the room?" Shade probed gently, not wanting to upset her again.

"No. I probably overreacted. I know how silly I sound."

"You didn't overreact. He had no business touching you," Shade said, his hand going to her hip, adjusting her so she sat more comfortably on his leg. Subliminally, he was giving her the message that he was the only one allowed to touch.

Several more minutes passed with him holding her, showing her he would release her when he was ready.

"Are you all right now?"

"Yes. Thanks, Shade."

After Lily opened the door, going back to work, Shade looked at the clock on the wall, seeing it was almost quitting time before he went to the work board to double-check that all the orders had been filled.

"Are you okay?" Bliss asked. She and Jewell had stopped by Lily's work station as they left.

"I'm fine. I just overreacted."

"Do you need anything before we leave?" Bliss offered.

Lily looked embarrassed before asking, "Would you mind getting me a number four green bean pack from the refrigerator?"

"No problem," Bliss said, turning to go to the back room to get the item.

"I'll handle it, Bliss. You two go on up to the club." Shade walked up to them, and the two women left after giving Lily a sympathetic glance.

"Go get the seeds. I'll wait here," Shade told her, understanding she had to face her fear while knowing he would be near.

She didn't argue with him and went to the room, and she was back in less than a minute.

Shade watched as she completed her order while the rest of the workers left for the day. When Lily had finished and cleaned her workstation in preparation for Monday, he dashed her hopes of going immediately home.

"Go get your bag while I lock up," Shade ordered.

"But I thought—"

Shade tilted his head to the side in question.

"I'll go get my bag."

Grabbing her shoulder bag, she followed Shade to the basement and went to get changed. Shade changed and was warming up on the mat when she returned.

She sank to the mat to begin stretching while Shade watched her for a few minutes before standing up and turning on the music. It was Friday, and the party upstairs would be getting started; the music would muffle any sounds.

Shade moved her into position to begin her defense training. Then he worked on her kick for several minutes, becoming irritated when she didn't connect with him. She was trying not to touch him.

Lily became distracted as the noise upstairs increased. The music he had put on wasn't able to entirely hide that the party had started. Her eyes went repeatedly to the stairway.

"Pay attention, Lily. If you used more strength, we would have been done ten minutes ago, and I would be upstairs drinking a cold beer," Shade said, deciding to see how she felt about him going upstairs after she left.

She managed to kick him on the side of his thigh.

"About fucking time." Shade smiled at her proudly, realizing she didn't like the thought of him going upstairs.

"Did I hurt you?"

"No, Lily, you didn't hurt me. Next time a dick like Gaige tries to touch your ass again, try that move."

Lily grinned back. "Okay."

"We're done for the day."

"Thanks, Sir."

Going for her bag, she picked it up before she hesitated a moment, twisting the handle of the bag in her hand. "Thanks for getting me to go get the seeds. I would have just avoided the room."

"I know. Lily, let's work on getting rid of the old fears before adding new ones. You're completely safe at the factory and here."

"I know that."

"Good. I'll see you Sunday." He waited to see if she would say whether she would be going to the diner after church.

"All right."

Shade smiled as he walked her to her car. She was walking with an added confidence she hadn't had before. The lessons were boosting her belief that she would be able to defend herself. She would, too; he would see to it. He would teach her how to defend herself against everyone except himself.

಄ ಅ

Shade carried two pizzas and a six-pack up the walkway to Lily's front door, pausing when he heard music coming from inside. Gazing around the neighborhood, he saw that most of the houses were dark before he stepped to the window and looked through to see Lily dancing around the living room.

He smiled at seeing her enjoyment and the sexy way she rolled her hips. Her sensual movements had his cock rising behind his jeans. Thank fuck she went into the kitchen at that moment.

When Shade went to her front door and rang the bell, Lily answered the door seconds later, wearing dark-blue fleece pajamas. He was going to have to have a talk with her about the fucking peephole.

"Move, Lily, before I drop the pizzas."

Unlocking the door, Lily took a step back, letting him enter.

Shade came in, setting the pizzas and beer on the coffee table.

"What are you doing here?" Lily asked, closing the door before walking barefoot back to the couch.

"I thought you might be hungry." Lily's stomach grumbled. "Go grab us a couple of plates."

She did as Shade told her then sat down on the couch as Shade opened the box, putting two slices on her plate. She immediately took a bite of the warm pizza.

Shade put two slices on his own plate and began devouring his. They ate quietly as Lily put a movie on for them to watch.

When he opened a beer, he felt her stiffen next to him, and the hand holding her pizza trembled as she lifted it to her mouth. Shade began to talk about the movie she had put on and the two others in the series. Eventually, she relaxed back into the cushions after taking another slice of pizza. He thought she must have worked up an appetite with the dancing.

Shade opened himself another beer as he took another piece of pizza, seeing Lily crowd herself closer to the side of the couch, pinning her gaze on the television.

Her mother had used alcohol against her like a weapon, yet Shade wanted her to realize she could be around it and nothing would happen. The brothers were constantly drinking at the clubhouse, and he had every intention of her being there more often, so that was one fear she needed to overcome.

When he finished, he cleaned the table and put the beer in the fridge before relaxing back on the couch. The movie ended, and they argued about what to watch next.

Lily was through half of the second movie when she dozed off, her head on the side of the couch. Shade lifted her, laying her next to him. He kept his touch impersonal while, at the same time, wanting to hold her close as she drifted toward a deeper sleep.

"Go back to sleep," he said with her stirring movements.

As her taut body relaxed against his with her bottom against his thighs, Shade held his breath, expecting her to wake up fully. He made sure to keep some distance, giving her personal space so he didn't overwhelm her. He was giving her the illusion of safety while the wolf held her in his arms.

Her back fell against his chest as she sank into an exhausted sleep, the shadows under her eyes all the evidence he needed to know she hadn't been sleeping well. His arm circled her waist as he pressed her closer.

He couldn't remember the last time he had slept deeply. For the past three years, he would go to bed tired and aching for Lily, and then he would wake up tired and aching for her.

⁎ ⁎

The couple sleeping on the couch didn't move when the key opened the front door. Beth and Razer came to a stop in the doorway with the early morning sun just coming up behind them. The Last Riders were going to the diner for breakfast and they had stopped by, thinking Shade would be awake and might want to go with them; instead, they found them sleeping.

Razer silently closed the door, expecting Shade to wake. They took a step closer to the couch to see Shade was holding Lily clutched to him as if she was a precious treasure. His usually fierce expression was softened in sleep, and his face was turned toward Lily. She was lying, facing Shade, with her head on his shoulder, her hands on his chest, and her leg thrown over his.

As Beth wiped a lone tear trailing down her cheek, Razer placed an arm around her shoulders, leading her back out the door and closing it quietly behind them, leaving the two on the couch alone. Tomorrow would come soon enough.

CHAPTER FORTY-THREE

Shade crossed his arms over his chest as he watched Beth and Razer eat their hotdog.

"Hurry up." They were taking their sweet time, which was irritating the fuck out of him.

"We're almost finished. Lily is just up ahead, looking at the blown glass," Beth told him, getting to her feet to throw away the trash. "You could have gone ahead and met her," she said, giving him a sly smile.

Shade almost rolled his eyes. Lily's sister could be a pain in the ass. Lily might have been adopted, but she and Beth were a lot alike.

He had already spent an aggravating day riding around town, trying to find Gaige. However, the fucking coward was hiding from him, so being irritated further by Beth trying to be funny was not what he needed.

Beth took her cell phone out of her pocket, frowning when she pulled up her messages.

"What?" Both Razer and Shade asked at the same time.

"Lily bought a piece of glass and took it to her car."

The sky was rapidly getting darker.

"Did she say where she parked?"

"No. She sent the message ten minutes ago. It shouldn't have taken that long. She should have texted me she was on her way back by now."

Shade took off, The Last Riders who were sitting at the picnic tables following behind him. When they heard a loud crash of glass breaking, Shade felt his stomach sink.

"Spread out!" Shade ordered the brothers.

He recognized Gaige who reached out, taking Lily's arm in his hand when she tried to take a step back. Shade and the brothers were able to see what Lily couldn't as three bikers about to become part of the action stepped up from behind her.

Shade walked hurriedly to the scene, watching the bikers exchanging words with Gaige as the obviously frightened man started to step back. He ran an experienced eye over the other three bikers. The blond one was the leader; the one with a scar running down his cheek the enforcer. Shade hadn't missed the subtle signal the blond one had given his men, and the lethal look of the other one spoke for itself.

The largest biker slung an arm around Gaige's shoulder as he said something to him, turning him toward a group of trees. Shade didn't feel any sympathy for Gaige, who looked scared enough to piss himself.

"Wait, he just lost his temper," he heard Lily plead as he moved along the side of a pickup truck, getting nearer.

Viper and Train were on the opposite side of the parking lot, stealthily moving through the shadows of the trees to get closer, while Cash and Rider were trying to sneak in behind them.

"That's okay, sweet thing. I'm going to help him find it." The large biker had no problem maneuvering a struggling Gaige away.

Lily took a step forward, but the blond biker slid an arm around her waist. "Let Max deal with him. He can't look much worse than he does now."

Shade was going to rip the bastard's head off. He was proud of Lily, though, for not having one of her panic attacks.

"Lily!" Beth yelled out, unable to wait for the brothers to move in.

Shade wanted to shake her as she rushed across the parking lot. Razer caught up with her. He had been left behind to watch her, not let her place herself in danger.

As Shade gave the signal for The Last Riders to come out, appearing in a circle around the three bikers, Razer handed Beth over to Evie and Jewell. The rest of the brothers were moving in as back-up.

"Want to take a bet on which one she belongs to?" the one with his arm around her waist spoke to his friends.

"Don't have to. I know," the dark-haired one said in amusement, moving in front of Lily and blocking her from view.

Shade's eyes narrowed. They didn't give a shit who she belonged to; they wanted to find out the strength of the club, identify The Last Riders' president and enforcer.

"Let me go." Lily tried to wiggle from the grasp the blond biker had around her waist.

"Calm down. I'm going to let you go."

Viper's harsh voice was low and filled with menace. "Let her go."

The blond one sent a critical eye over Viper. *There you go*, Shade thought. Strength can never take a backseat, and Viper wanted the situation over quickly with the women members and wives near.

The one with Gaige in a stranglehold turned back, moving closer to his friends.

"I have every intention of letting this sweet thing go. We're not out for trouble; just passing through." The leader nodded at Gaige and the one he had called Max. "Found him giving her some trouble." Nodding again toward Lily's car, he then said, "Decided to step in. Seeing she's yours, we'll step back." His arm slid away from Lily, releasing her.

While Lily took a step forward toward Razer, Shade didn't break eye contact with the scarred one who stepped to the side to let her pass. Shade didn't miss the gun tucked into his waistband under his jacket as Lily brushed past him.

"He's telling the truth, Viper. Gaige was angry that he got fired, and they made him leave me alone."

"Lily, go to your sister," Shade spoke.

She took off toward her sister and as soon as she was out of earshot, Shade gave his ultimatum.

"He's mine. Give him to me, and you can leave in peace."

"Peace is good." The leader spoke with a mocking twist to his lips. "But I'm just as willing for a good fight. Unfortunately, this fucker isn't worth it."

Max handed Gaige over to him, pleading with Shade that he hadn't been going to hurt Lily.

"Shut the fuck up, you pussy. You're brave enough when a woman has her back to you. Didn't you want her to see your small dick?" Shade mocked while his expression turned deadly.

Just then, Knox pulled his deputy car into the parking lot close to the men before getting out. "Beth called and said someone was giving Lily trouble?"

"He broke her windshield," Shade answered, indicating the asshole he was holding.

Knox took Gaige from Shade, putting him in handcuffs before placing him into the backseat of the cruiser. Shade didn't mind, though. When the deputy who was taking statements went home that night, Shade would be making a visit to Gaige's jail cell.

"They with him?" Knox nodded toward the out-of-town bikers.

"Fuck no. We're just passing through, stopped for some fun, and found him giving sweet thing a hard time," the blond biker said.

"Quit calling her that!" Shade couldn't hold back his anger.

"No offense." An insincere smile from the leader had Shade's hands clenching at his sides.

"Well, fun's over. You men need to be leaving town since you were passing through," Knox drawled sarcastically.

"You *telling* us to leave town?"

"That about sums it up," Knox agreed.

"Seems we don't have much of a choice, do we?"

"No," Shade answered.

The leader nodded. "Let's go, brothers."

The three bikers turned, going to their bikes.

"I'll make sure they leave," Knox said, going to the cruiser with Gaige inside.

As Shade and the rest of the men returned to where the women were waiting, Shade ran his eyes over Lily, making sure Gaige hadn't bruised her when he grabbed her.

"You okay?" Razer asked Lily.

"I'm fine," Lily assured her brother-in-law while her eyes avoided Shade's.

She began walking with her sister, looping their arms together. Shade had witnessed them walking that way before. Both women were very expressive with their love, and although Beth would take Razer's hand often, Shade couldn't imagine the day Lily would reach out to touch him voluntarily.

"Do you want to go back to the booth and get another figurine?" Beth asked.

"No," Lily said, changing the subject. "Let's play some games."

She walked up to one of the booths where you had to throw a ring around a milk jug, handed the worker some money, and he gave her several rings. Aiming, she missed pathetically. She tried again with the other two rings, throwing each one carefully, and missed them all. Shade wanted to help her yet hung back at the edge of the group, watching the members as they walked through the fairgrounds.

The members began splitting up, going to different games and playing. The brothers went to the shooting game, while Lily and the women moved on to another game, shooting water into a clown's mouth. She won and began jumping up and down, laughing.

After two more races, Lily earned a prize, picking a purple monkey, and the man behind the counter handed it to Lily.

"Here you go." Lily handed it to Beth.

"Don't you want it?" Beth protested.

"You're the one who likes stuffed animals."

Beth's face was confused as she took it from Lily. Shade had to walk away from the group, returning to watch the men shoot while staying close enough to keep an eye on the women.

Gaige had destroyed something Lily had let herself want; as a result, she was giving the stuffed animal away before it was taken from her. Shade knew it was what she was used to happening.

With the game over, the women came back to watch the men. While Train and Rider were shooting at the targets, Shade stood next to Viper, both watching.

"Why don't you take a turn, Shade?" Bliss asked loudly.

Shade shot her a look, which the small woman had no trouble understanding. Bliss was walking a fine line with him. She had been with the club long enough to have heard what job he had held in the military. She was trying to expose club secrets. He was growing tired of her attempts to draw his attention.

He felt Lily's angry stare at him and knew she didn't like that he wasn't friendlier with Bliss. Fuck, if she knew the truth about their past, she would understand Bliss was playing games she had no chance of winning.

"Let's go ride the bumper cars," Bliss suggested.

The Last Riders made their way through the fair, stopping and riding a few rides and playing several more games. Then they all came to a stop at the ride where they would get on a seat and go to the top and then be released to swing in a large circle.

"I'm going to go get something to drink," Lily told Beth, who was standing in line with Razer.

Shade, in line behind them, wasn't surprised Lily wasn't going to ride. He stood in line, keeping watch as she went to a food truck where she bought a drink and cotton candy then took a seat at one of the tables.

Shade got out of line.

"You want me to hold your place?" Razer asked with a snicker.

"Fuck you." Shade moved away.

He saw Beth bury her face in Razer's chest, her shoulders shaking. Those two had a warped sense of humor.

As he approached, Lily was delicately licking the sugar crystals from her lips.

Shade sat down on the bench next to her. "You don't want to ride?"

"Not that one, I don't," Lily replied, smiling.

Shade surmised the cotton candy had put her in a better mood. It sure as fuck was doing things to him.

She sat, eating her candy as The Last Riders got on their ride. Lily watched them while he watched her eat the sticky confection with his cock steadfastly reminding him it hadn't had a woman's mouth on it in three months.

She looked at him inquiringly when he shifted closer to her. His eyes dropped to her tiny pink tongue as it swept the sugar crystals from her bottom lip. He was about to take the job over for her when she turned away, taking a drink of her soda.

A smile came to her lips.

"What are you thinking?" Shade asked.

She turned to him with a start, giving him a sweet smile. "I was just thinking how happy everyone looked, like they belong together. I can see you all care about each other."

Shade turned to where she was staring. The Last Riders had gotten off the ride and were approaching, laughing and having a good time. He faced her again. He would rather watch her eat the cotton candy.

She tore another piece of the spun candy off. "You shouldn't be so hard on Bliss. I think she has a thing for you," Lily said, raising the confection to her lips.

Unable to take the temptation any longer, Shade's hand snapped out, catching her wrist in a hard grasp.

"What did I tell you about me not being your BFF? Bliss knows exactly what I feel for her." Shade brought her hand to his mouth where his tongue licked her fingers, taking the sugar off, and Lily shuddered, her eyes darkening.

Jerking her hand from his, she avoided his eyes. Then she got to her feet and dumped the cotton candy as well as the drink into the trashcan before making a beeline straight for Beth's side.

Shade watched her run to Beth for safety with a small smile on his lips, the taste of her still in his mouth. Her attraction to him was growing, and he planned on fanning that particular fire until it became all she could think about. Until her desire became stronger than her fear.

He rose to follow behind the group, keeping a watchful eye on his club members. Lily didn't stray from Beth's side for the rest of the evening.

He had thought Beth would be his biggest opposition, but surprisingly, Razer was playing the big brother. Shade was willing to go along with it, for a while anyway.

He watched as she looked back over her shoulder then moved closer to Beth. His gut twisted as he wondered if she would ever turn to him over Beth, if he would be the one she looked to for protection.

They managed to hit all the rides and most of the food trucks before heading to the parking lot. On the way out, Shade caught Viper's attention.

"I'll catch up with you later."

Once Viper sent him a curious look while he nodded, Shade went in search of one particular vendor, easily finding out there was only one which sold blown glass. The old man behind the table was polite yet wary. Shade was used to his appearance frightening some people, though.

"There was a young woman with long, dark hair and purple eyes here earlier tonight. She bought one of your pieces; which one was it?" Shade questioned, scanning the small figurines.

"It was one of a kind. I have something similar…" The old man began to reach across the table.

Shade shook his head, taking out his wallet.

"You make these?"

"Yes…but I only make one of a kind—" Again, he attempted to explain, but Shade cut him off.

"It was accidently broken." Shade handed him several bills and a card. "Make me another just like it and mail it to the address on the card. When you do, I'll send another hundred."

"But this is more than enough." The vendor counted the cash in his hand.

"Then it will give you the motivation to get it done before I change my mind, won't it?"

Shade walked away when he nodded. Lily was never going to lose what she wanted ever again.

ஐ ௸

Shade walked nonchalantly into the jail cell Knox had opened. He leaned against the wall as Gaige jumped to his feet.

"I'm going to make it simple for you. Get your ass out of town and don't come back."

"I have a wife and kids!"

"This the same wife and kids you had when you were sticking your hand up Lily's dress?"

"I was just playing around. If Lily told you any diff—"

Shade was on him in the next second, his fist punching him in the stomach. When he would have fallen to the floor, Shade jerked him up with his hands on his neck, throwing him to the wall then pinning him against it.

"You fucking coward, I will take your ass out if you say her name one more time. I don't give a rat's ass about your family any more than you do. When you get out of here today, Knox will give you an envelope with some cash in it, and you will sign an agreement to keep your mouth shut. Do you understand me?"

Gaige's face was turning purple, but he managed to nod his acknowledgement.

Shade finally released his throat. "Take your family and leave town, Gaige. If I ever hear or see you again, it will be the last time. I'm giving you enough money for you and your family to start over somewhere else. Do *not* make me regret my generosity."

Gaige bent over, trying to catch his breath. "I won't."

"Good." As Shade reached into his pockets, taking out his leather gloves, Gaige watched him with fear in his eyes.

"You really didn't think I was done, did you?" Shade mocked. "You destroyed something of hers then left a bruise on her arm. I drove that truck you're so proud of off Pine Mountain. Now, I'm going to break your fucking arm. Then we'll be even."

CHAPTER FORTY-FOUR

Shade sipped his coffee, watching Lily and Beth cross the street in front of the diner. If Lily had turned to walk home again, he would have worried she was trying to avoid him after his move the night before.

"What has you so quiet?" Rider asked, sitting next to him at the table inside the diner.

Train and Cash quit talking to listen to his answer.

"Just wondering how many beers Razer and Viper drank before Lucky's service so they wouldn't laugh out loud during it."

"You going to start going to church every Sunday when you and Lily get together?" Train questioned.

"What do you think?" Shade answered.

The table burst out laughing yet quieted when the women and Razer and Viper came in with their wives.

"Was the sermon good?" Shade asked sardonically.

Both men looked suspiciously at the brothers while they tried to hide their smiles. Shade noticed Lily took a seat between Razer and Winter at the end farthest away from him.

The waitress came to take the orders of the new arrivals. It didn't take long before the food was served. Shade had eaten earlier, but he got a refill of his coffee as the others ate.

When the door to the diner opened, Shade nodded to Viper so he would notice the men coming inside. The table went quiet.

"What's going on?" Lily looked up from her salad to ask Winter.

"The bikers from last night just came in," Winter answered.

"Oh."

The women began talking to cover the silence, but Shade and the men remained quiet as they watched the bikers take a table. There were more of them, they had brought in their own reinforcements.

As the women finished, The Last Riders rose to leave. Shade couldn't understand why Lily stopped at the cash register, opening her purse to take out some money. He was about to say something when Beth spoke up.

"What are you doing? Razer already took care of the check."

"I know." She gave her money to the cashier. "I want to pay for the men's ticket by the window."

After the cashier's mouth dropped open like his own did, she waited for Shade to nod before reaching out to take the cash from Lily.

"Lily, what are you doing?" Beth questioned in a lowered voice.

"Paying back a favor," Lily said, taking a deep breath.

Then, before he could stop her, she approached the men sitting at the table.

"I wanted to thank you for what you did last night. It could have gotten bad without your help."

Shade walked to stand behind her as she spoke to the man he knew for a fact was the president of the motorcycle club.

"Anytime, sweet thing." The man's hard eyes softened briefly when he looked at Lily, yet they resumed their hardness instantly. Shade's instincts kicked in, telling him something wasn't right.

Lily turned to leave, but her attention was caught by one of the men sitting at the table. Reluctantly, Shade had to admire the biker's ink work. It was some of the best he had seen.

"Hi, I'm Colton." He put out his hand for Lily to shake.

"Hi, I'm Lily." She placed her hand in his.

Shade glared at him, letting him know he wasn't happy with him touching his woman.

"Hi, Lily. That's Ice." He nodded toward the blond, telling Lily what Shade already knew.

He had found out who they were before he had lain down to grab an hour's sleep before getting up to come to the diner.

"The big guy there is Max, and the ugly one next to him is Jackal."

"It's nice to meet you." Lily smiled. "I didn't mean to disturb your lunch. I wanted to thank your friends."

"I'm sure they enjoyed it, knowing them. Take care, Lily," Colton said, putting out some strange vibes which Shade picked up on.

"I will," Lily replied, moving away and almost bumping into Shade.

He ignored her angry attitude at his interference, leading her away from the table and back to The Last Riders who hadn't moved away from the door.

They waited until she was outside before giving her hell.

"What were you thinking, Lily?" Beth started.

"I was thinking that I would do the polite thing and thank them for helping me out of a difficult situation," she explained.

"You can't get friendly with another motorcycle club," Evie said, taking the words out of Shade's mouth.

"I don't know why not." When several would have opened their mouths, Lily put up her hand. "I wasn't getting friendly. I was thanking them. I can be friends with anyone I want. I'm friends with Stud."

Shade lifted a brow at her lame excuse. She was no more friends with Stud than he was.

"They have more in the parking lot," Shade told Viper.

"I saw," Viper replied grimly.

"What do you want me to do?" Shade knew what *he* wanted to do. He wanted to get rid of the women then beat the living hell out of the mother fuckers. It showed disrespect for them to stay in town, wearing their colors. However, Lily and Beth were waiting for Razer.

"You two go ahead. I'll be there in a few," Razer told them.

Lily hesitated, moving toward Viper and touching his arm. "Leave them alone, please, Viper. They don't want trouble, and I approached them." Her purple eyes pleaded with his president.

"They came inside seeing our bikes were outside," Viper replied.

"Please, Viper."

"I'll give in this time, Lily, but don't ask me to back down again," Viper replied.

Shade wanted to rant at his president for giving in to her, the weak fucker. The woman needed to learn she couldn't use those eyes of hers to get her way all the time.

Lily reached up, kissing Viper on his cheek. "Thank you," she said before moving away.

Shade became even more pissed at her. First, she had talked to the other club, showing them her gratitude. Hell, he was the one who had beaten the hell out of Gaige. Now she was fucking kissing Viper for something he shouldn't have agreed to. He had been chasing after her for three fucking years, making an ass in front of the brothers numerous times, and she had fucking kissed Viper before him?

"Let's go home." Razer's voice was amused as he guided the women toward their home.

As soon as Lily's back was turned, Shade punched Viper in the stomach.

"Shade!" Winter grabbed her husband's arm when he would have punched Shade back.

"I just wanted to show him my gratitude for letting Lily kiss him."

"She was just being sweet, thanking him for—"

"Don't care," Shade snarled. "It should have been mine. If any other brothers decide to let her show them her gratitude, I'll show them my foot up their ass."

ॐ ☾

Shade watched the two men through his sights as they fueled their bikes. He debated firing a bullet in Joker's gas tank when he placed the nozzle in. He had the ability to make the shot from his custom-made Barrett rifle. It had been built to his specifications—with a range longer than any known rifle and a certain weight so it could be broken down in seconds. Shade knew the feel of every inch and could take the rifle apart in the dark as easily as in the sunlight.

He waited patiently for Joker and Dale to get back on their bikes. As much as he wanted to see them consumed in burning flames, he didn't want to endanger anyone inside the gas station. Besides, he never deviated from a plan once it had been made.

Shade had made it a point to find out about everything and everyone connected to the two.

Crazy Bitch had spent several hours giving him all the information she had on Dale. She hadn't paid much attention when she had mentioned Dale's cousin, but Shade had. He had contacted Jake, Dale's cousin, offering him more money than he would make in ten years strip mining to call him if Dale got in touch with him. And Jake had called yesterday.

Shade had already scouted out the area, his experience telling him it was the most logical place for the men to hide. When Jake had called, Shade had been ready, taking out his duffle bag from the place where he kept it hidden. Then he had ridden to his chosen spot to lay in wait, knowing it was the perfect place for them to refuel on their way. With his bike parked three miles away, he would jog there through the woods and eliminate all traces of his presence before leaving.

The two bikers who had almost caused Lily's death while trying to rob Sex Piston's shop rode back onto the curvy, mountainous road, and Shade's finger tightened on the trigger as Dale went around the sharp curve. He heard the bike spin out as the front tire exploded, sending Dale's bike spinning. His scream could be heard from where Shade was lying. Shade was an expert rider; he had known exactly how the bike and rider would react. It was unrecoverable. The bike hit the guardrail, and Dale went flying over the mountain's edge.

Shade didn't watch; he was changing the direction of his scope, pinpointing Joker's motorcycle. Again, with the slightest movement, a bullet left his rifle, hitting the targeted front wheel and causing it to explode. Joker didn't scream; he didn't have time. He was a better rider, but even he couldn't save himself. He died like Dale—flung from his motorcycle over the mountainside. The two bikes lay crumbled in a heap by the guardrail.

Shade sat up, tearing down his rifle then placing it carefully into his canvas bag. Standing, he placed the straps on his shoulder, his boots going to where he had been lying, stirring the leaves and twigs together before he tossed several rocks around. Even if someone guessed a sniper had taken them out, they wouldn't look that far away. No one could make a kill shot from that distance. Except him.

ﭏ ﬖ

"Lily."

For the first time since she had begun eating lunch with him, she didn't have a mutinous expression on her face when she entered his office.

Shade closed the door after she entered, going to sit at the chair beside his desk where he handed her the chicken salad.

"Thanks, Shade."

"You look tired today," Lily probed at his silence.

"Late night."

He had driven to Ohio so he could be seen there then had driven back during the early morning to be there when the factory opened. His ass was killing him from riding that many hours on the bike.

"Oh." Lily took a bite of her food.

A few silent moments later, she asked, "Are you mad at me for something?"

"Yes." Shade was going to tell her the truth even if she didn't want to hear it.

"Why?"

Shade gave her an angry glare, leaning back in his seat. "Why do you think?"

"Because I talked to those bikers?"

He was just as pissed off at her for kissing Viper, but he had to be content with blowing off half of his anger.

"You know better than being friendly with bikers like that. Remember the first time you saw us at the lake? You were petrified, yet you sashayed your ass right up to their table."

Lily winced at his description and then tried to explain. "Because I wasn't scared of them. I knew you were there."

Shade's anger dissipated. Well, fuck. How was he supposed to stay mad at her when she had just admitted to feeling brave because he had been there?

"They've left town, but if they come back, stay away from them." Shade gave her the warning in a cold voice, not *entirely* over his anger yet. It was going to take a while to get over Viper.

"I will," Lily promised.

She placed her dirty dishes back on the tray before going to the door. She was about to open it when he called out to her.

"Don't ever touch Viper or one of the other men again."

She twisted the knob and then went through hurriedly, closing it behind her. The woman *did* have a survival instinct. If she had turned around to argue with him, he had promised himself to throw her on his desk and fuck her silly.

Shade tossed the rest of his uneaten salad onto the tray, too disappointed to be hungry anymore.

❧ ❦

That afternoon, Shade spent his time walking the factory floor, managing the huge number of orders. If Georgia kept flirting with him, he was going to fire her or beat the hell out of Rider for hiring her. To make the afternoon worse, Train and Rider brought Kaley into the factory.

He had told them repeatedly to keep her on the down-low, but they had argued back that Kaley wanted to be a member, and she already had three votes. That was why the power of the vote was so important. If any member didn't want a woman to join, they withheld their vote. Kaley was never going to get enough votes to become a member. He believed she was joining as payback to a cheating husband, and he didn't think she would get along with the other women.

Shade could tell from Lily's blush she was uncomfortable with the way Kaley was dressed in a pair of shorts and a swimsuit top. She was going to have to get used to it, though. The women liked to dress seductively for the brothers, and as he had every intention of her becoming a member, she was going to have to get used to seeing a lot worse. Shade simply wanted to do it slowly and give her time to adjust, not have it thrown in her face like that.

Evie and Bliss came into the factory to see what was holding Train and Rider up, using the opportunity to try to convince Shade to go swimming with them.

He stood in the doorway while Lily kept working on her order, looking up at them every so often with a puzzled expression. Shade didn't try to interpret it. She was probably mentally fixing him up with them. She wasn't going to be clueless much longer, though; he was getting fed up playing Mr. Nice Guy, since she had kissed Viper.

After the women laughed, telling him he was missing a good time, Shade gave them an obscene gesture when Lily wasn't looking then went back in his office to clean his desk. At quitting time, he went to her workstation, coming up behind her.

"You ready?" Shade asked.

Lily jumped. "What for?"

"To work out." Shade couldn't understand why she was surprised. They worked out every day after work.

"I didn't bring my bag. I didn't know if you would be gone again today."

"I left a message for Georgia to tell you that I was out of town yesterday, and I would be back today."

"I guess she forgot."

That bitch never forgot anything. Not to mention, he had texted her what to tell Lily, and he had left a note on her desk.

"It doesn't matter. Winter always keeps extra outfits in her locker. You can have one of hers. You need a new one, anyway."

"There's nothing wrong with the one I have," Lily protested.

"Other than it's two sizes too big and meant to be worn during the winter, and you left it at home," Shade remarked.

"Fine," she snapped back at him. Shade was about two seconds away from paddling her ass when she apologized. "I'm sorry."

Shade nodded, pacified at her apology. "Go outside. I'll be there in a minute."

"Okay."

As soon as the door closed, Shade strode angrily to the back room where Georgia was placing the seed order which had been delivered, throwing them haphazardly into the refrigerators.

"Why didn't you give Lily my message?" he asked bluntly.

"I did. She must have forgotten."

"Don't fucking lie. Lie to me or any other boss here again, and you'll be fired," Shade said harshly.

"I'm telling—"

"Be very careful, Georgia. Remember those kids you have at home," he pushed. Georgia snapped her mouth closed. "Don't ever think for a second that I would believe anything you say over Lily. She doesn't know how to lie, unlike you."

"Okay."

Shade could practically see the steam coming out of her ears. As soon as he was finished with Lily's workout that night, he was going to have that talk with Viper.

"When you come to work in the morning, I want those seeds straightened out. You were putting them in the wrong refrigerator, and you've worked here long enough to know how to do it right."

"Is that all?"

Her sharp tone nearly had him firing her on the spot. If she didn't have so many children, he would have. Not that he cared, but Viper would.

"Yes."

When she hurried through the factory, her hands smacking the metal doors to the outside, Shade followed, turning off the lights and locking his office door. Then he came out of the factory, locking the door behind him.

"Why is she angry?" Lily asked as Georgia pulled out of the parking lot.

"When I leave a message, I expect it to be delivered," Shade answered grimly.

"Do you always have to be so rude?"

"Yes."

When they got to the basement, Shade made Lily wear Winter's much tighter and more appealing workout clothes, which Lily did not appreciate, throwing a tantrum and refusing to put them on until Shade put his foot down.

Their workout consisted of stretching until Lily gradually loosened up. He waited until her movements became more fluid to begin her defense lesson, taking her through the movements she had learned the week before. She became more adept at kicking him, making him take a step back. Once she had done that enough to make him happy, he taught her a different move where her knee would actually make contact with him.

"I almost got you," Lily bragged.

"Almost doesn't count." Shade intentionally raised her leg to his hip, her mound notching against his penis. Their workout clothes were thin, so Shade could practically feel the lips of her pussy. He exerted his control to keep his dick soft, wanting to be non-threatening, letting her feel him and see there would be no pain involved.

Shade held that position for a moment before his foot came out, sweeping the one she was standing on. She began to fall, landing on her back with him on top of her. She opened her mouth to scream but before a sound could erupt, Shade lifted himself off her in one fluid movement. Reaching down, he then snagged her hand and lifted her to her feet.

"Again. This time, I'll show you how to keep me from sweeping your foot out from under you."

Lily stood frozen, her eyes dark and unfocused. However, Shade had expected the reaction. He took her arm, leading her to the corner of the room, and then lifted weights until she was prepared to step out of the corner and continue.

"Go to the mat." Shade kept her waiting as he took off his shirt, using it to wipe the sweat from his forehead. .

Her first sight of the tattoos on his chest and stomach must have been startling because she looked away as he approached the mat.

"Eyes to me. Are you ready?"

Lily nodded and as soon as he was in position, she attacked, trying to take him by surprise. That time, when he caught her knee and pulled her off-balance, before her mind could spaz out again, Shade gave her instructions to keep her balance and avoid having her foot swept out from under her. He had deliberately picked that move because it required body contact to break.

He instructed her to place her hands on his shoulders to balance herself. Then he put his hands on her hips, explaining how to push off from him. As she completed the maneuver, she was awkward and didn't stand a chance in Hell of defending herself at her current level. However, it was a start.

"Good. That's enough for the day." He removed his hands from her body.

"Thank God," Lily muttered.

"What did you say?" Shade questioned. He had heard, but he wanted to see if she would be brave enough to repeat it out loud.

"Nothing, Sir."

"You can go get changed."

"Thanks, *Sir*."

Her sarcastic tone had him crossing his arms over his chest as he widened his stance.

"Would you like a lesson I give when I believe someone is being disrespectful?" Shade snapped.

"No, Sir." Lily rushed to the bathroom.

Shade was on his way to his bedroom to get changed when he heard her locking the door behind her.

CHAPTER FORTY-FIVE

Shade sat in the darkness of the truck he had borrowed from Cash after cashing in one of his IOUs. He was watching Lily as she walked next to the fucker who was courting a death wish if he didn't move his arm. He relaxed when he saw Lily move slightly away, keeping a few inches between them. He didn't like them holding hands, but he could handle it.

He had planned to come up with another lame-ass excuse to spend the evening with her, but Razer had told him Charles had beaten him to the punch. He hadn't had to deal with him before then because he had been out of town, but Charles was back and apparently thought he and Lily would continue dating.

Shade got out of the truck as soon as they had walked far enough around the lake that they couldn't see the car. Keeping to the shadows in case they doubled back, Shade made it quickly to Charles's car, kneeling down by the back tire. He slipped his knife out of his boot and thrust it into the rubber before moving to the front and doing the same. As soon as he heard the hissing air, he returned to the truck, sliding back behind the wheel.

Taking out his cell phone, he gave Rider a call to give him a heads-up that Razer would be calling him shortly, so he needed to finish his business with Kaley. He wanted his ass ready to roll when Razer called to give Lily a ride home.

Shade then sat back and patiently waited for the couple to return. When they returned only a short time later, he was surprised. He had thought they would be gone much longer since it was the first time they had seen each other in a long time.

Charles held the car door open for Lily, letting her slide inside, before he played the gentleman and tucked in her yellow dress so it wouldn't get caught in the door. He then walked around the front of the car, pausing when he was on the driver's side.

Charles bent down by the front tire then stood and walked to the back. After a minute, he got inside the car with Lily.

Shade knew exactly who they would be forced to call. Charles's daddy was out of town, and Lyle, the only one who had a tow truck in town, was always drunk after nine. If you were unlucky enough to need his services at that time of night, it was hit or miss whether or not he would pick up his phone. Often, if he did, you wished he hadn't.

His cell phone rang, and Shade answered it without taking his eyes off the car Lily was sitting in.

"Yeah?"

"Razer called, said Lily had a flat tire. I'm already in the truck. Be there in a minute," Rider said.

"Thanks, brother." Shade disconnected the call, the smile playing on the edges of his lips disappearing when he saw Lily lean across the seat and kiss Charles. Shade wanted to rip the steering wheel off. The only reason he didn't was because he needed the fucking thing to drive Lily home when Rider arrived.

Twenty minutes later, Rider parked his truck behind Charles's car, leaving the headlights on so, if they looked back, they would be blinded by the light.

Shade started Cash's truck and drove forward, parking it next to Rider's. As Shade climbed out, both Charles and Lily climbed out of the car.

"What's going on, Lily?" Rider asked as he walked to stand next to Charles and stared down at the car with the two flat tires.

"We went for a walk and when we came back, the tires were flat," Charles explained.

"I'll get it loaded onto the trailer and drop it off at the garage," Rider said.

"I'll give you both a ride home," Shade offered, moving forward.

Nobody said anything as the two men loaded Charles's car onto the trailer. When they finished, Rider climbed back into his truck while Shade went to Cash's truck and opened the passenger door for them.

Lily climbed into the truck first, holding her dress down as she slid across the seat, and then Charles jumped in. Shade closed the door, restraining himself from slamming it.

As Shade climbed into the driver's seat and started the truck, Lily tugged her dress down over her knees. He backed the truck up and turned around, making sure to brush his arm against her breast as he shifted the gears. She stiffened, but she couldn't shift away from his touch in the crowded confines of the truck.

The silence could be cut with a knife, and Shade saw Lily reach for the red rubber band; however, before she could snap it, his hand covered hers. She quickly slid her hand away from his, laying both on her lap.

"I appreciate you and Rider coming out." Charles broke the silence as they hit the outskirts of town. "We tried calling Lyle, but he didn't answer."

"That's because he was at Rosie's. I saw his truck as I passed." Shade's cold voice filled the cab of the truck. He had called Mick and told him to give Lyle an open tab for the night and to drive him home in the morning.

"That explains it," Charles muttered.

"Where to?" Shade asked, even though he already knew where Charles lived.

Charles gave him directions, and then silence resumed in the truck.

Shade made sure he took the curve to Charles's street sharply so Lily would fall against him, and moments later, he brought the truck to a stop in Charles's driveway.

Charles opened the door as soon as he put the truck in park. "Thanks, Shade. You and Rider come by the restaurant, and I'll buy you dinner."

"We'll do that," Shade lied.

"Goodnight, Lily. I'll see you in church Sunday."

"Goodnight, Charles."

Charles closed the door and Shade backed out of the driveway, his arm again rubbing against her breast. Lily tried to scoot over, but he had tucked her dress under his thigh while she had watched Charles get out of the truck. She tried unobtrusively to pull it out, but she gave up when she couldn't, sitting back against the seat.

"Did you have fun on your date tonight?" Shade asked, his jaws clenched to prevent him from saying what he really wanted to.

"Yes. We went to a movie and ate with my friend Miranda, Kaley's sister."

Shade didn't respond as they stopped at a red light.

"Beth and the others came into the diner when we were having coffee. You didn't go riding with them?" She looked at him questioningly.

"No, I wasn't in the mood for a ride tonight," he said honestly. Nor was he in the mood to stay home and watch Rider and Crash fuck Kaley.

The light turned green, and Shade shifted gears then pressed on the gas. The truck shot forward, and Lily fell against his side again.

"I'm sorry you ended up having to get out tonight," Lily apologized.

"You would have done better keeping your own ass home tonight." Shade couldn't hold his anger in any longer.

Lily stiffened next to him. "What do you mean by that?"

Shade turned the truck down her street. "I mean, you need to be cruel to be kind and quit leading him on," Shade replied, turning into her driveway.

"I'm not leading Charles on," Lily protested, turning to look at him as he came to a stop in her driveway.

Shade put the truck in park then turned toward her. "Yes, you are. When you went out with him tonight, were you planning on fucking him?"

"Of course not," Lily said, obviously shocked at his blunt statement. She tugged at her dress hard, jerking it out from underneath his thigh.

"Then that's leading him on, in my opinion." He wanted his bluntness to open her eyes. She needed to make it plain to Charles that they had no future together, or he would.

"Well, thank God your opinion doesn't count," Lily snapped, angrily sliding across the seat toward the door. "And you should know about being cruel." Lily slung that final comment as she opened the truck door, sliding down from the seat. Then she turned, damning him with her angry gaze as she slammed the door closed.

Shade took off after her, catching up with her as she reached her door. He pressed his body against hers, his hand planted against the door, not giving her an inch of breathing room and preventing her from moving to put the key in the lock.

"It's not a smart move not leaving your porch light on, Lily. You think I'm cruel? How was I being cruel by telling you that you should quit fucking with his head? Don't you think that, every time he goes out with you, he's wondering if that will be the time he actually gets to touch that soft skin of yours?" His mouth lowered next to her ear. "If you'll let him touch those firm breasts?"

He could practically feel her trembling as he carefully kept his body from touching hers.

"I'm a man, and I'm telling you without a doubt that, when he walks out of his door to go out with you, he is planning on spending the night between your thighs. I'm not the one being cruel; you are," Shade stated.

As Lily moaned, Shade took a step back. It took a moment before Lily unlocked the door and let herself in, and when she turned to slam the door in his face, he placed his hand on it.

"I'll have to teach you how to break that hold." He turned, leaving without another word.

He was playing with her, wanting her to think she was the only one affected by their closeness. She had looked like a startled doe when she had gazed back at him, her desire overriding the fear he had expected to see. She hadn't been afraid. She was becoming braver and braver whenever he came close to her, which was what he wanted. He needed her to lower her guard around him right up to the point she stepped willingly into his trap.

80 03

"Don't do it, Shade," Winter said as they watched Lily, Razer, and Beth leave the diner after their Sunday lunch.

Shade turned cold eyes on Winter for daring to interfere again. He had listened to her the day Razer and Beth had gotten married, but he was done listening to everyone.

He had been forced to sit and watch Lily and Charles eat lunch at the same table. Then, when the piss-ant had gotten up, he had kissed Lily while giving Shade a confident smile.

Shade had broken his coffee cup with his bare hand then thrown it to the floor, about to get up, but Beth had brought him back to reality by making the excuse she had dropped the cup.

Everyone wanted to protect Lily from him, while the real wolf was trying to steal her away. Fuck that. He had watched Lily put her mouth on Charles for the last time.

"Come to the lake with us. The whole club is going," Viper broke in between the building tension from his enforcer and his wife.

"No, thanks. I have something I need to take care of," Shade said, standing up.

"Shade." Winter's soft voice stopped him from leaving. "Be gentle."

Shade started to snap a reply to her for butting in yet again, but Viper's warning glare stopped him.

He nodded. "Always."

᠙ ᠗

Shade knocked on Lily's door. When she didn't answer, he unlocked it and went inside, worried Lily might have had an unexpected panic attack.

He found her outside sleeping on the lounger. Grinning wickedly, he walked closer, moving silently. He had only seen her once before in her swimsuit, and her body had matured since then.

Shade swallowed hard, forcing himself to wait. He went into the kitchen and began preparing them something to eat. After he had done as much as he could, he rewarded himself by picking up the bottle of lotion Lily had placed by her lounger. He rubbed the cold lotion onto her, knowing her hot skin would be sensitive.

She startled awake, her hands going to her side, ready to jump up from the lounge chair.

"Stay still. I didn't want you to burn." Shade rubbed more lotion onto the backs of her legs.

"That's enough. I was going to go in and get changed," Lily protested in a strangled voice.

"Stay and relax. I brought us some steaks to grill. When they're almost done, you can get changed."

Unable to resist, he rubbed his thumb against the bottom curve of her ass before he stood up, going to put the steaks on the grill.

"How did you get in?" Lily asked.

She isn't going to like this part, Shade mused, slapping the two steaks on the grill. "I have a key."

"What? How?"

"Beth gave me her extra key when you were in the hospital. She'd asked me to pack some clothes for you."

When she blushed, Shade knew she was remembering the red panties he had packed inside her suitcase.

"You can grab a quick shower. The steaks are almost done."

Shade nearly had a fucking heart attack when she rose up from the lounger. Her ass had been remarkable to look at and touch, but her breasts inside that tiny swimsuit were fucking magnificent. He almost lost his composure as they jiggled when she stood up and walked toward the house.

She kept her face averted from his, but Shade wasn't putting up with that. He slipped an arm around her waist as she passed, pulling her toward him.

"Wait a minute," he said, wanting to lick the bead of sweat trailing between her tits. He satisfied himself by pressing a finger on the skin just above the flesh of her breasts, instead. "You've gotten too much sun. Put some lotion on before you come back downstairs. I'll keep the steaks warm."

"I'm a grown woman," Lily snapped.

"I can see that for myself." His eyes didn't leave her tits.

"Jerk."

Shade released her when she started to wiggle away; a man could only take so much.

"Get changed." Shade grinned.

"I planned to." Lily stomped away, and Shade appreciated every step before she glanced back and caught him watching her ass.

"Don't say anything unless you want to learn my lesson on respect," he said, seeing the fire in her eyes. *Please, please, say something,* he silently begged.

Lily muttered something unintelligible under her breath.

"What did you say?" he asked with a warning glint in his eyes, almost licking his lips in anticipation.

"I'll be back in a minute."

"Damn," Shade muttered under his breath.

Going inside, he found a pitcher of tea and fixed a couple of glasses of ice then carried them outside.

He had already placed plates with baked potatoes on the table and was putting the steaks on a platter when Lily returned.

"Exactly how long have you been here?" Lily asked, taking a seat at the table.

"Long enough." Shade grinned, setting the plate of steaks down.

"I would complain, but the food looks too good," Lily said with wry amusement.

Shade placed one of the big steaks on her plate before serving himself. Lily cut off a piece of the tender meat then took a bite.

"It's delicious," she complimented.

"You didn't think I could cook?" Shade raised a brow.

"Why would you need to cook? You have a bunch of pretty women cooking and delivering it to you," Lily teased without an ounce of jealousy in her remark.

Shade had trouble swallowing his own bite of steak.

"I'll have you know that we all take turns cooking and sharing chores."

"I bet that's interesting. How often does Winter get stuck doing chores?"

"Not often, unless it's a punishment. She has a way of finagling things to get her way," Shade said wryly. She was becoming as good at playing cards as he was.

"I know. It comes from being a high school principal. She was a mastermind at making the kids do things they didn't want to do."

"Really?" Shade cut his steak, absently listening. He really didn't want to talk about Winter; she was a constant pain in his ass.

Lily nodded. "The seniors wanted to cut class on the first day of spring—it was a tradition at our school—yet students every year would manage to get into trouble. The previous principal had tried to stop it but wasn't successful. Winter, on the other hand, acted all gung ho for us to have the day off. She told us that, if we volunteered to clean the kitchen of the school's chef training program, she would let us have the afternoon off. What she didn't tell us was that the students had made pizza the day before and hadn't used pizza pans. It took us all day to clean those ovens. I had nightmares about burnt-on cheese for a month."

Shade stopped eating. That sneaky bitch had managed to trick him out of his marker by using the same trick on him she had used on high school students. Hell, he would have given her the marker, anyway; he didn't want to fuck her, but he would have made her work for it or held onto it for a rainy day.

Lily's laughter said she knew Winter had fooled him.

"Don't tell me she got you on that one?"

"Let's change the subject before I decide to stuff her into our oven."

Viper wouldn't let me, anyway, Shade thought grumpily.

They talked the rest of the meal about the different things people ordered through the factory.

"Diamond is becoming our best customer. We had a new shipment come in the first of the week. I had to be up early to help unload the truck. Diamond was sitting in the parking lot. She brought me breakfast so I wouldn't tell Knox on her."

"Did you?"

"Fuck no. She brought pancakes."

"Knox put Diamond on a budget," Lily told him.

"She's finally calmed down. She's too busy decorating her new house."

Shade got up to turn off the grill, making sure it was out before they went inside. Lily had already cleaned the table by the time he turned around, so Shade shut and locked the back door.

"I cooked; you can do the dishes," he said, opening the fridge to take out a beer, carrying it past her rigid body to the living room.

"What do you want to watch? Something scary or something funny?"

"Funny," Lily answered as she continued putting up the dishes.

"Scary it is," he teased while studying the titles of the movies.

"Don't you dare."

"Then you better hurry up."

She sat down on the opposite side of the couch from him only minutes later.

He had chosen a romantic comedy to watch with a fairly explicit sex scene. When it came on the screen, Lily jumped up and went into the kitchen, making the excuse that she wanted popcorn.

When she returned with popcorn and a beer for him, he was shocked. She hadn't been happy when he had grabbed a beer out of the fridge, but she had voluntarily brought him another one while she drank a soda.

She had subconsciously recognized that alcohol and pain didn't have to go together. It was only a tiny baby step for her, but for him, it gave him hope the size of the Grand Canyon.

"Thanks." He took the beer and popcorn from her as Lily returned to her seat at the end of the couch.

She didn't even stiffen when she heard the can pop that time, even though she couldn't bring herself to look at him when he lifted the beer to his mouth.

After the movie was over, Shade turned it and the television off while Lily carried the popcorn and empty cans to the kitchen. Shade was already at the door when she returned.

"Lock the door behind me."

"I will. Thanks for the steaks, Shade." Lily rose on her toes, brushing his cheek with a soft kiss before stepping back hastily. "Goodnight."

"Goodnight, Lily."

Shade closed the door behind him, waiting until he heard the lock click into place before he walked away with his fingers reaching up to touch his cheek.

He had believed he would have to be the one to initiate their first kiss, and his woman had proven him wrong. Hell, things were moving along faster than he had thought possible. By the end of next week, she might even manage to work up the courage to look him in the eyes when they had lunch.

‘ ’

Shade sat on his bike in the parking lot of Rick's Pub as the lights inside cut off and the workers exited, casting cautious looks in Shade's direction. Charles came out last, shutting and locking the doors behind him. When he turned to the parking lot and saw Shade, there wasn't any surprise in his expression; he merely walked toward the biker. Shade had to give the kid credit, too; he didn't even flinch from Shade's hard stare.

"If you came for that dinner, I'm afraid we're closed."

Shade let a wry smile touch his lips. "We both know that's not why I'm here."

Charles looked him over. "If you came here to threaten me to stay away from Lily, I won't. You're wasting your time. Even if you beat me up, all I have to do is show Lily, and it would turn her against you. There's no way you can win, Shade." The little shit smiled at him.

Shade smiled back affably before reaching into his pocket to pull some photographs out and hand them to Charles.

Charles took the photos from him, turning pale, then looked back up at Shade.

Shade leaned forward, taking the photos back, looking at the woman and child in the picture. "Amazing resemblance, isn't it? I think we both know what Lily would do if she found out you knocked up one of her friends. Miranda may have passed your kid off to the dumbass she married, but we both know it's yours. Not only would Lily not have anything to do with you, but it would break up Miranda's marriage, and the gossip would get back to your daddy. I believe her husband is a deacon in the church." Shade leaned forward, resting his forearm on his knee, his eyes pinning Charles in place.

"What do you want?" Charles asked, his jaw tight.

Shade smiled in satisfaction. "What I want is for you to go back to Lexington. I'll even give you a couple of weeks home before you have to leave. Just don't try to see Lily anymore."

With Charles's nod of agreement, Shade straightened, starting his motor.

"She won't ever love you. What makes you think you stand a better chance than me?" Charles looked him over as if he was trash.

Shade gave him his moment. Charles knew he had lost all hope of having Lily, and he sure as fuck was taking it better than Shade would have. He gazed back at the man yet felt no pity.

"The difference between us, Charles, is I would give my right arm for her. You, on the other hand, didn't take five seconds to put on a fucking condom." Shade drove off, leaving the speechless man behind.

CHAPTER FORTY-SIX

"Shade." Kaley was standing on the stairway, staring at him hungrily.

He paused in his stretching, looking toward the hallway leading to where Lily was getting changed into her workout clothes in the bathroom. "What do you want?"

"Rider said to tell you someone is here to see you." She shifted her weight to draw attention to her legs which were exposed by her tiny shorts.

"Why didn't he just call?" Shade asked, putting his T-shirt back on.

"I offered to come get you." Her eyes were practically licking his tattoos as he covered them up with the shirt.

He went to the steps which led upstairs and as he climbed up, she didn't move out of the way. Shade was the master of that game. The bitch wasn't going to manipulate him into playing a game he had no intention of participating in.

"Move, Kaley. Now."

Her hand reached out to touch his chest but Shade caught it, twisting her wrist until she had to sit down on the steps.

"Do not touch me without permission. I've told you this before," Shade reminded her. "I don't want what you're dying to give me."

When she nodded, Shade released her.

"Come down into this basement again when Lily is here, and I'll throw your ass out of the club. I don't care how many fucking votes you have. You got me?"

"Yes." Kaley rose to her feet.

"Good. Now get your ass upstairs," he ordered, following her up and into the kitchen where she hastily moved away from him into the other room.

Rider was leaning against the counter, drinking a beer. He tilted the bottle to the kitchen door, and Shade went outside to find Rachel Porter standing hesitantly by the picnic table.

"Greer's still in West Virginia, but he didn't want to keep you waiting, so he asked me to bring your regular Friday order." She held out a bag, which he took.

"He stay for a drink with The Blue Horsemen?"

Rachel smiled. "More like three or four."

"You walk through the woods?" Shade asked, seeing leaves and dirt clinging to the bottom of her jeans.

"Yes. I was checking on my roots, anyway. It's only a couple of miles."

"You need to be careful out in the woods by yourself."

"I know them like the back of my hand, and I have protection." She motioned toward a large dog sitting to the side, patiently waiting for her.

"I need to get back. Lily's waiting for me to work out." Shade turned to go back inside.

"Shade…"

Her concerned voice stopped him. He turned back to see her face filled with worry.

"I told you I would take it slow, Rachel. She's only here to work out. Be nice if you could work a little faster, though."

"It's not easy trying to work on her without her knowing it. I have to be careful because she knows I can heal with my hands."

"If she hasn't figured it out in the last month, she isn't going to," Shade told her.

"I told you I would do it when you bribed Judge Creech into dropping the possession charges against Greer, but it's hard to do when you won't tell me what I'm up against."

"Imagine your worst nightmare, multiply it by five, and you still won't be able to understand the Hell she's been through," Shade replied grimly.

"Jesus," Rachel whispered.

"He wasn't there for her then," he said snidely.

"Wasn't he?"

Shade wasn't about to get into a religious conversation with her. "Just keep doing what you're doing. She hasn't had a panic attack in a month, she's happier, and I don't think she's looking forward to going back to school."

Rachel shook her head at him. "She has a long way to go, Shade. As her mind heals, whatever she's burying in her past will try to come out. The only way she's ever going to truly heal is if she confronts her past, and Lily doesn't want to do that. She's too afraid to."

"You heal her mind, and I'll give her the strength to deal with the rest."

She gave him a sad smile. "I know you will, or I wouldn't have agreed to your terms. If I didn't believe you were the best thing for Lily, I would have let Greer rot in prison."

"I doubt that."

"Don't," Rachel replied firmly. Walking back to her dog, she reached down and petted its head. "She's not the only one who has to confront something inside of themselves," she said before leaving.

A chill ran down Shade's spine as he watched her go.

He went back inside, tossing the bag of reefer to Rider. The party was in full swing. Bliss was bent over the back of the couch as Cash fucked her from behind while Rider watched. Shade didn't have time to stay and watch, nor could he. It had been four months since he had fucked a woman; as a result, he couldn't watch them then workout with Lily without making his hard-on noticeable.

He was an expert at controlling his body, but it was getting beyond his capabilities to keep from showing his desire for her, especially since she persisted in treating him like a fucking friend. He could see the attraction for him in her eyes, but her mind refused to acknowledge what her body was telling her.

He went back downstairs, firmly closing the door to keep the loud noises of Bliss's climax from filtering down. He was glad he had put the music on when he had begun stretching out when he saw Lily on the mat, warming up.

"Sorry, there was something I needed to take care of."

"No problem," Lily said, bouncing up and down on the balls of her feet. "What are we going to work on today? Do you want me to try to knee you again?" Her eager face was lit up with excitement.

"You seem anxious to take my dick out of commission," Shade said wryly. He wanted to get off, and she wanted to pound his dick into the matt.

As Lily laughed, her eyes twinkling, he smiled back. It was worth the pain his dick was giving him to see her so happy. *Well, almost*, Shade admitted truthfully to himself.

He had painstakingly been painting a picture with Lily building her trust in him, and he wasn't going to stop until he had a masterpiece.

"We're going to work on something different today," he said, moving her closer to the wall at the end of the mat. "I want you to try to get out of a specific type of hold. For instance, if you're getting into your car and someone comes up behind you."

Lily nodded, her eyes watching him curiously.

"You ready?" he asked.

"Yes."

"Turn around."

Lily did as told and Shade moved closer to her, pressing his body against her back. Lily's hand automatically went to the wall to keep herself from being pressed against it, leaving her helpless. He felt the second she began to panic, but forced himself to wait for her next instinctive move.

One of her arms left the wall, going back to try to push him away, but his hand caught her wrist, bringing it backward to her lower back. Her other hand automatically went back but it was also captured, leaving her defenseless and pressed flat against the wall.

With his lower body flush against her butt, her breathing escalated and she went limp. Shade stepped back, and Lily began to slide down the wall without his weight holding her in place.

Shade had hoped she would have been able to tolerate the hold for a few seconds longer. Any time he took a step forward with her, he took two steps backward. He had to find a way to make her take more steps forward, or she would stay in the same place forever.

Once Shade took her arm, leading her to the corner and leaving her there to stand alone, she stood, gasping for breath, her hands going to her head and clutching her hair.

"Hands to your side. Stand up straight. Lily, by now you should know how I want you to stand."

She corrected her posture, her shoulders straightening as her hands obediently went to her side. Her submissive nature clung to his dominant voice for direction.

He took a drink from his bottled water before he went to the weights and began working out while ignoring her, giving her the time and space to analyze her feelings. He watched as her expressive face showed her resentment at being thrown into turmoil.

"Lose the attitude, Lily, or my hand is going to be on that bouncy butt." Shade was sitting on the weight bench with the weight paused in an upward position as he took in her look of shocked horror. "I didn't say I would beat you, Lily. But I *will* smack that ass if you don't behave." His blue eyes stared into her violet ones.

Lily gasped, turning her head toward the wall and breaking eye contact with him.

"Eyes forward," Shade said, continuing his arm curls.

Lily's eyes returned to him.

"I shouldn't have reached back," she said after a few moments.

"No," Shade answered. It hadn't taken her long to figure out her mistake, and she had recovered much faster than he had anticipated.

Lily took a step forward.

"Are you ready to go back to the mat?"

"Yes," Lily said determinedly.

"Turn around."

She met his gaze briefly then followed his directions. That time, when Shade grabbed her, pushing her against the wall, she braced herself with her arms.

"What do I do next?" Lily's voice trembled when he pressed his body against hers.

He talked to her firmly, giving her directions in a voice she could hold on to instead of the threatening darkness. She did exactly as he told her and while her movements were too timid, her initial terror had eased.

Shade released her. "Enough?"

"Yes." Lily turned around to face him then slid along the wall away from him.

"We'll work on that until you get it right. You need to learn how to defend yourself when someone comes up behind you. Men who attack women are confident that you'll panic, that you'll be too startled to be able to defend yourself."

"I'll work on it until I get it right."

"I know you will. You're learning fast. I'm proud of you," Shade complimented.

"Thank you, Sir." Lily reached out and hugged him. "I really appreciate all your help."

Shade had to use all his willpower not to drag her back when she pulled away.

"I'll get changed." She walked away with a spring in her step.

Shade nearly ran his hand over her ass as she passed him.

He was waiting for her next to the basement door which led outside when he got a text from Viper saying the Ohio brothers were asking about him. He sent a text back that Lily was about to leave, and then he would be up. When she came back within minutes, her eyes traveled up the steps to the closed door.

"It sounds like a football game is going on up there," she remarked.

"Several of the brothers from Ohio are down for the weekend," Shade answered, holding the door open for her, anxious for her to be gone. It was only a matter of time before some of the brothers came downstairs.

"Oh."

Shade was walking her out the door when his cell phone rang.

"Is she gone yet? The brothers are getting anxious, and the women want to play with the stripper pole," Viper's voice came over the line.

"Give me five. I need a shower and to get changed."

"You go ahead," Lily told him.

"You sure?"

"My car is just around the corner," Lily said dolefully.

"All right. I'll see you later," Shade replied, going back inside.

"Bye."

He closed the door behind him when he saw her turn the corner which led to the parking lot. Then he went into his shower as he heard footsteps running down the steps from the kitchen. Viper must have given the all-clear for the members to come downstairs.

Shade stepped under the shower just long enough to rinse the sweat off, barely drying off before tugging on clean clothes. He opened his bedroom door, going down the hall.

Evie and Rider came out wet from the room with the hot tub. Evie wasn't wearing a top, and her shorts had been left unbuttoned while Rider was wearing jeans.

"We were going to have some beer while we were in the hot tub, but someone must have taken the last one from the mini-fridge and didn't restock."

"I could send some down for you," Shade offered as he continued upstairs, following behind Evie and Rider.

"Don't bother. I forgot condoms, too, so I need to run upstairs to my room for more," Rider said.

"You shouldn't have used them all on Bliss," Shade joked.

"I have more." Rider tried to pinch Evie's ass as she went up the stairs first.

Evie opened the door to the kitchen and Shade saw her hesitate, but he merely thought the door was blocked with all the members and the brothers from Ohio. When Rider stopped, however, Shade knew something was wrong. Rider moved, and then Shade took the final step, entering the kitchen and coming face to face with something he had tried to keep from happening.

Lily was standing in the kitchen, her face a pale, tortured mask. His own face froze at her expression. He didn't have to be told what she had seen. The members' faces showed that Lily had seen it all. Her whimpers alone were ripping his heart to sheds.

Beth was in the doorway which led to the clubroom. She took a step forward at the same time he did, but Lily backed away from them. They both tried to speak at the same time, yet her whimpers of pain rose in volume, preventing her from hearing their words. Lily then ran from the kitchen and out the backdoor.

"Lily!" Shade yelled, running after her, but she didn't stop despite Beth's pleas along with his.

She ran down the path, her hair flying behind her and her screams filling the air. She almost fell down several times, tripping over her own feet as Shade ran like hell after her, his hand almost managing to catch her hair, but he didn't want to hurt her by grabbing her that way.

Ultimately, with a burst of speed, she jumped into her car, slamming and locking it before he could jerk it open. Her heartbroken cries spurred him to try opening the locked door.

"Lily, open the door. Please, baby, open the door."

Beth and Razer pulled him back from the car as she put it in gear, tearing out of the parking lot.

"Let me fucking go!" Shade jerked himself away from Razer and Beth.

He bent over, catching his breath. Not because he had winded himself running after Lily, but because of the look on her face when he had stepped into the kitchen.

"Shade…" Beth laid a hand on his back.

He straightened, turning around to see the brothers and women lined up on the walkway, watching. "What in the fuck happened? Why was she in the club?" he snarled.

Cash took a step forward, holding a wiggling Miranda by her arm. "Miranda came looking for Kaley, and when she couldn't get in the front door, she ran up the path and got in through the back. Lily was trying to stop her by coming after her. Brother, I'm afraid there's not much she doesn't know now. Kaley told Miranda about the votes and how the women get them."

Shade's hands clenched, wanting to rip the women apart.

"Viper," Shade spoke in a deadly calm voice which belied the hatred he was feeling at the moment.

"I'll handle it. Cash, take Miranda and Kaley to my room. I'll talk to them there in a minute."

Cash nodded, lifting a struggling Miranda off her feet while Nickel took Kaley's arm. When she would have jerked away from the rough-looking biker, he tossed her over his shoulder and carried her inside.

Beth and Razer moved toward Razer's bike, but Shade stopped them.

"You have to go get changed before you go home."

Beth looked down at her short skirt and fringed vest before nodding, her face going as white as Lily's. Then she ran back into the clubhouse.

"You going to ride your bike without shoes?" Shade asked Razer who was staring at him oddly.

"You calmed down?"

Shade nodded grimly. "Lily was going to find out sooner or later, though I never wanted her to find out this way," he replied grimly. "This shit is going to hit her hard, and she isn't ready for it. Truthfully, I don't think she ever would have been, and I probably would have put off telling her until she found out some other way. This way, it's out of my hands."

"Isn't that convenient for you? Lily, not so much," Razer snapped.

"Don't blame this crap festival on me, but don't expect me to cry over spilled milk, either. She found out, and now we have to fix it."

"That's not going to be easy," Razer warned, looking at the empty road Lily had driven away on.

"No, it isn't," Shade agreed. "But it's the only option I have because I'm not giving her up."

CHAPTER FORTY-SEVEN

"There she is," Shade told Razer when Lily turned the corner.

"It took her a long time to walk from class," Razer remarked.

Too fucking long, Shade thought.

Penni had given him Lily's class schedule. She had graduated in May, but the two women had remained in touch, having become good friends. Shade hadn't told his half-sister what had happened, because her usual good humor would have disappeared and Shade already had his hands full of upset women without adding more to the mix.

The women club members were upset that Lily had been hurt. Evie had wanted to call and talk to her, but Shade had told her to wait. If Lily didn't want to talk to Beth, Evie definitely wasn't going to be able to reach her. The only women who weren't troubled were Miranda and Kaley.

Shade had given Viper the information he needed to keep Miranda's mouth closed, but Kaley was a vicious bitch who didn't care about anyone other than herself.

Train felt guilty for introducing Kaley to the club. The man had a soft spot for women and couldn't stand to see them hurt. More than one of the women members had fallen in love with Train, but none had been successful in capturing his elusive heart. Shade doubted any woman would, but if they wanted his dick, then he was more than willing to oblige.

Beth stood, waiting for Lily by her dorm door, and Lily paused before continuing down the sidewalk, keeping her eyes averted from Razer and him. Shade knew damn well she had seen them, though.

While Beth and Lily talked for a brief moment before walking toward a bench under a tree, Shade watched the expressions of the two sisters. Lily's was hard, while Beth's was filled with hurt.

"It's not going well," Razer said.

"No shit."

Lily looked like she had lost ten pounds since she had left Treepoint, and the dress she was wearing needed to be cut into pieces and buried so it couldn't be sewn back together again. *Who in the fuck would make a dress in that ugly color?*

After Lily stood up then went inside her dorm, Beth sat there, watching her go inside.

Razer and Shade walked to the bench when they saw Beth bury her face in her hands.

"Beth, please don't cry, kitten." Razer sat down next to her, pulling her into his arms.

"I've lost her, Razer. I can see it in her eyes. She's so hurt. It's like looking into an open wound."

"She'll get over it."

"No, Razer, she won't. She thinks I've lied and deceived her, and she's right. I should have told her at least parts of it; she could have taken that. What she can't accept is the one person she trusted hiding things from her."

"Did she tell you not to talk to her anymore?"

"No, but she told me to give her clothes away. She's cutting herself off from me."

"Then don't let her," Shade said from behind them.

Beth looked over her shoulder at him. "She knows everything now, Shade. She knows that Razer and you both are original members. How the women get the votes."

"She was bound to find out sooner or later. When you, Winter, and Diamond found out, was it any less painful? But each of you got over it and moved on. Lily will, too," he said firmly.

Lily was stronger than any of the other women. She had endured Hell, surviving to become one of the sweetest, loving women he had ever known. He had no doubt she could make it through this.

"No, she won't, Shade. Lily is different. She'll believe that you and Razer took advantage of the women."

"That won't last long when she's around them," Shade said ironically.

Beth got to her feet. "You just don't get it, Shade. She's cut not only me, but us all from her heart. That's what Lily does. Lily doesn't give second chances with her love."

"No, Beth, it's you who doesn't understand. Lily's not going to be given the choice."

He started his motor, looking up at the dorm room and willing Lily to look out. However, it remained empty, and Shade's mouth tightened. What he had told Beth was the truth—he wasn't going to let Lily cut him out of her life without a fight. He had enough patience to outlast anyone or anything.

The problem was would Lily survive while he bided his time? Her fragility had shocked him. He couldn't stand back and watch her suffer. If it worsened, he would be forced to step in, and when he did, there wouldn't be any going back.

დ ርჳ

"Get in, Lily." Shade saw her look through the passenger window at him without saying a word, continuing to walk forward.

"You can either get in, or I'll put you in."

"Go away."

Shade opened the door, getting out of the truck and walking around the front to open the passenger door. "Get in."

"If you don't go away, I'll scream," Lily threatened.

"Try it and see what I do," he dared her.

He had ridden back the day before with Razer and Beth just to turn back around with Rider's truck and check into a hotel nearby. He wasn't leaving until he knew she would be fine and was eating something, because it looked like she had lost too much weight. He also wanted to make sure she understood everyone's need to keep her out of the loop.

Lily gave a long sigh, which had Shade wanting to paddle her ass. He wasn't Beth; his relationship with The Last Riders was one he had every intention of explaining to her, but he wasn't going to apologize for his relationships with them.

Besides, he wasn't in a relationship with her; he was free and single. However, as soon as he had decided to *begin* a relationship with her, he hadn't touched any of the women. His sexual past was his, and she was going to have to accept it, just like he was going to have to accept hers.

He had never anticipated being in a relationship, although if he had given it any thought at all, the woman would have enjoyed the same sexual freedom he did. He had never once entertained the thought that the woman would, at the mere thought of having sex with him, go into a full-fledged panic attack. He had never assumed he would fall in love, but she had driven those misconceptions out of his mind.

Now it was his turn to change her mind about the type of man she wanted.

She finally climbed into the truck, and then Shade slammed the door closed before going around the front and getting back inside. When he put the truck in gear, driving out of the parking lot, Lily sat staring out the window, refusing to talk as he drove through the small town.

It wasn't long before he pulled into a restaurant with a drive-thru, ordering food. He didn't ask what she wanted since she would have refused. Besides, he knew the foods she liked and didn't, because the lunches they had shared had shown him.

Shade took the bag of food, driving back onto the road without a word passing between them. As the aromas filled the truck cab, Shade noticed Lily turn a sickly shade of green, clutching her stomach. Hastily, he rolled down his window.

"Don't you dare throw up. Rider will be pissed enough when he sees his truck is gone."

Thankfully, after a few seconds of the fresh air, she regained a little color to her cheeks.

He pulled into the parking lot of the local hotel, stopping in front of the room he had rented. Picking up the bag, he walked to the room and unlocked the door before placing the bag inside then going back to the truck for Lily. If she fought him, he didn't want the food dumped in the parking lot.

He opened the door on her side to see her staring back at him with a stubborn expression, which was okay with him. It was better than the lifeless one he had seen her walking around campus with over the past couple of days.

"Get out."

"Quit ordering me around. I'm not going in there."

He wasn't going to argue with her. Lifting her into his arms, Shade then slammed the door closed with his shoulder before carrying her struggling form into the room.

The room was small but it held two beds, a small table, and a dresser with a television. He sat her down on one of the chairs by the small, round table in the room. When she would have jumped to her feet, he leaned down, placing a hand on each side of the chair she was sitting in, effectively blocking her in.

"Lily, I am a man with infinite patience, but you are trying me. I advise you to keep your ass on that chair. Do you understand me?" He would not allow her to keep neglecting her health. She was self-destructing, and he wasn't going to tolerate it.

Shade straightened, going to the other chair and sitting down. Then he opened the bag, pulling out a small cup of soup as well as several packs of crackers and setting them in front of her with a plastic spoon.

"Eat."

"Will you please quit ordering me around?" Lily asked again, her voice as cold as ice.

"I'll think about it." Shade's lips twitched in amusement at her frosty gaze.

As Lily took the lid off the soup and started turning green again, Shade remembered when he had been on an assignment and went without food. Afterward, his stomach had wanted to reject what it needed most.

"Eat a cracker first."

Lily's trembling fingers tore open a pack of the crackers, removing one. She nibbled on it slowly then ate another.

Shade ate the large burger and fries he had bought for himself, watching her as she struggled to eat her soup and crackers. Gradually, her appetite returned, and she began to eat more.

Shade finished eating then set a chocolate shake in front of her. It would give her some much needed calories. During their lunches over the summer, he had asked for whoever made their lunch to make her a milkshake a couple of times a week because he enjoyed watching her enthusiasm when she received the delicious treat.

She started to cry as she drank it. "I hate you."

"I know." Shade removed his sunglasses, letting her see his remorse. She wasn't ready to hear the words yet, but he wanted her to see that he hadn't wanted to hurt her.

She quit eating, sitting there with tears coursing down her cheeks, turning her face away from him.

Shade stood, picking her up and carrying her to the bed where he laid her down. "Sleep, Lily. You'll feel better when you wake up. You're exhausted."

Lily closed her eyes, curling into a small ball with her hand under her cheek, and Shade sat down on the bed next to hers as she gave a shuddering breath. When her body went limp and her breathing slowed, he stood up and took the blanket off his bed to cover her.

He leaned forward, brushing his lips across her cheek before lying down next to her, easing her back against his chest with his arm across her waist.

"Sleep, baby. I'm here. I'll always be here."

ℂ ℇ

She slept the rest of the day and into the night. Shade was sitting in the chair at the table when she woke, sitting up in bed.

"What time is it?"

"Ten o'clock. You've slept six hours."

"Oh." Lily brushed her hands through her hair.

"There are clothes for you in the bag. Go take a shower." He had purchased the items he had thought she would need before he had picked her up.

She picked up the bag he had placed on the bottom of her bed and then went into the bathroom without a word.

As she showered, he made sandwiches then ate his while she took her time in the bathroom. He had gone to the grocery store after he had rented the hotel room to purchase food he could make himself without having to cook, and the mini-fridge was stocked with enough food for several days. He had no intention of leaving Lily alone in the emotional state she was in.

Shade opened his mouth to demand for her to eat, but she forestalled him, holding up her hand. "I'll eat."

Pacified, he lay down on one of the beds and watched television, feeling her eyes on him while she ate.

When she was finished, she threw away the trash and the empty milk carton. "Will you take me back to my dorm now?"

"Later. Come here."

Getting up, she went to the phone on the bedside table instead of listening to him. However, before she could place a call, Shade jerked the phone from her hand then tugged her down onto the bed. Lily froze as he lifted and adjusted her until she was lying on the bed with her head on the pillow.

"I'll take you back in the morning in time for your eight o'clock class."

"I want to go now," Lily said between clenched teeth.

"Too bad." Shade lay down on the bed next to her, adjusting the pillow until he could see the television.

"You're unbelievable. You think you can do anything you want," she said resentfully.

When Shade ignored her, turning the volume up, Lily crossed her arms over her chest. He felt the silent waves of her hurt hitting him as she lay there stiffly, making sure she didn't touch him. Eventually, though, she was drawn into the old black-and-white movie and ended up falling back asleep before it was over.

Shade rolled her closer to him, pulling up the blanket to cover the both of them before turning off the television. He left the bedside light on, not wanting her to wake up in the dark. She had been through enough traumas lately without having to wake to old nightmares.

In the morning, he rose early to shower and dress. Then, going to the bed, he stood staring down at the woman who had captured his soul with her violet eyes.

"Move it if you don't want to miss your class."

Lily got up from the bed, following him outside, and neither of them said anything as they drove.

Shade went through a drive-thru, getting her breakfast and handing it to her before continuing back to her campus. She was finished eating by the time he pulled up outside her dorm.

Opening the door, she slid out of the truck, slamming the door behind her without saying a word to him. Shade watched her until she stepped inside her dorm, and then he drove away despite not wanting to leave her. He wanted to stay and walk her to class.

He snorted at himself. He had never walked a girl to class when he was in high school or college, arrogantly believing it was lame. It was funny how the inconsequential moments of his youth had come back to bite him in the ass.

ဆ ఴ

When Shade showed up the rest of the week, taking her to his hotel room every evening, Lily quit trying to argue with him and didn't speak a word to him once. He learned he couldn't wait in the truck for her; instead, he stood under a tree which had a view of both the front and back doors of her dorm.

Security approached him the second day, which he thought was bullshit. They should have noticed a hell of a lot sooner. He handed a card to the nervous guard and told him to leave him alone, and the security guard moved away, placing a call to someone Shade was sure was his supervisor. Five minutes later, the security guard was in his car and driving away. One advantage of doing certain jobs for the government was they made sure to keep him happy.

Friday, he waited in the truck. She had learned by then that there was no hiding from him.

After she climbed into the truck without him having to even get out, he put it in gear then drove away from the campus. She was still giving him the silent treatment, but she was about to break her stubborn silence in a few seconds.

He didn't slow down as he neared the hotel, going straight past it on the road which would take them to Treepoint.

"I don't want to go home for the weekend. I have a test Monday."

"Your books are in your backpack. You can study at home."

She sat with her arms crossed in front of her chest, fuming all the way to Treepoint. Shade could put up with her anger, though. At least she wasn't being as lifeless as a fucking doll.

When he came to a stop in front of her house, Lily's hand immediately flew to the door handle. Sliding out of the truck, she gave him a hateful glance.

"Enjoy your Friday night!" Slamming the door, she walked toward the house, her ass bouncing angrily up the walkway.

Shade jerked the truck door open and quietly came up behind the furious woman. When she unlocked the door, he propelled her forward with a hand on her arm before shutting the door behind them.

"What are you doing?" Lily tried to jerk away from him, dropping her backpack on the floor.

"Doing something I've warned you repeatedly about," Shade said grimly, jerking her to the couch where he took a seat then yanked her over his lap.

"WHAT?"

Shade firmly smacked her ass.

She tried to throw herself off his lap, but he placed a hand on her back, preventing her from getting away from her punishment. Then she kicked her legs, which earned her another smack across her bottom and caused her dress to slide up her thighs.

"You can't do this!" Lily screamed at him.

"Watch me."

His hand swatted her butt several more times until Lily stopped struggling and lay limply across his thighs, defeated. When he was done, he lifted her to sit next to him on the couch, gripping her jaw in his hand.

"Do not ever talk to me that way again. Do not slam doors to show your anger and throw me a fucking look like the one you did, or I will smack your ass with no dress and panties in the way. Do you understand me?" he demanded firmly.

Lily tried to turn her face away, her lashes hiding her eyes. "I understand."

"How do you fucking address me?"

"I understand, Sir."

As his hand released her jaw, Shade got to his feet, going out the door without another word. He wasn't angry with her, but he wasn't going to allow her to treat him disrespectfully, either. She could be as angry as she wanted, hit him, or throw something at him, but to be deliberately hateful when he knew she didn't have it in her was another matter.

He climbed back into the truck, wanting to go back inside and hold her. It didn't sit well with him to punish her and then not stay. However, Lily needed to return to normalcy, and she wouldn't be able to do that with him there.

Sighing, he pulled out of the driveway then went to the club for the first time in two weeks. It was a Friday night, and the members were probably already partying. The last thing he wanted to see when he walked in the door was the brothers getting laid and drunk, the very thing which had caused his mess in the first place.

"Fucking fantastic."

CHAPTER FORTY-EIGHT

Shade irritably answered his cell phone. "Yeah?"

"Where are you?" He recognized that particular tone in Lucky's voice.

"I'm at the factory, getting caught up with paperwork. Why?"

"Someone just tried to deliberately run Lily down with a car."

"Where?" he asked sharply.

"On the main road. She was crossing to get to her street, and it was parked in front of the hardware store. It sped out, only missing her by a few inches."

Shade was already locking the door to the factory. Once it was secure, he strode toward his bike. "You don't know who it was?"

"Never seen the car before, and the license plate had tape covering it."

"Shit." Shade started the motor.

"Where's she at now?"

"Home. I watched her go inside. Shade, I don't like the vibe I'm getting," Lucky warned.

"Understood."

No one had better instincts than Lucky. If he said it wasn't an accident, Shade believed him. Who could possibly want to hurt her, though?

A few minutes later, he looked around the area where Lucky had said he had seen the car parked. He walked to the hardware store and seeing the emergency number on the glass in front, Shade called the owner, checking to see if he had seen anything. Whoever had been in the car hadn't taken into account that, in small towns, people looked for things to talk about. The car hadn't gone unnoticed; he had a description.

He decided to check on Lily before going to have a talk with Knox. He rode his bike the short distance to her house, looking up and down the street for anyone who could be keeping watch from the front. He would check the back before he left. When he didn't see any signs, Shade knocked on the door.

"Who is it?"

"Shade."

She flung the door open. "Next time, come to the front door first. You scared me half to death."

"What are you talking about?" Shade asked, coming through the doorway.

"Weren't you just at the back door?"

Someone had tried to break in when she was awake. Whoever it was, they weren't afraid, and the chilling thought made him angry. They weren't out to hurt or frighten Lily; they were out to kill her.

"Stay here." Shade went to the back door, opening it and going out.

He looked around the backyard, careful to stay off the grass, not wanting to accidently step on their tracks. He was a good tracker, but he didn't want to take any chances with Lily's safety. When he didn't see anyone, he took his cell phone out of his pocket, calling Cash and quickly explaining what had happened and to get his ass to Lily's house. Then Shade disconnected the call, looking around one final time before going back inside.

"Someone was out there. They must have taken off when they heard my bike pull in the driveway."

Lily sank down on the couch. "Should I call Knox?"

"I will." Shade took out his cell phone and made the call.

"Shade," Knox answered his personal cell.

"I need you at Lily's house. Someone tried to get in using the back door."

"Shit. Did you call Cash?"

"Done."

"Okay, I'll be right there."

Shade hung up. "He's on his way."

"Who would try to break in the house?" Lily asked.

"I don't know, but I plan to find out."

It didn't take long for Knox to arrive. Minutes later, Cash knocked on the door, as well, coming inside to listen silently as Lily told them how she had been fixing herself something to eat when she felt someone watching and decided to lock the door.

"Are you sure you saw the handle move?" Knox questioned.

"Yes. At least, I think so. Maybe I was just tense. I don't know." Lily brushed her hair away from her eyes.

"What happened to your hand?" Shade asked sharply, seeing the road rash. He wanted Cash and Knox to hear the story Lucky had told him.

"I fell this afternoon when I was coming home from the church."

"How?" Knox asked.

"I was crossing the street, and a car was speeding. Pastor Dean pushed me out of the way, and I fell and skinned my hands and knees." Lily shrugged.

Shade didn't tell her Lucky had called him, not wanting to frighten her further. The men stared at each other in silence before Cash went out the back door.

"Where's he going?" Lily asked.

"To check things out," Knox told her. "I'm going to make a report then look around myself before going back to the station. I'll call Razer and let Beth and him know what's going on."

"Okay," Lily said.

"Shade?" Knox turned to him. "I don't think it's a good idea to leave her alone."

"I'll stay until they get home," Shade agreed, already having made that plan.

"Sounds good. Later." Knox went out the door.

"Do you think they'll be able to find anything?"

"Probably not, but Cash is good. If there's anything to be found, he'll find it."

Lily nodded before going into the kitchen where she began putting food away. She then started to eat a cold, grilled cheese when she saw him about to argue with her for not eating. Afterward, she placed the dirty dishes in the sink, leaning against it wearily.

"Go to bed. You look exhausted."

Lily turned to the steps, snapping out, "Don't you get tired of ordering me around?"

"No."

Lily began to make another comment when he raised his brow and crossed his arms against his chest, waiting.

"I can't believe I ever thought you were a gentleman."

Shade burst out laughing. "I'm no gentleman."

"No shit." Lily clapped her hand over her mouth. "You've driven me to cussing."

"Lily, cussing isn't going to be the worst thing I teach you." Oh, yeah, he was going to teach her plenty.

Shade couldn't help laughing some more when she immediately ran upstairs at his comment. She must have read the lust-filled fantasies going through his mind.

§¶ ¶§

Shade had finished his breakfast by the time Lily came in the diner with Diamond, Winter, Viper, Evie, Razer, and Beth. She took the seat farthest away from him, facing the door while the others crowded around the table.

Watching Lily, Shade thought her attitude toward Beth seemed slightly cool. It was going to take a while for that relationship to heal.

The harried waitress refilled his cup then took the orders for the rest of the table while Shade surveyed the room around him. The restaurant was packed, and several tables were filled with faces he had never seen in town before. When his gaze drifted over where Rachel was sitting with her brothers, her nephew, and Holly, she nodded at him and he returned it. Then Lucky came into the restaurant and joined them, bringing his focus back to his table.

Lily and Diamond were talking, and he could see the women becoming good friends. Despite Diamond being older, she was sensitive to other women's feelings, something Shade hadn't seen that often in the opposite sex.

As Lily listened to what Diamond was saying, their eyes met momentarily until she tore her gaze away to stare off somewhere in the restaurant. Shade shifted his attention to the table with a small family. He studied them, trying to see why Lily was focusing on them.

There was a little girl with dark brown hair sitting with her mother and father as the waitress set their plates in front of them.

"You want to go for a ride after lunch? I want to go to Jamestown. I'm thinking of asking Stud to build a bike for me," Rider said.

"I wouldn't mind the ride," Shade agreed.

Lily was talking to Evie as Shade listened to Rider describe his perfect motorcycle. Shade didn't want to know how many bikes the brother had. He kept them stored in the back of the factory and would change the bike he was riding as often as he did the women he fucked. He had one Shade had debated buying from him, but he had his broken in the way he liked, so he didn't feel the need for a change.

"Lily?" Evie said loudly.

Shade frowned, looking at Lily to see she had gone as pale as a ghost and was staring in terror at the table he had seen her watching before.

"Diamond. Please call Knox." Lily's hoarse voice had everyone sitting at the table going silent as her hand went to the rubber band on her wrist, snapping it repeatedly.

As Diamond called Knox, asking him to come to the diner as fast as he could, Shade scooted his chair out from underneath the table. Razer tensed, beginning to rise, and Beth moved her chair closer to Lily's side. Whatever was going on in Lily's head was leading to a panic attack.

"Lily, what's wrong?" Beth asked.

When Lily didn't answer, he stood up and walked toward her. Then Shade looked at the table Lily wouldn't take her eyes from.

The little girl's lips trembled when her mother's hand disappeared under the table. Her obvious pain had Lily moving to the end of her seat, about to rise, when the girl's father spoke sharply to the mother. He then reached out to soothe the little girl.

Shade's gaze went back to Lily when he heard her scream of pain. She was bent over, gripping her head.

"Lily!" Beth yelled her name.

Lily didn't try to reach for Beth like she usually did; she pulled away, rising blindly from her chair before trying to run from the restaurant. Shade caught her around the waist, but in her panic, she fought him, catching him off-guard. She managed to get loose from him as she screamed in agony before falling to the floor, writhing in torment.

Shade dropped down on the floor next to her.

"Lily! Baby, what's wrong?"

"Help me! Help me!" Lily screamed.

Shade gripped her hand tightly in his as the people in the diner began crowding around.

Shade thought quickly.

"Rachel!" he yelled, and then he turned to Razer. "Get them back!"

Razer and The Last Riders made the crowd move back while Rachel elbowed her way through the crowd, dropping down and pulling Lily's head onto her lap.

"Everyone shut up!" Rachel yelled, and the diner went silent.

Knox rushed in, crouching down next to him. "I called an ambulance. It's on the way."

Lily tried to roll away from the agony consuming her, but Shade held her hand tighter.

"Help me!"

Rachel placed both her hands on Lily's shoulders, and the next moments became the most surreal of Shade's life, causing goose bumps to rise all over his body as he heard Lily talk to a voice which never responded.

"Help me shut the door!" Lily screamed.

Rachel closed her eyes.

"Everything. Help me. She can't get out," Lily sobbed.

Rachel raised one hand, pushing at something no one but she and Lily could see.

After a few minutes, Lily said, "I have to lock it."

Rachel's face ticked.

"I can't remember what's behind that door," Lily sobbed.

A pause.

"Not ever," Lily replied to the unspoken voice, curling into a ball.

Rachel soothed her hands over Lily's face and Lily relaxed, her breathing returning to normal, her body going limp. She finally passed out, her mind seeking the only peace it could find.

"Shade, the ambulance is here."

He was forced to watch helplessly as the EMTs loaded Lily onto a stretcher and into the ambulance. He was about to climb inside when he turned back to Knox.

"I don't know what set Lily off in there, but something bad did, Knox. She was staring at the family with a young, dark-haired girl when it happened."

"I'll talk to them," Knox promised. "Go with her, brother. I'll find out what happened."

Shade gripped Knox's hand before jumping in beside Lily, taking her hand as the EMT slammed the door shut.

Shade didn't give a damn what Knox found out. The only reason he had asked for it to be checked out was he had a feeling that whatever it was would be important to Lily, and that was reason enough.

ଅ ଠ

Shade opened his bedroom door, coming to a stop when he saw Lily was awake and standing in the middle of his bedroom.

"Where am I?" Lily asked, taking a seat on the edge of the bed.

After she had been hurt back in the summer, he had purchased a whole new bed. None of the women had lain in the bed Lily was sitting on.

"My room," Shade replied, coming in and shutting the door, carrying a tray.

Walking across the room, he set the tray on the coffee table. "Come and eat."

Lily got up from the bed, going to a chair next to the coffee table and looking down at the tray of food.

"How did...? Why am I here?" She looked at him.

"What do you remember?" Shade asked patiently.

Lily sat down on the chair, her eyes on the tray of food. "I was at the church helping Rachel."

Lily licked her lips. Reaching forward, she took the bottled water and opened it, taking a long drink.

Fuck. Her mind had erased the car almost hitting her, the attempted break-in, and the diner. Her mind had completely wiped out anything which could hurt her.

Shade didn't say anything as Lily set the bottled water back down on the tray, keeping her eyes on him.

"Lily, you had an episode at the diner after church on Sunday. That was two days ago," Shade explained gently, wanting to be as truthful as possible.

"An episode?"

"You became hysterical."

"Oh, God. Where's Beth? Why am I here instead of my bedroom?" Lily asked, looking around the room as if Beth would magically appear.

"You had to be sedated, Lily. The doctor felt it was best that someone kept an eye on you. Since Beth works, we agreed this was the best place for you now." Of course, Shade had to persuade Razer with various threats to his safety to get Beth to agree.

"Where are my clothes?" Lily asked. "I want to get dressed."

"Eat first. Your clothes are in the closet and drawers. I'll show you when you finish."

Lily picked up an apple slice from the plate, chewing on it. Swallowing the bite, she then said, "I need to get back to school after I'm dressed. Would you—"

"Lily, you're going to be staying here for a while." Shade tried to break the decision he had already made to her gently.

Lily shook her head. "I have to finish school."

"You will. Beth talked to your school and arranged for a medical emergency so you can complete your coursework on the computer."

"But why can't I go back to school?"

"Lily, someone tried to run you over with a car and then tried to break into your house. We feel it's safer to keep you where we can watch who you come into contact with." Shade knew she didn't remember the events, but if he was going to convince her to stay, she had to have the information.

"I can stay at my house," Lily said before picking up her toast and nibbling on it.

"That won't work with Beth's work schedule. We need to figure out who tried to harm you twice."

"I just can't stay cooped up in your room," she argued.

"You won't. You can go back to work at the factory and finish your classes," Shade replied reasonably.

"I don't want to stay here at the club," Lily protested.

"A few weeks won't hurt you, Lily. By then, we may have some idea who is after you, and it will give you some time to figure out why you forgot the last few days."

Lily looked away from him. "Do you know what caused me to have the episode?"

"Yes. Actually, it was Diamond who figured it out. Do you want to know?"

"No." Lily got to her feet. "Where are my clothes? I want to get dressed. Do you mind if I use your shower? I could use the one in the other bathroom; it doesn't look as complicated."

Shade twisted his lips at her attempt of humor. "Use mine. I think you can figure it out."

"All right."

Shade opened one side of his closet, showing her the clothes he had brought for her from her house.

Lily took a step back. "Those are the clothes I boxed up to give the church. I bought new clothes. I was going to buy some more."

Lily tried to turn her face away but Shade caught her jaw in his tight grip, making her look him in the eyes.

"Those new rags you bought are the ones being donated. They look like what someone would wear to a funeral—all black, brown, and grey. Since I've known you, you've worn dresses with every color under the rainbow. Why have you suddenly stopped wearing color?"

"I don't know," Lily said, her eyes clouded over with confusion.

"Yes, Lily, you do. There are some things I'll let you hide from me for a while longer; others, I won't," he said implacably.

Lily stiffened, trying to turn away from his firm grip.

"Why the dark colors?"

She mutinously refused to answer his question.

"We'll stand here all day until you answer me."

Lily didn't answer as her hand went to her wrist to snap at the red band. Shade already knew what she would find. It was gone. He had taken it while she was still sleeping.

Her eyes widened when she found it gone. He wouldn't let her look at her wrist, though; his hand was still on her jaw, forcing her to maintain eye contact with him.

"I took it." At her look of horror, he spoke before she could. "I'll give it back on two conditions."

"What are they?" Did she know how desperate she sounded? Her red wrist showed how much she had come to depend on that band which could do nothing except inflict pain.

"You have to tell me about your clothes and secondly, every time you snap it, you have to tell me why if I'm there. If I'm not, then you have to write it down in a small book I'll give you. Each and every time," Shade stated his conditions firmly.

"All right."

Shade dropped his hand to his side.

Taking a step back, he demanded, "Tell me about the clothes."

Lily licked her lips. "I don't know how to explain it. When I wore my dresses, the colors made me feel happy. I would choose the color some days because it matched the sky or the sun or was the color of a flower I saw." She shrugged, seeming embarrassed by her confession.

Shade wasn't surprised. He had noticed the color of her dresses often matched her mood. She would always wear yellow or blue on sunny days, red if she was grumpy, and purple if she was content.

"The new dresses?"

"I don't know. I just guess…I don't know. The color is…I—"

"Do you feel sad?" he probed.

"Yes, but not like depressed sad, like someone died."

Shade nodded his head, catching her eyes with his. "Who do you feel like you lost, Lily?"

"Beth." A lone tear slid down her cheek.

"Anyone else?"

"Razer." Another tear joined the first.

"Who else, Lily?"

Lily remained quiet.

"Who else, Lily?" Shade's voice became firmer. He needed to know if he mattered to her. It wouldn't change what he was going to do, but he needed to know if he was making any headway with her at all.

"You," she whispered.

"Why do you think you lost me?" His voice went taut.

"I don't know. You were my friend. Then I saw you with Evie and Rider, and I knew that"—Lily took a shuddering breath—"I don't know you."

His thumb traced over her high cheekbone. "You know me, and you sure as fuck haven't lost me, even though I know you want to.

"Go take a shower then change into your workout clothes. I'll lay them out for you while you're in the shower. I'll meet you in the gym."

"Okay." Lily moved away. She seemed too relieved his questions were over, missing the brief expression that passed over his face.

He had gained a tiny portion of her trust, and Lily had taken it away much easier than he had earned it. Her trust in him was fragile and until it grew into something stronger, he would remain teetering on the cutting edge of a sword, precariously close to losing her permanently.

Chapter Forty-Nine

"Today, I just want you to stretch then work on your weight training."

"Okay." Lily warmed up then moved over to where the weights sat.

Shade handed her some weights. "From now on, when you feel uncomfortable trying something or you get scared, I want you to say a word that lets me know you're getting scared and want me to stop."

"All right. What's the word?"

"You make one up. That way, you'll remember it better."

"Blueberries."

"Blueberries?"

"Yeah, I like blueberries. Even saying it makes me happy." She smiled at him.

"Christ." Shade returned to work on his own weights.

"What's wrong with blueberries?" Lily asked curiously with innocence shining in her eyes. It made him feel guilty for wanting to fuck her.

"Nothing," Shade stated, his jaw clenched. *Other than it's a word a kid would use.*

Why couldn't she have picked a word which reminded him she was a grown woman? Red would have been good. He would have even taken strawberry. He could have worked with strawberry; it was sexy. Blueberries reminded him of when his dad would take him to pick them in the summer, making him imagine Lily picking them. It was a boner-kill. The more he thought about it, blueberries was the perfect safe word for her.

"Then why are you frowning?"

"I don't know. Most women would pick a color or an object, not a fruit."

Lily continued lifting her weights. "I can pick a color. I like pink."

"Lily, blueberries is fine," he snapped. It went from bad to worse. He would have seriously doubted Lily's maturity if he wasn't staring at her breasts as she lifted the weights.

"Why are you getting angry?"

"I'm not getting mad; you're just distracting me."

"Oh." Lily lifted the weight again. "I like baby blue."

Shade stopped and glared at her. "If you don't quit bugging me, you're going to be using your safe word in the next sixty seconds." He was going to prove to himself she wasn't a kid if she didn't shut up.

She did, though.

"You finish up while I get showered and changed," Shade told her after he was done with his workout, going to his room.

He took a shower long enough to remind his hard cock it wouldn't be getting any for a while before getting dressed in faded jeans, boots, and a black T-shirt with his dark hair still wet. After he went to the closet he had placed Lily's clothes in, laying his choice on the bed, he returned to the gym to find her still cooling down.

"Get showered. I laid out another outfit for you."

She threw him an angry glance over her shoulder as she left the room to go take her shower. Shade couldn't have cared less. He wasn't going to see her in another black dress which was not only three sizes to large, but represented the death of her friendship to him.

She was brushing her hair when he went to see if she was ready.

"Dinner's ready," Shade said. "Let's go."

"We're going out to eat?" Lily asked with hopefulness in her voice.

"No. We're eating upstairs like everyone else." He dashed any hope she was building to return to her house.

"But I'm not allowed upstairs," Lily argued, trying to pull away from him as he took her hand, leading her to the steps.

Shade stopped and looked down at her. "If you're going to get used to living here, that means you get used to going upstairs. You don't want to stay down here all the time, do you?"

"No, but I don't want to go up there, either," Lily insisted, her eyes wide.

Shade's mouth tightened into a grim line. Did she really think he would let her walk into the same situation she had before? The members were going to be themselves within reason until she could cope with more.

"Come on."

Lily tried to pull away again, her hand going to the rubber band on her wrist.

"Remember our deal," Shade warned.

"I already told you, I don't want to go up there."

"Lily, the club isn't going to hide itself from you anymore. That cat's already out of the bag. At first, you'll be uncomfortable, but then you'll become familiar with how things work around here."

Dinner turned out pretty well, considering Lily's initial hesitations. It took her a few minutes to warm up to everyone, acting like she was meeting them for the first time. However, she came out of her shell when she asked Rider about giving Killyama a ride yet.

Rider's previously amused expression disappeared. "Not yet. I've been busy."

"Pussy," Train goaded.

Rider's hand clenched on his fork. "That woman probably expects me to ride bitch," Rider made excuses for himself.

"If the panties fit, wear them," Train said, dodging the fork Rider threw across the table.

"I like Killyama," Lily said, cutting into her pork roast. The men stared at her in silence. "She saved my life, and I heard Star's mother had to have plastic surgery after she got in a fight with her. I can see where she might be too much for you."

Everyone at the table burst into laughter.

Rider turned to Shade. "Set it up," he ordered, all humor gone.

"Will do," Shade replied, keeping a straight face.

"Make sure you take protection," Train goaded.

"Which one are you talking about? Condoms or my gun?" Rider asked.

"Both," Train said truthfully.

Lily threw Train a reproving look. "I think you should volunteer to give Crazy Bitch a ride, Train. I think you two would have a lot in common."

Evie put her hand on her mouth while Bliss, sitting next to Lily, asked, "Is she serious?"

"I think so," Evie said, getting to her feet before she broke into laughter, taking the dirty dishes with her.

After dinner, Lily followed Shade nervously into the other room where everyone was sitting around and talking.

"I thought Beth would have been here by now," Lily stated when she became aware Train and Cash were pouring drinks at the bar.

"Beth won't be here tonight. Mrs. Langley had surgery to remove her gall bladder, and she's staying with her at the hospital," Evie said, taking a seat across from her.

Lily looked at Shade sharply, which he returned with mock innocence, before her eyes went back to the bar where several members were going back and forth, taking beers.

"But I need to talk to her." Her voice began to unconsciously rise.

"I'm sure you do, but it's not going to make a difference," Shade replied decisively.

Lily's hand went to her wrist as Viper and Winter came in through the front door. As a breath of relief left Lily, Shade knew Lily thought Winter would be her savior and drive her back to college or drop her off at her house.

Viper stopped at the bar long enough to take a beer before the couple came to sit down on the couch, forcing Lily to slide closer to Shade. He was more than willing to take advantage of the situation by sliding his arm along the back of the couch, touching her shoulders.

Winter sat next to Lily. "I'm relieved to see you up. How's it going?"

"Fine." She paused, and Shade saw her staring at Viper's beer. "Do you think you could give me a ride back to my house? I really need to get back to school."

"You're going to be staying here. Didn't Shade tell you?" Winter asked, meeting his eyes.

"He mentioned it, but—"

"Did he tell you why?" Viper asked, looking at Shade.

He shrugged. He didn't think Lily would believe him, but coming from Viper would have a greater impact.

"Yes, he did. Someone tried to hit me with a car then break in my house, but at school, I'll be perfectly safe."

"Lily, when Cash followed the prints of who tried to break into your house, they led to the house behind yours. Someone's been watching you for some time."

"That house belongs to a couple who vacation here a couple of times a year. It's usually empty," Lily explained.

"Knox traced the ownership of the house to a corporation, and that's as far as he can get. Cash said that whoever has been staying there is watching your house. There were video cameras, Lily."

As her face filled with fear, Shade was glad. He didn't want her to feel safe in her home; he wanted her to feel safe there at the club, where he was. He had no intention of taking something away from her without replacing it with something better.

Winter took Lily's hand. "That's not all."

"Your dorm room had listening devices planted there. There's really no safe place for you to stay other than here, for now. Cash and Knox are both trying to find out who could be doing this, but until they do, you have to be patient. At your home, you would inevitably be alone, but what if Beth or Razer's presence didn't deter them? You don't want them hurt because you didn't take our help, do you?"

Viper's harsh words had her shaking her head in denial. "Of course not."

"Good, then everything is settled," Winter said, leaning back against Viper.

"I was afraid you wouldn't listen to reason. I'm sure Beth will be relieved, too. She doesn't want you unhappy, but she wants you safe," Viper told her.

"I know." She bit her bottom lip, and Shade shifted closer to her.

Viper took another drink of his beer, and someone turned the music up louder. Winter and Evie started talking about Mrs. Langley while Lily's eyes wandered the room. The members had spread throughout the large room, giving her plenty to gape at. Shade debated telling her that her mouth was hanging open.

It wasn't long before her gaze caught on Bliss sitting with Cash. She had leaned forward, and her top had fallen open at her breasts. Cash was tracing the outline of her tattoo.

As Lily hastily turned her gaze away, joining into the conversation with Evie and Winter, Shade got up then returned, handing her a bottled water and sitting back down with a beer in his hand.

Lily ran her hand nervously through her hair. Shade was aware she was uncomfortable, but he wanted her to see the brothers could handle their alcohol, and no one would force her to drink or do anything she didn't want. The Last Riders believed in personal freedom, and that included not participating if it was the person's choice.

When her eyes followed Cash and Bliss as they went up the steps to the upper floor, Winter leaned sideways, breaking off her conversation with Evie.

Shade heard her whisper to Lily, "The members will watch how they behave around you for a while, but eventually, you'll walk into an embarrassing situation. Just do what I do: leave the room." Winter's face was blood red as she talked.

Shade appreciated her placing herself on Lily's level, showing her that she had been uncomfortable, too, when she had first become a member. It couldn't have been easy for her since she had been Lily's high school principal.

"At least she did the first few times," Viper corrected her, cutting into the conversation.

Winter threw Viper a dirty look.

"Bring it on, pretty girl," Viper warned.

Winter's face went an even darker shade of red.

Evie got up. "Anyone want another beer?"

"I'll take one," Viper spoke up.

Lily started fiddling with the rubber band around her wrist.

"Sorry, Lily. The men might refrain from acting inappropriate around you, but there's no way to keep them from their alcohol," Winter said.

Lily burst out laughing. "I guess beer outranks sex."

They all laughed in return, and the tension in the room lessened. Shade breathed his own sigh of relief when she unconsciously leaned back against him.

Evie sank back down in her chair, taking a long swallow of her own beer. "Don't knock it until you've tried it."

Lily's face went pale at Evie's suggestion of her taking a drink.

"I was only joking," Evie said in apology.

Shade's hand went to Lily's face. "Stop it, Lily. No one expects you to drink, okay? Evie was only joking like she would with anyone else."

Lily nodded, blushing. "I think living here for a while might be good for me. I need to get used to being around different people. This will make me quit being sensitive about people drinking around me. I wonder if cowboys drink a lot." Lily looked at Evie that time, being the one to make a joke.

"Like a fish," she answered.

CHAPTER FIFTY

Shade smiled as Lily stifled her yawn while she looked at her cards. They had been playing several games of poker with Winter and Viper.

"It's time for bed if you're going to start back at the factory tomorrow," Shade told Lily when Winter reached forward to claim her winnings, which were mainly IOUs for punishments.

Lily had been told they usually played for money, but Winter preferred to play for IOUs. That way, when she got in trouble and had to pull a punishment, she could cash in on one of the debts.

"I haven't had to do a punishment in six months," she bragged.

Viper ruffled his wife's hair. "Unless it was the ones you wanted."

Winter slapped his hands away.

Lily got to her feet, smiling down at the couple. "I'll probably have to find another way to pay you back for my IOUs. I probably won't be around long enough to pay all those back."

Winter looked doubtfully up at Lily, but replied, "I'm sure we'll work out an arrangement."

Shade thought about warning Lily that Winter was a card shark, but decided to let her find out on her own like everyone else in the club had. He wasn't worried that Lily would get in over her head, because he could bail her out of trouble if he needed to. He would always be the bigger shark in their pool.

"Goodnight," Lily told everyone sitting at the table before following him to the basement door.

Shade flicked on the light switch, and then they went down the steps together.

She went into his room, going to get her pajamas which were already sitting on the chair for her, and stiffened when he closed the bedroom door.

Shade went to one side of the bed, pulling off his T-shirt as he crossed the floor.

"What are you doing?" Lily asked, shocked.

"Going to bed."

"Oh, where am I sleeping?"

He had known she thought she would be sleeping in his room alone. However, she was about to find out exactly how things were going to change between them.

"In the bed next to me."

"No, I'm not." Lily shook her head.

"Yes, you are." He made his voice firm, not harsh.

"No, Shade, I'm not."

"I don't sleep on couches."

"Then I will," Lily said firmly.

"What are you going to do if one of the brothers stumbles downstairs drunk?"

Lily looked at the door fearfully as Shade continued mercilessly, using her greatest fear against her. "This room is off-limits, but the other rooms, not so much. We have an open-bedroom policy."

"Even Winter and Viper?"

"You think you're going to put Viper out of his bed?" Shade asked with a raised brow.

No one was going to make Viper do anything he didn't want to do, and Lily had been around him long enough to form that conclusion without any help from Shade.

"No, but maybe Evie?"

"Evie doesn't sleep alone; none of the women do." Which was the truth. "Go get changed, Lily. I'm tired. It's not like it's the first time we've shared a room," he reminded her.

Lily went into the bathroom, carrying her pajamas while Shade took off his boots and jeans before putting on a pair of shorts. He slid under the covers on the bed just before Lily came out of the bathroom, stopping in the middle of the floor.

Sighing, Shade got out of bed, moving the chair out of the corner. Taking her arm, he then led her to the corner the chair had been in, the one facing the bed. She would have to look at him while he could easily check on her.

"This is your safe place in the bedroom. Any time anything scares you or makes you feel uncomfortable, you can come here. I won't come near you here." Shade turned and walked away, feeling her gaze slide over him.

He climbed back into bed, pulling the thin blanket over him.

"Can I have a blanket?"

"No," he said, turning out the light. However, he kept the light in the bathroom on to avoid the room being completely dark.

He wanted her to be comfortable, but not too comfortable. He didn't want to make it a place she wanted to stay when he wanted her next to him in bed. She needed to get used to being close to him, learn she could touch him whenever she wanted or needed him, and she couldn't do that sitting a couple of feet away.

Shade restrained himself from getting out of the bed and tossing her onto it. It was a decision she had to make on her own.

She stood there for several moments before reaching out to pull the large chair toward her.

"Leave the chair where it is."

Eventually, she quietly slid down the wall, sitting on the floor. It was several minutes before she closed her eyes, leaning her head back against the wall.

Shade rolled to his side, watching as Lily dozed off. She woke several times during the night, trying to make herself more comfortable. Each time, Shade gripped the side of the bed, wanting to go to her. When he saw she was waking up, he closed his eyes, pretending to be asleep.

Stiffly getting to her feet without trying to be quiet in the least, she looked in the drawers, slamming each one closed until she found what she was looking for. She then went to the closet, opening the door.

"Wear the purple one."

Lily jumped, startled, and turned to see him watching her from the bed. She closed the closet with a snap then went to the bathroom, her bare feet stomping on the carpet.

Shade lay back on the bed, folding his arms behind his head, smiling as he stared up at the ceiling. He missed having the mirror up there. He wondered how long it was going to take him to talk Lily into putting one up after they became intimate.

Before his cock could get hard from where his thoughts were taking him, he went to the bathroom and knocked on the door.

"Unless you want to share, you need to hurry up."

It took her another ten minutes, and Shade was sure she was doing it just to aggravate him, just like when she had slammed the drawers. He'd had less sleep than she had, though, and he wasn't in the mood to placate her. He loved the woman, but he was determined not to become pussy-whipped like Razer, Viper, and Knox.

After she finally unlocked the door, Shade refused to move to the side, pressing her against the bathroom door when she tried to sidle past him.

"Lily, I'm coming to the conclusion that you're a little spoiled, and while I won't mind doing so occasionally after you've earned such rewards from me, now is not the time to piss me off." His hips pressed harder against her mound with just the material of the shorts and her dress between them.

When he saw the beginning of panic hit her, he stepped away, going into the bathroom. He walked to the toilet to take a piss, not caring that she was still standing in the doorway. Shade heard the bathroom door slam as he was about to relieve himself. He was still grinning when he stepped into the shower.

Shade opened the bathroom door five minutes later, coming out with only a towel wrapped around his lean waist.

Lily ran to the corner, obviously not appreciating his mocking laughter as he removed his clothes from the drawers. She turned to the wall when he started to drop the towel and get dressed in his jeans and boots, pulling on a T-shirt.

"Let's go eat breakfast, unless you want to stand there longer."

Lily moved to follow him but he stopped her with his hand going to her jaw, making her look him in the face. She didn't try to hide her resentment.

"That's two for slamming the drawers."

"Two what?" Lily asked in confusion.

"Two smacks on your ass. I'll keep a total, and Friday will be the day we clean the slate and start over," Shade said, ushering her out of the door.

"You have lost your mind if you think I'm going to stand still and let you spank me."

"You won't be standing; your ass will be turned over my knee."

"Sure, Shade. Anything you say, Shade," Lily said mockingly, too angry to be scared.

His eyes narrowed on her face. She believed it wasn't going to happen, that she would probably be gone before it could. Shade almost disabused her then decided to wait. *Let her build her punishments up.* It would give him something to look forward to on Fridays since he wasn't taking part in any of the parties anymore. Lily, on the other hand, could look forward to trying to escape him all she wanted to. She wasn't going anywhere. Her ass would be over his knee just like he had promised her.

⁞❦⁞

Shade spent the day setting a routine for Lily to get her emotions back to normal. She was extremely sensitive; as a result, anything that upset the balance sent her mental stability into turmoil.

After dinner, he offered her an excuse not to hang out in the clubhouse like the previous night, understanding too much might overload her if thrown at her all at once.

"I need to check on some work going on at my house. Do you want to come with me?" he asked.

"Sure." Lily walked out the back door with him into the huge backyard.

He led her up the new walkway, which had been laid a couple of weeks before. His house was being built behind Beth and Razer's. The new walkway led to Razer's house before splitting, each path going to a house.

His was nestled up higher than the main house and Razer's, with a wraparound porch that gave a view of the mountains from all sides, except the back which had the mountain behind it.

From his house, he could see the clubhouse, Razer's house, the factory, the parking lot, and even both sides of the road leading to them. It was a strategic stronghold which, if he had to, could hold off an army without worrying about anyone coming at him from behind. Once it was built, no one would be able to get near Lily without him knowing it.

Shade opened the door, coming into the living room and dining room combo. It was an open-concept house where you could see through the whole downstairs. The walls were all dry-walled, and the subfloors had been laid.

He walked into the kitchen where none of the cabinets or anything had been placed yet. There was a small, fold-up table and two metal chairs sitting in the room with several books lying on top. He had gone as far as he could without her input. He could have asked Beth for her opinions, but he was building the house for Lily. He was determined it was going to be her home, and he wanted her to pick her own preferences.

Shade looked around the room, moving from one area to the other.

Lily looked at him curiously. "What are you doing?"

"Trying to figure out where I want the island to go and which wall for the appliances."

"Start with where you want the sink, which is obviously by the window." She pointed toward said window.

"Why by the window?" he asked.

"So you can look out while you do the dishes," Lily explained.

Shade had to turn away, not wanting her to see his face. She had seen herself doing the dishes in his home.

"What about the stove?" He turned back around when he was able to regain his composure.

Lily looked around the room and pointed to the wall on the right. "That way, you can keep an eye on the room while you're cooking. The other wall you would have your back to the room."

"That's true, but the exhaust fan would break the line of sight."

Lily agreed, and Shade finally decided to place it against the wall she had pointed out. Then he sat down at the table, pretending to go through floor samples, and Lily indicated her preference for hardwood then the type of wood. Next, he randomly picked out cabinets. When Lily made a face, he turned over several more pages until she found one she thought would suit the style of the house.

"I'm surprised. I thought you would try to talk me into a country-looking kitchen, but you're guiding me into a more modern look." Shade had thought he would have to tolerate an old-fashioned house; instead, he actually would have picked many of the same options she had.

Lily smiled. "I'm surprised you know the difference. I like the modern look for the clean lines and angles."

"I do, too." Shade closed the books. "That's enough for today. It will take a couple of weeks to get it done; then I can pick out the fixtures for the bathrooms."

"Make sure you have one put in like you do now. Your shower is amazing."

"I like it, too, but I was thinking of going a little bigger here."

Shade was proud of that shower. He had designed it himself to be big enough for several members to shower in after they had a fuck session.

"How much bigger do you need? It's already big enough for several people." From her expression, Lily had figured out exactly what the shower had been used for. She closed the book she was looking at with a snap, getting to her feet without looking at him.

"Ready?" she asked. "If you need to stay, I can go back by myself."

"I'm finished," Shade replied, going to the door while turning off the lights on the way.

He didn't try to deny her assumptions; they were the truth. He wasn't going to blow smoke up her ass to keep her happy then have one of the women saying something to her later that would bite him in the ass for lying. He would live with the memory of her face when she had run away after finding out about the clubhouse for the rest of his life, and he never wanted to see her that hurt again.

They walked back to the house, and instead of going through the kitchen, he led her through the basement door.

Lily went to Shade's room, getting a fresh pair of flannel pajamas before she went into the bathroom to get changed. He was taking off his shoes when she returned. He had already removed his T-shirt, and his jeans were unsnapped.

He got up from the side of the bed then went inside the bathroom, closing the door. When he came out, Shade was disappointed to find her already standing in her corner. Hiding his displeasure, he got into bed, turning out the lamp.

Lily stood there several moments before she sank down onto the floor.

Shade placed his arm over his eyes, unable to watch while she was still awake. He waited until he heard her deep breathing before rolling over to gaze at her sleeping face. When her head fell forward then jerked back up and she didn't wake up, he knew she was exhausted.

Silently, he threw the covers back before slipping out of bed. He sat down next to her, pulling her into his arms and situating her until she could sleep more comfortably. Then he leaned his head back against the wall, running his fingers through her hair.

When the clock read six a.m., he gently slid out from under her. Standing up, he stretched before going into the bathroom to shower. He ran the cold water over his head, letting it wake him up. After two nights with no sleep, he would have to catch a nap in his office.

He leaned his forehead on the shower wall. It felt so hopeless with her sometimes, like she was never going to return any of his feelings.

A song came over his speakers, which he knew damn well he hadn't programmed in, shaking him out of his reverie. He listened to it as he finished showering and dressing. Then he went back into the bedroom to find Lily still sleeping. He decided to go upstairs and fix them some breakfast, hoping the woman who had dared to put the "Rose" on his playlist would be awake so he could give her Hell.

Shade opened the kitchen door, seeing the woman drinking her coffee while leaning on the counter. He walked to her, and as she looked at him curiously, he placed an arm over her shoulders and gave her a brief hug.

"Thanks."

"What for?" Evie asked.

"For being a pain in my ass."

CHAPTER FIFTY-ONE

He was cleaning off his desk when Jewell walked in his office. His cell phone rang, and he motioned for her to close the door. As he answered the call, he sat down on the side of his desk.

"Did you find anything out?" Shade asked Cash.

"Nothing new. After I tracked the vehicle's movement to a hotel a few cities away, I checked in with Knox about the photocopy of the license the man used to check in. It's the same one the car that tried to run Lily down is registered to, but the driver's license was in the name of a man who died two months ago."

"Fuck. Anything else?"

"The picture on the license doesn't match the face of the man he stole the ID from, which means he changed out photographs. So I called in a few favors, and they're running it through some computer programs. We may get a hit. I don't know. It's a shot in the dark. I'll give you a call when I find out anything else."

"Thanks, Cash."

"Anytime, brother." Cash hung up.

Shade returned his attention to Jewell who had laid paperwork down on his desk. Shade picked it up and set it in the appropriate tray.

Jewell laughed. "You don't want to take a look at it?"

"No," Shade said wearily.

Jewell raised a brow, sitting down on the edge of his desk. "You look tired."

"No shit," he snapped.

Jewell lifted her hands in the air. "Don't blame me because you're tired. Hell, when you fucked me, you always had energy to spare. Lily must be doing something right to wear you out," she teased.

Shade's face went hard. "She's sleeping on the floor rather than sleeping with me." Shade tossed his pen onto the desk.

"She'll come around, Shade. Who could resist you?" Jewell mocked.

"Plenty," he stated, standing up.

Jewell's face went mischievous. "I could talk to her and tell her you fuck like a dream, that she'll have an orgasm which will rock her fucking world. Then I could tell her there's more where that comes from. She'll be yours like that." Jewell snapped her fingers.

Shade couldn't help laughing at Jewell's antics. "If I tell her all that, she'll lock me out of my own bedroom."

"If she does, you can always come to my room. My door is always open," she said, gliding her fingers up his arm with a sultry look to her face.

Shade walked around her, opening the door. "The only door I'll be walking in is the one she's behind."

Jewell walked up to him in the doorway. "I guess the other brothers will have to pick up the slack," she joked.

"I think Rider can handle the job himself."

"I think so, too."

As they laughed together, Shade noticed Lily's eyes kept glancing over to them. He thought he might have seen a spark of jealousy, but he couldn't be sure.

He walked across the room to her workstation where Raci was talking to her.

"Ready?" Shade asked, coming to her side and touching her arm.

Lily jerked away from his touch. "Yes."

Lily turned to the door, ignoring him. Oh, yeah, she was jealous.

She went to the front door and he followed behind her, watching her flouncing ass as she went up the path angrily. He still couldn't believe she was jealous. Maybe Raci had said something?

On their way to the clubhouse, Train and Kaley were standing in the middle of the walkway, blocking them from passing. He could hear Kaley's big mouth as he walked up the path.

"Please, Train, talk to them." Her voice was pleading against Train's stony face.

Shade frowned. Viper was supposed to make it plain and simple that she wasn't ever going to become a part of The Last Riders.

Lily tried to pass the arguing pair, and Kaley's reaction at seeing her wasn't pleasant.

"This is all your fault," she said hatefully to Lily.

"Excuse me?" Lily asked, coming to a stop.

"Shut up, Kaley. It's not Lily's fault you didn't keep your mouth shut," Train said.

"No one would have cared if she hadn't been nosing in, like my sister."

"Miranda was worried about you," Lily protested.

"Miranda was just jealous. I was getting plenty of sex and she wasn't."

Her harsh words had Lily taking a step back, coming into contact with Shade who had moved closer to her. When his arm slipped around her waist, Lily tried to move away, but he held her still.

"That's not true," Lily tried to reason with the angry woman.

"It *is* true. Neither one of you would know how to have sex other than lying on your back and spreading your legs. And I doubt if you would even lower yourself enough to do that, Lily." She nodded at Shade. "He's fucking wasted on you, but he'll get tired of your shit, and when he does, he'll go back to fucking anything with a cunt."

"Lily, go on up to the house," Shade said calmly, his arm leaving her waist.

Shade waited until Lily was out of ear shot before he turned his gaze on Kaley. "Why are you here?"

"I wanted to talk to Train. I like it here, Shade. If you want me to stay out of Lily's way, I will. I'll even pretend to like the stupid bitch if you want me to. I don't have to become a member as long as you guys let me hang around. I'll do whatever you want." She ended with the seductive promise.

"You want me to handle this?"

Train hesitated. "I brought her in, so I'll take care of it."

"Do that, before I do," Shade said grimly.

He didn't turn around when he heard Kaley's sharp cry. The stupid bitch had underestimated Train. He always fooled everyone into thinking he was the easy-going one, which was true, but he had a button which shouldn't be pushed, and Kaley had pressed it a long time before. Train wouldn't lay a finger on a woman, but he would have no problem taking out anything she cared about.

One time, a prospective member had grown too attached to Train and had given Raci a black eye after she had seen Train fuck her. When the Last Riders had thrown her out of the club, everyone had thought Train wasn't even angry at the woman. Shade had known different and wasn't surprised when he heard her two brothers and cousin were in the emergency room with broken ribs and lacerations. Each of them had both of their eyes blackened after he had broken their noses. They never heard from her again.

Shade opened the door to the basement to see Lily already on the mat, working out in black leggings and a T-shirt which actually fit. He was glad to see he had gauged her size correctly, although he had asked Winter to buy them for her, knowing she wouldn't take them from him.

"I'll be right back," he told her as he went to get changed.

When Shade returned, she got into position. They always did a set of maneuvers, switching it up occasionally when she became bored. Shade made one of his practiced moves and Lily responded with more force than usual, almost managing to knee him in his privates.

"You're getting better. You almost got them that time," Shade complimented her, well aware she wanted to make him a her.

She had been trying to knock his nuts off since they had begun her defense lessons. He often wondered if it was all men in general or if it was only *his* nuts she wanted to hurt.

Lily gritted her teeth as she circled the mat, trying to get behind him. "You haven't seen anything yet."

Shade lifted his brow at her assertion, but he decided to take it easy on her. Lily's newfound confidence was hot as Hell.

That time, when he came for her, Lily responded unexpectedly, using a move he sure as shit hadn't shown her.

She used both of her fists to hit him between the shoulder blades after he let her wiggle away from his hold.

"What the hell?"

"I'm supposed to pretend you're attacking me, aren't I?" she asked snidely.

Shade's good humor disappeared. He was going to paddle that ass, which was driving him crazy, when he managed to get ahold of her.

"Yes, but I want you to learn to stop an attacker, not piss them off."

"As long as it works and I get away, that's all that counts," Lily said smugly.

"Is that so?" Shade said, placing his hands on his hips.

"Yes." Lily kept facing him, not letting him have her back like she usually did.

"Did Kaley go home?" she asked, her eyes a turbulent, violet storm.

Shade had started moving toward her, but his momentum stopped at her words. "Yes."

"Do a lot of women try to join?"

"Yes." Shade was beginning to get her message of anger, giving her a wary look. He didn't like the vindictive expression on her face.

"I bet that's fun for the men. Don't the women members resent the new members?"

"No. Why, are you interested?" Shade asked, making his move against her.

That time, her foot shot out, and she managed to nail him in the stomach, causing him to have to catch his breath from the force of the kick that had fucking hurt. He had always been careful not to hurt her, while the little witch staring back at him was filled with pleasure about doing what no one else had been allowed to get close to accomplishing.

Lily walked around the mat, gloating about her success. "You're getting slow, Shade." She bounced from foot to foot. "And, no, I'm not interested. You and the other men can have all the women in Treepoint who want to join your club. I won't be one of them. I plan to find me a man who can appreciate one woman."

"That's a joke." Shade said, deciding to make her angry enough to drop her guard.

"What do you mean by that?" Lily stopped bouncing.

"That you would ever let a man touch you. Tell me, how do you intend to catch a cowboy or any man when you have no intention of giving them anything? I bet Charles's balls are blue around you, but I'm sure he finds one of his daddy's waitresses to relieve him."

"That's not true. Charles is a gentleman."

"He likes his cock sucked as much as any man," Shade taunted.

"You're disgusting!" Lily screamed at him, turning to leave the mat.

"What's the matter, Lily? What really set off this little temper tantrum of yours?"

When Lily didn't reply, Shade blocked her path, wanting the truth from her before she ran away.

"Move."

"Make me. I'm already shocked as shit you haven't run to your corner like a scared little girl," he taunted, determined for her to face both of them with the truth. She was fucking jealous!

Shade almost shouted for joy. You were only jealous over something you cared about, something you didn't want to share with anyone else. She had to care about him to be jealous, right?

"You're a mean person. I hate you." Lily slammed her hands out, shoving his chest and trying to make him move out of her way.

Shade wanted her to recognize her feelings for him; however, she needed to cool off in order to think about why she was so furious.

His foot went out, sweeping her feet out from under her, and she fell to her back on the mat.

"You lose. Again." Shade looked down at her in triumph, unwarily standing over the woman.

He was about to reach down and give her a helping hand up when her hand reached up and viciously grabbed his balls, squeezing them in a vice. He fell to his knees as his hand went to his nuts, trying to jerk her hand away. Her hand tightened even further as she rose up on her knees, squeezing harder. Her satisfied smile widened at his pain-filled expression.

"How's this work for taking the attacker by surprise? Are you surprised? Don't underestimate me. I don't like it." Her hand twisted his balls viciously one last time before letting him go and getting to her feet.

"It's un-cool to talk about Charles like that. It's his private business, just like you and Jewell in your office. I don't care who either of you fool around with," she snapped.

Shade got to his feet, and Lily's face paled as she came to her senses. He was done with her bullshit. He was going to keep his promise and paddle that ass, which had been tormenting him, and then he was going to fuck her to make sure his dick was still working.

She wasn't stupid, though. She took one look at his face and took off running toward the stairs. Because his balls were killing him, the hellion managed to make it up several before he caught her ankle. He held her in a hard grip, not wanting her to get away.

Lily kicked her other foot out, balancing her hands on the upper steps and nailing him in the jaw. The surprise attack made him release her foot and she managed to escape him, going up the last steps to sling the door open. Then she ran into the kitchen and slammed the door in his furious face.

Shade had seen everyone in the kitchen staring at them before she had slammed the door closed on him. He gripped the door handle, wanting to rip it off. Instead, he turned it, opening the door with enough force it slammed against the wall.

The kitchen was full of members lined up for dinner, but Shade didn't give a fuck. She was going to get the punishment she deserved.

He moved toward her then came to a stop when he heard a familiar voice.

"Lily?" Beth's voice had both of them turning to the table where Razer, Winter, and Viper were looking at them in shock.

Razer and Viper both moved to the edge of their seat, correctly reading his expression.

Fuck, she was lucky.

CHAPTER FIFTY-TWO

"Been working out?" Beth asked, her gaze going back and forth between Lily and Shade.

"Yes. I think I'm finally getting the hang of it." Lily threw him a gloating look over her shoulder.

"That's great. I was so worried about you after the diner, but I knew everyone would look out for you, and Mrs. Langley doesn't have anyone. The doctor is going to release her in an hour. I'm going to spend the weekend with her, but I wanted to stop in to check on you."

"I'm doing great. In fact, why don't you stay here, and I'll stay with Mrs. Langley? No one will think to look for me there," Lily spoke in a rush, staring at Shade.

"Maybe when she's better, but she needs skilled care after just having surgery."

Shade smirked at Beth's answer. His woman had thought she was going to get out of her punishment. Not fucking likely! He would bar the doors if he had to in order to keep her inside.

"I'm glad you showed up. I have another idea. Since we don't know who was watching me, it makes sense for me to leave Kentucky. I can contact Penni and stay with her until the band she's working for goes on tour."

Shade lost his smirk at her quick thinking.

"I think that's a great idea. I know you would be safe with Penni, and I can understand that it's not comfortable for you to stay here." Beth's eyes went to Shade's. She had no legitimate excuse for why she couldn't go stay with Penni, and they both knew it.

"I need to go shower. I'll be back in a few," Shade said, turning on his heel as he heard Lily and Beth talking.

"I'll call her after dinner then let you know her answer."

"I can get Razer to drive you to the airport," Beth offered.

Shade closed the door then went down the steps to his room. Taking out his cell phone, he made the call he was already dreading.

"Hello, bro, what's up?" Penni answered.

"I need a favor."

There was a brief silence. "Does this involve Lily?"

"Yes, she wants to come stay with you," Shade said, already knowing her answer since the two had become firm friends during their time as roommates, which was what he had intended. However, the unexpected consequence was that, more often than not, she had sided with Lily against him while still taking his money.

"Cool! I miss her like crazy. I now this fun bar we can go to—"

"No," Shade snapped. "I want you to tell her no, or better yet, make up an excuse. You're good at that. I heard the whopper you told your mom on why you couldn't spend the summer with her."

"I'm not going to blow Lily off."

He heard the steel behind his half-sister's voice and knew there wouldn't be any changing her mind, unless...

"You know that old bike of mine you've been wanting? I'll give it to you. I'll even teach you how to ride it."

"Fuck."

Shade knew he had her. He merely needed to tighten the noose.

"I'll start your allowance back again." Shade had quit giving her money when she had graduated and found a job.

"Dammit! Why does she want to come down? And it better be the truth, Shade!"

He decided to give it to her. "Because she wants to run."

"If you've done anything to hurt—"

"I love her. I would never hurt her," Shade admitted. If he had to confess it to the world, he would to keep her. Then he unashamedly told the biggest lie he had ever told. "I'm trying to work up my courage to ask her out, but she's nervous about being around all the brothers."

"Awe. I can tell her their bark is worse than their bite. Let me talk to her and—"

"No!" Shade said sharply then made his voice soften with fake meekness. "If she knows I called, she'll get mad and never go out with me."

"All right," she agreed grudgingly. "But I'm going to come see her as soon as I can."

"Thanks, Penni."

"You're welcome. Just don't make me sorry I did this," she warned before hanging up.

After showering and changing, he went back upstairs and fixed himself something to eat. Beth was telling Lily how good she looked. Shade agreed; she was much healthier than when he had driven her in from college.

"You have color in your cheeks again. I hope being here this week has shown you that they really care about you."

"Yes."

Beth and Razer got up from the table. "Let me know what Penni says."

Lily stood up, hugging both Beth and Razer goodbye.

Shade was glad Lily was trying to put her hurt feelings behind her. Beth loved her and hadn't intentionally tried to hurt Lily. She had tried to protect her—they all had. It had backfired, of course, because they had smothered her with that protection. Then, when she had cut herself off from it, Lily hadn't been able to handle it.

After Razer and Beth left, she told everyone goodnight except him before going downstairs. Shade followed behind her, giving her enough time to reach his room and make her call. He wanted her to know all avenues of her planned escape were closed.

She had a big smile on her lips which fell flat when he casually walked into the room, shutting the door and locking it behind him then leaning back briefly against it. The cell phone was to her ear, but her eyes were on him.

Shade straightened from the door, going to the dresser where he took off his shirt then his boots, placing them to the side. Walking barefoot, he went to the large closet that was against the wall where her clothes were kept. He reached into his pocket and pulled out a keychain, unlocking the other side of the closet which held his neatly arranged equipment.

One after the other, he pulled out various items, testing their weight in his hands. He took out a thick ruler, which he smacked against his hand before putting it back in the closet. He then pulled out a flogger, which he slapped against his thigh before putting it back in the cabinet.

"Yes," Shade heard her strangled reply to something Penni must have said.

Shade lost track of the conversation while he debated which toy he would use on Lily first. He knew which one he *wanted* to use, but she would have a panic attack, and he didn't want that. He was going to have to start out slowly, despite wanting to give her a lesson a seasoned sub would cry over.

Shade pulled out his favorite paddle. It was thin and covered in leather. He smacked it against his palm, finding it was perfect for what he wanted. Happy with his choice, he shut the closet door then walked to the chair and sat down, staring directly into her eyes.

Her gaze tore away from his, going to the door. She was smart enough to realize she couldn't make it. Shade wasn't going to underestimate her again, already figuring out her next move by seeing her body tense in preparation.

"Make sure you do. I'm planning on coming for a visit." She spoke into the phone quickly.

All of a sudden, Lily jumped from the bed, making a run for the bathroom. She didn't make it, though. Halfway there, he had her around the waist, lifting her from the floor.

"Oh, no you don't."

"Don't you dare touch me!" Lily yelled.

"I am going to do more than touch you. I'm going to teach you a lesson that you will never forget, Lily," Shade promised.

She was about to scream, terrified, when he sat her down on her feet in her corner and took a step back.

He could feel her fear. *She should be afraid*, he thought grimly to himself. She had pushed him past his limits, but she was more than able to defend herself against him; she had proven that earlier. Therefore, it was time she faced her fears head-on, and come what may, he was going to rip away the barriers she used to protect herself from him. She needed to see the real Shade or as much of himself as he could show, anyway.

He pulled the chair to face her, taking a seat. "I think it's past time we straighten out a few things."

Her hand went to the rubber band as she pressed back against the wall.

"Cut it out. You're in your safe zone, and I won't touch you when you're there." Shade leaned back against his chair.

"I joined The Last Riders when I left the military. There are eight original members. When we started the club, we decided women would be members, too. Both the men and women have rules as to how they can join. The men, if they want to enter and we want them as a part of the club, pick four of the eight original members to go up against. If they can handle themselves, they become members. The women need six votes from the eight original members to join. To get the votes, the member either fucks them or has an orgasm as a result of their play."

"I don't want to know," Lily moaned.

"Lily, you're going to hear it all. No more pretending. Now, to continue, Beth and Winter earned their votes differently. They earned markers. That's not to say they didn't earn a few votes the normal way, just not the majority of them." He kept his voice dispassionate when he discussed Beth and Winter.

"I really don't want to hear this," Lily said, turning her face to the wall.

"After they gain their last vote, the women can get their tat with the date they earned it and became a member."

Lily turned back to face him. "Beth doesn't have a tattoo."

"I believe Beth and Winter both had their tats placed where no one would see them. I wouldn't know. I gave them both my marker. I also have never participated in any of their fun with the club. Diamond, also."

"Why?"

"Because Beth is your sister, Winter is your friend, and Diamond because I could tell that, when you eventually spent more time with her, you would become close friends. I didn't want you to feel uncomfortable around them."

"I don't understand." Lily shook her head.

"Yes, you do. You don't want to admit it, but you do." He stared directly into her eyes.

"No."

Shade sighed, realizing she was going to fight acknowledging any attraction between them.

"Lily, I've wanted you since the first minute I saw you coming out of the diner with Beth when we first moved to Treepoint. I took one look at you and knew you were mine."

Lily shook her head, still not facing him.

"Razer, unfortunately, made his move with Beth first, and I had to lie back and let him see where it was going. I also knew you were young and wanted you to have some time to yourself. I never intended to wait this long for you, but I let Winter convince me to let you finish school. So, I waited."

"You didn't suffer waiting, did you, Shade? With a club full of women at your beck and call," Lily snapped.

"I am no saint. I've enjoyed every woman here at the club, but they weren't you, Lily. Never you. I would fuck them for hours, trying to get me through the night so I wouldn't get on my bike and come for you." His voice was unintentionally harsh as remembered those lonely nights he had spent with the women, giving them his body while his heart and soul was already with her.

"You can't seriously believe I would have gone with you." Lily stared at him in astonishment.

He saw the moment when understanding finally began to dawn on her—that he wouldn't have given her a choice. She started shaking. Hell, he wasn't going to give her a choice now. That time had passed, and it was time to lay all his cards on the table.

"I am no longer going to hide anything from you, and you are going to have to learn to deal with what you can and what you can't. You have your safe space, and I gave you the summer to get to know me."

"I got to know too much: that you're bossy, you're mean, and you have sex with too many women."

"I'm no cowboy," he mocked, her words ripping his insides to shreds.

"You're no cowboy," Lily agreed.

"It doesn't matter what I am or not. I will be the one whose bed you will be in, who puts my ring on your finger, my baby in your belly, and you will let me, Lily," he told her with finality.

"No." Lily shook her head, denying his words.

"Yes, Lily, you will. You won't be able to help yourself. I'll make damn sure of that. Since I want to make sure there are no more secrets between us, I'm going to tell you that Penni is my sister. Actually, my half-sister, but she says that doesn't count."

As Lily sucked in a deep breath, Shade knew it cut deep, and he felt bad for that. He was already on the path he was determined to take, though. He was going to make her open her eyes and see him. He might not be what she wanted, but someday, hopefully she would see he was what she needed.

"Beth didn't know, and Penni thought I asked her to transfer colleges because of Beth. She has no idea of my interest in you." He gave that lie to protect Penni, not himself.

With her finally getting over Beth's betrayal, if she found out Penni had known, she would cut off all ties with her. Truthfully, Penni hadn't known all the machinations he had committed, so technically, it was only a half-lie.

She refused to look at him after that confession.

"Lily, look at me."

She turned her head to look at his grim face.

"I know that this is a lot for you to take in. You don't do well with surprises; however, there is one last piece of business we need to take care of.

"You have pushed me all week. After I told you that you had earned a spanking, you deliberately tried to raise my temper. I don't lose my temper, unlike you; instead, you have earned several more strokes. I will give you a chance to explain yourself, and you may be able to lessen your punishment if it's good enough. Otherwise..." Shade shrugged.

"I will not take a punishment from you. I'm not one of your women who actually care to please you. You can go to Hell. I'm leaving. If you lay one hand on me, I'll call the police." Lily frantically looked around his room.

Shade saw where she was looking and got up from the chair, walking across the floor to the phone and picking it up. Walking back, he handed it to her before going to the drawer, opening it, and then handing her an envelope. Afterward, he resumed his seat.

"Before you make a call, you should open that envelope."

Dread filled her eyes as she slowly tore the envelope open, pulling out the papers and then looking through them. They were ownership papers of The Last Riders' land, the factory, and the house. It showed all the separate names of the corporation.

Her eyes lifted to his, not understanding.

"My name is John Hunter."

Her eyes went back to the papers, going through them once again. Shade could tell from the horror on her face when she realized what the importance of the papers were. While the name of all the assets were divided equally among the members, the property everything was built on, including Beth's and Razer's new home, was owned by him.

Lily looked back up at him.

"When we all got out of the service, we wanted to start the business, but they had no capital. They had the ideas; I had the money. My money combined with what they had managed to save was invested in the business. The land, being in my name, was to ensure I wasn't left without anything since I took the most risk," he explained.

"Beth and Razer's home..."

"Is on *my* property," Shade confirmed. The money hadn't meant anything to him—he had told the brothers that—but they had insisted he take the property as collateral.

"Oh, God."

"There's no need to be upset. I have no intention of taking their home from them...if we come to an agreement," he clarified.

"What do you want, Shade?" A lone tear slid down her cheek.

He could have used that as leverage months before, but he hadn't. He could have found something when he had first met her to force her to his bed, but he hadn't. He had waited until she had almost died and lost her forever before he had realized he needed her, and by that point he wanted her more than the air he breathed. The only thing keeping him from being a true psychopath was his love for her. Without her, the empty void, which was his soul, would consume him.

"You."

Lily shook her head. "You can't be serious. You have to know this just makes me dislike you even more."

"Lily, you don't know what you want. You want a man who doesn't exist. One who will never touch you, pretend you don't have something seriously messed-up going on inside of your head, and be willing to put up with you constantly in some kind of trouble."

"I am not," Lily snapped.

Shade lifted his brow at her response and her inability to deny the truth of the other two statements.

"The man I want exists, and I know you're not him."

"I'm the only man for you." Menace poured from him before he regained control, shrugging and nodding his head toward the phone. "Make your mind up."

"Beth and Razer can build another house," Lily argued.

"They certainly can, but it won't be *that* house."

"Razer and you are like brothers; you wouldn't do that to him," Lily tried to call his bluff.

"Yes, I would," he stated matter-of-factly, letting her see the truth in his face.

"I can't do this." She pointed back and forth between them.

"I'm not going to rush you. We can go as slow as you want. I'm a patient man." *When you're not trying to rip my balls off.*

"I'm going to talk to Diamond."

"I'll take you to see her tomorrow after you get finished at the church."

Those papers had been written by the best lawyer money could buy. There were no loopholes other than his death. Shade would have to be careful turning his back to her.

"If I can find a way, I will leave."

"You can leave now, Lily. It's your decision," he reminded her. She might not like the consequences, but it was her choice to make, for better or worse.

"Okay." Lily gave in, staring down at the papers in her hand.

"Good, now that it's settled, we need to take care of your punishment for nearly ripping my balls off."

"I became caught up in our lesson," Lily defended her actions.

"You were pissed at me for something. Care to tell?" Shade waited to see if she would admit the truth.

Lily remained silent, however.

"All right." Shade leaned forward. "Let's begin with Jewell. She closed the door to my office when Cash called. Kaley broke the rules. I really didn't give a fuck if she tried to join the club or not. She would never have gotten enough votes to, anyway, so it's no loss.

"Now, let's talk about your punishment. I'm going to be lenient this time"—he paused at Lily's unladylike snort—"and give you your choice of punishment."

"What are the choices?"

Shade had no doubt she wasn't going to be happy with any of them.

"You can take the spanking you deserve, or you can sleep in the bed tonight, or you can give me one kiss. Take your pick."

"You're not serious?"

"Yes, I am being more than fair. It hurt like hell when you grabbed my nuts. None of your choices involve excruciating pain."

"That strap looks like it's going to hurt."

"I plan for you to enjoy that." Shade gave her a grin.

Lily shivered.

"Which one?" Shade prompted her. "Would you like me to pick for you?"

"No! I'll sleep in the bed," Lily said reluctantly.

"You sure?"

Lily nodded.

"Fine. You can get ready for bed." Shade got up from the chair, turning the television on. Since he had gotten the results he wanted, he needed to let her deal with the aftermath.

Lily gathered her pajamas before going into the bathroom. As soon as the door clicked shut behind her, Shade stood, placing the papers back in the envelope then setting them on the nightstand. He went back to the chair to sit down, listening to the shower running and knowing she was spending the time trying to figure a way out. There wasn't any; he'd had a long time to make his plans. Too long.

Finally, she opened the door, dressed in flannel pajamas which were ugly as shit, but Shade pretended not to take his attention away from the television as Lily climbed into the bed.

He gave her a moment to settle her nerves before turning the television off and going into the bathroom. Then he took a long shower, letting her have some time to herself before putting on a pair of shorts and returning to the bedroom.

He could tell she was only pretending to be asleep as he climbed in the bed then turned off the lights. She was hugging the side of the bed so tightly he was surprised she hadn't fallen off, and the whole bed was practically shaking with her frightened tremors.

Shade made himself comfortable. He had lost track of when the last time he had slept more than a couple of hours had been.

Her tense body gradually relaxed, and her fingers holding the side of the bed loosened to curl under her cheek.

Shade forced his body to remain still long after Lily had managed to drift off. When he was sure she had finally gone into a deep sleep, he rolled closer to her, fitting her against him as his warmth seeped into her chilled body. All his years of experience had led to that one moment: holding Lily close in his bed.

He was an expert at moving his body a centimeter at a time, slowly moving his fingers to play with the wisps of her hair on the pillow. A small smile tugged at his lips.

Chapter Fifty-Three

Shade followed Lily back to the club the next day after picking up her car from hers and Beth's house. He had driven her to work at the church store that morning then picked her up to take her to Diamond's house. He hadn't gone inside, letting her find out for herself the contract was ironclad. When she had come back outside, she hadn't said anything other than for him to take her to get her car, which Rider had gone to her college to pick up for her with his trailer.

As they drove, the sky darkened with storm clouds. Shade remembered Razer telling him Lily hated storms. The strong winds were buffeting her vehicle and his bike. He had almost asked her to wait until tomorrow to talk to Diamond, not wanting her out in the storm, but he didn't want her to think he was hiding something, so he had hoped the storm wouldn't hit until they were back at the club.

She pulled into The Last Riders' parking lot, driving toward the back where he motioned for her to park before he turned his bike around. Then he headed back toward the front where he parked his motorcycle with the rest. Shade walked over to her car when she got out, carrying a car cover.

He pulled it over the vehicle as she asked, "Why cover my car?" while watching him curiously.

"Just being careful. If someone is looking to find out where you're staying, they'll either have to follow you or come onto the property to see if this is your car."

"If they do?"

"Then we'll see them." Shade pointed to the cameras. "We placed a few in your home, too, so if they try to break in again, an alarm will go off at the sheriff's office and here, also.

"Maybe they gave up and moved on."

"Possibly, but I don't believe so. Whoever's been watching you has been doing so for a while." Shade tried to ease her fears. "Don't worry; we'll find out who it is and deal with it."

"You'll turn them over to Knox?"

"Maybe. Let's get some dinner." His answer was purposely evasive, because whoever had tried to run her down wouldn't be getting any protection from Knox.

By the time they walked up the pathway to the kitchen door and stepped in, most of the members had already been served. Lily took a plate before handing one to him, both of them getting into the buffet line. When she finished filling her plate, Shade followed her to the table Winter and Viper were sitting at with Bliss and Raci. She took a seat next to Winter, and Shade sat down across from her, next to Bliss.

They ate while listening to Winter and Viper argue over him donating money so she could buy computers for her students at the alternate high school where she was principal.

"It's not fair, Viper. They deserve the computers as much as the high school students do."

"If they had kept their asses out of trouble, then they wouldn't have gotten thrown out of the school district."

"That's unfair. Both schools should have the same standards," Winter argued.

Viper shrugged. "I gave you two large chunks of money already this year. You've reached your limit with my generosity, but that doesn't mean you can't hit the other members up for donations. Their pockets are deeper than mine since you've already robbed me twice."

Winter turned her eyes to the members sitting across from her.

"Raci?"

"Don't ask me. I'm not an original member; I earn a paycheck like everyone else."

Shade almost snorted. The woman worked more hours than almost anyone at the table and earned more bonuses for completed orders than any of them combined.

"I do the payroll; I know what you make." Winter gave the woman a narrow-eyed stare.

"I can buy a couple," Raci conceded reluctantly.

"Bliss?"

"Put me down for two." Bliss wasn't even going to fight Winter. She didn't want her paycheck up for discussion, either. She was paid for many hours she hadn't put in, constantly telling Viper she would make them up.

"Thanks. Shade?" Winter turned her greedy gaze on him.

Shade paused with the fork halfway to his mouth. "No."

Lily shot him a reproachful look.

"Don't look at me that way, Lily. I've already bought that school two pieces of expensive equipment for their auto shop, a confection oven for the cooking class, and paid the salary of the auto shop teacher, so no computer from me. Maybe next year, if you don't hit me up for something else before then." Shade had no problem returning Winter's stare.

"Have you asked Razer?" Lily broke into their staring contest.

"No," Winter said.

"Why not?"

Because Razer is the biggest donator of all with Beth adding her own pleas to Winter's, Shade thought to himself, seeing Winter would play that card with him, too, as soon as she managed to get Lily alone.

"Because he coughed up the money to pay for the afterschool tutors. Her chances of getting any money out of Razer are nil," Shade answered, taking a drink of his beer. Lily sent him another reproachful look.

"Rider and Train?" Lily asked.

"New bus to drive the kids and lab equipment," Shade replied after Winter's continued silence.

"Knox?" Lily asked hesitantly.

"Media library."

"Ouch. I could buy two. I have some money saved up," Lily offered.

Everyone at the table looked at her. The woman had less than anyone in the club, yet she had made a generous offer.

"No, Lily. I couldn't take your money. I have one other member I haven't hit up yet."

"Who?" Lily asked.

"Lucky."

When Bliss looked at him from under her lashes, Shade wanted to snap at the woman, but it was too late—both Lily and Winter had noticed her behavior.

"I haven't met him yet," Lily said, glancing across the table at Bliss and him.

Shade kept his face impassive. However, as her hand went to her chest, resting on top of her heart, Shade wanted to jerk Bliss up from the table.

He was going to have another talk with her, and that time, he was going to be firmer. He hadn't wanted to get too hateful with her, because they had shared a sexual relationship for several years, and she was a member of The Last Riders. Lily was the newcomer and was taking the place Bliss had wanted. Shade had kept to the rules of the club, but it was Bliss who had hoped for something more from him.

"Are you all right?" Shade asked, looking across the table at Lily with a frown.

"Yes, I must have eaten something that gave me indigestion," Lily said, getting up from the table.

"Yeah, I feel a little nauseous myself," Winter commented with a warning look at Bliss.

"You're probably stressed out, worrying about coming up with the money for the computers. Let me know how much they cost, and I'll write you a check for two of them. I wish I could do more," Lily said, not looking at the people sitting at the table.

"I'll ask Lucky. If he doesn't, then I'll pay for them," Viper conceded, taking Lily's hand as she reached for his plate. "We'll take care of it. Keep your money, Lily."

Lily gave his hand a squeeze before letting it go and picking up his plate then Winter's.

"Okay, but if you decide you need it, let me know. I'm going to bed. I'm tired tonight. Goodnight, everyone." Lily left everyone sitting at the table, carrying the dirty dishes to the sink.

Shade turned to Bliss. "Next time you act like that in front of her, I'll drag your ass out of the club and throw your clothes out in the yard."

Bliss gasped. "You're not serious?"

"Try me, Bliss," Shade snarled. "The brothers would miss your pussy, but not enough to fight me to keep it." Bliss paled. "See that woman standing there washing dishes?" Shade nodded at Lily doing dishes with Jewell until Nickel took over for her.

Lily left, telling them goodnight, and again, Shade waited until she was out of hearing. "Lily would never intentionally hurt another soul—she's incapable of it—while you didn't give a fuck who you were hurting with your behavior."

Shade stood up, picking up his dirty dishes. "Now ask me why I care about her and not you," he said sarcastically, leaving the table to take his dishes to the sink.

Shade heard Lily in the bathroom blow-drying her hair when he walked into the bedroom. He was removing his T-shirt, having already taken his boots off, when she came out of the bathroom.

Lily started to go to the corner.

"Bed, Lily."

"But—"

"You agreed when you chose your punishment last night," Shade reminded her.

"I thought that was just for last night," she protested.

"No. Go to bed. I'm going to take a shower." He didn't want to argue with her tonight.

The storm was getting closer—he had listened to the warnings before coming downstairs—and he wanted her asleep before the worst of it hit Treepoint.

He showered then changed before going back to the bedroom to see Lily was already asleep. He turned off the bedside lamp, leaving the bathroom light on, then laid down next to her, propping his back against the headboard.

Shade reached into the nightstand drawer, pulling out his tablet. He was in the middle of the fourth game, shooting zombies, when the bathroom light began to blink. Shade turned off his tablet, moving closer to Lily's side.

The light blinked again, but that time, it didn't come back on. He unconsciously held his breath, hoping Lily slept through the blackout, but the lights hadn't been out a minute before she jerked straight up in the bed, screaming in terror.

"Lily." Shade spoke calmly to her in the darkness, giving her his voice to cling to in the pitch black. "The power went off. The generator will kick on in a minute. Just take a deep breath with me and let's count."

She couldn't concentrate enough to count.

"Lily! Concentrate. Count with me. One…two…three…"

Lily finally calmed down enough to join him. "Four…five…"

Shade kept reassuring her that the generator would cut on and she was safe as she continued to count through sobbing breaths until the lights flickered briefly then came on. Then she turned to him, laying her head on his shoulder and crying in relief.

"I have you, sweetheart. Shh…I have you," Shade promised, his voice thick.

While he soothed and rocked her in his arms, holding her tightly, Lily's arms circled his neck. She burrowed closer to him, searching for comfort, which he gave her without hesitation.

Fine tremors shook her body while his firm hand stroked her back as he continued to rock her, repeating over and over soothingly that it was only a storm.

After she gradually relaxed, exhausted, lying limply against him and falling back asleep, Shade pulled her closer, rubbing her cheek with his.

"I've got you, Lily. Nothing's ever going to hurt you again. I swear."

CHAPTER FIFTY-FOUR

"Here you go." Shade placed his laptop on the desk in front of Lily. She wanted to get started on the class assignments she had missed the previous week.

Giving her privacy, he worked out so she could be alone and concentrate.

Afterward, she didn't even raise her head from the computer when he passed through the bedroom to take a shower. When he got out, he pulled on a pair of jeans, going barefoot and shirtless.

She was frowning at her assignment when he reentered the bedroom.

"Hungry?"

"A little, but I want to finish this."

"Go ahead and finish. I'll bring you a plate."

"Sounds good, thanks," Lily said absently.

Shade left the room to go upstairs where several members were in the kitchen, sitting around and talking after dinner. Shade made himself and Lily a plate of food, seeing Winter stacking the dirty dishes in the dishwasher.

"What did you get in trouble for this time?" Shade asked.

Winter looked at him with a dejected air. "I wouldn't quit bugging the members to buy computers, so Viper made me pull the punishment when Rider told on me. He has over twenty motorcycles, and he got mad at me when I suggested he should donate a computer for every bike. The freaking tightwad!"

Shade looked over his shoulder at Rider sitting at the table with his arms crossed over his chest. The brother was sensitive over his bikes. He was notorious for being a cheapskate over everything other than the motorcycles he bought. Winter had been lucky to have pried open his wallet as much as she had.

Shade set the tray of food down to get drinks. He was walking by Winter when he came to a stop.

"Order the computers you need. I'll cut you a check in the morning."

The plate Winter was holding slipped through her fingers, landing with a thud in the dishwasher. Then she threw herself into his arms, hugging him.

Shade felt uncomfortable since Viper was watching from the table as his wife cried her 'thank yous' against his bare shoulder. He finally managed to break free, placing the drinks on the tray.

"No problem," Shade said, heading for the basement door.

"Shade," Viper drawled. "I see what you mean about watching your woman in another man's arms, but for the amount of money you just forked over, I'm thinking of hugging you, too. I was going to break and buy them."

Shade mock-shuddered. "I'll pass, brother. Winter's was enough." He closed the door on Viper's 'fuck you' gesture, chuckling as Winter smacked Viper on the back of the head for flipping him off. The price of the computers was worth seeing that sight alone.

He carried the tray into the bedroom, setting it down on the table in front of the television. Then he picked up the plate he had prepared for Lily and her drink, placing them in front of her.

"Thanks," she said briefly, typing something on the computer.

Shade sat and watched the television while eating his own meal. Afterward, he sprawled out, relaxing and enjoying his day off from the factory. If anyone had asked him what his idea of contentment was, it would be having Lily close-by where he could see her whenever he wanted.

"Is the television distracting you?" Shade asked when she gave a frustrated sigh.

"No."

Shade turned back to the movie, though his concentration was broken when her chair scooted back from the desk.

She stood up, grabbing her plate from the desk. "Do you need anything while I'm upstairs?"

"A beer would be great."

He frowned when she left the room. Maybe her classes were turning out to be harder than she had anticipated. He would offer to help her, but she seemed to be in a grumpy mood and he didn't think she would accept his offer.

She came back a few minutes later, empty-handed.

"Where's my beer?" Shade asked.

"I forgot it." She was flushed, looking down at her empty hands as if surprised nothing was there.

"I'm going to take a shower," Lily said, grabbing her pajamas and then disappearing into the bathroom.

Shade frowned at her behavior. Standing up and stretching, he then carried the tray of dirty dishes to the kitchen.

He went through the kitchen door, hearing a moan as he entered. Looking toward the television room, he saw Bliss and Train were fucking on the couch. Lily's behavior explained, Shade placed his dishes into the sink before going to the fridge to take a beer. Leaving the two to their fuck session, he returned downstairs to the bedroom, turning his movie back on.

Shade was taking a drink of his beer when she returned to the bedroom.

"It's a little early to go to bed, isn't it?"

"I have a headache. I guess it's from staring at the computer screen."

"Possibly. Will the television disturb you?"

"No." Lily was about to climb into bed yet stopped, coming to stand in front of him instead.

"You need to let me go. I'm never going to fit into this club."

"What makes you say that?"

"You know why." She waved her hand at the beer. "Bliss doesn't try to hide that you both have shared a relationship. She doesn't want me here. She belongs here; I don't."

"You will."

"No, Shade, I won't. You're only going to hurt everyone involved. I'm never going to adjust to your lifestyle. You're not a one-woman man."

"I already am," Shade said softly.

"Don't claim I'm the woman for you when you smell like another woman's perfume."

"I smell like perfume?" Shade asked, not trying to hide his amusement.

"Yes," Lily said angrily.

"That's because Winter hugged me when I told her I would pay for the computers for her school."

"Well...heck." Lily paused. "I'm sorry," she apologized.

"You were awfully harsh to me, don't you think? I mean, I was nice enough to fix your dinner and bring it to you, and then you forgot my beer. Then you rant at me about other women. I'm beginning to think you're jealous. I never took you for the jealous type," Shade said in mock-seriousness.

"I'm not jealous," Lily snapped.

"I believe you are, and I don't believe you're sorry. Do you know how much those computers are going to cost me?" Shade tried to appear affronted.

"I am not jealous, and I apologized."

"I don't believe you." Shade gave her a reproachful look.

"I really am."

"Prove it."

"How?"

"Kiss me and make it better."

"No." Lily shook her head.

"I knew you didn't mean your apology," Shade said, turning back to the television.

"I did—I do," Lily corrected herself. "But I'm still not going to kiss you."

"Why? You've kissed before, haven't you?"

Lily didn't say anything.

"Lily, have you kissed before?" He stared at her in surprise. Shade couldn't believe she had never kissed Charles, since they had dated throughout her high school years. The part inside him which held jealousy toward the bastard suddenly died.

"No," Lily admitted.

"What about Charles?"

"Just on the cheek or a brief peck on the lips. I guess I could do that," she said unenthusiastically.

"Don't knock yourself out. I've been told I'm a good kisser. I could teach you how," Shade offered, trying to appear innocent.

"I bet you could," she said sarcastically. "Who told you you're a good kisser?"

"I don't kiss and tell," he said, grinning at her wickedly.

While Lily gritted her teeth in aggravation, Shade decided to push a tiny bit more, seeing she was battling her conscience.

"Come on, Lily. What's a little kiss between friends?" He rose to his feet and put his hands behind his back. "I won't touch you with anything other than my mouth. You can experiment and see how you like kissing." He tried to appear non-threatening, not staring at her directly, as if it didn't matter if she kissed him or not.

Lily froze, her face a mask of indecision, but then she took a timid step forward. Shade didn't say anything, appearing bored.

It took several seconds for her to take another step. Shade never became impatient as she steadily drew closer until a mere inch separated them.

She cautiously raised herself onto her tiptoes, and then her mouth briefly touched his before breaking away and taking a step back.

Then, like a moth to a flame, she fluttered closer again. That time, her hands rested on his chest as she touched her mouth to his, letting hers linger a mere breath of a second before leaning back to study his face.

Shade kept his expression impassive as her eyes searched his face for a reaction.

She leaned forward again, pressing her lips harder against his mouth before she lifted herself away, but she didn't move from his body that time. Shade wanted to snatch her into his arms when her tongue licked his lips to taste him. Her lashes lowered as she studied his mouth, and only the years he had spent being a Dom allowed him to remain in control.

She came back for more, pressing her lips harder against his mouth until he opened to her slightly. And that's when Lily jumped away as if she had touched fire.

"That's enough for tonight. You're not a fast learner. It may take weeks for you to catch on to how it's done." He stepped away, going back to his chair while praying his shaking legs wouldn't betray him.

He clenched the arms of his chair to make himself remain seated as she lay down in his bed, pulling the covers over her. He wanted to rip them away and give her a lesson in kissing she would never forget.

Shade gritted his teeth, trying to get his body back under control, forcing himself to keep his eyes on the television screen.

Out of the corner of his eye, he saw her hitting her pillow in frustration, and his hands clenched by his side. The woman didn't know the meaning of frustration, but he was about to show her if she threw him another one of her pissed-off looks.

He was trying to go slow, not frighten her away, but even he had his limits. That innocent kiss he had gotten from her had nearly been his undoing.

When he was sure she was asleep, he got up and left the room. He didn't trust himself to climb into bed with her at that point. He had to calm his body down.

Going upstairs, he grabbed a bottle of whiskey and poured himself a generous amount. His wall of patience was crumbling. It was time to heat up his efforts with Lily. He didn't think it was fair to be the only one suffering. Lily needed to discover exactly what she was missing out on, which was him fucking her until she begged him for mercy.

Shade poured himself another whiskey, his hand shaking as he picked up his glass.

ഇ ങ

Lily was dressed and ready to leave for work when Shade entered the room. She wrinkled her nose as he crossed the bedroom floor.

"You've been drinking!" she said accusingly.

"Don't worry; I'm not drunk."

She paled at his words, flinching away as he brushed by her.

"Aren't you going to work?"

"I'm taking the morning off. Rider is managing the factory until this afternoon."

Shade went to the side of the bed, taking his shoes and T-shirt off. He started to take his pants off yet stopped when she didn't leave as he had expected. He stared at her with bloodshot eyes as she stood, unmoving.

"Um...you must have started drinking after I went to sleep."

Shade cocked an eyebrow at her question. "Yes, I went upstairs for another beer, and Cash and Rider were having a card game, so I joined in. I wasn't ready for bed as early as you."

If he had climbed into that bed with her, he wouldn't have gotten out until he had fucked her. He had drunk two bottles of whiskey to keep from coming downstairs and waking her up. He told himself he wouldn't have taken her unless she wanted him, but Shade was smart enough not to put his control to a test because he wasn't sure he would be happy with the outcome.

Lily fiddled with the rubber band on her wrist. "I didn't expect you to be. I guess I'll see you this afternoon."

She started out the doorway yet turned back when he spoke.

"It was just us; none of the women were there." He didn't want her spending the day flicking that fucking rubber band, wondering where his dick had been the night before.

"I didn't ask."

"You didn't have to," Shade mocked, seeing her relief.

She fled the bedroom, leaving him staring after her.

He stood up, pulling off his jeans and kicking them across the floor viciously. His spending the night drinking hadn't touched the fire in his dick she had started.

Going into the shower, he turned on the music, letting himself picture her in his mind as his hand stroked his cock, sliding back and forth as he imagined her lying naked on his bed, begging for him. His hand was no replacement for her body, but his cock didn't care. It had been at a fever pitch since her lips had touched his. He groaned as he climaxed.

When he finished showering, he returned to the bedroom, finding it as empty as he had left it. Somewhere in the part of him that he didn't allow himself to acknowledge, he felt the brief hope die that Lily had come back and would be there waiting for him.

CHAPTER FIFTY-FIVE

"They lay down the hardwood floors today. The men want to install the cabinets tomorrow," Rider told him.

Shade, Rider, and Bliss were standing in the basement talking as Bliss did the laundry. He and Lily had finished their workout, and she had left to take a shower.

Shade used his T-shirt to wipe the sweat from his chest.

"When are you going to tell Lily you're building the house for her?" Bliss asked, and Shade could see the hurt in her face.

He was about to answer when Lily came back through after showering. Still not speaking to him, she went upstairs without a word. She was giving him the cold shoulder after she had come to his office earlier in the day, asking for Georgia's brother to be given her job. He had refused, telling her they didn't want the brother and sister working together.

She had turned the conversation into an attempt to get him to see he didn't need her, that he only wanted her, saying she wouldn't be able to be with him then watch him be with another woman and remain friends. She was placing herself on the same level as the women members when Shade had been trying to show her he wanted more from her than he did the other women. It was frustrating that every-one else could see what was right before her eyes.

"I'll tell her when she's ready to hear it." Shade pulled a beer out of the mini-fridge and sat on the couch.

Raci and Cash came downstairs to hang out. He never went upstairs to eat, relaxing with the others. He didn't go upstairs to check on Lily, either, sensing she needed time to herself in order to come to grips with the emotions she was battling. It couldn't be easy having your body betray you with a sexual attraction to a person you disliked. Hated. Lily didn't dislike him; she *hated* him. However, her body wanted him, and with her past, it had to be terrifying.

He had to get her to the point where her body's demands outweighed her fears. He was going to have to use his years of experience to build her desire until she couldn't think of anything except him. He planned to get her so needy that, when she walked and her thighs rubbed her pussy, she would think of him.

Bliss turned on the music after she had folded the last load of clothes. Then Raci and Cash slid the workout mats out of the way and began dancing.

When Lily came back downstairs, she paused, watching Raci and Cash.

Rider and Bliss were kissing on the couch after playfully tossing the clothes back and forth, and he was sitting next to them on the couch, watching Raci and Cash dance.

Raci was dancing seductively, grinding her butt back into Cash's pelvis. His arms were on the pole, trapping her between them.

Lily tried to rush past but as she did, Shade reached out, snagging her wrist and pulling her down on the couch next to him. She started to protest, but he cut her off mercilessly.

"You can sit out here with me or you can run and hide in the bedroom, wondering what I'm doing out here with them."

"I don't care what you're doing," Lily snapped.

Shade straightened away from her. "Then run away." He lifted his beer to his mouth, leaning back against the couch. Expecting her to run from the room, he was surprised when she didn't.

Rider was sitting with Bliss on his lap with his hand under her T-shirt, the tanned expanse of her stomach showing. Then Rider started sucking on the flesh of Bliss's neck while his hand slid farther up her top.

Cash's hand went to the waistband of Raci's short skirt, his fingers sliding underneath.

Shade watched Lily tense, her eyes going back and forth between the two couples, ready to fly off the couch.

"Look at their faces, Lily."

Shade's words had her eyes flying up to his.

He leaned closer to her, his chest just brushing against hers. He felt her nipples tauten against him, and she began to breathe faster. Shade dropped all pretenses with her, letting her see the desire he had kept carefully hidden. Since the first time he had seen her, he had been swimming in an ocean of longing for her. But right then, he was dragging her into the ocean with him, letting her see for herself how it felt to want someone until you felt like you were drowning.

Lily turned her head, her eyes going to Raci as Cash's hand completely disappeared under her shirt.

"Does she look frightened?" Shade asked her.

Lily's eyes lifted to Raci's face. There was no way Lily could mistake fear for the excitement Raci expressed as her hips wiggled back against Cash, her head falling back against his shoulder.

Lily's eyes moved away, going to Bliss whose breasts were uncovered with Rider twisting her nipple. Her eyes dropped to Bliss's tattoo with four daisies and a date in the middle. Her face paled and then she turned, glaring at him.

Lily tried to get up, but Shade used his body to stop her. She sank farther back into the couch cushions, trying not to come into contact with his body. Shade allowed her to keep that space so she would still be able to see Rider and Bliss. The two were erotic as hell to watch. The only thing hotter was when Rider wanted to play Dom.

"You understand that tattoo, don't you?" Shade asked, staring down into her eyes.

"You disgust me," Lily spat.

"You're not even going to ask me if one of those daisies is me?" Shade mocked.

"I don't have to." Lily tried to turn away, but he kept her pinned in place as her hand covered the flesh over her heart. Shade saw the tell-tale sign yet didn't back off. He had to be cruel to be kind. He wasn't going to let her discover any secrets which would drive her away from him once he had her. And he was close to having her.

Shade moved her hand away, letting his replace it. "I was, and Winter wasn't any happier to find out Viper was, too. Evie and Cash were the other two." His hand rubbed against her flesh, seeing the stabbing pain of betrayal his words elicited as if it was his own. "Bliss likes to show off, so it was only a matter of time before you saw it now that you're living here."

"For now."

Shade almost snapped "Forever," but Raci's moans drew their attention.

Cash picked the woman up, throwing her over his shoulder before carrying her up the steps.

"I'm not stopping you. You can leave anytime, Lily. I'm sure Beth won't be heartbroken for long. On the other hand, you could start enjoying living here. Look at Bliss. I don't think there's any place else she wants to be." His seductive comments had her focusing on the lone couple as they became bolder in front of her.

Rider's hand was no longer under her shirt but beneath her skirt, which had ridden up to show Bliss was naked underneath. He was rubbing her between her splayed thighs, and her hand had gone into his jeans as she unzipped them.

Shade placed his mouth against Lily's throat and saw her eyes begin to roll back. He wasn't going to let her escape into her mind this time.

Using the tip of his tongue, he barely touched the flesh of her throat. Her attention was so focused on Rider and Bliss he didn't think she even noticed as he traced a path to her ear.

"See how wet she is? She isn't afraid to let him touch her. She's enjoying every minute of it." One of Rider's fingers slipped inside of Bliss, and her moan had Lily shuddering. "She loves to fuck," he whispered into her ear before rising up to stare down at her flushed face.

"Give her another finger, Rider," Shade ordered, hearing Lily's soft gasp as she watched, entranced.

Bliss moaned louder when Rider's two fingers slid in and out of her pussy.

"See? She's enjoying his fingers in her pussy," he said, lowering his mouth to her ear once again before he pulled back and directed Rider once more. "Rub her clit harder, Rider. She enjoys a little pain."

Lily's thighs pressed together, and Shade's cock thickened when he felt that needy movement against his hip.

"Shade..." Bliss moaned, lifting her hips and pumping them, riding Rider's fingers, her juices easily visible to Shade and Lily.

"Let her come, Rider."

Rider's fingers stroked even faster, and Bliss raised her hips before plunging herself down on his hand. Her small scream had Lily jumping up from the couch, tearing her body away from his.

"Run, Lily. It's not going to change the fact that you're mine. And the next time a woman moans my name, it will be you," Shade promised without sympathy.

He winced when he heard the bedroom door slamming shut.

Bliss stood up unsteadily, and Rider held her hand until she quit shaking.

"You want me to take care of that for you?" Bliss asked, nodding at the bulge in his jeans.

"No." Shade finished his beer, throwing it across the room into the trash can. It made a loud thud when it landed inside.

He reached into his pocket and pulled out four slips of paper, handing one to Bliss and three to Rider.

"You can give Raci and Cash their IOUs for me."

Rider looked at him curiously. "You didn't have to give us the IOUs for something we would have done for free."

"Would you have stopped at only finger-fucking Bliss if I hadn't offered the IOU?"

"No," Rider admitted. "If I didn't know how you like holding those fucking slips over our heads, I don't think I would have. I would have definitely fucked Bliss when I saw Lily press her legs together." He laughed.

"You like to show off." Shade shook his head at the brother. "One day, that's going to get you in trouble," he warned.

"I'm not afraid of trouble. I'm more afraid of not finding enough." He laughed.

"I didn't think Cash was going to stop for a minute." Bliss giggled.

"Cash would have stopped. He knew I would rip his dick off if he pulled it out. I wanted to get Lily horny, not give her a panic attack."

"She ever tell you why—" Rider began to ask.

"No."

"Message received, brother." Rider looped his arm around Bliss's shoulder. "Want to go to my room and you can finish what Shade wouldn't let me have down here?"

Bliss nodded, her eyes on Shade. "Unless you want us to stay? Lily left."

"No, thanks. The only other show I plan to watch tonight is on that television on the wall." Shade stood. Going to the cabinet over the dryer and opening it, he took out a full whiskey bottle.

ഇ ന

"How's Georgia doing?" Rider asked as they waited for the few remaining employees to leave.

"Better. Razer managed to scare her better than Viper and I did. After she insulted Beth at church, she's trying to be more careful with what comes out of her mouth. Unfortunately, Lily's right; Georgia's not a nice person. She's a fucking bitch," Shade said.

"I know Lily didn't call Georgia a fucking bitch." They both laughed yet stopped when they saw Lily running down the path from the clubhouse.

She was barefoot, wearing sweats and a T-shirt. Shade recognized she was having a panic attack instantly. He started toward her as she ran to him. He barely had time to hold out his arms before she was throwing herself into them, clutching him tightly and shaking. She tried to burrow into him as tightly as she could, her black hair surrounding them.

"What's wrong?" He held her to him tightly, giving her the security she needed.

"I don't know," Lily cried.

"Couldn't you get hold of Beth?" he asked.

"What? I didn't try," she said, trembling harder.

"You didn't try to call Beth? You came to me first?" Shade's hand smoothed her tumbled hair away from her face.

Lily nodded against his shoulder, whimpering. "My head hurts," she moaned.

Shade lifted her into his arms, handing Rider the clipboard he had been holding. He then carried her back to the house, closing the door she had left open in her terror. In the bedroom, he sat down with her on the bed and Lily curled into the safety of his arms, laying her head on his shoulder.

"I think I'm losing my mind," Lily confessed.

"No, you're not." Shade rubbed the back of her neck, easing the tension from her shoulders. "Lily, your attacks are coming less, but they're becoming stronger. I think your mind is trying to tell you that you're strong enough to remember."

Shade didn't believe what she had seen the previous night had triggered this panic attack. Her attacks were usually immediate, not delayed, so something else had triggered it. She had proven she was getting strong, managing to keep the darkness from taking her long enough to find him. A few months before, she would have been paralyzed with fear.

Lily jerked upright, her hands going to the sides of her head.

Shade's hands went to her wrists. "Look at me, Lily."

Her violet eyes lifted to his.

"Look at me," Shade repeated.

She stared at him mutely while he held her gaze with sheer will, wanting her to see he was with her. There, in the room, together. Forever.

"What's in here can't hurt you anymore." Shade tapped the side of her head. "The world around you"—his hand circled the air around her body—"I've got that." He brought his hands back to hers, holding them in his. "No one will ever hurt you again," he promised in a steely voice.

It was a promise he intended to keep for a lifetime.

CHAPTER FIFTY-SIX

Lily was brushing her hair out in the bedroom when Shade walked in. She had woken up the morning after her panic attack without remembering what had triggered it, or she had deliberately forgotten. Shade didn't know which; he doubted she did, either. The rest of the week had passed as if it had never happened.

She twirled her skirt around her legs, showing off her outfit. Her black hair was long and loose, and she had several chunky necklaces on.

"You look great. What are you supposed to be?"

"A gypsy."

"How is it any different than what you usually wear? You should have at least been adventuresome enough to raise the hemline above your ankles," Shade said, taking a change of clothes out of a drawer.

Shade saw Lily looked down at herself.

He walked to her, cupping her cheek. "You look gorgeous. Who got it for you?"

"Beth," Lily said, twirling away.

Shade looked at her dress closely. "Remind me to thank her."

He was going to have a long talk with Beth to thank her for buying Lily the gypsy costume for the Halloween party. The dress had a shimmering fabric which was practically see-through when the light hit it.

"Why?"

Shade merely shook his head, going into the bathroom. "Never mind. I won't be long." If he told her what he could see, she would take it off. He wasn't about to deny himself a glimpse of that ass.

Shade took a quick shower then changed before going into the main room of the basement and taking a seat on one side of the couch.

Several club members were already there. Beth was sitting on Razer's lap next to Evie on the couch, eating snacks. Viper and Winter were dancing among others who had toned down their usually more suggestive grinding.

"How was Georgia this week?" Beth asked Lily, putting her arm around Razer's shoulder.

"Fine."

"Lily, would you mind getting me a beer?" Shade requested. "The new prototype came back today with suggested changes from the manufacturer," he told Razer.

"Figures. What do they want done now? It better not change the cost of production."

Lily got up from the couch to go to the table where the beer had been set up at and got him one. When she came back and handed it to him, Shade reached up and pulled her down on his lap. Lily tried to wiggle off.

"Sit still," Shade ordered.

Lily quit wiggling.

Shade ignored her rigid posture, resuming his conversation with Razer about the production of one of the tools which was selling well.

"The only way to increase production is to go with another manufacturer," Razer said.

Their conversation continued while Lily and Beth talked about the church store Lily had volunteered to put together with Rachel Porter.

It wasn't long before Train and Jewell came downstairs and started dancing alongside Viper and Winter. Train wasn't wearing a shirt, but he had on a bandana over his hair and a patch over one eye. Jewell was wearing a pirate wench outfit which left most of her breasts bare, and the short skirt showed the long length of her shapely legs.

As the song changed, Razer got to his feet. "Let's dance."

With that, Beth and Razer joined the couples dancing.

Halfway through the song, Evie came downstairs dressed as a French maid with Cash dressed as himself.

Lily laughed, looking into Shade's eyes. "Train is the only one who dressed up?"

Shade shook his head. "Rider dressed as Tarzan, but I threatened to kick his ass if he came down here."

Lily's giggles were cut off as Shade got up, setting Lily on her feet before taking her to the dance floor. She tried to get away but he snagged her around the waist, pulling her close.

"Dance with me, Lily."

"I don't know how," she protested.

"That's okay. They don't, either." Shade pointed his hand at Evie and Cash.

She began moving, and by the third dance, Shade could tell she was relaxed.

The other members came and went, moving back and forth between the two floors, everyone seemingly enjoying themselves.

Shade pulled her closer as someone turned off a couple of the lamps, dimming the room without making it too dark. The thin material of her dress let him feel every inch of her body. Yes, he had a lot to thank Beth for.

Beth, Razer, Winter, and Viper had gone upstairs while Cash, Evie, Train, and Jewell were still dancing. She seemed to have grown comfortable enough around the members to have a good time. It was definitely a party unlike any at the clubhouse. While upstairs the usual 'anything goes' was in effect, the downstairs was tame in comparison.

"Are you having a good time?"

Lily smiled up at Shade. "Yes, I am."

"Don't seem so surprised," Shade said, his thigh sliding between her legs as his hand dropped to circle her waist.

"I just thought it would be wilder."

"It is, upstairs."

Lily blushed, turning her eyes away. "If you want to go upstairs, I won't mind."

"Shut up. I'm exactly where I want to be."

Lily smiled.

Shade lowered his head then, his lips briefly touching hers. Lily didn't move away from the brief encounter, so he did it again, lingering against hers. He increased the pressure on her lips, trying to get her to part them. When he slid his tongue along the seam of her lips, she gasped and Shade took advantage, sliding his tongue inside her mouth.

Lily's hands grabbed his T-shirt, but she didn't push him away; therefore, he gently explored her mouth, giving her the first kiss from him, one she would remember. He wanted to replace each memory from her childhood with something which could be cherished.

Then Shade lifted his head, breaking the tender kiss, continuing to dance as if nothing had happened.

The music ended, and Shade stepped back. "Want to get something to drink?"

"Yes."

As they moved off the dance floor, an out-of-breath Evie plopped down on the couch next to Jewell.

"I love your outfit, Lily. It looks all demur. Then, when you move, it shows that rockin' body of yours. I might need to borrow it for the next party," Jewell complimented.

Lily's mouth dropped open as she glared at Shade. It was time to beat a hasty retreat. She obviously hoped he would feel guilty for not telling her the dress was sheer, but she was shit out of luck. A person had to have a conscience for that crap.

"The drinks are all gone. I'll go get some more," Shade said, making his move to get out of Dodge.

He climbed the stairs, going into the packed kitchen. The parties were getting larger every weekend, and he noticed a couple of new women he hadn't seen previously at the club. He didn't let his eyes rest on any of them as he moved across the room, taking a large pack of beer and soda out of the fridge.

Train and Cash came upstairs, foraging for what food was left. Cash swiped a pizza away from Nickel, and Train took a bag of chips out of the pantry.

Heading back down, Shade saw Lily on the pole when he reached the halfway point of the stairs, his feet automatically moving to the bottom as he watched her unconsciously seductive movements.

"It's great not only for the thighs, but your stomach muscles, as well. Just don't let your arms do the work for you; let your tummy and thigh muscles do it," Lily was telling the women.

When no one said anything, Lily rose and turned to see Shade standing there.

"I was just showing Evie an exercise I learned in my pole class," Lily said, jerking her leg down from the pole and straightening her skirt.

"Could you show me that move again? I have a few pounds I need to lose," Train asked seriously.

Shade shot a threatening glare at him as he set the drinks down on the side table.

Lily went to get one, picking an orange soda. Shade pulled her back down on his lap. That time, she didn't try to wiggle away.

Stori came down the stairs dressed in a bunny outfit which was even more suggestive than Jewell's wench costume. She began dancing with Hound, a brother from Ohio who was putting his hand on her ass, grinding her closer to his hips.

"You never told me you knew how to pole dance."

Lily turned bright red. "My gym at college taught an exercise class using the pole."

"Lord have mercy," Shade muttered.

He wasn't embarrassed to admit to himself that he enjoyed watching strippers perform. It was highly erotic watching the way they moved. The really good ones had a sensuality which was hard not to appreciate, and he had shown a great many of them his gratitude. Lily, on the other hand, was unaware of her sexuality, but once she learned to accept it, she would be able to drive a man to his knees.

Lily laughed at his expression as she playfully hit his chest. Shade's hand went to the back of her neck, tugging her head down to him so he could catch her mouth, feeling her relax against him. They were in a dark corner, and no one was paying attention to them.

Her arms slid around his neck as she kissed him back. Shade felt her breasts against his chest as he gave her another kiss to remember. Then his hand flattened against her flat stomach before sliding up to her shoulder, raising her back up to a sitting position.

"Let's dance."

"Okay." She got to her feet and they went to the dance floor, spending the remainder of the evening dancing.

The rest of the members spent the night continuing to go between the two floors. Viper and Winter both showed up a couple more times before eventually saying they were going to bed.

It was getting late as Shade talked to Train and Evie while Lily talked to Beth. When she yawned, Shade noticed.

"I'm going to bed. I have to be up early to go to the church store."

After everyone told her goodnight, Lily went into the bedroom.

80 03

He stared down at Lily sleeping in his bed before taking a shower. The smile playing on the corners of her lips affected him in ways he never knew were possible. Her peaceful sleep was deep, unmarred by the nightmares she was constantly trying to outmaneuver. Then his smile slipped when he thought about how he was going to kick Razer's ass for not telling him Lily knew how to swing on a pole better than any stripper he had ever paid for.

His backstabbing brother knew there were three things he enjoyed in life: whiskey, pole-dancing, and Lily. He could finally enjoy all three.

He whistled low as he took his shower then dried off. He blow-dried his hair, not wanting to get Lily's pillow wet, then shaved before going to bed.

His arm went around her waist, pulling her close. He rubbed his cheek against hers as he thought about how Lily had discovered she could fit in his world that night. He just had to convince her he belonged in hers.

Shade fell asleep with Lily against him, breathing in her scent. However, sometime later, his predatory instincts woke him, alerting him to danger. He gently moved away from Lily, not wanting to wake her until he found out what the issue was. He didn't doubt the pervading sense of alarm sending out warning signals—his instincts were never wrong. He had seen too many soldiers who hadn't trusted their instincts end up in a casket, so he didn't hesitate when it came to his own.

He quickly pulled on his clothes and boots then went to the bedroom door, already smelling the deadly smoke on the other side. Going back to the bed, he started shaking Lily awake. There was no time to lose since there were no windows in his bedroom.

"Wake up, Lily!"

She jerked upright in the bed. "What's going on?"

"Get up. The basement's on fire!" He grabbed her from the bed.

Shade ran to the bathroom while she put her shoes on, coming back with a fire extinguisher he kept under the sink. There were sounds of screams from upstairs and running feet as the fire alarm went off.

"How are we going to get out of here?" She looked frantically around the room, seeing they were trapped inside.

"The brothers will get us out," Shade said grimly.

Going to his dresser, he pulled out a couple of shirts and then ran to the bathroom again to wet them. He came back with the wet clothes, tying one across her face then his own.

Just as he finished, they heard the sounds of a fire hose and an extinguisher from outside the bedroom door.

There was a loud bang on the door, and Shade opened it. Viper stood on the other side with just jeans and boots on.

"Let's go!" he yelled.

Shade took Lily's hand, pushing her behind Viper as he followed. It was pitch-dark except for the dying embers of the blackened walls. Viper was carrying a flashlight as the brothers put out the fire with water hoses, spraying the smoking couch. The steps to the upstairs were destroyed, the blackened door closed.

Viper led them out the side door as Lily started to cough, choking on the smoke.

Shade picked her up into his arms, carrying her back to the main part of the house and into the living room before removing the cloth he had tied around her face.

Beth handed Lily a glass of water while Shade stood near her as she quit coughing long enough to take a drink. Then the glass was falling out of her hands, crashing to the floor as she grabbed her head. The crowded room went quiet the instant Lily began screaming.

Shade dropped down to his knees in front of Lily, knowing it was going to be bad. He had witnessed the gradual, spiraling ferocity of her panic attacks and knew this was the worst he had seen. Seeing Beth's terror for her sister, his assumption that it was indeed the worst was confirmed.

"Razer, call Rachel and tell her to get here as fast as she can. Beth, call her doctor." Shade could do nothing except hold on to the woman he loved more than life itself as her tortured screams scored his soul with an agony he couldn't stop.

His friends stood back, giving him space as she fell to the floor. All he could do was hold her, repeating her name as soothingly as possible.

Beth returned, falling to her knees beside him, calling for Lily as she held her hand. It seemed like forever, each minute ticking by endlessly, until Rachel ran through the door Cash was holding open.

"Move out of her way," Cash ordered everyone.

Shade didn't make a move to release Lily whose voice had broken from her screams of terror until Rachel motioned for him to move over, and he complied shakily. She sat down on the floor by Lily's head, pulling it onto her lap. Her graceful hands went to Lily's temples, pressing her fingers along them while rubbing in soothing circles.

Then everyone went silent as Rachel's hushed voice spoke to Lily. "Lily, what do you need me to do?"

"Shade will come." He tensed when he heard her hoarse voice.

Lily was staring blindly up at the ceiling, lost in a world of terror where he couldn't reach her. He wanted to snatch her up and drive her to the hospital, but the doctor was on his way and he would get there quicker than taking her to the hospital.

"Where is he? Shade? Shade! Where are you, Shade? Was I bad? Is that why you're not here? Shade, please help me. I'm so scared.

"Beth, please, I won't be mad at you anymore. I'll be good, I promise. Please, Beth. I want to go home. Please. Beth!

"Shade! Help me!"

While Shade nearly broke down in front of The Last Riders, Beth cried, her shoulders shaking as she held Lily's hand.

"Razer? Razer! You promised me no one would hurt me. You broke your promise. Razer, please help!"

Razer fell down next to him. The tough brother had tears sliding down his cheeks.

"Shade! Shade!

"Pastor Dean! Please, help me!

"Vida? Sawyer? Where are you? Why did you leave me? Vida! Sawyer! Please, help me."

Shade didn't recognize the names and Beth shook her head, indicating she didn't, either.

Cash let the doctor in who had been treating Lily since she had almost died and again after she had the panic attack at the diner. They had told him then what Rachel had done for Lily.

The doctor crouched down, taking Lily's vital signs.

"Shade...Shade..." She kept repeating his name over and over.

Shade picked up the glass she had dropped and threw it across the room, feeling helpless to do anything for her. He had promised to protect her but he couldn't, not from her own demons.

All of a sudden, Lily seemed to calm down, like she was hearing something no one else could. Shade hoped that somehow Rachel had finally reached her.

"I'm here! I'm here! Help me!"

Rachel's face twisted as if she actually saw the horror Lily was seeing in her mind.

"Help me! I'm lost! I can't find my way back!"

Beth sobbed at Lily's tortured declaration.

The doctor sat on his knees, watching carefully, his hand on Lily's pulse.

"The flames won't let me pass, and I'm afraid to go the other way in the dark. I'm afraid I'll get lost!" Lily screamed in terror.

Rachel's brows furrowed.

"But you're on the other side of the flames!" Lily cried out.

The members in the room stared at each other then looked back at Rachel. Everyone came to the same conclusion: Lily actually believed Rachel was with her.

"How did you do that without getting burned?"

Rachel shook her head.

"I want to get out of here," Lily whimpered. "Can you help me?"

There was a pause.

"Then we're both lost. I want to go home." Lily started crying again.

After another pause, Lily screamed, "I can't go through there!"

Rachel's hands tensed at Lily's temples, her face appearing heartbroken.

"No, I can't!"

"Lily, your memories have broken free. There is no locking them away anymore. The only way to avoid it is to stay lost. You have to go through the flames," Rachel spoke aloud that time, barely whispering.

"They'll hurt me again!"

"No one is ever going to hurt you again. Didn't The Last Riders save you tonight? They're not going to let anyone hurt you again. You know that deep in your heart." Rachel raised a hand in a turning motion then dropped it back to Lily's forehead.

"I can't," Lily sobbed.

"Not alone, but together we can. I'm beside you. I won't let you go. Shade is here and so are Beth and Razer."

As Rachel spoke, Shade moved as close as he could to Lily, placing his hand on her shoulder. Next to her, Beth and Razer each held her hands tightly. "We're all here for you, Lily. Lead us home."

The doctor moved to the side, opening his bag and taking out a syringe before inserting it into her arm.

"It will relax her," he said quietly so Shade could understand what he was doing.

Lily cried softly, her legs scissoring on the carpet as if she was actually walking.

Suddenly, a tortured scream filled the silence of the room as she withered on the floor.

Shade was about to yell at the doctor to give her something to knock her out when Rachel spoke loudly over her screaming.

"The pain will lessen as you go through the flames. You'll leave the pain behind, Lily, because they can't hurt you anymore. Keep walking."

Lily began talking, revealing the monsters she had lived with while hiding them from the ones she loved. She had suffered alone with the memories of her childhood. Shade had heard most of it the night he had turned the lights out in the hospital. However, it wasn't any easier hearing it again; it was actually worse because, this time, others were listening. He almost made them leave then decided against it.

For Lily truly to heal, she had to have others around her who loved and under-stood the horror she had survived. Keeping it a secret was driving her to lose her mind. The Last Riders were a family, and it was going to take a family's love and compassion as strong as them to destroy her monsters.

CHAPTER FIFTY-SEVEN

Shade carried Lily upstairs with the doctor following on his heels. He opened the third door down, thinking Raci could sleep with Rider or Jewell. He wasn't letting Lily sleep in his basement room until the situation with the fire was sorted out.

He laid her on the made bed, brushing her hair back from her face.

"Go downstairs while I check her out," the doctor ordered, pissing Shade off, but then Beth came into the room.

"Go ahead, Shade. I'll stay with her in case she wakes," Beth urged, coming to stand by the bed.

He nodded. "I'll be right back. I want to shower and get some clean clothes on. I don't want her to smell the smoke on me when she wakes up. Find something to change her into and wash her off when the doctor leaves."

"I will," Beth said, sitting down on the side of the bed.

Shade left the bedroom, going to Razer's room where he showered quickly, looking through Razer's clothes for jeans and a T-shirt to borrow before getting dressed.

Then he went downstairs to see if Viper had discovered where the fire had started, finding The Last Riders still standing in the living room. Viper was holding Winter who was crying. Bliss was sitting on a chair with her head buried in her hands, also crying. Train was holding Jewell while Rider had his arm around Evie. The rest were shell-shocked.

"We're not going to let Lily know that we know she was abused when she was a kid." Shade placed his hand on the banister, wanting to rip it to pieces at the things she had talked about happening to her. "She was too young to defend herself then. Fuck, she was too young to even know she was *supposed* to defend herself. We're going to act as if nothing happened unless she wants to talk to us about it."

Viper looked at him. "Anything you need for her, you tell me, and it's yours. We're going to find out who fucked with her, and then we're going to fuck their lives up permanently."

The members all agreed.

331

Shade nodded. "I've already been looking into it. Beth doesn't remember much, and we can't find her adoption papers. That's why Lucky wanted the basement cleaned to see if we could find Beth's father's legal papers. Nothing's turned up so far."

"Lucky knows?" Razer asked.

"Only that it was important to Lily's safety that we find out about her adoption."

"You knew how bad it was before tonight, didn't you?" Razer asked.

"Yeah, I knew."

Razer ran a hand through his long hair. "I'd heard some of it a couple of times when the lights went out or she had a panic attack, but I didn't think it was to that extent." Razer turned from the group, giving them his back as he raised a hand to his face. "I promised to protect her...but I was too late, wasn't I?" he said in a choked voice.

"We're here now, Razer. We all are. She'll never have to go through that shit again," Shade vowed.

"That's for fucking sure," Train muttered fiercely.

The doctor came down the steps, carrying his bag.

"She's sleeping comfortably, for now. When she wakes up..." He shrugged.

"Thanks."

"If she needs—"

"I'll call," Shade said, shaking his hand.

After the doctor left, Shade turned back to the brothers and women. "Let's get the basement cleaned and cleared out after Knox gets here. Cash, Viper, let's find out what started that fire."

Shade followed the brothers toward the kitchen, looking up the stairs where he saw Beth standing with clothes in her arms. She had heard them talking.

She nodded to him as he passed underneath, saying without words her gratitude that she wasn't alone in her battle to save Lily. The Last Riders would stand with them to the last man and woman. Beth knew that, and soon, Lily would, too.

80 03

Shade opened the back door to Knox's car. Then He reached in, taking several pizza boxes before he closed the door after Knox reached in to grab the rest.

"It's going to be a mess to get that smoke odor out of there," Knox griped as they went up the steps.

"We're going to rip out and replace anything that was damaged. The carpet is destroyed from the water, so that was the first to go, and the brothers have already started ripping out the walls that were burned," Shade replied as they went in the door. "With all of us working together, it shouldn't take long to make the repairs."

Shade opened the kitchen door, moving to the side to let Knox enter as they both carried pizza boxes inside. Shade glanced at Lily before setting the pizzas on the counter, quickly going to her side.

She had slept most of the morning away, missing the action of the men tearing up the damage from the destroyed basement.

"Hungry?"

"I could eat," Lily admitted, getting up from the table while avoiding his eyes.

Getting in line, she took a slice of pizza before resuming her seat. Shade filled his plate then sat down next to her.

"Evie said someone deliberately set the fire," Lily told him.

"Yes. Knox came out this morning and took the evidence he needed. Whoever it was slipped into the party last night with a hanger-on. We have a description. It's only a matter of time before we find her."

"Her?" Lily repeated, shocked.

"Yes," Shade answered.

"Why?"

"We think it was another attempt on your life," Shade told her.

Knox sat down at the table as she asked, "Why does someone want me dead? I don't understand." Lily looked back and forth between the two men.

"We don't know yet but when we find who started the fire, we will," Knox assured her.

Everyone finished eating then Viper organized them all into one team as a cleanup crew and another to put up new drywall.

Lily got up to go downstairs.

"No. You stay up here and start dinner for everyone," Viper ordered as he went down into the basement with the men following behind him.

Shade hung back once the other members had left. "You need anything?"

"No. Shade, maybe it would be better if I left. I don't want to endanger anyone."

"You're not going anywhere," he said, pulling her to him. "It's because you were here with all the security we have that it wasn't much worse. We slipped up because we didn't think someone was brave enough to actually make a move on you in the house. We won't make that mistake twice."

"Beth will be back soon. Go shopping; get out of the house for a while. Razer will go with you two," he suggested.

"That sounds good. I'm ready to get out for a while."

Shade touched his mouth to hers briefly before going downstairs. She needed to get out of the clubhouse and have a good time. He texted Beth as soon as he was down the steps.

"Rider, hand me a couple of those trash bags."

"If you're going to put the pieces of drywall in them, you'll need the heavier ones," Rider said, handing him two bags.

"No, I'm using these to throw away Lily's clothes. Tell Razer I need to see him before he leaves."

There was going to be something good to come out of the fire after all.

„‛ ‘’

Shade was standing in his office at the factory when Beth's SUV pulled in and parked. He went outside as Razer was opening the trunk, and they all stared at the small mountain of bags.

"I think we may have overdone it a bit," Beth said jokingly, turning to Lily.

"You think?" Lily laughed. "I'm already planning on taking most of it back."

"Don't you dare," Beth reprimanded her.

"She won't," Shade spoke up from behind them, reaching inside the vehicle to take several of the bags.

Razer followed suit, pulling out a large number for himself. Lily and Beth split up the remaining packages, and then they all carried them up the steps to the house and into the room Shade had put Lily in. They set the bags on the floor in front of the bed, and Shade smiled as Lily looked down at the bags as if she didn't know how they had gotten there.

"I'll see you at church in the morning." Lily hugged and kissed her sister goodbye.

Razer gave her a tight hug. "Goodnight, lil' sis."

"Night, Razer."

The door closed behind them.

"I'm not staying in the basement anymore?"

"No. If someone tries to hurt you again, they'll have to get past every brother in the house with you up here," Shade replied grimly.

"I see." She took a deep breath. "Beth told me at dinner that you paid for all this. I'll pay you back."

"No, you won't, and you won't take anything back. Quit worrying and go get your shower."

Lily went to the bathroom, taking a gown, while Shade undressed then lay down on the bed, waiting for her. He was tired, but he didn't want to go to sleep until Lily was in bed with him.

When she finished, she climbed in bed beside him, pulling the covers up as she gave him a smile.

"What was that for?"

Confusion marred her brow. "What?"

Shade turned off the bedside lamp, checking first to make sure the bathroom light was on with the door left half-open. "That smile you just gave me."

"I don't know. I was just happy you were here. I thought you might be sleeping in your room."

Shade rose on his side, his serious face cast in the shadows of the bedroom. "Lily, the only bed you'll be in is the one I'm sleeping in." His finger traced down the fragile line of her cheekbone.

He bent down, kissing her, and when Lily parted her lips his tongue entered her mouth, searching its depths. Her tongue timidly touched his, and he sucked it into his mouth, sliding his own against hers, tempting her to explore the warmth of his mouth.

When her arms slipped around his shoulders, Shade raised his head, breaking off the kiss.

"When I kiss you, it's like touching perfection." Shade placed soft kisses on her neck.

Lily's arms dropped to her side. "I'm not perfect," she replied, turning her face away.

"You're perfect for me," Shade corrected her.

"Shade..." Lily began hesitantly.

"Not tonight, Lily. Tonight, I want to hold you in my arms, knowing that you're taking one breath after another. That, when I wake in the morning, your beautiful face will be on the pillow next to mine, and tomorrow night, when I go to bed, you'll be by my side again. Day after day, night after night." Shade's vow expressed how seriously he had taken almost losing her.

Lily's lips smiled against his throat. "What about when I snore?"

"Angels don't snore."

CHAPTER FIFTY-EIGHT

"What's going on?" Shade asked, coming up behind Lily. He had seen first Beth then Winter go downstairs, followed by Razer and Viper.

He was glad she was standing and talking with the women in the kitchen. He had been worried about her when she had acted strange as Lucky had come into the diner after church, wanting to leave in a rush. She had worked on her course work in the bedroom upstairs while he had helped the men in the basement. By dinner time, she was fine, his concern for her leaving when the women had started talking about their 'dream weddings.' The other brothers had tuned out, but he had listened carefully to Lily's idea of a dream wedding.

"There was a wedding in December and it was snowing just a little bit. They got married in the backyard of a tiny church. It was beautiful," Lily had breathed with dreams in her violet eyes for once.

"What kind of dress?" Evie had asked.

"My mother's. I have it packed away. It's stunning with long sleeves made of lace, but they're off the shoulder, and it has a long, lace veil."

Afterward, Lily and Beth had left to go see Beth and Razer's house for the first time. They were finally back, and everyone was standing around, talking.

"She told Beth about your shower and then Beth told Winter. Winter's been wanting to redo the bathroom in Viper's room. Want to bet he's going to be shelling out some cold hard cash?" Evie answered.

Shade looked down at her, and Lily gave him a mischievous smile which had his dick getting hard.

"You're not causing trouble, are you?" His arm went around her shoulder.

"Can I help it if that shower is a work of art?" Lily said jokingly.

Winter and Beth came back upstairs with determined expressions on their faces. Viper and Razer, on the other hand, sent accusing looks toward Lily who unsuccessfully tried to hide her laughter.

"I can't blame them. That shower has given me many pleasurable moments," Jewell joked.

Shade's instincts told him his night was headed for the shitter. Maybe it wasn't such a great idea for Lily to become friendlier with the women.

"Me, too. That rainfall showerhead is gold-plated," Evie agreed. "Shade designed it himself when he moved to the basement after Beth moved into the club."

"I love the music that plays to the beat of the water," Dawn shuddered.

Lily stiffened at the second comment, and by Dawn's, she had pulled away from him; all her amusement had died. Yep, he was right. The shitter.

"It's getting late. If I'm going to work tomorrow, I need to get some sleep," Lily excused herself without looking at him. "Night, everyone."

The members mumbled their goodnights to her as she left.

Shade glared at the women. "Thanks."

Jewell shrugged. "Are you honestly going to blame us? We weren't alone in that shower," she reminded him.

Shade ran his hand over his head. "Next time, think before you open your mouth with comments like that. She might know I've fucked you all, but she doesn't need to hear the details about it, either," he snapped.

"You haven't fucked me," Evie said, opening a beer.

Shade folded his arms over his chest, glaring at her.

"Me, either," Beth laughed.

Shade frowned in her direction.

"Me, either," Winter spoke up, biting into a brownie.

"Anyone else have something to say?" Shade asked snidely.

"No, I think you fucked everyone else," Raci giggled.

Shade jerked his head at Viper. "You're not going to help a brother being ganged up on by the women?"

Viper took the brownie away from Winter, sitting down at the table next to her. "Nope. I have problems of my own to deal with, unless you want to pay for the new shower Winter is going to make me put in. You do that, then I'll have your back."

Shade looked at Razer who raised his own hands in the air. "I'm going to have to keep Beth from ripping out a perfectly good shower which my woman was happy with before she saw yours, so no. Sorry. I can't open my mouth, anyway." He placed an arm around Beth, giving her a wink before turning back to him. "I've fucked more women here than you have."

Shade flipped the men off as he left the kitchen to go upstairs.

Lily was hanging her new clothes in the closet when Shade walked into the bedroom. "What are you doing?"

"Hanging up my new clothes," Lily replied, stepping back from the closet and closing the door.

"Why didn't you hang up the rest?" Shade asked, eyeing the numerous bags still on the floor.

"Because I'm not keeping them." Lily turned away from him, going to the dresser to brush her hair.

"Why not?" Shade asked, confused.

"Because I can't afford them."

"I paid for them."

"Exactly. *You* paid for them; I didn't."

Shade's mouth tightened. "If you're angry, that's fine, but you're keeping the clothes."

"No. I. Am. Not! I'm taking them back." Lily went to the chair, picking up the nightgown and robe before going to the bathroom.

Shade wanted to go back downstairs and yell at the women, but he was afraid they would kick his ass.

"Fuck this." Shade emptied all the bags on the bed, hanging up all the clothes in the closet and putting away the rest in the drawers Raci had emptied out for her.

He was placing the shoes in the closet when he saw the price tags on them. He almost thought about letting her take those back until he opened the boxes then thought, *She definitely needs to keep these.* Giving a wicked smile, he finished stacking the boxes in the closet before closing the door.

He went to the bedroom next door where Raci was about to climb onto the bed with Rider when he walked in.

"I need to keep these in your closet for a while." Rider and Raci both looked at his arm full of shoes.

"Help yourself." Rider motioned toward the closet while reaching for Raci.

Shade dumped the shoes in the closet then turned to leave.

"Just a minute." Raci broke away from Rider to go to the closet. Shade slammed the door shut, standing in front of it.

"No," Shade said firmly, remembering he had been drunk off his ass when he had voted years before to let women become members. He had learned then to never make a decision whenever he had more whiskey in him than common sense. Tonight, the women were proving to him it had been a mistake.

"But…" Raci protested, looking longingly at the closet.

"If she goes near that closet, spank her," Shade ordered Rider who grinned back.

"I'll handle it," he promised, staring greedily at Raci's naked tits.

Shade sighed. All Raci would have to do was shake her tits at Rider, and he would open the closet door for her.

"I'll buy you a pair if you leave those alone. You can't wear them, anyway; I have the match in my room."

"I just want to try them on," Raci said. "But if you buy me two pairs, I won't touch them. Plus, I won't tell Lily where you hid them."

Shade gritted his teeth.

"Fine," he agreed, striding back to his room. He had to get out of there before he spanked Raci himself.

Back in the room, he had to sit down at the desk to calm himself down, wondering when he and the brothers had lost control of the club to the women.

He was still sitting at the desk, going through his email, when Lily came out of the bathroom. He pretended to ignore her as she walked across the floor and noticed the empty store bags sitting on the chair. When she lifted one of them, the tags fell to the floor. She then stormed angrily to the closet, opening the door to see all the new clothes hanging up. The shoe boxes were even neatly stacked on the floor.

"I can't believe you did this! I told you I was taking the clothes back." Lily stood with her hands on her hips.

"And I told you that you weren't," Shade replied coldly.

She bent down, opening one of the boxes and staring in shock at what he had done. Going down on her knees, she opened each of the boxes, finding each one contained only a single shoe.

She rose to her feet, holding one tennis shoe in her hand. "Where are the other shoes?"

"I've put them away. When you want to wear a particular pair, I'll get you the match."

"I'm not keeping the shoes."

"Doesn't look like you have much choice, does it?" he said, satisfied that he had outmaneuvered her.

"You think you have it all figured out? Fine, I'll keep them and the clothes, too. In fact, I'll share them with all the women in the house. They all share clothes. They'll love the shoes."

Shade laughed, refusing to feel bad for what he was about to say.

"They wouldn't be seen dead in those clothes."

Unless the clothes showed off ass, tits, or both, the women wouldn't wear them.

"That's fine, then." Lily did an about-face. "I'll give you the money for everything. I don't want to share anything with them, either. Not their clothes, not their shampoo, and certainly not you." With that, she threw a tennis shoe at him.

Shade couldn't believe she had actually thrown it until it almost smacked him in the face. He had barely managed to dodge it.

Lily crossed her arms over her chest, obviously proud of herself.

"Do you mind getting me the match?" Lily unwisely mocked him. His little pacifist had snapped.

Shade got up from the chair, his face impassive. "That robe belongs to Bliss. She didn't need it because she doesn't wear it."

Lily shrieked in anger, jerking the robe off before she threw it at him. He grabbed it, tossing it to the chair.

"The nightgown belongs to Raci. She sleeps in the nude, so she lent it to you."

Lily wasn't so far gone that she was about to tear the gown off. Instead, she went back to the closet, getting one of the new pajama sets.

She was jerking it off the hanger as he came up behind her so when she turned back around, she ran into his chest.

"I thought you didn't want them?" he mocked her.

"I don't, jerk-face, but I have to wear something."

"I don't see why." His hands went to her hips, clenching the material of the gown in his hands, bunching it until it came up to her calves.

Lily's eyes snapped violet fire at him. Losing her temper, she used one of her favorite moves, raising her knee.

Not fucking going to happen. Shade wasn't about to let her bust his balls twice in his lifetime; he didn't care how cute she looked mad.

"Oh, no, you don't." Shade moved his thigh, blocking her knee and throwing her off-balance so her body fell against his.

Lily was a creature of habit, so Shade already knew the move she was going to make next.

Determinedly, she reached out with her hand to grab his nuts. The feisty woman had lost her fucking mind. If she had her way, he would never be able to give her all those kids she wanted in the future. He was going to have to talk to Rachel to see if she could fix Lily's psychological need to rip his dick off when she became angry.

"Nuh-uh, you little wildcat." He used his leg to swipe her foot out from under her, making her begin to fall to the floor. However, he twisted so he fell first, and she landed on top of him.

"You're a mean, mean person. I don't even know why I like you." Lily beat on his chest with her fists. "The only women you haven't been with in Treepoint are the ones who are either happily married or dead."

He laughed up at her, rolling her onto her back then wedging himself between her thighs as he took her wrists in one of his, locking them above her head and holding her in place beneath him.

"You don't hate me; you're jealous," he said smugly.

"I'm not jealous of you. You're a...a—"

"Exactly what am I?" Shade look down at her in amusement at the extent she was letting her jealousy show.

"A man-whore," Lily spat angrily. "I do not think you being promiscuous is funny. I don't care who you have sex with as long as you leave me alone."

"But you're the one I'm the most interested in, Lily. I wouldn't want to leave you out in the cold," he murmured seductively.

"Leave me in the cold! Better yet, why don't you forget all about me?"

"Forget about you? That's not going to happen, especially since I've thought of nothing but fucking you since the moment I saw you. Don't you get tired of sitting on that moral throne of yours? Don't you want to come out and play?"

Lily stiffened underneath him when he slid a hand under her nightgown, moving determinedly toward her panties. Her eyes widened, and Shade could tell she expected him to stop. *Not fucking likely.* She was the one who had taken the argument to a physical level. If she wanted to get physical with him, he was going to show her the right way to do it. One which didn't involve pain—at least, not his.

His hands slid under the wispy pink underwear she was wearing, his finger sliding through the dry skin of her pussy.

Lily arched against his palm. She wasn't aroused yet, but he was going to fix that problem.

"I'm going to play. Feel free to join in anytime." He lowered his voice to a more intimate level.

She opened her mouth, but he closed his over hers before she could gather her stunned thoughts. His tongue thrust into her mouth as his fingers began playing with her clit, stroking the little nub with an experienced touch which had been perfected over many years. A rush of wetness moistened his finger, enabling him to glide slickly against her sensitized flesh.

She tried to wiggle away from him but Shade kept his fingers firmly on her clit, stroking harder. Lily quit moving, her hands gripping his shoulders as he continued to rub her clit. She wiggled her hips timidly, her eyes going from angry to curious, and then he felt another rush of moisture against his fingers.

Shade's mouth left hers, going to her neck and sucking a tiny amount of the sensitive flesh into his mouth as Lily's hips rose off the floor, grinding her pussy against his palm.

His finger slid wetly along her flesh as she began twisting beneath him. He sucked harder on her neck then pressed between the folds of her clit.

Lily shuddered, her thighs clenching his hand tightly against her pussy as she stiffened then trembled underneath him. When she lay still, Shade raised his head from her throat, removing his hand from between her clenched thighs. He brought his fingers to his mouth and sucked the nectar of her from them, staring down into her embarrassed face.

Lily pushed him off her, going toward the bathroom.

"Lily, *now* I've had every pussy in town that's not happily married or dead."

Lily slammed the door on his mocking words.

Shade rolled onto his back, his arm covering his eyes. *That went well*, he thought sarcastically to himself. It was not how he had imagined her first orgasm with him.

Sighing, he rose to his feet then turned back the covers and lay down. Nothing was ever easy with Lily. She wanted to be treated like a child, but Shade wasn't going to go along with that shit. She was a grown woman and that was how he was going to treat her. If any other woman had thrown a shoe at him, she would have been dealt a punishment which would have left her crying. She certainly wouldn't have been allowed to climax a few minutes later.

To Lily, however, that *was* a punishment. He had shown her she was a woman with a woman's needs. And Shade would bet the property the houses were sitting on that she wasn't happy with the discovery.

He turned the bedside light out, relaxing against the mattress as he waited for the next storm to hit.

The bathroom door opened, and Lily walked barefoot to stand by his side of the bed.

"I want you to leave. I'm not sleeping with you anymore. There's nothing wrong with your bedroom, so go sleep down there."

"Lily, get in the bed and go to sleep. You're mad because you lost our first fight, but it's over." Hell would freeze over before he let her throw him out of her bed.

She tugged at his arm. "I am *not* sleeping with you."

"That did it, Lily. You're going to learn your next lesson in how to behave with me." Shade rolled to his side, almost gaping at her expectant look that he would give in to her demand. *My woman is too used to getting her own way.*

He sat up on the side of the bed and before she could get away, he flipped her over his knees. Lily screamed in surprise, but he knew damn well she wasn't frightened when she threw him an angry look over her shoulder.

His hand smacked down on her butt, her thin gown and underwear no protection against the pain of the swat.

"Don't you dare!"

Shade smacked her bottom again. He didn't like being dared not to do anything, especially if it showed her who had the dick in their relationship, despite her best attempts to rip it off.

Another and another rained down on what he hoped was her burning bottom.

"Stop it!" she yelled back at him.

Another hard smack.

"Blueberries!"

"Don't you dare use your safe word to get out of a punishment," Shade snapped.

He was hurting her pride more than her ass; he wasn't spanking her hard enough to hurt a fly. Bliss would have laughed in his face if he had spanked her with the swats he was giving Lily. Her ass might be pink when he was finished, but it wouldn't be the bright red Bliss had often left his room happily satisfied with.

After another hard smack, she quit struggling and lay quietly across his lap.

Thwack.

"I'm sorry!" Lily wailed.

He stopped the spanking immediately then flipped her up and set her down hard on her stinging bottom on his lap.

He grasped her face, making her look up at him. "Don't think you can order me out of your bed when you get mad at me." Shade's voice was coldly furious.

"Okay!" Lily yelled.

Lily found herself flipped back over his thighs, receiving two more punishing smacks.

"I'm sorry." That time, her voice was tearfully remorseful.

He again sat her upright on her stinging bottom, keeping his expression cold and remote.

"Apologize to me correctly."

Lily was confused. "I'm sorry?"

"I'm sorry, *Sir.*"

Lily's face turned mutinous. Shade was more than willing to spoil Lily rotten within reason and give in to her when it was important, but his woman would give him respect.

He started to flip her over his lap again, and Lily hastily changed her attitude. "I'm sorry, Sir."

"I give you a lot of leeway, Lily—more than I have ever given any woman—but I'm also not going to let you twist me around your finger like you did Charles."

Lily opened her mouth.

"I advise you to go to bed before you say something else which makes me angry. You'll learn what I'll allow you to do and what I won't. It'll just take a little time."

Shade released her, and Lily crawled into the bed without looking at him. He ignored the expression of anger she tried unsuccessfully to hide. At least she had made the attempt, and he could appreciate that.

Shade lay back down, pulling the covers over both of them.

He felt the bed shake from the force she was punching the pillow. She had a habit of doing that when she was angry at him. It took her several minutes to lie still, and then he realized she had buried her face in the same pillow she had taken out her frustration with him on and was sniffling.

"Are you crying?" Shade asked, rolling closer. He rubbed the flesh of her ass which he could have sworn wouldn't be hurting, his thoughts turning to those of guilt.

"No."

"All right, why *aren't* you crying?"

Lily shrugged in the darkness.

His loud sigh of frustration filled the room. "Lily…"

"It was the first time I…" She wasn't bringing herself to finish her sentence, and only one thing shut Lily up—talking about sex.

He couldn't help laughing, relieved he hadn't spanked her too hard.

Insulted, she started to climb out of bed but his arm circled her waist, preventing her from getting up.

"Go to sleep, Lily. I promise it won't be the last." For the spanking or the orgasm, but he kept that thought to himself.

CHAPTER FIFTY-NINE

Orders were coming in at so fast a rate many of the members were working over-time, trying to get them out. Lily didn't want to take off that Wednesday to work at the church store, but Shade told her to go. He drove her into town, telling her to call when she was finished and he would pick her up.

"Do not leave, even to go to the diner to pick up a drink." He stared at her seriously, not wanting to frighten her; however, he wanted her to understand her safety was at risk.

"I won't," Lily promised, going inside.

As soon as the door closed behind her, he left to go back to the factory. He did the paperwork then pitched in to fill the orders backing up. All the members were there working; plus, the staff was working overtime.

Shade took a quick break to call Lucky, asking if he would bring Lily home for him. When he agreed, Shade went back to work so he would be able to spend some time with Lily that night. The last two, she had already been asleep before he had finished work.

He was taping a box closed when his cell phone vibrated in his pocket, showing an alarm was going off. He dropped the tape and went to his office, shutting the door. Going to his computer, he pulled up the camera feed.

His breath stopped when he saw Lily enter her house alone.

His cell phone rang then.

"You seeing what I'm seeing?" Knox asked.

"If you mean do I see my woman doing what I told her not to, then yes, I'm watching."

"What do you want me to do?" Knox asked.

Shade watched as Lily went through the house, his heart in his throat. He was about to tell Knox to go get her out when Lily went to the door and left.

"She's out. I'll deal with her when she gets home," Shade said grimly.

"She's yours to deal with, brother." Shade heard his muttered "Thank God" before he disconnected the call.

His lips tightened as he punched a button on his cell phone while walking out of the factory toward his bike.

"What the fuck!" Shade yelled when Lucky answered.

"What's up your ass?" Lucky snarled back.

"I thought you were smarter than to let Lily go into her house alone! I'm going to smash that pretty face of yours when I see you—" Shade broke off when he saw a car pull into the parking lot he recognized.

"Later." Shade hung up on a cussing Lucky, not giving a flying fuck. He would deal with him later, after he dealt with Lily.

He strode angrily toward Rachel's car, opening the door as soon as the vehicle stopped, taking the bag out of Lily's hand.

"Thanks, Rachel," Shade said.

Before the stunned woman could say anything, Shade shut the car door, ushering Lily up the steps to the house and straight to the bedroom they were sharing, shutting and locking the door behind them.

"What's the matter with you?" Lily asked.

"Didn't Dean tell you I asked him to give you a ride home?"

"Yes, but—"

"But what? Someone almost killed you the other day! I asked Dean to bring you home because I knew he would be able to handle anything that could happen. If I had wanted you to ride with Rachel, I would have called Rachel.

"Not only did you not come straight here, you went by your house and Rachel sat in the car. Someone could have been waiting and killed you inside the house, and Rachel wouldn't even have known."

"I didn't think," Lily confessed.

"You sure as fuck didn't. What was so important? Beth and Razer could have picked it up for you."

"I wanted to get a few of my things," Lily told him.

"I asked you days ago if there was anything you wanted. What was it?"

"Shampoo."

"Shampoo?! You got to be fucking kidding me!" His raised voice was interrupted by a knock on the door.

"What?" Shade snapped, opening the door to see Beth's white face.

"Is there a problem? Maybe I—" Beth was cut off.

"No, Beth, I don't need your help. Lily and I are having a discussion. You can see her at dinner."

"But—" Beth began to argue.

Shade opened the door wider to take a step out into the hall.

"Razer!" he shouted. The two sisters were determined to make him lose his cool, and they were succeeding.

Shade wasn't pacified when he heard footsteps running up the steps and saw Razer coming down the hallway. He stepped back into the bedroom.

"What's going on?" Razer asked, seeing his wife's pale face and Lily standing in the middle of the bedroom.

"Your wife is interrupting a discussion I'm having with Lily. Out of respect, I'm letting you handle your woman, but she needs to understand that, when Lily and I are arguing, she needs to back the fuck off."

"Razer, he was yelling at her," Beth defended herself.

"I'm not that crazy-as-fuck father of yours. I am not going to hurt her, but I *am* going to spank her because she took an unnecessary risk."

Beth gasped. "Are you listening to him, Razer? He is *not* going to spank my sister. She's a grown woman."

"Yes, she is, and it's time you realized that. Razer and I are brothers, and you and Lily are going to be sharing this house and our lives together for a long time, so we need to set some boundaries. One is that, when our door is closed and we're arguing, you mind your own business. She can cry on your shoulder later, but you do not interrupt me again. I keep my nose out of your shit; you need to keep your nose out of mine."

Razer put his arm around Beth. "He's right, Beth. Deep down, you know he's right. I would be pissed as hell if Lily or Shade came knocking at our door when I was giving you hell."

Beth looked up at Razer.

"It was my fault," Lily admitted. "I asked Rachel to drive me home after Shade had already asked Pastor Dean. Then I stopped at our house."

"Lily, it's not safe there for you." Beth's worried face gazed back at her from the doorway.

"I wasn't thinking about that. I wanted my shampoo."

"Your shampoo?"

At Beth's dumbfounded expression, Lily explained. "I didn't want my hair to smell like Jewell's, Bliss's or Evie's. I wanted it to smell like mine."

Beth's eyes flew angrily to Shade, her mouth snapping open.

"We're leaving," Razer said in amusement. "I'll handle her. Your door is off-limits when you're pissed. Got it. Later, brother." He turned a red-faced Beth away from the door, closing it behind them.

"I will never understand you, will I?" Shade said, crossing his arms over his chest.

"How would you like it if I doused you in Charles's cologne? If every time you breathed in, you smelled like him?"

Shade winced at her words as she drove her point home.

She took a step forward, sliding her arms around his waist, laying her head on his chest. "I'm sorry. I didn't think. I'll be more careful in the future."

Shade's arms tightened, drawing her nearer. "Next time, will you at least call me and tell me there's been a change in plans? I almost had a heart attack when the silent alarm went off, and I saw you on the camera."

"I will. I'm sorry, Shade." Lily looked up at him, smiling in apology.

"Let's go eat dinner. You can sit there and gloat while Beth throws me dirty looks," he said in resignation.

Fuck, he was going to have to call Lucky back and apologize, too.

He shut the bedroom door behind them, seeing her happy expression. She thought she had manipulated him into forgiving her, and he begrudgingly admitted to himself that she had. It was a sad day when he found himself wrapped around a woman's finger, and he hadn't even fucked her yet. He was going to be in deep shit when she learned she could manipulate him with sex.

"Fuck," he muttered as they went down the steps.

"Did you say something?" Lily asked, looking back over her shoulder with a soft smile.

"I think I'm having crow for dinner."

ᔕ ᔓ

Shade watched Lily, Beth, and Winter do the dishes as he played cards with Razer and Cash at the kitchen table. Lily blushed when she caught his gaze on her.

Before dinner, they had been playing around, and she had run up the stairs ahead of him. He had then caught her watching Raci and Train fucking in the room across from theirs. He had seen nothing except embarrassment and curiosity at her catching sight of Train and Raci. For a brief second, he had thought he might even have seen a brief flash of longing, but he couldn't be sure. However, she hadn't spiraled into the panic attack the sight once would have once caused.

It was almost Thanksgiving, and the woman had made huge strides since Halloween. He hadn't touched her intimately since the night he had spanked her;

instead, he had used every opportunity possible to fuel her desire without giving her the pleasure he expertly judged she wanted to experience again.

Viper walked into the room and threw Winter over his shoulder, leaving with her yelling at him to put her down. Shade's grin widened when Lily winced in sympathy at the sound of the loud whack from the other side of the door.

"Brother, you've got it bad," Razer muttered, throwing a bill into the pile of cash in the middle of the table.

Shade raised a brow, throwing his own bill in.

"You're one to talk. How's the new bathroom look?" Shade said snidely.

Lily took out a bucket of champagne on ice with a ribbon tied around the bottle. Turning, she handed it to Beth. "I wish you many years of happiness, sister."

Razer got up from the table, throwing down the cards he had been dealt. "Ready? I'm done with these card sharks. If I don't leave now, Cash will be riding my bike tomorrow."

He walked to Lily, pulling her close for a hug. "Thanks for the booze, lil' sis. Thanks for the green, Shade. We'll see you guys Sunday." He grabbed a squealing Beth into his arms, and Lily rushed to open the side kitchen door for them.

"You're joking about the green, right?"

Razer winked at Lily on his way out the door.

Lily shut the door behind them then threw the dishcloth at Shade.

He caught it in midair. "What did I do now? Did I say anything about you giving booze to your sister?" Before she could say anything, he added, "I know, I know. It's legal."

She had seen him come back to the clubhouse with weed earlier to give to the brothers. *It is Friday*, Shade thought as he shrugged to himself. She should be happy that was all he had planned for the night. His plans went up in smoke as fast as the weed would when he saw her expression, though.

Lily went toward the living room, taking a few steps forward before coming to a stop. They had spent a long time in the kitchen after dinner, so the party was in full swing.

"I don't think that's legal," Shade said from behind her as they watched Jewell giving Rider a blowjob while Train was sitting behind her, smacking her on her bare bottom.

As Lily walked to the steps, Shade admired that she didn't run screaming toward them, but then his good humor vanished at seeing the two blondes heading toward him with seductive smiles pasted on their lips.

The two were not only the biggest sluts in Treepoint, but were also the nosiest. They were a fountain of information that Lucky needed, so he had made the request for the twins to be allowed back in. He hadn't been happy about it when Viper had told him, and he was even less now with them heading his way.

"We've been looking for you. Jewell said the kitchen was off-limits and your room. What's up? We've missed you, Shade. Hook us up with a room and give that flogger of yours a workout. The last marks you put on us are gone; we need a refresher."

Shade's face went cold at their damning words.

"You can have the third bedroom on the left; no one is using it anymore." Lily spun on her feet, heading back toward the kitchen, but Shade caught her within a few steps, lifting her into his arms and carrying her struggling body back to the steps.

"Shade?" Stacy whined.

"Cash!" Shade snapped.

"I'll take care of it." Cash ushered the women away from Shade, giving him room to pack Lily up the stairs.

Lily tried to get away as soon as they were off the steps. When he refused to let her go, she froze in his arms. He closed the door behind them, he set her down on her feet, and Lily hurriedly moved away from him.

"Lily."

Lily held her hand up as she sat down calmly on the bottom of the bed, facing him. Shade's blood went as cold as the ice dripping from her voice.

"What do you want from me, Shade?" she asked, startling him with her bluntness when she usually wanted to avoid any type of discussion about their relationship. "Are you wanting a platonic friendship, friends who have sex, or were you wanting me to fall in love with you? Exactly what do you want?"

"I told you. I want *you*," Shade answered truthfully.

Lily nodded.

He watched as she stood up and went to the dresser, pulling out her ponytail holder then brushing her hair while staring at herself in the mirror.

"You don't even know who you want." Lily reached out and briefly touched the mirror she was staring into. Her lips twisted ironically. "You want me because you think I'll be the perfect submissive for you. That weak-minded Lily can be guided and manipulated into being exactly what you want."

She strode angrily across the room to stand in front of him, sinking to her knees. In perfect posture, she knelt with her back straight, her head lowered, her hair falling against her face. She laid her hands palm-up on her lap.

The perfect submissive pose. Shade angrily wondered who she had learned it from.

"I could be everything you ever dreamed of having in a woman." Lily's impassive voice didn't show an ounce of emotion. "You and those women downstairs play games for a few nights a month, but I have dreams, and they don't include being your little pet," she snarled at him, getting to her feet.

No, Lily wasn't anyone's pet.

"I hope you enjoyed that because I will never"—she poked her finger into his chest—"*ever* do that again, you big jerk." With that, Lily started to gather her pajamas.

"Those blonde Barbies are more plastic than the dolls," Shade commented drily before staring, stupefied, as she stomped across the floor to the bathroom.

"What are you doing?" she snapped when she saw the direction his eyes were focusing on.

Shade stood with his arms across his chest, watching her as she yelled at him. "Watching your ass jiggle."

"My ass? That's all you can say?" Lily's mouth opened and closed. "If I said what I really wanted to, I would have to pray for forgiveness every night for a week." Lily went into the bathroom, slamming the door closed.

Shade gave a wicked grin as he stared at the closed door. Then he took off his clothes, throwing them on the chair. He went to the bathroom door, opening it and going inside. His woman needed a refresher course in respect as well as a little something to take the edge off her anger. He had warned her about yelling at him, hadn't he?

She was rinsing off when he opened the shower door and stepped inside.

"What are you doing? I'm naked." She looked wildly around the shower for an escape, but Shade stood in front of the door, blocking the only exit.

Shade's voice turned seductive. "I can see that."

Lily covered her breasts with her hands, her eyes traveling down his body. Shade was a confidant man; he had been with a lot of women. However, he felt a moment's worry when she saw all of his tats at one time. His whole body was covered except his dick, which was hard enough that a touch would easily make him come. He released a silent sigh of relief when he didn't see revulsion on her face.

Shade grinned when he saw what she was staring at. "Ignore it. Come here."

"Ignore that thing. You're joking, right? Get out! Didn't you understand a thing I just said to you?" Lily kept moving her hands back and forth, trying to cover her tits and then her pussy.

He wasn't the least modest. He loved fucking in the shower, and when he was done with her, she would have a new appreciation for the one which was being installed in his house.

Reaching to the side, he picked up the body wash and began washing his body.

"You're seriously not getting out?" Lily screeched.

"No. You take forever in the shower."

"Fine, you can have the shower." Lily tried to pass him, but he refused to move. "Move your hands."

Lily's hands were trembling against her wet flesh.

Shade deepened his voice. "Eyes to me, Lily. Move your hands."

She lowered her hands to her side.

Shade crowded her closer to the shower wall, his chest brushing the pointed tips of her breasts. He lowered his mouth to one, gently licking the drops of water away from her nipple. The tip tautened, becoming a hard little nub, and Shade sucked the nipple into his mouth, lifting her breast with his hand and squeezing the plump flesh.

She turned her head to the side, and Shade lifted his. "Look at me while I suck your breast. I don't want you to take your eyes off me."

Lily nodded in response.

Shade brought his mouth back to her breast, and Lily moaned as he teased the tip with his teeth.

"You wanted to know what I want. I want these breasts to suck." Shade lifted his head from her breasts and then went to his knees, his face going between her thighs, using his hand to widen her stance. "I want this pussy." His tongue went to the cleft, sliding between the folds and searching the moist warmth of her silky flesh.

Lily eyes fluttered closed. He bit down on her clit briefly before releasing the tortured flesh.

"I told you not to take your eyes off me." He licked at the flesh, soothing the sting and building her desire to a fever pitch. He wanted to stroke his cock while he licked her yet kept both hands on her, denying himself to give her pleasure.

His tongue went to her opening, entering a tiny bit then withdrawing. Then Shade slid his hand up her leg, going between her thighs and parting her flesh, finding the wetness his tongue had been playing in.

"You're nice and wet, Lily. Do you know why?"

It took Lily a moment to find her voice. "Yes."

"Tell me why."

"Because I want to come."

"That's right, baby, and I'm going to let you. Do you know why?"

"No," Lily whimpered, her hips arching into his touch.

"Because you're mine, and I take care of what's mine. I don't need a pet. I want a flesh-and-blood woman, and yes, Lily, you *will* kneel in front of me again because it will be one of my needs, just like I plan to satisfy all of yours. Every single one," he promised as he placed a feather-light kiss against her pussy which she was too far-gone to even feel.

As his finger slid deep inside her, Lily's legs gave out but Shade stood up, bracing her body with his against the shower wall. His finger slid deeper as her hands went to his chest, her nails digging in.

He then began to pump his finger in and out of her slick pussy while he kept her eyes pinned with his. He pressed his nearly bursting cock against her silky belly. When he looked down, her eyes were filled with need, so Shade pumped his finger deeper inside her.

"Those other women downstairs are no comparison to you. I fucked them, made them beg for me, but they weren't you. No matter how hard I tried to pretend they were."

Lily began beating at his chest, not appreciating him talking about the other women he had fucked.

He slid his finger in her faster. "Not one of them could give me as much pleasure as you're giving me now with just my finger inside of you." He couldn't help remembering the tormented nights he had spent without her.

Her hands quit beating at his chest, rubbing the flesh, instead. He placed one arm above her head, bracing himself over her, letting her nipples tease his chest while his cock pressed harder against her stomach.

"It hurt so bad waiting for you, Lily. I thought I would lose my mind. No amount of liquor, women, or pot drove you from my mind. I would ride on my bike all the way to your dorm and sit outside just to watch you go to classes in the morning, then drive home and start the whole fucking thing over again.

"That night you were stuck in Sex Piston's beauty shop was the worst night of my life. I didn't get stuck in that traffic jam because I was already on the way to your dorm when Razer called me and told me what was happening.

"I swore when you were in the hospital ER that I was done waiting. Everyone knew I was waiting for you but you. I'm *still* waiting," he groaned against her neck.

Lily shuddered and cried out as her body gripped his fingers tightly. Shade felt her muscles contracting as she came with the water cascading down on them.

Shade got out of the shower, drying her shivering body and then helping her dress in her pajamas before sliding on his shorts.

Lifting her, he carried her to the bed, lying down next to her before he pulled the covers over them, wrapping them in a snug cocoon and keeping her close to his side.

"Shade?" Lily whispered.

"Yes?"

"Can I see your flogger?" Lily giggled.

"Not tonight." As much patience as he liked to brag he had, there was no way he could put that flogger anywhere near her without fucking her.

After she fell asleep with her head on his shoulder, Shade heard the sounds of the members fucking next door and across the hall.

He gently rolled Lily over so he could climb out of the bed, going to the bathroom to finish what he couldn't with Lily. He hadn't jerked off so much since puberty. Shade shuddered as the cold water hit him. They had used all the warm water with the earlier shower. He just couldn't catch a fucking break.

CHAPTER SIXTY

Shade followed Lily into the kitchen, packing another stack of dirty dishes left over from the huge Thanksgiving dinner which had been prepared with everyone pitching in to help Lily and Beth.

"You were quiet at dinner." He studied her remote expression.

"Just tired, I guess. It's been a long day," Lily said quietly.

Shade leaned against the counter, watching her face carefully. "Bliss said she had a talk with you this morning. Did something she said upset you?"

"No, we're fine," Lily replied as she loaded the dishwasher.

Shade nodded. Maybe he should have another talk with Bliss. When she had stopped him on the way downstairs that morning, she had told him she had apologized to Lily for her behavior. Could she have said more than she had told him?

"Ready for some football?" Rider asked as the rest of the club came through the kitchen to go into the television room.

"Go ahead. I'm going to head to bed when I finish," Lily urged, waving her hand at him to go.

"I'll be up after the game."

"Okay."

Shade left, going into the room to find a space on the already overflowing couch, listening to Beth talk to Lily.

"Need any help?" Beth asked.

"Nope, I've got it covered. I'm almost finished. Go watch the game."

"I think I will. I'm exhausted." Beth sat down on the arm of the couch next to Razer, who reached up and tugged her down onto his lap. Beth then laid her head on his shoulder.

Shade saw the way Lily stared at the two and felt a sense of disquiet. She had acted too quiet over the course of the day.

He frowned in concern as he watched her doing the dishes. She seemed so alone, lost in her own world.

When she slipped out the kitchen door, he rose.

"Aren't you going to watch the game?" Razer asked, looking up at him.

"No. You can tell me who won later."

Shade left, going outside to see Lily several feet in front of him as she walked toward his house. He stepped off the path, walking through the trees silently as he watched her climb the steps to sit on the porch. He had observed her often going there to sit, looking toward the mountains. He didn't like her out alone, but he sensed her need to be so; therefore, he would stay back and give her time to herself.

It would become easier once they moved into their house. All she would have to do was walk out her front door. He needed to remind Cash to tell his grandmother to buy an old rocking chair during her yard sales. He thought Lily would like the history of an old piece of furniture on her porch, something which could withstand the test of time.

It was beginning to get cold. Shade was about to step forward and tell her it was time to go inside when he saw Lucky coming outside and walking up the path.

"You're going to get sick sitting out here in the cold without a jacket." Lucky came to a stop at the bottom of the steps, looking up at her.

Lily stiffened when she heard Lucky's voice.

"I was just about to go in," Lily replied.

When Lucky walked up the steps, taking a seat next to her, Lily turned her face away from him.

"Why have you been avoiding me?" Lucky asked quietly.

"I haven't been avoiding you. I saw you last week at the store and Sunday at church," Lily prevaricated.

"You hide behind Rachel at the store, you take off as soon as church is over, and you haven't said two words to me today. What's wrong, Lily?"

She leaned her head against the wooden rail next to her, hiding her face in the darkness. "Because I'm so ashamed," Lily's voice trembled.

Shade's hands clenched by his sides. Lily had never mentioned her abuse other than when she was having a panic attack or when Rachel had helped her those two times. She had never talked about it even with Beth.

"What on Earth have you got to be ashamed of?" Lucky's stunned voice had Lily trying to scoot farther away from him.

"Because I don't belong in your church." Lily paused. "I'm not the person you think I am. I've done things, Pastor Dean. Things I know God's not going to forgive me for."

"Lily, don't. Please don't think like that." He reached out to touch her shoulder but Lily moved away, not wanting him to touch her.

"It's true. I...I..." Lily's voice firmed. "Before I came to Treepoint to live with Beth's parents, I lived with my mother. She...she wasn't a nice person. She had me do things, Pastor, to men she would bring to our apartment." She shuddered.

Shade wanted to step forward and hold her in his arms, but standing still, he acknowledged Lucky was what she needed to find the peace he wanted her to find.

"I didn't want to, but she would make me drink liquor so I wouldn't fight them. I quit fighting what she wanted me to do so she wouldn't make me drink it anymore. Do you think God will forgive me for that? She told me that, if I told my friends, she would kill them. I knew she would because I was her daughter, and she didn't care if I was dead or alive. She just wanted the money they would give her for me."

"Dear God. Lily, stop..." Lucky's voice was hoarse.

Shade moved a little to his left, knowing Lucky would see the small movement. When he looked toward him, Shade shook his head. Lucky wouldn't want to hear Lily's dark confession, thinking it wasn't his place, but it was. If anyone could help Lily find solace with her God, it was Lucky.

"If she couldn't find someone for me, she would send me to apartments where she knew the men lived alone and make me ask if they wanted company for the night. I learned how to do what she wanted, or she would beat me so bad I couldn't go outside and play with my friends until I healed. If anyone came to ask about me, she would tell them I was too sick to play."

"What happened to your mother?" Lucky's voice was harsh.

"Her boyfriend moved in with us. He was nice for a while. He paid the bills and gave her money to spend. He even bought me my first doll, but she would get mad at him because he wouldn't give her extra money for her pills, so she would wait until he went to work and sneak men into the apartment.

"One day, he came home early and saw me in bed with a man. Marshall pulled a gun out and made them sit on the bed and told me to get dressed. I heard him call someone, but I was too scared to listen. He made us all sit there until someone knocked on the door."

"Who was it?"

"I don't know. I'd never seen him before, but he was big and scary to me because, when Marshall told him what he'd seen when he came home, he took the gun and killed my mother and the man on my bed." Lily took a deep breath. "Then he turned to me, asking me if Marshall had ever touched me, and when I told him yes, he killed Marshall. He lit a fire on my bed and made me leave with him. I didn't try to scream; I was too scared."

"I bet you were," Lucky said grimly.

"He took me on a long drive. I slept most of the time. When I woke up, I was in Beth's house, and he was gone. Her parents told me they were adopting me and to forget about my mom and the life I had before, so I did. I made myself forget every dirty thing I had been forced to do. I forgot the men. I forgot my mom. I forgot Marshall. I forgot my sitter who always smelled like chocolate chip cookies. I forgot my friends, Sawyer and Vida, who were like sisters to me. I forgot every single ugly detail of my life until I forgot me."

"Lily, look at me."

Lily didn't.

Shade ached for her, wanting to give her the comfort she deserved.

"Please, look at me," Lucky pleaded.

Lily broke, crying as if her heart was breaking. Shade fought back his own tears as Lucky put his arm around her shoulders, letting her cry until she lay quietly against him.

"I promised myself I wasn't going to cry anymore," Lily said.

"I think that one was well deserved. That's why you wanted to become a social worker, isn't it, to help children like yourself?"

Lily nodded. "Yes, I think so."

"Lily, do you plan on judging children if you find them in situations like you were in?"

"Of course not," Lily said, clearly shocked that Lucky thought she would.

"When people start coming into the church store tomorrow, are you going to judge them for being in need?"

"No," she repeated. "They need our help."

"Yes, they do, like you needed help and no one was there for you. You chose to survive, Lily. You're the kindest, most compassionate woman I know, and it's a true miracle that part of you wasn't destroyed. As your pastor, I couldn't be more proud. You make my Sundays worthwhile because when I look out into my congregation and see your face, I know God has graced my church with your presence.

"You have done nothing to feel ashamed of. The ones who *should* be ashamed are the ones who are responsible for hurting you. You don't have any lessons to learn from me, but I have many to learn from you, Lily, because as God is my witness, I would have killed every single one of the bastards who touched you."

"Thank you, Pastor." Lily smiled at him with relief.

"Go on inside. It's freezing out here. I'll see you in the morning."

She stood up, pausing when he didn't follow. "Aren't you coming in?"

"In a minute. I want to say a prayer."

"Would you like me to stay and pray with you?" Lily asked.

"No, you've been out here long enough. I won't be long."

"Goodnight."

"Goodnight, Lily."

When Lily had walked down the path and out of hearing, Lucky spoke up.

"You don't deserve her," he said, standing up.

"I know," Shade stepped out of the shadows, not taking his eyes off Lily as she walked back toward the clubhouse.

"It's a good thing they're all dead, or we would be riding tonight."

"It seems they're all dead but one," Shade said thoughtfully, turning to his brother.

Lucky frowned at him. "Which one?"

"The one who gave her to Beth's parents."

"You think something from her past may be why someone is trying to kill her?"

"Whoever has been watching her house has been doing it for years. Who else could it be?" Shade said, coming to the only conclusion which made any sense.

"Damn."

"Talk to Knox, tell him what we found out tonight. I'm going to talk to Beth again and see if she remembers anything from when Lily first came to live with them. At this point, any adoption papers, even fake ones, would be a lead." Shade's only hope of finding the papers was Beth.

"I'll talk to him before he leaves tonight."

"Let's get inside. I don't want Lily alone tonight."

They walked up the path together. Shade was about to go inside when Lucky's hand on his arm stopped him.

"Promise me one thing."

"What?" Shade asked.

"If we find out whoever took her could have stopped that shit, I get him first."

Shade couldn't make him that promise; he didn't make promises he couldn't keep.

₭₭

He heard her teeth chattering when he opened the door. Closing it, he quickly undressed then pulled the covers back, scooting closer to her in the bed and holding her shivering body to his.

359

"Shade?"

"Yes?"

"That day in the diner when I had that panic attack, there was a little girl at one of the tables. What happened?"

"I had left with you, but Knox told me Diamond had seen you staring at the family. Knox talked to them. The little girl was placed in her grandmother's custody."

"It's funny how things turn out, isn't it?"

"I don't think it's funny at all," Shade said, pulling her tighter.

"I believe sometimes it's meant for us to have to bear trials so we can recognize how to help others." Lily's voice grew drowsy.

"Go to sleep." Shade's voice was soothing.

It was then Shade realized the room was encased in darkness. She hadn't turned the bathroom light on.

Her hand laced through Shade's, and he pulled her closer, his cheek resting on her damp one.

The little girl in the restaurant had been abused by her mother. If Lily hadn't recognized the signs, it would have continued. Lily's suffering had changed that girl's life for the better, but no one had been there to save Lily.

Shade raised his face from hers when he realized it wasn't her tears on her cheeks. It had humbled him that her beautiful soul held no bitterness, trying to make the best out of what cards life had dealt her. He, however, was a mean moth-erfucker, and he was going to exact the revenge which she had been denied.

Chapter Sixty-One

He heard the music at the top of the steps. Lily must have turned it on after he had left her washing clothes in the basement.

He had expected her to be finished when he was done, but he had wanted to make sure she still wasn't in the basement before he went upstairs. He knew she was all right in the club but he couldn't keep himself from checking, making the excuse to himself that he would pack the clothes back upstairs for her.

Shade stood at the bottom of the steps with his mouth dropped open. She was on the pole, making experienced moves a stripper wouldn't be able to perform. He quietly went to sit down on the couch to watch the show she didn't know she was giving.

Lily was at the top and using her arms as leverage, she pushed her legs out from the pole. He could see the fine trembling of her arms and almost stopped her, afraid she would hurt herself, but she kept a firm grip before circling the pole with her thighs, making his cock harden at the sensuous movement.

Sliding down the pole, she stopped her momentum a few feet from the floor. Using her thighs, she held on to the pole, going backward until her hands touched the floor. Releasing her grip, she flipped her body, doing a brief handstand before continuing to flip until she stood straight, facing the steps. Then the buzzer for the dryer went off, and she moved toward the machine.

Thinking herself alone, Lily walked confidently with seductive grace across the floor, coming to an abrupt stop when she saw him sitting on the couch and staring at her. All her sexual confidence disappeared, and the shy woman was back.

"How long have you been there?" she asked suspiciously.

"Long enough to see you climb then come down the pole."

"Oh." Lily went to the dryer, pulling out the clothes and putting them in the basket. She didn't meet his eyes as she jammed the clothes into the basket.

He made her nervous, which was a shame because she made him horny as hell.

"Come here, Lily."

"Uh, no," Lily said firmly.

"Why?" He tilted his head to the side, studying her reaction.

"Because I can tell by the way you're looking at me that…you're in a mood," she finished helplessly.

"You're right. I'm in the mood to fuck. Come. Here."

Lily's trembling hands set the basket down on the dryer before she slowly walked toward him. "Shade…"

"What do you call me when we're down here?" He wanted her to have the same confidence with him that she'd had when she was alone. To do that, he had to build her trust.

Lily stopped in front of him.

His hand came out, cupping the back of her knee, touching the flesh below her workout shorts. He was well aware of how sensitive the flesh there was. Many men thought only the pussy or tits were sensitive to pleasure, whereas he had discovered a whole woman's body could be used to raise her pleasure if touched the right way.

"Answer me." Shade's firm expression wasn't harsh; however, he left no doubt that he expected her to obey him.

"Sir," Lily answered.

He raised her knee, pulling it toward him until she had to lift the other on the other side of his hip, making her have to come closer. Shade maneuvered her body until she was kneeling over him while he stared up at her.

He slid his hands up the sides of her thighs, curving around toward her butt until his hands cupped her bottom, pulling her closer to him.

"Kiss me."

He was pleased when Lily bent down, touching her mouth to his. Shade parted her lips, sucking her tongue into his mouth, letting Lily explore timidly.

His hand slid forward from behind, rubbing her crotch through the thin material of her shorts. He teased her clit with a brief touch before sliding back, not giving her a full caress, only a promise.

Lily moaned against his mouth as he slid his hand back and forth until her butt was pushing back against his hand, and her arms circled his neck.

Shade leaned forward, rising to his feet with her thighs clenching his hips as he carried her back to his bedroom. He opened the door and then closed it with his foot. Bending down, he laid her on the side of the bed before rising and standing between her spread thighs.

He turned to the bedside table, turning on the small lamp in the dark room. He wanted to see her face when she came.

In a split second, she had turned and scrambled off the other side of the bed, breathing heavily. Her breasts lifted and fell with her erratic breathing. She pushed her hair back from her face, her erratic movements causing the flesh of her tits to tremble. When she lifted her arm, Shade waited expectantly to see if they would spill out of her top.

"Cut it out, Shade." Lily blew out a deep breath, unconsciously rubbing her tummy. "I can't do that." She motioned to the bed.

"Why not?" he asked, staring at her in amusement. His eyes dropped to her hand's tell-tale movements. Mentally, she might not be ready to fuck him, but her body was begging for it.

Lily quickly dropped her hand to her side. "Because I'm not ready yet. I haven't made my mind up if I want to and," she paused, "I've always planned to wait until I was married." Lily lowered her eyes to the floor. "It means a lot to me," she spoke softly, seeming embarrassed about telling him her feelings.

"I see." Shade walked toward the door, opening it for her. The only way she was going to build trust with him sexually was to see he could stop when she wanted him to without freaking out on her.

She walked toward the doorway, giving him a relieved smile. "Thanks, Sir."

"No problem." Of course—he narrowed his eyes on her ass—that didn't mean he had to keep building trust at her speed.

What had she meant that she hadn't made her mind up yet? If they were in a relationship or not? He had a newsflash for her: they had been in a relationship for several months already. He was going to help his woman make up her mind.

Lily gave him a curious look as she went through the doorway but Shade kept his face impassive, not letting her see she wasn't free. He was merely moving her seduction to a less-threatening room.

Shade carried the laundry basket to their bedroom, his lips twitching at her morose expression as she went to shower and change. He used the shower in the hallway, anxious to get downstairs.

Evie had fixed a huge roast with all the trimmings. Shade talked to the others at the table during dinner while Lily kept giving him angry glances.

"Train isn't back yet?" Lily asked with a frown.

Shade had noticed the brother wasn't back. As a matter of fact, he and Rider had joked that he had driven Killyama back to Jamestown to get Stud's help to get rid of her.

Train had offered to give Killyama a ride on his bike when she had insulted the club about keeping promises when Rider's bike wouldn't start, and Viper had been gone with the keys to the metal door where Rider kept his extra bikes. Train was probably going to kick Rider's ass for constantly losing his own key.

"Who are you worried about? Killyama or Train?" Rider questioned Lily with a grin.

While the whole table cracked up, Lily threw the members an angry glance, her lips tightening in disapproval. Shade was happy someone else beside himself was on the receiving end that time.

The door opened and closed with a slam. They all sat watching as Train fixed himself a plate, piling on food, and then sat down at the table.

"Well?" Rider asked.

"Well, what?" Train asked with a glare.

"How did it go?"

"How the fuck do you think it went? The woman is a fucking lunatic. She thought I would let her drive my bike."

"What happened when you told her no?" Lily asked.

"She tried to climb in front of me. I almost wrecked my bike." He tore the top off his beer, taking a long drink. "When I brought her back here to her car, she actually thought I was going to fuck her." He shook his head in disbelief.

"What happened when you told her no?" Lily asked again, apprehensively.

That time, Train remained quiet.

The shocked silence had Train lifting the beer to his mouth, finishing it in a long swallow.

Lily's giggle had Shade hiding his own smile. He was smart enough not to goad Train when he was simmering to a boiling point.

"Did you manage to tame the bitch?" Rider asked with a smirk.

At that, all Hell broke loose. Train's fist flew out, hitting Rider in the jaw and knocking him backward, toppling the chair and him over. Lily screamed, standing up from the table, about to go to Rider's aid, but Shade took her arm and pulled her away.

Train threw himself on Rider when he attempted to stand up. Then the two fought on the floor, throwing their fists viciously at each other, striking whatever body part they could reach while Viper and Nickel tried to pull them apart.

"Stop!" Winter yelled. "You two are scaring Lily."

Everyone except Winter froze, looking at Lily in trepidation, waiting for her to have one of her panic attacks.

Shade stared down at her, frowning. She didn't seem upset.

Beth relaxed first, familiar with Winter's machinations. Lily's twinkling violet eyes had the other members turning to Winter suspiciously. She shrugged, sitting back down at the table then continued to eat. Lily joined her. Shade sat down next with the others gradually retaking their seats, as well. Finally, Train held his hand out to Rider, helping him to his feet. Both returned to their seats to finish their own dinners. Eventually, the atmosphere relaxed, and no one else dared to ask about either of Train's rides.

After dinner, Shade, Train, and Rider began a game of cards while several others played pool in the corner of the room. Lily and Beth cleared the table as Winter and Ember started the dishes.

The brothers were behaving themselves, so Lily couldn't make an excuse to disappear upstairs. However, when Raci and Jewell came back downstairs after changing, Shade read her intent to leave.

As she passed the card table, Shade reached up then pulled her down to sit on his lap while he continued to play cards. He made sure to seat her so Lily's back was to the room, unable to see what was going on behind her.

She relaxed against him, looking down at his cards. Nickel put some music on as Crash moved the furniture so they could dance.

When Shade won, she clapped for him, and Shade motioned for Rider to begin another game.

"Do you want to play?" Shade asked.

"I don't know how," Lily said regretfully, her eyes filled with disappointment.

"I'll teach you," Shade offered. True to his word, he spent the next hour teaching her how to play.

Rider got up from the table, going into the kitchen and then coming back with beers for the men, placing a soda in front of Lily.

"Unless you want a beer?" he joked.

"No, thanks." Lily opened the soda, taking a drink.

Raci's moan sounded behind their backs, and Lily started to get up. Shade didn't have to turn to see who had moaned; he was familiar with all the sounds each woman made when they fucked.

"It's your turn," Shade reminded her, trying to distract her.

Lily took her turn, and he watched as she tried to concentrate.

Shade wished Raci would hurry and climax before Lily couldn't take it anymore and darted from the room. Nickel liked to play around with the women before they came. Shade was going to beat his ass if he ruined his plans.

Lily was winning steadily with a pile of cash sitting in front of her. Shade could see the little wheels turning in her brain on how many people she could help at the church store with that wad of cash. She had already sweet-talked him out of two large donations at Thanksgiving.

She scooted her latest winnings into the pile sitting in front of her.

"Sucker." She grinned at Train across the table.

Shade smiled at her gloating.

"Beginner's luck," Train mumbled, dealing another hand.

Shade was going to give him an extra IOU for his performance. He knew it was killing the brother to deliberately lose.

Lily looked down at her cards, unsuccessful at stifling the grin which threatened to break loose.

Shade rolled his eyes. The woman was a lousy poker player.

"Can I join?" Jewell came up behind Train, circling his neck. He reached around to pull her down onto his lap, and then he dealt her a hand.

"Ante up," Rider said. His own acting job wasn't going so well.

Shade threw him a threatening glare at his lackluster performance.

"I don't have any money. How about we play for favors?" Jewell's hand went to Train's lap.

"Okay with me. I need my room cleaned," Train teased, pulling at her top.

Jewell playfully hit his shoulder.

"Okay with you, Lily?" Shade asked, his arm circling Lily's waist, using the movement to kick Train under the table. He changed his mind; the brother wasn't getting the extra IOU. He wasn't going to get any at all if Lily left before the game was over.

"I'm in," Lily said.

"I don't like that vindictive look in your eyes, but I'm in," Rider agreed.

Lily looked expectantly up at Shade.

"Are you sure you want to play?" he questioned her, soothing his conscience by giving her a chance to leave the table.

She nodded eagerly, and that was all his conscience needed.

"Deal," Shade said.

Train dealt the cards.

As Lily gazed down at her cards, still smiling, Shade rolled his eyes again.

When it came time to place the bets, Jewell got a pad and paper and wrote household services. Ripping the paper off, she threw it onto the middle of the table.

"Of course, that means a lot of services I can perform in the house."

Train wrote on the paper "An hour of my time," throwing the slip of paper into the pot, as well.

Rider did the same then Shade. When they handed her the paper, she wrote what the men had, "An hour of my time." Lily tore off the paper, throwing it in the growing pile.

The game continued. When it came time to bet again, the pen and paper made the rounds again. Everyone's IOUs stayed the same except for Jewell. Lily's mouth dropped open when Jewell read hers out loud. "An hour of fucking."

She was about to throw it into the pot when Lily spoke up.

"Uh, excuse me. It's nothing personal, but I don't want that." Lily shook her head.

"Are you sure?" Jewell didn't try to hide her disappointment.

"I'm sure," Lily replied firmly.

"Perhaps you should just bet what we are?" Shade suggested.

Jewell wrote down "An hour of time."

The game resumed with more calls to ante up. Lily was practically bouncing on Shade's lap she was so excited. He scooted her forward an inch. The woman wanted to bust his balls even when she was in a good mood. Shade almost hated to spoil her good time, but then eased his conscience by telling himself he would show her a better one.

He leaned forward, making his move.

Minutes later, Shade grinned as he raked his winnings across the table to set them in front of himself.

"I'm done for the night. Good game," Shade lied.

He lifted Lily off his lap so he could rise to his feet. Then he reached down onto the table, stacking his papers and sliding them into his pocket before reaching back to collect Lily's winnings and handing them to her.

"Thank you," she said, taking the cash from him.

"It was my pleasure. Later." Shade nodded to the table.

Lily turned to go upstairs.

"Lily." He shook his head at her. "We're going downstairs for a couple of hours first." Lily stopped. "Unless you want to renege on a bet?"

Everyone at the table paused, looking at her.

Lily cleared her voice. "Of course not."

"I knew you were honest, going to church as often as you do." Shade ruthlessly used her honesty against her. Thank fuck he didn't have that problem.

Lily reluctantly followed him downstairs, lagging slightly behind. He held the bedroom door open for her then closed and locked it when she stepped reluctantly across the threshold.

"Shade…" Lily began.

"Take off your clothes," he said sternly.

Lily didn't move.

"So you don't plan to keep your word?" He lifted a brow, keeping his face impassive.

She sucked in a sharp breath. "Yes, but choose something else."

Shade reached into his pocket, pulling out the slips of paper, flipping through them. He found the one he wanted and showed her the piece of paper.

"There are no exceptions or exclusions on this paper. You should have made that clear."

"I thought stuff like that would only count when it was worded like Jewell did. I didn't…"

"Then you should have asked. Again, there are no exceptions. I won several hours of your time. Do you or do you not plan to keep your word?"

"Yes," Lily finally answered.

"Good. Now take your clothes off."

When she didn't move, only stared at him helplessly, he sighed.

"Lily, do you trust me? I mean, really trust me?"

Lily took her time answering, and he was about to give up and hand her the slips of paper she had signed when her words stopped him.

"Yes, I trust you." The truthfulness in her voice released the tight vice around his stomach.

"Good, now take off your clothes. This time, I'll let you leave your bra and panties on. Will that make you feel better?" He let her see a glimmer of his approval before erasing it from his expression. She needed to become familiar with what would and wouldn't earn his praise.

She slowly undressed, pulling off her clothes and laying them on the chair.

As she undressed, Shade pulled off his T-shirt and removed his socks and boots. Then he went to his closet, unlocking the door to search through his toys.

"Lie down on the bed."

Lily climbed on the bed, sitting on her knees and waiting.

Shade turned on his stereo, and the room filled with soft music. When Shade got on the bed beside her, his finger traced down her cheek to her throat. She swallowed nervously as his hand lowered, and he traced the edges of her bra above her breasts. Her breathing escalated at his touch.

"You have beautiful breasts." Shade's lips traced the same path his fingers had followed, from her check to the flesh above her plain white bra. He lifted her hand to buckle a fur lined leather cuff onto her wrist.

Her mouth opened to protest.

"No exclusions, Lily," Shade reminded her once again.

She closed her mouth as he fastened another on her other wrist.

"Lie down," he ordered.

She lay down on the mattress as he reached for the thin chains he had placed on the bedside table. He clicked the chains into the metal loop on the side of the cuffs. One at a time, he locked each of the chains to a hook positioned on the bottom of the headboard that the mattress had kept hidden.

Again he reached to the nightstand, picking up two plain silk scarves. Shade could tell from her frightened look that she had expected something else.

Shade tied the silk scarf around her eyes, knowing darkness was Lily's greatest fear. To conquer it, he wanted her to experience the pleasure she could find within it.

His hand slid across her stomach, her muscles quivering at his touch. He remained silent as his hand traced over her body, lingering at her ankles, brushing his lips over the delicate flesh. His hands explored her calves and thighs until he reached her hips, and then he brushed his mouth along the same path his hands had taken.

Patiently, he explored every area of her body with his hands and mouth except for her breasts and pussy. He familiarized her with his touch until her nervous quivering stopped, and she relaxed back against the mattress.

When he gently removed her panties, sliding them down her legs, Lily tensed. His hand went between her thighs, holding his breath in anticipation for what he was going to discover, only releasing it when he found she was wet. He had been just as nervous as her, afraid he would find that she didn't want him.

He explored her slick flesh, easily slipping his finger against her clit until her legs tried to close to press his hand harder against her. He touched her as if her pussy was a delicate flower which would tear if handled too roughly.

The music started getting louder, the beat faster, and Lily's hips twisted on the mattress as she tried to capture his touch.

"Shade, please..."

He carefully placed a slap against her clit, making Lily shudder.

"How are you supposed to address me when we're in this bed?" he explained why she had been given the slight punishment, which really had been no punishment, but a guide to the climax he was leading her toward.

"Sir."

"Now, ask me how you're supposed to."

"Sir, please, I want to come."

Shade moved his hand away from her pussy, sliding his body down until he was lying between her thighs. He lowered his mouth to the pink flesh which was driving him crazy. His tongue found and slid between the lips to her clit, rubbing the already-sensitive nub until she arched upwards.

He first licked and then sucked her clit into spasms he felt against his tongue, which had her screaming her climax out as the music rose and then ended abruptly before going back to a soothing rhythm. He continued to stroke her body, bringing her down from the orgasm while still leaving an ache. He didn't want Lily completely satisfied. Oh, no; he wanted his woman to want more and more.

He rose, releasing the chains and taking the cuffs off before removing the blindfold.

"Thank you for trusting me, Lily." He brushed a tender kiss against her cheek.

"You're welcome, Sir."

Shade grinned at her, helping her off the bed and back into her clothes. He dressed as she put her shoes back on before storing everything back in his cabinet, locking it and then leading her from the room with an arm around her shoulders to their room upstairs.

Lily changed into her pajamas then climbed into bed as soon as she came out of the bathroom. Shade went in the bathroom, closing the door behind him. He leaned his forehead against the door, breathing deeply, clenching his hands at his sides.

No other woman had ever given him as much pleasure in bed as what Lily had just given him, especially when he still remained hard, holding his own desires back to give her pleasure.

He turned to the shower, staring at it balefully; even Viper was joking about the fucking water bill. He showered, which didn't take long and that made him even more upset until he went to bed and Lily turned to him, laying her head on his shoulder and placing her hand over his heart.

Wrapping his arm around her, he decided to go online and buy stock in the local water company.

Chapter Sixty-Two

"Dammit!" Shade placed the coffee pot back on the burner. The machine was older than he was.

"What's wrong?" Viper asked from over the phone. They had been discussing orders when Shade had tried to pour himself a cup of coffee.

"Order a new coffee machine. I'm throwing this one out," Shade told him.

"I'll take care of it, and the Maloney account," Viper laughed, hanging up.

Shade went to his office door.

"Lily, the coffee pot isn't working. Could you go to the house and get me a cup?"

"Get it yourself!" she snapped, slapping the tape dispenser down onto the worktable.

While the room went silent at her sharp remark, Shade stared back at her.

"I'll get it for you, boss," Georgia offered with a smile which gave him the willies. He would be too afraid to drink anything she gave him.

"No, thanks, Georgia. I'll take care of it. Lily, come here." His jaw tightened when he saw her about to refuse. Luckily for her, she changed her mind at his expression.

She came into his office, closing the door behind her while Shade resumed his seat behind the desk, swiveling his chair to face her in the doorway.

"Want to tell me what burr has crawled up your ass?"

His blunt question didn't have her backtracking. "No, I don't." She even had the audacity to place her hands on her hips as she snapped back at him, silently challenging him. She was brave with the factory at her back.

He grinned, loving a challenge. "Lock the door."

"Fine." Lily went to the door, about to make her escape.

"From the inside, Lily. And, if you think to disobey me, have no doubt I will punish you in the other room in front of every man and woman busy working. We really don't want to disturb their work even further, do we?"

"I don't suppose so." Lily reluctantly locked the door.

"When I asked you to lock the door, you knew which side I wanted you on, didn't you?"

"Yes." Lily slowly turned back to face him.

"I see. You were being cute. I like cute; you being a smartass is *not* cute. For future reference, it pisses me off."

"I'm sorry, Sir."

Shade's eyebrows rose at her fake meekness.

"Good try, but I appreciate the effort." He grabbed the ruler he kept on his desk. "Come here."

Her feet carried her around the desk, standing next to his chair.

"Lean over my desk," he ordered.

Lily did as told, her posture one of angry defiance.

"Now, if you answer my question, you'll get a pass. If not, well, your bottom will tell you that answer, won't it?"

Lily nodded.

"Why were you snippy with me?"

"Because I didn't want to get your coffee?"

Lily's attitude had the Dom inside of him bristling, but he had a feeling what the problem was because he was suffering from the same one.

He raised the back of her skirt and Lily threw him a heated glare, making the blood rush to Shade's cock.

He stood up, looking at what he had uncovered. Shade froze, staring at her perfect ass.

Every man, whether he admitted it or not, had a part of a woman's body that lit a fuse to their dick. He was a definite ass man, and damn, hers was the best he had seen.

He stared at it hotly, imaging just how he was going to fuck her from behind so he could feel that ass against his stomach, but then Lily shot straight up, her skirt falling back in place before she hurried to the corner of the room.

Shade burst out laughing. "Smart move." He sat back down at the desk, leaning back casually, linking his hands together over his flat stomach. "You're quite a surprise with your sexy little panties. Those red ones of yours always drove me crazy imagining them on you. Now that I've seen you in that pair of purple lace, I have a new favorite color."

She flushed angrily as she stared at him across the small distance of his office.

"So, are you going to tell me what's wrong, or are you going to stand there the rest of the day?" he probed.

"I don't know what's wrong with me," Lily burst out. "Everything is bugging me: you, Georgia, Jewell, the church. Name it."

Shade leaned back farther in his chair, his smile widening. His woman didn't deal with frustration well. He was able to give himself some relief, while she was too innocent to give it to herself. He wasn't about to enlighten her, though. He had never been accused of being stupid.

"How about we take one issue at a time. How am I bugging you?"

Her mouth opened and closed. "You're getting on my nerves, bossing me around. You never do what I expect you to."

"Like what?" he asked curiously.

"Like not cashing in my IOUs, not touching me, and when you come in a room, you just set my nerves off," she finished.

He hadn't touched her for the past two weeks, waiting for her to decide when she wanted more. He understood her convictions; while they weren't his own, he was aware they were an integral part of her personality. Her beliefs had helped her survive a nightmare, and he wouldn't tarnish the very thing that had saved her for him.

"Okay, we'll tackle that problem last. What has Georgia done now?"

"She made a face at me this morning when I came in late. She's not a nice person."

Shade nodded. "I can agree with that. She isn't, but she is a good worker. Were you late?"

"Yes," she said sulkily.

"Why?" His eyes narrowed on her face. She looked worn-out and pale.

"I was tired," Lily admitted.

"So you're angry at Georgia because you were late, and she made a face at you when some bosses would have at least said something to you about being late," he reasoned.

"I may have been wrong," she admitted after a brief pause.

"Now that's settled, let's move on to Jewell. What did she do?" Shade had to admit that that one had him stumped. Georgia soured his stomach, but as far as he knew, Jewell was friendly with Lily.

"Nothing," she admitted grudgingly.

"Then how is she bugging you?"

"You have her IOUs." She stopped talking suddenly, narrowing her eyes on his expression. "Or do you?"

"I do. And that bothers you?" Shade pinched his lips together to keep from laughing.

"Yes."

"All right." Shade opened the desk drawer before reaching in and pulling out the slips of paper. Opening them, he counted out several of Jewell's IOUs before putting the remaining ones back in his drawer. "Here, you can have them." He handed the slips of paper over.

Lily stepped out of the corner, taking the papers before hastily returning to her safe space. Shade didn't burst her bubble of satisfaction by telling her he didn't need to use an IOU for what Jewell would eagerly be willing to give him. Lily's reasoning sometimes boggled his mind, although the longer he was with her, the more he was coming to understand her naïve thinking.

"Next up, what's bothering you at the church?"

Lily stared down at her hands. "Pastor Dean can't find anyone to run the church store. No one outside the church wants the position because it doesn't pay. No one *in* the church who would do okay at it wants it because it doesn't pay, and the few people who *did* volunteer did terrible. Jordan Douglas told everyone in her bible study class how much money someone made who came in the store. Marie Newman told Lark Jackson he didn't need a new coat, that the one he had was just fine. He had on a thin jacket! Laverne Thomas told Willa to keep the clothes she was donating because the way her weight fluctuates, she would probably need them again in a couple of months." Lily blew out an angry breath.

"So the job needs someone who is qualified to judge based on financial need if the people coming in require help, be sensitive to their privacy, and work five days a week all for free?"

"Yes! Oh, and they need to be nice."

"I know the perfect person," Shade said ruefully. Lucky had been right; he had mentioned a month ago that Lily wouldn't be able to walk away from the church store.

"You do?" Lily asked hopefully.

"Yes—you. I can't think of anyone more qualified."

"Me? I can't take the job," Lily protested.

"I don't see why not. It will give you the opportunity to use your degree in a way which will really benefit those in need, especially children, which is what you wanted to accomplish. You'll have a better sense of what's going on in their homes than a social worker with limited time. Anyone who arouses your suspicions, you can tell Knox about. You would be sensitive to their privacy, and you never gossip. But, most of all, you have the most important qualification—you're extremely nice."

Lily smiled at his compliment.

"But what about the pay?"

"I have enough money for the both of us." He held up his hand before she could interrupt. "But, since I know you want your own money, I'll ask the brothers to each donate enough to pay your salary for the year."

"I couldn't ask them to do that."

"You won't; I will. Anyway, I already have a couple of their IOUs."

Lily stepped out of the corner, giving him Jewell's IOUs back. "Don't forget to ask the women members," she reminded him.

"I won't. Feel better?"

Lily nodded then bit her lip.

"What?"

"There is a family who comes into the store. They have two kids. Could the father have my job? I know there is a wait list, but since you said my job is extra, could you?"

Shade groaned. "Give them my number."

"Okay." Lily happily went toward the door.

"Lily, we aren't finished. Come here."

She let out a loud sigh. She had apparently forgotten the issue that he had saved for last—the most important one to him.

She started to go back to her corner, hesitating, but then she walked back around the desk, coming to stand next to him.

He stood up, causing her to lean backward until her hands went behind her back to press against the desk.

"I think I've also figured out what it is about me that's setting your nerves off."

"You have?" Her eyes widened as she stared up at him.

"Yes, I have. You see, sometimes when a woman wants a man, her body lets her know by becoming...How shall I put it delicately? Horny. Yes, that's the word I'm looking for. You're horny."

"I'm not horny!"

"I can prove that's what's bothering you," Shade said smugly, leaning over her, pressing her back against his desk. His hand went to her thigh, bringing it up around his hip. "And I can fix that problem for you, too."

"How can you fix the fact that you're an arrogant ass?"

"I can't, but I can fix it where you won't care," he said confidently, sure about his ability to satisfy the woman whose breathing changed the second he drew closer to her.

His mouth covered hers, cutting off her smart-aleck reply. She immediately opened hers wider, letting him take what he wanted, and she needed to give him.

He slipped his hand under her skirt, pushing it up to her waist, and then he stepped back, pulling off her panties. Lily didn't even tense, lifting her leg to help him slide them over her shoes.

He then went to her pussy, finding her wet and needy, her clit engorged and begging for his touch. He stroked it and Lily pressed herself harder against his hand, trying to get him to exert more pressure.

Shade lifted his mouth away from hers. Gasping for breath, Lily ran her hands through his short hair, drawing him closer to her. His hand left her cunt, lightly snapping the waistband of her skirt against her taut stomach before sliding her loose shirt up, exposing her matching purple bra.

Shade tugged her breasts out of her bra, his eyes gazing down at her taut, pebbled nipples. Then he bent over, sucking one into his mouth and laving it into a pointed tip.

"Am I still bothering you?"

"Not so much," Lily moaned as he teased her nipple.

Shade rose, standing straight. His cock was about to burst his zipper as he went to his belt buckle, unbuckling and unzipping his jeans.

Lily froze on his desk, fear coming to her eyes.

"Eyes to me, Lily."

He leaned over her, seeing the fear disappear to be replaced with need then acceptance. Her face and breasts flushed as her desire built.

Shade placed the head of his cock between the lips of her pussy, and she lifted her hips to help him slide deep within her, opening herself to him without reservation. His hard hands on her hips held her to the desk, pinning her in place.

He began sliding his cock back and forth against the outside of her cunt, butting up against her clit, giving her the stimulation she needed until she was writhing as her climax played out.

He continued to hold her tightly, careful his cock didn't slide into the sheath he wanted to desperately thrust himself inside.

Her scream was stifled by his mouth as his cock pulsated his release against the outside lips of her pussy.

She was still trembling as he reached over his desk, pulling several tissues out of the box. She lay across the desk, looking up at him with wonder as he gently cleaned her before throwing the tissues into the trashcan. He then helped her into a sitting position before cleaning himself and zipping his jeans back up.

Lily pushed her breasts back into her top then pulled her shirt back down to cover herself.

Shade gently grabbed her jaw, tilting her head back to give her a brief and gentle kiss, silently thanking her for the dream she had been willing to give up for him.

She didn't want to have premarital sex, and Shade was aware of how important her convictions were. He didn't want her breaking it for him, but he had taken it a step further than petting, hoping it wouldn't rub her conscience too raw. It was the best he could do since he wasn't a fucking saint, even though he felt like one right then. It was a miracle he had been able to stop himself from thrusting inside of her.

Stepping back, he started to help her to her feet.

"Ready to go back to work?"

Lily nodded happily as she slipped off the desk. She was almost around the desk when she turned back, looking around the floor.

"What are you doing?"

The resignation in Shade's voice had her looking swiftly to his eyes, a flush coming to her cheeks.

"I was looking for my panties." Her eyes swept the floor again.

Shade pulled his hand out of his pocket. "These are now mine." He then pushed the panties back into his pocket. It was the least he deserved until he could get his hands on the red ones.

She blushed as she stared at him. Shade knew what was going on in her head. The thought of her working the rest of the day without underwear was going to be an added perk to his workday, though.

It was short-lived when he read the intention in her violet eyes.

She went through the door and was reaching back to shut it when he said, "By the way, while you're at the house getting another pair of panties, could you get me a cup of coffee? Please."

Lily's only response was to slam the door.

Shade grinned at the closed door. He might need to call Viper and tell him to hold off on buying a new coffee pot.

CHAPTER SIXTY-THREE

Shade took a drink of coffee, ignoring the others sitting at the table as he waited for Lily. She had stayed after church to ask Lucky if she could run the church store. She had been talking excitably about it that morning as she dressed, confiding she was nervous about asking the pastor.

Shade had turned onto his stomach on the bed to keep her from seeing him roll his eyes. Lucky was going to accept her offer so fast she would be fortunate if she didn't get whiplash.

He was able to see clearly out of the diner window. He hadn't liked the thought of her alone with Lucky. He didn't worry that Lucky would try anything with Lily, though; his principles were too strong for that.

They had served in the military together when Lucky was a chaplain and Shade had seen firsthand the commitment Lucky had for what he had said he had been called to do.

The change in Lucky had started slowly, beginning with Knox's first wife Sunshine's death. By the time his service had ended, Lucky had been replaced by another man in the same body.

No, Lucky wouldn't violate the trust others placed in him. However, women tended to think of Lucky as a sheep—mild-mannered and easy-going—when, in reality, he was a wolf biding his time. Shade recognized it because he was a wolf, too; he just didn't pretend.

Lucky and he were alike yet different. Lucky would attack you and leave you staring at a missing hand with nothing except a bloody stump remaining while you wondered what in the fuck just happened. Shade would simply rip it off while you screamed for mercy.

Lily came out, taking Lucky's arm as they crossed the street. Shade unconsciously stood as she laughed happily up at the man, making Shade's hands clench at his sides.

Viper and Razer broke off their conversation, turning to see what he was staring at out the window.

"Fuck!" Viper yelled, getting to his feet and taking Shade's arm.

"Shade, she's coming inside. Do you want her to see you acting this way?" Razer asked.

"I don't give a fuck. I'm going to tie his dick around his balls," Shade snarled, trying to break Viper's hold.

"Shade! For Christ's sake, it's only Pastor Dean!" Beth snapped.

Shade started to snap back at her then caught the warning looks from Viper and Razer. Gathering his control, he blasted a threatening glare at Lucky as he came inside the diner.

Lily looked up at Lucky with happiness shining in her eyes before reaching up and hugging him. Shade tried to knock Viper away, but he pulled him back.

"Cool it. You're going to scare the shit out of her. Look, Dean's running for his life. Calm down and paste a smile on your fucking face before she realizes you're a crazy motherfucker."

Viper kept his restraining hand on Shade's shoulder as Lily approached.

"What happened?" Lily immediately went to Shade's side, her hand going to his forehead.

"He's fine now. He choked on his breakfast," Viper said, resuming his seat by Winter.

"Thanks, Viper. I'm glad you were here," Lily said with concern.

"Me, too," he said grimly.

Lily told everyone the good news about "Pastor Dean" letting her run the church store and received their congratulations. Shade listened as he took out his cell phone, texting Lucky, "Later." It was only one word, but Lucky would get his message.

"Are you sure that's what you want to do?" Beth asked, leaning closer to Lily's side.

"Yes, I do. I'm happy we settled it before Christmas. Do you think we have enough time to push for another toy drive? The store is already running low."

"I'm sure we do," Beth said above the groans at the table.

"I'm going home and hiding my wallet. Not only do we have Winter constantly after our money, now we have Lily after it for toys. Jeez," Rider moaned.

"It could be worse," Lily suggested.

"How?"

"If I don't get enough toys, I was going to ask Killyama if she could help take donations," Lily said, taking a drink of her hot chocolate.

"How much do you need?" Razer asked, reaching for his wallet.

Shade felt his tension slowly easing. Lily had steadily become more comfortable with the men, able to talk and joke with the brothers where before she would only talk with the women.

After lunch, Shade asked Lily to go furniture shopping with him while the others went back to the clubhouse.

The local furniture store had a vast assortment to choose from. After only a couple of hours, he had managed to find furniture for the entire house and appliances Lily had approved of. He would pretend to look at the different furniture, but the ones she would gravitate toward, he would buy. The ones he couldn't tell which she liked, he would pretend to be uncertain about and ask her help to choose. It took two hours to accomplish, yet he finally had enough to furnish the house.

"Is that all I can help you with today?" Leonard asked, carrying the handheld computer which had rung up the purchases he had made. The sales clerk had lost his snobbish attitude after the first ten minutes, although his new kiss-ass attitude was just as annoying.

"That will be it," Shade replied, putting his arm around Lily's shoulders when she would have kept looking at the furniture.

"But you haven't picked out your bedroom furniture," Lily reminded him.

"I don't need bedroom furniture. I have bedroom furniture."

"The set in the basement?" Lily questioned, looking up at him.

Shade nodded before turning to follow the clerk to the cashier. Lily hung back, though, her feet not moving.

"But that furniture won't match the furniture in your house," Lily protested. "Just look at the bedroom furniture. You might find something you like better."

"I like what I have," Shade said, again trying to follow the sales clerk.

Lily refused to move, looking down at the floor. "It won't match."

Shade gave a frustrated sigh, motioning for the clerk to wait for him at the register.

"Eyes to me, Lily." She reluctantly raised her eyes to his. "Are you crying?" he asked, stunned.

"No, I don't cry anymore. Haven't you noticed?"

"I can't say that I have," Shade replied drily.

"Well, I don't," she snapped back.

"Okay. We'll debate that later. Why won't my bedroom furniture match the rest of the furniture I bought? That happens to be an expensive set, which I custom-ordered," Shade explained. He loved that fucking set and had been forced to wait three months for it to be made and delivered.

"I don't care how expensive it is; it's still different from the rest of your furniture."

"How?"

"It isn't new."

"It isn't new?" Shade repeated.

"It's not freaking new!" Lily whisper-screamed so no one would hear her.

Understanding came to Shade, and he bent down to whisper in her ear. "I bought that bedroom set after you were hurt last summer, Lily. It's still new."

Lily's eyes widened. "It's *all* new?"

"All of it, including the mattress and sheets. And, before you can ask, everything in my cabinet."

She turned red yet didn't try to avoid his amused gaze.

"Then I guess it matches after all."

CHAPTER SIXTY-FOUR

A knock sounded on the door.

"Come in," Lucky said, setting his pen down on the desk.

Shade walked into the room, dressed in slacks and a button-down shirt along with shiny, new, expensive shoes.

Lucky sat, uncomprehending exactly what he was staring at. As understanding dawned, an unholy grin came across his face, and he sat up straighter in his chair.

"Before we start, I'm warning you that, if you make one wisecrack, you'll be giving your own eulogy," Shade threatened.

"Shade, you have to at least give me one."

A warning gleam appeared in his deadly eyes. "Like I said, it's your funeral."

"It might just be worth it," Lucky replied, hastily raising his hands in surrender when Shade took a step forward. "I promise I will behave to the best of my ability."

"You do that," Shade said, still not relaxing his threatening manner.

Lucky stood up, coming from around his desk. He reached out his hand for Shade to shake. "I told you I didn't think you deserved Lily. Let's see if you can change my mind, John."

"Pastor"—Shade shook his hand back—"I want to marry Lily tomorrow."

"Congratulations." Lucky slapped him on his back. "When did you ask her to marry you? I saw her at the church store today, but she didn't say anything."

"I haven't asked her yet," Shade admitted grudgingly.

"You haven't asked her yet?" he repeated in astonishment.

"No. I'll tell her in the morning," Shade said, taking a seat in front of Lucky's desk as he stared down at Shade in shock.

"You can't spring something like that on Lily."

"She wants to get married during December when it's snowing, and I'm not waiting another year," Shade said stubbornly.

Lucky stared down at him, frowning, and Shade looked right back up at him.

"Lily has strong moral convictions."

"I know; I'm her pastor." He crossed his arms over his chest. "I still don't—"

"She has *very* strong moral convictions," Shade stressed.

"You mean…"

"Yes." Shade turned red in anger when Lucky's lips began twitching. If he didn't love Lily so much, he would have decked the man five seconds ago.

Lucky went behind his desk and sat down. "I see." He cleared his throat several times before saying, "You would like me to perform the ceremony?"

"Yes." Shade unclenched his hands. One day, he was going to make Lucky pay for this. "And I want you to tell Lily you've given your permission."

Lucky's face went serious. "Shade...I know you and the brothers don't take my role as pastor here seriously, but I do. And Lily is special to me. When she sits through my sermons, I know at least one person is listening and receiving God's word.

"I decided when I took this job that my decision about how I wanted to live my life would be postponed until my work is completed. When I'm no longer a pastor, it won't be because I lack faith in God, but because I lack faith in myself to follow the path God wants of us. Until then, I have made a commitment to serve this church to the best of my abilities. It's been difficult, time-consuming, aggravating, and rewarding, and that's only been for a few years.

"Couples who come to me before their wedding want their commitment to be lifelong, as their faith in God will be. Before I give my permission to couples, I counsel them for at least six months. With Lily, I have no reservations that, when she gives her vows, she will be able to keep them. You..."

"*Pastor Dean*," Shade mocked, "if you were to ask me if I share Lily's convictions about God, I'd say no. If you ask me if I intend to start attending church with Lily regularly, I'd say hell no. If you were to ask me if I plan to lead a Christian life, I'd say no and laugh in your face. If you ask me if I love Lily, I'd say with all of my heart. If you ask me if I will support Lily when she does things important to her, like go to church, work in the church store, or give to the needy, I'd say yes.

"I plan on being a good husband, provider, and being faithful to her until the day I die. I know you and everyone else say I don't deserve her, and you're all right, but no one does. She's special. I recognize that and will treat her like she is until—"

Lucky held up his hand, stopping him. "Shade, if you would have let me finish, I would have told you that I don't know of another man who can give Lily the life she deserves. I've known you several years, and while you're a cold-hearted bastard and crazy-assed, you are, without a doubt, loyal. If you give Lily a fourth of what you have given to The Last Riders and our country, then Lily is in good hands.

"I've come to think of Beth and Lily both as sisters, and if I could have chosen men for them both, it would be you and Razer. I've never believed you had to sit in church every Sunday to deserve God's blessings. You and Razer are proof of that because both of you have been truly blessed with the gift of those two women's love."

Shade asked, "You'll give your permission?"

"Yes."

Shade stood as Lucky took out his cell phone. "What are you doing?"

"Taking a picture of you. If you ever fuck up, I'm going to show you this picture and remind you of the promises you made me."

"You won't need a picture," Shade told him. "I've never forgotten or broken a promise, and I won't start with Lily."

∓ ∔

Shade felt Lily's excitement as she bounced off the mattress, jumping out of the bed and to the windows, pulling back the curtains.

"It snowed, Shade."

"I know. It started getting heavy last night," he grumbled from the covers.

The day before, he had gathered the brothers and even Lucky had worked to pull together Lily's dream wedding in the backyard of the church. Thankfully, the church had chairs for them to set up and cover with tarps to be pulled off just before the ceremony.

Beth and the women had shown up to set up the tables and decorations in the warmth of the church after dinner when Lily had gone to bed. They would arrive an hour before the ceremony to place more decorations outside.

When Knox had arrived with the sheriff's car filled with fresh flowers, Shade had stared at the vehicle in amazement. "How did you manage this?"

Knox had grinned. "Told old man Carter I had to confiscate them."

Shade had burst out laughing. "For what?"

"Illegal flowers. Came into the country without being taxed. It's a thing now."

"It is?"

"Shit no, but it was the best I could come up with. He didn't argue when I handed him the cash."

Shade hadn't thought it was anything other than Knox's fierce appearance which had kept the florist from arguing.

"Who were they meant for?" Shade had asked.

"Betsey Watson's wedding. She's getting married at the country club the day after tomorrow."

"She's going to be pissed."

"Don't really care, do you?"

"Fuck no." Shade had slapped Knox on the back. "Let's get them unloaded before Betsey comes looking for them."

Back in the present, Lily jumped on the bed again. "I love snow."

"I know. You told me." Shade grinned, pulling her back down.

Lily circled his neck with her arms. "Does your family open presents on Christmas Eve or Christmas Day?"

"What?" Shade asked, not understanding what she was getting at.

"Each family does it differently. Some families open their presents on Christmas Eve, others Christmas Day. We always opened them on Christmas Eve because I couldn't wait."

"We opened ours on Christmas Day," Shade told her.

"Oh." Her face fell in disappointment.

"But I can open it on Christmas Eve." He smiled.

"No, I'll wait until tomorrow. I don't want to break tradition. It might be bad luck."

"I don't believe in bad luck."

"I'm still not giving you your present until tomorrow," she taunted.

Shade got out of bed, going to the bathroom to shower and dress after telling Lily she took too much time, so he was going first. Lily lay on the bed and was still waiting for him when he came out.

He had taken the time to not only shower and shave, but to dress in a new pair of jeans and a dark blue muscle shirt.

He walked to the window to look out, seeing it had snowed another couple of inches since he had come in the night before.

"It's supposed to quit snowing this afternoon." He turned toward the bed. "Come here, Lily."

Lily climbed out of bed to stand by him in front of the window.

Shade went to the bedside table and opened it, removing an envelope before coming back to her and placing it in her hand.

"This present isn't technically for you. Open it," he urged Lily when she stared down at it in her hand.

Lily tore the envelope open, reading the words on the paper. Then she looked back at him with pure joy on her face.

"Look at the date."

The paper signing over the land which Beth and Razer's property was built on had been signed the day after she had visited Diamond at her home.

"I don't know what to say, Shade. Thank you."

"You're welcome." Taking the papers away and setting them on the chair by the window, he reached into his pocket and pulled out a tiny box, placing it in her hand. "This present is for you."

Nervously, he watched her face for her reaction, trying to brace himself for her rejection as she slid the ribbon off and then opened the box. Inside, a diamond ring lay on a bed of black velvet.

"Will you marry me?" Shade went down on his knees in front of her.

She began crying. "Yes, I'll marry you."

Shade stood up, kissing her so passionately it had her arms circling his neck. He pulled her away just as quickly as he had begun to kiss her.

"Good. Now, you need to get showered and dressed. We're getting married in two hours." He walked to the door and started to open it.

"Wait. What are you talking about? We can't get married in two hours. Weddings have to be planned and—"

"I've already planned everything and what I couldn't, Beth and Winter took care of. You want a snowy, winter wedding. Look out the window. You know Kentucky weather; it could be another year before it snows again. I'm not waiting a year to get married. Besides, how do you schedule snow?"

"I don't know," Lily said in bemusement.

"I don't, either. So everything is a go for today, even the snow. I talked to Pastor Dean and got his blessing."

"You did?" Pleasure filled her eyes.

"I did. So are we going to do this?"

"Yes. Do you need me to do anything?"

"No, everything is ready. The brothers and I spent half the night getting it set up. But I do have a quick question."

"What is it?" Lily asked.

"Do I have to invite Sex Piston and her crew?" Only for her would he put up with that group of man-eaters.

"What do you think?" Lily giggled.

Shade went out the door, closing it behind him. "Fuck."

He groaned, taking out his phone. Before he punched the number in, he looked upward.

"God, if you are up there and listening, remember it's not only Lily's wedding day, but mine, too."

Taking a deep breath, he pushed the dial button.

Chapter Sixty-Five

Shade stood beside Lucky on one side and Razer next to him with a video camera as he waited for Lily to come out of the church. The Last Riders had made an arch for them to stand under with flowers woven through and fairy lights. Candles were placed intermittently around the podium.

The church door opened and Lily came out, her arm in Beth's as she walked down the aisle where a white runner had been laid. Shade's breath caught at his first sight of her as the music played softly in the background.

She walked slowly toward him, wearing a lace wedding gown which hugged her body and a veil which lay on her black hair, trailing behind her and brushing the snow.

"She's beautiful," Lucky said reverently.

"Yes, and she's all mine," Shade reminded him, stepping forward to take Lily's hand as she came to stand beside him.

Beth remained standing next to Lily.

Lucky waited until everyone retook their seats before beginning the ceremony.

"The marriage ceremony is the most sacred ritual a pastor performs. I am blessed to be able to stand here today to join Lily Cornett and John Hunter into the Holy union of wedlock.

"Ruth 1:16-17. Entreat me not to leave you or to return from following after you. For wherever you go, I will go, and where you lodge, I will lodge. Your people shall be my people, and your God, my God. Where you die, will I die, and there will I be buried. The Lord do so to me, and more also, if anything but death part you and me.

"This beautiful expression of love and loyalty is why Lily and John are standing here today to give their vows before family and friends—so all will know their commitment to each other.

"Who gives this woman in marriage?" Lucky asked.

"I do," Beth answered with tears in her eyes.

"Shade and Lily, marriage is a sacred relationship and should not be entered into lightly. The road which has brought you here today hasn't been an easy one. It's been filled with many challenges and obstacles which both of you have overcome.

Instead of using these challenges as excuses not to love, you have chosen to use them as a reason to love each other.

"Lily and Shade, the vows you are about to make in your own words will be a promise to keep the commitment and love you both share for each other now and forever.

"Lily, you may give your vows first."

Lily smiled at him with such love that Shade felt tears brim in his eyes.

"Shade, I give you my heart, willingly and without reservations. I give you my promise to always love you, be the mother to your children, and to be the strong wife you deserve. I pledge my devotion and faith to you. I swear to keep all these in my heart for you through sickness and health, through our successes and our sorrows, for the rest of our lives together."

"John," Lucky prompted.

Shade had to clear his throat before he began.

"Lily, I promise to be your lover and friend, not only a husband. I will be your partner in this life we will share. I will be your warrior when you cannot find the strength to fight for yourself. I will be the father to your children. I give you my hand and heart to hold as we walk through life's struggles. I will remain yours long after my body turns to dust and our names are just a memory. Together. Forever."

A cross between a laugh and sob escaped Lily at the end of his vows. Shade used his thumbs to wipe away the happy tears coursing down her face, grinning at her and trying to hold back his own, happy to finally be tying his woman to him forever.

"What will be the symbol of the vows you have pledged to each other?" Lucky asked.

"These rings," Shade and Lily both answered at the same time.

"These rings will serve as a reminder to the both of you and to others of your vows.

"John, place your ring on Lily's left hand and repeat after me.

"Lily, I give you this ring as a symbol of my love."

Shade repeated the words after he placed the wedding band on her finger.

Lucky then turned to Lily.

"Lily, place your ring on John's left hand and repeat after me.

"John, I give you this ring as a symbol of my love."

Lily repeated the words, placing the wedding band on his finger. When she finished, Shade gripped her hand in his.

"Lily and John, you have now exchanged rings and vows, marrying in the presence of God, your family, and friends. By the authority vested in me by the state of Kentucky, I pronounce you husband and wife.

"You may kiss the bride." Lucky smiled as he finished the ceremony.

Shade pulled Lily closer, lowering his mouth to kiss his wife for the first time.

ༀ ༀ

The freezing guests left immediately after the ceremony while drinking the cups of hot coffee or cocoa that had been waiting for them inside the church. Shade invited only Lucky and Killyama, who was the only psycho of the bitch pack able to attend, back to the clubhouse for the private reception; both had refused. Lucky had Christmas Eve service that evening, and Killyama wanted to get back to Jamestown before the weather made the roads even worse.

Lily and the other women climbed in Beth's SUV, while Shade and Train were riding with Rider in his truck.

Train had climbed into the back seat when Killyama came out of the church, going to her car, but then Shade and Rider turned, startled, as Train jumped out of the truck and approached the woman before she could get in her car.

Shade rolled his window down, unashamedly listening to the budding argument.

"Why are you ignoring my calls?" Train asked.

Killyama didn't answer his question, asking one of her own. "How did you get my fucking number? I sure as hell never gave it to you!"

"I asked Stud for it."

"Bastard."

Shade wondered who she was calling the name—Stud or Train.

"So, why didn't you answer my calls?"

"Why in the fuck would I want to talk to you? I wanted a fuck, and you gave it to me. Then, when I asked if I could come to one of your parties, you said no. If you thought your dick was too good for me, then you shouldn't have given it to me."

"That wasn't what I meant!" Train snarled.

"You had your shot, but you didn't want it. Now, fuck off."

Shade watched as Killyama got in her car, ignoring Train who was still trying to talk to her. Train had to jump out of the way to avoid being hit by her before finally climbing back into the truck.

"That bitch is crazy."

"Nope, that's her friend," Rider laughed, putting the truck in gear and backing up.

A car sped into the church parking lot, barely missing Rider as he continued to back up.

"Who the fuck was that?" Rider asked angrily.

Shade looked out his window at the woman getting furiously out of her car and slamming the door shut.

"Betsey Watson." Shade turned his back to the window so she couldn't see him.

"Why is she here? The wedding's over," Rider asked, pulling out onto the road toward the clubhouse.

"She didn't come to see the wedding; she's here to see Knox."

ဆ ‍ေ

With everyone back at the clubhouse, the men ended up carrying the women up the steps since they were so icy. Then several of the men went back out to clear them and the pathway for anyone who came by later.

As soon as Shade set Lily back on her feet, she escaped to their bedroom to change while Shade and the men were standing at the bar, congratulating him with shots.

Shade saw Lily standing on the steps a few minutes later, watching him with a curious expression on her face, and went to her. She had changed into a green sweater and brown slacks. His hands circled her waist, lifting her off the last two steps and holding her against his chest.

"What are you doing?" he asked.

"Watching you." She smiled, touching his cheek.

"Why?" Shade smiled down at her.

Lily's face got solemn. "Shade, we need to talk. We should have talked before we were married this morning."

Her serious tone wiped his smile away. Shade didn't want anything bad to tarnish their memory of today.

"Not today."

"But I really need to tell you—"

"Not today, okay? Today is Christmas Eve—our wedding day—and we're not going to talk about anything else except that today."

"Okay." Lily gave in to his demand.

"I'm going to go get out of this get-up. I'm never going to live this down."

"I think you'll survive," Lily teased.

Shade bent down, brushing his lips with hers, but before he could start up the stairs, a knock sounded on the door behind them.

Shade gave her a quick grin. "I have another surprise for you," he said, turning to open the door.

As it opened, Shade caught the second Lily saw Penni standing on the porch, her whole face lighting up.

When Penni saw Shade, she threw herself into his arms, something Shade hated yet decided to let go since it was his wedding day.

"You big doofus. Only you would give me a day's notice to get here. My stupid flight got cancelled, and I didn't think I would ever get through the roads from Lexington. I didn't even know you two were seeing each other. How come neither of you told me?"

Shade set Penni back on the floor. "Slow down, Penni. If you hadn't been so occupied with your new job, you would have known," he told her.

It hadn't taken Penni long to figure out the real reason he had wanted her to switch colleges. The nights he had spent watching their dorm room had both concerned her and provided ample opportunity to tease him, which was why he hadn't told her his and Lily's relationship had progressed until he had called and left a voicemail that they were getting married.

"Lily!" Penni squealed when she saw her from behind Shade and then grabbed her, pulling her into a tight hug. "I missed seeing you in your wedding dress. I was supposed to be there," she wailed.

"It's all right. Razer took a video for us." Lily said with mild resentment in her tone.

Penni's eyes flashed her hurt, but she wasn't one to take anything without giving it right back.

"I know you're probably mad at me for not telling you Shade is my brother, but he threatened to take the car back if I told."

Shade's face went blank at his sister's revealing words then tuned the two women out as they chatted until Lily corrected his status as Penni's half-brother.

"That doesn't matter. Our families both get along. It wasn't an ugly divorce. His mom was just sick of moving every couple of years. Our parents are pretty cool, our dad especially."

"We'll save that for another day. He couldn't make it to the wedding. He and my stepmother are in Florida, taking a long vacation. He just retired," Shade explained to Lily. "Why don't you take Penni into the kitchen and let her see everyone while I go get changed." He didn't need more of the lies he had spilled to Penni unraveling like the one he had used to prevent her from running to Penni when she had first come to the clubhouse.

The girls continued talking as they made their way to the kitchen, and Shade went to change out of his uncomfortable suit.

When Shade came back down, everyone was together in the kitchen. They spent the next hour eating and talking, and Shade found out Penni's boss had connections to the Predators, the club which had come through town and Lily had acted friendly with after they had helped her when Gaige had gone after her at the fair.

Shade put his foot down and demanded Penni to stay away from them, but he could tell she was hiding something from him about them. Their bickering about it continued for some time and then settled down as everyone talked throughout the rest of dinner. When the meal was over, the women left to go to Christmas Eve service while the men got busy.

CHAPTER SIXTY-SIX

"We finally done?" Knox asked, coming in the kitchen door to see the brothers all sitting around.

"Yeah, we're done." Shade tossed him a beer as he leaned against the kitchen counter.

They had just finished hauling his bedroom set from the basement to his new house. He was going to surprise Lily when she returned from Christmas Eve service. Shade smiled.

"Damn, I don't even want to know what he's thinking about," Train told Viper.

"Can I help it if I'm in a good mood on my wedding day?" Shade asked.

"Fuck no. I just wished it would last," Train laughed.

"About as long as you lasted with Killyama?"

Train's laughter died abruptly. "What in the hell do you mean by that?"

"Stud told me when I called to invite them all to the wedding that Killyama has been telling anyone who will listen that"—Shade had to smother his laughter—"you're a little quick on the draw."

Train stood so fast his chair fell backward. "That bitch! I'll show her how long I can last. Next time I fuck her, I'm going to make her beg me for twenty minutes before I let her come."

Viper pushed him back down in his chair after picking it up. "You aren't going anywhere. I'm not starting a war with the Destructors and The Blue Horsemen just because you can't perform," Viper joked, sitting down next to Train.

"Oh, he performed, just not long enough," Shade reminded Viper helpfully.

Train turned red, clenching his fists on the table. "I'm going to pay her back some way," he promised.

"Brother, I don't think you're up to the job," Knox joked.

Train went for Knox, having enough of the kidding, but Viper and Shade held him back as the women returned. Train sat sulkily back down at the table, drinking his beer.

Shade looked for Lily and didn't see her.

Beth came in the kitchen, wrapping her arms around Razer from behind.

"Where's Lily?" Shade asked her.

Beth nodded out the backdoor. "She wanted to go for a walk before she came inside. Shade, Georgia gave her a hard time at church tonight." Shade started to question her, but Beth raised her hand. "Lily handled it. She had Georgia running out of the church."

"She's fired," Razer snarled before Shade could.

"I'm not going to argue—Georgia stepped over the line tonight—but, Shade, I don't think that's all that's bothering Lily. When we were in my car today, she asked the women who the worst one in the club was." Beth looked toward Train. "She thought it was Train, but she figured out it was you."

The women in the room looked guiltily away from him.

Shade nodded, going toward the door. "Thanks, Beth. I'll handle it."

"See, Lily knows I can last a long time. I'll get her to tell those bitches the truth—" Train broke off when Shade turned back to stare at him.

Train hastily changed his mind when he saw Shade's expression. "Then again, maybe I won't."

Shade went out the backdoor.

"I told you his good mood wasn't going to last," Train muttered.

❧ ☙

Shade found Lily leaning against the front porch post of their house, staring out at the mountains.

"Why are you out here?" Shade asked, coming to the bottom of the steps, looking up at her.

"You couldn't have picked a better spot for your home. The view is…perfect. When I stand here from this viewpoint, I feel like I could reach out and touch the sky. It sounds silly, but it's so high here I think God might hear me a little better."

She gave him wry smile. "When I was a little girl, I would pray and pray at night. My real mother wasn't much of a church-goer. If it wasn't for my friends, I wouldn't even have known there was a God. They told me about Him. My mother didn't believe, explaining as much to me."

"Lily, stop. I told you, not today. Not on our wedding day," Shade begged her. He didn't want her dream day spoiled with nightmares from her past.

"I have to tell you today, Shade. Today's the day you made me your wife." Her arms circled the post she was leaning against.

Shade wanted her to lean on him for the strength she needed, but he remained at the bottom of the steps, sensing her need to talk. She thought he didn't know the woman he had married; however, he had known from the first time he had looked in her eyes.

"I didn't know what a daddy was, so my friends tried to explain it to me. When they told me, I started crying because I wanted one. I didn't have a lot—no dolls or toys—but I never cried for those. But when they told me what a daddy was, I really wanted one of those. My friends didn't know what to do, but then one of them ran into her apartment and came out with a Bible, and they told me about God, how He was everyone's Father. I would talk to Him whenever...whenever I needed Him. I don't know if He could hear me. I don't think I was close enough.

"That's why I love the mountains. I feel closer to God. When I came to the mountains, He gave me parents who loved me. He gave me Beth, and He gave me you, Shade. My husband.

"Do you know why I didn't want to have sex with my husband before I married? Because I wanted it to be clean and new, because I'm dirty, unclean—"

"Don't you ever fucking say that again!" Shade's foot came up on the first step.

"It's the truth, Shade. I've slept with more men than any woman in that house, and you deserve to know that. I can't give you my virginity; I lost it long ago and everything else from that life that I forgot until Halloween night."

"I wish you had never remembered." Shade's voice held all the anguish he felt at what she had lived through.

"I don't. It was destroying me, Shade."

"There was nothing worth remembering."

His harsh words had her straightening from the pole.

"Oh, yes, there was. There were three little girls who were like sisters. When my mother would finally crash and sleep, she would take me to a babysitter. I know my mom didn't pay her; she spent all her money on anything other than me. I was raised with two beautiful little girls. They loved me enough to see that I had food to eat, that I had toys to play with, that I had a normal touch. They would hold my hand constantly when we went out. They were constantly afraid they would lose me.

"We would sit on the playground and pretend that we would run away when we grew old enough. Vida was sweet and sensitive. She loved animals. She wanted to live on a farm. Sawyer was more adventurous. She wanted to have fun. She chose Disneyland, and I wanted to see the Northern Lights."

"That was why you wanted to go to Alaska," Shade wondered aloud softly.

"I had the farthest to run," she said softly. "That night we were looking through those books must have triggered a memory. My mind was trying to remind me of my past. A past I don't belong to any more than I belong here."

She stood straight, standing on the top step, looking down at him. "You thought I was a young, innocent woman, that I've never touched alcohol. You don't know that I was sold for pocket change. I've done things which make me sick. How can I belong anywhere when I know how disgusting I am?"

"Lily, look at that house behind you. I built that house for you—every room, this porch, these steps, is for you, for us and the children we will have." He put every ounce of the passion and love he felt for her in his voice so she would understand her past wasn't a burden she had to carry alone anymore.

"I love you. When I say it, I don't say it lightly. I say it because, when I look at you, I see an angel who God let slip through His fingers to leave behind just for me.

"Lily, you belong. You belong to me. You will always belong to me." Shade walked up the steps, sweeping her up into his arms. "Always."

He took her to the front door of their house, carrying her inside and slamming the door behind them. Reaching beside the door, he balanced her while he flipped on the lights.

Lily stared around the living room filled with furniture. "When did you do this?" she asked, seeing the furniture they had just picked out the day before.

"While you were in church tonight. The brothers and I busted our balls getting this done while you were gone."

"How did you get the furniture delivered so fast?"

"I threatened Leonard, but I also gave him a big tip," Shade said ruefully.

"We did good," Lily said, trying to wiggle down so she could look closer at her house. "Let me down; I want to see the kitchen," Lily said, exasperated.

"Later. I'm going to show you the bedroom first." His gave her a wicked grin, and she grinned back, laying her head on his shoulders.

Shade took her upstairs to the bedroom where the door was already open. He carried her through, setting her down in their new bedroom. There were candles set in various places throughout the room, giving it a soft glow, and the bed was made up with the covers pulled down. On the bed was the present she had bought Shade the day before.

"Beth made me promise to have it on the bed waiting for you," he told her when her eyes fixated on it.

"What time is it?" Lily asked.

Shade glanced down at his watch. "Eleven-thirty."

"That's close enough. I think it's time I gave you your Christmas present," she said mischievously.

Lily went to the bed, picking the package up, and then headed toward the bathroom.

"Wait, I thought you were going to let me open it?" Shade asked, confused. If it was meant for him, why was she taking it away?

"I will. Give me ten minutes." Lily disappeared into the bathroom.

Shade took his clothes off while she was in the shower then laid down on the bed to wait for her. The bathroom door opened some time later, and he saw his wife standing in the doorway.

"That is the best present I've ever had. Come here and let me open it." His intense eyes didn't lift from the gift she had bought him.

The white lace corset she was wearing had no straps. It hugged her chest in sweetheart cups which pushed her full breasts up and showed how tiny her waist was in comparison to her flared hips. The lace ended just above the tiny white lace panties.

Lily slid into the bed next to him, her shy eyes going over his naked body.

"Come here." Shade put his hand behind her neck, drawing her closer to him.

His mouth went to her breasts, grazing against the top.

"I don't get a kiss?" she asked playfully.

Shade lifted his head, giving her a brief, hard kiss before returning to her breasts.

Lily burst out laughing. "You can't do better than that?"

"Angel, these breasts are...I'm trying to think of a word that's good enough to describe them." His hand went to the tiny hooks that went down the lace corset, unfastening them. When he finished, he spread the corset apart. "Fucking magnificent." He pushed one globe up, finding the tip with his lips. He sucked just the tip of the nipple into his mouth before releasing it. His hand then went to the other breast, grasping it before he lowered his mouth to the tip, sucking it into his mouth then releasing it. "Fucking gorgeous."

"I take it you're a breast man."

"All men are breast men," he replied, looking at her tits in awe. They were as good as her ass. It was hard to choose. Of course, since she was his wife, he didn't figure he had to.

Lily stretched before her arms reached out to him. Shade bent down, covering her mouth with his, giving her the kiss she had wanted. She needed gentleness and tenderness from him, and Shade felt it as if she was screaming it at him.

Lily had pictured her dream wedding since she was sixteen, so she had to have envisioned her wedding night, as well. Shade wanted both of her dreams to come true. That morning, he had given her the wedding day she wanted; now he was going to give her the wedding night.

He parted her lips with his tongue, seducing her with the wildness of his taste and the gentle glide of his against her own. His mouth then went to her neck, exploring her flesh with tiny flicks of his tongue while his hand slid up her thigh, gliding straight to her pussy, finding her nub and rubbing it with strokes that were already close to making her climax.

"Shade, I need you," Lily moaned, one of her legs rubbing against his as she tried to tell him what she needed.

"You're not hot enough yet." Shade moved his mouth to her breast again, taking her nipple back into his mouth.

"Yes, I am," Lily disagreed.

Shade traced her opening, finding her damp yet not nearly enough to take him. Lily was an innocent to desire. When he touched her, she always laid still, never touching him back. He wanted her to see that making love was different than having sex.

Her hands left his shoulders, exploring every inch of his skin, discovering his body. He trembled when her lips grazed the flesh at the base of his throat as her fingers explored his muscles, smoothing over his body.

She grazed his nipples with her teeth and stroked his back when he shifted to lie between her thighs. He gently slid his cock deep within her, feeling her palms slide along his ribcage, circling his waist and holding him tight.

He felt her nipples brush his chest when she arched, lifting her hips to take him deeper. He lowered his body to her, giving her his weight slowly so he wouldn't frighten her, crushing her breasts beneath his chest.

Shade gave her his body as he took hers slowly, wanting her to remember their night instead of the other times she was forced to lie under someone else. He wanted his kiss, his touch, his image to be the only one she would remember, so when any thought of sex came to her mind, she would remember tonight and only tonight. Their wedding night. Their first time.

Lily leaned her head into his and whispered in his ear, "I love you, John Hunter."

His heart soared at hearing her words.

"Lily, I didn't know a man could love a woman as much as I love you. I don't deserve you, but I'm never going to let you go. I couldn't survive without you in my life. I wouldn't want to."

He kissed her again as his thrusts increased, carrying them both into a climax which gave as much as it took. It gave them a way to express their love and took a part of their souls as it receded, crashing the two into one, forever entwined.

Shade rolled over afterward, pulling Lily onto his chest.

"That was beautiful," she said, nuzzling his neck.

"Did you enjoy it?"

"Yes, I never expected...Yes, I enjoyed it a lot." She laughed against his neck, sending goose bumps over his body.

"Good. That was for you. This time is for me," Shade said, sitting up.

"What are you doing?" Lily asked curiously.

Shade slid out of the bed, picking her up and carrying her into the bathroom then down the three steps which led into the massive shower. He turned the water and music on, and the water began to pulse to the beat.

"Oh, heck no," Lily said, giggling as she tried to get out of the shower. "I just blow-dried my hair."

"I'll help you when we get out, if I'm not too tired." Shade's hand went into her already-wet hair, turning her mouth up to his. His hand was already going for the lotions on the side of the shower.

"Lean up against the shower wall," he ordered her after lifting his mouth away from hers and stepping away.

With a grin, Lily went to the wall, doing as told.

He opened the bottle of lotion, spilling some of it on his hand before reaching out and rubbing it into her tiny, black curls.

Lily tried to smack his hand away. "What are you doing now?"

"I'm going to shave you," he answered, his hand returning to the tiny curls.

"Oh, no, you're not," Lily protested.

"Yes, I am. Now stand still or I'm going to go get my paddle. It's my turn."

Lily stood still, though Shade had seen her indecision.

Her safe word didn't leave her mouth as his hand went to the shelf again, pulling out a long, old-fashioned razor.

"Let me do it. I'll get a regular razor," Lily attempted to stop him.

"But that won't be any fun for me." Shade went to his knees in the shower. "Don't worry; I'm good at this. Not as good as Razer, but almost as good." He scraped the first few curls away. "See. That didn't hurt, did it?"

"What do you mean, *as good as Razer*?" Lily asked, his remark diverting her attention from what he was doing.

"This is how Razer got his nickname." Shade scraped away even more curls.

"Eww, that's TMI. I didn't need to know that about my brother-in-law. Wait a minute; does Beth know how Razer got his nickname?"

"What do you think?" The wicked amusement in his voice was muffled with laughter.

"That's definitely TMI, Shade. He used to shave the women in the house?"

"Yep."

"So you're almost as good as him now. I guess I don't need to know who took over for him, do I?" Lily asked snidely.

"Nope." Shade spread her legs, one at a time.

When he finished, he took the showerhead, spraying the now clean-shaven pussy.

"Damn," he said in appreciation.

"I thought you were a breast man?" Lily teased.

"I don't play favorites." She didn't need to find out about his fascination with her ass yet.

"Let me do you now," Lily said with saccharin sweetness.

"No, it's—"

"Not my turn," Lily finished for him.

"Angel, when it's your turn, you can do anything to me you want," he dared her.

"I'm going to hold you to that."

That time, he used his mouth to divert her attention from the revenge she was planning for him. He buried his mouth in her pussy, sliding his tongue through the fleshy pink lips of her cunt.

Lily's hand grasped the back of his neck, pushing him closer as his tongue teased the opening of her pussy, plunging deep inside of her then pulling out before plunging back in again. He tongue-fucked her until her thighs started trembling.

Dragging his tongue away with a final sweep across her clit, he stood up. He then turned her until she was facing the shower bench that was against one wall of the shower.

"Bend over," he groaned, looking down at perfection.

Once Lily bent over, placing her hands on the bench, his hand on her back pushed her down farther until her head lay on her hands.

Shade rubbed the tip of his cock through the silky wetness of her pussy, sliding the long length between the lips. He placed the tip on her clit then slid it away, feeling her quiver. He changed directions on his next forward thrust, the momentum sending his cock tunneling through her cunt, burying himself deep within her. He leaned over her back, pushing himself inside of her to the hilt.

Lily screamed over the loud blast of the music as he pistoned inside of her, driving himself in and out until her screams became whimpers. His foot moved her bare feet, widening her stance. She wiggled her hips, trying to adjust to his cock, but he held her still. He wanted the head of his cock to brush her g-spot with every thrust.

"Stay still." He found the tender flesh of her neck with his mouth. "I'm going to fuck you deep and long enough that you're going to always remember tonight. I'm going to leave my mark on your pussy so you will never, ever doubt in your mind that you belong to me. Do you understand me?"

"Yes," Lily gasped, tiny climaxes driving her back on his cock.

His hand slid around her ribcage then upwards, grabbing her breasts in a tight hold to pull her back onto his thrusting cock.

"How long, Lily?" he demanded.

"Always, Shade. I'll always belong to you."

CHAPTER SIXTY-SEVEN

"The fucking bitch. I was looking forward to firing her today." Razer kicked a rock across the parking lot.

"Cool it; here comes Lily," Shade warned.

He, Razer, Rider, and Train all stood around in a circle by the end of the factory building.

Lily was walking down the pathway from their house, heading to the parking lot. He had left her in bed still sleeping because he had to be at work two hours before she had to open the church store at nine. He had dressed quietly so he wouldn't wake her, since he had kept her up late the previous night and he didn't want her going to work tired.

It was the fourth day of their marriage. He wondered how long it would take before he would stop counting the days. Hell, he had been lucky he had made it past their second day when Lily had caught Raci wearing his jacket. She had been furious at him and had stormed back to their house where they had made up.

Shade promised himself he would pick a fight with her the following Friday night. He wanted to ease her into the many scenes he had planned for them.

"What's up?" Lily asked, walking up to them with her coffee cup in hand.

"Nothing. We came out here so we could talk without being overheard. Georgia has several friends in there," Shade replied.

"What about Georgia?" Lily stiffened. Shade had told her the night before at dinner that he and Razer were planning on firing Georgia that day.

"She quit. When she didn't come in this morning, I called her. She told me she wasn't coming in to give us the satisfaction of firing her. Then she told me what to do with the job, so I hung up on her." He'd wanted to jerk the woman through his cell phone so he could tell her personally what she could do with his fucking clipboard. Instead, he had hung up, ultimately glad to be rid of the vicious bitch.

"It doesn't make any sense to me," Lily said, blowing on her coffee.

"What doesn't? That she's a fucking bitch or that she quit?" Rider asked grimly.

"Both. Not a month ago, she was giving me heck because she thought I took her brother's job. Now, suddenly she's calling one of her bosses' wives bad names in front of a large group who will spread it all over town so she wouldn't be able to deny it. It's almost like she *wanted* to get fired," Lily answered, blowing on her coffee again.

She reached up, giving her husband a quick kiss on the lips. "Later." She grinned, walking away, not paying attention to the stunned looks on the men's faces as she left.

঺ ଊ

Shade was standing next to Razer in his office when his cell phone rang. The caller ID showed Lucky was calling.

"Yeah?"

"Thought I'd let you know that your new wife found a lock box in the basement this morning. Want to take a wild guess what was inside?"

"Lily's adoption papers?"

"Yes."

"Fake?"

"Yes. I'll take them by Knox's office when I go to lunch."

"Thanks. Want to hear something interesting?" Shade asked before Lucky could hang up.

"Hit me."

"Georgia quit this morning. Beat me to firing her ass. Thing is, Lily came up with this idea. She seemed like she wanted to be fired, so we checked it out. Seems the bitch had a chunk of money put in her checking account the day after Halloween."

"How much?"

"Fifty thousand. Not only that, another deposit of thirty was put in first thing this morning. This is the first day the banks have been open since Christmas. Someone paid her not only to start the fire, but to start an argument at the church," Shade concluded.

"Why start an argument at the church?"

"I think to try to rattle Lily into running out of the church. A month ago... Hell, two weeks ago, it would have worked. Whoever wants her dead is getting desperate to try to get to her. We don't leave her alone, so someone was trying to make their own opportunity."

"I'll call Knox to come here and pick these papers up. I'm not going to leave the church from now on when Lily's here." Lucky's voice was grim over the phone line.

"I'll call you if I find anything else out. Once Knox has the proof from the bank, he's going to arrest Georgia. I took him her coffee cup, so if the DNA matches the evidence found from the fire, we have her ass, and we may be able to find out what the fuck is going on," Shade's anger carried through the phone line.

"All right, I'll talk to you later, Shade."

"Later, Dean."

        ℬ℺ℭℬ

"Why the truck?" Lily asked, climbing inside Rider's truck. Usually, Shade rode his motorcycle to pick her up.

Shade stared back at her from behind his sunglasses. "I wanted to talk to you on the way home," he said, making no effort to put the truck in gear.

"Is something wrong?" Lily questioned, frowning.

"Knox arrested Georgia this afternoon."

"Why? What did she do?" Lily's breath caught in surprise.

"She's the one who set the basement on fire."

"What? Why would she do something like that?" Lily asked, shocked.

"Someone paid her fifty thousand dollars. The same person who probably tried to run you down on the street and attempted to break into your house," Shade explained.

"Who?"

"I don't know. Knox is questioning her now. He's going to be at the club tonight, so we can find out more then."

She sat quietly, staring out the window as he drove them home.

"You better tell Knox to keep an eye on her. When she was younger, she tried to kill herself twice. This is going to humiliate her, Shade," Lily warned.

As soon as he parked the truck, Shade made the call to Knox. Then they went to their house to get changed before going over to eat dinner at the clubhouse. This was their first party since they had gotten married, and she had made an effort to dress up for him.

She had worn a skirt which he was surprised she owned. Almost all her dresses and skirts came down to her calves. This one came barely a half an inch above her knees.

Shade grinned. He was willing to bet she considered it risqué. He liked it, though, because it hugged her perfect ass.

The soft pink sweater she wore with it showed the top globes of her breasts when it slid off her shoulder. Shade wanted to tug it down all the way yet decided to save that deed for later.

"You look pretty tonight," Lily complimented Beth after they had walked into the clubhouse.

Shade frowned behind her back. She had been glowing with confidence before they had walked in the door. It finally clicked with him that she was trying to be sexy. His angel just had to walk in the door to get his attention. He didn't give a shit how she dressed.

"You do, too. I might have to borrow that sweater," Beth said enviously.

"You can have it. It won't quit sliding down my shoulders." Lily pulled it back up in frustration.

"That's what makes it so pretty," Winter said, coming up behind her.

Shade fixed himself a plate of food, letting the women bolster Lily's ego for the moment; he would show her later how much his dick appreciated her effort.

The women decided to play cards, ignoring the men. Shade and the brothers sat on the chairs and couch, talking quietly about who could have hired Georgia and if the money in her account could be traced.

Shade was sitting on the end of the couch with his feet on the coffee table while Viper sat at the other end. Razer was sprawled on the chair next to the couch.

He saw Lily approaching and warned the other two men. She wore an angry frown, while Winter was sending sneaky looks his way. She must have spilled the beans about the card game being rigged.

Lily noticed they had stopped talking and turned to leave but Shade caught her hand, dragging her down to sit on his lap.

Viper began talking about their clubhouse in Ohio and the new recruits they had wanting to join.

"Got one wanting to go for the patch here," Shade said, lacing his hand through Lily's.

She lost her angry expression, rubbing her thumb back against his.

"Who?" Viper asked, his eyes going around the room.

"Dude against the left wall with the eight-ball tat," Shade answered without turning his head.

Lily started to turn her head, but Shade's hand tightened on the hand he was holding. Lily took the hint and remained still. That time, it was his thumb rubbing hers.

"Name?" Viper didn't take his eyes off the recruit.

"Eightball."

"How original," Viper said wryly.

"I thought so. He had to think a couple of seconds when I asked," Shade said, his voice unemotional.

"Anything else?"

"He's good. Knows how to handle himself and his bike." Shade paused, looking at Lily. "Too good for someone not patched."

"Stud?"

"No. Stud doesn't play that game, but even if he did he wouldn't with us. He wouldn't want to take a chance on Sex Piston finding out; she and Beth are too tight. He's not going to get his old lady upset when she's carrying his kid."

"I agree, so who?" Viper demanded.

"Don't know, but I'll find out," Shade promised his president.

"Now," Viper commanded.

Shade remained sitting. The best part about being an enforcer was letting someone else do his dirty work.

"I'm on it," he replied, nodding toward Cash at the bar who was watching Shade for his signal.

At Shade's gesture, he set his glass of whiskey down then said something to Nickel who was standing next to him. When both men moved toward the left wall, Shade's hand tightened on Lily's, again silently warning her not to look.

Lily started trembling, and her bottom lip began quivering at the sound of the scuffle going on behind her between Eightball, Cash, and Nickel.

"Shade…"

He leaned forward, brushing his lips against hers as his hand picked up his beer.

"Angel face, I like that sweater on you," he murmured against her lips.

"Don't hurt him," she pleaded softly.

"Have to find out if he's here because of you," he whispered before kissing her. It was too much of a coincidence that someone was trying to find out information on their club when someone was trying to kill Lily.

He lifted his mouth away from hers, leaning back against the couch as he took a drink of his beer.

Train came up to them then.

"Lily, a buddy of mine gave me two pieces-of-shit bikes he wanted to get rid of. I fixed them up. Don't want them; none of the brothers do. If you want them, you can have them to sell for your store, or maybe someone needs a ride for work."

"Thank you, Train." Lily jumped off his lap.

Shade could read her intention to hug him. He leaned forward, sliding his arm around her waist before she could take another step, sweeping her back down onto his lap. She stared up at him with her mouth hanging open.

"Stop doing that shit. Do. Not. Touch," he told her with his jaw clenched.

"What? But I was only going to thank him," Lily protested.

"Then thank him, but Do. Not. Touch. And quit kissing," he added as an afterthought.

"Quit kissing? But I like kissing you. I don't want to stop that," Lily protested. She turned red when Viper and Razer began laughing. Train was still standing, unmoving.

"That's not what I meant." Shade gradually regained control. "I meant when you kiss men on the cheek."

"Who did I kiss on the cheek?"

"Viper."

Lily looked thoughtful before she reproached, "You scared Pastor Dean,"

"You do not touch anyone, especially Pastor Dean," Shade told her sharply, still glaring at a pale Train.

Lily looked at him. "Okay."

She relaxed against him, rubbing his chest with her hand until his breathing returned to normal.

"Thank you," he said, relaxing back against the couch.

"No problem." Lily smiled gently up at him.

"Thank God. At least we finally got that shit straight. I didn't think I'd have a brother left after Christmas."

She had given each and every one of the brothers a peck on the cheek with a present she had picked out for them.

"You didn't?" She looked at him suspiciously.

"No, but it was close," Shade said unrepentantly.

She was shaking her head at him when Knox came in with Diamond. She was like Lily; she hadn't dressed overtly sexy, either. She was wearing a dark jumper and a black pair of leggings with high-heeled boots.

Knox took a seat on the couch next to Shade, pulling Diamond down onto his lap. He wasn't wearing his uniform, just jeans and a T-shirt. His huge frame crowded the large sofa. Lily sat up straighter, curling her legs on top of Shade's.

"I put Georgia on suicide watch. Had to hire an extra policewoman from Jamestown, but at least I don't have to worry about walking into her cell and finding her dead," Knox said, looking at Lily. "You were right; I saw the marks on her wrist."

"I wouldn't have ever said anything, but I didn't want her to hurt herself because she'd made a mistake."

"It's more than a mistake. She fucked up bad. She's going to do some hard time for arson unless she can come up with a name. Cash is trying to trace the account, but he said whoever set the account up knows what they're doing. He said it's one of the best he's ever seen," Knox informed them.

"Fuck," Shade exclaimed.

"Not only that, but Georgia says she doesn't know the man who gave her the money. Said she was at the grocery store, and he drove a dark car up to her when she was putting groceries in her car. Handed her twenty thousand to do it then promised her the fifty thousand after it was done."

"Did you check the store surveillance?" Viper asked.

"Sure did. The store erases the tapes after a month. I looked through them just in case we got lucky, but no such luck."

"Damn," Shade said. "I was hoping she had more information than that."

"I'll see if she can remember anything more in the morning. Maybe spending her first night in jail will jog her memory," Knox responded, adjusting Diamond on his lap.

"We need to catch a break somewhere before whoever they are makes another move against Lily," Shade said grimly. It was disconcerting to have someone so determined to hurt someone you love and not know why.

"I like your boots," Lily said to Diamond.

That started a whole conversation about shoes which caused Knox and Shade to share a what-the-fuck look and roll their eyes. Finally, Shade could take no more of it.

"Let's dance," Shade interrupted them, his hand lifting her legs off his.

Shade saw her looking toward Train who had his hand between Bliss's thighs as she sat on a stool at the bar. Several of the women who were allowed in the house were dancing suggestively with the members on the floor. Nickel was standing behind one, pulling her breast out of her top.

Lily hastily turned away.

"I think the floor is crowded enough." she stood up.

"It isn't downstairs," Shade said, taking her hand. "Knox?"

"Coming."

Shade turned to Viper and Razer. "Later."

"Happy New Year, brother," Viper said, lifting his beer up.

"You, too."

Shade led Lily downstairs where he turned on a couple of the lamps then the music. He pulled up the workout mats, placing them against the wall before holding out his arms for her. She stepped into his arms without hesitation.

Knox and Diamond came downstairs, closing the door behind them, and then they began dancing next to them.

Shade was aware of Lily's wariness to be around Knox. He was the one she had spent the least amount of time around her in this setting.

They danced several dances before Shade went upstairs, getting beers for him and Knox, bringing sodas for Lily and Diamond.

After sitting and talking for a while, Knox and Diamond went to the dance floor to dance again.

"Are you having fun?" Shade asked, sitting down on the couch next to her.

"Yes. I like Diamond." Lily lowered her voice. "Shade, she really doesn't believe that zombies are going to take over the world, does she?"

Shade laughed. "I have no idea. I think she just watches too many zombie movies."

"See, that's why I don't watch scary movies." She gave him an I-told-you-so look.

"Why? Are you susceptible to movies?"

"Scary ones. They give me nightmares."

"Porn?" Shade leaned over her.

"No." Lily hit his shoulder, laughing. Her laughter broke off when he stared down at her breasts.

Her sweater was barely on her shoulder, the cleft between her breasts slightly visible.

His mouth touched hers, parting her lips with a firm thrust of his tongue, demanding her response. She widened her lips, letting him take what he wanted from her.

He brought his hand to her shoulder, brushing the sweater off it. His mouth followed the path of the top while his other hand slid it off the other shoulder. Only her breasts held up her sweater.

Then Shade leaned closer to her, pressing Lily against the corner of the couch. His hand went to her thigh, sliding underneath her skirt and finding the edge of her panties.

The music changed to a different song and she pushed him off her, sitting upright. Lily looked quickly toward the dance floor. The couple dancing wasn't paying any attention to them, lost in their own world.

Knox was standing behind Diamond, grinding his hips into her ass, his arm around her waist to pull her back against him. Diamond was dancing with her eyes closed, listening to the music, and Knox was only looking at Diamond.

Shade stood up, pulling Lily to her feet before lifting her into his arms. He carried her back to the bedroom where he set her on her feet next to the bed then turned on the bedside lamp.

He took off his clothes then reached out, taking off her sweater and bra, his lips kissing each nipple when he pulled it off.

"Sit down."

After Lily sat down on the edge of the bed, Shade bent down, pulling off her shoes and then kissing each foot. He then stood up, tossing her shoes out of the way.

Bending over, he kissed her, giving her the passion she had been waiting for. His teeth nipped her bottom lip, giving her a small sting of pain, which he laved away with the tip of his tongue before he pressed her back against the mattress.

Lily tore her mouth away from his. "Where did this furniture come from?"

"I ordered another set. It came yesterday."

"Oh." Lily looked thoughtful for a second. "Why?"

"For when I want to play over here," he explained, taking a nipple into his mouth.

"Ohhh," Lily moaned as he bit down on the tip of her breast.

Just as her thigh came up, rubbing against his hip, Knox came in, carrying a wiggling Diamond on his shoulder.

"Bed or couch?" Knox asked, pausing long enough to shut the door with his foot.

"Bed."

Diamond and Lily both squealed; however, Shade covered her mouth with his.

The bed lurched as Diamond was dropped onto the opposite end.

"Shade, I—" Lily started to protest.

"Lily, it's my turn," he said with a smile. "And I'm cashing in another of my IOUs."

He returned his mouth to play with her breasts, not giving her time to think.

The mattress underneath them shook as Knox undressed Diamond.

Shade straightened, standing up. "You got your cuffs?"

"Always," Knox grunted.

Shade grinned when he saw Diamond slap Knox's bald head as he pulled his handcuffs out of his pocket. He reached into his nightstand for his own pair while Lily lay staring in disbelief up at him as he slipped one cuff onto her wrist then stretched, snapping the other to Diamond's wrist above her head. Shade then lifted her other wrist and handcuffed it, also stretching her arm above her head so Knox could handcuff them together.

They started wiggling and when Diamond tried to lower her wrists, it stretched Lily taut on the mattress. When Lily tried to lower hers, it stretched Diamond's body taut. Shade could come simply from watching them do that. It was sexy as hell.

"Fuck," Knox's groaned, just as turned on.

Lily stared up at him as Shade stared down at her, his eyes filling with desire for her. Only her.

Lily understood his silent message, relaxing back against the mattress. Shade saw the resolve in her eyes and grinned, knowing she was going to let him play.

The mirrors on the walls reflected the four of them. Lily and Diamond were lying on opposite sides of the huge bed, handcuffed together, Shade was naked, and Knox was getting undressed.

Lily's mouth dropped open, and she squinted her eyes at Knox's cock.

Shade frowned. She had never stared at his cock the way she was gaping at Knox's. Shade was big himself, yet Knox's cock was big and pierced. He couldn't have her staring at Knox's cock like that. Fuck, he didn't mind getting any tat she wanted him to get, but he wasn't getting a piercing.

Shade opened the nightstand again, pulling out several silk scarves and tossing a few to Knox. Shade wound a scarf around the inside of Lily's cuff so it wouldn't scratch her before he did the same to the other wrist.

Turning to the wall, he turned on the music.

"You have a thing for music, don't you?" Lily teased.

"It inspires me," Shade replied, smiling before stepping back between her legs and reaching for the waistband of her skirt. Then he pulled it and her panties off.

Shade reached for another silk scarf, placing it over her eyes and tying it behind her head as Knox tied one on Diamond.

"I could jack off just looking at you like this." Shade's voice was hoarse as he stared down at her body. He lifted his eyes briefly to see Knox sliding his hand up and down his cock as he stared down at Diamond.

Shade placed his mouth on the curve of her stomach, his tongue tasting her flesh. Diamond moved, bringing Lily's arms up, stretching her taut on the mattress.

Lily gasped as his lips and tongue explored the bare skin of her pussy, his tongue dipping inside the slit, licking the top of her clit before sliding underneath, searching for the nerve endings which were screaming for attention.

Shade cupped the back of her knee, bringing her leg up until her heel touched the mattress. Then he pressed her leg down sideways, the movement widening her. His tongue then slid through the opening of her cunt.

Diamond groaned, and Lily apologized for something.

"That's okay. You can do it again if you want to," Diamond moaned.

Lily giggled.

Shade smiled against her pussy when, a second later, the bed started shaking and Diamond began laughing, too.

"I think the next time I'll bring a couple of gags to the party," Shade threatened the women.

"I'll take care of it," Knox promised.

Both of the women's laughter died immediately.

Shade played with her clit with the head of his cock, teasing her and himself before steadily stroking deep inside of her, groaning at how wet she was.

Lily reached up to his shoulders, sliding her hands to his chest and lingering on his nipples. Shade gritted his teeth; her hands on him had every animalistic need in his body wanting to fuck her so hard he would imprint himself on her soul.

Her hands were jerked away when Diamond tried to reach Knox, her loud moans escalating, telling everyone in the room she was enjoying Knox fucking her. Her screams filled the room a second later.

Shade began toying with Lily's clit as he pounded his cock inside her slick pussy. He couldn't let Lily hear Diamond having a better time than her. Although, he was still a little pissed at the way she had stared at Knox's cock. He didn't care if it was the first time she had seen one pierced.

He lifted her thighs, pressing them to her sides as Shade gave her more of his weight.

"Want to switch?" Knox asked, looking at him over the women writhing on the bed.

"Fuck yeah," Shade answered.

"WHAT?" Diamond yelled.

"No!" Lily squealed.

The men ignored them.

Shade slid his cock out of Lily's pussy, feeling the sudden drop of her desire at the thoughts he was sure were flying through her mind. Shade put his hands on her waist, rolling Lily onto her stomach at the same time Diamond was being turned onto hers. He had turned her so her face was on top of the mattress, their hands now palm down.

"Very funny," Diamond's irritated voice sounded over Knox's laughter.

Shade brought his hand back to her hips, raising her bottom in the air before sliding his cock back inside her in a hard thrust which had her screeching almost in Diamond's ear.

The mattress shook as the men pounded the women. Lily's hands grasped the sheets. Each stroke, he slid deeper, going farther inside her. Shade rebuilt the fire in her pussy one thrust at a time until her moans filled the room.

"I've never seen something so hot," Knox groaned, reviving his own efforts to heighten Diamond's desire. The brother never could stand to be shown up.

Shade began rubbing Lily's clit as the sounds of slapping flesh began to overtake the music he had put on.

He pinched her clit between his thumb and finger, the slight pain lifting her ass higher against him so it was flush against his flat stomach. Then he ran his hand over the smooth flesh, swallowing hard.

"Fuck me back," Shade grunted.

Lily began shoving her ass back at him as he thrust forward while he teased her clit, rubbing away the small sting of pain in a move that had her panting.

"Shade, I need to come," Lily begged.

He pulled his cock out so only the tip was inside her. "You going to come by my office before you go to work Monday and give me this pussy?"

"Yes!" Lily screamed when his cock filled her tight pussy again.

Diamond began screaming as well, clutching Lily's hands. Lily grabbed her back as Shade's fingers reached underneath her, taking a nipple in his hand.

He began squeezing her breast so it would become tender and sensitive from the blood rushing to the tip. He twisted the tender nipple, giving her that slight edge of pain she needed to make her come. Lily was his perfect match—she liked a small amount of pain when he fucked her, and he liked giving it to her.

Shade felt her climax rippling through her pussy. Looking down at her ass again, he let himself thrust one final time, burying his cock to the hilt and coming inside of her with such intensity that it took several seconds to get his breath back. Knox hadn't fared much better, his hand shaking when he reached up to wipe the sweat off his forehead. The men smiled at each other as they unlocked the handcuffs.

Shade pulled off Lily's blindfold, kissing her on her parted lips as her eyes opened to stare dazedly up at him. He gazed back at her, not ashamed to let her see how much he loved her for trusting him enough to try something which was completely out of her comfort zone.

Her hand gently touched his cheek. "How do you keep your face so cleanly shaven?" Only Lily would ask something so mundane after her first experience of group sex.

"I shave a couple of times a day," he answered, lifting her up into his arms.

"Why so often?" she asked, laying her head on his shoulder.

"Because you like to touch my face." Shade carried her into the shower before setting her down.

"Why don't you do that for me? " Diamond asked Knox.

Lily looked up with wide eyes when she heard Knox behind him. Shade deliberately blocked her view of Knox so the only thing she could see was the brother's back and head.

Lily tried to make an escape out of the shower, her face an amazing shade of red, but he turned the water on, handing her the soap.

Lily quickly washed then hurried out of the shower. Shade let her, staying right behind her as she practically ran back into the bedroom. Grinning as he dressed, he watched Lily throw her own clothes on, trying to get dressed before Knox and Diamond returned.

He was putting on his boots before she finally calmed down and realized they were giving her time to dress. Diamond wouldn't be any more anxious to get dressed in front of him than Lily was Knox.

"Thirsty?" Shade asked when she finished dressing.

⁎⁎

Lily's eyes were closed when Shade slid under the covers, pulling them over their bodies. When he tugged her to him, she rolled over, burying her face in his neck as she lay against his chest.

"Shade…" Lily began.

"Knox will always be a brother, but being Sheriff, he has to keep a low profile. Diamond is a lawyer. She's a good one. She's going to move up.

"I like to play; Knox likes to play. We all know how to keep our mouths shut. That's why Viper and Razer talked club business in front of you. You kept Georgia's secret even though that bitch trashed you all over town. The only time you talked was to protect someone else and to save Georgia's life after she almost killed you.

"I think Diamond's an attractive woman, but I don't want to fuck her. Do you understand what I'm saying?"

"Yes," Lily whispered.

"If you want to play sometimes with them and only them, we can. You don't, we won't. It's your call." Shade yawned, putting his arm behind his head. "I thought you and Diamond would get along since you're not close friends, but you can become friends. You're both kind of...sweet," he said tactfully.

Lily lifted her head. "That wasn't what you were going to say." She glared down at him. "I don't know if you or Winter is the most devious."

"I am, but she thinks she is," Shade said smugly.

"Heaven help the person you two gang up on; they wouldn't stand a chance."

CHAPTER SIXTY-EIGHT

Shade was sitting at his desk when the first call came.

"You have something of mine, and I want it back."

"And would this be Ice or Jackal?" Shade replied.

"You know?"

"I know something is going down, and you know what it is. And you're going to tell us what we need to know, or you're going to have one less brother under your command."

"We need to meet."

Shade gave him the address.

"Bring my brother."

Ice could demand all he wanted; however, he wasn't getting anything until he produced the information Shade needed.

"You'll see Eightball when I decide you get him back." Shade emphasized Eightball's name to let Ice know they were aware it was as fake as shit, and it had been a stupid fuckup to get caught by.

"Oh, you'll bring him, and I'll bring that pretty little sister of yours."

Shade didn't lose control of his temper. He had fucked up himself; he should have expected the move.

"I'll bring him." Shade had no choice other than to relent.

"Now that's more like it. We'll be there in an hour." The line disconnected.

Shade got up from behind his desk, opening his door. "Jewell, take over. Rider, Train, you're with me."

They were halfway across the parking lot when the second call came in. Shade paused to answer it.

"Later, Lucky. I'm busy—"

"Shade, it's Lily. She's gone. I was on my way to my office when someone knocked me out. When I came to…she was gone. I called Knox; he's on his way over."

Shade disconnected the call.

"Shade?"

He looked at Rider. "We'll talk in the house. Gather all the brothers and meet me in the kitchen."

They ran up the flight of steps. Shade found Viper in the kitchen. It took very little time to have the brothers gathered in the kitchen and the television room. The door stood open toward the living room so all the members could hear.

Shade quickly explained about the meet with Ice and that Lily was missing from the church.

Viper took control. "Razer, call Beth. Tell her to get here and stay here. Train, call the brothers in Ohio, tell them to haul ass here, then call Stud and tell him the same thing. I'm calling in my marker. We'll meet the Predators, we find out what they know, and then we'll find out how to find Lily.

"We have to shut the town down so whoever has Lily can't get away. We have to have someone who knows every way in and out of town. Call Knox and tell him to call the Porters for help. There's no place in town or the mountains they don't know. Everyone's got five minutes to get dressed and packed for war. We'll meet at our bikes. Move."

Shade went to his house and came back carrying a canvas bag. When he got to the parking lot, everyone was getting on their bikes. He threw his bag into Rider's back seat with Nickel. Unzipping it, he took out his .50 caliber Desert Eagle, shoving it in the back of his jeans. Then he reached in, taking out several magazines and putting them in his jacket pocket, zipping it back up. Slamming the truck door, he went to his bike, climbing on. Only then did Shade cut on his motor, ready to ride.

The brothers were all moving their bikes behind Viper and Cash at the beginning of the parking lot.

Viper's voice sounded strong and clear over the roar of the bikes. "Last Riders, we ride!"

A few minutes later, The Last Riders were pulling into the parking lot of Rosie's bar where the Predators were already waiting.

Viper and Cash pulled to the front while Shade rode his bike to the other side of Viper. The three waited.

Ice and Max rode their bikes forward, and the men faced each other down.

"Where's Rip?" Ice's cold eyes searched the riders behind them.

"You mean Eightball?" Viper asked sarcastically. He pointed to the mountain ridge to their left. Two men moved to the edge, one held with a gun to his head.

"Are you going to tell us why you planted a traitor in our club and what the fuck it's got to do with Lily? Or is your brother going to take a leap of faith?" Viper finished, turning back to Ice.

Ice gave a whistle, and two bikes at the back of the lot moved. Penni stood with a gun to her head. The terrified look on her face made Shade want his rifle; however, he knew the men wanted their brother as much as he wanted his sister.

"Ice, man, this wasn't part of the plan." Two men toward the back got off their bikes, walking forward.

Shade remembered the one with the goatee from the diner. The second one was recognizable to anyone who could turn a television set on.

"I told you I would let you talk, Colton. You got ten minutes before I do my own fucking talking."

The one named Colton walked a step closer to Viper before the large man next to Ice put an arm in his way, stopping him.

"My name is Colton; this is Kaden. Our wives were friends with Lily when she was a little girl. A man named Digger runs a sex ring; he kidnaps young women then sells them as slaves. Digger is in a power struggle with a man named King. Last year, my wife was kidnapped and held hostage by Digger to gain information to destroy King."

"What did she know?" Shade asked.

"That King had a daughter, Callie. Your wife, Lily. It was only when Penni started working for us that we discovered Callie was still alive. Unfortunately, so did Digger."

"That must be who's been trying to kill her," Shade said thoughtfully.

Shade saw the men pause and look at each other. "We weren't aware someone had tried to kill her yet. We didn't know until Friday, when Digger escaped, that he was aware of Callie. They found information that he had taken a hit out on Callie.

"Our wives have been tortured by this information. They love Callie and want to be reunited with her, but didn't attempt to do so because they didn't want to lead Digger to her. Ice was doing me a favor by trying to put a man in to keep an eye on Callie, and to be honest, make sure she was happy. That's important to them.

"If you bring Callie here, she can confirm that she knows them. She was just eight, but she should have been old enough that she would recognize one of them. We have them waiting. When you bring Callie, I'll send for our wives to be brought in."

"What're your wives' names?" Shade questioned.

"Sawyer and Vida. Are you willing to bring Callie?" Colton asked.

"There's a problem with that. She's missing," Shade said, carefully watching their reaction.

Shade could tell from their faces that they didn't have Lily. They had told them what they knew. Viper could tell, too, which was why he lifted his hand. The two men disappeared from the edge of the cliff.

"You can have your man back. Any idea where Digger would take her?" Viper asked.

"No. He's been in prison. We don't know where the houses he operates are or which routes he still has open. The FBI have been trying to find information and can't. That's why they didn't kill the bastard when they took him into custody."

The sound of a motorbike filled the air as Train pulled into the lot behind Viper. Rip got off the back of the bike, going to his brothers who started cheering.

"Aren't you forgetting something?" Shade's voice snapped out.

"Jackal!" Ice yelled.

The man holding the gun moved it away from Penni's head, and he gave her a shove forward.

She turned around and spat into his face. "Asshole."

The men around him broke into jeers as she walked through their midst. When she reached Kaden and Colton, Kaden reached out to touch her, but she jerked her arm away, going straight to her brother and climbing on the back of his bike.

"How long has she been gone?" Ice asked.

"Since this morning," Shade answered.

"Need some help?" Ice questioned, reaching his hand out for Viper to shake in truce.

Viper shook his hand. "Couldn't hurt. Tell us what you know about Digger."

Shade listened to the men, gradually coming to the conclusion that only one man had the power to save Lily.

It was time to call Lucky.

Shade took his cell phone out of his pocket, punching the dial button.

"Hello?"

"I need to see you. I'll be there in twenty." Shade disconnected the call, turning to Viper.

"You got this? I'm going to go see Lucky."

"Go, I can handle this. The Porters are on the way. We'll divide the town and county up and begin searching," Viper told him.

419

"I'll meet up with you after I drop Penni off and talk to Lucky. I'm going to get us some help," Shade said.

"We're going to need it."

৪০ ৪৪

The knock came ten minutes earlier than he'd said he would be there, but Shade didn't have time to waste.

"Come in."

Shade walked into his office, seeing his brother standing by the window.

"Lucky, I wouldn't ask if I had a choice." Shade's harsh voice sounded hollow in the room.

"I've stood looking out this window for a lot of years, Shade. It took me over a year after your father opened the investigation into the pipeline going through here to find a connection. Then I had to find a way into the community which wouldn't arouse suspicion. I'm a month away from closing down a pipeline which runs through nine states, carrying drugs and guns, and you're asking me to blow my cover for one woman when the men I'm getting ready to arrest have killed hundreds while I've had to sit and wait to get enough evidence to bring them all down. We have all the warrants, everything gone because of one woman."

"Lucky," Shade said, forced to do what he had never done before. "Brother, please. I can't lose her. I'm not like you and the others. I can pretend I have emotions, but they're not there for anyone. There's nothing inside of me except shadows. Lily drives the shadows away. She feels everything. She can't even stand to crush a fucking flower under her foot, and I don't feel anything unless I'm with her. I can't lose that. I waited so long for her. I've loved her for years; she's only loved me for a few weeks.

"When I first saw her, all I could think about was fucking her. Then I saw her at the lake with Beth and I felt her fear, but I saw the look she gave to Beth. She loved and trusted her, knew that Beth wouldn't let anything happen to her." Shade swallowed hard, uncomfortable opening himself up to anyone, especially Lucky. "I wanted her to look at me that way, *needed* her to look at me that way. I wanted to give her a life away from the darkness I saw had touched her beautiful soul."

Shade's face twisted into a painful mask. "I've taken countless lives and never felt an ounce of emotion. That's why they recruited me in the military. One psychologist even joked after my evaluation that I had been born without a soul, and it was true until that day at the lake. I fell in love with her that day. There is no other woman for me; there never will be. Lily is my gateway to Heaven. Without her, the only thing left for me is Hell.

"You used to believe in something more important than that badge you carry. I'm begging you to save me, brother, because as God is my witness, I will kill you if you don't help me."

"I wouldn't do it for anyone else. Not my mother or any brother, not for a million fucking dollars, and especially not because of any fucking threat of yours. But I will for Lily."

"Thank you." Shade's mind caught on something. "Wait a minute. You said you have the warrants? I think I know how we can get Lily back and serve those warrants at the same time. Call your boss."

It took less than thirty minutes and several phone calls from both Lucky and Shade where they made promises which would have to be kept later when the government wanted their skills. However, neither man argued, agreeing to their terms.

"Lily is worth the price," Lucky conceded then hung up the phone. "It's all set. In thirty minutes, the warrants will be served." He looked down at the phone. "We just sold our souls to get her back."

Shade smiled grimly. "Then they got the short end of the stick. They'll have to go to Hell to collect."

CHAPTER SIXTY-NINE

Shade stood outside Knox's office, waiting for Lucky. They had found Lily, and she was safely inside with Beth. His hand still shook with the thought of being in the police car with Knox and Lucky when the call had come over that she had been found, and there was a shootout in progress. Knox had floored the pedal, flying toward the location.

When they had arrived, he had been forced to wait for the FBI to give the all-clear and then gone ballistic when the Porters, who had managed to beat all the law enforcement officers there, had asked for an ambulance.

The moment he had walked in and seen Lily safe would remain in his memory for the rest of his life. Afterward, they had brought her to the sheriff's office for a statement. As soon as they were done, he could take her home. It was going to be a while before he was going to let her out of his sight again.

Unfortunately, Lily was about to find out that another person she trusted wasn't what they seemed.

"Ready?" Knox asked as he approached.

"Where's Lucky?"

"He's finishing up a call. He'll be right in," Knox said, opening the door.

"How did the Porters find me?" Lily was asking.

"I have no idea," Shade heard Beth answer.

"I can answer that question." Knox took a seat behind his desk.

Lily waited expectantly. "Well?"

"We're waiting on someone. We promised we would until he arrived." Shade walked to stand beside her chair, taking her hand.

Razer came into the office then, shutting the door behind him.

"What's wrong?" Shade could tell Lily had figured out the news they had wasn't going to be good.

"Nothing. There's just a few things Razer and I haven't told you. It's not because we didn't want to; it was because we couldn't," Shade answered as Razer moved to stare down at his wife.

A knock sounded on the door.

"Come in," Knox called out.

The door opened and Lucky came inside, closing the door with a serious expression instead of the affable one he normally wore around Lily and Beth. He was wearing jeans and a T-shirt, which Shade was sure was a hell of a lot more comfortable than the suits he usually had on.

The women gaping at him in shock weren't staring at the jeans and shirt, though; they were gawking at the ATF jacket and hat he wore.

"Beth, Lily."

"Why are you wearing that?" Lily asked, standing up, her face turning pale.

"Because I'm an ATF Special Agent. I've been undercover since I took over your father's church. It's taken me this long, and over forty agents, to shut down a pipeline which carried drugs and firearms through nine different states."

When Lily's pale face flushed with color, Shade knew she was remembering the different times she had confided in the pastor she admired.

Lucky continued, "When Cash joined the military, he never forgot you two. He was especially sickened with Beth's treatment, and he knew it wouldn't be much longer before Lily would be receiving the same. Shade's father, Will Hunter, had retired, so Cash asked him to stop by Treepoint to check on you two."

Lily's eyes flew to Shade at the mention of his father, the former sheriff.

"I was going to tell you when Dad came back into town next week. Think, Lily; why would I hide that from you when I've confessed to much worse than that?"

Lily nodded. Thankfully, she seemed to believe he was telling the truth.

"When he stayed here those few days, Will decided he liked it enough to stay indefinitely. He and his wife both were tired of moving around so much and wanted a break from it.

"They settled here, and as you both know, it wasn't long before he gained enough respect to become sheriff. That's where his military training came in handy. He soon discovered the pipeline and notified the proper authorities." Dean walked farther into the office, leaning against the corner of Knox's desk.

"This is where the conversation becomes confidential." Lucky stared at both of the women, giving them a silent warning. "I had left the military and joined The Last Riders. I had been in the Seals and had served as a military chaplain, but when I left the service, I no longer felt the call to serve as a pastor, so I left that part of my life behind. But I wasn't content. I missed the action of being in the military, so when the CIA approached The Last Riders to become a paramilitary group, we accepted.

"That's how we ended up in Treepoint to begin an investigation. The ATF offered me a position as a Special Agent to lead the investigation, but I had to go undercover to do so. The people who had begun developing leads ended up dead, so I waited for a way to enter the community that would be above suspicion."

Beth cut in. "Our parents' deaths created the perfect opportunity." Her face had gone as white as Lily's as she gazed at Razer.

"Sadly, yes. I'm sorry." Dean paused then continued, "I became Pastor Dean and began my investigation. It's taken me all these years to gather enough evidence to win my cases. I was a week away from making my arrests. I even had the warrants ready to go, but it all came crashing down today. "

"Why today?" Beth asked.

Shade silently watched Lily's reaction to Lucky's bombshell, knowing Lily only wanted to get away.

"Because of Lily. We pooled all our available resources together, but to do that, I had to break my cover."

"I'm sorry," Lily said. Even after learning she had been betrayed by Dean, she was apologizing.

"Thanks to Shade's quick thinking, we were able to serve the warrants in a two-hour mass bust and arrested three-fourths of the people we were after, and we're confident we'll be able to locate the remaining ones."

"How?" Lily asked, visibly relieved.

"We had interagency cooperation. It was one of the deals Shade made for The Last Riders. In return, they sold the pending patents' right to a technical computer system for pennies on the dollar than they would have made.

"One of the conditions was that they had to use their technology to help find you."

It was the use of the planes which had cost both him and Lucky. It required special clearance and technology which were only used to find terrorists in other countries. Unless the agencies all agreed, with the permission granted by an office of extreme power, they would have never found her in time. When Lily's location had been pinpointed, the Porters had been close by and had moved in with enough fire power and skill to save her.

"When you were located, the Porters were the closest. That's how they got there first. They're never going to let us live it down. They want Dustin's record expunged for their cooperation. I'll see they get what they want. They deserve it." Lucky stood up straight, looking at Lily.

Lily took a shuddering breath, stepping forward. She reached up, kissing Lucky on his cheek. "Thank you."

Shade stood hastily. No matter how hard he tried and what he owed for Lucky's help, he couldn't stand to see her touch him.

"Don't you dare," Lily said, pointing a finger at him.

Shade managed to control himself, taking a seat back in the vacant chair.

"I think you just returned the favor," Dean said, smiling at Lily.

When Beth would have gotten up, Razer pressed her back down in her chair with a hand on her shoulder.

"I have to go. I still have a lot of reports to finish today. I also have to find a new minister for the church." Lucky smiled wryly.

"You never know…You missed the military when you left it; you may miss the church," Lily said hopefully.

Dean looked at both sisters briefly before going to the door and opening it. "Perhaps. I was blessed to meet two angels, so miracles can happen. We'll have to wait and see," he said, closing the door behind him.

"Show-off," Shade said, standing up. "I called you an angel first, remember that."

Lily laughed, breaking the tension. "Can we go home now?"

"Yes," Shade said, still irritated

"Can I make a stop on the way and see my dad?" Lily asked.

"Yes." Shade personally thought the man who had kidnapped Lily deserved to be behind bars. He didn't give a fuck if he had only done it to keep Lily safe from his enemy. Lily's father King had been the one the ambulance had been called for, having been shot before the Porters had arrived.

Lily laughed at his short responses, reaching up to kiss him on his cheek. "Does that make it better?"

He smiled down at her as he put his arm around her shoulders. *Fuck no*, he thought to himself, *but it will do until we get home.*

Lily turned to her sister. "Would you like to go, Beth?"

"Yes. I'm looking forward to meeting him. When I first saw him, when he brought you, Dad said he was from the adoption agency."

"That reminds me, Lily. That strongbox you found contained your fake birth certificate. Cash sent it off to a buddy of his, and they tracked down your real one. It came in the afternoon mail." Knox handed it to her.

Lily took the envelope and stared down at it. Shade placed his arm around her shoulder, leading her out of the office. She didn't need the paper. Lily was Beth's sister, his wife, friends with a group which had sacrificed millions of dollars to keep her safe. No, she didn't need it any longer. Shade had already known that when he had told Knox to send for a copy of it for her. Lily would have it for when she needed it, but other than that, it was just a piece of paper.

Neither parent listed on that certificate deserved the child they had created. One was dead, and the other deserved to be for the childhood Lily had suffered.

She wanted to give King a chance, and because Lily wanted it, Shade would try to bury his feelings. If the fucker screwed up again, however, then he would be the one buried.

‴ ″

Shade lay on his side in the bed, watching Lily brush her hair.

"What's going to happen to him?" she asked.

"Not much, since you've already told Knox you weren't kidnapped, and it was just a family reunion. Several government agencies aren't very happy with you right now."

Lily shrugged, not concerned. "How about that man who was after him?"

"He's a different matter. Since he believes in letting everyone do his dirty work for him, he wasn't hurt. He's in Knox's jail, waiting for the Texas Rangers to come and get him. I imagine he's planning more song and dance, holding the where-abouts of those women to himself."

Digger, the man responsible for the attempts on Lily's life, was a piece of shit who had mistakenly assumed he was capable of outsmarting everyone.

"I hope not. I'm going to pray for him to let those women go tonight."

"You do that, Lily. I have a feeling he's going to need your prayers tonight," Shade said, stroking her back.

Digger was going to need more than prayers; he was going to need a miracle.

Lily set her hairbrush on the table then stood up, her violet eyes staring down into his. "It's my turn."

Shade's grin widen as he scooted over on the bed, patting the mattress. During the short time they had been married, when they had sex, Lily preferred for him to make love to her gently. The newness of their relationship and being around the women club members had her instinctively needing the reconfirmation of his feelings for her. He understood and didn't care how he had her.

Lily shook her head. "Uh-uh. I want you to stand up."

Shade was puzzled by her behavior. Lily had never been the one to initiate having sex.

He rose to stand next to her. She walked across the room, turning the overhead light off yet leaving the bedside lamps on. Shade was shocked when she opened his cabinet, which he no longer kept locked since it had been moved to his house.

Turning, she walked to stand directly in front of him where she took off her robe and tossed it onto the chair by their bed. She stood completely naked before gracefully lowering herself into a kneeling position, placing her hands on her lap, palms up.

He stood staring down at the perfect submissive pose she had voluntary presented him, struggling for several seconds to find his voice.

"You did very well, Lily. Thank you." He cleared his throat. "The other night, I told you that you were not allowed to kiss other men to show your gratitude, yet you did so today, didn't you?"

"Yes, Sir."

"I also said one man in particular you were not allowed to touch. Who was it?"

"Pastor Dean, Sir."

"Have you got anything to say for yourself?"

"I'm very sorry, Sir. I won't do it again."

"Thank you for your apology, but that won't get you out of your punishment."

"I didn't think it would, Sir. I deserve your punishment for disobeying you."

Shade went to his cabinet, finding it hard to keep his face impassive. Her wanting to please him didn't keep that worried frown from her face as he sorted through his toys.

"Lie down on the bed."

Lily obeyed as Shade readied the contents of the package. He came over to Lily, bending between her spread thighs, sliding the metal balls inside of her.

"Sir?"

"I didn't give you permission to talk."

"I'm sorry, Sir."

Shade climbed off the bed, going to the bathroom then coming back to stare down at her naked body on his bed.

"You did very well, Lily. Since this is the first time I used them on you, I will tell you that I inserted two metal balls inside of you. They will add to our enjoyment tonight. Now, I want you to get up and get dressed."

Shade handed her a new pair of tight, black jeans, a sweatshirt, and then a thick jacket and boots, no bra or panties. They dressed without talking.

They left their house, walking behind it and down the pathway. When Shade got on his bike, Lily hesitated then grinned, getting on behind him. It was the first time he had let her ride with him without a helmet. The night was about being bad, and he wanted Lily to be very bad. He wanted her to feel free after being held hostage. Although, with the balls inside of her, he planned to go slower than his usual speed.

She circled his waist with her arms, gripping the front of his jeans as he pulled out onto the road. The metal balls inside of her would feel the vibrations from the road and his bike. Shade knew her pussy would be on fire by the time they arrived at his intended destination.

It was one of the warmer days of winter—cold, though not unbearable.

Shade slowed his bike, turning into a clearing in a private cove off the lake where Lily had first seen him. Shade cut the bike off, not far from the water. They sat there in the quiet for a few minutes, but Lily couldn't sit without moving around on the seat.

"I remember the day I saw you here in the lake. I've thought of how beautiful you were and how frightened you looked. I wanted to protect and fuck you at the same time. I thought the years I had to wait for you were a nightmare, but all those days and years combined didn't equal the torture of not knowing where you were today and that I couldn't protect you."

Lily got off the bike, coming around to face him. She touched his face, rubbing her thumb over his cheek. "Shade, I'm not going to say I'm not afraid of dying, because I am. Everyone is. But today, what I was most afraid of wasn't dying; it was the fear of being separated from you. I prayed that, if I died, I would forget you because I knew, if I remembered you, I would be in Hell."

Shade jerked her to him, thrusting his tongue inside her mouth, exploring every part and memorizing the feel and taste of her. When Lily's mouth broke away from his passionate kiss, gasping for breath, her hands full of his shirt, Shade was gasping as much as she was.

Lily leaned forward, placing butterfly kisses against his throat, tenderly kissing the curve. Her hands slid under his T-shirt as her mouth traveled to the base of his throat before tracing to the side where his neck and shoulder met, sucking a piece of his flesh into her mouth.

Shade groaned as she unzipped his jeans, pulling out his cock. She slid her hand up and down it as her teeth bit into his shoulder. Her tongue then brushed against the barely-there teeth marks.

She lifted her head as her hand began to slide even faster on his flesh. Lily bent over him, placing her mouth over his cock, sucking him deeply then sliding her mouth up, letting her tongue tease the tip of his cock.

"Damn, angel, quit teasing. Suck my cock," Shade groaned.

Lily stopped torturing him, sucking on him harder as he buried his hand in her hair, pushing her down on him as she used her tongue. Seeing her lips around his cock had him sucking in air to keep from coming. He didn't want the pleasure to end too quickly. Hell, he didn't want it to ever end.

She thrust her hand deeper inside his jeans to play with his balls while Shade lifted her hair to grasp behind her head so he could watch every move, tugging her hair to make her go faster or slow down.

He sucked in his breath sharply when she took the tip of his cock to the back of her throat. She went down even farther the next time and his hips jerked upwards, trying to storm into her tantalizing mouth. He held her head in place as he came, leaning over her as his cock jerked in her mouth.

"Did I do okay?"

Shade put his cock back into his jeans, zipping himself up with shaking hands. "So good I'm going to let you do it again in the morning," he joked, starting the motor.

Once Lily climbed on behind him, wrapping her arms around his waist, Shade turned the bike toward home and they flew back through the night.

The night seemed almost surreal to him. It wasn't that many hours before he had been worried frantic for her. For the same woman to then give him the best blowjob of his life was a little hard to take in, even for him.

By the time Shade pulled into the parking lot, Lily was squirming on the seat behind him, unconsciously rubbing her breasts against his back. He admired her restraint, that she hadn't begged him to fuck her before they reached their house.

With each step, he noticed Lily gritting her teeth and shooting him looks of retribution, which he ignored with a grin.

Shade made it back to their house a few steps ahead of her, leaning against the doorway, waiting for her as she finally made it to the porch, gasping. He arched his brow, daring her to speak her thoughts out loud.

When she remained quiet, he stepped back, giving her the room she needed to go inside, closing the door as soon as she managed to step through.

"Do you need anything, angel face?" He lowered his voice seductively, adding more fuel to her desire to come.

"Take them out or fuck me, Shade," Lily moaned, leaning back against the door.

He stared at her as she rubbed her thighs together. The jeans he had bought her were a size too small so the seam would rub her clit without her panties.

"If you want my dick, all you have to do is ask for it," Shade teased.

"Please, Sir. Please, can I have your dick?" she begged with a flushed face and wild eyes.

He would give his woman his dick; she didn't need to beg. Thank fuck she didn't realize she could be the one to have him begging with little effort.

"Come here."

Shade pulled off her sweatshirt, dropping it to the floor. Placing his hands on her hips, he turned her until she was facing a chair before pressing her down over the back. It was waist-high, and her belly was against the thick material.

He slid his hands between the chair and her belly, unbuttoning her jeans and then tugging them roughly down her hips and legs before he stepped on the middle of them.

"Step out of them." His hand was pressed against her bare back, holding her down over the chair.

When she lifted her feet up, he impatiently kicked them out of the way before he pressed down harder on her back, making her ass come up higher.

"I'm going to give you what you want now. I can't give it to you hard because the metal balls are inside of you, but I'll give it to you hard later after I let you rest," he explained as he stared down at her ass. He placed his hand on the smooth flesh, sliding it down between her thighs to find her pussy.

"You're wet, angel. So wet. All I have to do is give you my dick."

He slid his cock in inch by slow inch, causing the balls to rub against the walls of her pussy with his cock sliding them up and down as he slowly fucked her. It only took a few strokes before she had an orgasm which had her screaming.

His fingers found her clit, rubbing her as he slid his cock in and out. By the time he ground a second orgasm out of her, she was crying his name.

When she lay too spent to move, he lifted her off the chair, carrying her upstairs to the shower and turning on the water.

"I love this shower," she said as he pushed her down onto the bench.

He pulled her ass to the edge of the seat then delved his fingers inside her, pulling both balls out. He placed them in a small, plastic, red container, snapping it closed.

He then pulled her off the bench, washing her off. They took their time before getting out and drying off.

Lily was asleep before her head hit the pillow.

Shade slid into bed next to her, pulling the covers over them. He rolled over to turn the lamp off on his bedside table when a swatch of color caught his attention.

Sitting up in bed, he reached out, picking up the object. In his hand lay a red rubber band.

Chapter Seventy

"Shade came out of his office, motioning to Evie who had been heading back to her workstation.

"What's up?" she questioned as she walked up to him.

Shade opened his office door wider and Evie walked in, taking a seat on the corner of his desk. He closed the door as he came back inside.

"I need you to do something for me."

"What do you need me to do?" Evie asked curiously, taking a sip of her hot coffee.

"Beth has been changing King's bandages, but she's tied up with Mrs. Langley and a new patient. She wanted to know if you would be able to stop by and take care of it for her."

"No problem. I'll stop by after lunch." She paused. "I thought he would head back to his home," she said as an afterthought.

"He wants to stay and spend some time with Lily before he goes back."

"How's that working out for you?" She didn't try to hide her amused grin.

As Shade sat down behind his desk, staring at her, Evie lost her expression and was about to get up.

"He nearly got Lily killed. The stupid bastard couldn't protect her when she was a kid, but he thinks he can make up for it now." He leaned back in his chair, his deadly gaze pinning Evie in place. "He's supposed to go back to Queens City in a few weeks, though, so I can tolerate him that long. I'm planning on taking Lily to Alaska the first of the month anyway, and we're going to be gone for a few weeks, so there won't be any need for him to stay."

"Lily will love it."

"I haven't told her yet."

"I won't say anything." And she wouldn't.

He and Evie had shared many confidences over the years, many they had never shared with the rest of The Last Riders.

Shade nodded. "Penni has decided to go back to work for Kaden Cross. I'm not happy about it, but I can't change her mind. The only stipulation I was able to get out of her was that The Predators have to stay away from her. I want you to drive back with her and spend some time with her."

"To make sure she's safe?"

"Partially. Penni has always managed to watch out for herself, but I have another reason."

"Which is?"

"King. I want you to find out exactly what shit he's involved in and if it could touch Lily."

"And if it can?"

Shade remained quiet.

"All right. Let me know when she plans to head back, and I'll get packed. What reason did you give her for why I'm going back with her?"

"Brotherly concern."

Shade didn't feel emotions the way everyone else did; however, Penni was his half-sister, and she had earned her own place with him. He would protect her, although there were easier ways to accomplish it instead of sending Evie. With a phone call to his stepmother, Penni's ass would be sitting at home with the parents.

Evie snorted. "That works for me. I could use a vacation. Besides, Lily said her dad runs a strip club; I can always pick up a few new pointers."

"I doubt that. You could probably teach them a thing or two."

"I do try." Evie grinned, sashaying her ass to the door.

"Evie?"

She turned her head back to him. "Yeah?"

"Anything, one little piece of dirt that can get Lily hurt, and I want to know."

She lost her smile, seeing the grim resolution on his face. "Sure thing."

⁜ ⁝

The next day, Evie was again sitting in his office. Beth had asked her to change King's bandages for her again, which had worked out well for Shade. Beth wouldn't share any information on King with him. She wasn't stupid; she knew Shade wouldn't tolerate anyone being a threat to Lily or The Last Riders.

"That was all he said?" Shade's enigmatic gaze rested on her, waiting for her response.

King had mentioned Friday nights to her, like he knew what the club did those nights. It had made Evie nervous, and she had immediately called Shade the minute she left King with a message that they needed to talk. He had also asked Evie to join them Friday night for a dinner Lily and Beth had set up with King. Shade had suspicions King was up to something with the invite.

"Yes, I think he knows about the club."

"Perhaps. It wouldn't be difficult with Kaley telling everyone in town."

"You think that's all?"

"No, I think he's checked us out. I'm sure he has the resources to find out what he wants."

"It doesn't bother you?"

"No, Lily knows the truth about the club. He's not going to tell her anything I haven't."

"You've told her everything?" Evie asked in shock.

"Not everything, no. Just the parts King can use against me. The rest about my jobs with the military, no."

"Did you tell her about me?" Evie licked her dry lips.

"No."

He didn't know how much longer he would be able to keep that part out, thanks to Lucky. Shade was going to talk to him, though. Maybe another pastor could be found before Evie learned who was taking over for him.

"Thank you. So, what are you going to do?"

"Nothing. I'm going to let him make his move."

"You don't think he can come between you and Lily?" she asked hesitantly.

"No. I'm really not worried about some bullshit he thinks he's going to pull out of the closet. If he does, Lily and I will deal with it."

"Cool. I could just picture you beating the shit out of him with Lily watching. That's why I accepted his dinner invitation."

"When I deal with King, Lily won't be around. I can deal with him, man to man, whatever he pulls. It's the garbage which could get Lily killed that concerns me."

"When is Penni going back to Queens City?"

"The week after next. The same week Lily and I leave for Alaska. I told her last night."

"Is she excited?"

"That's putting it mildly." A smile lit his face briefly as he thought about Lily's excitement the previous night before it disappeared.

It actually benefited Evie that they were leaving. King would return to his hometown, and Evie would follow along with Penni. When she found out who Merrick Patterson had married, she would be thankful for the excuse to leave Treepoint for a while.

"You finished for the day?" Evie asked, breaking into his thoughts.

"Yeah, I just have to lock up."

When they walked out of the office, Evie stood by his side as he locked the factory door before going up to the clubhouse together.

Dinner was already starting when she turned to go upstairs. Shade paused.

"You're not going to eat?" Shade asked.

"No, I'm not hungry. I'm going to have an early night. See you in the morning."

"Night." Shade watched Evie going upstairs.

He had seen the growing discontent the past few months. A few weeks away would give her time to think. She wouldn't be the first woman who had eventually left the club. Evie would always remain a Last Rider, her loyalty without question, but she had healed enough to begin searching for a lifestyle she couldn't find there, something to call her own. Whether that was a man or a different life away from The Last Riders, it was a choice only she could make.

೮ಬ

The next day, Shade was going around his desk to leave his office when he looked out the window. Lucky was in the parking lot, unloading his things from a car. He would probably sell his "pastor wear" or donate them to the church store as soon as he could.

The brother had waited a long time to ride again.

He watched as Evie and Jewell came out of the factory. Evie ran forward, throwing herself into Lucky's arms.

Shade left his office, going outside to greet the brother.

He crossed the parking lot to stand beside them. "I see you're not wasting any time."

"No. I wanted to make Merrick comfortable. I'll hand over the church to him Sunday, and then I'll be free of all my commitments to the church."

"We need to talk," Shade said just as Lily pulled into the parking lot. There were a couple of things they needed to discuss.

"Fuck," Lucky said, his eyes on Lily with a grim expression on his face.

Shade wanted Lucky to enjoy being back at the club, but he didn't want Lily hurt, either. The brother was going to have to find a happy medium, one which kept Lily happy while also keeping Lucky happy. Shade had kept Beth and Winter out of his business, so Lucky could be circumspect and still have his fun, too.

"Be cool," Shade warned Lucky.

"Pastor Dean, hi. I was wondering where you were today," Lily said as she came up to the group.

"I'm outta here," Jewell said under her breath.

"Coward," Evie teased.

"I'm a lover, not a fighter. Arguments tense me up."

Jewell left, but Evie didn't. The woman loved to sit back and watch drama unfold around her.

"Hi, Lily. I was going to come back and introduce you to the new pastor because you were at lunch with King when I came by the church store earlier."

"You went to lunch with King?" Shade asked sharply.

"At the diner," Lily answered.

"Why didn't you tell me?"

"I wasn't aware I had to tell you my every move since the danger is over."

"We'll talk about this later."

"No, we won't. It was lunch, just across the street."

"Lily, we still don't know who Digger hired to hurt you. Until we make sure he's stopped, you're not completely out of danger." Shade knew exactly who the guy was, and he had plans for that motherfucker.

"Oh." She paused. "Next time, I'll tell you when I leave the church."

Lily turned back to Lucky expectantly. "Are you staying for dinner?"

"Actually, dinner and breakfast. I'm moving in."

"That's great. I was worried you would move away, and I wouldn't see you anymore."

"I think you're going to be seeing a lot more of Lucky than you ever expected to see."

Evie just couldn't help herself, Shade thought. He and Lucky both gave her silent warnings. It seemed their talk wasn't going to take long concerning Lily.

"Let's go home, Lily," Shade said, taking Lily's arm and moving her toward the pathway to their house.

"Spoil sport," Shade heard Evie call out as they left.

"What did she mean by that?" Lily asked curiously.

"Nothing," Shade answered, changing the subject to asking about her lunch with King.

Keeping Lily's world safe and happy was becoming more difficult to manage than he had anticipated. Lucky and King were both threats. One he could handle without difficulty, while the other would take a little time.

CHAPTER SEVENTY-ONE

Shade drove Cash's old truck with Lily sitting in the middle and Evie by the passenger door. He would rather be going anywhere other than King's house for dinner. Neither King nor Shade thought the other belonged in Lily's life, and they were both right. The evening was going to be a fucking disaster, one he had every intention of having Lily make up for when they returned home.

A huge fucker opened the front door for them.

Shade hadn't lost time by finding out all he could about King. He hired the best, and Henry, his bodyguard, was known to be lethally efficient at his job.

He led them into the living room where King was sitting. Evie and Shade both silently watched as Lily greeted her father, bending down to hug him and brushing a soft kiss on his cheek.

King then turned to him. "Shade."

"King." Shade gave a small nod.

Shade had dressed in his good jeans, boots, and a nice black shirt. King's eyes flicked over Shade's relaxed attire. Shade stared back just as critically, scanning over the expensive suit and shoes King had dressed in for the dinner. Then the two powerful men glared at each other, neither afraid.

"Evie," King greeted.

Shade stiffened at the condescending tone King addressed her with. His mouth snapped open to say something, but he was silenced at her own tone. Evie hadn't earned her rank of being over the women by allowing herself to be pushed around.

"King."

A twist of King's lips showed he had received her message.

"Henry, get everyone a drink."

Shade placed his arm around Lily's shoulder at her wary look as they sat down on the leather couch. While she was around liquor more constantly at the clubhouse, she would never lose the fear it inspired; her scars ran too deep. She was still uncomfortable being around it, and King had just showed how little he knew about his daughter.

After the doorbell rang again, Beth and Razer were shown into the living room. Beth was much more casual with King, giving him a hug and inquiring how he felt.

"I'm almost back to normal."

Shade was barely able to restrain his snort. The fucking bastard wasn't normal when he was in tip-top shape.

"Dinner's ready." Henry's voice broke the silence in the room.

Shade held Lily's hand as they went into the dining room. The table had been set lavishly. Both Shade and King sat on opposite ends, Lily sat next to him, Evie sat next to King, and Beth and Razer sat across from them.

He was forced to admit to himself that the food was good—a standing rib roast with fingerling potatoes and asparagus tips. Afterward, Henry brought out a chocolate mousse which had Shade wanting to take Lily's portion. Only the sensuous way she was eating the damned stuff kept him from swiping it.

King was deliberately flaunting his wealth in front of them. Shade could have told him it was a wasted effort. Lily didn't care about money other than how it helped others.

"Would you like more?" King asked Evie.

"No, I think that was enough," Evie replied coldly.

While Shade sensed chemistry between the two, she wasn't a pushover. If King thought she was, he wasn't as experienced as Shade had read.

King nodded then turned his attention to Lily. "Would you like more?"

"Yes, please. I have a weakness for chocolate."

Fuck! Shade didn't know if his dick could take him watching her eat another bowl of that stuff.

After they finished their dessert, they went back into the living room. Shade resumed his seat next to Lily on the couch, sitting tensely.

The dinner had gone well. King had fed them good food in a relaxing atmosphere, luring them in like all good predators did.

"How do you like working in the church store, Lily?" King asked.

"I love it. The Christmas holidays have left our shelves almost bare, though, so we're having a clothing and food drive this Sunday after church. There's supposed to be a break in the weather. Pastor Dean—I mean, Lucky—thought it would be a good way for the new pastor to meet the congregation."

"I'll have to attend. It will be a good time to meet the rest of your friends."

"That would be nice."

"You're content at the store instead of using your degree? After all, anyone can be a cashier."

And so it begins, Shade thought, stiffening at the indirect insult.

"No, I really like it. It's more than being a cashier. I have to approve of the needs of the people coming in—"

"I'm glad you don't feel like you're settling with the job opportunities available in Treepoint."

King's interruption of Lily talking didn't sit well with Shade, or Beth by her expression. Razer wasn't much happier, but he was able to hide it better.

"Lily's excellent at her job. Several families in the community have benefited from Lily working there. She's also helping them find jobs." Shade's arm went around Lily's shoulder, and her eyes smiled up into his. He smiled back, his thumb rubbing the delicate flesh behind her ear.

"So, how did you two meet?"

"We met at the lake when I was in high school."

Lily's choice of words had King straightening in his chair, his indolent attitude disappearing.

"You allowed her to date a man of his age while she was still in school?" His accusation was directed at Beth, who paled at his harsh words.

"Of course not! I started dating Razer when Lily was in high school. As they were friends, naturally she met Shade. However, Lily and Shade didn't start seeing each other until last summer."

"A whirlwind courtship?"

"We had known each other for years." Shade's voice equaled King's in attitude.

Lily's head went back and forth between the men until her eyes settled on King. "I didn't feel rushed, if that's what you're getting at." Lily took Shade's hand in hers, gripping it tightly.

"I didn't mean to insinuate it was. I'm sorry if I implied otherwise."

Bullshit, Shade thought, gritting his teeth.

"I'm very happy, King. Shade and I are looking forward to a long and happy marriage with children."

"You're not pregnant, are you? You've only been married a month."

At Lily's hurt expression, Shade's hand went to her jaw, raising her face to his. He leaned over, giving her a kiss which would reassure Lily while at the same time pissing off King. Lily's face was bright red when Shade let her lips go.

"Lily and I are both anxious to start our family, but no, she isn't pregnant. Yet." Shade kept his face impassive as he stared at King.

He intended to get Lily pregnant as soon as possible. She wanted children, and she would make an exceptional mother. Not only that, but it would tie her to him irrevocably for the rest of their lives.

King opened his mouth to reply.

"I think that's wonderful, Lily. You're going to make a great mother," Evie said, cutting in before King had the chance.

King's mouth snapped closed at her words, and Shade saw his hands clench on the arms of his chair. He hadn't appreciated Evie butting in to the conservation.

Beth rose to her feet. "Tomorrow may be Saturday, but I have to be at work early. Lily, you and Evie have to be at the church early, too, remember? The luncheon we're having for Pastor Patterson and his wife?"

"Yes. Rachel is helping, too, and Willa is bringing dessert. You're right; we should go. I don't want to tire you, King." When Lily got to her feet, thanking Beth silently for stepping in, Evie, Razer, who had remained quiet almost all night, and Shade rose to their feet, also.

Lily went to King, reaching up to brush his cheek with a kiss. "I hope to see you Sunday."

When Lily would have turned away, King took her hand. "You haven't called me Dad since I was shot."

Lily looked at him warily at his statement.

Shade was about to intercede at her discomfort when Evie took a step forward, reaching her hand out for King to take. He released Lily reluctantly.

"Thanks for dinner, King." Evie maneuvered her body, and Shade took the opportunity to lead Lily away from the manipulative bastard.

"Will I be seeing you Sunday, too?" Shade heard him ask Evie as they waited for her by the door.

"I'll be at the church," Evie confirmed.

"Good, I'll look forward to it."

Shade was damn sure Evie couldn't say the same. However, Evie was an attractive woman, and from his research, King enjoyed women. That was one of the few things they had in common.

Shade helped the two women into the truck after they said their goodbyes. It was a good thing they were leaving Monday for Alaska, and King would be heading back to Queens City. If King stayed, he would do his best to try to destroy his and Lily's relationship, uncaring how it affected his daughter.

Shade hated the bastard, already regretting his decision to give him a chance to redeem himself to Lily. There were some men who couldn't be saved. He and King had that in common, as well.

The clubhouse had all the lights on when they returned and got out of the truck. Beth and Razer pulled in next to them and instead of heading into the clubhouse, they waved as they took the path to their own house.

"Lily, go on to our house. I'll be there in a few minutes. I need to talk to Lucky for a few."

"All right. I need to talk to Rachel about next week's schedule," she agreed, looking up at the clubhouse. They could hear the music from where they were standing.

She kissed him on his cheek before walking up the pathway.

Evie and he both watched her until she turned the corner.

"She's never going to get used to the parties, is she?" Evie asked.

"No," Shade answered, going up the front steps with Evie.

Opening the clubhouse door, they entered to see the party was still going strong.

"See Lucky anywhere?"

"Yeah, he's over there." Evie pointed.

The newly retired pastor was making up for lost time. He was sitting on the couch with Stori bent over his lap, giving him a blowjob while his mouth was on Ember's bared breast.

"Later," Shade told Evie as he left her to take a seat in the chair across from the couch.

Looking at his watch, his lips tightened as Lucky took his time coming.

Five minutes later, Shade decided he'd had enough.

"Brother, we need to talk. Either finish up or start over later," Shade told him.

Lucky gave a groan, shooting him a dirty look. "Should you even be in here without Lily?" he asked sarcastically as he rammed his dick farther down a gasping Stori's throat.

"That's what we need to discuss," Shade told him, watching as Lucky tugged at Ember's nipple with this teeth.

"Dammit," Lucky groaned, shuddering.

Shade gave him a minute to recover before standing up. "Kitchen."

Lucky stood up, buttoning his jeans. "I won't be long," he told the women as he followed after Shade.

"What's so important?" Lucky asked as Shade took a beer from the fridge.

He opened it, standing and staring at Lucky who was wearing only jeans. His tats, which would shock both Lily and Beth, were easily visible.

"We need to talk about how your behavior is going to affect Lily, and I don't think Beth is any more ready to see your dick than Lily is."

Lucky ran his hand through his already tousled hair. "I agree. I knew you were all out tonight, but when they're here in the house, I'll make sure I keep my business upstairs."

"I know it's a pain, but I would appreciate the effort."

"No problem. I care about Lily and Beth, too. I don't want to hurt them. I've waited a long time to live my life, but I can get what I need without throwing it in Lily and Beth's faces."

"What about Winter?"

"That's up to Viper."

Shade nodded his understanding.

"If that's it, I—"

"It's not." Shade stopped him from leaving. "We need to talk about Merrick Patterson."

Lucky frowned. "What about him?"

"I like to keep track of my enemies. Fortunately, most of mine are six feet under. Unfortunately for you, I became caught up in club business and Lily and let one slip through my fingers."

"How does this affect me?"

"I have some history with his wife. Pick someone else to take over for you."

"I can't; it's too late," Lucky told him. "He resigned from his other church, and his wife's in Atlanta, putting their home up for sale. Besides, Beth and your wife were on the pastor search committee. They hired him."

"Fuck." Shade set his beer down on the counter.

"What does it matter? If you fucked his wife, it's not like you're going to be in church staring at her every Sunday."

"I never fucked her. You have no clue of the woman she is. She's an evil bitch, and that's being nice referring to her that way. She's a fucking psycho."

"I have friends who are, too."

Shade sighed, ignoring his jab. "This doesn't only concern me. She's hurt Evie in the past and will again. She's dangerous," Shade warned.

"Dammit." Lucky went to the refrigerator, taking a beer for himself and opening it. "Shade, it's too late. Merrick has already moved into the church, and his wife will be there in a week or two. There's nothing I can do."

As the men stared silently at each other, Evie came into the kitchen, carrying a laundry basket.

Shade looked at her curiously. Since when did Evie start doing her laundry during the Friday parties?

Evie, seeing where his eyes were, shrugged. "I need to get caught up with the clothes so I can pack. Penni wants to leave Tuesday."

Shade took a deep breath. He was going to have to tell her. "Let's sit down."

Evie, Lucky, and Shade all sat down at the table.

"This doesn't seem to be good news." Evie stared back and forth between him and Lucky.

"It's not," Shade said grimly. "You know the pastor taking over for Lucky?"

"He came to the church to do a 'in view to a call' sermon, but I didn't take the time to meet or speak to him directly, so I only vaguely remember him. He was a chaplain who worked with Lucky before I was discharged."

"That's right, but there's something about him that you don't know. He's married to Brooke."

Evie's face whitened at his words. "You have got to be shittin' me."

"I wish I was," Shade replied grimly.

"She's my evil twin," Evie told Lucky.

Shade silently agreed. Truer words had never been spoken.

"I'm sorry, Evie. I didn't know," Lucky apologized.

"It's not your fault," Evie told him before her face dropped even more. "Crap. I told Lily and Beth I would go to the church tomorrow to meet the pastor."

"She won't be there. She's in Georgia, closing up the sale of their house."

"Thank God for small miracles. Brooke didn't come with him when Merrick came for his interview sermon. I overheard Merrick say his wife had wanted to make sure he was given the job before she came to Treepoint. I'll be leaving on Tuesday, so I can avoid her. When I come back, I'll find another church to attend. Maybe I'll try the one Willa's gone to a few times."

Lucky frowned. "I wish I knew why she didn't like me as her pastor."

"Other than you're too good-looking for a pastor and single, and she's really shy?" Evie said, rolling her eyes at Lucky.

"You mean...?"

"That she has a crush on you."

Shade laughed at the reddish tinge which came to Lucky's face at Evie's sarcastic voice.

"I didn't know."

"No shit, Sherlock. You're the only one who didn't. You're as blind as Lily was. I think, in both cases, neither one of you wanted to see what was right in front of your face," Evie said shrewdly.

Lucky stiffened. "I know how women act when they want to attract a man. Hell, she did everything she could to avoid me. It's not like I would notice, otherwise."

Evie threw Lucky an angry glance. "What the fuck does that mean?"

"It means she's not my type," Lucky stated, obviously confused by why Evie was becoming angry.

"If she's a woman, she's your type," Evie said snidely.

"That's not true. I like a particular type of woman. I like—"

"Women who are thinner? Prettier?" Evie was breathing fire at the clueless brother by that point.

"She's not a slut," Shade answered with what Lucky was being too polite to say.

"What?" The fire in Evie extinguished.

Shade nodded when Evie turned to him. "He likes sluts. The sluttier, the better."

Lucky looked pained at Shade's explanation.

"Willa isn't a slut," Lucky answered, damning himself with his own words.

"No, Willa *isn't* a slut," Evie agreed, leaning back in her chair, her shoulders beginning to shake.

"What's so funny?" Lucky asked, finding the anger Evie had was now lost and believing she was making fun of him.

"How in the hell did you stay celibate for all those years?"

"It wasn't easy," Lucky admitted with a smile. "When I see myself settling down, it's with a woman who's like Jewell or Bliss."

"Poor Willa," Evie said sympathetically.

Shade didn't say anything, preferring to stay out of other people's business, but then he just couldn't help himself.

"Maybe she's a slut in the bedroom." He stood up. It was time he went home. After watching Lucky with Ember and Stori, he was ready for his own woman.

"I doubt that. She's afraid of her own shadow," Lucky said.

"There's only one way to find out," Shade told him. "Fuck her."

CHAPTER SEVENTY-TWO

The shadows around the house allowed him to blend in with the background as he waited patiently for Lily and Beth to leave. When their SUV turned the corner, Shade moved stealthily through the night.

Earlier that day, there had been a luncheon at the church to welcome Pastor Merrick and, surprisingly, his wife, the demon bitch Brooke. Shade, Lucky, and most of all, Evie were surprised to find her already in Treepoint.

Shade had been informed after the luncheon that Brooke was already showing her demon, chasing Willa out of the church with her snide, backhanded comments.

Then the reason for the night visit—Evie had told him about her conversation with King when he had made comments about Evie fucking Shade, asked if Lily and Beth participate in orgies, and then insulted Evie, which then led to Lucky pummeling him into the ground. That was when Shade and Lily had come upon the scene, having heard the commotion from the church's store where Shade had been keeping Lily busy and far away from Brooke.

Lily and Beth had then taken King to the hospital because he was bleeding at his gunshot wound, something Lucky must have caused when beating the shit out of him. Shade stayed back, getting the story from Evie and Lucky, his suspicion and dislike for King growing.

King had a state-of-the-art alarm system, which didn't make it impossible to enter, only more difficult. He worked efficiently on it, taking his time so as not to set the alarm off, and was rewarded when he heard the click of the lock. He kind of liked the new locks which had keyless entry. Finding the right frequency made it easy to gain access.

He soundlessly entered the house, hearing Henry in the kitchen. He could have taken him out without a chance to defend himself, but he didn't.

Coming at him from behind, he grabbed Henry around the throat, cutting off his oxygen. He had given him a chance, and it had still ended with the same result—him lying on the floor, unconscious.

He searched for King, finding him in his bedroom, smoking a cigar while staring out the window.

"Should you be out of bed?"

King remained still, not bothering to turn around; instead, he looked at Shade's reflection in the glass.

"I needed to move around. You just missed Lily and Beth."

"I saw them leave."

King took a deep draw of his cigar. "Henry okay?"

"He'll wake up in a few minutes."

King turned to face Shade. "Say what you want to say."

"Stop, King. Go back to Queens City. Live your life. If you want to play father, call Lily once a month. Come and see her for a week in the summer. But stay out of our lives the rest of the time."

"And if I don't? I'm not someone you can make disappear without Lily asking questions."

"I don't have to make you disappear, King." Shade held the promise in his eyes while his features remained emotionless.

"I see, like how the two bikers who nearly killed Lily ended up at the bottom of Black Mountain?"

Shade let the stony silence fill the room. Then an ironic smile came to his lips.

"I understand your desire to protect Lily from me, but I will never hurt Lily—I would die for her. You, on the other hand, have always placed your own needs above hers. You were the one who left her in the care of a mother who sold her. You were the one who placed a child molester in her home. And you were the one who nearly got her killed three weeks ago. Lily needs protection from only one person—you."

King crushed his cigar out. "You don't need to remind me of the mistakes I've made with her. I plan to do better by her."

"The only way you can do better is by staying out of her life. You're not going to fix your past mistakes now. It's too late." Shade went to the bedroom door.

"You're not going to keep me out of her life. You're wrong for her, and we both know it. When I prove it to her, she'll leave you behind. You don't frighten me, Shade. It's been a while since I've had to get my hands dirty, but that doesn't mean I've forgotten how."

"Go home, King." Shade went out the door as quietly as he had entered.

He hadn't wanted to confront King yet, believing their battle could wait. After all, he was leaving tomorrow. However, King's stunt at the church had proved he would use any dirty method to break him and Lily apart. He had used Evie and Lucky to start a fight which Lily would witness in order to draw sympathy toward himself. It wouldn't work. Lily and Beth were fiercely loyal to those who had earned it, and Evie had.

Walking back to where his bike was hidden a block away, Shade climbed on and then rode home.

He put away his treat in the kitchen then found Lily in the bedroom, packing their clothes.

"I thought you were going to help me pack." She stared at him with mock frustration.

"I will." He crossed to the chest, pulling out three pairs of jeans, a handful of T-shirts, and some socks. Tossing them onto the suitcase, he then lay down on the bed to watch her. "I'm done."

"Jerk." Lily smiled down at him as she refolded his clothes and continued placing hers inside the suitcase. "You're going to get the comforter dirty with those boots."

"Take them off." Shade stretched out on the bed, placing his folded arms behind his head.

Lily paused then reached down to tug one then the other off.

"Come here," Shade said as he saw her nipples peak under her thin gown.

"I need to finish packing…"

Shade rose one foot, kicking the suitcase off the bed. "Come here."

Lily trembled, licking her bottom lip. She placed a knee on the mattress then the other before crawling forward until she was above him. Shade brought his hands to her hips, bunching the material up until it was at her waist and exposing her ass. With her over him, her modest gown hung down, showing her tits.

Shade took his hands away from her waist, going to her shoulders where he slipped the capped sleeves over her arms. Lily raised her hands one at a time until the gown hung from her waist, her tits as bare as her ass.

Shade lifted his head, sucking a nipple into his mouth.

"Shade…I really need to pack," Lily panted.

His hand came out, placing a hard smack on her ass. "I'll finish packing for you when I'm done fucking you. Unbutton my pants."

Shade took Lily's nipple back in his mouth, torturing the sensitive tip with his teeth while Lily bit back a moan, her fingers unbuttoning his jeans and pulling his zipper down.

"Take out my cock."

As Lily slid her fingers inside his jeans, it brought an exquisitely painful sensation to him, especially as she took out his engorged cock.

He stared up at the beautiful woman staring down at him. "Do you have any fucking clue what you mean to me?"

Her lips lost the seductive smile playing across her lips, turning serious. "I want to be the woman you want me to be. I know I'm not as experienced in how you like to make love, but I'll try, Shade—"

Her words broke off as Shade lifted her, rolling over until she was the one underneath him with him above her. Taking her hands in his, he raised them then pressed them down into the mattress above her head.

"Shut up." He slid his thigh between hers, wedging himself between her spread thighs, his cock brushing her shaved pussy. "I enjoy making love with you any way I can get you to give it to me."

One of her legs curled over his hip, pressing him down to her, as her anxious eyes stared up into his. "If you want me to do something, all you have to do is ask."

Shade frowned. "Why are you talking about this? Usually, you avoid talking about sex like the plague."

"No, I don't," Lily denied anxiously.

Shade frowned down at her, arching a brow.

"I won't anymore," she hastily clarified. "We can talk about it now, if you want to."

"I don't want to talk about it right now. Right now, I want to do it." Shade smiled gently down at her.

"Oh." Her eyes filled with disappointment.

"Lily...?"

"You were at the clubhouse a long time...last night."

"Yeah, so?" Shade said.

She remained silent.

Understanding dawned on him, and his smile widened. "Angel, I needed to talk to Lucky and Evie."

Relief had her sinking deeper into the soft mattress.

"Why did you wait a whole day to say something?" Shade ran a finger over her cheek.

"I needed to think about it first."

"You mean you needed to worry about it."

Reluctantly, she nodded.

"Can you do a couple of things for me? Actually three, now that I think about it?" Shade asked.

"Of course. What are they?"

"The first is, you need to trust me. I'm not going to fuck around on you. I'm going to be at the clubhouse a lot when you're not there. I'm telling you I won't touch, and I'll keep my word. Okay?"

Lily nodded.

"The second is you need to tell me when something's bothering you."

"I will, some of the time," Lily partially agreed.

"*All* the time," Shade corrected her firmly.

"I can't tell you every time something bothers me. That's ridiculous."

Shade tightened his lips. "All the time, Lily. You thinking about shit isn't good. You come up with crazy ideas, like me fucking around on you. You worried about nothing for a whole night and day."

"All right, I'll confide in you more."

"Cool. Now the third thing is the most important, and I want you to give me your full attention on this."

"All right."

"Stay still; I'll be right back."

Shade got off the bed, going into the kitchen then coming back within a couple of minutes. Lily hadn't even turned her head to watch him leaving and entering.

"My sweet angel obeyed her husband."

He climbed back onto the bed, placing a dollop of chocolate mousse on her chest between her breasts. Lily started to look down.

"Stay still," Shade said sharply. "It's a spoonful of chocolate mousse. I'm going to fuck you, and if it moves, I'm going to quit fucking you and go to sleep. If it doesn't, then I'll reward you."

"Shade…"

"Quiet, Lily."

Shade slid his aching cock into Lily's warm pussy, driving himself in to the hilt. His woman already wanted to move, her eyes melting with desire. He bent over her, delicately licking a peaked nipple, and felt her tremble slightly.

"Careful," he warned, switching to the other nipple as he began to steadily fuck her.

Lily's thigh curled over his ass, pressing him down harder against her as she began whimpering. Shade bit down gently on the nipple in his mouth, and she sucked in a breath. The mousse trembled yet didn't move. He let the slick nipple slip from his mouth, returning to the other one when she stiffened, preparing herself for his small bite. He made her wait for it as he began to fuck her harder, and her hands clenched in the comforter above her head.

"You are so fucking tight and wet," Shade groaned against her tit before giving her the bite she was waiting for.

She moaned, remaining still.

Shade hooked his hands under her knees, raising them to her chest and completely opening her pussy to his plundering cock.

He raised his head from her nipple, seeing the mousse was still in the same spot he had placed it. He lowered his head, licking the small amount from her chest then laving the area until the mousse was completely gone.

"Fuck me back," Shade ordered.

Lily lowered her arms, sliding them over his tattoo-covered shoulders as she raised her mouth for his kiss. Shade licked her lips, parting them before sliding his tongue inside to explore her mouth as if he had never kissed her before. She arched her hips, her pussy clenching in a series of climactic ripples.

Unwilling to hold back any longer, Shade allowed himself to come, grinding his climax out into her until he collapsed, surrounding her with his body, his cock still inside of her.

"That was...that was..."

"That was pretty good," Shade finished the sentence for her.

Her mouth dropped in disappointment. "But I thought it was amazing," she said softly.

"Nope, only pretty good," Shade said, lifting his body off hers then lifting her until she lay propped up on the pillows against the headboard of his bed. "We've only been married a few weeks and we start our honeymoon tomorrow, so the best is yet to come. If it's already amazing, what have we got to look forward to?"

Lily giggled. "In that case, it was just okay."

"That's my angel. Now, for your reward." He reached over to the nightstand, picking up the chocolate mousse. He placed a small amount onto the spoon then lifted it to her lips. Lily obediently opened her mouth, her eyes widening.

"That's the mousse we had at King's the other night."

"Yes." Shade took a spoonful for himself then scooped another spoonful for her, lifting it to her mouth again.

"That was nice of King to give it to us." Lily opened her mouth, sliding the rich mousse from the spoon.

He moved the spoon away. Lowering his head, he licked the tiny spot of chocolate which had been left behind.

"I thought it was a perfect way to apologize for his making an ass of himself today," Shade stated, taking another spoonful for himself.

"I'll have to call and thank him," Lily said as Shade fed her another spoonful.

"You do that. Tell him I enjoyed it, too."

CHAPTER SEVENTY-THREE

Shade frowned as he came out of the kitchen. He was going to paddle her ass when he found her. She had caught him busy in the kitchen and used the opportunity to go outside.

Going to the bedroom, he jerked the blanket off the bed then put on his jacket and boots before going out. He stood briefly on the porch, just long enough to see her standing on the first rise almost half a mile away. His mouth tightened in anger. His woman was constantly putting herself in danger.

He walked off the porch, moving as quickly as he could through the snow. He had warned her several times about how dangerous it could be outside; not only from the cold environment, but from deadly predators. One of which was stalking her now.

She didn't even jump when he placed the blanket around her shoulders.

Lily stood on the snow bank, shivering despite being dressed warmly. She kept sneaking out to look at the mountains. Shade shook his head at her, knowing it was a lost cause. She would never change; she would always be Lily, so sweet it made him ache.

Her hand had been out when he had come up behind her. She had confessed shyly the night before when he had caught her doing the same thing that it was like holding the Northern Lights in the palm of her hand.

"What did I tell you about sneaking out of the cabin, Lily? I'm going to punish you when I get you back inside," he whispered into her ear.

"I couldn't resist, Shade. Isn't it beautiful?" Lily whispered reverently. "I didn't know anything so beautiful could exist."

"I didn't, either," he said, rubbing his cheek against hers. His tone was just as reverent, but he wasn't watching the sky; he was staring down into her face.

"All these years, I've waited to see this. It's more spectacular than I ever believed possible."

He swept her into his arms, packing her back inside the warm cabin, shutting and locking the world outside.

Shade had hot chocolate on the table in front of the couch and a warm fire blazing a few feet away. He heard her sip her chocolate as he threw a log onto the fire.

He stood up, going into the bedroom then coming out with a small package, handing it to her.

Lily opened the tiny package. Inside was the exact replica of the flower Gaige had destroyed at the fair so many months before. He had saved it to give her at the right time. Wanting it to be special, he had chosen their honeymoon.

"Happy Valentine's Day."

"Thank you, Shade. I love it." She reached up, kissing his cheek.

"I'm going to go take a shower. Can I trust you not to sneak out again?"

"Yes." She curled her legs under her, sipping her hot chocolate.

She was still sitting and staring into the flames when he came back wearing only a pair of sweatpants.

He sat down next to her on the sofa, his arm on the back of the couch. "What are you looking so serious about?"

Lily shrugged, avoiding his question.

"Lily?" He bore his gaze into her, demanding an answer.

"Nothing, really. I was just thinking." She looked up at him.

He cupped her cheek, his thumb wiping away the lone tear clinging to her lashes. "About what?"

"It's just that I waited such a long time to see the Northern Lights...It would have been disappointing if they hadn't been as beautiful as I thought they would."

"I'm sure it would have," he said gently.

"I was just thinking that you said you had waited for me since Razer had met Beth, and then I thought that...What if I wasn't what you wanted? You might've become disappointed."

"You did a lot of thinking while I was in the shower."

"I know." She nodded.

"Lily, you only saw the Northern Lights in pictures. It's different having expectations of something you don't know anything about. I grew to know you over the years; what a warm, loving woman you are, how you can't stand anyone hurt, and how strong you were to survive a childhood which would have seriously fucked-up anyone else.

"Angel, I didn't have expectations. I knew I wanted that sweet girl whose beautiful soul I could see in her eyes. The more I grew to know you, I wasn't disappointed—I was captivated by everything I had learned. It was like unwrapping a pretty Christmas package and finding a work of art inside which was priceless. So, no, I wasn't disappointed."

"You're definitely not what I expected. Giving me flowery speeches on Valentine's Day, a trip to Alaska to make my dream come true, even being a nice guy and giving Georgia's brother her job so he would be able to support his kids and hers while she's in prison.

"The first time I saw you, all I could think about was how scary you looked with all those tattoos. Then they ended up being the reason I fell in love with you," Lily said ruefully.

"You fell in love with me because of my tats?" Shade asked, surprised.

"I understood their meanings." She reached up, touching the stars on the side of his neck. "The stars are your guide, so you always know what's important. The compass, so you never lose your way home." Her fingertips brushed the one on his collarbone. "'Strength and Loyalty' means someone strong enough to always protect me." Her hand glided down to the tat scrawled across his chest. "'Only Death Can Stop Me,' someone who will always be there for me. When I realized their meaning, I realized I had found him."

"Who?" Shade's asked tenderly.

"I knew I had found my cowboy." Lily circled Shade's neck with her arms, touching his lips with hers in a kiss which showed how much she had come to love him.

Shade lifted her into his arms, laying her down on the blanket in front of the fire. She smiled as she opened her arms to him, his beautiful wife staring up at him with dreams in her eyes. He was no dream man—that was for fucking sure—but he loved her, and he finally had her.

"Why do I always feel each time with you is like the first?" he murmured against her throat.

She rubbed her cheek against his. "Are you sure you're not going to get tired of me after a few years?" she teased.

"Fifty years of being married to you wouldn't be enough," Shade said, pulling down her top so he could trace the cleft between her breasts with his tongue.

"Fifty years is a long time." She ran her fingers through his hair.

"I can prove it."

"How?"

His lips smoothed away the frown on her forehead. "Ask me again in fifty years."

Chapter Seventy-Four

The cell phone rang as he was running a towel through his damp hair. They had been home from Alaska only since the night before, and it seemed like everyone had something they wanted to say or needed from them. When they had gotten home, they had been surprised by an excited Razer and Beth, who told them Beth was pregnant with twins. Now it seemed like Evie had news to impart.

Shade picked up the phone. "What's up?" he asked, leaning casually against the dresser as he watched Lily frantically dress for work. It might have been their first day home from their honeymoon, but he had already started the routine of making her late for work, again.

"Guess who your sister has a date with next Saturday?"

"Who?"

"Lily's ex, Charles."

Shade disconnected the call without saying goodbye then punched in Penni's number.

"Hey, bro," she answered.

"That date you have next Saturday? Cancel it," Shade said ruthlessly without explanation.

Lily bent over to put on her shoes, and Shade narrowed his eyes on her ass.

"With Charles?" Penni asked.

"That's the one. Cancel it, now."

"Okay," Penni agreed. "Anything else?"

"No, that's it. Be safe," Shade told her then hung up.

Lily stood up straight, blowing her hair out of her eye with frustration.

"What was that all about?"

"Nothing, just a small problem I needed to take care of. How late are you for work?" Shade asked, casually walking to the bedroom door as she picked up her purse.

"Two hours. Rachel's a sweetheart; I'll buy her lunch…" Lily came to a stop in the middle of the bedroom floor, her mouth dropping open when she saw him leaning against the door, still naked with his arms crossed against his chest.

"Uh, Shade, what are you doing? I really need to get to work."

His hardening cock swelled, pointing upwards to his tatted belly.

"You have two options. I can fuck you, in which case you're going to be another two hours late because I'm off today, and I told you to take off also," he reminded her. "Or you can give me a blowjob, in which case you'll be only thirty minutes later than you are now." He shrugged. "It's totally up to you which one you decide."

As Lily snapped her mouth closed, staring at him, Shade stubbornly stared back.

She sighed, tossing her purse onto the bed, then walked seductively toward him, dropping to her knees in front of him.

He groaned when she took him in her mouth. "That's the one I hoped you would pick."

⋇⋇⋇

The sound of a car pulling into to the parking lot had all the men staring at the ugly, puke-green car. Their expressions turned apprehensive when they saw the woman getting out.

"That's all I need right now," Cash muttered.

Shade watched Killyama approach, narrowing his eyes on her determined expression.

"I need your help." The bitch didn't believe in beating around the bush.

"Why should we help you?" She deserved Train's smart-ass comment after the way she had been making fun at the brother's expense.

"Because if you don't, I'll ask Beth, Winter, and Lily for help."

Shade didn't like to be blackmailed; it was a pet peeve of his, actually, because it showed vulnerability. Lily was his, and Killyama knew it.

"What do you want?" Viper snapped, not any happier at being blackmailed than he was.

Razer was the only one who had stayed silent, his clenching hands showing he was debating strangling her.

We're all pussy-whipped, Shade thought glumly to himself.

"Fat Louise has put herself in a fucked-up mess, and I need you to help me get her out."

"What kind of trouble?" Train asked suspiciously.

"She sneaked into Mexico to get her half-sister out."

The men stared at her blankly, completely surprised by her answer.

"Fat Louise? She doesn't even take a piss without one of you by her side," Razer commented. "Besides, why did she have to sneak? The *federales* want her?" he joked.

"You think this is funny?" she snapped, taking a step toward him.

"No." Razer didn't step back, but Shade almost laughed at his expression.

He could tell the woman was proud of herself for standing up to Razer, not realizing the man was an inch away from throttling her.

"Her dad is a government employee, doing some kind of secret shit for them. Employees and their families aren't allowed to travel in certain areas. He alerted Border Patrol, trying to stop her before she went inside, but he was too late."

"What in the fuck are we supposed to do?" Viper asked, diverting her attention from Razer. You had to be cool and calm to deal with this bitch.

"You have connections. I need them to get me inside so I can find her."

"You're not going after her," Train stated angrily.

"Since when do you think you can tell me what I can do?" Killyama glared at him.

Train didn't back down. "Since you came up with a crazy-assed plan to try to enter a country which has made a career out of kidnapping and killing people," he snapped.

"Back off, lover boy. I'm going after her. Are you men going to help me or not?" From the way she said the word "men", it was obvious she meant it as an insult.

"Do we have a choice?" Viper asked snidely.

"No, but don't worry." She curled her lip. "I have a plan. Where's Dean?"

"Probably hiding if he saw you," Train said grimly.

"Get him. We're going to need him," Killyama ordered. "Knox, too. They'll have the contacts we need to find Jane. Beth told us the strings he had to pull to find Lily when she went missing."

Shade wasn't about to volunteer his contacts.

"Anything else?" Train asked sarcastically, pulling his phone out.

"Yeah, you can shove that phone up your ass when you're finished making those calls."

Train lowered the phone to his side, his face turning cold. As he took a step toward her, Killyama held her ground.

"We don't do jobs for free. If you want our help, you'll pay for it like everyone else."

Shade raised a brow at Train's comment. He himself didn't like any of the women. Truthfully, there weren't many people he would give a fuck if he never saw again in general, but Fat Louise was the most tolerable of Sex Piston's crew.

Besides, none of the women would be happy if Train charged her an outlandish sum of money for helping Fat Louise.

"What's your price?" She placed her hands on her hips.

"I'll let you know when I decide."

"You're just going to hold it over my head until you decide?" she snapped.

"Yeah."

"I don't have a choice, do I?"

"No. Sucks, doesn't it?"

Lucky came down the steps from the clubhouse.

"You needed me?"

Viper filled him in about Fat Louise sneaking into Mexico, and unlike the rest of them, he voluntarily agreed to help.

"Go get some sleep. If we need you, I'll call," Shade ordered Cash as his exhaustion becoming more apparent.

"Thanks, Shade."

He nodded in response.

Cash left as Shade turned back to the group.

"Let's go inside the factory. I don't want to go to the clubhouse, because the women will want to know what's going on, and I don't want Lily worried." Shade unlocked the door for everyone to go inside.

Shade went into his office and picked up his iPad before going back to the main room and setting it down on a worktable.

Pulling up a map of Mexico, he handed it to Killyama. "Tell us where she went in, and where she is now."

Killyama took the iPad.

Shade listened closely, his eyes meeting Train's. Killyama was very detailed, telling them Fat Louise's last-known whereabouts as well as some intel of where she had been heading. The woman, to his knowledge, had never been in the military, yet she talked as if it was normal to handle an operation of this scope.

Shade had never looked into the past of any of Beth's friends; he hadn't seen the need. However, Killyama handled herself a little too well for her not to have any special training. She was overly confident of her skills, and that kind of self-assurance didn't come unearned. After she left, Shade would be making some calls to his contacts to find out more about the woman ordering them around.

Lily was in the shower by the time he was able to make it home. Shade took off his clothes, stepping into the shower with her. The water was almost too warm for him, but he didn't say anything as he pressed his chest to Lily's back, slipping an arm around her waist.

Lily leaned back against him. "You're late."

"Sorry, I had some paperwork to finish."

"You work too hard."

Shade brought his mouth to her throat. "It will slow down soon. I have to go out of town on Thursday, and I'll be gone a couple of days."

Lily nodded, going up on her toes as his hand slid between her thighs, finding her clit. He gently stroked it, discovering her already wet.

"Already missing me?"

"Yes," she admitted softly. "Where are you going?"

"Mexico."

"Mexico?"

"Mmhmm...Fat Louise needs a ride home, so the brothers and I are going to pick her up."

He would tell Lily when he returned exactly why Fat Louise needed the ride home. There was no way Fat Louise wouldn't spill the beans when she got back. She was the biggest tattletale in Jamestown and Treepoint.

"That's nice of you all."

"I thought so. As soon as Killyama asked, I offered. I had to talk the rest of the brothers into it, but they eventually gave in."

"That's so sweet."

೮೦ ೦೩

"Do you see them yet?" Shade asked Killyama over the radio in his hand.

"Dude, when I see them, you'll be the first to know," she snapped back at him.

Shade flung the radio down on his lap. Taking his cap off, he ran his hand over his hair before putting it back on.

Train was sitting at the control of the helicopter, waiting for a signal from either Killyama or Viper, who was on the roof of where the helicopter was with binoculars. The latest intel they had received had said they were thirty minutes away, and that had been over an hour ago.

"Shit!" Viper came running across the roof. "Let's go."

Shade put the radio in his front pocket then picked up his rifle. Train started the helicopter, lifting off with Cash talking over the radio he had in his ear.

Shade looked out, seeing Killyama running toward Fat Louise and the man who had been hired to bring both her and her sister home. They were racing toward the border,

Killyama was running toward them with soldiers parallel to her. The soldiers had the advantage of being closer and were going to reach them first.

"I'm going to beat her. She was supposed to stay out of sight," Train said over the intercom.

"You really didn't expect her to listen to anything you had to say, did you?" Cash's amused voice was heard next.

"Shut up with the chit-chat and get us lower so we can fucking fire before they're all dead," Shade snapped.

Train dropped the helicopter, blocking the Jeeps.

"Get in!" yelled Rider, giving cover fire to the fleeing women and Cade.

Shots rang out as the soldiers began firing at the helicopter. Shade lifted his rifle, returning the fire with Viper by his side, giving them time to get inside.

Bailey threw herself into the helicopter, and then Fat Louise was lifted in by Cade who flung himself inside with his body covering hers.

Shade, Rider, and Viper kept firing, waiting for Killyama to get her ass inside. As soon as she jumped in, she yelled, "Go! Go!"

Train lifted the helicopter, flying back toward the United States' side of the border.

Shade sank back into his seat right as Fat Louise threw herself into Killyama's arms, bursting into tears.

Shade studied Killyama's reaction. Her expression was rigidly controlled. If he hadn't seen the bitch's arms tighten around the sobbing woman, Shade would have thought her unaffected.

Killyama was saying something to Fat Louise which had her nodding then talking. They went back and forth for a while before Killyama pulled out a protein bar and handed it to her.

She had told them of Fat Louise's medical condition, and they had used it shamelessly to get the government's aid in helping locate her.

Killyama stared at Cade. The poor fucker didn't know what he was in for. He probably had thought he was home free when he had jumped into the helicopter.

"He wasn't doing a great job, was he?" she sneered, yelling to be heard.

Cade stiffened. "I was doing fine until Bailey took off like a bat out of Hell."

Bailey flushed yet defended herself. "It worked out fine, didn't it? We're all safe now."

"No thanks to you," snorted Killyama.

The two women glared at each other.

It was twenty minutes later when they safely set the helicopter down on the roof of a hotel.

"Everybody out. I have to get this baby back before someone notices it missing," Train yelled over the loud noise.

Cade jumped out first to help the women out. Bailey took her time, clinging to Cade much longer than necessary, and Shade rolled his eyes at Viper as Cade lifted Fat Louise out next. Then he turned back to help Killyama, but she ignored his and Rider's helping hands as she started to jump out.

"Killyama!" Train yelled loud enough to be heard over the blades of the helicopter, stopping her. "Remember our deal. I'll be calling it in soon."

"Deal with this!" Killyama shouted above the roar of the blades, making an obscene gesture before jumping out of the helicopter.

"You can handle her later," Cash told Train over the intercom. "I want to get back to Treepoint."

Train gave him a thumbs-up, but his angry expression showed he had been about to shut down the helicopter and show Killyama how badly she had misjudged him. He was possibly the only other Last Rider who could equal him in the number of kills made. Shade's had been made with his rifle, whereas Train had been trained to kill with whatever he had on hand.

"What are you laughing at?" Viper asked.

"I'm thinking I need to start collecting Train's IOUs. I've got to watch when he finally gets his hands on Killyama."

"I think she can take him," Rider snorted, chiming into the conversation.

Viper and Shade both shook their heads.

"Killyama will chew him up and spit him out," Cash said over the intercom.

Shade gave each of the men an innocent look. "Wanna make a bet?"

CHAPTER SEVENTY-FIVE

Shade answered the phone on the first ring.

"Can you talk?" Evie asked.

"Hang on." Shade stared down at Lily lying on the bed. "I need to take this call. I'll be right back. Don't move."

He went outside the bedroom door, shutting it behind him. Walking down the steps, he went to the kitchen where he poured himself a glass of whiskey before coming back on the line.

"Go ahead."

"I had a meet with Rabbit today. Remember him?" Not giving him time to acknowledge that he remembered him from the service, Evie continued, "He's a middle man now, does transactions involving illegal commodities. He makes the buys and pays for what's wanted then delivers the goods to whoever purchased his services.

"He confirmed what my other sources have told me. King's been slowly turning control over to Ice, although Desmond Hart will be the one in charge as a silent partner. He's even transferring ownership of his strip club to Henry. He's getting out of the business, Shade."

He took a drink of whiskey, hearing a tone in her voice he didn't like.

"Then what's wrong?" Shade asked.

"There's a deal going down which could go bad. I have to see how it ends to know if he can walk away clean."

He didn't say anything. She was defending King to him, which meant Evie had become close to King in the two months she had been in Queens City.

"Shade, he's not involved in the deal. Someone's trying to piss on his doorstep."

"If he cared about Lily, he'd let them piss then hose the door down after they left."

"Give him a chance. He's trying."

"Evie..."

"Please, Shade?"

"What do you care?" Shade probed.

461

She didn't say anything for a minute. "I don't want to see Lily hurt, either, and losing her dad would hurt her, Shade."

"Let me know when the deal goes down and what happens. Do you need me to send a couple of brothers down as backup?"

"No, I'm good."

"Tell me the truth."

"I'm good, I swear. If there's any trouble, I'll call."

"Okay, you better. I won't be happy if you get hurt," Shade warned.

"I won't."

"Later."

"Bye, Shade." Evie disconnected the call.

Shade finished his whiskey then set his glass down on the counter. He climbed the stairs to the bedroom, opening and closing the door quietly behind him before walking silently to the bed. He looked down at his wife who lay on the bed with a red scarf tied around her eyes and her hands cuffed to the hooks at the bottom of his headboard.

He reached up, letting the tips of his fingers brush her flesh from her ankle to her pussy, finding her wet.

"Did I keep my woman waiting long?" he crooned seductively.

"Shade, I need you," Lily moaned.

"I know, angel. I'm going to make it up to you. I was gone six minutes, and that's exactly how long you're going to come for me."

⮞ ⮜

"You left your tackle box on the porch." Lily handed him the small box.

Shade took it from Lily, placing it in the back of the truck before turning back to her.

"I didn't forget. I was going to come back and get it. I wanted to say goodbye in private." He curled his hand across the back of her neck.

"I guess I missed out." Lily rolled her eyes at him.

Shade let a small smile touch his lips. He had taken an hour to say goodbye before he had started carrying his things to the truck. He didn't want his inquisitive wife snooping through his things.

"How long are you going to be gone?" she asked, placing her hands on his chest as he started propelling her backward, leading her into the shadows of the factory building.

"A week," Shade reminded her. "If the fish aren't biting, maybe more." He brushed his lips across her cheek before catching her mouth in a kiss which would have her missing him five minutes after he left.

"Remember what I told you?"

"Yes, Shade. How could I forget when you've reminded me a million times? Stay home, let Rachel handle the church store until you get back, and tell Razer or Viper if I need anything. If I don't want to tell them, ask Beth." Lily playfully smacked his chest. "I'm not a child. I can take care of myself."

Shade didn't want to leave, but there were things which needed to be done. While he took care of that, he wanted Lily away from the church store so she didn't have a run-in with Brooke. So far, that had been successful. However, he wasn't taking any chances of that happening when he was out of town. He had confided other worries to Rachel who, knowing Lily's past, had promised to hold down the store until he got back.

"No, you can't," Shade disagreed, enjoying the light-hearted teasing.

"Can, too." Her eyes narrowed dangerously on him.

"Did you or did you not give all your cash to Anna Barr the other day in the grocery store?"

"I had my debit card," she argued.

"Which didn't have a cent in the account. When were you going to tell me you gave Lark Jackson money to pay his back-rent plus enough for the next two months?"

"How did you find out? I was going to tell you."

Shade just shook his head at her.

"Are you mad?" Lily bit her lip, staring up at him.

"No, angel. I don't get mad at you."

Lily looked at him suspiciously.

"Really." He shrugged. "I even put a little money back in your account for you."

"I don't need it; you pay for everything. Besides, I get paid next week," she stated angrily.

"If I don't get mad at you, then you can't get mad at me." Shade bent down, giving her another kiss when Cash yelled his name.

"Gotta go. See you in a week."

Lily frowned at him as he turned to leave. "Exactly how much did you put in my account?"

"Enough to do you until I get back," he laughed. "Try not to give it all away."

He climbed into the front seat of the truck as Lily was pulling out her cell phone.

They were pulling onto the road when he heard her yell his name in frustration.

"Want me to go back?" Rider asked.

"Fuck no. We need to keep to the schedule." He had everything timed to a precision. Any delay would cause him to miss an opportunity to exact his justice, and for some, it had already been delayed too long.

Lily would let him have it if they turned back, and he wouldn't be able to resist her. She was sexy as fuck when she was mad, and she let her guard down.

Damn, he was already regretting not having Rider turn around. He would just have to prod her memory when he returned.

ℝ ℞

Shade lay on his stomach in a ventilator shaft, two hundred fifty meters away from the building his target was being kept within. He had lain there for the last two days, watching as the police had swept the parking lot that morning, placing barriers so no one could get through. He hadn't eaten and had drunk sparingly. There was barely enough room to take a piss in the tight confines of the vent he was laying in.

He trained his rifle on the passenger window of an SUV as several officers jogged forward, moving in synchronized formation as they protected a man who didn't deserve them putting their lives on the line.

The ones in front slid into the vehicle while the others still kept his body covered with their own.

Shade adjusted his sight a millimeter as Digger took a step up into the SUV. Then he squeezed the trigger, and the bullet soundlessly left the rifle before hitting his target between the eyes. Shade regretted the son of a bitch wouldn't have felt a thing; just lights out, sending his soul on its way to Hell.

Shade was already sliding backward and was almost out of the shaft before the officers realized Digger was dead. He dropped out of the shaft, landing on his feet in an empty closet used by maintenance. The janitor had called in unexpectedly sick after receiving an inheritance from a long-lost relative.

Shade retrieved his canvas bag where he had hidden it behind a large shelf containing cleaning supplies. He placed the cap on his head, dumping his canvas bag into the trash can then putting the lid on top. He opened the door, wheeling the trash can down the hall as he heard the sirens.

"Hey, Marcus. How are you liking the new job?"

"Fine, sir. Anything I can do for you?" Shade asked humbly, keeping his head down.

"I left a box by my trash can; would you make sure it gets taken out?"

"Sure thing. I'll do it right now."

"Thanks."

"No problem. I'd be happy to take care of that for you," Shade said, whistling as he went down the hall to the supervisor's office, which was conveniently next to the exit.

᮰ ᳱ

Shade lay on his belly on top of a railroad car, staring through the night scope at the group leaving the warehouse.

He had tracked Rabbit the day before, knowing the sneaky shit would lead him to the buy. Cash had texted him, telling him Evie wasn't answering her messages. It didn't take a fucking rocket scientist to figure out why Rabbit was acting cocky. He had insurance—Evie.

He had followed Rabbit, realizing it was his only hope of finding Evie. When Rabbit had arrived at the warehouse and Shade had seen the Predators in hiding, watching the same building, he had known his theory was right.

He had quickly surveyed the surrounding area, finding the best spot. He believed in planning every detail, but that didn't mean he couldn't get the job done on the fly.

He shifted the rifle slightly, adjusting his trajectory for the hellacious wind.

After Evie and King, Rabbit and then the Predators came out of the building, Shade saw Max, another Predator, come out holding several bags.

Shade moved the rifle a fraction of a centimeter. His target stopped, saying something, but he would never hear what Evie replied because Shade pulled the trigger and Rabbit fell to the ground.

Shade sighed; the wind was a motherfucker. He had aimed for the back of his head, but the bullet had hit the side. He would compensate more on his next target.

The Predators were running like ants. Most were running for their lives, but Shade easily saw a couple of them heading his way, trying to discover where he was shooting from.

Shade moved the rifle to his next target—King.

Frowning, he saw Evie had thrown herself in front of King, plastering herself against him. Then she yelled out, telling them not to move. Shade's brow arched over his scope.

King pulled away from her as his car stopped by them and then opened the door. Evie shook her head, refusing to get in. King didn't budge.

Evie turned her head, staring in his vicinity.

"Please," she mouthed. "Please, don't."

"Fuck," Shade hissed.

Taking out his pin light, he gave her a quick flash, acknowledging he wouldn't kill the son of a bitch.

Evie reluctantly climbed into the car while King paused, staring in the same direction Evie had before getting inside.

"Don't tempt me," Shade muttered, moving backward.

Dismantling his rifle, he placed it back in the canvas bag. He saw the Predator who had kidnapped Penni and Ice drawing nearer. He silently dropped between the railcars, crawling on his stomach underneath, stealthily moving forward under them until he reached the end.

Shade heard running footsteps pass by, freezing in place. He pulled his .50 caliber Desert Eagle he had tucked into his pants. The first one who looked under the rail car was going to get his face shot off. The second would get one in the artery of a leg. Shade saw the two pairs of feet moving closer to his position.

"Hold up, Jackal."

"Max, keep your voice down," Jackal hissed.

"Ice texted. He said King told us to haul ass out of here."

Shade shook his head. The Predator had barely lowered his voice.

"I saw," Jackal said, "but I want to find the shooter."

"Doesn't matter what you want. Ice ordered us back to the clubhouse. We're lucky the cops aren't here yet."

Shade saw one pair of booted feet moving away.

"Coming?"

"Fuck, I'm coming." The second pair of boots moved away.

Shade remained still for the remainder of the night, slipping out before dawn to run toward his hidden rental car. Changing in the car and placing his canvas bag in a specially made suitcase, he then pulled out, driving to the airport.

Returning the rental car, he wheeled his suitcase to the front of the airport. He stared at several employees behind his sunglasses, standing out front. He wheeled it toward the one standing by the closest door.

"Bruno?"

"Yes, sir?"

"How's the food here?"

"A little salty for my taste."

"I like mine salty."

"Can I check your bag for you?"

"Thanks." Shade let him take the handle of the suitcase. An envelope of cash was placed in his pocket as he brushed against his side.

"Elmo will meet you at your destination," Bruno said, holding the door open.

Shade nodded, going inside the airport to check in.

The plane was on time and Shade boarded, handing the stewardess his coat as he went to first class while ignoring her flirting smile.

After the plane took off, she leaned over provocatively, showing her full breasts.

"Did you enjoy your business trip, Mr. Burns?"

"It could have gone better," Shade said, looking out the window.

She lowered her voice seductively. "Would you like something?"

Shade turned back to face her, his eyes dropping to her tits before rising to her eyes. "Just a whiskey," he said coldly.

ಐ ೞ

Shade sat on his haunches on the roof of the supermarket, watching the man Digger hired to kill Lily place his groceries in the car. He had taken the money to kill Lily, and he had a reputation of always finishing the job. He was good, just not good enough. One simple mistake had led to his downfall. Knox had tracked him down, giving Shade the information he needed.

Shade felt not an ounce of regret when Ray raised his head. He took the kill shot, placing the bullet in the exact same spot he had put Digger's.

His wife screamed as he fell to the pavement. Shit, he had done her a favor. Her husband had been stashing the money he made for his assassinations in offshore accounts. Shade was willing to bet, when he retired, he would have disappeared and left her behind as his last victim.

Crawling across the roof, he tore his rifle apart and placed it in the metal box. When he was finished, he stood and picked up the box, before climbing down the metal ladder. The supervisor stood below, waiting.

"Well?" he asked impatiently.

"All done. I took care of the problem. The motor that keeps the freezer cold had a clog in the coolant line. I flushed it out, and your freezer should be cold enough to freeze your balls off before you get back inside."

"Thank Christ. I lost my bonus this month and had to run a meat sale the last two days to get rid of the meat in the freezer."

"Well, it's all fixed now." Shade reached in his pocket, pulling out a pre-made bill then handing it to him. "You can pay that online if it's easier for you."

"Thanks. I will."

"Have a nice day." Shade placed his metal box in the back of the borrowed truck before climbing inside then shutting the door. He would clean it down and dump it not far from the owner's house. They would think it had been taken out for a joyride, and it had.

🕉 ☪

Shade held his rifle steady, slowing his breathing one heartbeat at a time, focusing only on the woman sitting at the picnic table. Watching her smoke the cigarette, he let her take six puffs before he pulled the trigger. It was the longest shot he had ever made at almost three hundred meters.

When her head hit the table, he knew he had succeeded in making the kill. Loosening his legs which had been gripping the tree trunk for sixteen hours, he slid the strap of his rifle over his shoulder then climbed down the tree to land on his feet.

Hurriedly, he broke down the rifle, placing it carefully in the canvas bag as he heard the loud blasting of the sirens.

He took a brief glance at his wristwatch before smoothing out the leaves beneath the tree. Jogging in a zigzag pattern through the wooded area, he increased his speed, jumping over the water to land on the other side of the creek. Once on the other side, he walked downstream several feet before deftly jumping sideways into the creek. Turning in the other direction, he began walking upstream.

He was two miles up before it started getting deep. Shade pulled on the straps of his bag so it would ride higher on his shoulders. When the water became waist-deep, he came to the tree he had been looking for. Jumping up with all the strength in his legs, he managed to grip the low-hanging limb and climbed up onto it until he could reach the trunk of the large tree. Shimmying down, he took off running through the woods for three miles. As he turned the bend, he came to a campfire with two men sitting on the riverbank, fishing.

"What took so long?" Rider asked, taking a hit from the joint in his hand.

"Kiss my ass," Shade said, going inside the tent where he took off the canvas bag and placed it in a trash bag, zip-tying it closed before placing it inside the cooler. The fish inside were four days old. Shade had to hold his breath when he opened it. Anyone opening it would puke their guts out from the smell, assuming it was rotten fish inside the trash bag. If the dogs did track him there, the fish inside the cooler would throw them off the scent.

Shade slammed the cooler shut then took off his camouflage pants and shirt. He dressed in jeans and a T-shirt before packing his wet clothes back outside, throwing them into the campfire after dousing them with lighter fluid.

Placing a metal grate on top, he set a frying pan with fish in it onto the fire. It didn't take long before the smell of frying fish filled the air.

Shade stood up, stretching before walking toward Rider. He crouched down next to him, taking the joint held out to him.

Cash tossed him a cold beer, which he caught with the other hand.

"We heading home in the morning?" Cash asked.

"Yes."

"What are you going to tell Lily if she smells weed on your clothes?" Rider joked.

Shade grinned back. "I'll tell her I didn't inhale."

CHAPTER SEVENTY-SIX

When Rider pulled his truck to a stop in The Last Riders' parking lot, Shade opened the passenger side door and got out as Rider and Cash hopped out alongside him. Shade opened the back door, reaching inside and pulling out his canvas bag, looping it over his shoulder before slamming the truck door closed. He then moved around to the bed of the truck, helping Cash pull out the big ice cooler.

"You go ahead. We got this." Rider grinned, coming around the back of the truck.

"You sure?"

"Yeah. Have fun." He smiled mockingly as he reached inside the truck bed for the fishing poles.

"Later," Shade said to both men, turning toward the path which led to his house.

He was halfway there when he saw her running toward him down the path lined with spring flowers she had planted, her purple dress and black hair blowing in the breeze.

His somber expression broke into a smile as he came to a stop, lifting his shades to the top of his head so he could see her clearly. When she got close, he held out his arms and Lily jumped into them, her mouth already turned up for his kiss. He gave her the kiss he knew she wanted; he'd take his when he got her inside their home.

"Did you have a good fishing trip? Did you catch anything?" Lily asked, gazing up at him with love shining in her violet eyes.

"Yeah, two big fish and a small fry."

"Was it fun?"

"Always." He looked down into her shining, violet eyes. "Did you miss me?"

"Always."

Shade grinned down at her, placing his arm around her shoulder as they walked up the path toward their house.

"Anything exciting happen while I was gone? Find anyone to give all my money away to?" he reminded her, keeping the promise he had made to himself when he had left.

"I'm not going to get angry with you today. I missed you too bad." Lily shot him a glare then slipped her arm around his waist. "Are you hungry? I can fix you something to eat," Lily changed the subject.

"Sounds good. I'll shower and change. I'll help you fix dinner, and then you can help me later," Shade teased.

"I don't think that's an even trade. Cooking is easy, while you require a lot of hard work." Lily's idea of dirty talk didn't match his.

"Angel, I promise to do my part tonight, too. While you're giving me a blow-job, I'll suck that pretty, pink clit of yours."

Lily blushed bright red, rushing into the kitchen.

"I'll go get changed." Shade climbed the steps, grinning when he heard a pot drop on the floor.

He took a couple of minutes to place his canvas bag in the hidden compartment of his cabinet before changing.

₧ ₨

Shade was about to sit down to eat lunch at the clubhouse when his phone vibrated. Taking it out, he stared down at the text message.

"Viper, I need to borrow your computer for a minute."

"Help yourself," he said, staring at the same text Shade had read. "Door's open."

Shade left without another word, running upstairs to Viper's room. He went to the computer, going to their security footage, smiling when he saw Evie until he saw who she was talking to. Closing the computer, he went back downstairs to the kitchen.

"Evie's back. Anyone want to go welcome her home?"

"Hell yeah!" Train said.

"Let's go." Raci bounced out of her chair.

The members all stood up one by one.

"I have a PTA meeting. I'll stop by and see her afterward," Winter said, picking up her dirty plate.

Shade followed the rest of the members outside.

They rode to Beth's and Lily's old house which Evie had purchased before she had left for Texas.

As they pulled up in front of the house, the door was flung open.

Evie came running outside, and Jewell and Raci jumped off the backs of the bikes they were riding on.

471

"Why didn't you call? We would have picked you up at the airport," Jewell complained.

"I didn't want to get you guys in trouble for missing work. I know what a slave-driver Shade can be," she teased as he sat watching the commotion of her greeting everyone from his bike.

"How did you know I was back? I was getting ready to call," Evie asked him.

"I saw you when the security alarm went off," Shade stated matter-of-factly while his eyes searched her face.

"I forgot to key in the code."

"Your visitor must have distracted you." He caught her eyes with his.

"She didn't stay long."

"Who stopped by?" Jewell asked curiously.

"No one important."

Knowing better than to push for answers Evie wasn't going to give, they all filed inside her new home. All the members had areas of their lives they wanted to remain private.

"So, what's first?" Raci stared around the empty room.

"The first thing is the furniture store. Want to go with me?"

Raci, Jewell, and Ember all agreed to go, while the brothers were going to head back to the clubhouse.

"You going to come by tonight?" Train slung an arm around Evie's shoulders.

"Not tonight. I'm tired from the trip and want to get unpacked," Evie replied evasively, moving away slightly. She smiled at Train's frown. "I'll be there for work bright and early tomorrow, though, so don't worry."

"It wasn't work I was thinking about. I've missed having you around."

"I missed you guys, too," Evie admitted with a smile.

"If we're going to get this house furnished, we need to get to the store," Raci reminded her.

"I'm coming."

Evie picked the keys up off the counter. Beth had dropped Evie's car off for her the day before. Razer and Shade had followed her and drove her back in Rider's truck.

"Let's go spend some money."

The women yelled while the men groaned as everyone trailed out of the house.

Shade was the last one out the door and waited for her to lock it. "Brooke cause any problems?"

"Same old Brooke. What can I say? Shade, she's really sick. I can't believe she's my sister."

"She's not sick; she's an evil bitch. I wish I had known who she was married to. I would have talked Lucky out of letting Merrick take over for him."

"It's too late now. We'll just have to deal with her."

Shade turned to walk back to his bike, but Evie grabbed his arm. "Shade, she's still fixated on you. Watch out. I'm worried with Lily being around her so often."

Shade's face darkened. "I didn't want to talk to Lily about Brooke until I spoke with you first."

Evie sighed. "You're going to have to tell her everything. I understand. I don't want her hurt because you want to respect my privacy."

"Are you sure?"

"Yes. Lily won't talk about my past with anyone, and she of all people will understand me not wanting to talk about it."

"I'll talk to her tonight."

"The sooner, the better. I don't want to give Brooke any opportunity to damage what you and Lily have."

"If that bitch causes you any more problems, you tell me immediately."

"I will. I promise."

Shade gave her a brief nod before going to his bike, watching as the excited women left to go shopping. Sighing, he sat down.

He had mistakenly believed he and Lily would have a peaceful life after their honeymoon. King was no longer trying to break them apart, and Lily was no longer in danger from her past. He had thought their troubles were over. According to Evie, however, they were just beginning.

೫ ೞ

Lily rolled over to face him, her hand reaching out to cup his face. "You're the best husband."

"I hope you always think so, Lily," Shade said seriously. "I really do." He sat up in the bed, turning on the lamp.

Lily blinked at the light.

"Sorry," Shade apologized. "But I need to talk to you."

"Is something wrong?" Lily sat up in the bed.

"You remember when I told you Evie and I went to high school together?"

"Yes."

"I went to school with her sister, too." Shade stared at Lily. "I didn't want you to feel uncomfortable in church, and I wanted to make sure there was a need to tell you before I did."

"Shade, you're frightening me." Lily's voice trembled.

"Lily, Brooke is Evie's sister." When Lily's expression turned angry, Shade raised his hand, stopping her angry outburst. "She and Evie do not get along. Evie hasn't spoken to her in several years, and I didn't think it was my place to talk about Evie's relationship with Brooke. I have only talked to her a few times, which I couldn't avoid, and I have never touched her, nor have I ever wanted to."

"I can understand Evie not wanting to talk about her past. I don't like to discuss mine, either. I thought you were going to tell me you had a relationship with her. I learned to accept the women at the club, but I'd feel strange looking at my pastor knowing you and his wife...Well, you know." She waved her hand in the air.

"Fucked each other?" Shade asked, trying to keep a straight face.

"I don't think you should talk like that about a pastor's wife. God might punish you," Lily said seriously.

"I'll take my chances where Brooke is concerned. She's an evil bitch."

"Shade..."

"Listen, I wasn't finished," Shade interrupting her. "While I didn't care for Brooke in high school, unfortunately she developed an obsession for me. Evie had a boyfriend. Levi and I hung out together, we played football, and both of our fathers were in the service. It was through him that Evie and I became introduced. We would even party and double-date together. Brooke always tried to butt in, which I didn't pay much attention to until it was too late. I had believed she was trying to bug Evie. At one point, I even thought she had a thing for Levi."

"But it was you she was interested in, wasn't it?"

"Yes." Shade's voice became unconsciously harsh. "She began to flirt with me."

Shade would never forget the night he had showed up at Evie's house. He was meeting Evie and Levi there to watch some movies. When Brooke had answered the door, he had gone inside thinking Evie and Levi were waiting. They hadn't been. When he asked Brooke where they were, she explained they had gone out to dinner with her parents.

"Why did Evie text me to come over then?" Shade had asked impatiently, turning toward the door.

"She didn't. I did, on her phone when she was getting ready," Brooke had admitted, gleefully proud of herself.

Shade had turned back to see Brooke removing her T-shirt and jeans.

"They won't be back for a couple of hours." She was wrapped around him the next instant, rubbing her naked tits against his chest. He had jerked her arms away from him, taking a step back.

"I don't care if they don't come back until tomorrow. I'm not fucking you."

"Why not? You fuck everyone else," she had snapped. "I'm prettier than any girl you go out with."

"No, you're not."

Brooke's ugly expression proved his words; however, she deliberately softened it in an instant, trying to look sexy. "I can do things for you they can't." Brooke had licked her lips, staring down at his jeans before raising her eyes to his. "I'll even let you hit me if you want to." She reached down on the couch, picking up a plastic rod that was used on blinds.

"Why do you have that?" he asked, raising a brow.

"Bethany told me how you like sex. I wanted to know why you saw her more than the other girls you go out with."

"Bethany wouldn't tell you." His eyes narrowed on the bitch holding the rod casually in her hand. "Touch her again, Brooke, and I'll take more than that belt to you," Shade threatened.

The girl actually shuddered at his words.

"I mean it, Brooke. I'm not going to fuck you. I'm *never* going to fuck you, but I'll wring your fucking neck if you touch another one of the girls I see." Shade went to the door without looking back.

Brooke tried to catch his arm, but he jerked it away, going out the door. *Brooke is crazier than I am*, Shade had thought then, and he still believed it.

Shade saw Lily was expectantly waiting for him to finish.

"I had several girls I was dating and she would bully them at school, making it miserable for them. One was Bethany. I saw her a little more often than the rest, and that was why Brooke picked on her the worst.

"Prom night, Levi, Evie, Bethany, and I were coming out of a restaurant. Levi and I went to get the car while the girls waited at the door. We weren't even at the car yet before we heard the girls screaming and ran back. A car had jumped the curb and hit Bethany and Evie. Evie had a couple of broken ribs and a broken leg."

"And Bethany?" Lily prompted.

"She was paralyzed from the waist down."

"Oh, my God."

Shade nodded. "It was a hit and run. It was so quick, the driver disappeared before Levi and I could get back."

"You believe Brooke did it, don't you?"

"Yes, but I could never prove it. I left Georgia after graduation, and I haven't seen Brooke since. Evie was attacked when she was in the service. Levi was dead a month after that; he got in a fight with Evie's attackers. One of the men had a connection with Brooke. I believe she was responsible for that, also. Evie had come home with me during a short layover, and she had told her mother."

"It could be coincidences."

"Maybe, but I don't believe so. You have to be careful around her. I don't want you to go anywhere that someone else can't see you with her in the church," Shade stated firmly. "I wish you would quit, but I know you won't," he added when he saw she was about to protest.

"I won't, but I'll be careful. I promise," Lily said, lying back down.

Shade turned the lamp off, lying back down with her.

Lily laid her head on his shoulder, her hand massaging the tension out of his muscles. "Shade, do you know what happened to Bethany?"

Shade rolled to his side. His angel always was more concerned with someone else rather than herself. She was the one in danger now. Brooke had hurt Bethany for no reason other than he had fucked her more than the others because she enjoyed being dominated by him.

"She's still living in Georgia, happily married with two children." He had made sure when he began making money that Bethany had the best care and had given her a sum of money she would be able to live off for the rest of her life.

"Good." Lily stroked down his arm. "I bet she still misses you. You would be hard to replace."

"Not so hard. She managed to find someone."

"I wouldn't. If you left me, I would still be waiting," Lily murmured drowsily.

"Angel, me leaving you isn't going to happen."

CHAPTER SEVENTY-SEVEN

Shade was facing his wife while she leaned against one of the large oak trees, waiting for him to finish his conversation with Viper and Rider. It was the Fourth of July picnic, which he'd had no intention of attending, nor had he been planning to let Lily until she had told him Brooke had returned to Georgia for a visit with her mother.

Shade thought it suspicious the way Brooke kept going back and forth between Georgia and Treepoint, but he really didn't give a fuck other than wishing she would keep her ass there.

"When are you going to fill the club in on what's been bothering you the last couple of days?" Viper asked.

Shade kept his eyes on Lily who had started looking pale recently. He had been deliberately trying to get her pregnant since their wedding night. Only when she had his child would he feel less threatened by the thought that she would leave him.

If she found out his final secret, that he was a cold-blooded killer, the child would tie her to him. He felt no rush of emotion at the thought of his child. He would be a good father and simply pretend like he did with everyone else.

He shrugged.

Lily was staring at him with a soft smile on her face. For a flash of a second, her face turned to one of heated desire before she blushed, regaining her composure. Shade caught the look and returned it with one of his own. With her not feeling well, he hadn't touched her the last week, wanting to give her time to rest and regain her strength.

"Had a couple of things on my mind, nothing to worry about. I'm going to go back to the clubhouse. Later." Shade didn't wait to hear their replies.

He strode across the yard to his wife who was frantically looking around to make sure no one was watching them. He gave her a wicked grin as he drew closer, and she tried to escape to the picnic table.

"Come here." He caught her around the waist, pressing her against the tree.

Shade slid his hand across her flat belly. If she didn't feel better in a few days, he was going to make her go to the doctor.

Bending down, he whispered, "Going somewhere?"

"I was going to get something to eat," Lily murmured shyly.

"You ate just a little while ago. Let's go home and have dessert. I have some chocolate mousse in the refrigerator. I made Evie get the recipe off Henry."

Once Lily nodded her acceptance of them leaving as she smiled, Shade placed an arm around her shoulder, maneuvering her through the crowd.

As they approached the gate to the backyard, King reached out to open it with Evie by his side.

"Leaving early?" King searched her face as Lily turned a bright red.

"The heat is getting to Lily. We thought we would go home until it cools down then come back for the fireworks," Shade explained with an impassive face.

King smiled down at Lily. "I'll see you later tonight, then."

"You two have fun," Lily said quickly as Shade led her to his bike.

"They make a cute couple."

Shade rolled his eyes at her. "Cute doesn't come to my mind when I see them together." Shade said, getting on his bike.

"Really, what does?" Lily asked, getting on behind him.

Shade looked at the couple still watching them. Evie had been the happiest he had seen her these past few months since high school. King had returned to town not only to get to know Lily better, but to continue the relationship with Evie which had started in Queens City.

"Never mind. They are cute together," Shade said, starting his bike. He could just imagine King's expression when he told him Lily's choice of words. "We need to invite them to dinner," Shade suggested to his wife. He would have to cash in another of Winter's IOUs to get her to make another batch of mousse, but it would be worth every spoonful.

ༀ ༃

They had been out on the water for over an hour. Shade and Rider both had their fishing lines in the water. He looked over at King as he lit a cigar. The man was hopeless at fishing. Shade had to give him credit, though; he had never really expected King to show for the fishing trip.

Evie was giving Beth a baby shower at her house, and Sex Piston was attending along with her crew. Those bitches had been a powerful motivator for the fishing weekend the brothers had organized.

Stud had fucked it up for the men when he had attended Sex Piston's baby shower; therefore, the brothers had decided the fishing trip would save Razer's ass from having to go.

Lily had pressured him into inviting King. Bonding with King wasn't high on Shade's to-do list, but Lily had promised him a night of sex when she would do anything he wanted. That was all Shade had to hear to move King up his list. Shade consoled himself with the knowledge that he wasn't the first man to be bribed by pussy, nor was he going to be the last.

"We could go back to shore and get you another pole," Rider offered.

"No, thanks. I would probably lose that one, too," King stated, biting down on his cigar in frustration.

Shade's lips twitched. King had lost his pole when a fish he was trying to land took off with it. King's face had been priceless when the pole had disappeared under the water.

"Don't feel bad. We've all lost poles. Of course, we were all drunk as shit at the time," Rider joked.

King looked toward Shade, who was sure he was waiting for a smart-ass comment to come from him; instead, he kept his eyes on the lake.

"How's Lily adapting to the new minister and his wife?" King asked.

"She's adjusting, but there's not a connection with Merrick like Lucky."

"Dean's living at the clubhouse now?" King broached the subject Shade was sure he was the most interested in.

"Yes," Shade answered.

"How's that working out?"

Shade sighed while turning to look at him, noticing Rider had a smile on his face as he listened.

"If you want to know if he participates in the club's activities, yes, he does. Not that it's any business of yours. Lily and I have our own separate house. Neither of us want Lily to see him when he's partying, so I text him when Lily's in the house. Dean cares about Lily and has no desire to tarnish his image to her."

"That's a lot of work for you two to make sure Lily isn't uncomfortable."

"She's worth the trouble."

"Yes, she is. Now that I'm in town, I want to get to know her better." King hesitated before adding, "Both of you. I don't want to invade your lives, just become a small part of it. I want to be able to have a relationship with my grandchildren when you two have a child."

Shade could imagine the hit it took to King's pride to admit he wanted a relationship with the children he and Lily would have.

The boat went silent; the only sound was the water lapping against the side.

"Got another cigar?" Shade eventually asked. If the man wanted to end the silent war between them, he wasn't going to say no. He wasn't the one who had started it, and King had something Shade needed more than he wanted to maintain the antagonism between them.

"Yes, I do." King pulled his stash out of his tackle box, offering one to Rider and him.

King relaxed on his seat while they talked, the atmosphere lightening on the boat. Shade actually managed to talk to King a couple of times without wanting to rip his arrogant head off.

Shade and Rider both managed to catch six fish before the sky darkened, and they decided to go back to camp. They docked the boat, carrying their tackle boxes and poles as they walked to the cabin. The others had fished from ashore and had already begun frying their catches.

"Where's your pole?" Viper asked King from the grill.

"He lost it," Rider volunteered the information.

As The Last Riders broke into laughter, making jokes at King's expense, King took it good-naturedly. If he was going to maintain a relationship with Evie, then King was going to have to get used to the brothers giving him a hard time. Fuck, they were going easier on him than if Shade had been the unlucky bastard to lose his pole.

Viper and Cash served up the fish. Then, after dinner, they all pitched in to clean up outside before going inside to get away from the insects and play some cards.

Shade looked up at the flashes of lightning as he went inside the cabin, frowning. Lily was still terrified of storms.

He managed to play three games, listening to the thunder get closer and closer. By the middle of the fourth hand, a loud burst of thunder shook the cabin. Shade stood up, going to his bunk. Every instinct in his body was screaming that he had to get the fuck out of here.

"What are you doing?" King asked when he saw him gathering his things.

"I'm going back."

"Why?" King looked down at his watch. "It's after midnight."

"I know what time it is. The storm is getting worse, and Lily is afraid of storms."

"She's with Evie and Beth; she'll be okay. We're heading back in the morning, so there's no need to hike back a mile to the truck in this storm. Call her if you're worried," Cash advised, throwing two poker chips into the pile in front of him.

King didn't say anything; instead, he crushed his cigar into the ashtray and got to his feet.

"What are you doing?" Shade stopped putting on his jacket.

"Going with you." King put on his boots then his jacket.

"There's no need for you to leave."

A sense of urgency filled him, and King would slow him down. The storm was nearly overhead, but Shade didn't believe that was what was causing it. He had been outside during too many storms to attribute that to his instinct to protect Lily.

"We're going back in a few hours, anyway. Might as well go now," King stated.

Shade didn't argue further as King reached to open the door after grabbing one of the flashlights.

"Wait a minute. Let me get my things. I'm going, too," Razer said, getting up from the table and gathering his things.

"Fuck, if you guys go, then I have to go. Winter will throw it up to me that you came running back to your women, and I'll never hear the end of it."

"You pussy-whipped bastards are ruining all the fun," Cash said, getting to his feet.

As they gathered their things, Shade wanted to snap at the brothers to hurry. King caught his eye, and Shade knew the man was beginning to feel his anxiety. Shade didn't care if everyone thought he was crazy as hell; he needed to get back to Lily.

Cash locked the door behind them as a loud burst of thunder sounded from directly above.

Shade traveled at a fast pace which was hard for any of them to match. He was the first one back at the vehicles and was waiting impatiently for them as he sat behind the steering wheel of the truck when they finally came out of the woods. As soon as King, Cash, Rider, and Viper closed the door, he peeled out of the parking lot, leaving the rest of the brothers to the other truck.

"Fuck, what's the hurry, Shade?" Cash asked from the backseat.

"The girls aren't answering their phones," Shade said grimly, peeling out onto the slick road.

He expertly straightened the truck before pressing down on the accelerator to speed the truck up. He clenched his jaw.

King was hanging onto the door. Shade shot him a glance.

"Try Evie's cell phone."

King took his cell phone out, punching the number in, while Shade concentrated on the dark road ahead of him.

"She didn't answer," King told him, worry in his voice now.

Shade's mind went to the night Evie had been raped. Brooke had been miles away that night, also.

"Cash, reach into my bag and hand me my gun. It's in the side pocket."

Shade heard the zipper of his backpack being undone.

"Aren't you overreacting?" King asked when Cash leaned forward, handing him his Desert Eagle. Shade tucked it into the waistband of his jeans.

None of the brothers questioned him. As enforcer for The Last Riders, they didn't doubt his skills; it had saved their own asses too many times.

"If I am, then we can all get a good night's sleep," Shade said, seeing the lights ahead which showed they were close to Treepoint. "If not, then we're prepared. I would rather have my gun even if I don't need it. If I need it and don't have it, then it will be the last time I need one."

King grunted as the truck went over a pothole, his head hitting the roof of the truck cab.

"I can agree with that."

The truck went on two wheels when Shade turned the corner to Evie's house. Turning off the headlights, he brought the truck to a stop.

"The lights are out," Shade said grimly, opening the truck door.

"What? Probably because of the storm," King said.

Shade didn't answer; Viper did.

"They're on in the house next door."

Shade was out and running as soon as his feet hit the ground, heading for the front door. He took out his gun when he found it was open. Shade heard Viper and Cash running and the sound of Rider's truck coming down the street.

As he entered the house, he heard the women's screams from above and the crashing of a door. Shade ran up the stairs two at a time. Seeing one man enter a room at the end of the hall, Shade didn't hesitate. He moved forward and brought his gun up as he came to the doorway.

There were three men inside, one standing over Lily as she held a crying baby.

"Please, don't hurt the baby," Lily begged for the baby's life and not her own. "Please."

Shade fired three times, one bullet for each man. He didn't need to check to see if they were dead. He didn't miss.

"Lily!" Shade ran across the room to her.

"Call an ambulance!" Evie screamed as the room filled with The Last Riders. "And get my medical bag out of my bedroom closet."

A minute later, King had the bag and was next to her.

"The ambulance is on the way," King stated, moving away.

"Beth!" Razer tried to get to Beth, but there wasn't enough room.

The room erupted with movement as the men moved the bodies then the bed out of the way.

"Beth." Razer's voice broke as he managed to reach her hand.

Evie glanced up at him. She didn't have to say anything; the blood seeping everywhere said it all.

Shade swallowed hard, lifting Lily to her feet.

"I can't leave her, Shade."

"You're not. I'm just moving you so they can bring the stretcher inside." Shade held her in her arms as the lights came back on.

Train came in soon after, and Shade knew he had been the one to fix the lights.

Lily didn't want to give the baby up, crying as she handed it to the medical technician who wrapped a warming blanket around its body. Lily turned, burying her face in his chest.

"Angel, get some clothes and get dressed. I'll drive you to the hospital," he said as they wheeled Beth out on the stretcher.

Lily nodded against his chest. "Thank God you came back in time."

"I've told you, I will always be here when you need me." Shade smiled, releasing her so she could get dressed.

She nodded again, moving away to get her clothes.

Shade looked away from her, meeting King's eyes he walked forward, holding out his hand. Shade shook it, both of them realizing they could have lost the women they loved that night. They could and would learn to tolerate the other for her.

⁎ ⁏

The large hospital waiting room was filled with silence. Evie sat next to King, holding his hand tightly. Razer sat on her other side, and Shade sat next to him with Lily on his other side.

"Do you need me to get you something?" King offered Evie.

"No." Evie brushed her tears away.

They hadn't even come out to tell them if the babies were doing okay, but they had informed them Razer's second son had been delivered in the ambulance.

"I've known some scary situations in my life, but when I heard those gunshots and couldn't get to you and Lily..." King's hoarse voice had Shade's hand tightening on Lily's as he relived those seconds of seeing someone with a gun pointed at her head.

"I'm fine, King," Evie said.

Razer sat next to him as if turned to stone. He hadn't said a word since the nurse had forced him to take a seat in the waiting room.

One by one, each of the members of The Last Riders entered the room. Shade stiffened when Sex Piston and her crew came in, followed by a grim-faced Stud. He hoped the bitches knew it wasn't the time for their crazy-ass antics.

The door to the waiting room remained open, revealing a line of bikers down both sides of the long hallway. Not only were there The Last Riders which couldn't fit in the room, but the members from The Blue Horsemen and the Destructors.

Beth's friendship with the bitches had formed an alliance with the two clubs. Like him and King, The Last Riders, The Blue Horsemen, and Destructors would get along to preserve the friendship which had begun that day at the gas station.

Sex Piston knelt in front of Razer, placing her hand on his thigh. "When I met Beth, I thought there was no way she could be for real. No one could be that sweet or clueless. As I got to know her, I realized she was the most real person I have ever met.

"The last month of my pregnancy, I was scared, afraid of the delivery, the pain, of being a mom." Tears coursed down Sex Piston's cheeks. "She told me not to be afraid, that I had to have faith that everything would be all right.

"Razer, we're both going to listen to Beth and have faith that she and those precious babies are all going to be fine."

Razer's composure broke as he took Sex Piston into his arms. Shade put his arm around Lily when he heard her begin to cry along with Evie.

"Evie, listen to her. Beth is going to be okay," King murmured, trying to soothe her.

"I was a terrible friend to her," Evie cried.

"You saved her life—*our* lives," Lily contradicted her. "Tonight, when those men came, you didn't leave her side. You delivered her son, and the doctor told us it was your skills as a Corpsman which kept her alive until the ambulance came. Beth considers you more than a friend. She loves you like a sister, and I do, too."

"Excuse me." The exhausted doctor standing in the doorway eyed the rough-looking crowd waiting for news.

Razer rose shakily to his feet.

"Your wife is in recovery. It will be at least an hour before you can see her." He motioned to the nurse. "Shelley will take you to the nursery. There are two boys waiting to meet their dad."

℧ ℥

King nodded to Shade, who gently clicked the door shut before Razer could catch them. They had been listening to Razer tell his wife their boys were fine. Shade was standing sentry as Razer lay in bed with Beth. They were both emotionally distraught and needed the time to hold and comfort each other after their nightmare of a night.

Nodding, King walked away.

Shade turned to Lily as she approached with a bottled water in her hand.

"She's awake," Shade told her, moving away from the door as Razer came out.

The brother looked haggard, as if he had aged ten years overnight.

Lily hugged Razer, whose arms went around her. "Thank you, Lily."

"I didn't do anything. Evie's the one who delivered the baby."

Razer shook his head. "You..." Razer blinked back the tears both Shade and Lily saw in his eyes. "You offered your life for my son's." Razer's voice broke. It took a second for him to regain his composure. "It's a debt I can never repay, but if you ever—"

"You're my brother, Razer. You don't have to thank me," Lily said softly, stepping back.

"I'm going to go get the nurse to bring the babies in for Beth to see. You two go inside."

Shade nodded, receiving the message that he didn't want Beth left alone.

Lily's face lit up with joy, immediately going inside the room.

"Shade...If you hadn't decided to come back—"

Shade cut him off. "Brother, if you start crying on me, I'll punch you."

"All right. Just wanted you to know that plan you have that you don't think we know about, I'm in, and the rest of the brothers are, too."

Shade looked at him in surprise. "How...?"

"You think you're the only one who wants revenge? Been doing the same searches you have. Knox told me because he was tired of repeating the same information four times."

"Who else wanted the information?" Shade asked.

"You, me, Lucky, and Viper."

"Fuck. I was looking forward to doing it on my own."

"Sorry, brother; we're too used to sharing all the fun." Razer slapped him on the back before moving away to find his babies.

Shade opened Beth's door, seeing the two sisters hugging each other. He silently closed it again, leaving the two alone. He would wait for Razer.

CHAPTER SEVENTY-EIGHT

Shade reached into the ice cooler, pulling out a beer then carrying it to King who was determined to man the grill, despite the heat. Shade handed him the beer, seeing the sweat dripping of him.

"Thanks." King took a long drink of the cold beer.

"Want me to take over for a while?" Shade offered.

"Don't even think about it. Evie doesn't think I can do anything macho. This is me about to prove her wrong."

"Grilling is macho?" Shade's eyes took in his sweaty T-shirt.

"Isn't it?" King asked, wiping the perspiration from his brow with a paper towel.

"You're not going to feel very manly when you suffer a heat stroke," Shade advised.

"Just keep the beers coming. The burgers are almost ready."

The crowd had gathered in the backyard of the clubhouse for the baptisms of Beth and Razer's sons. Many were waiting to be fed, already making their plates from the buffet the women had put together.

King looked like he was about to pass out as he pulled the meat off, placing them on platters.

"Go find a seat in the shade. I'll take these to the tables," Shade told him as he picked the platter up.

King nodded, taking his beer to find a cool seat.

Shade carried the plates to the tables, setting them down, then got out of the way as the hungry members grabbed plates. He took a beer for himself as he walked around the yard, talking to the brothers while waiting for Lily to come outside. She had told him she would be out in a little while, that there was something she needed to do. It had been an hour already, though.

Shade passed Evie who was holding one of Beth's sons while Razer stood not far away, keeping him within his eyesight. No one could tell the babies apart other than the parents. They had named one Noah and the other Chance.

Evie had grown attached to the baby she had delivered. With her and King now married, if King wasn't careful, his father-in-law would be carrying around his own bundle of joy soon.

Shade laughingly joked to himself. *The man can barely handle a grill, couldn't fish worth shit...I hope, if King does have another kid, it's another girl.*

Lily came out of their house, carrying a large book. When she saw her father, she walked over to his table. She sat down next to King, placing the book in front of him.

Shade had watched her working on the scrapbook over the last week. She had shown him several of the pictures inside.

While King opened the book and began looking through it, Shade gave them their privacy as he threw his beer bottle away.

He saw sadness in King's face until he turned through most of the book then joy filled his expression. Then Lily said something to King which had the man practically in tears.

Shade figured he had given them enough time. Besides, if he didn't break it up, King was going to have every brother in the backyard making fun of him.

King closed the scrapbook as he approached.

"Are you ready to eat?" Shade asked Lily, frowning when he saw King wipe his tears away.

Maybe he should take another look at the scrapbook. The pictures inside shouldn't be causing that kind of reaction from her father.

"No. Would you mind going to the car? I left a pack of diapers on the backseat. I thought we could..." Lily began mischievously.

"No. I am not making another diaper anything. I don't care who it's for." Shade broke off his rant, taking a good look at King's face. "Is Evie...?"

Hell, he felt bad about making fun of King's crying.

"No." King smiled widely at him.

Shade looked back and forth between Lily and King. His face broke into a smile as he lifted Lily from her seat, twirling her around in his arms.

"What's going on?" Evie asked as she came to stand next to King. "Have you been crying?"

Shade heard her when he placed Lily back on her feet, kissing her then picking her up to twirl her again.

"Yes," King admitted.

"Why?"

"Lily called me Dad."

"Do you know why Shade's crying?" Evie asked.

"Yes, because he's going to be a dad."

›‹ ›‹

Bernard used his cane to hold the door open for the man entering the bar. He nodded toward the same card he had in his pocket.

"I see you won one, too."

"What?" The man stopped as he was about to enter.

Bernard walked in, looking around. There were about twenty men watching the stripper shake her tits at the men in the bar.

"I got one. It's for a free lap dance, isn't it?"

"Yes. You won, too?"

Bernard nodded, losing interest in the man he was talking to.

"We must be on the same mailing list," he said, taking a seat at an empty table.

"Maybe." He shrugged, taking a seat at the same table.

"Here you go." A server placed two whiskeys down on the table in front of them.

"We didn't order these—"

"Don't worry; they're on the house."

"Damn, why haven't I come here before?" He smacked the table before picking up his drink.

"Name's Jason."

"Mine's Bernard." The two men shook hands.

The stripper walked off-stage as the door at the top of the stairs opened, and a huge man walked down the steps.

"He must be the bouncer," Bernard wise-cracked. "Damn, those are some mean-looking fuckers in the corner by the door." Bernard nodded at the group of bikers.

Jason turned his head, his expression growing pale when he saw the men. Hastily, he turned to face forward when the one with the scar stared at him. The creepy fucker made his skin crawl.

"That's the Predators." Jason lowered his voice.

Bernard turned to stare at them again rudely. "I've heard of them. They don't look as badass as I thought they would. In my day, me and a couple of friends of mine could have taken the whole bunch of them," Bernard bragged loudly.

"Sh...I don't want any trouble with them," Jason muttered.

"You a pussy?" He hit the table. "You're in the right place. Jump on the stage."

Jason looked around the room at the men sitting at the tables and standing at the bar. Some of them looked vaguely familiar.

The door to the outside opened, and another group of bikers entered. They looked just as lethal as the ones sitting at the table.

"Fuck, how many free coupons did they give away?" Bernard muttered.

Jason ignored him, staring at their cuts.

"The Last Riders," Bernard answered his unasked question.

Jason had never heard of them, and he didn't intend to get caught in a turf war. He finished his own drink, setting the glass down on the table.

He was about to stand up and leave when the last biker came in. When the door closed, he locked it and stood in front of it. He was as big as the bouncer, but he was bald. He crossed his arms over his chest, blocking the door.

Bernard slammed his empty glass on the table. "Where did that waitress go? I need another drink. Think they'll give me another free one?"

"I don't think the first one was." Jason sat on the edge of his chair. "Where did all the waitresses and strippers go?"

Bernard stared around the room. "Don't know. Guess they're taking a break."

"All at the same time?" Jason said sharply.

"They're coming back. See, the lights on the stage are coming on."

Jason looked to the stage. Everyone in Queens City would recognize the man walking across it. His harsh features and elegant suit were his trademark.

"I know him. That's King. I remember him from when he was first starting out."

"You're from King's neighborhood?"

"Used to be. I moved in with my son and his wife ten years ago. You, too?"

"Yeah, I moved away twelve years ago when I got married. I live with my daughter and her kids after my wife died, and she got divorced."

"You have grandkids? How old are they?" Bernard asked with a gleam Jason recognized too easily.

"I'm getting the fuck out of here." That big son of a bitch might be at the front door, but the place had to have a back exit.

A hand landed on his shoulder, and Jason looked up into the creepy biker's face.

"Sit down. The show is just beginning."

Jason nodded as he felt a drop of piss roll down his leg. He sat back down, but the man's hand didn't leave his shoulder.

Jason's attention was drawn back to the stage where King began talking. "Good evening, gentlemen. I want to thank you for showing up for the free lap dance. Please show your card if you have one. Anyone here who doesn't have a card?"

While the cards were being waved eagerly in the air by the others, Jason left his lying on the table.

"Good. I see we only have one missing tonight. The turnout was much better than I expected. You can place your card down now. I'd like to turn the stage over to my son-in-law."

Jason thought the biker standing behind him was scary; however, the man walking out onto the stage was the stuff of nightmares.

"I'm not going to say a lot to you filth. You've already taken too much of my time." He walked to the stage to a large square which was covered by a cloth. Then he reached out, removing the white cloth and dropping it to the floor. "Remember her? Each of you should."

Several men tried to make a break for it, but the bikers had spread throughout the room. They knocked the men down to the floor as they tried to escape.

"Tonight, each and every one of you are going to die, and I want you to remember her face. The little girl you raped and paid money for is King's daughter and my wife. Her name is Callie, so when you enter Hell tonight, you'll know why you're there." He reached down to his boot, pulling out a lethal-looking knife. Taking a step forward, he jumped down from the stage.

Screams and yells filled the bar as the group of men were beaten. Jason didn't feel anything after the first ten minutes.

He was being kicked in the ribs when he saw Bernard's cane laying on the floor and him trying to crawl away from the blond biker kicking him. When the biker reached down and picked up the cane, smashing his head in, Jason started crying.

"Please don't kill me...Please don't kill me."

The one on the stage who said the little girl was now his wife crouched down next to him, staring down mercilessly into his eyes.

"Did she beg you not to touch her? Did the thought even cross your mind to help her? I'm going to show you the same mercy."

The flash of a knife was all he saw as his shirt was ripped open. Jason felt the first cuts then the sensation of the warm blood leaving his body until the darkness came and carried him away.

ॐ ॐ

Shade stood, looking at the motionless bodies lying on the floor. King stood, as well, having finished with the last one before walking across the room to stand next to him.

"Damn. You better hope that comes up or Henry will be pissed," he said, commenting on the pool of blood at their feet.

"Sorry," Shade lied.

"If you're all done, Ice and his men will get them loaded into the truck out back."

"I'm done. We'll help load them. It'll be quicker."

It only took them twenty minutes to get the bodies loaded. Then Ice sent several women in through the back door to begin straightening and cleaning. One even had a shampooer.

"You ready to head home?" Lucky asked, wiping the blood off his leather jacket with a bar cloth.

"Yeah, I'm ready. Where's Razer and Viper?"

"Over there by Ice. They're thanking him for his men's help."

Shade nodded as The Last Riders gathered by the door. Shade watched as King shook Henry's hand then the Predators' before joining him at the door.

They started to go outside, but King's hand on Shade's arm stopped them.

"You used the excuse last time that you went hunting, so what reason did you give Lily for leaving town this time? I told her and Evie that I had to sign some papers, selling the bar."

"I told her we were going to a funeral."

CHAPTER SEVENTY-NINE

"Everyone here?" Viper asked, coming into the kitchen.

"Yes," Shade answered, leaning against the kitchen counter.

Having missed dinner, Viper was finally coming downstairs to the meeting he had called. The room was filled with only the brothers since the women had left after dinner.

Viper walked to the front of the room. "A few weeks ago, Stud asked for a meet with Cash. Once I gave the go-ahead, they met, and he asked Cash to find out what he could about a new biker club which had recently moved into his territory. Stud wanted to be cautious before he made a move to drive them out. He was smart.

"Cash found out they call themselves Freedom Riders. Their leader is called Scorpion, and Vaughn is his vice. They are anti-government, and their numbers are large—bigger than what Stud is going to be able to handle even combining The Blue Horsemen and Destructors."

Viper paused briefly before continuing, "They want to buy a large piece of property to train their men, land which is isolated and easily defended. Once the purchase goes through, they'll bring in even more men, assuming Stud won't be able to stop them."

"Who owns the property?" Shade asked.

"Curt Dawkins, the football coach here in town," Cash answered.

"Cash told me they' are fanatical and deadly," Viper continued. "So, the question is, do we back Stud up with our numbers or leave this mess in his lap? I've thought about this all last night and today. Truthfully, I made my decision only a few minutes ago before I came in here."

"Which is?" Shade asked, already knowing the choice Viper had made. Not only would the brother never turn his back on someone who had asked for help, but Stud had also helped them a couple of times; therefore, Viper wouldn't leave the debt unpaid.

"We'll stand with Stud. I studied the map of where the property is they want to buy, and it's not far from Treepoint, so there isn't going to be a way to avoid fighting them anyway. I think they just want to get Stud out of the way before they turn their attention to us."

"I agree," Shade said.

The other brothers stated their agreement, as well.

"Shade, I want you to handle Dawkins. I don't want him selling that property to them, even if you have to buy it. I don't care how you do it."

Shade nodded.

"There's also something else we need to discuss." Shade saw the flash of anguish which crossed Viper's face before it was hidden. "I have refused to name a VP out of respect to Gavin. It was his idea to begin our club and I didn't want to name another, but Gavin wouldn't have wanted it that way. Shade, you're too valuable to me as an enforcer to give you that title, though you deserve it."

"Fuck, I wouldn't have wanted it anyway. I have enough on my hands as it is, saving your asses," Shade joked, easing the tension in the room.

"Razer, you're our best rider, so I need you at our back," Viper stated. "Plus, you have kids. I need my vice to put the club first."

The members waited for Razer's reaction.

"Don't blame you, brother. If I needed decisions made, I would want the man making them not to be worried his wife will marry a jackass after he's dead and gone." Razer shrugged.

Viper smiled. "Rider and Train, you're my soldiers, always will be. I need men I know can carry out my orders and see the other brothers do, too, without question."

Both men nodded.

"Knox, you're too valuable as the sheriff."

"Diamond would kick my ass, anyway," Knox stated.

Viper paused, clearing his throat. "Lucky, the job's yours if you want it. You've put your time in longer than any brother here, and I think Gavin would be proud if you took his spot by my side."

Lucky stiffened next to Shade while the room waited expectantly for his answer.

He stood up straight, walking forward to stand by Viper's side. Then he held out his hand to shake Viper's. "I'd be honored, brother."

Viper smiled, jerking Lucky to him and hugging him before slapping him on the arms. "Rider, get the women back in here. Nickel, pass out the beer. We're going to celebrate."

The women came back in the room and Lily came to his side, slipping an arm around his waist.

"What's going on?" she asked worriedly.

Shade smiled, taking a beer from Nickel. "Viper just made Lucky his vice president." Shade purposefully left out the issues with the Freedom Riders.

"Oh."

Shade had thought she would be relieved the meeting was over; instead, her troubled gaze went to Lucky who was being congratulated by the other brothers.

"I take it you don't agree with Viper's choice."

"I guess I was hoping Lucky would eventually realize he missed the church." Lily shrugged sadly. "I miss having him as my pastor; a lot of the church members do."

"Angel, the only reason he remained a pastor so long was for his investigation."

"Perhaps, but I think it was an excuse, too."

"For what?"

"For what he was called to do," Lily answered softly.

"Yeah? Well, he's getting called to do something else now, and he looks a lot happier doing it." Shade motioned to Lucky, who was opening his beer and kissing Raci on the mouth as she congratulated him.

"Does he?" Lily said.

༄ ༅

Shade and Curt Dawkins looked around the heavily wooded property in Jamestown that Friday. It would be useless to The Last Riders.

Shade didn't like the thought of forcing the man not to sell, but he really didn't want The Last Riders to spend half a million dollars on a property which would take years to resell.

"What do you think?" Curt asked.

"I think you need to reconsider putting it up for sale," Shade told him.

"Why would I do that? I have an offer for the asking price—"

"From a buyer who belongs to an anti-government organization. Think you'll be able to keep coaching if the school board finds out?"

"If I sell this land, I won't need to work," Curt boasted, but Shade didn't miss the glint of worry in his eyes.

"You get to keep the money all to yourself, or do you have to split it?" Shade asked.

"I have to split it. My mom gets the biggest chunk then my brothers and me."

"How much is your part?" Shade questioned.

"Sixty thousand."

Shade stared back at him. Sixty sounded a hell of a lot better than five hundred thousand.

"The Last Riders will give you seventy-five for your part." He shrugged. "That way, we get what we want, and you get some extra cash and keep coaching."

"What will I tell my family?" Curt frowned.

"That's up to you. We have a lawyer who can draw the papers up. You can sign and have the money in your hands by tomorrow. Of course, the stipulation will be that the rest of the property can't be sold for five years."

"Make it three, and we have a deal."

"Fine." Shade would have gone down to a year. He didn't think the Freedom Riders were going to hang around that long and wait for the property to become available again. They would either move on or try to find another piece of land. This was going to get expensive if they did the latter.

The men shook hands, and then Shade, Lucky, Rider, and Cash walked back to their bikes.

"That was easier than I expected." Cash nodded his head as Curt drove away.

"I'm just grateful we didn't have to drop that kind of cash on this place." Shade started his bike. "Lucky, when we get back to town, call Knox and tell him to have Diamond draw up the papers. Make sure she puts in there that we have access to hunting up here."

"Damn, this might have a bright side after all," Rider said. "I saw a couple of deer trails while I was looking around."

"Not only that, but we can take it as a tax deduction." Shade grinned. "We can have survival workshops out here."

"Damn, Shade, I like the way you think," Lucky laughed.

"Let's head back to town. Since I saved the business so much money today, you can buy my lunch."

They were still joking around when they went inside the diner. Shade had turned to say something to Cash when his expression went cold. He was staring at a table by the window where Rachel and Willa were sitting with a group of bikers Shade recognized from Cash's files.

They took a table themselves. Unfortunately, it wasn't close enough to hear what was being said, although Rachel was smiling and talking and Willa seemed her usual nervous and shy self, uncomfortable with the attention the men were showing her.

The waitress came and took their order. Shade and Rider both ordered sandwiches and fries, while Lucky and Cash only ordered coffee.

"I thought you two were hungry?" Rider said, putting sugar in his coffee.

"I've lost my appetite," Cash said.

Shade ate his sandwich thoughtfully as he watched the table. He knew of only one thing which made a man lose his appetite, and that was a woman. . He decided it had to be Rachel he was interested in; not because of the looks, but because of the attitude. Cash had never been attracted to shy women; the bolder a woman was, the more Cash liked her.

Shade turned his attention to Lucky who was talking to Rider without looking at the table at all. As vice president, he should be studying them and memorizing the faces of the men with Scorpion and Vaughn.

"Did Willa just give her card to one of those sons of bitches?" Lucky snarled.

Shade looked up, understanding dawning on him. Lucky had been watching the table using a mirror placed in the corner of the ceiling for the waitress to see if anyone had come through the door when she was out back.

"I believe she did. Maybe he wants to get something sweet off her." Shade picked up his coffee cup to take a drink.

"Shut up, Shade. Willa isn't that type of woman."

"Brother, they're *all* that type of woman; it just depends on who's asking." Shade picked up the check, tossing it toward Lucky.

As the women left, Shade could see Rachel holding a to-go order he was sure was for his wife. *It better not be another burger and fries.* The woman was constantly craving hamburgers and junk food. He had put a strict limit on how many she could have in a week, and she had reached her quota when she had sent him out at one a.m. for one the previous night.

"Rachel should know better than sitting with strangers. Someone should tell her brothers." Cash looked toward Shade.

"If you're wanting me to tell 'em, you're shit out of luck. I'm not pissing off Rachel—she's the one who bags our weed. I've heard they add stuff when you piss them off."

"I've heard that, too," Rider confirmed, dropping another sugar in his fresh cup of coffee.

"With your sweet tooth, I'm surprised you aren't chasing after Willa," Shade said to Rider, watching Lucky's reaction from the corner of his eye.

Rider sat back in his chair, as if considering the thought. "I'm not into virgins." He grinned cockily. "They get too serious, and I don't want to set a standard another man can't match."

"Jesus," Lucky said, looking heavenward.

Shade stood up. "Rider, I'm going to leave because I have nothing I can say to your asinine remark."

Shade had passed his chair, headed for the door, when he heard Rider's next comment.

"He's lucky I didn't fuck Lily first," he boasted.

"You did not just say—fuck, Shade, let him go!" Lucky yelled as both he and Cash tried to pull him off Rider.

Shade threw them off him, banging Rider's head on the table then putting his hand in his hair to jerk his head back so Rider was staring up into his deadly eyes.

"Do. Not. EVER! Think it's okay to mouth off like that again about Lily, you got me? Brother or not, I *will* take you out."

"Shit, Shade, I was only kidding around!"

"Don't care." Shade released him, still furious.

"What in the fuck are you smiling about?" he snarled at Lucky.

"Because you can dish it out, but you can't take it," Lucky laughed.

Shade took a second then regained his composure. "I was trying to get one of you jackasses to make a move on her."

"Why?" Lucky asked with a puzzled frown.

"Have you tasted her cupcakes? None of the women at the club like to bake, and I'm tired of running out in the middle of the night for cupcakes and hamburgers."

CHAPTER EIGHTY

The women were standing at the counter when Shade entered the church store, his mouth tightening into a thin line when he saw Brooke was standing beside Lily. He took off his glasses as he went behind the counter, placing a kiss on his wife's lips while ignoring Brooke.

"Rachel told me she saw you at the diner. I thought you would have already gone home." Lily smiled up at him.

"I thought I would stop by and see if you wanted to close the store early and take a nap before the party."

Rachel was throwing Mrs. Langley a birthday party. She was Winter's aunt, so she was basically extended family to The Last Riders, and Beth cared for her; therefore, they had all been invited.

Lily bit her lip. "We haven't had a customer in two hours."

"Go ahead, Lily. I'll stay," Rachel offered. Shade noticed she hadn't missed the look of envy Brooke had quickly concealed.

"Are you sure?"

"Of course. Go. I have to stay in town anyway," Rachel urged.

"All right then." She gathered her purse.

"Go ahead. I'll be right behind you," Shade said.

Lily shot her husband a curious look yet left without question.

"Do you mind excusing us, Brooke?" His tone implied he really didn't give a damn if she did. Brooke wouldn't expose her true colors in front of Rachel. She wanted to keep up the pretense of being the sophisticated wife of a pastor when she was nothing more than a snake in the grass.

Brooke's face blushed bright red. "Not at all." She turned on her high heels, leaving with an expression that said she would pay him back for being rude to her.

"Anything wrong?" Rachel asked.

"Could be. You tell me." He said anger tightening his lips.

"What about?"

"The men you had lunch with, how long have you known them?"

"An hour. Willa and I were having lunch and the restaurant was crowded, so they asked if they could sit with us. Is there a problem with that?"

"Those men are bad news, Rachel. Stay away from them," Shade warned.

"Let me get this straight. You're telling me not to talk to them again?" she snapped.

"Yes."

"Shade, I can talk to anyone I want. I don't even let my brothers tell me what to do anymore," Rachel argued.

"Listen, Rachel. They aren't someone to get involved with. You've never dealt with men like them before. You're a friend of Lily's, so I'm giving you a heads-up."

More calmly, Rachel said, "As Lily's friend, I'll take it under consideration. Willa and I shared our booth with them. We ate, we left. It was that simple."

"And Willa gave them her card?" he probed.

"They want her to make some desserts for them for their next cookout."

Shade nodded.

"Satisfied?"

"Not really, but I guess it's all I'm going to get. You might drop a word and tell Willa to think twice about going out with one of them. You'll handle it better than me."

"Of that, I have no doubt." Rachel gave him a wry smile.

"All right, then I'll see you tonight."

She was a friend of Lily's, and without her using her gift on Lily, he didn't know if her mind would have remained intact, so he had tried. However, she wasn't going to listen, and like her brothers' stubbornness, it was going to get her in trouble.

"Bye, Shade."

Shade nodded then left the store, crossing the street back to the diner's parking lot where the brothers were waiting for him on their bikes. Viper had showed up while he was in the store.

"What did you find out?" Cash asked impatiently as he approached.

Shade came to a stop by his bike. "That Rachel and Willa have never met them before. They were having lunch, and the Freedom Riders asked if they could sit because the restaurant was busy," Shade repeated what Rachel had told him.

"That was convenient," Cash snarled.

"We didn't have trouble finding a table," Lucky agreed.

"You warn her?" Viper spoke up.

"Tried to." Shade shrugged.

"She didn't listen, did she?"

"Nope. Willa gave them her business card because they want her to make desserts for their next cookout."

"Fuck." Lucky's hands tightened on his handlebars.

"Let's go back to the clubhouse. I don't like that they came into Treepoint. Curt might have turned their offer down by now, so they may have come into town to scout for new property," Viper said grimly, pulling his bike out in the lead.

Shade climbed on his bike, starting the motor. "Looks like someone is going to steal your cupcake away," Shade needled Lucky and Rider. "Look on the bright side, though."

"Shade...." Lucky warned.

Shade gave him a mocking grin. "When they're done with her, she won't be a virgin anymore." He gunned his motor, riding away from the furious brother.

⁂ ⁍

"I better go break this up," Rachel excused herself, rising from the table as Shade approached his wife.

"What's going on?" Shade asked, sitting down next to her then taking the remaining piece of hotdog away from her, popping it into his mouth.

"I think Holly doesn't like the way Greer's new girlfriend is acting in front of Logan."

"Greer's an ass."

"I think everyone in town shares that opinion."

"You don't?"

"I don't know him well enough to cast judgment," she said reprovingly. His wife was determined to find the best in everyone.

"I do. He's an ass," Shade remarked.

The escalating argument between the two was easily heard in the back-yard in direct contrast of the balloons and fairy lights which had set a party atmosphere.

"You deal with her!" they heard Greer yell at Rachel, who was trying to get him to shut up. "I'm done listening to her sanctimonious bullshit." Greer jumped back into the pool, spraying both women with water.

"I told you he was an ass," Shade said, seeing Lily's angry expression. "Come on, they want to cut the cake." Shade took Lily's hand as they walked toward the large table which had gathered a crowd to watch Mrs. Langley cut her cake.

Beth was standing with the knife, but she was motioning for Rachel to do the cutting. Shade turned to see what the holdup was, spying Rachel heading to another argument which was building between Greer and Cash.

"Be right back, angel," Shade told Lily, giving her hand a squeeze before moving toward the end of the pool where Cash was sitting.

Greer's new girlfriend Diane, who he easily recognized as having attended several of the Friday parties, was sitting next to Cash. The stupid bitch was trying to start a fight with the way she was pressing up against him.

"You never could keep your hands off another man's woman. What is it with you; can't you find one of your own?" Greer climbed out of the pool to glare down at Cash and Diane.

When Cash stared back impassively at Greer's tantrum, Shade stepped closer so Cash could see him give a warning shake of his head.

"I know it's hard, Greer, but be smart. Go have a piece of cake and leave me alone."

Tate and Dustin came out from the house, coming closer to see what had Greer's voice raised loud enough to be heard inside.

"You just can't leave women alone, can you, Cash? Like father, like son," Greer jeered.

Shade sucked in his breath as Cash got to his feet. Then Shade and the other Last Riders moved closer to back him up if he needed it.

"Keep cool," Shade muttered to them under his breath.

"This is a birthday party! Let's go eat some ice cream and cool down." Rachel tried unsuccessfully to end the fight, but Greer wasn't having it.

"Shut up, Rachel," Greer snarled at her attempt.

"Don't talk to her that way," Cash growled.

"I can talk to my sister any way I want to."

"Talk to her that way again, and I will—"

"What are you going to do? Rachel is none of your business. She's the only woman in this town of ours you haven't fucked."

"Wanna bet?" Cash grinned. "I fucked her under your own roof."

The horrified looks on Rachel's brothers' faces as they turned to her had Rachel taking a step back. Shade tensed, knowing the three brothers weren't going to take Cash's comment without retribution.

"You son of a bitch!" Greer threw himself at Cash, nearly knocking him into the pool, but Rider managed to grab his arm and steady him. After Greer's fists flew out, one nailing Cash in the stomach, Shade moved, blocking Cash from returning the blow.

"This is how you repay us for saving Lily's life? You motherfuckers can go to Hell!" Tate tried to go for Shade, who went stiff at his damning insult.

"We *are* paying you back. We're not beating the shit out of you right now! Back off." His brusque order was ignored.

Rachel made an attempt to stop her brothers one more time, grabbing Tate by his arm when he moved toward him again. "Tate! Stop. Please!"

Shade restrained himself from knocking the fucker in the pool, aware of Lily watching. Beth had placed a hand on her arm, keeping her away from the fight.

"Don't fuckin' touch me." Tate shoved Rachel from him, jerking his arm away.

Rachel stumbled but Tate caught her, realizing what he had nearly done. Pulling her to his side, his furious eyes glared down at her in disgust.

"Get Logan and Holly, Dustin. We're leaving." Tate jerked Rachel toward the patio doors as Dustin and Greer followed.

Shade was disgusted by the brothers' treatment of their sister. He might be a cold bastard, but he would never have treated Penni to a public spectacle the way the Porters were Rachel, who was crying, humiliated by them.

Mrs. Langley and half the town at the party were witnesses to the woman's embarrassment as they escorted Rachel from the party.

Lily started after them.

"Hell no, you're not getting involved in that mess." Shade took her arm, pulling her back.

"But…"

"No, Lily. If they don't care how they treat their own flesh and blood, they aren't going to care how they treat you. Do you think I'd be able to stand back and watch if they were rude to you?"

Lily bit her lip, shaking her head.

"Go help your sister cut the cake. She needs your help." Beth and some of the women were storming away from Cash at that moment, Beth making her way back to the cake and seeming to apologize to Mrs. Langley. "Rachel will be fine," Shade told her, hoping it was the truth.

He walked back to Cash. "I'm going to fucking kill them after the way they treated her." Cash's voice was low and deadly.

"Brother, I don't know what you were thinking when you said what you did, but I've known you long enough to know that shit spewing out of your mouth wasn't by accident. You wanted to fuck with her brothers, and you accomplished your goal."

"I didn't expect them to go ape-shit!"

"Then that was your bad. You both provoked each other, and Rachel was the one hurt. You think telling her you're sorry is going to make a difference?"

"No, I don't. She'll never talk to me again. Did you see her face when I told her brothers I fucked her?"

"I saw. Go get a drink," Shade advised.

Once Cash nodded, going to the ice cooler, Shade motioned for Rider and Train to stay with him before going back to Lily.

She was standing beside Beth, already having served the cake and now eating a slice. Lily's plate had two pieces.

Shade casually reached out, taking the plate away. At Lily's crestfallen expression, Shade picked up the plastic fork, spearing a piece of cake with a generous amount of frosting before placing it in front of her mouth. Lily opened, taking the bite he fed her, and the frown disappeared.

He took the next bite for himself. "Damn!"

"What's wrong?" Lily asked.

"Lucky and Rider are idiots."

CHAPTER EIGHTY-ONE

Shade looked up from his paperwork when his office door was opened. As Lily rushed inside, leaving it open, he could see Cash and Rider coming inside the factory door, quietly closing it behind them. Lily had her back turned, so she didn't see them enter.

The workers had all left for the day, and he wouldn't have still been there if he hadn't needed to finish up the day's paperwork.

"You have to find her, Shade!" She was upset, twisting her hands together.

Cash was unashamedly listening, his jaw tightening when he heard her words.

"Lily, calm down and start over. What happened?"

Lily took a deep breath, her body shaking. "Pastor Patterson came to the store this morning and told me Rachel had called to tell him she wouldn't be volunteering anymore. I was concerned because I knew Rachel would have a hard time facing everyone, but I thought she would just take a couple of weeks off! I didn't realize until Tate came into the store, looking for Rachel, that no one has seen her since Friday night."

"You said Pastor Patterson told you he had talked to her?" Shade asked.

Cash's face had gone pale at Lily words. The women had given him hell Friday night for what he had done, and he had told Shade that morning that he was trying to avoid town so he wouldn't run into Rachel.

Lily nodded.

"Then we know she's okay if someone has heard from her," he reasoned, calming his wife.

"Okay."

"What did Tate tell you?"

"He said she was gone the next morning when they woke up. She left them a note, but he didn't tell me what it said. He's worried sick, though. He was going to see Knox when he left the store."

"I'll call and talk to Knox to see if he's found anything out."

"Thank you. I'm so worried about her, Shade. I saw her face, and she was so humiliated. She didn't deserve Cash and her brothers treating her that way. She helps everyone. She gives her skills and usually doesn't even charge people.

"Mary Owen's little girl had something wrong with her stomach and couldn't even hold food down. Rachel gave her a supplement, and she's gained five pounds. Mrs. Willis had the shingles and when Rachel made a cream for her, she was able to go back to work. Rachel helped me, too, Shade. I don't know what would have happened if she hadn't pulled me out of that nightmare."

Shade got up from behind his desk, taking her into his arms. "Don't worry, Lily; I'll find her, but be prepared. She may not want to come back to Treepoint."

"You made me come back," Lily argued.

"There's a difference between you and Rachel. You belong to me."

"I didn't then."

"You did. You just didn't know it." Shade smiled down at his wife. "Now, go feed my baby, and I'll call Knox."

"All right." Lily turned, coming to a stop when she saw Cash and Rider. Throwing them an angry glare, she moved between them, leaving the factory.

Shade picked up his phone as soon as she was out the door while both Rider and Cash entered the office.

"Knox, Lily told me Rachel's disappeared. What do you know?"

"Not much. I've been making a few calls. Tate showed me the note she left. Told them she was leaving and not to come looking for her. It said she wouldn't be coming back, and she was sorry for shaming them." Knox's voice became harder as he read the note.

"If you find where she's at, call me or Cash."

"Will do." Knox hung up.

Shade looked at Cash, relaying the information he had just received.

"I'll kill them." Cash turned to find the doorway blocked by Rider.

"Sit down, Cash," Shade ordered.

Cash turned angrily yet didn't sit down. "Don't tell me what the fuck to do. Do you know how badly they must have treated her for her to run off?"

"And that surprises you? You knew Friday night when she left with them what she was facing. I didn't see you running to her defense then."

Cash picked up a chair and threw it against the wall.

"*Sit down!*"

Cash sat.

"How do you want to handle this?" Shade said calmly.

"I'm going to find her, of course," Cash stated angrily.

"I'm not the enemy, brother."

Cash stood to his feet. "I know," he said, running a hand through his hair. "I'm a fucking idiot."

"Piece of advice. Take it or leave it, but I'm going to give it anyway. Figure out why you want to find her before you go looking."

Cash gave an abrupt nod before leaving his office.

By the time Shade had finished his paperwork and was locking the factory, Cash had changed his clothes and was on his bike, leaving the parking lot.

"Thank fuck the days of me having woman trouble are over," Shade said out loud to Rider who was working on Cash's truck.

"Don't jinx yourself, brother." Rider poked his head out from under the hood.

"I don't believe in luck, and I sure as shit don't believe in jinxes," Shade snorted, heading to the steps.

"I hope you're right, because you just tempted fate to prove you wrong."

"I don't believe in fate, either."

Shade made his way up the walkway and to his house where he found Lily in the shower. He quickly took off his clothes and stepped in behind her. She turned around to face him, wrapping her arms around his shoulders.

Shade placed his hands on her hips, lifting her until her pussy was over his cock. Slowly, he lowered her, sliding inside of her. Taking a step forward, he pressed her against the shower wall as he gently stroked inside her.

Lily ran her hands over his shoulders. "Harder," she moaned.

"You want me to fuck you harder?"

Lily frantically nodded.

"I think you can say the word fuck and not go to Hell, Lily."

"It just seems so…I don't know…"

"Dirty? Sexy? Fun?" Shade laughed at her embarrassed expression. They had been married almost a year, and Lily still found it hard to completely relax her guard.

"Yes," she admitted, moaning as her pussy started clenching on his cock.

Shade began to fuck her more forcefully, driving himself deep while drawing out her climax and building his own. He groaned into her throat as he felt his nuts tighten until he thought they were going to explode.

When he lifted her nipple to his mouth, biting down, her soft whimper had his cock jerking its release as he came.

Lily was placing soft kisses on his shoulders when he finally managed to give her breathing room, placing her back on her feet.

He held her arm as they walked out of the shower.

"I'm not going to fall, Shade."

"I don't want you to shower unless I'm in the room," Shade told her, drying off.

Lily gaped at him as she dried off before putting on her nightgown. "You're being ridiculous." She shook her head. "Am I supposed to go without a shower when you're not home?

Shade frowned. "Of course not. You can call Beth and have her come over." Shade lay down on the bed, flipping on the television.

Lily stood staring at him with her hands on her waist. "For a minute, I thought you wanted me to call Razer," she snapped.

"Now *you're* being ridiculous," Shade stated.

Lily left the bathroom door open as she blow-dried her hair. The show he was watching was almost over when she came to sit on his side of the bed, gazing down at him with a frown.

"I'm not going to wait to shower until you're home or call Beth. I'm very careful when I'm in the shower, so nothing is going to happen."

Shade studied her serious expression, his hand going to her belly. "I don't want anything to happen to this baby."

Lily's frown disappeared. "Nothing's going to happen. I'm fine; the baby's fine. You need to keep from overreacting."

"I'm not overreacting," Shade denied.

"Yes, you are, and I love you for it, despite the fact that you're driving me crazy." Lily leaned forward, brushing his mouth with hers, her hand cupping his smooth cheek.

Shade caught her troubled expression as she started to rise. He took her hand, pulling her back down.

"Is there something wrong?"

Lily didn't try to avoid his question, asking one of her own. "Why do you still shave all the time?"

"I told you before, because you like to touch my face."

"I thought men who were married eased off trying to be so perfect, but you haven't."

"And that's a bad thing?"

"It's not only that, Shade. Sometimes, I think you do too much for me and not enough for yourself."

"Like what?"

This time, Lily hesitated. "Sex."

Shade laughed. "In case you missed it, I was just as loud in the shower as you were."

Lily's lashes lowered, but Shade saw the hurt in her eyes. He reached up, cupping the nape of her neck and tugging her down to him. "I'm very happy with our sex life, Lily, if that's what you're trying to ask." The tip of his tongue came out to trace her bottom lip before parting them and plundering her mouth in a passionate kiss which dissolved her doubts.

He rolled over until she was beneath him.

"Very happy."

80 03

"Any luck?" Shade asked Cash.

He had just arrived back at the clubhouse, and he, Razer, Viper, and Train were about to go up to the house after getting out a large order when Cash had pulled in.

"No," Cash answered grimly. The brother looked exhausted. He had been out all night and the entire day, searching for Rachel.

"Get some rest," Viper ordered. "I'll ask Winter to call some of her former students to see if they have any idea where Rachel would go."

"I'd appreciate it," Cash said before pausing and informing, "Viper, I'm going to Lexington to make sure Rachel isn't there. She has a couple of friends who live there, and Lily's old boyfriend lives there, too. Maybe she's staying with one of them."

Viper nodded. "You want us to go with you?"

"No need for all of us to waste our time. I won't be long. If I can't find her, I'm going to try to talk to Tate."

"Good luck with that," Shade said sardonically.

"If he's half as sorry as I am for running her off, he'll listen. If not, I'll make him."

"Ride safe, brother." Viper turned toward the clubhouse, and Shade followed behind. He almost turned back to go with him, but he knew Cash didn't want his help, preferring to search for her alone.

As they walked up the path, Viper said to him, "It shouldn't take Cash long to track down his leads."

"It might take longer than he thinks," Shade replied.

They heard Cash restart his bike and turned to watch him leave. Neither man knew it was going to be a long time before Cash came home.

CHAPTER EIGHTY-TWO

"How is Cash?" Shade asked Viper who had come into the waiting room.

Shade had been in bed with Lily when Viper had called to tell him that Cash had crashed his bike. He had made Lily stay at the house with Beth, despite both of their arguments.

Viper shook his head. "Truthfully, I don't think he would want to live in the shape the doctors say he's in, if he even makes it."

The women were sitting on the chairs, crying. King was standing behind Evie with his hand on her shoulder.

"He'll live with whatever shape he's in. Cash is a fighter," Shade said forcefully.

"Yes, he is, but there are some battles which can't be won, and you know that, Shade."

"I do, but this isn't one of them."

"You can't fight the inevitable."

Shade knew Viper was remembering his brother Gavin.

"No, but I know someone who can. I just have to find her."

⸾ ⸾

Shade watched Rachel as she carefully stepped down the steep path on the hill. When she got to the bottom, she looked up, coming to a stop as she saw him.

"Hi, Rachel." He was leaning against the door of her car with his arms folded across his chest.

"Shade. What are you doing out here?"

He gave her a mocking smile. "Knox told me you used to come here every weekend. I knew, eventually, you would come by for a visit, so I had the place watched. Old habits die hard."

"Evidently. What do you want?"

"I want you to fix Cash," Shade said determinedly.

Her mouth dropped open. "I'm not capable of fixing him, Shade. I don't have super powers." She brushed a tendril of hair away from her cheek. "Besides, I already tried."

"Then try again."

"It's not that simple."

"You're just going to leave him lying in that bed without trying?" Shade asked brusquely.

"I tried! What don't you understand?"

Shade straightened away from the car. "Rachel, do you feel any better since you left town?"

"No," she admitted.

"Then, if you're going to feel like shit, why not stay in town near Cash? Even if you can help him deal with the pain, then wouldn't it be worth it?"

"I don't owe Cash any favors," she responded stubbornly.

"Don't act like you don't care, or you wouldn't have come back to town. No one says you have to move back into your brothers' house."

"Where would I stay?"

"You could stay with Cash's grandmother. No one goes near that old bitch's house."

A slight smile touched her lips. "She's not that bad."

"Yes, she is. Well?"

"All right." Rachel agreed to what they both knew she wanted to do, anyway.

"Good. She's expecting you."

Rachel rolled her eyes.

"I owe you, Rachel."

"That's the same thing you said when you asked me to go to work in the church store to help Lily. I would have helped Lily regardless, but it would have been nice if you would have broken up that fight before Cash opened his big mouth."

Shade climbed on his bike, turning on the motor. "I paid you back when I helped Viper hold Cash back when Tate dragged you away. If he had gotten near Tate, he would have killed him. Welcome back, Rachel."

Shade felt Rachel glaring at him as he rode away. She could hate him as much as she wanted as long as she stayed and healed Cash.

80 03

Rachel stayed by Cash's side, although Shade would see her slip out the door whenever any of The Last Riders visited, avoiding talking to them.

Cash's doctor gave them regular updates on his condition, and each time, he was less optimistic about Cash's recovery.

511

"We decreased his medication, so he's in more of a deep sleep versus a coma."

Shade stood next to Lily as they listened to Cash's doctor explain his condition.

"His spinal injury is quite severe, and we're going to begin to wean him off the ventilator." The doctor paused. "I do not anticipate him walking again."

At his proclamation, several of the women began crying. Viper put his arms around Winter, Knox pulled Diamond closer, Shade pulled Lily into his side, and Evie turned to King. Everyone there stood stupefied at the doctor's prognosis that the consequences of the wreck would be life-changing for Cash.

The Last Riders began making plans as soon as the doctor left.

"We can put him downstairs. It's accessible with a wheelchair and has the exercise equipment and hot tub," Viper stated.

"I'll call Donna as soon as he's out of the rehab center," Winter said.

Each and every one of them discussing how they would help Cash heal and adjust to his new life was why Shade was loyal to The Last Riders. They stood together to face any challenge thrown their way.

"I need to go talk to Rachel." Lily wiped her tears away as he released her.

"I'll go with you," Beth said.

Both women walked to Rachel who was standing at the edge of the group. Shade went to get a bottled water, waiting for Viper to come out of Cash's room so he could go inside for a few moments.

Viper walked out, and then Shade motioned to Lily that he was going to go see Cash.

He went into Cash's room, staring down at the brother fighting for his life.

"Brother, your woman is here, but if you want her, you're going to have to wake up." Shade continued talking to Cash as if he was awake until the door opened and Pastor Patterson came into the room.

"I'm sorry to interrupt, but Cash's grandmother asked me to stop by and pray for him. I'm Pastor Merrick Patterson." He reached out to shake Shade's hand, which he didn't take. The pastor dropped his hand to his side.

"Have we met before? You look familiar?"

"We met once in the service briefly. I served with Dean."

"Ah…That explains it. My wife tells me I have a terrible memory, and I have to agree with her."

"Your wife is a fucking lunatic. While everyone in town believes she has the wool pulled over your eyes, I just don't believe anyone can be that clueless unless they want to be."

Pastor Merrick paled.

Shade didn't feel the least bit of sympathy for the man. He was the one who had brought Brooke back into his and Evie's lives.

Merrick gave a nervous laugh. "I know Brooke is a little high-maintenance for a pastor's wife, and she hasn't learned to fit into small town life yet, but she will adjust. The church congregation will learn to love her as I do."

With that, Shade knew he had been right. Merrick Patterson was a man who loved his wife. He wasn't blind to her evil; he tolerated it and turned a blind eye to keep her.

Shade stared at him coldly before he walked toward the door. "You need to pray for yourself more than Cash. When Brooke no longer needs you, neither you nor that kid of yours will be safe. I'd pray hard if I were you."

He went out the door, closing it behind him. One of the two men in that room was facing death, and it wasn't the one lying on the bed.

CHAPTER EIGHTY-THREE

"Could you come to the hospital and pick me up?" Lily asked.

"Give me ten minutes." Shade disconnected the call.

He tracked Rider down, finding him in his room with the bedroom door open. Rider was lying on his back on the bed with Jewell and Stori. The brother was watching the women have a clit fight while he jerked himself off.

"Can I borrow your truck?"

"Keys are on the nightstand," Rider grunted.

Shade walked into the room, picking up the keys, then turned to leave.

"Sure you don't want to join?" he asked.

"I'll pass. Have to go pick up Lily."

Stori gave a small scream, twisting on the bed.

"I won," Jewell gloated, sitting up and running her hand down Stori's thigh.

"Come here." Rider motioned for Jewell.

She crawled across the mattress to Rider who was putting on a condom. Jewell threw one leg over Rider's hips, plunging herself down onto his cock.

Shade was going out the bedroom door as Winter came out of Viper's bedroom. As she passed Rider's bedroom, she heard Jewell's moans, automatically looking inside, and her eyes met his.

Shade dangled the keys. "Just borrowing his truck," he said mockingly.

"Did I say anything?" Winter shook her head. "I don't doubt your devotion to Lily."

They walked down the steps together.

"How's Cash?"

"The doctor called Viper. He crashed again this morning. That makes twice that we've almost lost him. If he crashes again, the chances are slimmer that he'll pull through."

Winter blinked back tears, "I'm going to start dinner. Viper is on the way to the hospital. When I'm done, I'm going to join him."

"Lily went there after work. She wants me to pick her up. After dinner, I'm going back and staying with him until Train comes."

"Cash is lucky to have you all." Winter reached up and kissed his cheek.

Shade frowned.

Winter laughed. "I won't tell Viper if you won't." She turned toward the kitchen.

"Winter, I don't understand…"

She turned back. "Why I kissed you?"

Shade nodded.

"Because I know you're responsible for Rachel staying, and you've made sure one of the men is always at the hospital. You're a nice guy, Shade."

"No, I'm not."

Shade's sharp reply had her shaking her head at him, turning back to the kitchen. "Yes, you are."

"No, I'm fucking not!" Shade went out the door, slamming the door to prove it.

The drive to the hospital didn't take long. Shade pulled up to the hospital door, expecting Lily to come out. When she did, he threw the truck in park and jumped out.

"What the fuck is wrong with her."

"Help me get her in the truck." Lily struggled to push the wheelchair Rachel was sitting in, looking deathly pale.

Shade took the handles of the wheelchair, pushing it toward the truck, then lifted her inside. Lily climbed inside the driver's side, scooting over toward Rachel.

Shade took the wheelchair back inside the lobby, angrily coming back to the truck and climbing in.

He pulled out, driving to Cash's grandmother Mag's house, where Rachel was staying.

"What's wrong with her?" Shade snapped out.

"She saved Cash," Lily spoke breathlessly. "I still don't believe it. If I hadn't seen it with my own eyes…Her blood pressure dropped too low."

Lily went on to explain Cash was awake, and his vital signs were better. Her jumbled words were filled with excitement, relief, and worry over Rachel.

Shade packed her inside Mag's house with the old woman staring at him from her wheelchair as he carried Rachel to the room she was staying in.

Lily took off Rachel's shoes. "I'm going to stay with her for a while. I'll call when I need you to pick me up."

"All right. I'll go back to the hospital and stay with Cash until you call." Shade kissed Lily briefly.

Rachel caught his hand as he was about to leave. "I want your promise not to tell him I was there."

"Why?" he asked curiously.

"Because," she said stubbornly, unwilling to explain.

"I'm not going to make a promise I can't keep." Shade raised his hand when she would have interrupted. "I won't say anything unless he asks, but that's the best I can do."

Rachel reluctantly nodded as she began shaking so hard Lily had to cover her with a blanket.

Shade left the two women alone, going through the house and outside to the porch where Mag was sitting in her wheelchair.

"I want to go see Cash."

Shade stared silently at the old woman then went down to the truck and opened the passenger door before walking back up to the porch. Leaning down, he lifted her, carrying her to the truck then gently placing her into the seat. Reaching up, he buckled her in.

"I could have done that," she snapped.

He didn't respond, closing the truck door before going back to get her wheelchair. Shade expertly folded it before placing it in the back of the truck.

Once behind the steering wheel, he drove out of her driveway and then turned toward town.

"You don't talk much, do you?"

"Not when I don't have anything to say," Shade replied.

"Had to do some talking to catch that pretty wife of yours." Mag snorted. "She must like the strong, silent, asshole type."

"You talk to Cash this way?"

"Hell no, Cash is my grandson. I don't have to pretend to be nice to him." She laughed, hitting him on the arm.

Shade's hands tightened on the steering wheel. Maybe Cash would have been better off in the coma.

☙ ☞

Fat Louise was sitting on a bale of hay as she watched her friends lead Sex Piston's kids through the field to pick out pumpkins. She didn't look much happier since the last time he had seen her on the helicopter, and back then, she had been crying on Killyama's shoulder.

Shade knew something had happened since she had returned, but Lily refused to tell him. Truthfully, he hadn't been interested enough to badger her for the information. He would remedy that when they went back home, though.

The smile on Fat Louise's face disappeared as Lily came into view. She was holding Chance, one of Beth's twins, looking beautiful. She was just beginning to show her pregnancy, and she glowed with health and happiness.

T.A. came up to her, snagging the child away and Lily laughed, brushing her windswept black hair away from her face. Then Shade watched her go inside the store attached to the pumpkin patch.

His attention returned to Fat Louise who was digging her boot in the dirt, casting furtive looks at Cade sitting on his motorcycle. Shade had been surprised when they had parked and he had seen Cade ride in on his bike with her at his back.

The man was watching Fat Louise the way he had just been watching Lily. The only difference was the sadness in his eyes. Fat Louise might be doing him, but she wasn't a sure thing. That kind of longing look only came from being tortured about whether feelings were returned. Shade remembered when he had suffered from the same problem. *Thank fuck those days are over.*

Lily came out of the store, carrying two cups. Smiling, she headed toward Fat Louise, who scooted over on the hay bale to make room.

Shade was leaning against a tree not too far way, so their voices easily carried over to him.

"You looked like you were cold. I thought this would warm us up."

When Lily handed Fat Louise one of the cups she was holding, she took a sip. "Thank you."

"You're welcome. The kids are all growing so fast," Lily said sadly.

"Thank goodness. I'm on everyone's speed dial for babysitting. How is Cash recovering from his accident?"

"He's been moved to a rehabilitation center. He's doing better. Shade says he's getting stronger every day."

"It won't be long before he gets out and makes up for lost time with the women in Treepoint," Fat Louise wisecracked.

Lily laughed, tilting her head toward Cade. "Your boyfriend seems nice."

"He's not my boyfriend."

"Does he know that?" Lily teased. "He reminds me of Shade. He never lets me out of his sight, either."

Shade let a smile touch his lips at Lily's words.

"He's nothing like Shade. Shade loves you. Everyone knew how he felt about you before you did. Cade doesn't care about me. He just feels guilty and trapped." Fat Louise's voice was filled with hurt.

Lily went quiet, her eyes gazing back at her in compassion, before she said, "I didn't see it, and maybe you don't, either. Sex Piston told me about your loss. I'm really sorry."

Fat Louise turned away from Lily. When she did, she was facing him, and he could see the tears in her eyes.

"I didn't mean to bring up something so painful," Lily apologized.

"It's all right."

"No, it's not. You looked so sad sitting here, and I wanted to cheer you up, not make it worse." Lily started to get to her feet.

"Don't go. It really wasn't anything you said. It's me." Fat Louise licked her lips. "I was sitting here, watching you, and I'm so jealous I can't stand it. I see you looking absolutely beautiful and healthy, pregnant with your baby while I lost mine." Tears slid down her cheeks.

Shade swallowed hard. His worst fear was losing their child, losing that connection with Lily. Now Shade understood why Fat Louise had been staring at Lily.

Lily enfolded Fat Louise in her arms.

"I know I should be getting over it since I was only two months along, but I had already picked out names, and I was pestering Crazy Bitch to take me shopping for a crib. I love babies. I've always wanted a lot, and I didn't miss Cade as much when I felt his baby in me."

After several minutes, Fat Louise managed to gather herself.

Lily released her, taking her hand. "There's no need to be jealous." She placed Fat Louise's hand on her stomach. "We can share. I know nothing will replace the one you lost, but when you want one to hug or love, you can hold this one. He needs a godmother," Lily said hesitantly.

Shade felt a lump in his throat as he stared at his wife. She amazed him more each day. Lily didn't have a selfish bone in her body. She was willing to share the most precious thing to her with a woman who had lost her own. Lily's first instinct was to help heal the void left behind.

He knew Fat Louise was hurting; however, he hadn't felt any emotion for her other than the increasing fear he had about Lily losing the child she carried. He had known all along he wasn't worthy of Lily yet had always swept the thought away. It would not change anything, because the one thing he couldn't and wouldn't do was let her go. Ever.

"I would be honored."

"That's settled then." She looked toward Cade before dropping her voice. "Cade is throwing me dirty looks. He thinks I've upset you."

Shade straightened, walking toward Cade. Stud and Dozer were talking to him, but they broke off when he neared.

"Shade," Stud greeted him.

"Stud, Dozer." Shade returned the greeting.

"You met Traveler yet?" Stud asked.

"Briefly." Shade gave him a nod.

"He was one of the men on the helicopter who rescued us in Mexico," Cade explained briefly.

"Your kid picked the biggest pumpkin," Shade remarked to Stud, watching Sex Piston struggle to lift the large pumpkin.

Stud stood up. "I better go help." He grinned as he left.

Dozer stood up also, going to help with the pumpkins Stud's girls were struggling to carry.

Shade turned back to Lily, seeing Fat Louise smiling at her.

"She yours?" Cade asked.

"Yeah, she's mine." Shade lifted his hand with his wedding ring. "You and Fat Louise?"

"Depends who you're asking."

"I'm asking you." Shade lifted a brow.

"Then, yes, she's mine."

Shade's lips quirked. "How you getting along with the rest of the crew?"

"Depends on what day of the week it is."

Both men were still laughing when Lily stood, throwing the cups away before coming toward him with a mischievous smile.

"I wish Jane would look at me that way," Cade said softly.

"Wishes are like rainbows; they're always going to be out of reach. Jane is sitting right there, so there's nothing stopping you from putting that smile on her face."

CHAPTER EIGHTY-FOUR

"How was the drive back with Cash?" Lily looked up from doing the dishes.

Shade walked behind her, slipping his arms around her waist and placing his hands on her abdomen. Every time he touched her, he felt a surge of possession go through his body.

"Pretty well considering he spent four months in a rehabilitation center. We stopped and he went in to see his grandmother before we brought him back to the clubhouse." He released her as she dried her hands on a dish towel.

"I love his grandmother. I bet she was happy to see him."

"I couldn't tell. She was too busy giving him a hard time over Rachel."

"She's grown attached to Rachel since she's been living with her," Lily defended her.

Shade shook his head at his wife, hugging her close. "Could you just once agree with me about someone?"

Lily giggled. "I will when you're right. Was Rachel there?"

Shaded nodded. "She didn't say more than she was glad he was out."

"I can't say I blame her after he humiliated her at Mrs. Langley's party."

"Cash let his temper get away from him, and he regrets it. Rachel might as well get over it and move on."

"It's not so easy for women to get over being hurt that way. This is a small town, and Rachel's dealt with the gossip about her family selling weed her whole life. She didn't need Cash making her first time fodder for the local gossips," Lily snapped angrily.

"Why are you getting mad at me? I wasn't the one who did it."

"You're the one taking up for him."

"I'm not taking up for him. What's going on between Rachel and Cash is between them."

"There is no Rachel and Cash."

"If you say so. How was work at the church store today?"

When Lily sighed, moving to the living room then going out the front door and closing it behind her, Shade followed.

"Why did you just walk off and leave without answering me?"

"I thought that was what you wanted."

Shade sighed.

Lily angrily spun around to face him. "Don't do that!"

Shade stared at her in surprise. "Do what?"

"Patronize me. I'm not a child," she snapped, stomping her foot.

"Then don't act like one."

Lily stormed past him, running into the house and up the stairs to the bedroom.

Shade followed her again, swallowing down his anger and trying to figure out what had set her off. He had heard pregnant women became overly emotional, so perhaps her behavior was hormones. He was going to have to research it and find out.

"What are you doing now?"

"I'm going to take a shower and go to bed. I have a headache."

"Oh, that's why you're acting—"

"Like a child?" Lily finished for him. She sat down on the side of the bed, staring up at him with unhappy eyes. "You treat me like one all the time. If I become angry about something, you change the subject. If I don't like something, you fix it. You're constantly trying to make me happy."

"And all of that is what's making you angry?"

"Yes, because it's not normal the way you do it."

Shade went ice-cold at her words.

"You don't try to make yourself happy. You're going to become bored and find someone else who does things the way you like them without giving me a chance to prove I can handle things on my own." Lily stared down at the nightgown in her hands.

Shade knelt down in front of her. "I didn't realize I was doing that."

Lily reached out to touch his cheek then let her hand fall to the bed. "Shade, you've already won my heart, so you don't have to keep fighting for it anymore. There's nothing left to win."

"Yes, there is," Shade said softly. "Lily, are you happy?"

She nodded, tears in her eyes.

"Then I'm happy. Go take your shower, and when you come back, I'll show you how to make me even happier." He smiled, taking her hands then helping her to her feet.

Her troubled gaze caught his as she went into the bathroom, closing the door behind her.

Shade took off his clothes then lay down on the bed, staring up at the ceiling. For a brief second, he had feared she had found out about him. If he wasn't careful, his smothering attitude was going to have the opposite effect he wanted. Instead of making her not want to leave him, it might be what drove her away.

He couldn't bring himself to treat her like his other women, because she was more than that to him. He couldn't treat her like a true submissive, because he was constantly worried something he did would trigger a memory. The few times he had taken her the way he wanted, he had gone gently with her, wanting to ease her into it, but that had stopped when she had become pregnant. He had gone too far being overprotective after the break-in at Evie's house and had become worse as her pregnancy had advanced.

They had married on Christmas day, and like a kid who was finally given a toy he had wanted for a long time, he had been excited about getting it yet afraid of touching or playing with it because he didn't want to damage it.

Lily was asking him to trust her, to have faith that their marriage couldn't be broken apart.

The bathroom door opened and Lily came out dressed in her nightgown, brushing her long, black hair as her eyes gave a soft apology.

To give her what she wanted, he would have to be willing to take the risk of losing her, and that wasn't a risk he was going to take.

❧ ❧

"You done for the night?" Train asked when Shade stretched from his bent position at the workstation.

"Finally." Shade packed the order he had filled, placing it in the mail cart which the truck would pick up and take out early in the morning.

"You're looking tired."

Shade grimaced mockingly. "Guess I'm getting old."

"Or you're not getting enough sleep," Train said shrewdly. "I thought your sleepless nights would be over when you married Lily."

"I've been putting a lot of hours in since Cash wrecked his bike. The last month since he's been home, he's doing better, so I'm hoping he's well enough that he can start working a few shifts soon."

Train nodded. "You go ahead. I'll finish this order I'm working on and lock up."

"Thanks, Train."

"Welcome. Shade…You know, if you need anything—anything at all—we're all here for you, right?"

Shade cocked his head to the side. "Where did that come from?"

"Brooke has to be a thorn in your side, and with a kid on the way, it would be hard to handle that kind of problem."

"If I find proof that Brooke had anything to do with Evie's break-in last summer, believe me, brother, I won't have a problem dealing with her the way she deserves," Shade said ominously.

"When you make the decision, remember we're here to have your back."

"I will. See you tomorrow." Shade went out of the factory, sucking in a deep breath. Thinking about Brooke brought back his frustration.

They hadn't been able to tie her to the three men who had broken into Evie's house. He was furious at himself for not leaving one alive to get information, but he hadn't wanted to take a chance with Lily's safety if bullets had started flying around the room.

As he walked up the path, he heard the blaring music from the clubhouse, but he wasn't even tempted to go inside. He was too fucking tired.

He saw Cash leading Bliss into the gazebo. The brother had surprised him, since he had thought Cash would have made more attempts to see Rachel. Instead, he was seeking solace from the women in the clubhouse.

Shade opened the door to his house and saw Lily and Rachel sitting in the living room. As exhausted as he was, he couldn't help smiling when Lily got up to give him a kiss.

Rachel rose to her feet. "I'd better go. It's almost Mag's bedtime, and I don't want her to lock me out."

Shade went into the kitchen to make him a plate of food as the women said their goodbyes.

"Would she really?" Lily asked in shock.

"No," Rachel laughed. "But she would make me wish she had by the time she quit fussing at me for making her get out of bed." She reached into her pocket and pulled out the keys. "Here you go. I'll stop by the store tomorrow to pick them up."

"All right. Thanks again, Rachel."

"Dinner more than made up for it," Rachel replied, giving her a hug. "Bye, Shade."

He nodded to her while spooning chili into a bowl, mentally debating with himself whether he should stop her. Cash would still be in the gazebo with Bliss.

Coming to a decision, he let her leave.

"I forgot something at the factory. I'll be right back," Shade told Lily.

"All right. I'll put the chili back in the pot so it won't get cold."

He went out the door, easily seeing Rachel walking down the path and coming to a stop by the gazebo. She froze on the pathway for several seconds, and then she started walking again until she barreled into Train.

Shade leaned on the porch rail, watching the show as Train and Rachel talked briefly before they walked together down the pathway.

Bliss came out of the gazebo a minute later, stomping toward the clubhouse. When Cash came out, he didn't go to the clubhouse, walking down toward the parking lot instead.

Shade stayed on the porch until he saw Train and Cash coming back up the pathway toward the clubhouse. Then he walked down his steps, wanting to have a word with Cash yet coming to a stop when he heard the two men talking.

"Train, I...I..."

"Brother, if you don't want me to touch her, all you have to do is ask."

"I'm asking."

"Cool, I'll leave her to you then."

Cash slung his arm around Train's shoulder, and then Train helped Cash inside.

Shade waited a minute before entering behind them, giving Train enough time to get Cash upstairs. The brother was the most dependable of them. Train always managed to be there when he was needed; however, because he was so quiet, he tended to be overlooked. If Shade was in a life-or-death battle and could only pick one brother to back him up, it would be Train. His skills were as sharp as when he had left the military, and he had been lethal then. His skills as a chopper pilot were unequaled. He was a fucking legend.

Once, a helicopter he had been flying was transporting troops when he had been shot down behind enemy lines. The helicopters in the Navy were pieces of shit, but Train had managed to bring it down without any loss of life. He and the troops had spent five days behind enemy lines, and they had all made it out alive except one, a woman.

After Train came back downstairs, throwing himself down on the couch next to Jewell, Shade went up the steps, noticing the members' eyes on him. He went to Cash's bedroom door, rapping on it with his knuckles.

"Go away," Cash snapped from inside.

"I want to talk," Shade snapped back, opening the door.

The room was dark, and Shade heard the mattress squeaking as Cash rose up to turn the bedroom light on.

"It couldn't wait until morning?" Cash asked.

"Brother, you used to fuck all night and work all day then start all over again," Shade said, leaning casually against the doorway.

"I haven't gotten all my strength back yet."

"If you've gotten enough to fuck Bliss in the gazebo, then you have enough to start taking a couple of shifts a week. Starting tomorrow morning." Shade tossed him his set of factory keys.

"No problem," Cash said, catching the keys in his hand. "You pissed at me for not pulling my weight, you should—"

"I'm not pissed at you, Cash. Brother, I'm glad you're back and doing well. It's just I haven't spent that much time with Lily lately, and with the baby due, I'd like to," Shade admitted, telling the partial truth.

With Brooke going back and forth from Georgia to Treepoint, his sense of foreboding told him she was up to something. The next one she took, he wanted to follow her and to do that, he needed Cash back at work. He had talked to Cash's physical therapist, and she had told him she was getting ready to release him.

"I'll be there bright and early."

Shade nodded.

"Shade?"

"Yeah?"

"Why was Rachel at your house tonight? She's never been there before."

"Lily called and told me she had lost the church store's keys, and she was going to run into town and borrow Rachel's. Since Rachel would be closing the store, and she's still staying at Mag's, I suggested Lily call her and see if she minded dropping them off to her."

"She saw me with Bliss in the gazebo."

Shade narrowed his eyes on Cash, studying his reaction. "Did it matter what she saw? She's the wrong type of woman for you. Besides, you'd have to put up with her brothers," Shade warned. "She's the type of woman who would never fit in the clubhouse...unless..." He stopped, bending to pick up an empty condom wrapper which must have fallen out of Cash's pocket before tossing it into the trashcan.

"Unless?" Cash prompted.

"Hmm...? Oh, unless she loved you. Then I think she would do anything for you. She's a Porter, though, so remember that."

"What does her being a Porter have to do with anything?"

"They're hot-headed, hot-blooded, and they don't give a shit what anyone in town thinks. Now that I think about it, I think she would fit in just fine. I might mention that to Rider, Lucky, or…Train. They're always looking for new women to come to the parties."

Cash stiffened on the bed before shaking his head at him. "You're a dick."

"Don't tell Lily," Shade joked, going out of the bedroom.

"Believe me, brother; she already knows."

CHAPTER EIGHTY-FIVE

Shade came in the clubhouse around three in the morning to find the brothers sitting around, drinking beer. He studied the men's bruises and beat-up faces.

"Who in the fuck did you get in a fight with?" Shade snarled. He was already in a foul mood, and seeing the brothers had gotten into a fight without him had only added salt to the wound.

Viper winced, taking a drink of his beer. "We went on a ride today so Cash could break in his new bike. Stopped for a drink in Jamestown, and the Freedom Riders were there. It was Rider's fault."

Sitting with Bliss on his lap, Rider was shaking his head before Viper finished his sentence.

Shade narrowed his eyes on Rider.

"I was provoked," Rider defended himself.

"How?" Shade growled.

"He asked me to scoot my chair over," he said defensively. "Then the fucker threw the first punch."

Shade strode to the bar, taking a bottle of whiskey and pouring himself a glass. He had been gone for a couple of days, and this was what had happened. He took a long drink before setting his glass down on the counter.

"Some good came out of it. Cash found a source who will call if she hears anything, and we got to beat the shit out of Scorpion and a few of his men," Viper said.

"I'm glad you had such a fucking good time," he said, taking another drink. "Where the hell *is* Cash, by the way?"

"We dropped him off at Mag's," Rider replied.

"Your trip didn't go well?" Lucky's amused voice came from between Jewell's tits where his face was buried.

"No, it didn't. Brooke stayed at her mother's the whole time. She didn't leave once. It was a completely wasted trip." He poured himself more whiskey into the glass.

"I wouldn't say that. How was the convention?" That time, it was Viper's amused voice which had spoken up while he tried not to smile.

"How the hell do you think it was? A convention room with over a thousand doomsday preppers. I'm never doing one again. The swag was gone in an hour, I've got orders I don't know how we're going to fill, and I'm not going on a road trip with Nickel again."

"Where is he?" The brothers looked around, only then realizing the brother hadn't come into the room with him.

"I made him get out of the truck in town. I couldn't take another five minutes with him. The brothers got the bladder of a pea and had to stop to take a piss every five minutes. I left when he went in the diner to use the restroom. One of you can go get his ass."

Rider stood up. "I'll go get him."

Shade set his glass down yet picked the whiskey bottle up. "I'm going home to Lily. Don't call me unless the clubhouse is on fire or one of you fuckers decides to get in another fight."

"Uh, Shade." Viper stopped him with his hand on the door to the kitchen. "Lily's home, babysitting Razer's kids. Beth needed a break from them, so Razer's giving her one upstairs." His president couldn't keep the snicker out of his voice.

Shade's lips tightened into a tight line. Walking back to the bar, he set the whiskey bottle back down on the counter before walking silently out of the room, wondering if the Freedom Riders needed a new enforcer.

ഌ cള

He was crossing the parking lot after leaving the factory early, since Train had said he would finish the day when he noticed Cash, who seemed to be getting off his bike. However, when he saw him, he sat back down.

"I'm going to Rosie's for a drink. Want to go?"

Shade hesitated, seeing the manipulative gleam in Cash's eyes. Did the brother seriously think he could pull something on him?

"Sure, Lily won't be home for a while." Shade got on his bike, interested to see what Cash had up his sleeve.

Rosie's had a few vehicles out front when they pulled up. He was surprised Cash voluntarily wanted to go in with the Porters' truck parked outside.

Climbing off his bike, he then followed Cash in.

The Porter brothers were sitting in Rosie's, having a beer.

Shade saw the determined expression on Cash's face as he walked over to their table to greet them. Their hate-filled expressions and lack of response had Cash gritting his teeth loud enough for him to hear. Shade wanted to laugh at Cash's predicament. Hell, he had only had to deal with Beth when he had wanted Lily, but Cash was stuck having to deal with not one but three assholes.

"Mind if we join you?" Shade asked, tempted to let Cash handle this on his own for trying to trick him into helping, but he couldn't desert a brother who was facing a firing squad.

They didn't wait for acquiescence, both of them taking a seat at the table. The Porter brothers might hate Cash, but Shade was their regular customer, so he would be harder to piss off.

The men looked like the beer in their stomachs was turning sour as Cash and Shade both ordered their drinks.

"What do you want, Cash?" Tate didn't hesitate to ask why Cash would be willing to sit down at the table with them.

Cash decided to take the devil by the horns and be honest with the three brothers. "We need to come to an understanding and cut out this bullshit between us." Cash began his talk to get in the good graces of Rachel's brothers.

"Why? It works for us." An evil grin came to Tate's face. "This has to do with Rachel, doesn't it?"

"Why does his talking to us have anything to do with Rachel?"

God, Dustin has to be the slowest of these idiots, Shade thought in pity.

While his two older brothers rolled their eyes at the question, realization slowly hit Rachel's youngest brother.

"Hell, no." Dustin's reaction mirrored his older brothers'.

"We can keep fighting between us, and we'll all lose Rachel, or we can pretend to get along and keep Rachel in Treepoint. It's up to you. I'm willing to tolerate you three for Rachel."

Without another word, the three brothers got up from the table, leaving Cash and him staring at their backs as they left the bar.

"That went well," Cash said drily.

"Did you expect any different? You four have spent years pissing each other off. It's going to take more than a meet to change that."

Cash studied Shade speculatively. "I gave Lily my vote for your marker."

Shade's amusement died. "Yes, you did. So?"

"I want your help to bring those assholes around," Cash laid out his terms.

"I promised you my marker, not a fucking miracle."

"Shade, you're the most manipulative bastard I know. If anyone can get those assholes to tolerate me, it's you. Can you think of a bigger challenge for your skills?"

"Actually, no."

Mick set the beer down in front of them.

"You're buying," Shade told Cash, picking up his.

⊱ ⊰

"What are we doing here?" Cash asked as they sat outside the movie theater.

"Trying to pay you back."

Before Cash could ask any more questions, the movie let out and the moviegoers came through the doors. They sat in silence while Shade searched the exiting crowd for the one he was wanting to talk to.

"You sneaky son of a bitch." Cash's voice was filled with admiration of Shade's skills.

As the two boys they were waiting for drew closer to where they were sitting, their gazes were all for the bikes.

"Hi, Shade, Cash." Jace and his friend came to a stop at the bikes.

"Hey, Jace, Cal," Shade responded to their greeting.

Jace and Cal were friends who came from opposite sides of town. Jace's father had been one of the wealthiest men in town until The Last Riders had arrived, while Cal's parents were lucky to put dinner on the table. It was a mismatched pair, but the two were close friends.

"Can we talk?" Shade deliberately made it seem as if he was taking the boys into his confidence.

"Sure." Jace puffed up his chest at the thought of someone like Shade seeking him out, while Cal's expression became impassive and watchful.

"Your dad will be here any minute."

Shade had to admire the kid for trying to watch out for his friend.

"This won't take long. I have a favor to ask. Cash here wants to make friends with those cousins of yours. I was hoping you could hook him up with a helping hand. Of course, I could help you out with something you're wanting real badly, too. I have an extra bike I don't need any more. You would have to get your dad's permission and get your motorcycle license, but it would be yours, free of charge."

"Why do you want to become friends with them? They hate your guts." Of course the boy was a Porter, and he was suspicious of their motives, despite the gleam in his eyes when the motorcycle had been mentioned.

Out of the corner of his eye, Shade saw Cash wince at the blunt question.

530

"I was hoping you could help me out with that problem. I'm going to be straight with you: I don't give a shit about your cousins, but Rachel won't go out with me without their permission," Cash admitted.

As the two boys looked at each other and burst into laughter, Cash shifted uncomfortably on his bike.

"You have a whole clubhouse of chicks, and Rach is giving you trouble?"

At Cash's silence, their laughter continued.

"Do we have a deal?" Shade intervened before Cash made another relative of Rachel's an enemy.

"Yeah, I'll help. But let's be clear: if he hurts my cousin again, I'll tell my dad, and believe me, if you think Rachel's brothers are a pain to deal with, he will become your own personal nightmare."

"I have no intention of hurting Rachel," Cash said through clenched teeth.

"Cool, it's settled then," Shade intervened once again, seeing Cash's temper wearing thin. He shot him a warning look.

"I'm going hunting with them this weekend. We've been dying to hunt on your private land. We could stay the night at your cabin. That would win some brownie points with them."

"All right. Set it up. I'll pick you guys up Saturday morning at five a.m."

"We better go," Shade warned.

Everyone in town knew the cherry-colored Porsche at the red light, ready to pull into the theater's parking lot, was Jace's father's car.

"Later," Cash said, starting his motor.

While both men rode out as Drake pulled in, Cash lifted his hand in acknowledgment. Shade shook his head, not missing the gloating look on Cash's face. The poor fucker was actually looking forward to getting the Porters on his side; however, Shade would rather make friends with a pack of rabid dogs.

ಌ ಌ

He opened the door to his house later that night, seeing Lily sitting on the floor beside the couch, going through her purse.

"What are you doing?"

Lily looked up, smiling at his worried question. "You're going to be mad if I tell you, so before I do, could you help me up?"

Shade hastily walked to her, bending down then easily lifting her to her feet.

"Thank you."

"Now tell me what happened."

"Nothing. I over-estimated the size of my belly. I didn't realize that I couldn't move the table back once I scooted down from the couch."

"You actually wanted to sit on the floor?" Shade asked patiently.

Lily nodded. "I was looking for my driver's license. I must have dropped it the other day when I switched purses."

"Did you find it?"

"No. I must be getting careless, trying to get everything ready for the baby. I'll go into town tomorrow to get a new one."

"Why didn't you wait until I came home?"

"Because I can do some things for myself," she said stubbornly.

"It didn't seem like you were doing so well when I walked in the door."

"Don't pick on me. I'm pregnant," Lily teased, reaching up to kiss him. "How was the movie?"

"It was good," Shade said, picking her up into his arms then carrying her up the steps.

Lily laid her head on his shoulder. "I didn't know Cash was a fan of romantic movies."

"I didn't, either, until he asked me. He was afraid the brothers would bust his balls if he asked any of them to go see it with them."

"You're a good friend."

"I try." Shade took her shoes off, noticing her feet were swollen. "You need to stay off your feet more."

"I will, but we were busy today." She yawned. "There's so many in town needing our help, and more and more people are coming in each day. Brooke asked us to make several bags of clothes and household items for a new couple that recently moved to town."

"You don't seem too happy about it," Shade said, surprised. Lily never seemed to resent giving to people who came into the store whether they attended church or not.

"I'm happy she was able to help them. It's just that she gave them so much, I don't know how I'm going to replace it all at one time."

Shade's hands went under Lily's dress, pulling off her underwear before helping her to sit up. When she did, he tugged off her dress, laying it carefully on the bottom of the bed before reaching behind her back and unsnapping her bra.

"Shade, I can undress myself." Lily watched as he took off his own T-shirt before toeing off his boots.

Unsnapping his jeans, he saw her smile widen.

"I fixed dinner for you. Aren't you hungry?"

"I'm very hungry." Shade pushed her back to the bed, parting her thighs.

Lily had grown more beautiful every day of her pregnancy. Her breasts had become even fuller, and even better, it had an added benefit of making them more sensitive. He could bring her to climax merely by playing with her nipples.

Teasing the tip of one with his tongue, he brought it to a peak. "Close your eyes."

Lily obediently did.

Shade rose up. Sitting on the side of the bed, he reached for his jeans where he pulled out a small box, placing it on top of her stomach.

"Open your eyes."

She followed orders, seeing the jewelry box perched precariously on her tummy. Reaching out, she took it and opened it. Shade watched her reaction as her gaze returned to his.

"They're beautiful, but I don't usually wear earrings. They're clip-ons?"

Shade reached out, taking them away from her. "They aren't earrings; they're nipple clamps." He took them out of the box. "I had them specially designed to match your eyes. I bought the purple diamonds from Australia and then had a jeweler add them to the nipple clamps I bought." Shade placed one on the hardened tip of the breast he had been playing with, bending down to tease the other one before placing the nipple ring onto it. He placed them loosely. He would gradually get her used to them being tighter after the baby was born.

"Ouch."

"Did I hurt you? I didn't…"

"They pinch, but they don't hurt. Your baby just kicked. I don't think he approves."

Shade ran his hand over the mound of her stomach, his voice lowering and gentling. "Go to sleep, little one. Daddy wants to play."

Tears filled Lily's eyes. "That's the first time I've heard you call yourself that."

"Daddy?"

Lily nodded at his question.

He bent lower, kissing her stomach before rising. "I guess you're not the only one who's getting ready. It won't be much longer, just a couple more months." He smiled down wickedly at her. "We better take advantage of him still being inside of you while we can." He reached out, pressing on the side of the nipple clip.

"Oh!" Lily moaned as the clamps began to vibrate.

Shade nudged Lily's thighs apart, sliding between them. He placed his cock at her opening, letting himself glide inside her wet pussy and she arched underneath him, taking him deeper. Their eyes met, each sinking into the whirlpool of desire which drove their bodies together.

"Harder, Shade," Lily moaned.

He moved more forcefully inside of her while still restraining himself from pounding into her the way he wanted. It took all his restraint to keep their love-making subdued so as not to hurt her or the baby.

Shade sensed as she was nearing her climax, taking off the nipple clamps.

"Shade!" Lily screamed as she came.

He thrust deep, giving in to his own climax as her thighs circled his hips, pressing him harder against her.

He set the nipple clamps on the nightstand as Lily moved closer to his side.

"I really liked my present."

"I thought you might." He tweaked a red nipple, producing another shudder from her.

"Are you ready for dinner now?" Lily yawned.

"In a little while. Go to sleep." He ran his hand down her smooth back, enjoying relaxing with her on the bed.

He was content to just lie there and hold her. Each time he did, it replaced a memory of him lying alone without her. He wanted to savor every moment and wasn't going to take any of them for granted.

CHAPTER EIGHTY-SIX

Shade and Razer were in the diner having coffee as Beth and Lily shopped for the twins when they saw Knox, Willa, and Rachel enter the sheriff's office. A few minutes later, Cash pulled up in front and went inside.

"Something's up. Call Knox and find out."

Razer took his phone out, placing the call. When Knox didn't answer, Razer left a short message to call him back before disconnecting. That was when Tate came running into the sheriff's office.

"Guess we'll have to wait."

Knox didn't return the call until after Rachel, Willa, and Tate were seen leaving.

Razer's face was grim when he finished the conversation with Knox, turning toward Shade. "Willa shot Lewis at her house. Brooke had asked Lily to pick some texts up for Bible study, and Rachel offered to go instead because Lily was going shopping with Beth. When Rachel arrived, Lewis was beating Willa with a belt. She tried to stop him, and he attacked her. Willa shot him when he was strangling Rachel."

"Damn, Willa shot Lewis?" Shade was shocked the meek woman had even had it in her to shoot anyone.

Razer nodded.

"How bad?"

"He's dead."

Not only had she found enough courage to shoot him, but she had killed the crazy-assed fucker.

Razer looked down at his phone again. "The women are done shopping. We can load the packages in the SUV then follow them home."

Both men rose to their feet, going to the register to pay their bill with their minds on Lewis, Rachel, and Willa. Shade was sick to his stomach at how close Lily had come to being involved. If Rachel hadn't gone, then...

"Did Brooke know Rachel was going to Willa's house instead of Lily?"

"I don't know. You'll have to ask Lil—what the fuck!"

Razer and Shade both stared at the carnage which was the only thing left of their bikes. The motorcycles had been destroyed as if they had been hit repeatedly.

"We'll load the packages up and ride home with the women. Rider and Train can come pick up what's left of our bikes." Shade was trying to remain calm and collected, taking deep breaths through his nose.

"How in the fuck did someone do this without anyone seeing?"

"Because the fucking dumpster hid whoever did this." Shade pointed to the dumpster in blame. "Whoever did it was mad as hell. They must have been waiting for an opportunity to strike out."

"You think it was deliberate?"

"Yes. Whoever did this took their time. They wanted to hurt us. Tell Rider when he picks up the bikes to check the diner's security camera. I don't want the women to know about this. Lily will worry over who did it, and I don't want this shit on her mind when the baby's so close to coming."

"Do you think it was Brooke?"

"I think it's a hell of a coincidence, don't you?"

"Yes."

"Look on the bright side," Shade said, smacking Razer on the back. "We can borrow a couple of Rider's bikes until we buy new ones. Cash has been gloating about the new one he bought, so we'll buy a couple that will make his look like a tricycle."

⁖ ’

"What are you reading?" Lily looked up from her reading device at his question.

"Just a book I asked to borrow." Shade saw the faint blush on her cheeks.

They were sitting in their living room, watching television before they went to bed. He was leaning over to see what she was reading when her cell phone rang, and she dropped it on her lap to pick the phone up.

"Hello."

Shade's attention went back to the television until Lily stiffened next to him. Then he began listening to her end of the conversation.

"He didn't." Her lips thinned into a tight line, her violet eyes sparkling with angry fire.

"I'll call you back." Lily dropped her phone on the coffee table as she struggled to rise from the couch.

"Where are you going?" he asked curiously, wondering what had made her so angry. Lily didn't become angry often, and he hadn't seen her that mad unless he was the one provoking her temper.

"I'm going to have a talk with Cash, and you're not going to stop me," she snapped, going out the door.

Shade rose to his feet, walking out behind her and shutting the door she had left open. He watched her heavily pregnant body stomp toward the clubhouse. She went in the back door, going through the kitchen while ignoring the curious looks of the members.

Cash was sitting at the bar with a drink in front of him and Bliss leaning against him, running her tongue over Cash's bottom lip. She was wearing a lace vest which left nothing to the imagination; you could see her daisy-chain tat on her bared breast. Her hands were curled into his T-shirt, trying to pull him closer. Cash had his head tilted to the side, not giving her his mouth.

Lily stormed up to him, ignoring Bliss.

"Beth told me you were over here when she came home. I can't believe you took Rachel out then came back here to get...get..."

"Laid?" Shade said helpfully.

His wife threw him a quelling look, which he responded to with a raised brow. Lily took a step away from Shade, giving him her back.

"After everything she did for you, I thought you were smarter." Lily suddenly lost her fury, turning melancholy. "Beth and I owe a debt of gratitude to you, Cash. If you hadn't sent Shade's father here to Treepoint, then we may never have met Razer and Shade. You showed compassion and concern for Beth when you saw she was being mistreated at church. I just don't understand how the same man could treat Rachel the way you have."

"Lily, I wasn't—" Cash began.

"She sat beside your bedside from the moment she heard you were hurt. Did you even know that?"

"No." Cash rose from the bar stool.

"Well, she did," Lily said empathically. "The doctors didn't think you were going to make it. She had already tried to help you the way she does her clients, but it hadn't worked. She told Shade her gift wasn't powerful enough to help you. I think whatever she does comes from inside her. I can't explain it. The times she helped me, it's like a part of her went inside of me to give me strength. When she touches you, you feel the strength of her love and caring. I think, when you and her brothers hurt her at the party, it damaged that part of her. After the doctor told us all that you weren't going to make it, I went back to your room to talk to her because I could tell she was upset by what the doctor had told us."

Lily paused, taking a shuddering breath. "She didn't even know I was in the room. God, I don't even know what I witnessed, Cash. What I saw was a man dying, but then she touched you. When she started touching your body, I could feel a presence in the room. I saw you gradually begin to move, and then she passed out.

"I ran to get a nurse and when we came back, she was sitting in the chair, and you were coming to. The nurse started helping you while I took her to Mag's house. She was in bad shape; she was shaking and freezing. I stayed with her and saw what she suffered through for helping your ungrateful ass!"

Lily waved her hand at Bliss. "She certainly doesn't deserve for you to be two-timing her. She was so nervous about going out with you tonight. She does everything for everyone and doesn't ask for anything in return."

"Why didn't anyone tell me she had been in my hospital room?" Cash asked hoarsely.

"Rachel asked us not to; that was her price for helping you," Shade answered, pulling Lily back against his chest.

"Do you know where she was when she disappeared?"

Lily remained mutinously silent.

"I wasn't going to touch Bliss or any of the other women. I was pissed off, but I cooled down before I got here."

"I promised I wouldn't tell." Her bravado was wavering at his explanation.

"Please, Lily. I need to know." Cash played on Lily's soft heart.

"I can't break my promise, but if you figure it out for yourself, that's not my fault, is it?"

"No." Cash's lips twitched in amusement.

"Rachel was in high school, but wasn't in high school," she hinted.

"I don't understand—" Cash began.

"I do," Winter broke in. She laid down the cards she had been playing in the game against Viper and Crash. "Rachel took accelerated courses in high school. By her sophomore year, she was taking college classes. She stayed at the high school because Tate had worked it out with me so she could still stay with her own age group.

"By the time the students her age were graduating, she had a Bachelor's in Biology. I believe, for the last four years, she's gotten her Master's and is now almost finished writing her thesis for her doctorate in Aquaculture. I'm willing to bet she was able to find housing in the dorms at the university." She shrugged at Lily's accusing look. "I didn't promise her. I figured it out."

"So, both you and Lily knew where she was?" Viper carefully laid his own cards down on the table.

"We talked about it. It wasn't rocket science for anyone who knew her." Winter's snide tone had Viper, Cash, and Shade all turning red.

"Then why didn't Tate know?"

"Because she didn't tell him she was working on her doctorate. Seems that was why Greer had gotten busted selling weed to that undercover cop. They were trying to sell extra to pay for her tuition. She'd told them she had dropped out; she didn't want them to go to jail to pay for her education," Winter answered.

"So, how's she been paying for it?" Viper questioned.

"Her parents left each of them a plot of land. She sold hers," Diamond spoke up from Knox's lap on the couch. "I handled the paperwork. After the clients left, she went to the restroom, and I heard her crying. She told me that property had been in her family for generations."

"It has. Who bought it?" Cash asked.

"Drake Hall," Diamond answered.

"So, let me get this straight. While we were all looking for her and her brothers were worried sick, none of you told?" Viper glared at his wife then each of his men's insubordinate wives.

"It took us a while to figure it out. We didn't think they deserved to know," Winter explained cautiously, seeing the furious look Viper was sending her. The women began to sense the undercurrent of their husbands' angers.

"Do you have my tat on you?" Viper growled out through gritted teeth.

"Yes, but women should stick together." Winter tried to soothe her husband with her explanation, but she failed.

"So should Last Riders," Viper snapped. "Did Beth know, too?"

Winter snapped her mouth shut.

"I'll take that as a yes. All four of you will be pulling from the punishment bag next week." The women wisely remained silent, staring at their husbands in trepidation.

"And I'll deal with you upstairs." Viper's eyes on Winter were promising retribution.

"Thanks, Lily." Cash reached out to cup her cheek. "I sent Shade's dad here not only because of Beth, but you, too. I lost every bit of faith I had because of Saul Cornett. He might have adopted you, but he was a sick son of a bitch. It was only a matter of time before he hurt you, and I couldn't stomach watching Beth be hurt one more time."

Lily grasped his wrist. "You changed our lives. Thank you."

As Cash's eyes met his over Lily's shoulder, Shade gave him a small nod.

"You're welcome." Bending down, he brushed his lips against her cheek. "Now, go on home. I promise Rachel won't know you talked to me."

"Okay," Lily said happily.

"I'll be there in a minute. Don't go to sleep; we need to have a little chat before you do." Shade's deep voice wiped the smile from her face.

"I'm tired. I have to get up early for church," Lily said evasively.

"You can go to the evening service," Shade countered amicably.

Lily flounced angrily out of the room.

"Ten to one she's calling Beth as soon as she gets home." Cash grinned.

Shade grinned back, taking his phone out of his pocket and quickly texting a message to Razer before putting the phone back.

"Lily's going to be furious at you for telling on Beth," Cash warned.

"I'm counting on it," Shade said with an anticipatory grin.

₧ ₨

Shade was talking to Jewell and Bliss as they filled their orders to speed things up. If the women worked as hard filling orders as they did fucking, he would be a happy man.

Cash came inside the factory, nodding toward the office, and waited.

"What did you find out?" Shade asked as they went into the office and closed the door.

Cash had been investigating whether there was a connection between Lewis and Brooke. It was too much of a coincidence that she had asked Lily to stop by Willa's house then have Lewis show up in a murderous rage. Shade knew only one woman capable of arousing that emotion.

"Nothing concrete. I talked to Jewell. She said Lewis received a phone call about twenty minutes before he got off work, and he finished his order and left. You talked to her?"

"Yes, she told me the same thing."

"I checked his phone records; it came from a 'pay as you go' phone. I couldn't find out who bought it," Cash said grimly.

"Find anything at his house?"

"He was fucking someone. He had a bag filled with sex toys and condoms."

"Willa?"

"I don't know. If so, she wasn't giving it to him; he was taking it. She hated him, but I don't think it was her."

"Why not?"

"Because he had an underwear set in the bag, and I'm pretty sure it wouldn't have fit Willa. I checked the local hotel then Jamestown's. No one recognized his picture."

"Go farther. Start with the towns closest to the Virginia border. If you don't get a hit, try the Tennessee border," Shade ordered.

"He wouldn't be able to drive far. With the kids, he would've needed to stay close," Cash reasoned.

"Unless he had a sitter."

"Thought of that. Beth is going to ask around church to see if any of the women there were babysitting for him."

"That it?" Shade asked.

"Pretty much. If I find out anything, you'll be the first to know." Cash went to open the door.

"Cash, while you're flashing around Lewis's picture, show them one of Brooke. She may be the more memorable of the two."

"Will do." Cash closed the door behind him.

Shade sat down behind his desk. If anyone could find the information he needed, it was Cash. The sooner, the better. He wanted concrete proof that Brooke was trying to kill Lily, and once he had it, Brooke was going to get what she wanted. Someone was going to die.

CHAPTER EIGHTY-SEVEN

"Can I ask you a personal question?" Lily asked as he was cutting a piece of steak.

They were at King's restaurant, enjoying lunch. He had surprised Lily by taking the afternoon off since she had been acting strangely the last few days. Whenever he had tried to probe about what was wrong, she had evaded his questions. Shade had begun to think it was nerves as her due date neared.

Shade looked up from his plate. "Go ahead." He took the bite of steak he had just cut.

"Are you a *Dom* Dom or a Dom?"

The bite of steak in his mouth went down the wrong way and he began choking, needing several seconds to clear his throat. Taking a drink of his beer, he blinked back the water in his eyes as he stared across the table at his wife.

"Are you a *Dom* Dom or a Dom?"

"I heard you the first time," Shade said hoarsely. "Quit saying that. It sounds like a sucker."

Lily laughed, taking a bite of her own steak. "Are you embarrassed?"

"No, but I think we should talk about this when we're at home."

Lily looked at him from underneath her lashes, shrugging. "I want to talk about it now."

The restaurant was crowded with customers eating their own lunch. King was standing beside the door, greeting the customers and seating them. It dawned on Shade why she was asking him right then. It was a neutral environment where the subject could be changed or diverted if it became uncomfortable for her. She could find an excuse to leave the table to talk to King.

He laid his fork on his plate. "What do you mean by a *Dom* Dom or a Dom?"

His wife straightened in her seat, trying to appear collected; however, her trembling fingers played with her water glass, exhibiting how nervous she truly was about his answers.

"I meant do you consider yourself a Master or someone who only does it occasionally?"

Shade considered her question carefully. "I am a Dom all the time. Although some men only do it when they want—when they feel the need to release the Dominant side of themselves—it's not something I switch on and off."

Lily licked her bottom lip, staring at her plate. "I don't understand. Sometimes you're bossy, but other than the few times when we've made love and it was your turn, you don't seem overtly Dom-like to me, not compared to the relationship you shared with Bliss."

"How would you know about the relationship I shared with Bliss?"

"I asked her." Lily's voice dropped to a whisper. "During Beth's baby shower, a few of the women were talking about the men."

"I was a topic of conversation at a baby shower?"

"No! Bliss and a few of the women became a little inebriated and began talking. Killyama was talking about Train, and then she asked me about your tattoos. She really wanted to know—"

"I know what she wanted to know. Did you tell her?" His jaw was clenched so tight he could barely talk.

"Of course not! But Bliss did then Jewell. Don't be angry. They didn't know I was listening. They had offered to pack Beth's gifts to her car. I took one out, and they didn't see me."

"You could have told them you were there," Shade snapped.

"I could have...but I didn't," Lily readily agreed. "I want to understand you."

"All you had to do was ask me instead of listening to gossip."

"I've tried, but you always make me feel as if I'm imagining things or blowing things out of proportion. I wanted to understand that side of you better."

"What did you find out?"

"That you treat me differently than them."

"Each submissive is different, and you're my wife."

Lily took a drink of her water before continuing. "She said you're a master with a whip, that you can leave patterns without bruising that go away in a few hours. She said you made several on her back, but you haven't with me. I looked. Why?"

"I told you, each submissive is different, with their own particular needs. Bliss enjoys pain; she craves it. You do not."

"How do you know? You haven't really tested my limits, have you?"

"No," Shade admitted.

"Why? Because of my past?"

"Partially..." Shade continued, despite the flash of hurt that crossed her face. "And partially because I knew you would ask when you were ready for more."

"Like the other women in the clubhouse did?" Lily looked away from him, staring at the doorway of the restaurant.

When King frowned, taking a step forward, Shade shook his head. Lily had broached the subject, and he wasn't going to let her end it before it was settled.

"Eyes to me, Lily," Shade said firmly. He was tempted to give her one of those patterns she was jealous over when they went home. If she wasn't so far along, he would have left no doubt in her mind that she was his submissive.

She turned her gaze back to him. "I told you I've had sex with the women in the clubhouse, so why are you bringing it up now?"

"Because you don't treat me like you're my Master like you did the other women! Am I doing it wrong? Is it because I'm pregnant?" Lily's lips trembled. "I'm not special to you at all, am I?"

"Lily, I married you, so of course you're special to me." He lowered his voice. "Are you upset because I don't treat you like your idea of what a sub should be treated like?"

"Yes! You don't treat me like one at all."

If he lived to be a hundred, he would never understand his shy wife. Her convoluted thinking would stump a rocket scientist.

"Why do you have my dinner on the table when I come home?"

Lily frowned, believing he was changing the subject. "Because you frown and go to eat at the clubhouse if I don't."

"You hang my clothes in the closet the way I like, why?"

"Because you go behind me and do it the way you like. The last time I messed up, you washed your own clothes for two weeks before you let me do it again..." Her voice trailed off.

"And when I want to fuck my way, do you turn me down, or are you looking forward to it?"

She didn't answer, her face turning angrily red.

"Now you're getting angry because you realize I *have* been treating you like my sub," Shade mocked. "There are several different kinds of Masters, Lily. I don't need contracts or whips unless I feel it's what the sub needs. I guide you into finding your own personal fulfillment while I also find mine. That's what makes a good Dom/ sub relationship."

"Lily." Both of them looked up to see King standing next to their table. Her father bent down to kiss her on the check. "How was lunch?" King asked, his eyes going to Lily's still full plate.

"It was good, but I'm not very hungry. I need to get back to work." Lily started to rise from the table.

"Just a minute. King, will you ask the waitress to bring the check? Tell her to add a piece of Willa's cake to go. Lily can't have her cake and eat it right now, so I'll save it for her for later."

Lily's eyes sparkled at his play of words.

He paid the bill and took the cake when King handed it to him before escorting Lily outside to the truck. Lily climbed in, sitting with her arms crossed in front of her breasts.

Shade sat down behind the wheel, his wife's stubborn silence amusing him. She had been jealous when she had believed he had differentiated his relationship with the women at the clubhouse and her. However, now that she knew he had been treating her the same, merely with a different method, she wasn't any happier.

When he pulled up in front of the church store, Lily climbed out, ignoring the hand held out to her. He placed it on the truck door, blocking her from moving away.

"Enjoy the rest of the day at work. Tonight, you can tell me which pattern you want me to put on that pretty little ass of yours." He dropped his hand, moving away, and Lily slammed the truck door.

"I won't be home until late. Beth and Razer are going out, and I offered to babysit," Lily said smugly before rushing into the church store.

Shade stared at the store, debating going after her. Eventually, he got back inside the truck, not wanting to give Brooke the satisfaction of hearing an argument between him and Lily. Lily also needed time away from him to think.

Driving back to the clubhouse, he didn't regret responding to Lily's questions the way he had. When she had said she wasn't special to him, it had cut through him like a knife. She was challenging his feelings for her, feeling as though he was holding a part of himself back, and he couldn't fault her instincts when she was right.

 ఎ ∞

"This is ridiculous. Rachel is going to know this is a set-up," Beth snapped from the backseat.

"Not if you two are there, she won't," Shade replied, looking at his quiet wife in the rearview mirror.

The wives were all furious at their husbands for going along with Cash's plan. He had asked them to come to show Rachel she could fit in. When the women didn't feel it was right to trick Rachel and had denied Cash's request, he had gone to Viper. Then Viper had reined the women in, making it part of their punishment for not telling Cash where Rachel had been when she had disappeared.

Lily looked away from him, turning to look out the window. She had jumped into the backseat with her sister when Beth had angrily climbed back there, but she had been the only one to agree when Cash had asked them to go.

It had surprised Shade, but when he had asked her why she had avoided the question, leaving the room. She was doing a lot of that lately. Shade's lips tightened. Lily still remained an enigma to him in some ways.

Shade parked the truck beside the motorcycles, jumping out to help Lily before she could open her door. She hesitated before placing her hands on his shoulders as he lifted her down to the ground. Shade closed the truck door and was about to move away when he looked down to see tears in her anxious eyes.

"I'm sorry I've been such a brat."

Shade motioned for Razer and Beth to go on without them as he pressed Lily back against the side of the truck. His hand cupped her check, rubbing his thumb against the soft flesh.

"Angel, I love you."

"I love you, too. I just want to make you as happy as I am. Instead, I created a rift between us."

"No, there isn't. I'm not going to let anything come between us. I understand it's your first relationship, Lily. I rushed you into marriage then into having my child."

"Shade, you didn't rush me—"

"I could have waited until you had dated a few more men, lived a little more on your own, but I didn't. I couldn't watch you dealing with your past anymore. Truthfully, it wouldn't have made a difference, anyway. I couldn't live without you in my life anymore, and I wouldn't have been able to watch you become involved with another man when I knew I was the one for you."

Lily gave a low laugh. "You're very confident of yourself."

Shade shook his head. "I've never been overly confident of you, Lily." Shade let her see his vulnerability for a brief second before closing down again and stepping back to hold out his hand.

"You ready to welcome Rachel into the club?"

"Let's do this." Lily grinned, taking his hand.

They walked to the group sitting near the lake where the men had laid down blankets. Shade was holding onto Lily as she sat down on one when they heard the approach of a motorcycle.

Cash pulled in and parked with Rachel on the back of his bike. They got off, immediately coming toward where they were sitting. As they neared, Shade could see Rachel was nervous being there with so many of The Last Riders.

"Hi, Rachel." Lily's soft voice had Rachel's tense expression relaxing as she saw Lily sitting next to him. Then her eyes traveled to Beth who was sitting on the other side of her, next to Razer.

"Hi." Rachel walked closer to the blanket they were sitting on.

Lily scooted closer to him, giving Rachel enough room to sit down next to her. Beth then edged closer to Razer on the opposite side, giving enough room for Cash to sit down next to Rachel.

"It's beautiful out here at night, isn't it?" Lily smiled, handing her a soda out of the cooler. "Rider came out earlier to set out the torches."

"It's nice here. Holly and I bring Logan." Rachel looked at Beth cuddled up into her husband's side. Razer and Beth must have had their own talk because Beth no longer was acting angry with Razer.

"Who's keeping the babies for you?" Rachel asked Beth.

"Evie and King. I think she would actually keep them if we let her," Beth said wryly.

Winter came out of the water with Viper's arm wrapped around her waist. Winter sank down on the blanket across from Rachel while Viper reached into the cooler, pulling out two beers and giving one to his wife.

"I'm surprised you're out on a school night, Winter," Rachel teased.

"I usually don't. I hate being tired first thing in the morning, but we all punish ourselves sometimes for a good cause." Winter threw Viper a sidelong glance which he ignored, lifting the beer to his lips.

A sudden squeal filled the night air as Rider threw Bliss into the water, going in after her and pulling her into a passionate kiss, gradually edging her over to the darker side of the water. As Rachel lowered her gaze, embarrassed, Razer cut into the sudden silence.

"Let's go for a swim," he said, helping Beth to her feet.

All the couples stood except Lily, Shade, Viper, Winter, Rachel, and Cash. The air rang out with splashing and laughter.

"I'll open the store tomorrow. I need to organize a few things for Willa," Lily said. "Lewis's younger children need a few things, and I thought I would make a couple of bags for them and deliver them when you come in."

"I'm sure she's going to need several things. I picked them up some games to keep them occupied."

"I offered to take them to the Saturday matinee to give her a break." Winter's husky voice was due to Viper's determination that his wife wasn't going to stay angry with him. He was kissing her neck, uncaring that Rachel was watching.

They all wanted Rachel to become more comfortable around them, and to do that, they would act normally. The husbands were all constantly touching their wives, and the brothers were not shy about touching the women. Cash wanted Lily, Beth, and Winter there to show her she would have ready-made friends in the club, not pretending they acted differently than they did.

Shade bent down, capturing Lily's mouth with his hand on the back of her neck, holding her in place.

"Let's go for a swim." Cash rose to his feet, holding out his hand.

Rachel took it, standing up. "I don't have a suit."

"Lily brought you one. You can go into the trees and get changed."

Shade shrugged when Lily sent him a reproving look. He had given the suit to Cash when he had asked. His wife easily was the most modest of the women. If she showed her shoulder or calf, she felt as if she was exposing too much. Shade didn't mind, though; he liked that he wouldn't have to kill any fucker caught staring at her.

Lily buried her face in his shoulder when Cash changed into shorts in front of everyone.

"You don't want to get a good look? You didn't mind staring at Knox's," Shade teased.

Lily raised her head. "You know I only looked because he had that piercing."

"Yeah, sure," Shade laughed.

Lily sent him a quelling look as Rachel walked out, timidly approaching the water where Cash was waiting for her.

Crash took the last two beers out of the cooler before standing.

"Anyone want to go on a beer run?" No one spoke up.

Razer sighed, kissing Beth on the cheek before rising.

"I'll go with you. We can take the truck. I'll ride my bike back."

Shade tossed him the keys.

"She's going to have a hard time when she finds out about the club," Lily said, drawing his attention back to her.

Shade reached for the beer Train was handing him.

"Yes, she will, but you did, too. It depends how much she wants to be with Cash, but I think she'll get over it. It's not easy for him, either. He likes women who like to play and play a lot. They both are going to have to do some giving and taking."

"Like us?"

"Like us," Shade agreed.

"Is it worth it to you, Shade?"

Shade saw Beth's anxious face when she heard Lily's question.

Shade stared back at Lily. "Lily, you're worth me giving up the club if I was left with no choice. You mean everything to me. Are you not happy with the club in our lives?"

The other members quieted, listening in to the conversation going on between them.

"I can't imagine them not being in my life," Lily answered softly. "It would be like losing a part of myself if I lost them. They make me feel safe and cared for."

Shade nodded, taking her hand.

"Don't worry, Lily; you're never going to lose us. Once The Last Riders claim you, we don't let go of what's ours." Viper spoke for the whole group who all nodded at his words.

Bliss and Rider had come out of the water and had paused behind them, listening to the conversation. Beth handed her a towel, which she used to wrap around herself before crouching down behind Lily, hugging her from behind.

"We would never give you up. You're too special to us."

Lily placed her hands on Bliss's, squeezing them in a return of affection.

"I'm not going anywhere. I'm exactly where I belong."

CHAPTER EIGHTY-EIGHT

Lily was practically skipping ahead of him. Shade reached out, taking her hand and making her wait for him.

"Quit being a slow-poke," Lily chastised him with a grin. She was already impatient. She had been ready long before the rest of The Last Riders who were following along behind them.

"The town festival isn't going to be gone before we get there."

"No, but the best food will be. I'm hungry," Lily complained.

"You're always hungry," Shade teased her as they neared the tables that had been set up for the crowd to sit at. It was surrounded by booths which had been set up to serve food made by the townspeople.

"Hi, Rachel!" Lily called out when she saw her friend sitting at one of the tables.

When Cash took a seat next to her, Shade and Lily shared a look, wondering why Cash was giving Rachel a heated glare.

"Hi, Lily," Rachel greeted Lily, ignoring Cash.

"You're not eating?" Lily asked, looking down at the empty place in front of Rachel.

"I'm afraid to. There's enough fatback in those dishes to take down a horse," Rachel joked.

"I'm starved. I'll be back in a minute." Lily left, going to the different booths.

Shade and the rest of the men remained seated.

"Exactly when did you sneak out?" Cash asked, breaking his silence.

"Around two. Don't worry. I didn't walk home; Cheryl gave me a ride," Rachel told him.

Cash didn't look any happier with her answer. Rachel shrugged, clearly not concerned that Cash was still angry.

Beth gave her a wink while Shade and Razer shook their heads at each other. Beth was protective of Rachel because she was Lily's age.

"You're not hungry?" Rachel asked Beth.

"I'm with you. Thank God I'm not pregnant anymore and don't get the cravings Lily does."

The women turned to watch as Lily went from booth to booth, getting samples of everyone's food.

"When did Brooke learn to cook beans and greens?" Rachel asked.

Shade was surprised the evil bitch could boil water.

"I have no idea," Beth said then added, "You going to try it?"

"No, it would be too depressing if she can cook as good as she looks."

Lily came back to the table with a huge plate, sitting down between her and Mag.

"Aren't you going to eat?" Rachel asked Cash.

"Later." Cash was staring at the Freedom Riders who had sat down a few tables away.

"You don't like them, do you?" Rachel questioned when she saw where Cash was staring.

"No."

"Why? They seem friendly enough."

"So was Ted Bundy."

Shade agreed with Cash's harsh comparison.

"I can't eat anymore." Lily pushed her plate away, looking queasy.

"You only ate a biscuit." Rachel said.

Shade frowned, bringing his attention back to Lily. Her plate was practically untouched.

"I guess it's not agreeing with the baby." Lily turned green, getting up from the table with his help. Seconds later, she darted to the nearest restroom inside the church.

Shade stood beside the table. Lily hadn't had an upset stomach since the early stage of her pregnancy. If she didn't come out soon, he would check on her.

"No need wasting food." Mag reached out, pulling the plate toward her.

"I heard things didn't go well last night," Beth broached the subject tentatively of Rachel attending her first Friday night party.

Rachel made a face. "That's putting it mildly."

"I was shocked the first time I went, too. I ended up leaving." Beth's face was red from embarrassment. "Lily ran back to college."

"I tried to run, but Viper wouldn't let me," Winter gently butted into the conversation. "It was after my attack. Believe me, if I'd had use of my legs, he wouldn't have been able to catch me, either."

"I would have caught you," Viper stated.

At that moment, Shade saw Mag pass out at the same time Beth screamed, her chair falling back.

"No!" Rachel screamed at the same time Beth yelled for someone to call nine-one-one.

Shade already had his phone out, dialing the number.

Mag had turned deathly pale and had passed out, her head falling back over the wheelchair. The men quickly pushed it back from the table, laying her on the ground. Beth frantically took her pulse while Shade moved Lily back as she came out of the restroom, turning her so she couldn't see what was going on. Cash knelt by his grandmother, holding her hand.

"Her heart is racing," Beth told Cash.

Rachel was staring down at Mag, crying. Going to her knees beside Mag, she laid her hand on her heart.

Shade could see she was going to try to help her the way she had helped Lily and Cash.

They all watched in amazement as Rachel used her gift to save the old woman. Whimpering cries passed her pale lips as she focused on her.

Shade moved Lily farther away as the ambulance arrived.

"What happened to her? She was fine when I went to the restroom," Lily asked.

Shade looked down at her pale face. "Are you feeling better?"

Lily nodded, wincing. "I threw up. Something I ate must not have agreed with me."

His eyes narrowed on her. "Stay here. Don't move," he ordered. Seeing Knox and Diamond on the edge of the group, he quickly walked toward the brother.

"Knox." Shade stopped a few feet away.

Knox excused himself from his wife, coming toward him.

Shade didn't waste time. "Lily was sick right before Mag passed out after she ate off Lily's plate. I want the food tested."

"You think it's food poisoning?" Knox said, pulling out his cell phone.

"No, I don't. Lily and Mag got sick too fast. You see anyone else getting sick?"

"No, I don't. I'll call my deputies in and get the food checked out."

"Make it fast. It could help save Mag's life. I'm going to drive Lily to the hospital and get her checked out."

As Shade strode back to Lily, they were loading Mag into the ambulance. Lily was crying helplessly as another paramedic worked frantically on Rachel.

"They called another ambulance. Rachel's heart went out of rhythm."

Shade let her stay long enough for the other ambulance to arrive. Then they watched as a paramedic shocked Rachel's heart. When they loaded her into the other waiting ambulance, Shade turned to Lily.

"We're leaving. I'm taking you to the hospital."

"I'm fine, Shade," she protested.

"I want to make sure." Shade took her arm, leading her back to the truck and passing the booth Brooke was in.

Once Brooke turned away, avoiding his gaze, he tore his eyes away, his hand tightening on Lily's arm. He didn't need Knox's test results to know she was guilty. Her fucking face when the crowd had parted and he had glimpsed it had said it all. The malice emanating from her was dangerous, and Shade wasn't going to put off the inevitable any longer. Brooke had sealed her own fate, and he was the executioner.

80 CB

When Cash opened Rachel's hospital door, stepping into the hallway, Shade was waiting on the other side.

Beth had come to the emergency room when he had called Razer and told him he and Lily were there. Beth and Razer had taken Lily home for him because he wanted to talk to Cash before leaving.

"You got my text?"

Cash had sent him a text telling him Brooke had been in Mag's house with her husband when a plant had gone missing. Rachel hadn't thought anything of it at the time, but she and Cash had made the connection when the reports had come back on what had nearly killed Mag. Trace amounts had also been found in Lily.

"Yes. You sure Brooke is the one responsible?" Shade asked menacingly.

"We have no concrete proof of the poisoning other than she was there the day the plants disappeared from Mag's house, but I found the motel she and Lewis were using. She was manipulating the stupid bastard." Cash's harsh voice stated his own hatred of the woman.

"She's an expert at that."

"What are you going to do?"

"Nothing for now. I can't take care of personal shit until the mess with Scorpion is cleared up. As soon as it is, I'll deal with Brooke. I'll keep Lily home for now. She's far enough along that she shouldn't put up too much of a fuss."

"Good luck; you're going to need it."

"Lily won't jeopardize our baby; she'll listen."

"I'll ask Rachel if she'll take over the store," Cash offered.

"Thanks, brother."

Both men stared at each other, reading each other's intentions before they shook hands and parted. Cash went back inside to Rachel, while Shade rode Razer's bike back to the clubhouse since Razer had driven the truck to take their wives home.

Cash hadn't stated his intentions out loud, but it was going to be a race to see which one of them took Brooke out first, although both of them had a commitment to the club to deal with the Freedom Riders before they took care of their own personal grievances. He wasn't going to have to dig out some of Cash's IOUs, though. There was no way he was going to let him have the pleasure of killing Brooke. That pleasure was going to be all his.

※ ∽

"What's wrong?" Lily asked, walking out of the kitchen.

Shade was at the top of the steps, about to come downstairs for dinner, but paused when he heard Lily's concerned voice.

"Nothing," Beth denied, taking a seat on the couch.

Lily had told him Beth and Razer were coming to dinner. Evie and King were babysitting, so the sisters could spend the evening together alone with just their husbands.

"Don't lie to me, Beth. I can tell something's wrong. Are you and Razer having problems? Where is he?"

Beth was already shaking her head. "It's not Razer. He's coming. He's in the shower. I wanted to see if you needed help with dinner."

"No, I made a roast, and everything's done. So, if it's not Razer, what's wrong?"

"It's nothing important," Beth prevaricated.

"If it's not important, then tell me. I'm getting tired of everyone treating me like a child."

"Okay, okay, you win," Beth said, giving in to Lily's demand. "I received a text message today, and I don't know who it's from."

"What did it say?"

Beth took her cell phone out of her pocket, pulling the message up.

"Oh, my God. They called you a slut," Lily whispered.

Beth nodded, taking the cell phone back. "If Georgia was still alive, I would think it was her. Could it possibly be one of her friends?"

"Possibly. They were just as mean as she was, but why would they send that message to you?"

"I don't know. I showed Razer when I came home this afternoon, and he said he would check it out."

Shade was willing to bet that was what he was doing right then and why he had sent Beth over ahead of him.

"Then I'm sure he'll take care of it. If he doesn't, I'll tell Shade to," Lily said reassuringly. Standing up with difficultly, she looked down at her sister. "Help me set the table?"

Beth stood up, smiling wryly. "You think Shade can solve everything, including world hunger," she teased.

"He probably could if everyone would listen to him. He's very smart," Lily said, making her way into the kitchen.

"Yes, he is," Beth stated, looking up the staircase and meeting his eyes, only breaking contact when a knock sounded on the door.

While Beth opened the door for Razer who came inside and hugged his wife, Shade came down the steps.

"Dinner ready?"

"Almost," Beth answered her husband before going into the kitchen.

"You hear?" Razer asked in a low voice.

"Yes."

"When I find out who sent that message, I'm going to rip their throat out." Razer kept his harsh threat subdued so the women couldn't hear.

"Any luck?"

"Disposable phone," Razer answered, watching the women chat as they set the tables. "We never did find out who fucked our bikes up, and now someone we don't know is texting Beth. Someone tried to poison Lily. Could it be possible that someone is targeting us? The Freedom Riders?"

"I don't fucking know. I'm sure Brooke is the one who tried to poison Lily, but I can't imagine the odds of them not being connected. It's too much of a coincidence that this is happening at once."

"I agree."

"Dinner's ready," Lily said, trying to lift the heavy roast.

"Don't you dare," Shade snapped.

Lily hastily stepped away as Shade picked the heavy dish up.

"I could have managed," Lily said, rolling her eyes as she took her chair.

"That's a pretty dress you have on tonight, Beth," Shade complimented, ignoring Lily's crestfallen expression when he didn't mention how pretty she looked in her new maternity dress.

"Thank you, Shade."

"I love the pattern. It really suits you." Shade took his seat, staring with determination at Lily. "I'll have to remember it. It would look fantastic on Lily."

While his wife glared at him, Shade picked up a roll, biting into it. He was keeping count of his lovely wife's punishments, and she was on number sixteen. When the baby came and she had regained her strength, his dear wife was going to be reminded of every time she had misbehaved. She wanted proof that she was special, so he was going to give it to her one stroke at a time.

CHAPTER EIGHTY-NINE

"We're out of eggs. Do you want to eat breakfast at the clubhouse?" Lily asked when he came downstairs.

"Sounds good." Shade opened the door for her as they went outside.

"Looks like there was a large crowd at the clubhouse last night."

The front porch had a view of the parking lot where there were row after row of motorcycles lined up, ready to ride when Viper gave the word.

Viper had given his order, and the brothers from Ohio had arrived the day before after the Freedom Riders had beaten up Drake Hall when he had refused to sell a piece of property to them. Viper and Cash both shared the opinion that whatever attack the Freedom Riders had planned was imminent, and Shade agreed.

When it went down, Viper wanted him with the women instead of the brothers, which chaffed at Shade, but he also had to agree he was right. If the Freedom Riders couldn't be stopped in time, the lives of the women were going to be left in the hands of the man who stayed behind, and Shade didn't want Lily's life in anyone's hands but his.

Viper and Cash were in the kitchen when they opened the back door, but they quit talking when Shade and Lily entered.

Lily went for the refrigerator to pour herself some orange juice while Shade drank his coffee, ignoring his wife's baleful glances. The woman loved coffee yet hadn't drunk any since she had found out she was pregnant.

"What has you two looking so serious?" Shade asked.

"We just got some information that Scorpion might have an interest in Molly's Valley. It doesn't make sense to buy property there. There's no..." Cash broke off, watching his words so Lily wouldn't become alarmed.

"No one can buy property in Molly's Valley," Lily stated, sitting down at the table. All three pairs of eyes fixated on her. "Well, they can't." She shrugged. "Ask Rachel; she's the one who wrote a huge paper on it in high school. She wanted to do her paper on the effects of mining on the water, but she was too afraid she would be run out of town."

"Why can't anyone buy property in Molly's Valley?" Cash asked, trying to keep her on track so they could get the information they needed.

"Because it's a depository for nuclear waste." As the men at the table paled, Lily nodded. "I know. It's frightening what happened. From what I remember from Rachel's report, there was ground seepage. They have to monitor it forever."

"Why aren't there any signs? How didn't I know this?" Cash asked, sounding surprised.

"I have no idea." Lily shrugged. "Like I said, ask Rachel. She got an A on her paper. None of us could hardly understand a word of it, but she gave lists of the companies who stored their waste there. She's writing her doctoral dissertation on it. She had to get special permission from the state and federal governments to take soil samples. She's writing about some kind of isotopes."

"Transuranic?" Cash asked sharply.

"That's it!" Lily exclaimed. "I would call her and ask to make sure, but there's no cell reception there. She went there today to get some samples; her paper is due next week."

"Holy fuck!" Cash yelled, getting out of his chair to run after Viper. "Shade, call Lucky. Tell him everything and to notify Homeland Security."

Inside the kitchen, Viper's commands to the brothers could be heard with the sounds of the men hauling ass to leave.

Shade called Lucky.

"What in the fuck is going on?" Lucky asked. He had taken over the bedroom in the basement. "I'm getting dressed. Why's Viper—"

Shade cut him off. "You need to call Homeland Security now. Tell them to get to Molly's Valley ASAP. The Freedom Riders are going there, and Rachel's there, too."

"What's wrong with that? There's nothing there, and no one even lives there."

"No one fucking lives there because it's a nuclear waste dump, and one of the things they dumped there was isotopes."

Lucky hung up on him before he could say another word.

Lily was staring at him with her eyes wide until the basement door was flung open as Lucky came running through, wearing only his jeans and boots. In one hand, he had his cell phone, which he was yelling into, and in the other hand, he held a T-shirt. He ran through the kitchen, slamming through the door to the front room.

"Is Rachel going to be okay?" Lily's gaze was still on the door Lucky had gone out.

"Yes, Cash will take care of her."

Lily nodded, turning back to him and looking stunned.

"What?" Shade asked.

"Pastor Dean has tattoos."

Shade's eyes narrowed on her. "He has as many as I do."

"No, he doesn't. He doesn't have any on his neck and hands."

"He has as many tattoos as I do," Shade repeated.

"You mean..." Lily's eyes dropped.

"Exactly."

ಔ ಚ

Shade sat at the kitchen table while the brothers were being patched up by the women. Even his wife was helping out, cleaning a cut on Lucky's forehead. They were all watching their words, but the atmosphere was gloomy as they talked about the three who had been killed.

"Hound pulled him off me. When he did, the fucker stabbed him then Stache," Train said, staring into the whiskey bottle in his hand.

"It wasn't your fault; Hound didn't see the knife."

Train didn't reply. Shade knew he would take the deaths hard. He was already living with the burden of feeling responsible for someone else's death.

"I'm going to miss Cruise. He was a crazy son of a bitch, but whenever anyone wanted to party, he was always up for it," Rider stated morosely.

"That wasn't the only thing he was always up for," Jewell wise-cracked in a tearful voice.

That set the whole room off as they began talking about their memories of the men.

Shade watched as Lily carefully applied the Band-Aid to Lucky's scratch.

"That's enough, Lily. Come here. It's just a fucking scratch."

Lily threw him an impatient look as she moved away from Lucky. "I think it might need stitches." She turned her back to Lucky, facing Shade with her hands on her hips.

"Which you can't do, so there's no need with you fussing over it."

Lucky flipped him off and Shade's jaw tightened as he snaked a hand around her waist, pulling her down onto his lap. Shade flipped him back off with the hand behind Lily's back.

"Where's Cash?" Shade asked, changing the subject.

"He was going to make a stop in Jamestown then head back," Viper answered, placing an arm around Winter's shoulders. "I'll ride back to Ohio with the brothers and handle the funeral arrangements, so I'll be gone a few days. Lucky, you'll be in charge while I'm gone. The rest of you can come the day of the funeral, and I'll ride back with you."

He and Lily stayed at the clubhouse until late. When they went home, Lily showered first. After Shade took his, he lay down on the bed and she rolled over to him, wrapping her arms around him and hugging him close.

"Is it awful of me that I'm glad you weren't there?" she whispered.

"No." His hand went to her ass, massaging the firm flesh. "You think it's awful I wish I was?" he whispered back.

Lily placed gentle kisses against his throat. "No. You wanted to protect the men you lost, and you weren't there, so you wouldn't be you if you didn't feel bad about it."

Shade shook his head in the dark, rising up on an elbow. "Lily...I don't..."

"You don't what?" Lily stared up at him with the same look she had since the day she had married him—complete trust.

"Nothing. Night, angel." He turned the light out, lying back down.

"Good night, Shade."

⁂ ⁖

He stood in the doorway of the church, watching Cash put on the performance of a lifetime.

"Seems to me it would have been a lot simpler to propose," Train said.

"Must have been worried about getting a yes," Shade stated as Lucky performed the wedding ceremony between Rachel and Cash.

"Another brother bites the dust. There must be something in the water," Train joked, but Shade heard the envy in his voice.

He was aware that Cash had let him join in with him and Rachel a couple of times.

He might live with Lily in a separate house, but that didn't mean he didn't do his job by seeing to the members' safety. He was fucking ecstatic that he didn't have to follow Rachel home anymore to make sure she arrived safely when she snuck out of Cash's bed every morning. Shade supposed he could have called and told Cash she was leaving, but the brother had always appreciated things more when he had to work for them. He hadn't given a shit about his promotion in the military until it had been denied. Then he had worked his ass off, pulling extra duty until he had been promoted a year later. He didn't slack off once he had the promotion, either. Rachel was a smart woman, and she would keep Cash on his toes.

Train was different than any of the other brothers. They all loved pussy and lots of it, but Train more than any of them. The difference was the man wanted a wife and kids. He wanted to settle down. He just hadn't met the woman yet who could give him what he wanted. The brother was fucking eye-candy to women, like that fucking Conner whose ass he had sent back to Texas. Most women wanted Train for his dick, not seeing the tortured soul underneath.

"Enjoy yourself while you can. Once you put a ring on their finger, your life's never the same again," Shade told him.

Train looked at him sharply. "You regretting getting married already?"

Shade saw Lily crying as Cash slid the ring onto Rachel's finger.

"I'll never regret marrying Lily. It was the best moment of my life. If it lasts fifty years, it won't be enough time with her." Shade was aware he was opening himself to the brother, but he was also aware of the load he was carrying. "It's like cutting your soul in half. You can either give it up voluntarily or fight it all the way."

"Which was Cash?" Train said, nodding toward the happy couple kissing to the cheers of the church congregation.

"He fought it long and hard."

"How about you?" Amusement filled Train's face.

"Me?" Shade slapped Train on the back, pushing him forward to congratulate the newly married couple. "Hell, I was easy. I gave it up without her having to ask for it."

Shade stood in the shadows, remembering his words to Train two days before as Brooke turned the bedroom light off.

Viper and the others had returned from the funeral a few hours ago. He had remained behind with Lily, Winter, Beth, and Diamond. Knox had made Diamond stay at the clubhouse while he was out of town.

As soon as the brothers had returned, he had gone to talk to Evie before coming over. The Freedom Riders were taken care of, and it was Brooke's turn. All he needed was the opportunity.

Brooke was going to Georgia the following week. She had told Rachel when Rachel had requested that Pastor Merrick find someone who could help out in the store for a couple of days so she and Cash could have a short honeymoon. Lily wanted to, but he had put his foot down. There was no way she was stepping foot back in the church store until Brooke was no longer a threat.

With her due in two weeks, it barely gave him enough time to do what he needed. Brooke would be leaving for Georgia, but she wouldn't be coming back.

CHAPTER NINETY

"What's the rush?" Viper asked when he saw Shade come out of the factory in a hurry.

"I left Lily at the obstetrician's office when her appointment was delayed because the doctor was delivering a baby, so I'm going back to pick her up. If we didn't have that special order to get out, I would have waited with her."

"I'll see you later then."

Shade nodded, getting inside the truck and driving toward town. He had texted Lily that he was on the way before he had left the factory.

He drove the truck to the front of the doctor's office and was about to get out of the truck when Lily came rushing out, practically jumping inside the truck, which wasn't an easy accomplishment at her late stage of pregnancy.

"What's the hurry? You in labor?" Shade asked, noticing her pale cheeks and frightened eyes.

"No." She remained quiet after that, staring out the window.

Shade put the truck in gear then drove back toward the clubhouse, shooting her several glances along the way. She was being uncharacteristically quiet, and her fingers were trembling.

When he pulled up in front of the clubhouse, she climbed out without waiting for him before going up the pathway as if she was trying to outrun him.

A sense of foreboding struck Shade. Something was wrong for Lily to be acting that way.

He followed behind her, concerned yet wanting to wait until they were alone at their house. She didn't go to their house, though. She went to Beth's and Razer's, knocking on their door.

"Lily, what...?" Shade started.

Beth answered the door, her eyes going first to Lily's frightened face then Shade's concerned one. Before she could speak, Lily held out her hand.

"I need to borrow your car keys."

"Okay." Beth left the door briefly before coming back. She was about to hand Lily the keys when Shade cut in.

"Lily, if you want to go somewhere, I'll take you." Shade tried to take her arm but she jerked away from him, still not meeting his eyes.

Razer came to the door of his house, watching silently. When he would have said something, Shade turned to him and snapped, "Don't interfere."

"Lily, come inside and tell me what's wrong."

"If you don't give me the keys, I'll call a cab. It's what I should have done, but a cab wouldn't drive me to the airport in Lexington."

"You're too far along to get on a plane," Beth reminded her.

"Then I'll drive to where I'm going."

"Lily, what is fucking wrong?" Shade couldn't keep the harshness out of his voice because he was too worried. His guts twisted at how she was ignoring him as if he wasn't there. She hadn't acknowledged his presence until he had reached out to touch her.

Bliss and Train had been sitting on the picnic table, drinking beers. Shade felt them watching. The kitchen window was open, and when the door opened and the members started coming out, he knew they were hearing their raised voices.

He reached out to touch Lily's arm, but she moved out of his reach again jerkily.

"I'm leaving you, and as soon as possible, I'm going to divorce you." Her voice was emotionless, unlike anything he had heard come from her before.

"The hell you are!"

"You can't stop me. You've lied to me the whole time we were married. I'm the only one here who didn't know your secret, because you knew I wouldn't marry you if I knew the truth." Lily walked agitatedly back and forth across Beth's porch.

"What are you accusing me off?" Shade asked quietly.

"You're an assassin, hired by the highest bidder to kill people. Did you kill Digger?"

"Yes."

"Georgia?"

"Yes."

"Oh, God." Lily shook, crying and grabbing onto the porch rail.

Beth took a step forward, but Shade blocked her. Razer took her arm, pulling her back and holding her around the waist.

"I'm not going to apologize to you for anything I've done. I've never killed anyone who didn't deserve it."

"You're not God! It's not up to you to make that judgment."

"Whose is it, then? What justice did their victims get? They don't even have a fucking body count on how many women Digger killed or know where their bodies are. Their families will never be given the chance to bury them. Where's the justice in that?

"Georgia tried to kill you twice, and do you think she would have shed one tear if she had succeeded? The night she started the fire, she could have killed not only us, but the whole club. It was full that night, so over sixty people could have died."

"She was in prison."

"The bitch had three kids, and her lawyer was filing a petition to get her out," Shade said remorselessly.

"You don't even care that those kids are orphans now."

"I gave Lewis a job so he could support them."

"He's dead."

"Which I'm not responsible for. I'm searching for their father."

"That doesn't matter. You killed their mother."

"Which they're better off without," Shade said ruthlessly.

"You don't even care, do you? But that's not a surprise, is it? You already know you're incapable of emotion, don't you?"

"Yes, I've known since I saw a kid in second grade get hit by a car, and I didn't feel anything. I knew before then something was wrong with me, but I couldn't understand what the psychiatrist was telling my parents.

"He told them I have an attachment disorder, either from the constant moving around my father had to do in the military or the copious amounts of alcohol my mother drank while she was pregnant. Take your pick; it could have been either or both."

"You lied to me. You told me you loved me! Everything—all of it—was lies."

"None of it was lies. I love you, and I have from the first moment I saw you," Shade said truthfully.

Lily turned away from him, holding her hand out to Beth. "I'm begging you for those car keys. Please, Beth," Lily pleaded.

Once Beth held out the keys, giving them to Lily, she turned, leaving the porch and going down the walkway.

Shade didn't say anything as he followed silently behind her, his cold heart filled with anguish which was slowly breaking him inside.

"You bitch!" Bliss moved to block her path. "Do you even know half of the things he's done for you? If it wasn't for him, you would have been in a psychiatric ward by now."

"Shut up, Bliss," Shade ordered.

"No, I'm not going to shut up. I've loved that man for years! Fucking *years*! But he never once gave me an ounce of hope that I was anything except a pussy for him to get off in. For you, he works a job he hates, kisses your ass as if you're a fucking princess, and do you appreciate it? No, you're leaving him and taking his child, too. Go! You don't deserve him."

"That's enough, Bliss," Winter said, stepping forward. "Lily, please stay with Beth or in town and think this over. Don't be rash in making a decision."

Lily stepped around her and kept walking; however, she turned around when Shade kept following her.

"Stop! You can't change my mind. I'm leaving!" Lily screamed at him.

"I know. I won't stop you from leaving, but I'm coming with you."

"No, you're not! Our marriage is over, I'm going to file for a divorce..." She twisted her hands together.

"Then take off my ring, I'm surprised you're not throwing it at me. You like to throw things when you're mad, so why aren't you throwing my ring?"

Lily lips trembled as she turned to go back down the path. "Go away!"

"Where you go, I will go," Shade repeated. "I won't break my vows to you. I promised." Shade stared at her, seeing the tears well in her tortured eyes.

She fell to her knees, crying while holding her stomach as she rocked back and forth.

"Oh, God, help me. Please, help me. I can't do this," she prayed.

Shade crouched on his knees beside her without touching her. "What can you not do, Lily?"

"Leave you." Lily buried her face in her hands, crying helplessly. "I told her I wouldn't even after she told me all about you and showed me proof. I told her I wouldn't. She showed me your military records, and she told me Digger and Georgia were both killed by a sniper."

"Who?" Shade asked, already knowing the answer.

"Brooke. She told me, if I didn't leave you, she would turn over the proof to the sheriff in Jamestown. I told her we would get a lawyer, and she laughed at me. She told me..." Lily cried harder, raising her face to him. "Brooke told me she would kill you by hiring someone better than you, and that, if she couldn't have you, no one would. She even said she had taken precautions so that, if anything happened to her, you would be blamed for it. I didn't know what else to do but leave...I don't want you hurt because of me," Lily cried heartbrokenly.

"Angel..." Shade reached out, gently pulling her into his arms. "Without you, I'm dead anyway."

Lily buried her face in his shoulder, unable to stop crying. "I'm so sorry. I'm so sorry," she kept repeating.

Shade spoke soothingly to her, repeating he loved her over and over until she was lying spent against him.

"How did Brooke get to you?"

"She came inside the room the nurse showed me into."

"How did she get in?"

"I don't know. I just assumed she snuck inside. Evie was off today, and I didn't know the nurse working."

"Let's go home." Shade was going to the doctor's office as soon as he was able to get Lily inside.

He started to lift her from the ground, but Lily frantically shook her head.

"I can't. Brooke said, if I went home, she would know. Please, Shade, I can go stay with Penni until after the baby is born. We'll talk to Knox and see what we can do to stop her."

When Shade's eyes caught Viper's concerned gaze, he nodded silently, motioning the members to engulf the couple in their midst.

"Lily, listen to me carefully. We'll stay in the clubhouse—"

She shook her head. "Brooke will know—"

"I'm going to see Brooke is taken care of. Trust me, angel." Shade stood, helping Lily to stand. He started to take her arm to help her into the house but she gave a sudden cry, clutching her stomach and crying out in pain.

"Shade!"

He picked her up, carrying her toward the parking lot. He placed her in the truck while the brothers were climbing on their bikes with the women jumping on behind whoever was closest.

Her water broke as he was getting into the truck. He started the motor before backing up then followed behind Viper and Lucky as they pulled out onto the road. A long line of motorcycles rode behind the truck.

"Rider isn't going to be happy with you," Shade teased.

Lily gave a gurgling laugh. "Tell him he can put my name in the punishment bag."

ಬಿ ಛ

"Will you quit pacing? You're making me nervous," Lily moaned between labor pains.

Shade gave his wife a baleful look. "Should you sit like that?"

Lily was sitting cross-legged on the bed with a sheet over her while she rubbed her belly. "It eases the pain."

The nurse came into the room, looking at the monitor. "You're progressing nicely. We'll be giving the doctor a call soon." The nurse turned to leave again, and Shade moved to block her path.

"He isn't here yet?"

"No, Mr. Hunter. This is the first child your wife has had, so I'll explain once again." Her condescending voice grated on Shade's nerves. "Labor can take several hours. As soon as she's dilated to a certain point, we'll call the doctor, and he'll be here within ten minutes."

"And I told you I wanted him here now. Call him and tell him for me that, if his overpriced ass isn't here in the next ten minutes, I'll have the sheriff come and get him," Shade growled.

The nurse flew out of the room.

Lily giggled. "That wasn't nice."

"I have a newsflash for you: I'm not fucking nice," Shade said, beginning to pace again.

A soft knock sounded on the door.

"Come in," Shade snapped, frustrated it wasn't the doctor when Beth came inside.

"Can I stay?" she asked hesitantly.

Lily held out her hand for her sister.

"I don't want to intrude on your special moment, but I'd like to stay."

"I couldn't imagine doing this without you." When Lily's soft voice came out laced with pain, Shade ran his hand over his closely cropped hair. "Besides, I might need you in case Shade gets thrown out of the room."

"I'm not going anywhere." He crossed his arms across his chest. He dared any motherfucker to try to get him to leave. He would kick their ass out of the window.

It wasn't long before the door was flung open and Lily's doctor came in, still putting on his white coat.

"I'm here now. Let's see how the mother-to-be is doing." The doctor looked at the monitor before moving to the foot of Lily's bed. "I'm going to check and see how much you're dilated."

Shade held Lily's hand as the doctor checked her. When he was done, he removed his gloves.

"We're almost there. I have two other patients to check on, and then I'll be back."

"I would feel better if you stayed here," Shade stated.

"I can't. Other patients—"

"He can't. He's busy…"

Shade ignored Lily's protest, his expression impassive as he stared down the doctor. "Those are my brothers out in the waiting room."

The doctor's eyes widened at Shade's silent threat. "I'll call another doctor in and go over my patients with him. I'll be right back."

Shade nodded.

"Shade! You can't threaten a doctor, or they'll throw us out of the hospital. They'll call the police…" When Lily's head fell back to the pillow and she began panting, Shade counted her through her contraction.

"Okay?" Shade said when it was over. "I'm going outside to talk to Viper for a second, but I'll be right back. We have a couple of minutes before your next contraction." Shade started to release her hand.

"Don't leave me." Lily gripped his hand tighter, refusing to release him.

"Lily, I'm right here. Let Shade tell the others how you're doing. They're worried."

She stubbornly kept his hand, pulling it tighter and pressing it against her chest. "I don't want him to leave."

Shade could feel her pounding heart under his hand.

He bent over the bed, catching her mouth with his. "I will be right back. I'll stay by the door. Nothing is going to happen to me. I promise." He stared deeply into her eyes. "Angel, no one is better than me."

Her hand reluctantly released his.

Shade looked back at the monitor. "I'll be back in one minute."

As soon as she nodded, watching him leave with frightened eyes, Shade stepped out of the door to where Viper and Lucky were both waiting.

"I don't have much time. I want brothers in the hospital at all the entrances and exits, outside her door—" Shade began.

"Already taken care of. We called Knox. He went to the church and found out Brooke and her baby are in Georgia. Pastor Merrick told Knox she's been there for two days, that she couldn't have threatened Lily."

"How convenient," Shade said snidely.

"That's not all. Knox went to the obstetrician's office, and the security camera's footage for the whole building was off for the four hours Lily was there."

"Son of a fucking bitch!" Without that footage, they had no proof Brooke was in Treepoint.

"Parking lot?"

"That, too," Viper confirmed.

"Who has Brooke found capable of doing all this shit?" Lucky asked with a worried frown. "As soon as Lily is able, take her to the clubhouse in Ohio and stay with her there until we can take care of Brooke. Cash wants her. He's on his way to Georgia now, so let him deal with her," Lucky advised.

"Tell Cash to just watch her. I'll take care of Brooke," Shade said grimly.

"You heard what Lily said. If you make a move—"

"I won't make a move unless all my bases are covered."

"How did she find out the information she gave Lily?" Viper questioned. "There's a leak somewhere."

"I'll deal with that," Lucky said.

Shade nodded. Lucky could find out who the traitor was and deal with them. Brooke was the one he wanted.

"I need to get back inside."

Viper stopped him. "Take care of your woman, and let us handle the rest." They gripped hands.

"Is she doing all right?" Lucky's concerned gaze stared into his.

Shade opened the door, holding it open. "Would you like to see her for a minute? I know she would want to see you."

Lucky was inside the room in a second.

"That was nice of you." Viper held his hand up. "I know, you're not a nice person," he countered as he laughed.

"I'm not," Shade snapped. "But I will always give Lily what she needs."

Both men stood in the doorway, watching as Lucky, Beth, and Lily prayed. Most things, he would be able to give Lily himself, but this was not one. Deep down, he knew it was the reason for his jealousy of Lucky. He filled a part of Lily's heart Shade couldn't. For that, she had Lucky and always would. Whether Lucky was a pastor or not, he would give Lily the spiritual reassurance she needed. Hell, Lucky had almost made a believer out of him.

Lily stiffened on the bed, beginning to pant again.

"Go get that fucking doctor. Tell him time's up." Shade rushed back to Lily's side, taking her hand as they began counting again.

When it was over, he looked at Lucky, who was videoing it on his phone.

"What are you doing?" Shade growled.

"Videoing this for Lily. I'll show it to her when she's thinking of having another baby."

"I'm going to shove that phone up your ass."

"Shade!" Lily screamed.

Lucky beat a hasty retreat.

Shade stared at his wife without remorse. "He deserved it."

Lily groaned again, and Shade looked at her worriedly then the monitor. He was going to kill that fucking doctor as soon as the baby was born.

"I want you to promise me something," Lily moaned.

"What?" Shade held her hand tighter.

"I want you to promise me you won't kill Brooke."

Shade shook his head. "I won't make you a promise I can't keep."

"Please, Shade, please. If she dies, then you'll be blamed, and my baby isn't going to be raised without a father the way I was. Please, Shade, promise me…" she cried, holding her stomach and crying out in pain.

"Okay," he snapped. "I promise I won't lay a hand on her." When she frowned up at him, he continued, "Nor will I shoot her."

"Or The Last Riders."

Shade remained quiet until she began whimpering. He gave in only when a tear slid down her cheek. "All right."

"Thank you." Lily lay back on the bed, relaxing.

His eyes narrowed on her face before going back to the monitor.

"Did you just manipulate me into getting your way?"

She grinned up at him unremorsefully. "I learned from a Master."

CHAPTER NINETY-ONE

"Isn't he beautiful?" Lily breathed, stroking his son's cheek with a gentle finger.

"Yes," Shade said, staring down at her.

"You did great, Lily," Beth complimented as she reached out to hold her nephew.

Lily was about to hand him over when the door opened. Fat Louise stood at the door with Cade by her side.

"Can we come in?" she asked hesitantly.

"Yes," Shade answered, stepping back from the bed to lean against the wall as the couple entered.

Fat Louise went to Lily's side and looked down at his son. "He's gorgeous. He looks just like Shade."

"Would you like to hold your godchild?" Lily offered.

"May I?"

Both Lily and Beth were smiling with affection at Fat Louise as Lily lifted their child to the woman. She tenderly took him, cradling the baby to her chest. As emotionless as Shade was, even he felt a twinge when the woman stared at the baby.

Cade's face was filled with concern for his woman yet gradually relaxed as Fat Louise told Lily everything she had bought for her godchild.

"It's in the car. I figured it's too much to fit in the room with all the visitors I'm sure you're having."

"Cade and I can go put it in the truck," Shade offered, already heading toward the door.

"Hi, Shade. Congratulations," Rachel greeted him on her way in as they were leaving.

"Rachel." Shade nodded. "Go on in. I'll be back in a few," he said, sending Lily a reassuring glance before going out the door.

Once outside, he stared in dismay at the loaded backseat and trunk.

"Don't blame me." Cade raised his hands in the air. "Some of this is from the rest of the crew who are coming over later. I'm just the delivery man."

"At least I didn't have to sit through a baby shower," Shade grunted, lifting one heavy box.

"You dodged the bullet on that one. They had one planned for tonight," Cade told him as he followed him to Rider's truck with an armful of stuffed animals.

"My kid's already saving his father's ass."

When they finally went back inside to Lily and the baby's hospital room, it was unnaturally quiet and Shade sensed the tension in the room. Beth's face was pale, while Fat Louise and Rachel both looked troubled. Lily was the only one acting normal as she held the baby, chatting about breastfeeding.

Shade and Cade hastily left the room, going to the lobby for a cup of coffee.

Fat Louise and Rachel came out a few minutes later, and Fat Louise placed an arm around Cade's waist as she stood next to him.

"Anything happen when we were gone?" Shade asked curiously.

"Nothing important." Fat Louise lowered her lashes. "Cade, we need to go. I need to get back to work."

Shade frowned and was about to ask Rachel what had gone on inside the room when his cell phone rang.

He answered it, seeing Cash's name on the caller ID. "Yes?"

"We have a problem. Brooke isn't here in Georgia, or if she is, I can't find her. I'm going to stay a couple of days to make sure she isn't hiding out at her father's instead of with her mother. I'll check on what friends she has, too. Evie is texting me some names, and she's also going to call her family members to find out where she may be hiding."

"Thanks, Cash. I know it's hard being away from Rachel when you just got married."

"Brother, I owe that bitch, too," Cash said, hanging up.

Shade slid his phone back into his pocket. It would be hard for Evie to talk to her family again, so Shade wouldn't have wanted her to unless it was important.

The brothers were taking shifts to protect Lily, and when Shade returned to his wife's room Train was standing outside, keeping guard. Until Brooke was found, not only Lily's safety was at risk, but also his son's.

When he went back inside the room, Lily was holding the baby as Beth sat on the bed next to her. Shade was about to probe further into the women's strange behavior when the door opened behind him. The three people entering the room had him staring in surprise.

"How did you get here so fast?" Shade asked.

"Dad flashed his old badge. There's three people stuck in Florida, cursing us right now for taking their spot on the plane." Penni laughed, throwing herself in Shade's arms. Shade hugged Penni back as his father reached his hand out to shake.

"Had to get here to meet my new grandson," his dad said with a grin.

Rachel, his stepmother, moved to take Penni's place within his arms when she moved away to the bed. Shade placed his arm around Rachel's shoulder, leading her to Lily's side.

"Can I hold him?"

"Of course." Lily lifted the baby to her, and Penni grabbed and hugged her as soon as she released the baby.

"Your timing couldn't have been better. I was taking my vacation with the parents when Shade called and told us you had the baby. Have you decided on a name yet?" Penni asked.

"No. I like several, but Shade says they'll kick his butt in school if we picked any of them. I really like Brandon."

Penni and his father both grimaced at that name.

"I told you so," Shade reminded her.

"I know the perfect name," Penni offered with a mischievous smile.

"What is it?" Shade asked cautiously.

"Lily's favorite cowboy, John Wayne."

"John Wayne Hunter," Shade's father repeated. "I like it."

"So do I," Lily said, staring at Shade hopefully.

Taking the baby from Rachel, he held his son as he walked to stand in front of his father. "Meet your grandson, John Wayne Hunter."

His father reached out, taking the baby into his arms as Shade went to Lily's side, reaching down to place a kiss on her pleased face.

"You don't mind?"

"No, a cowboy name beats a pussy name. Did you really think I would let you name him Brandon?"

Lily laughed, giving Penni a conspiratorial look when she didn't think he was looking. "I was going for Colin."

୫୨ ଓଃ

The roar of his motorcycle going down the street never failed to give Shade a shot of adrenaline. He was on his way back to the hospital after going to the clubhouse to shower and change. He had snuck out while his family was there so Lily wouldn't worry.

The light ahead turned red. Slowing down, Shade came to a stop. As he waited for the light to turn green, he casually looked down the neighborhood street to his side, seeing a large group arguing in a yard and on the sidewalk. Recognizing a familiar figure, he turned down the street when the light changed.

His mouth almost dropped open when he saw a little girl kick out at the biker dressed in leather.

He parked his bike a few feet away from them and climbed off, striding forward as Willa came rushing out of a house.

"You a-hole!" Shade lifted a brow as the girl who looked to be the oldest among the group of kids yelled at Lucky.

"Sissy!" Willa moved between Lucky and the girl, handing Lucky a towel and a plastic bottle.

"What am I supposed to do with this?" Lucky snapped, staring at the items in his hand.

"I thought you could use them to clean it off," Willa said, pointing at his bike.

Shade's eyes went to Lucky's bike sitting in the driveway next to Willa's house.

He went closer, staring at the motorcycle that had been spray-painted with the word "Blasphemer," while Willa grabbed the items from Lucky's hands and went toward the bike.

"I'll clean it for you." Willa was about to spray the words with the cleaning solution when Shade stopped her.

"What happened?"

"Lucky thinks one of the children or I did this while he was inside Jenna's house. I told him they didn't, that they were playing in the backyard, but he doesn't believe me." Willa's lashes blinked furiously, trying to hold back the tears brimming in her eyes.

Shade stared back angrily at Lucky who was flushing a guilty shade of red.

"I didn't say they did. They"—Lucky pointed at the little boy and older teenager—"were both out front when I came outside, and Willa was going inside her house when I got here two hours ago. I was just trying to ask if they had seen who did it."

"That wasn't the way it sounded to me," Willa said, contradicting Lucky's explanation.

"Then I'm sorry." Lucky pointed at his bike. "I was just angry when I saw that. Maybe I over-reacted."

Willa ignored his apology, again moving to clean the word written across the entire frame of Lucky's bike.

"Don't touch it, Willa. I'm going to call Knox and get him to come and take pictures and see if he can find any prints."

A frightened look came to her eyes as she stared at the children behind his back. "That's not necessary. I can pay for the damages."

"Why would you pay for something you're not responsible for?" Lucky snapped.

"I don't want you thinking we did it. There's no need for a police report."

Shade was guessing from her worried frown that one or more of the children had been in trouble since the death of Lewis.

"I'll take care of it," Lucky said as the front door to the house that Lucky was parked in front of opened, and Jenna came outside.

She was dressed in a short, black skirt and a red, silky blouse. She used to work at Mick's until King's new restaurant had opened, and then she had been hired to work there. Shade had recognized her house when he had pulled out. Several of the brothers had partied there throughout the years since they had come to Treepoint. Jenna at one time had even tried to become a member of The Last Riders, but her temperament with the other women had kept her from getting all the votes she had needed.

"I thought you left," Jenna said, coming to Lucky's side and placing an arm around his waist.

"I was side-tracked," Lucky said without moving away from the woman.

Shade didn't miss the hurt look that flashed briefly across Willa's face, and he was sure Lucky hadn't missed it, either.

"Who...?" Jenna stared at the bike sitting in her driveway then at the children standing near. "You fucking brats. You need to have the—"

"Shut up, Jenna!" Lucky interrupted. "They didn't do it."

"Then who?" Her eyes went to Willa. "You jealous bitch." Her hand flew out, smacking Willa across the face before Lucky or Shade could stop her.

Willa cried out, her hand going to her cheek.

Lucky grabbed Jenna back while Shade stepped forward, fury storming through his body.

"Go to work, Jenna. I'll deal with you later," Lucky said harshly.

Jenna paled. Nodding her head, she went to her car and got inside, but not without shooting a retributive look toward Willa as she drove away.

"If she touches Willa again, we're going to have a problem," Shade warned. "She's a friend of Lily's."

"I'll talk to her tonight," Lucky said, reaching out to pry Willa's hand away from her face, but Willa jerked away from Lucky's touch.

"Since you don't want my help cleaning the paint off, there's no need for us to be here. Shade, go ahead and call Knox. I'll talk to him when he comes. Let's go, kids." Willa bustled the kids inside her house, the flaming red hand print on her cheek standing out starkly.

Lucky winced at the sound of her front door closing. Any other woman would have slammed it shut, yet the quiet sound of the door closing was a testament to the embarrassment the woman had just suffered.

"Don't say a fucking thing," Lucky said between clenched teeth.

Shade simply took out his phone, calling Knox and asking him to come to Jenna's house.

"On my way," Knox said, hanging up.

"I have to get back to the hospital." Shade slid the phone back into his pocket. "You going to send Knox over there?" He nodded at Willa's house where the two older girls were staring out the curtained windows.

"No, they didn't see anything. If they had, they would have said something."

"They didn't do it. Whoever trashed mine and Razer's bikes did this."

"I figured that out too late. I let my temper get away from me when I saw that word," Lucky confessed.

Shade could understand how it would have struck a sensitive cord in Lucky.

"I'll stop by in a day or two to apologize, since I don't think she wants to hear anything I have to say right now."

"I don't think that woman wants to ever see you again, much less hear anything you have to say."

"I won't be getting a cupcake from her anytime soon; that's for sure," Lucky agreed glumly.

"I've had Jenna's pussy and Willa's cupcakes. I know which one I would've chosen, but you were never the smartest brother in the club."

CHAPTER NINETY-TWO

Lily sat on the couch, playing with John, while he worked on the laptop next to them.

"Can you watch him while I go upstairs to get changed? He spit-up on me."

"Of course," Shade said, closing the computer before taking John from her.

"It always surprises me how easily you handle him," Lily said, rising.

"I helped with Penni," Shade told her as she went up the steps.

Shade bent his leg, placing it on the other one then laying his son on his lap. The baby's blue eyes stared up at him as he sucked on his fist. Everyone who saw him remarked on how much he looked like Shade but he disagreed, seeing Lily in his cheeks and eyes. The blue was gradually fading, and a purple tint was beginning to appear. His son was going to have Lily's eyes.

Over the first two months of his son's life, Shade had become adept at pretending around Lily that he felt all the fatherly feelings he was supposed to have. Instead, when he looked at him, he felt the same void he did with everyone except his wife. However, he had been successful at keeping everyone in the dark about Penni when she was a baby, so he saw no reason he couldn't do the same with John.

Lily came back downstairs, going into the kitchen and beginning to fix dinner.

"I'm heading into town to go shopping with Beth tomorrow. One of our church members is ill, so we're going to take some food and a few other things to her. It's Cal's mother."

Shade opened his mouth to protest but at her next words, it snapped closed.

"She's dying, so I'm going," Lily stated in a tone of voice which said she was going whether he wanted her to or not. "Besides, Razer's going with us, so we'll be perfectly safe."

"You could have said that from the beginning."

"I could have, but then I wouldn't have seen that look on your face," Lily teased.

Shade smiled wryly. Lily had become adept at teasing him. Motherhood suited her, giving her a confidence he had never seen in her before.

She had also become even closer to Rachel, the two spending large amounts of time together since Rachel had moved into the clubhouse while Cash remodeled their fishing cabin into a home for the two of them.

Lily had even gone to Mag's house a couple of times. He had dropped her and John off then returned to pick them up when she called. No one would be crazy enough to attack Lily at that old bitch's house.

No trace had been found of Brooke, and her family hadn't given Evie any information they could use. To top it off, Pastor Merrick seemed unworried by his wife's absence when Knox had questioned him several times.

"That fucker gives me the creeps. I don't care if he's a pastor or not," Knox had told him.

"He's not concerned she's missing?" Shade had asked sharply.

Knox had shaken his head. "Said she goes on trips with her friends. Seems to think she's laying on a beach somewhere, that the kid is with the grandmother. We're checking it out. I've never seen a man deluding himself to the extent he is."

"That's why Brooke picked him; he's easily fooled and believes every word out of her lying mouth."

"If she goes for that type, why is she so hung up on you?" Knox had joked. Shade hadn't thought it funny then, and he didn't now. He should have taken care of Brooke after Evie's attack.

John wiggled in the bassinet as they ate a quiet dinner. After they had loaded the dishwasher, Shade packed him upstairs and played with him on the bed as Lily showered.

She blow-dried her hair before lying down next to him on the bed. Then she lowered her gown and picked John up. He rooted for a brief second before latching on to his mother's nipple.

Shade laughed at Lily's wince, rising off the bed. "I'm going to take my shower," he said.

Going to the bathroom, he stepped into the shower and turned the water on cold. He hadn't touched Lily since before she had delivered the baby; as a result, his cock was nearly bursting after watching her nurse their child. The doctor had given them the go-ahead to have sex again, but Shade felt Lily wasn't ready.

Neither of them had brought up the details she had found out about him; therefore, Shade felt he should let Lily take the lead. She deserved to have time to think things through before they came back to the level of intimacy they'd had before. It couldn't have been easy finding out you were married to a monster the same day you gave birth to his child.

Shade managed to get his raging hard-on under control. When he went back into the bedroom, Lily wasn't there. For a second, Shade's heart stopped until he heard her singing from the next room.

She sang to John every night when she put him to sleep, not that he would sleep long. He awoke every three hours like clockwork.

Shade was watching television with Lily sleeping next to him when he heard John waking. Shade quietly got out of the bed without disturbing her as he went to the nursery.

"Sorry to disappoint you, little man, but it's just me."

Shade changed his diaper and laid him back down before going downstairs to make him a bottle.

Lily had diligently pumped her milk, telling him it was so he would be able to give John the occasional bottle. She believed it would help them bond.

Shade went back upstairs, lifting his wailing son into his arms then sitting down in the rocking chair with him. Shade placed the bottle in his mouth and watched him suck the milk down.

Lily was wrong; he felt no different than when he had given a bottle to Penni or one of Razer's kids.

His son's eyes drooped as he sucked.

"Twinkle, twinkle little star…" Shade sang.

His son's blue eyes opened, tearing up before jerking his mouth away. Then he began to scream.

"I think you scared him." Lily giggled, walking forward.

Shade gratefully relinquished his wailing infant. "I scare everyone."

"Not me," Lily said, taking his place in the rocking chair. "At least, not as much anymore," she clarified at his raised brow.

"I'll do some work while you show up my singing talents," he teased, watching the two of them together until he made himself leave. The look on her face when she stared at their child always captivated him. It was like she was holding a miracle in her hands.

Shade was working on his laptop when Lily came to bed. He shut it before turning off the light. Lily rolled toward him, laying her head on his chest and her arm over his stomach.

Shade gave a brief laugh as he twirled a tendril of her hair around his finger.

"What's so funny?"

"I was just remembering, when we first started sleeping together, I was the one who held you, but now you're the one who holds me."

Lily started to rise. "I didn't—"

"Stay," Shade said, pressing down on her back until she lay relaxed against him again.

"Shade, I don't believe those reports."

"Lily..." He wasn't going to let her believe another lie about him, and he wasn't about to go back to the last year of fearing she would find out the truth. Her finding out had been a relief in a sense, taking the weight of fear away.

"Don't tell me you don't care about The Last Riders. I won't believe it. Don't tell me you don't care about Penni, Beth, or our child, either." Lily's voice trembled. "I won't believe you. Not everyone loves the same way. You just show and feel it differently from the rest of us."

"I buy that I'm different," Shade agreed as Lily began kissing his chest, moving down toward his stomach.

"You are." Lily leaned over him, slipping the sheet down from his hips and baring his hardening cock. Her hand gently explored him, her tongue licking the tip before she placed only the head into her mouth.

Shade groaned. "Lily...If you're going to suck my cock, suck all of it." His hand went down to her head, his fingers threading through her hair.

"If you love me, how can you not love all the different pieces of me? John, Beth, Razer, and everyone else in that clubhouse have a piece of my heart. You may own the largest part of me, but you'll have to share it with the rest of the people I give my love to.

"You don't have to love them as much as I do. Say, for example, if you can't find it in that heart of yours to love Bliss"—her mouth glided over his cock, going down on him farther before sliding back to the crest—"or Jewell"—down her mouth went again, that time taking him deeper before going back up again—"or Stori"— Shade groaned when she took his cock to the back of her throat before repeating the move again—"or Ember, I'm cool with that."

Shade's laugh was cut off abruptly when his wife's teeth grazed the sensitive underside of his cock. His hips arched when Lily's mouth came down on him as she quit teasing him and began to suck on him the why he liked.

"I'm going to come," Shade warned.

Lily lifted her head, rising to her knees on the bed and placing her legs on each side of his hips while she bunched her gown up to her waist.

Shade stared at her bare pussy as she poised herself over his cock. Watching her slide herself down onto his cock was the most erotic thing he had ever witnessed. He watched her reaction carefully to make sure she wasn't hurting herself, and the only thing he saw was ecstasy as it filled her expression when she began to move up and down.

Shade reached up, sliding down the straps of her gown until the top was bunched at her waist, leaving her breasts bare as she fucked herself on his cock. He started to thrust up into her, but she stopped with her pussy flush against his pelvis.

"If you move, I'll stop," Lily threatened with mock seriousness, repeating the words he had often told her when they were having sex.

Shade nodded, bringing his knees up so she could lean back against his thighs as he let her have her way. Thankfully, she began moving again.

"I love having your dick in me. Have I told you that before?" Her breasts swung as she fucked him while she licked her bottom lip. "I do, almost as much as I love sucking your dick."

"Woman, I don't know how much longer I can take you talking dirty to me while you're fucking yourself on my dick."

"Then you're going to love this." She leaned down, pressing her nipples into his chest, her teeth nipping his ear. "Fuck me."

His hands went to her hair and jerking her head forward so her mouth met his, he devoured the warm recesses, dueling with her tongue for control. Then he flipped her until she was lying on her back, his cock plunging to the hilt as her thighs gripped his hips, pulling him to her tighter.

"I want to get a tattoo."

"You're telling me that when I'm fucking you?" Shade took a nipple into his mouth, biting down.

"Is that a good thing or a bad thing?" Lily's nails dug into his shoulders as she came.

"Angel, with me, being bad is always a good thing." The thought of his mark on her nearly drove him insane.

He plunged his cock inside of her, pounding her hard enough to shake the lamp on the bedside table. His mouth went to the curve of her breast, sucking on her flesh as he gave her the release he had been holding back for the last two months.

He shuddered as the last of his climax played out. Then, when he was able, he rolled off his wife to give her breathing room and began brushing the hair back from her face.

"I'm going to have to talk dirty to you more often."

"Just make sure we're alone when you do, or you're going to be embarrassed."

Lily's expression turned serious. "I made myself a promise when I was in the hospital with John. If I was strong enough to go through giving birth, I'm strong enough to handle anything. I'm never going to forget your face when I walked down that path." Lily buried her face in his neck. "I should have trusted that you could handle Brooke. I'll never forgive myself for that. She's insane, Shade. She truly is."

"I'm not going to argue with that assessment."

"Every time you walk out that door, I'm afraid you won't be back. I should have told you in the truck what she said to me. I hate myself for that and walking away from you, and the members all hate me now because of it, too." Lily's bottom lip trembled.

Shade tugged her face upward. "Don't you dare say that. It was my fault. I should have told you the whole truth about my past. Actually, it's a relief that we don't have any more secrets between us."

Lily lowered her eyes. "No more secrets," she agreed. "And I'm going to become strong and capable like Rachel and Killyama."

Shade rolled his eyes, recalling how she had been unsuccessfully channeling Sex Piston the previous year. "Let's not get carried away. Killyama might be more than I can handle."

"Aww, you could handle Killyama," Lily bragged confidently.

Shade shook his head in disagreement, thinking his wife had entirely too much faith in him. "Angel, I'm man enough to admit that I'm not up for that job."

CHAPTER NINETY-THREE

"You ready?" Beth asked as she and Razer waited patiently for Lily to grab her purse and jacket.

"Yes, thanks again, Fat Louise. I really appreciate you babysitting."

Fat Louise was holding John as he sucked on his pacifier.

"No problem. I'm going to enjoy taking care of him."

"I'll be right outside in the yard. The men and I are going to tie some things down before the storm hits tonight," Shade told her, walking outside with the others as they left.

"Damn." A strong wind struck them as they walked down the pathway.

"Make sure you don't stay in town long. You should wait until tomorrow—"

"We'll be fine, Shade," Beth said. "It will be good for Lily to get out and get some fresh air."

"She'll get plenty of that today," Shade said sarcastically, watching a hard breeze blow the women's hair into their faces.

Lily reached up, giving him a brief kiss before getting inside Beth's car. "We'll be fine. We'll be back in a couple of hours."

"You better be. If you get caught out in this storm, I'll be pissed. The forecasters are predicting tornadoes a couple of towns away."

"I won't let them stay long," Razer promised, setting the Crockpot on the floorboard of the backseat before climbing behind the steering wheel. "We're going to stop and pick the twins up at Evie's after they visit Cal's mother. I don't want them out in the storm any more than you do. The clubhouse has a basement; Evie and King's house doesn't."

"Bye. Love you." Lily blew him a kiss as they pulled out.

Shade would have reached out and caught it, but he knew an amused Train and Rider would never let him live it down.

"Get to work," Shade snapped. "Where's the rope? We have to get all this shit tied down before the storm hits, or that gazebo everyone loves fucking in will be torn apart."

Shade and Rider went to the backyard to secure the gazebo.

"Think the picnic tables will be okay?" Rider asked.

reached out, easily lifting a corner of it into the air. "We should tie it

Shade reached out, easily lifting a corner of it into the air. "We should tie it down to be careful. I'd rather be irritated tomorrow having to untie all this than have it blow down the hillside into the road and cause someone to wreck."

They placed a couple of stakes and tied it down as Train gathered the trashcans, placing them in the shed which held the lawnmower. It took them over an hour to secure everything. When they finished, Rider went inside to grab them some beers.

Shade frowned down at his watch. The sky was beginning to darken, and the wind was getting stronger.

"Son of a bitch. This is going to be a nasty storm," Train commented.

Lily, Beth, and Razer should be back any minute. If they weren't back soon, he would call. He surveyed the yard critically for anything they had missed. His house was against the hillside, but he had reinforced it against mudslides before he had begun building it. The huge trees were swaying. Although he had taken down a couple of them, there was one he knew he should have taken down. However, the tree cutter he had hired had assured him that, if it fell, it wouldn't touch the house.

A vicious wind struck just then, nearly knocking them off their feet.

"The winds are getting stronger. I'm going to call Fat Louise and get her to—" Shade's words ended in horror as both he and Rider began running toward his house. Train came outside, dropping the beer and yelling to the brothers inside for help.

The tree cutter had been right; the tree hadn't fallen on his house directly, but a massive branch had broken loose from the trunk, landing on the back of the house and causing it to crumble like a foot on a tin can.

Shade was unaware of the sounds coming from his chest as he began to dig in the debris, looking for his child.

Viper tried to pull him back. "Let us, brother."

Shade jerked away, his hands a bloody mess as he dug through glass and broken wood. He had volunteered for several natural disasters, digging family members out for terrified relatives, never dreaming that one day he would be doing the same for a member of his own family.

Viper had everyone organized in a matter of minutes, sending Cash and Rider for the equipment they needed from the factory while Lucky called for an ambulance and Knox.

They were in the living room when Shade stepped back outside where they had been digging first. "Everyone quiet!" he yelled.

The members stopped digging, listening. The faint sound of Fat Louise could be heard, and they rushed to the side where the kitchen was located, digging hastily as her voice became clearer. Finally, they pulled back a board and found her lying with debris covering her.

She rolled back, and Shade saw his son, still sucking his paci. He quickly and carefully bent down to pick him up, holding his son close to his chest as he moved away, his heart aching as his son's arms waved in the air. His trembling hands ran gently over John's body, checking him for any cuts or bruises.

"Little man, you scared the fuck out of me," Shade croaked. "You're not allowed to take that particular trait after your mother."

"I was fixing us both something to eat when the house crashed around us," Fat Louise said shakily.

"The ambulance is here," Lucky told him.

They went down to the parking lot to have the baby and Fat Louise checked out. Other than a scratch on Fat Louise's arm, both of them were fine. The EMTs cleaned and bandaged Shade's hands when he refused to go into town to the hospital. He wasn't willing to let go of his son just yet, holding him close and switching hands as they worked on him.

Shade took his phone out of his pocket. "I'm going to call Lily. I don't want them pulling in and seeing the ambulance, or she'll freak out." He frowned when her phone went directly to voicemail.

He was calling Razer when Lucky's phone rang next to him. He stepped away as he talked.

Razer didn't answer his phone, either, and his heart began to pound in the same fear he had experienced when he had seen the tree limb fall onto his house.

He called Beth. When she didn't answer, he knew something was wrong. One of them should have picked up.

The EMT found him as he was hanging up the phone. "They're fine," he said, nodding his head toward John in Shade's arms, "but we can take them in for a doctor to check out if you want."

Shade shook his head, looking down at John. "I'd rather he stay here if you're sure he's okay."

"Doesn't have a mark on him." The EMT grinned. "I wish all my calls ended this way."

Fat Louise climbed out of the ambulance. "I'm fine, too. There's no need for me to go to the hospital, either."

Shade swallowed the lump in his throat as he handed his child to her. "I need a big favor from you, Jane. Could you stay at the clubhouse with him until I get back? Lily isn't answering her phone, so I want to go into town."

"I can do that."

"Stay in the basement. Jewell, take the rest of the women."

The sounds of a tornado siren were going off in town, and the sky had turned ominously dark.

"Now! All of you, go!" Shade yelled.

The women ran up the pathway to the house while Viper yelled for the men to get inside as Shade went to his bike.

"Where in the fuck are you going?" Viper yelled at him.

"I have to go into town. Lily, Beth, and Razer are there, and they aren't answering their phones."

"The winds probably took down a cell tower."

"No, it wouldn't have rung if it had. Something's not right. They should have been back by now. Call Rachel and tell her to text me Cal's address. I'm going to call Evie and see if they've picked the twins up."

Shade was about to call Evie when he looked up, seeing Lucky's face as he approached.

"They haven't. I just called." Lucky's fierce expression told him the person on the phone hadn't been the bearer of good news.

"Who called you?" Shade asked, placing his key in the ignition.

"My contact with the FBI. He sent me the satellite pictures of who trashed yours and Razer's motorcycles." Lucky stared down at the picture on his phone before turning it so Shade and the brothers standing near him could see.

"Who the fuck is...? I've seen him before..." Suddenly, it clicked where he had seen that harsh, egotistical face before; however, Cash got his name out before Shade could.

"That's Saul Cornett, Beth's father."

CHAPTER NINETY-FOUR

Knox led the way in the squad car with the blue lights flashing. It was crazy as fuck to be headed into the storm with tornado sirens blaring. Shade had told Viper and the others to go to the clubhouse, and he would call when he was at Cal's. The brothers didn't listen, though, climbing on their bikes and following him to town.

The house was on the outskirts of town, up at the end of a rutted driveway they had to ride up carefully. It was easier to park the bikes and run the rest of the way. Hail pelted them the last few inches.

The door was standing wide open when the men went inside. The smell of the place was horrendous. Dirty clothes were everywhere, unwashed dishes were in the kitchen with rotting food sitting on the counter, the coffee table was broken as if there had been a fight, and the Crockpot with its contents were spilled onto the floor. It sickened Shade that Cal was forced to live in this environment.

A search of the house found it empty. No one was there.

"Take cover!" Viper yelled from the doorway as he slammed the door.

Shade saw the tornado touchdown in the yard a few feet away.

"Get in the hall." Shade pushed and shoved the men toward the hallway just as the tornado struck the house.

The home shook, and the sound of breaking glass filled the air as the men covered their heads with their arms. The furniture in the room was tossed around by the wind screaming through the house.

He was crouched down next to Train when a lamp flew toward them. Shade jerked him out of the way a bare second before it crashed against the wall where his head had been.

"Hold the fuck on to each other!" Viper yelled over the roaring noise.

All the brothers linked arms and scooted farther down the hallway, bracing themselves against the shaking walls. A picture fell down, hitting Shade on the shoulder. He grimaced yet brushed Viper's concern away, more worried about the time they were losing.

It only lasted a few seconds, but it seemed like minutes as the brothers huddled together. When it passed, more than one man stood in disarray as they came out

587

of the hallway to see that, fortunately, only part of the brick walls and front porch were gone.

The men filed out with the wind still blowing, but the sky was gradually clearing.

"Where could he have taken them?" Shade asked harshly, not shaken by the ordeal and near death experience they had just gone through, only concerned with finding his wife.

"I've called the FBI in, but they're over an hour away and the storm is slowing them down. We can't use a plane like we did last time for the same reason. Saul Cornett was a pastor in Treepoint for years, so he could be holed up anywhere with another of his followers," Lucky said with frustration lacing every word.

"I think I know where he is. This time every year, he would always go to a sister church. It closed years ago, but I believe the building is still there." Cash quickly called his grandmother who confirmed the church was still standing.

The men ran back down the driveway toward their bikes, gaping as they drew closer to the destruction the tornado had caused. They had to climb over one tree which had fallen across the driveway, and as they did, the carnage of their motorcycles hit them like a slap in the face.

"Can I please catch a fucking break?" Shade yelled up at the sky before he looked at the mangled motorcycle he'd had delivered only two days before. He didn't care about the bike, only the delay its destruction would cause.

"Look and see if any of them are still able to ride," Viper ordered the men.

Out of forty bikes, three were working.

"Shade, you, Lucky, Rider, and Train ride with Knox. Knox, call and have your deputies give the rest of the brothers a ride back to the clubhouse. I'll stay here with them then follow."

Shade saw the conflict in Viper's eyes as he directed the men. He wanted to go with them, but he had a responsibility to the brothers left behind.

"Cash, you take one of the working bikes. If the roads are blocked, you might get through easier on it. I'll call the FBI and give them the address. Maybe, with the weather clearing, they can get there to back you up."

The brothers climbed into the sheriff's car as the others threw the pieces of their bikes out of the way for Knox to back out of the driveway. Once on the main road, Knox turned on his lights and siren, speeding through town.

Shade looked out the window at the passing town. Most of it had been spared. It seemed the destruction had only happened toward their side of the valley.

It took an hour for them to reach the sister church. Knox turned the siren and lights off two miles before they reached the large building sitting on the hillside.

"Don't get to close, or they are going to see us coming," Shade warned. "Pull over here and let me out."

Knox pulled off the road behind two large trees, and Cash parked the bike he was riding behind the squad car.

The men went to the back of the car where Knox opened the trunk. Shade and the men reached inside, pulling out weapons. He hadn't taken the time to run to his house for his own, knowing it would take too much time to find them in the wreckage.

Cash took out a rifle, loading it, and Shade tucked a Glock into his waistband before reaching for the M4.

"You need a gun?" Cash asked Train.

"Fuck no. I had mine in my saddlebag." Train pulled his leather jacket back to show his revolver.

Knox slammed the trunk closed.

"Take no chances, brothers. Shoot to kill." Shade changed his mind. "Except for Beth's father if you can. If not, then blow the motherfucker's brains out."

The men took off at a fast clip. Knox, even being the biggest, kept up with Train and Rider, who were the fastest; however, the rest of the men weren't far behind. Each had diligently kept their bodies in the same shape they had been in during their military service.

As they came up on the building, Shade motioned the men in the direction he wanted them to take. As they moved into their positions, the growing darkness did what Shade had thought would be impossible: provided cover enough to allow them to go unseen.

Shade nodded to the side of the house. Using the tree line to shield him, he stopped by the largest one. Handing Knox his rifle, he shimmied up the tree and reached down for the rifle then climbed several more inches before he stopped moving.

Bringing the rifle up, he used the scope to look through the church window. Quickly counting, he raised his hands, showing five fingers then another four, indicating there were nine people he could see.

Shade recognized a few of the faces inside, many he had seen on Sundays when he would wait for Lily at the diner after church. Some of those same people she had attended church with were inside watching something, their fanatical gazes turned toward the front of the church.

Shade had learned earlier from Knox that the diner's owner had explained how his and Razer's bike had been destroyed without it being caught on video. Then Dr. Jones, who was in practice with Lily's obstetrician, had showed how they had managed to get near to Lily at her appointment. However, it was from the bitch standing toward the front of the church—Kaley, that really set his trigger finger to itching.

He couldn't see Lily or Razer, but he could see Beth.

Shade's hand tightened on the trigger as he watched Saul use the belt in his hand to beat Beth. Her dress had been torn down the back, and her head had fallen forward. She was unconscious.

He almost fucking shot everyone through the window when he saw one woman standing in the group, watching Beth being beaten. The only reason he didn't kill the evil bitch before he climbed down was the promise he had made Lily.

"Each of you get to a window. We'll attack at the same time."

"Weapons?" Knox asked.

"I only saw two," Shade answered. "One by the front door and one by the back."

"A church with a lot of windows isn't the brightest place to hide out," Rider commented.

"Saul needed a church to carry out his judgment," Cash reasoned. "The sadistic bastard uses God as an excuse to do what he gets off doing—hurting someone."

"It will be the last time that bastard touches Beth." Shade took off, heading for the left window. It would be the hardest to get through, but it was the one closest to Beth. If he could get to her, he could untie her and get her behind the podium for cover, if she was still breathing.

Shade raised the rifle in his hand, taking aim. He pressed the trigger as Saul began to hit Beth again. He had told the men not to kill Saul, but he had no compunction about shooting him in the hand.

While the minister screamed out in pain, grabbing his blood-soaked hand, Shade flipped the gun around, using the butt of the rifle to break the rest of the glass. Expertly spinning the rifle back around, he raised it to fire at the man by the front door who had raised his own gun to fire at him. Shade shot him between the eyes then jumped through the window.

Once Knox kicked in the door, pushing the dead body out of the way, the women in the church began to run and scream, trying to find somewhere to hide. He heard shots and looked up to see Rider had killed the one by the back door. Then Train killed two who tried to pull guns from their waistbands. They were inept, the members relying on the pastor who was kneeling on the floor, believing he would protect them.

Shade ran to the cross where Beth had been tied, checking for a pulse. As soon as he felt the weak beat, he cut Beth down, carrying her behind the podium to lay her flat as Lucky ran to stand over him, giving cover.

He looked up in time to see Cash backhand Brooke as she tried to run away. Then he dragged her to the podium where both he and Lucky were standing.

Rider, Train, and Knox forced the ones still alive onto their knees in a circle. Rider and Train stood over them, watching to make sure no one ran away or tried to save their pastor while Knox placed zip-ties around their wrists, securing them until backup could arrive. Train ignored Kaley as she begged him not to tie her up, his face a furious mask.

"Where's Lily and Razer?" Shade asked Brooke.

"She's dead!" Brooke screamed at him, her eyes crazed.

Shade raised the handgun. If Lily was dead, he had no promise to keep any longer. Rage filled his mind as agony tore through his heart. He forced back the crushing grief, taking aim at the woman who had finally succeeded in destroying his life.

"Shade…" Beth whispered, drawing his attention. "They're locked in the basement. Dad was going to punish us one by one. He saved Lily for last. Razer…he's hurt, Shade. Please help him."

Shade took off, looking for the basement door, flinging them all open and checking for anyone else hiding until he came to one which was down a small hallway. It was locked, so he took the Glock out and shot the lock off before flinging the door open. It was pitch-black inside.

"Here's a flashlight," Cash said, coming up behind him.

Shade carefully went down the old steps. When he took the last one, he used the beam of the flashlight to sweep the room, finding Razer lying on the dirt floor.

His hands and feet were tied, his shirt had been torn off, and he appeared to have been severely beaten. He was covered in cuts and lash marks with blood seeping from them. Razer's nose had been broken, and the son of a bitch had even carved "Sinner" on his chest.

Shade took off his jacket and covered him before Cash could see then, knowing Razer would want it that way, then turned his gaze away.

"Lucky's already called for some ambulances," Cash told Shade, bending down to Razer and untying his hands and feet. "He's still alive."

Shade nodded.

"Lily?" Shade yelled then went quiet to listen.

When he heard banging, he went to an old wooden door in the back of the dark basement and shot at the chain locking it closed. Opening the door, he saw Lily tied to a chair with a gag in her mouth. He untied her, ripping the gag away.

Smoothing back her tumbled hair, he studied her appearance. Other than the terror in her eyes and her clothing torn where she had struggled, the only bruises he could find were on her wrists. Thank God he had reached her in time.

"Shade." Lily's voice was a painful croak.

"Woman, just one time I'd like you to leave the house without me having to come and rescue you," he teased, lifting her into his arms.

"Razer and Beth?" she asked with wide and terrified eyes.

"They're in bad shape, but they're alive. Let's get out of here." Shade led her into the other room where Cash was lifting a now conscious Razer to his feet. His painful groan had Shade wishing he had remained unconscious until they had been able to get him out of there. Cash held him steady as Shade helped him put his jacket on.

"Shade…"

Shade cut him off. "Later, brother. Let's get you and Lily out of here."

He helped Lily out of the basement first, afraid the steps would collapse under the brothers' combined weight.

When they came around the corner, Lily saw Beth and pulled away from him to run to her. "Beth!"

Beth took Lily's hand in hers. "I'm okay, Lily. He's given me worse before. I'll heal."

A tear slid down his wife's cheek as she smoothed Beth's hair from her face and pulled her dress back up her shoulders.

"Why did you make him take you after Razer? I begged him to take me, but you called him that name—"

"Because he *is* an old douchebag." Beth gave a soft laugh.

"It should have been me," Lily cried.

Beth shook her head against the dirty floor. "There was no way I was ever going to watch him hurt you. You're my little sister."

"The ambulance will be here in five, the FBI in ten," Lucky told him.

"Knox, you and Train take these so-called Christians to the front of the church and get them lined up for them." Knox nodded. "Cash, Rider, take Saul," Shade ordered.

Lucky laid his revolver down on the podium. He took off his do-rag and used it to staunch the blood coming from Saul's wounded hand.

"We don't want him to bleed to death, do we?" Lucky said sarcastically.

"Get your hands off me! I didn't do anything. I was trying to stop them!" Brooke yelled as Train approached her.

Shade turned to stare at the lying bitch. She was already planning her defense.

"Shade, you have to see how weak she is! She can never be the woman you deserve."

"Like you?" Shade snarled.

"Yes! She can't understand you the way I can! She'll never love you the way I do!" Brooke's crazed eyes stared into his.

"Get her out of here before I kill her," Shade ordered, not wanting to waste another second on her. Train pushed her toward the doorway.

Brooke was going out the front door beside Train when she shoved him, catching him off-guard. As he stumbled, off-balance, she bent down and picked up the gun of the man Shade had killed. Turning, she pointed it at Lily.

Shade lifted his rifle, taking a split-second to aim, remembering his promise to Lily as his finger tightened. A shot rang out next to him, and Brooke's shocked expression went blank as she fell outside the open doorway with blood pouring from her chest.

Shade turned in stunned surprise to see Lily holding a gun, still pointing it at Brooke. He carefully reached out and took the gun away from her limp hand.

"Lily...?"

"I hit her, didn't I?" Her voice trembled with hysteria.

"Yes, angel. You shot her in the chest."

"I know. It's what I was aiming for." Lily's legs gave out, and Shade managed to catch her as she fainted.

ဆ ೞ

"Do you remember that time you fixed dinner and burned the meatloaf? You didn't want to admit you had burned it, so you said it was the way you liked it. You managed two bites before you had to admit it was inedible." Shade picked up Lily's hand as he talked, picking another story to tell her.

"Do you know why I have so many tattoos? It's because I felt invisible, as if I didn't exist. The tattoos made me feel like I wasn't a shadow."

"Shade..." King came inside the room. "I'll stay. Go home and get some sleep. I talked to the doctor..." King's voice was hoarse, and his eyes were bloodshot.

For the last two days, neither King nor Shade had left her side.

593

"I'm not leaving her. You go home to Evie. I'll call when she wakes up."

King sat down in the chair beside Lily's bed. Burying his head in his hands, he cried. "They think she's had a psychological break," King said. "They want to start her on medication."

"She's breastfeeding." Shade had repeated it several times before and would continue to do so.

Rachel had come by that morning, leaving in tears. She had told him that, when she had tried to reach for Lily, she couldn't find her.

Lily had confided in him that, as she was growing up, she had hid all her fears behind a door. Shade believed *she* was the one hiding behind that door at the moment, too afraid to come out and face that she had possibly killed someone.

"Please, angel, come home. I need you."

Shade's phone lit up with a text message. He read it before placing it back in his pocket. He went to the hospital door, opening it and finding Jane on the other side. She came inside the room, and Shade made no effort to touch the baby, going to the opposite side of the bed than Jane.

"Lily, I brought John. You told me you were only going to be gone a few hours, but it's been three days. I need to go home. Cade's waiting for me." Jane's soft voice filled the room as she talked to Lily.

Jane gently laid John down next to Lily. "I told you a few months ago that I envied you. Truth is, Lily, I don't think anyone could have survived what you've had to face in your life. If it was me, I'd want to escape for a little while to rest, too, but it's time to come home.

"John needs you. As much as I love him, he's yours, not mine. John is yours and Shade's, and he needs you." Jane broke off, crying as she stepped away from the bed.

Shade stared down at his wife and son. "Rachel told me this morning that you had asked her to teach you how to shoot the day she came to visit you when John was born. You did target practice at Mag's when you visited her. Lily, something inside you told you that you needed to protect your family. That's what I've been doing since the day I met you.

"You were right; I *can* feel love. I thought I couldn't all these years, but I could. I confused loyalty with love. It took us almost losing John for me to understand what you've been telling me all along.

"The last time you tried to leave me, I could follow you. I can't follow you where you are now, so you have to come back here to me and John."

As his son began to whimper, Shade didn't try to give him his paci or pick him up.

Jane stepped forward. "Let me."

"His mother will get him. Won't you, Lily? The nights I went in to check on him, you were already there, watching over him.

"You didn't want me to kill Brooke, because you didn't want him to be raised without a father, but he needs a mother, too. I won't raise him without one." His voice lost its gentle tone, becoming harsher. "I'll move Bliss in to take care of him. If she does well, I'll marry her."

Jane gave a shocked gasp.

"Who's going to make sure he's warm? You know I like to keep the house too cold.

"If you don't wake up, we're going to have to give him formula. I'll pick the best one I can, but that shit's expensive, and cheaper is always better.

"Who's going to keep him from riding the motorcycle I'm going to buy him when he gets old enough to ride?"

John began to cry louder.

"For God's sake, Shade, pick him up." King stood.

"When King gets too old to take care of himself, I'll put his ass in a nursing home."

Shade gave it a final try. "When John turns eighteen, he can join The Last Riders with Chance and Noah. They'll have a fucking blast."

"Shade..." King took his arm, trying to move him away from the bed.

"Let me go!" Shade snarled, picking his crying son up and placing the paci back in his mouth.

"You didn't kill that bitch. You missed her heart. If you don't come back, she wins, Lily."

Tears fell down his cheeks as he stared at her. "Lily, I'm begging...please come back."

When Lily remained unmoving, Shade turned his back to the bed and began rocking his son, placing him against his shoulder as he crooned to him the song Lily always sang to put him to sleep.

"Twinkle, Twinkle, little..."

John began to cry harder.

"Shade!" King's voice had him spinning around.

Lily was watching him from the bed.

Shade walked back to her.

"I told you it scares him when you sing."

CHAPTER NINETY-FIVE

"Are you sure you want to do this?" Shade warned as they walked up the pathway to the clubhouse.

"I'm sure. I want to see our house before I go inside," Lily told him, carrying John as they drew near the corner of the clubhouse to see what remained of their home.

Most of the wood was already broken apart and moved to the side so they could try to recycle as much of it as possible. The Last Riders had already begun the clean-up, moving what furniture could be saved to the storage room of the factory and throwing the rest away.

Lily stood, looking at her destroyed home.

"I'm sorry, angel. I should have listened to my instincts and had that tree cut down before I had the house built."

"It wasn't your fault." Lily leaned against his side, and Shade wrapped his arm around her shoulders. "We didn't lose anything which couldn't be replaced. We'll build it back. That house was built for a woman who didn't know who she was by a man who was afraid to *show* who he was. That's why it was broken. The house we build now is going to be stronger, and nothing is going to break it apart."

"You sure about that?" Shade teased.

"Yes," Lily answered firmly, handing him John who was wrapped in the blanket Shade had dug out from his crushed dresser. It was the one Lily's mother had made for her.

"I know someone who is going to be very happy with this," Lily said as she started going through a box of pictures the women had found.

"Who?"

"Leonard, the man at the furniture store. I bet he retires after we repurchase our furniture."

"You ready to go inside?" Shade asked, turning her toward the clubhouse.

"Are you sure it's okay? A crying baby in the middle of the night is going to be hard for them to listen to until we get our house built," Lily worried as they went inside the kitchen from the back door. The kitchen was completely empty as they walked through it to the club room.

596

"I'm going to lay John down then go see Beth and Razer..." Lily came to a stop in the kitchen doorway, staring in surprise at the club room.

Blue balloons were everywhere. There was a cake and food sitting on the bar counter, and the pool table was filled with presents. All The Last Riders, Sex Piston and her crew, Willa, and Beth standing with Razer filled the room.

"What's going on?" Lily asked, staring up at Shade.

"They decided not to listen to me and threw you a baby shower," Shade complained with a grin.

Pleasure filled Lily's face. "I just have to ask; did you make anything?"

Shade left her side and going behind the counter, he pulled out a motorcycle with a stuffed teddy bear at the wheel. It was made out of diapers.

Lily released a giggle of laughter. "It's a masterpiece."

"No. John's my best work so far, but give me time. I get better each time I make something."

୫୦ ୯ଓ

"Where do you think you're going?" Shade glided the towel over his wet body.

As Lily paused while putting on her lipstick, he felt her eyes slide over his body in the bathroom mirror. His cock began hardening at the desire easily visible in the violet orbs.

"I'm going to work." Her jaw was set determinedly as she stiffened at the bathroom counter. She was ready to get into an argument as to why she couldn't go.

"Who's going to watch the baby?"

"I am. He's going with me. The store's never really busy, and I can breastfeed him in the back room."

"Are you ready to go back?" Shade rubbed his wet hair with the towel.

Lily's eyes went to his abdomen. "Yes." She licked her bottom lip.

His cock lengthened at her concentrated stare. He hadn't fucked her for two weeks, wanting to give her time to recover from having her adoptive father kidnap her and then her breakdown.

"Okay." Shade tossed the towel into the hamper, walking into the bedroom to get dressed. Lily's look of disappointment followed him.

Taking out a pair of jeans and socks, he pulled on the jeans before sitting on the bed to put on his socks.

Lily put on her white sandals. She was wearing a pale pink dress, looking as pretty as the sunny, early summer day outside.

597

Shade reached for one of his boots, tugging it on. As he stretched for the other one, Lily kneeled, handing it to him.

"Can I ask you something?" The troubled look in her eyes warned him that it was a topic he had avoided since she had returned from the hospital.

"No," he said sharply.

She lowered her gaze to the floor.

"Eyes to me, Lily." He reached out, snagging a tendril of her hair and gently tugging it.

She did as told, scooting forward until she was kneeling between his thighs.

"I am not going to have any more lies between us; do you understand me? So don't ask me questions I'm going to answer with a lie."

"Why did he hide from us? As mean as he was, we would have welcomed him home. He was our father."

Shade reached out to cup her cheek. Lily hadn't asked about Saul before, and Shade was certain it was because her mind hadn't been ready to hear the answers. Lily's gentle soul still fought to forgive and understand evil, even after it had nearly destroyed her. She had been pushed to learn to defend herself, not because of her own needs, but because of the love she had for John and him.

She was feeling strong, which was why she wanted to return to work. Shade thought it would be good for her. There was no danger for her there anymore. With Brooke in the hospital under armed guard, Merrick Patterson had resigned as pastor, returning to Georgia to be with his son. Apparently, Brooke had gone to Georgia long enough to drop her child off with his grandmother before she had returned to Kentucky.

Brooke would never understand the love Lily felt for him. Hell, he hadn't believed Lily loved him as much as he did her until Brooke's revelations the day at the doctor's office. That day had showed that his wife was able to look past the man he had been. Brooke had also underestimated Lily's strength to do what it took to keep her family safe and happy, which was why he hadn't touched her in two weeks.

She was stronger, so he would talk to her that night. He didn't want her submissive to him if she was only doing it to please him. He would miss that aspect of their relationship, but he would suppress that side of himself if she was doing it only to make him happy. *She'll avoid the conversation, but it's one we are going to have*, Shade thought determinedly.

"I will tell you what we know. Your mother was killed in the flash flood with the rest of the village he was ministering to. Then he traveled from village to village, preaching to whoever would listen and give him and a place to stay.

"He made no attempt to come back until recently. He had come to a village where a Christian group was visiting, and they helped him get paperwork to get back in the United States.

"He showed up at the church one night when Brooke was there, and Merrick was visiting someone." He watched her reaction carefully to Brooke's name and gave a silent breath of relief as she continued to listen. "She told him how his congregation had fallen since he left. The egotistical bastard believed he would find it as he left it—too afraid to commit any sins."

"He's mentally ill."

"No shit," Shade snapped then calmed at seeing the hurt she tried to hide. "Angel, he's more than mentally ill; he's a sadistic whack job. Brooke fed that craziness, telling him about Beth's and our relationships before we were married, that we belonged in a motorcycle gang. She fueled him into striking out then told him she would help him get his church back from Merrick, but it would take time. He would have to prove to his congregation that he deserved the church again. She stashed him at Cal's house after she asked him who his most faithful followers were."

"I remember Cal's parents went there from the time they were little. They were very upset when they heard he had died."

"They believed Saul could heal her cancer. They placed all their belief in him and even went so far as to stop her chemo, which was why she was slipping so fast. Cal wanted to tell someone, but he wanted to make his mother happy during her last days. Saul slowly contacted more members of his congregation, and they began meeting at Cal's house."

"Poor Cal." Lily's soft voice was filled with sympathy.

Shade agreed with Lily that time. The kid had wanted to give his mother peace in her last days; instead, it had been horror-ridden. She had died two days before at home, still believing Saul would save her.

"Cash has talked to him several times and warned his father to stay away from him. Because he needs the job Drake gave him, he's signed over guardianship. He's living with Drake and Jace."

"I'm glad." Lily laid her head down on his thigh. "The day we went there, it was filthy. I can't imagine Cal living there." She shuddered.

Razer had told them they had known something was wrong when they had entered Cal's house. The front door had been opened by Cal, and Razer had been carrying the Crockpot. Cal's father had slammed the door shut behind them, attacking Razer as more men jumped them. Then they had grabbed Beth and Lily, threatening to hurt them if Razer didn't stop fighting. Saul used the storm outside to work them into a religious frenzy as proof God wanted him to punish them. They were tied up, thrown in the trunks of their cars, and driven to the other church.

"It's over, angel," Shade reminded her.

Lily rose to her feet. "Yes, it's over."

John cried from the other side of their bed.

"He's hungry."

"When isn't he?" Shade joked, going to the chest to get a shirt while watching as Lily sat down on the rocking chair to nurse the baby.

They had moved back into the basement while their house was being rebuilt. He hadn't wanted to move back downstairs after the fire, but after one night upstairs, the members coming to work the next day bleary-eyed had convinced him it was for the best. He had asked Lucky if they could use it until their house was finished and he had agreed, moving back upstairs for the time being.

Shade had alleviated his worries about his family being trapped in the back room by pulling the workers off the house for long enough to build a trap door which they could crawl through to the club room. It had only taken a day, and he was much more at ease since they had an emergency exit.

Lily switched breasts and John latched on quickly, making Shade laugh. Lily grinned down proudly, rubbing his head with a gentle hand. He took his cell phone out of his pocket, snapping a picture.

"What are you doing?"

"Taking a picture so when I want another one and you need convincing, I can show you."

"I won't need convincing." She smiled softly, staring back at him with love shining in her violet eyes.

Shade took the baby, dressing him as Lily finished her makeup and brushed her hair. When he was finished, he buckled him into the carrier which would slide into the base already in Lily's car.

"Ready?" he asked, holding the door open with the carrier in his hand.

Lily picked up the bright blue diaper bag with a big picture of Elmo on the side.

"Did Sex Piston pick the ugliest one she could find?"

"That's not nice," Lily reproved him. "I think it's cute."

"I'm not carrying it, ever," Shade warned her. "Get another one."

"No, it would hurt her feelings."

The ugly thing is going to disappear, Shade determined as they went out.

"It's beautiful outside."

Shade smiled as he walked her to the car and placed the car seat inside.

When John started to cry, Shade expertly slid his paci in his waiting mouth.

"You're giving him that too much. He would have stopped when I started the car. You're making him a paci baby."

"There's nothing wrong with that, is there, my man?" Shade bent down, kissing his son's soft cheek before closing the door and turning to his wife. "You need me to follow you to work and pack him in for you?"

"No," Lily said exasperatedly. "I can manage. I'll take him into the store, and then Rachel can watch him when I go back to the car to get his bag. Satisfied? I carried enough that I can leave it there and bring it home once a week to refill."

"Good. I won't have that little fucker staring at me all the time," Shade said, glaring balefully at Elmo as Lily placed the bag in the backseat before getting in behind the wheel.

Shade bent down, kissing her mouth. "Drive careful."

"I will. I'll see you tonight. Evie and King want to keep him tonight. I think they're worried about the Friday parties corrupting him." she teased.

"Angel, if my son takes after me, then the Friday parties are going to be the least of our worries." Shade stood.

"If our son takes after you, he'll be fine. I can't think of a better man I would want him to be like."

Shade had to look away from Lily to blink several times before saying gruffly, "I love you."

"I love you, too. Now I have to get to work. I'm late."

Shade laughed, shutting the car door. "Later."

Lily waved as she pulled out onto the road to town while Shade stood still, staring until the car was out of sight.

"Ready?" Viper asked, coming out of the factory followed by the rest of The Last Riders.

"Yes."

ॐ ೞ

The brothers formed their circle in the clearing as the brothers from Ohio who had asked to attend out of respect for Razer pulled into the hidden area. The original members waited as they walked the mile to the clearing.

Shade stared at the harsh expression on Razer's face. His friend had waited patiently for this day to avenge his wife.

When the brothers from Ohio took their places, Cash untied the man who had been bound to a tree. Cash jerked him forward mercilessly, pushing him into the circle before removing his blindfold and untying his hands, uncaring about the scream of pain coming from his infected hand. Viper had refused to give him any relief other than making sure he wouldn't die of blood poisoning before they could kill him.

Saul Cornett stared defiantly, arrogantly believing God was going to save him.

Viper took a step forward. "Saul Cornett, you have been found guilty of crimes against The Last Riders, and your judgment is death." Viper's cold voice was loud enough for all the brothers to hear.

"Razer and Shade, he tried to kill your wives. Razer, he tried to kill you. I determined Razer has the right to go first, but Shade holds Razer's IOU, and he's using it to go first." Viper stared at Shade in disapproval.

Shade kept his face impassive as Viper stepped back so he could take his place in the circle. Shade ignored Razer's angry glare as he stepped forward, staring into Saul's eyes.

Raising his fist, he smashed it into Saul's face. The old man then held his face as blood gushed from his broken nose.

"That's for Lily. I wanted you to feel that before Razer killed you, because there's not going to be anything left of you when it's my turn." Shade stepped back into the circle.

"I give Razer my turn!" Shade yelled.

Razer stared back in surprise before his eyes narrowed on Saul. Stepping forward, hatred blazed from his face as he spat on Saul.

"I've seen the marks on my wife's body. You made her stand on fucking nails when she was just a little kid, you sadistic bastard. Is that why you stayed overseas, because they let you beat the crap out of their kids? Times were changing too fast for you here, with the sheriff watching every move, weren't they?"

Saul's eyes went to Knox who stood in the circle, wearing his uniform.

"I bet you thought the new sheriff would let you slide back in, but you had to take your time to accomplish that, and Brooke gave you the perfect opportunity. Tell her Shade said hi when you see her in Hell!" Razer held his hand out to Viper who handed him a large stick. Shade saw that nails had been hammered at one end until the points came out the other side.

Razer walked behind Saul, swinging the stick at him like a baseball bat, striking him on the back. Saul fell to the ground, crying out and begging for mercy, but

Razer ignored him, swinging the bat over and over until his back was covered in blood.

"I need a doctor!" Saul screamed. "Help!"

"*You* need a fucking doctor after you convinced a woman to die in agony instead of taking a pain pill? Where was your compassion, *you fucking asshole?* Get his damn shoes off!" Razer yelled.

Shade stepped forward, pulling the man's tennis shoes and socks off before stepping back.

Razer brought the stick down on his feet repeatedly, only stopping when they were a bloody mess and Saul was unconscious.

"Throw some water on him," Viper ordered.

Knox stepped forward, tossing a bucket of ice-cold water on him. He came to, crying as Razer stepped back in the circle, his eyes still blazing with hatred.

Viper stepped forward. "He passed out, so it's someone else's turn. Shade, you gave yours to Razer; it's my turn now. I hate the bastard, and as much as I want my turn, I'm giving it to you, Razer." Viper stepped back in the circle.

Razer stepped out of line, going to Rider's truck and taking out a box. He carried it back inside the circle and took off the duct tape before he kicked the box over, spilling the contents onto the ground.

"Shit!"

"Fuck!"

Several more obscenities followed as the brothers took several paces backward, widening the circle as two rattlers slid out of the box.

Saul began screaming when their tails started shaking. He swatted at them as one struck his arm and the other struck his face several times.

When one would have slithered away, Cash stepped forward with a metal pole, slipping a noose over its head. Using a boot, he placed it back in the box before grappling the other one then placing it back inside the box, as well. He then packed it back to the truck.

Shade watched as Cash carefully taped the box closed again then saw Rider's worried gaze. The brother didn't want those mean fuckers getting loose on the ride home.

"Aren't you going to pray to be healed?" Razer snarled. "You didn't give a shit when you let your own daughter be bit every fucking year. You didn't take her to the doctor once when she was a kid. She didn't even have medical records until she was pregnant!" Razer squatted down next to him, watching the poison take effect. "You're going to die knowing the pain you put Beth through."

Saul's eyes rolled to the back of his head as Razer stepped back in line.

Viper stared down at Saul mercilessly. "Train."

Train stepped forward. "Razer can have my turn."

"Mine, too," Lucky called out.

"He can have mine," Knox said.

"Damn, you all are taking all the fun out of it. He can have mine," Rider complained.

Razer left the circle, going a few feet away to pour gasoline onto the wood which had been placed at the bottom of a large pit. Taking out his lighter, he took off his do-rag, setting it on fire then throwing it into the wood. Flames soared from the pit.

Razer walked back to Saul, picking him up from under the shoulders then dragging him toward the pit and dropping him at the edge. Reaching down, he felt for a pulse.

"I'm going to give you the last prayer you're ever going to hear." Razer looked up at the bright blue sky. "I pray to God there's enough left in you to feel this, you son of a bitch!" With that, Razer kicked him over the edge and into the fire.

Shade stepped up to him, placing his arm around the brother's shoulders. Razer's chest was heaving with unspent rage.

"Go home to your wife and kids," Shade stated over Saul's screams. "I'll take care of this."

Razer nodded, turning to leave, but then he spun back. "You used all your IOUs to get them to give me their turns, didn't you?"

Shade remained silent, staring back at his friend who had stood by him through the years while he had denied to himself that Razer was as close to him as any blood brother.

"Thanks, Shade," Razer said huskily.

"Anytime, brother."

Chapter Ninety-Six

Lily was dressed in a robe, brushing her hair, when he entered the bedroom later that night.

He was tired as fuck. He had stayed to cover the hole with five other brothers and then had to drive to the Porters to argue with Greer for extra weed for the night's party. The brothers from Ohio had cost him an hour of his time as well as an argument with Greer.

The angry Porter had made out like a bandit for his weed, claiming it was meant for another buyer. Shade had to give him more money to get him to give him the order, and then the stubborn asshole hadn't wanted to give it up until Shade had threatened to find another supplier. He would make sure not to smoke any until Greer was over his anger. He didn't trust him. He had probably pissed on it when he was growing the plant.

"You look tired tonight," Lily said, putting her arms around his neck then taking a hasty step backward.

"I'm taking a shower now," Shade apologized, taking off his shirt.

"Want me to join you?" Lily smiled.

"No," Shade said, unintentionally abrupt. He was so horny he would fuck her before they could have the talk he was determined they would have.

"Oh." Lily looked down at her feet then up into his face. "Are you afraid I'm going to have another break if you make love to me the way you want?"

Shade stared at her in horror that she believed that. "Of course not," he denied. "Let me shower, and then we can talk. I had planned to have this conversation with you tonight."

"You did?" Lily's eyes filled with hurt.

"Yes. Lily, you're misunderstanding me. Just give me a few minutes."

"Okay."

Shade hesitated yet knew he reeked. He needed the shower.

He showered, washing his hair and body twice to get the smell of gasoline off. Then he spared the extra minutes to shave.

He opened the door, ready to talk, only to find the bedroom empty. Frustrated, he dressed.

His wife had probably run to Beth's house to complain to her sister that she wasn't getting any. Shade laughed to himself as he put on his boots.

Going to the bedroom door, he opened it then walked down the hallway. The Friday party had taken over the upstairs and had gradually overtaken the downstairs, too. He had shut his bedroom door, but he would be lucky if no one was inside fucking by the time he was able to get Lily to leave Beth's.

The pole in the workout area was surrounded by a large group of brothers. Shade took the first step upstairs, casually looking over to see which woman was drawing all the attention. He nearly fell up the steps when he saw Lily swinging from the pole.

He turned, watching as his wife hooked a leg around it, falling backward and giving the brothers a view of her tits which nearly fell out of the tiny, red leather top she was wearing. It was tied in a bow between her breasts.

She raised herself with only the strength of her thigh muscles, and Shade saw Lily was wearing a pair of matching red booty shorts which showed the bottom curve of her ass.

She turned, using her arms to lift her up the pole, her thighs clenching it as she climbed toward the ceiling.

"Holy fuck!" Lucky said, coming down the steps, his mouth hanging open.

When Shade glared at him, starting to go up the steps, Lucky took one look at him and ran off, running upstairs and slamming the door behind him.

Shade went to the music, turning it off. The men turned, about to yell, only to see Shade's furious face.

"Get out, now."

The brothers left, going up the steps as they threw him envious looks.

"Doesn't the brother know we're about sharing?" one brother from Ohio complained.

"Why don't you go remind him?" Rider suggested as they went up the steps.

The brother snapped his mouth closed, the others following behind him.

"Rider, shut the door!" Shade yelled up behind the brother who was lingering at the top of the stairs.

He waited until he heard the door slam before he turned the music back on then walked back to stand next to the pole.

"You can finish your performance now," Shade told Lily who was holding onto the pole at the top.

"I'm not in the mood anymore," she snapped. "The only ones who would have appreciated it are gone."

"Angel, I appreciated watching your ass climb that pole, believe me. What I don't appreciate is that the brothers from Ohio saw it, too."

"So, you wouldn't have minded if it had been the men here?"

"I would have minded, but they would have been smart enough not to watch."

"Rider watched," Lily taunted.

"He doesn't count—he can't help himself," Shade said. "If you're not going to continue, why don't you come down?" Shade asked conversationally.

"Because you're mad at me," Lily explained.

"Isn't that what you wanted?"

"I've changed my mind."

"Come down, now," Shade said through gritted teeth. "Or I'm coming up to get you."

Lily loosened her thighs, sliding down the pole.

"Are those the shoes I bought you last year?"

"Yes."

Shade stared down at the gold high-heeled shoes which had cost almost as much as a bar of gold.

"You need to buy another pair," Shade told her, his eyes going over her taut body. "Go to the bedroom."

Lily sidled past him, walking through the basement and down the hallway. Shade followed behind her, his eyes never leaving her ass.

His wife had a perfect ass. He had to admit it was one of the reasons he had fallen in love with her, right after he had seen her eyes. It was her ass which had sealed the deal, though.

Shade closed the door, leaning back against it with his arms crossed in front of his chest, watching as his wife shifted nervously from foot to foot.

"Would you like to go to your safe spot?" Shade asked.

"No."

"Do you remember your safe word?"

"Blueberries."

"Good. By the way, before I forget, where did you get that outfit?"

"Vida bought it for me. It came in the mail last week."

"She the one who showed you those new stripper moves?"

Lily reluctantly nodded.

"You have me debating whether we should join them for vacation this year. You'll have to earn that privilege."

"Fuck you," Lily snapped. Then horror filled her eyes as she slapped a hand over her mouth.

Shade guessed it was okay to use the curse word when playing around, but not in anger. He shook his head. Trying to figure Lily out would give him a headache, and he had another ache to take care of first.

"We'll deal with your disrespect later. By the way, that's number twenty-four."

"Twenty-four?" Lily questioned.

"Twenty-four times you have disrespected me since you found out you were pregnant. It's time I brought your punishments up to date, which I will rectify after we're done talking."

"There's nothing to talk about, is there?" Lily said, turning her face away from him. "You think I'm too emotionally unstable to talk to or have sex with. Even when you *did* have sex with me, you went easy on me because you were afraid I couldn't handle it, didn't you?"

"Yes and no." Shade raised his hand. "Never having experienced a Dom/sub relationship, I wanted to find out how you would deal with one. I didn't want to throw you in the deep end if you couldn't deal with the lifestyle. I wanted to find the parts you liked and give that to you, and then we could go further slowly."

"What if I didn't like any of it?"

"Then I would have stopped."

"You can't stop being who you are for me." Lily's anger had her flushing. Her hands went to her hips. "You do that all the time. Why do you work at the factory? Bliss said you hate it; do you?"

"Yes," Shade admitted truthfully.

"Then why are you doing it?"

"Because when I asked Viper for the job the summer you wanted to work there, that was the deal. I couldn't toss it away when I was done with it unless I found someone to replace me who does it just as well."

"Then find someone," Lily said with frustration.

"Who? Name me one Last Rider who can do it as well as I can. I'm not bragging; I'm actually good at it. It's hard and time-consuming, and you have to deal with the brothers and women who would rather be in bed than filling orders."

"Razer," Lily blurted.

Shade shook his head. "He hates it as much as I do."

Shade could see her thinking of the rest of the brothers.

"Lucky?"

"He's been tied down for years with the church and dealing with the demands of others, so he deserves a break for a while. Besides, he's Viper's VP, and he's staying pretty busy with that job. Viper has his hands full with the two clubhouses, and he handles the business side of the factory. Lucky is actually with him on that."

Lily went quiet then an inexplicable look crossed her face.

"I know someone who can handle the job."

"Who?" Shade asked, ready to shoot her idea down. He had already thought this over several times before he had accepted. He was stuck with the job for the foreseeable future.

"Jewell."

Shade opened his mouth to come up with a reason she couldn't then closed it when he realized she was right. Jewell was tough but fair. She was often on time more than he was, and she was always willing to pitch in when help was needed. She was also extremely smart.

"I'll talk to her."

Lily's face glowed. "What are you going to do if you don't manage the factory?"

"I'll still have to work there two days a week. We all have to put that time in. The other three days, I could work on my projects more. Some of the patents The Last Riders have were developed by me, and I'd like to spend more time doing that," Shade admitted.

"Why didn't you suggest any of the other women?" he asked, his lips twitching. "Bliss, for example?

Lily rolled her eyes. "We're not exactly on speaking terms right now. Besides, she's never on time and fills the orders too slowly. If she were to run the factory, it would be backed up with orders in two days."

"Why aren't you on speaking terms?"

"Did you know she was in love with you?" Lily asked instead of answering him.

"I suspected that she was, but neither of us talked about it, and she was aware I didn't return her feelings."

"You didn't feel bad about having sex with her, knowing you didn't return her feelings?"

Shade remained silent, raising a brow.

"I'll take that as a no." Lily blew her tumbled hair out of her face. "You're a..."

"Whatever you're about to call me, think about it and decide if it's worth another stroke."

"Ass. Jerk," Lily continued defiantly.

"Aren't we little Mrs. Spitfire tonight? That's twenty-six." Her fiery look had him struggling to retain his impassive expression. "Suppose you tell me what you want from me."

"I want you to treat me like I'm your freakin' wife! I want you to treat me as if I won't break if you play too rough with me!" She stomped her foot in the high heels, almost toppling over. "Forget the safe word. I know the words 'no' and 'stop'! I know the difference between those men raping me when I was younger and Saul whipping us. There's a difference. You love me; they didn't! I would never confuse you with them."

"You sure?"

"Yes."

Shade grinned, straightening. "Then let's see how you deal with your first real punishment."

Lily's dueling expressions had him going to the new cabinet he had purchased. He unlocked the side with his new toys, taking out his whip and flogger. Laying them on the foot of the bed, he then went to the wall beside the bed, taking down the two pictures and propping them against the wall several feet away.

Going back to the cabinet, he pulled out a set of chains, deciding on a thicker set than he had used on her before. The thinner ones were more like jewelry; these were not. Each time she moved, she would be aware of their weight.

Taking a pair of handcuffs which were padded, he closed the cabinet.

"Come here," Shade ordered.

Lily walked toward him in the stripper outfit. Red was definitely her color.

Reaching out, he pulled at one of the strips of cloth coming down from the bow. It easily came untied, the cups of the top barely covering her nipples.

"I'm surprised you had the courage to walk through the room in this outfit."

"I was angry," Lily confessed.

"That makes two of us," Shade said. "I'll be right back."

He left the room, coming back a few minutes later carrying the workout mat. He closed the door with his booted foot.

Lily's eyes widened, watching as he used the loops on the end to hang the mat against the wall on the hooks the pictures had been hanging on.

"That's convenient," Lily snapped.

"I thought so." Shade turned to face her when he was finished hanging the mat.

"Take off those shorts."

Lily started to take off the heels.

"Leave those on," Shade instructed her.

Lily paused then went to the chair, holding on to it as she pulled the tight shorts down her hips. Shade nearly had a heart attack when he saw what was underneath it.

A tiny black patch of material barely covered her pussy lips, and it was held in place by three tiny strings.

"Turn around," he ordered hoarsely.

Lily obediently turned. He wanted to bend her over the chair and fuck her when he saw the black string between the cheeks of her ass. From his view, he could see her pussy.

"You can turn back around."

Once Lily turned, her hands went to her hips to pull the tiny thong off.

"Leave it on. Come here."

Lily walked seductively toward him, coming to a stop in front of him. He reached out to touch the patch, feeling how damp she already was. A blush filled her face when his finger went to his mouth, licking at the taste of her.

"Take my shirt off. From now on, you're going to undress me every time we're in this room," Shade ordered.

"Yes, Sir."

He studied her expression, seeing only acceptance.

Raising his arms, she took off his shirt. When it was in her hands, she folded it then placed it on the chair before coming back to him.

Shade took off his boots, leaving the jeans for her. Her hands went to his zipper, lowering it, and then she pulled the pants down. When he stepped out of them, she folded his jeans and placed them on the chair.

Shade drew her toward the mat, turning her to face him. "Give me your hand."

When she held her hand out, he lifted it over her head after placing the cuff on her wrist, attaching it to the hook on the wall. Then he did the same with her other wrist.

He stepped away just long enough to turn his music on then returned to Lily, admiring the seductive picture she made.

With her arms cuffed above her head, the cups of the top of her bra left her tits bare. Shade took one of the ties used to make the bow, raising it as his other hand lifted her breast. He twined the tie over and under her breast, not too tightly, but enough to give her the sensation of being tied. He held the end with his teeth while he wrapped the other breast with the other tie. When he finished, he lifted his head. Then, taking the end of both ties, he tied both ends together in a knot.

Her nipples poked out from the cords and her tits were pushed together, creating a deep cleavage.

Using his foot, he used it to make her widen her stance. He took a step backward again to observe his handiwork.

"If I didn't want to fuck that ass so bad tonight, I would fuck your tits," Shade stated darkly, stepping toward her then bending down to lick each nipple, making them tighten.

Lily whimpered. Shade ran a finger under the cords to make sure they weren't too tight. Then his hand went back to her pussy, rubbing it through the black patch.

Going to his knees, he ran his tongue under the material, only giving her the barest touch of it against her pink flesh before standing again.

His hands went to her waist. "Your safe word?"

"Blueberries."

Shade spun her to face the wall, turning the hook so it would flip.

His cock swelled as he ran his hand over her ass before going to her hair, tugging until her head fell back.

He stared into her eyes, letting the Dom in him have something it had never had with Lily—full reign.

"If you ever walk out of my bedroom like you did tonight, I will drag you in here then punish you in front of them."

"Yes, Sir."

"I'm getting sick and tired of you running every time you're mad at me. Do it again, and I'll chain you to my wall and fuck you until I come, and I'll make fucking sure you won't for a week."

"Yes, Sir."

"How many strokes did I say you deserved?"

"Twenty-six." Lily's voice was calm, and Shade heard no fear.

Stepping back, he picked up his whip, taking the position he wanted. He raised the whip, sending it forward. The last time he had used his whip on her, he had gently led her into her seduction. This time, it was what it was.

The sting he gave her had her going to the tips of her toes. He waited to hear her safe word, and when she remained silent, he raised it again. The first five strikes were little stings which would string together, giving her a light burning sensation.

He moved his trajectory of the whip to her other cheek, giving it the same treatment.

"How many is that?"

"Ten," Lily answered.

"How many more?"

"Sixteen."

Shade raised his whip again, that time making her back his target. The whip flew across the room too quick for the eye to catch. Each time the snap of the whip hit her flesh, it sounded throughout the room.

"How many?"

"Twenty."

"How many more?"

"Six."

Shade walked back to the wall, flipping her forward so she would be able to witness the last of her punishment. Going back to his position, the whip flew out again, hitting the cords which tied her breasts. Lily moaned. He gave her two more strikes, and she began whimpering.

"If you come, I will stop, and I will sleep on the couch tonight," Shade threatened. From her reaction, she really didn't like that threat. "If you deny something I want, I will deny you something you want." Shade could practically see her trying to gain control of her impending climax. When he saw she had it, he cupped her pussy, rubbing his thumb over the patch which covered it.

Shade unhooked her arms. Taking off the handcuff and chains, he unwound the cords from her breasts, tracing a finger along the faint red lines.

"Who do you belong to?"

"You."

"Do you flaunt yourself in front of other men?"

"No."

"You want to flaunt yourself in front of anyone, I'll call Knox and invite him and Diamond over."

"Yes, Sir."

"How many more strokes do you deserve?"

"As many as you think I deserve, Sir."

"That was a good answer. I'll have to reward you for that one. Get on the bed on your hands and knees."

Lily went to the bed as Shade went to the nightstand, taking out the tube of lubricant before getting on the bed behind her.

"Do you have any idea how much I fantasize about your ass?"

"No, Sir."

Shade ignored her pussy, squirting the lubrication on her tight hole. Using his finger, he thrust inside, working it gently in. Her hands and legs trembled but when she would have crawled forward, his hand came down on her ass and she froze in place.

He inserted another finger slowly, beginning to finger-fuck her to stretch the tight opening. He moved closer to her from behind, his other hand going to her belly before slipping under the thin string, gliding under the patch to rub her clit. Lily moaned.

"Don't come," Shade warned her again.

Removing his fingers from her ass, he put on a condom then placed his cock at the entrance and slid inside her inch by inch, feeling his own climax building to almost an uncontrollable point.

"I'm going to make you beg me for it," Shade said, sliding inside of her until his balls rested against her. He leaned over her back, his mouth going to her neck. "What do you want me to do?"

"Move...please, move," Lily pleaded.

"That's not enough. Give me what I want...and I'll give you what you want."

"Fuck me! Please. Please...fuck me." Lily buried her face in the blanket.

"Eyes, Lily. Turn your head and watch me fuck you."

Lily's head tilted to the side, watching as he slid his dick out then pounded it back inside her ass from the mirrors on the wall. A small scream escaped her as he lost control, giving her everything he had, driving himself deep.

Just as he felt himself about to come, he pulled out. Ripping off the condom and her thong, he rammed his cock into her pussy, stroking it roughly inside of her. Her screams intensified as Shade pinched her clit.

"I have to come...please, can I come?"

"Come for me, angel."

Shade released her clit at the same time he surged forward, grinding his cock inside of her. Unleashing his passions, he spilled his own release in her throbbing pussy.

Lily was crying when he turned her to face him.

"Are you all right? Did I hurt you?"

Both of them were on their knees facing each other.

Lily shook as she stared up at him. "Is that what you've been holding back from me?"

Shade nodded, waiting for her slap or recriminations for hurting her. She shoved him hard against his chest, toppling him over onto the mattress before leaning over him, lowering her face to his.

"The next time I think you're holding back on me, I will be the one sleeping on the couch."

Shade laughed as her long hair fell forward and surrounded them. He lifted a hand, twirling a tendril around his finger. "I promise I won't hold back with you anymore."

Content, she dropped to his side, laying her head on his shoulder and placing her hand on his heart.

"I agree with you," Lily said.

"Of course you do," he stated arrogantly.

"Don't you want to know about what?" Lily teased.

"I'm always right, but you can tell me which time you're talking about," he teased her back.

"Fifty years won't be enough time." Lily rubbed her cheek against his.

Shade lost his good humor.

Turning his head on the mattress, he said, "Don't joke about that, or at least wait a while before you do. I haven't recovered from you being in the hospital last time." His eyes clouded at remembering how close he had come to losing her.

"I won't." She glided her hand over his chest, soothing him.

"Ouch! What the fuck was that for?" He stared at the bright red bite mark on his shoulder.

"Did you threaten to marry Bliss?"

"I might have, but I was desperate. I had already tried everything else."

Lily rose up on her elbow. "And did you say you would give our son cheap formula?"

"You already knew I'm a tightwad." Shade shrugged, moving his shoulder away from her vicious teeth.

"You ass!" Lily's head fell forward as she burst out laughing.

"You're not going to say anything about what I said about him joining The Last Riders?"

"Shade, he already belongs. We both do."

CHAPTER NINETY-SEVEN

Shade woke and glanced at the clock before sliding silently out of the bed. Going downstairs, he fixed a bottle before treading back upstairs to the nursery. He opened the door then went to his son's crib where John was wiggling, his hands waving in the air.

"Daddy's here." Shade lifted his son, changed his diaper, and then sat down in the rocking chair. He placed the nipple in John's searching mouth as his foot set the chair rocking back and forth.

"You're getting bigger every day. Your grandpa King brought you a fishing pole by today, said he was going to teach you how to fish." Shade stared at the different sized colored fish he had painted on the nursery walls.

"Don't worry; I'll go with you and show you how to catch them. Your grandpa can't fish for shit. The only thing he's ever caught worth keeping was Evie."

His son stared up at him with sleepy eyes that were now the exact color of Lily's and King's. Shade cupped his hand behind John's head, ruffling the silky black hair.

Shade would never forget the day he had thought his son had been crushed underneath their house. The Last Riders had worked hard to help them rebuild it, only taking three months to complete. He was sure having a baby in the clubhouse had sped up the process. Not one Friday party had taken place while they had stayed there, despite Shade telling them it was unnecessary since he kept Lily and John downstairs. However, no one had wanted to. Instead, they had usually spent the Fridays grilling burgers and hanging out in the television room with the women fighting over who would hold John.

Shade lifted his son to burp him. When John finished, Shade made no attempt to put his son back to bed, cuddling him against his chest as he rocked his son back to sleep.

Staring down at his perfect son, he didn't have to wonder at the emotion that filled him whenever he shared these private moments. It was contentment.

"You're going to spoil him," Lily warned softly from the doorway

"You can't spoil a baby by holding him too much." Shade lifted John closer to his chest as Lily came farther into the room, dropping down to the carpet where she rested her head against his leg.

"Do you miss it?"

Shade didn't have to ask what she was questioning him about. It was their first night in their new home, and you could still hear the noises coming from the clubhouse. Shade was sure they were celebrating not having a baby in the clubhouse anymore.

"No, and if I do, we can always get Evie or Fat Louise to babysit." He stared down at her with a wicked smile, not missing the shiver that coursed through her body and the tightening of her nipples against her thin gown. "Or I can wait until John's asleep and tie you up to have my way with you then."

"You don't have to tie me down to do that."

"Would you enjoy it as much?"

Lily laughed, shaking her head at him as she wrapped an arm around his leg and laid her cheek against his thigh.

"Anyway you take me, I enjoy," Lily confessed, staring up at him holding their child.

A serious look crossed her face before she laid her head back on his thigh. Shade reached down to smooth her tumbled hair.

"Thank you."

"What for?" She looked up at him in confusion.

"For John."

"You're welcome, even though your fifty percent responsible for him being here. It's not cramping your style being a dad?"

"Hell no, but I do have to admit to one thing," Shade said in mock seriousness, leaning forward to hand her their child.

"What's that?" She smiled worriedly, taking John into her arms. Then her nose wrinkled as she began laughing.

"Not crazy about changing his diapers."

ಬ ಛ

Shade jogged across the beach, feeling the warm sand under his bare feet. Drawing closer to the attractive woman sitting on the lounge chair in a dark blue bikini, he came to a stop.

"Mind if I join you?" he asked, staring down at Brooke's surprised face which quickly turned pale. She sat up in her chair, looking around the exclusive beach resort. Seeing several people nearby, she relaxed.

"Yes. I'll call security—"

"Why would you do that? Unlike you, it's not my method to kill anyone with witnesses around."

Shade sat down in the chair next to hers, and the waiter immediately approached for his order.

"Bring me what's she having. A mojito?" Shade looked at her questioningly, and Brooke nodded. "Charge it to my room."

Shade leaned back on the chair as the waiter left, feeling her eyes greedily taking in his tattooed chest. The sunglasses hid his eyes which were blazing with hatred for the woman.

"Did you really think you could hide from me when you skipped bail?"

"How did you find me?"

"Because I'm a nice guy, I'll tell you. It was easy. All I had to do was follow the money trail. Merrick and your parents are providing you with ample funds, even enough to take care of that pesky scar Lily gave you, I see. It was smart to pick a place where the United States doesn't have extradition."

"I thought so. I left a letter in case…" Brooke replied smugly.

"In case you were killed? Yeah, I know that's what you told Lily. Kaley told Train where he could find it. He said it only took one lick to her pussy before she was singing like a bird. You should have picked someone better to confide in. Needless to say, I destroyed it and the rest of the information on me you managed to fuck out of the poor sucker you had wrapped around your finger in the CIA. He no longer works for the agency, by the way." Shade nodded to the waiter to place his drink on the table between the two chairs where Brooke's drink was sitting.

"Why are you here?" Brooke took her sunglasses off, glancing around the beach once again.

"Don't worry, I didn't bring any of The Last Riders to drag you back to jail. You have nothing to fear from me. I promised Lily I wouldn't lay a hand on you or shoot you."

"You did? I'm beginning to wonder what I ever saw in you. You've become just like every other man I know—a pussy," she said nastily.

Shade shrugged. "It was never my intention to impress you, anyway."

Brooke's eyes were caught by the striking woman walking down the beach toward them in the tiny, black bikini which barely covered her gorgeous body. The bottoms barely covered her front.

"You ready for lunch, Shade?" The woman had Brooke flushing in anger as she came to a stop by Brooke's chair, forcing her to look up into the bright sun.

"Does your wife know you have a new whore?"

When the woman took a step forward, Shade got to his feet and caught her arm, holding her back.

"Here, take my drink and go over there and wait for me." Shade handed her his drink then watched her walk away in appreciation.

Bringing his focus back to the sole reason he was here, he stood up. "Goodbye, Brooke."

"You're leaving?"

"Of course. It's a beautiful day, and I don't plan on spending another second of it with you." Shade stood up and walked a few feet before she stopped him.

"I don't understand. Why...?"

Shade paused, turning back to her. "What? Oh...I forgot to tell you. Evie said goodbye, too." He began to walk away again. "Enjoy the sun, Brooke. It's the last day you will ever fuckin' feel it on your face."

"Shade...wait!"

He didn't stop. Walking away, he could hear the fear and frustration at his presence when she had thought she was out of his reach.

Shade dropped down in the lounge chair next to the woman who had helped him exact his revenge by being the perfect distraction.

"Finish your drink. Our plane leaves in a couple of hours."

Killyama picked up her drink, staring in puzzlement at Brooke who was finishing her Mojito.

"That's it?"

"Yes. I'm ready to go home."

"So, we're even now for you saving Fat Louise?"

"I told you that, if you came here with me for a week, the slate would be wiped clean."

"I know, but I didn't expect us to be staying in separate rooms when you said it."

"Did you really expect me to cheat on Lily?" Shade asked with a raised brow.

"No, but I thought..."

"That it would be Train here when you arrived?"

Killyama remained silent, taking another sip of her drink.

"For what it's worth, Train wasn't happy when I called in all his IOUs. He's going to be even madder when I tell him about that swimsuit you have on. He'll probably never play poker with me again, and he's my second best mark."

Killyama grinned evilly. "I'll let you take a picture to give the fucker something to think about. So, The Last Riders all know we're here this week? How did you explain that to Lily?"

Screams and yells filled the air as people ran to the lounge chair where Brooke was hunched over, her body twisting and turning in excruciating pain.

Shade watched in pure fucking pleasure as she died.

"I told her I needed to set up a trial study for Rachel's plant."

Epilogue One

Four Years Later

"I told you so," Shade said, coming up behind her to place his arms around her protruding belly.

"What about this time?" Lily said softly.

"That Evie would have her baby first."

"You bet against your own child?"

Shade shrugged. "King did, too."

Evie shook her head at the two men as she settled on the couch. Lily handed her baby Sophia, who was sound asleep.

"John, don't you dare eat that. It's almost dinner time. Go tell Aunt Beth and Uncle Razer dinner's ready." Lily took the cupcake away, watching as John put on his coat before he ran out the front door. Then she pulled the wrapper off and took a bite of the pink cupcake.

"I'm telling," Shade said, taking the cupcake away just to place the last bite in his mouth.

Evie and King shook their heads at the couple.

"You two shouldn't fight on your anniversary." Evie handed the baby to King.

Evie wasn't the only one to blink back the tears at the expression on King's face in that moment.

Shade handed his wife a napkin when she asked, "Can you take the turkey out of the oven for me?"

He went to the oven, pulling the gigantic bird out. "Couldn't you find a bigger one?"

"That was the biggest." Lily set the platter on the counter for him to transfer the turkey to before she went to place the sides on the table.

Shade watched to make sure she didn't try to lift anything too heavy.

John ran back in, holding the door for Beth and Razer and their children. He was glad he had listened to Lily's suggestion when she had asked for a bigger dining room when he had rebuilt their home.

Shade relaxed during dinner. They had decided to have a family dinner before Lily and the others went to church. The following day, they would share Christmas dinner at the clubhouse.

Shade stayed home alone when everyone else went to church, using the opportunity to put together a few of the toys Lily had bought for John. He had barely managed to do half before they were back.

As Lily finished cleaning the kitchen, Shade took John upstairs for his bath where he shaved while his son played.

"Daddy?"

"Hmm?"

"Mommy said you married her on Christmas Eve."

"That's right."

"I'm going to marry her on Christmas Eve when I grow up."

Shade laughed, splashing water on his face then drying off with a towel. Picking another one up, he dried off his son before helping him dress in his pajamas.

"You can't marry your mother when you grow up," Shade said as they went into John's bedroom.

"I can, too!"

Shade pulled the covers down, giving his son a stern glance.

John's bottom lip trembled as he climbed into bed. "Why can't I marry her?"

"Because she's already taken. You have to catch your own."

"How do I do that? Do I sneak up behind them and grab them?"

"No, that might get you arrested by Uncle Knox, so don't do that. You have to be sneaky. You have to make them like you first, a whole lot. Then, when they think you're the most special thing on Earth, like Daddy did to Mommy, you tell her your secret."

"I do?"

"Yes."

"What's the secret?"

"That you love her and think she's the most special thing on Earth, too."

"I can do that."

"I know you can." Shade ruffled his hair before bending down to place a kiss on his son's cheek.

"Night, son."

"Good night, Daddy."

Shade turned to the door, seeing Lily standing in the doorway. She gave him her smile as she passed by him to kiss John and tuck him in bed.

Shade waited for her in the hallway, closing the door behind her when she came out.

"Happy anniversary, Shade."

"Happy anniversary, Lily."

"Do you still think fifty years isn't going to be long enough?" Lily teased.

"Yes," Shade admitted. "Not nearly long enough." He lifted her into his arms, carrying her into their bedroom where he placed her on their bed. Then he lay down next to her, enjoying the peaceful tranquility of the night. It wouldn't be much longer before their nights of sleep were interrupted with the sounds of a crying baby.

"What are you thinking about?"

"Wishing my baby girl would hurry and get here."

"I love the rainbows and unicorns you painted on the nursery walls. It's beautiful. Thank you."

"You're welcome." Shade smiled down at her before nuzzling her neck.

"Shade?"

"Hmm?

"I think you're the most special man on Earth, and I love you."

Epilogue Two

Another Fourteen Years Later

"John Wayne Hunter!" Lily scolded.

His son turned around, avoiding his cousins' amused eyes as he turned back and walked back to his mother.

"You forgot your backpack."

John blushed, picking up the backpack.

"Be safe, John."

His son's face gentled as he stared back at his mother, who was doing a horrible job keeping it together. John grabbed her for one more hug, "I will, Mom. I've promised you a thousand times."

"I know, I know." Shade placed his arm around Lily's shoulders, pulling her close to his side.

"You three watch out for each other, and you'll be fine," Shade advised his son.

"We will, Dad. I have to go; our plane's boarding. Chance and Noah are already on board."

When Shade held his hand out to his son, John ignored it, reaching out to hug him one more time.

"Bye, Dad."

"Bye, son." Shade stood there, watching his son board the plane which would take him, Noah, and Chance to basic training. He wouldn't see him again for six months, and then John would only be able to stay for a few short days before he was given his first assign-ment.

"We should have never let him enlist."

"We both agreed to let him make his own decisions, Lily."

"That's where we made our first mistake. The rest of our children, we're telling them no," she said firmly, getting inside the car.

It was a three-hour drive home, and Lily cried most of the way back. Shade pulled into the parking lot, bringing the car to a stop.

"You going to let the kids see how upset you are?" When Lily didn't answer, he shook his head at her. "Well?"

"I'm thinking about it," she snapped. "That way, if they think about joining, they'll know how upset I was when John did it."

"Do you want them to make their decisions based on how much it's going to upset you?"

"Yes." Lily crossed her arms over her chest.

Shade slid out of the car, going to the other side to open the door for her. She got out of the car but instead of walking up the pathway to their house like he expected, she wrapped her arms around his waist and buried her face in his chest.

"I'm going to miss him so much."

"I know. I am, too," Shade told her, hugging her close.

Eventually she nodded, stepping away so he could close the door.

"What are you going to do with his bike while he's gone?" she asked as they walked up the pathway, hand in hand.

"Put it in the storage room where Rider keeps his."

They passed Beth's and Razer's house, which was dark. They had decided to stay in Lexington for the night and come back in the morning.

Shade held onto her hand as they walked up the steps to their porch.

"Shade?" He paused as he was about to open the door. "I'm sorry I cried all the way back. I'll try harder not to be a crybaby. I promised myself I would be more like—"

"What have I told you about trying to be like those bitches?"

Lily laughed. "I was going to say like Beth."

"Oh, that you can do."

"I bet you're regretting wanting fifty years of the trouble I've put you through."

"Lily, where you're concerned, I only have one regret." Shade bent down and kissed her.

"What's that?" Lily stared back at him with the same love in her eyes and expression as she'd had that long-ago spring day.

"That I didn't catch you sooner. I should have sneaked up behind you and carried you away."

"I would have had you arrested." Lily shook her head.

"I knew the sheriff and had a lawyer who ended up becoming Attorney General. I would have gotten off."

EPILOGUE THREE

Another thirty-two years later

Shade walked behind John as his eldest son packed his mother to sit on the bench they had placed in the yard over twenty years before so Lily could sit and stare at her mountains.

John carefully placed her on the bench, moving aside so Shade could sit down next to Lily.

"You need anything, Dad?"

"No, thanks. We'll be fine. Go enjoy the picnic."

Shade leaned back against the bench, placing his arm around her shoulders. She laid her head against him.

"I shouldn't have let you talk me into coming outside," Shade said, seeing the pain she was trying to hide.

"It's beautiful out today. I wanted to watch the grandkids play before they went home. I wish we could have gone to the picnic in town."

"Everybody's here," Shade told her. It was the first Fourth of July picnic they hadn't attended.

Lily shivered next to him.

"Are you cold?" he asked in concern.

"I'm fine, Shade."

Her hand reached for his as they sat watching their children and grandchildren enjoy the sunny afternoon.

Piper brought them both a bottled water.

"She looks just like you," Lily said when their granddaughter ran off to play with one of Chance's children.

Lily watched the huge crowd. "Did you ever dream our family would become this large?"

"Angel, my life with you exceeded any dreams I had," Shade told her, brushing her lips with his.

Lily brushed the tears from her cheek then stared down at her wedding ring.

"Did I ever tell you about the day you said you saw me at the ice cream store?"

627

"No."

"Beth had picked me up from school that day, I usually walked home, but her client had called and asked Beth to pick up a prescription for her. While they were filling the prescription, she decided to pick me up. As we drove to get the prescription we passed the ice cream store. I suddenly wanted an ice cream cone." Lily laughed self-consciously. "I don't even like ice cream. How many times do you ever remember me eating it?"

"None, actually," Shade said, going back through their years together. Lily nodded at his answer.

"I just had to have it right then." Lily relaxed against him. "I think it was meant for you to see me that day."

"Angel, Treepoint is small, and I saw you again at the lake. All I needed was one look." Shade tenderly picked up her hand bearing his ring. "Besides, I was only slightly interested in you that day," he teased. "I actually didn't fall in love with you until I saw you in that pink bikini at the lake."

They watched as the men gathered to set off the fireworks, sending the children to stand on his porch so they would have the best view.

"They bought a lot." Lily laughed, commenting on the fact that John, Noah, and Chance had purchased a lot of illegal fireworks. It had taken them over an hour to set them up, and they would be shooting them off when it was dark enough.

"Ridge is just like his dad. He always had to be a show-off," Shade said wryly as they watched him performing wheelies in the parking lot.

His eyes were caught by a movement at one of the picnic tables. His face went ice cold, and he started to get up from the bench. However, Lily's hand caught his, preventing him from going to the couple sitting at the picnic table.

"Shade, leave them alone."

"Hell, no, that shit's not going to happen!"

Lily shook her head at him. "She loves him. Don't spoil it for them."

Shade watched his granddaughter sitting with the president of The Last Riders. He wasn't embarrassed to admit that Violet held a special place in his heart. She was almost an exact replica of Lily. If he had ever wondered what Lily would have been like nurtured in a healthy and loving environment, Violet had answered those questions. John and his wife had done an excellent job raising their daughter. No one could resist her loving and sweet personality. Evidently, not even the man who had taken over as president.

Looking at the succeeding president, Shade reminisced to that night, so many, many years ago, when Viper, Gavin, Razer, Rider, Knox, Cash, Levi, and himself had sat in that motorcycle bar, planning their own motorcycle club. It had been the birth of The Last Riders and the start of so many memories, both good and bad...

Shade wrapped his arm around the stripper's shoulder, leading her off the dance floor to the table the others were sitting at.

Taking a chair next to Viper, he sat down and pulled the stripper onto his lap.

The men spread around the table stared at him balefully.

"You trying to get our asses maimed so we can't go back on duty?" Levi shook his head at Shade.

"What?" Shade asked, lifting the beer the stripper handed him to his mouth.

"You know what," Viper said sarcastically. "She belongs to those bikers over by the bar. We're already on their shit list for being in here, anyway."

Shade shrugged. "It's a biker bar, and we're bikers, aren't we?"

"Occasionally, when we're not getting munitions thrown at us." Gavin grinned.

Viper shot his brother a glance. "In a few months, we'll be riding all the time. I never want to ride in another DPV again. Every time I get out, I feel like my balls are going to fall off."

"I kinda of like it," Gavin said, hitting his brother on the back. "Calm down. If Shade starts a fight, we'll deal. I'm bored, anyway, since he managed to grab the only woman in this dump with a decent pair of tits.

"We ever live to see the end of our tour, we'll have our own bar and beat the shit out of assholes like us." Gavin winked at Viper.

"You're planning on starting a biker club?" Rider grinned, his hand going under the table to the thigh of the stripper.

Shade shifted her closer to Rider. He didn't want to take the chance he would grab anything that was attached to him.

"Hell yes. Want to join when you get out?" Gavin asked.

Shade hid his smile when Viper rolled his eyes.

"Fuck yeah. Just let me know where, and I'll be there as soon as I get out," Rider told him.

The stripper's head fell back on Shade's shoulder.

"You in, Levi?" Gavin turned to him next.

Levi watched Rider and Shade with the stripper, shaking his head. "No, Evie and I are getting married when we get out. She'd kick my ass if I tried to join a biker club."

Gavin frowned. "What about you, Cash?"

"Count me in. I have no place I want to go back to."

"Train?" Gavin asked, motioning for the waitress to bring them another round.

"I'm with Cash. I haven't got anything waiting for me, either. Sounds better than what I had planned."

"What did you have planned?" Shade asked, his hand going to the stripper's waist and sliding under her see-through top. The men could easily see him playing with her nipple.

"Re-enlisting."

The men at the table laughed.

"Knox?"

"No thanks. Me and Sunshine are going to buy a house and start having kids when we get out."

"Shit, you and Sunshine are getting married?" Rider asked.

The stripper was moaning loudly now. Several of the men at the table were forced to shift in their chairs to adjust themselves.

"Shit, quiet her down, Shade," Viper hissed.

Shade saw the angry glares focused on their table.

Bending down, he whispered in her ear, *"Make another sound, and Rider will stop."*

She immediately shut up.

"I wish I knew how you did that," Levi said.

"What about you, Shade? You going to join us?" Gavin asked.

"I'll think about it."

"What's to think about? Bikes, bitches, and fighting all the time." Gavin leaned back in his chair. *"Viper can be the president; I'll be his vice; Cash can be his lieutenant; and you can be his enforcer."*

"That does sound tempting." Shade gave Gavin a half smile. *"What about you Reid? You in?"*

"Yeah, he had me at the bitches," Reid laughed.

"Well?" Gavin prodded.

"I'll give it a try. If I like it, I'll stay," Shade told him.

"I'm glad you're in, Shade," Viper snapped. *"Your first duty as our enforcer is to get us out of here alive."* He stood up as four of the bikers who had been glaring at them started coming at them as the stripper began shaking with her climax.

Shade sighed, standing up to set the woman on his chair.

"Sorry, that's all you'll be getting tonight," Shade said regretfully. He had been looking forward to fucking her. It was his own fault. He should have taken her to the back ten minutes ago and fucked her in the bathroom.

He waited until the bikers were almost on top of them before picking up Viper's empty chair. Spotting the biggest one, Shade left him to Knox. The one in front was the leader, so that was the one he needed to take out.

Before the biker could open his mouth, Shade crashed the chair down on his head.

"Fuck! Next time, give us some warning," Viper snarled as the bar broke into a brawl that left the bikers with bloody injuries and the furniture broken. They didn't stop until the cops arrived, pulling them off the unconscious bikers.

"They started it!" Levi yelled as he was getting cuffed. "You're explaining this to Evie, Shade."

Shade grunted as two officers threw him to the ground, handcuffing him before lifting him to his feet and dragging him outside.

"If anybody gets a phone call, call Lucky and tell him to come bail us out." Viper groaned when the cop slammed him against the patrol car.

They were all driven to the local police station and placed in a holding cell.

"Damn, the bikers didn't touch me. The cops did more damage with that fucking taser," Knox groaned.

Gavin started chuckling.

"What the fuck is so funny?" Viper glared at him, pissed.

Gavin placed his arm around Viper's shoulders. "We were the last ones standing. We were outnumbered three to one, and we still kicked their asses."

"That's what we should call our club," Shade said, shifting to try to make himself more comfortable. They hadn't taken his cuffs off.

"What?" Gavin asked.

"The Last Riders."

"Remember when King had the same reaction to you?" Lily reminded him, bringing Shade back to the present.

"I don't give a fuck. Brick makes me look like a saint," Shade snarled.

"I wouldn't go that far." She laughed.

Shade gritted his teeth, staring at the man who had stolen his granddaughter while he had been recovering in the hospital.

"Where's Lucky? I may not be able to kick Brick's ass, but I can his grandfather."

"The men would laugh at two old men fighting in the backyard." Lily shook her head at him.

"They won't laugh long," Shade threatened.

"Shade, look at her. She loves him."

His lips tightened. Violet's eyes gazed at him with tears in her eyes at knowing he was upset with the two of them together. She had been living in Tennessee until about a month ago and only came to Treepoint when she had found out he was being operated on.

Brick stared back, looking at him much the same way Shade had looked at King. Lily was right; it was too late. Brick wasn't going to let anyone take Violet away from him.

"I'll accept it on one condition."

"What?" Lily asked.

"You have to give me another fifty years," Shade bargained. Lily pressed her face into his shoulder.

"We only celebrated our fiftieth a few months ago, and you think we'll make in another?" Lily's face softened. "Haven't you had enough of me yet?"

"No," Shade scowled. "Brick put a ring on her yet?"

"No, he already talked to John, but he wanted to talk to you before he proposed."

"Good, then I can tell him hell no to his face."

"Shh...they'll hear you, Shade. And you know you don't mean it, anyway."

Oh, yes, he fucking did, but he wanted Violet happy, and that bastard would make sure that none of life's ugliness would touch his granddaughter. For that reason only, he nodded at the man staring back at him so resolutely.

"Dad, we're going in. Mom, are you ready for me to carry you back inside?" Clint interrupted the staring contest.

"In a little while." Lily pressed harder against Shade's side.

"I have my cell phone. I'll call when she's ready," Shade told his youngest son.

He nodded, giving his father a smile that reminded him of himself when he was young and full of shit. Shade watched him bend down and kiss his mother's pale cheek.

"I love you, Mom."

"I love you, too."

After their son walked into the house, it gradually quieted, and the crickets began to chirp again.

"I'm sorry," Lily whispered.

"What for?" Shade turned to look at her.

"I'm not going to be able to give you another fifty years."

Shade stared down into her tired face. They were both aware they weren't going to make it to their fifty-first, though neither one wanted to speak the thought out loud.

He knew the only reason she had held on as long as she had was because of him. He still remembered the day the previous year when her doctor had told him Lily was dying. The doctor had sat behind his desk, crying, while Shade had held his own tears back. He had called him to come into town without Lily in order to tell him what he hadn't been able to tell her: she had only a few months to live. Neither of them had to tell her; she had known without being told.

When she had found out Shade's own doctor had wanted to operate on his heart, and he had refused, she had cried. How did he expect her to fight when he wouldn't fight for his own life? He hadn't argued with her, not wanting her upset, so he had the surgery, recovering as he watched Lily slip farther away.

"You still going to marry Bliss?" Lily teased.

"No, her husband will beat me with his cane." Shade swallowed the lump in his throat.

Lily laughed, the joyful sound still able to twist his stomach in knots.

"Shade…Thank you for a wonderful life. I love you. You've given me everything out of life I could ever want. Then, when I didn't think there could possibly be more, you showed me there was. You gave me the faith to believe I was strong enough to handle anything, hope that somehow in this crazy universe we'll never be apart, and you gave me your love.

"You once told me that nothing in here"—she tapped her forehead—"could hurt me." She circled the air around them. "Then you told me that you had the rest, and you did. For all the years we spent together, you made sure me and our children were taken care of beyond my wildest expectations." She tapped his heart with a gentle finger. "Don't be worried about us ever being parted." She looked up at the dark starry sky reverently. "I've got that."

"Lily…"

"The mountains are beautiful tonight. I feel as if God can hear every word we're saying," she whispered, her hand tightening on his.

Shade wiped her tear away with his thumb.

"I do, too."

Her violet eyes stared at him, the same ones she had passed on to their children and grandchildren. She was still staring at him when her eyes lost the special light they had always held.

"Where you go, I will go," Shade said, holding his wife closer. "I love you, Lily. Always."

Shade listened to the night, focusing on the sounds around him until he could separate each sound, searching for the one he wanted—the sound of his heartbeat.

He concentrated on the speed of his pumping heart then each single beat. Gradually, he slowed his heartbeat, one beat at a time, just how he had learned to do all those years ago as a sniper. It took time and concentration on each…single… beat…before there was nothing other than complete and utter silence"

BOOKS BY JAMIE BEGLEY:

THE LAST RIDERS SERIES:
RAZER'S RIDE
VIPER'S RUN
KNOX'S STAND
SHADE'S FALL
CASH'S FIGHT
SHADE

BIKER BITCHES SERIES:
SEX PISTON
FAT LOUISE

THE VIP ROOM SERIES:
TEASED
TAINTED
KING

PREDATORS MC:
RIOT

THE DARK SOULS SERIES:
SOUL OF A MAN
SOUL OF A WOMAN

ABOUT THE AUTHOR

"I was born in a small town in Kentucky. My family began poor, but worked their way to owning a restaurant. My mother was one of the best cooks I have ever known, and she instilled in all her children the value of hard work, and education.

Taking after my mother, I've always love to cook, and became pretty good if I do say so myself. I love to experiment and my unfortunate family has suffered through many. They now have learned to steer clear of those dishes. I absolutely love the holidays and my family puts up with my zany decorations.

For now, my days are spent writing, writing, and writing. I have two children who both graduated this year from college. My daughter does my book covers, and my son just tries not to blush when someone asks him about my books.

Currently I am writing four series of books- The Last Riders, The Dark Souls, The VIP Room, and Biker Bitches series.

All my books are written for one purpose- the enjoyment others find in them, and the expectations of my fans that inspire me to give it my best. In the near future I hope to take a weekend break and visit Vegas that will hopefully be this summer. Right now I am typing away on my next story and looking forward to traveling this summer!"

Jamie loves receiving emails from her fans,
JamieBegley@ymail.com

Find Jamie here,
https://www.facebook.com/AuthorJamieBegley

Get the latest scoop at Jamie's official website,
JamieBegley.net

Made in the USA
Monee, IL
11 November 2022